THE SINNER OF SAINT AMBROSE

By ROBERT RAYNOLDS

Novels

BROTHERS IN THE WEST
SAUNDERS OAK
FORTUNE
MAY BRETTON
THE OBSCURE ENEMY
PAQUITA
THE SINNER OF SAINT AMBROSE

Drama

BOADICEA (verse)

The Sinner of Saint Ambrose

by ROBERT RAYNOLDS

THE BOBBS-MERRILL COMPANY, INC.

INDIANAPOLIS   *Publishers*   NEW YORK

TO THE FIRST AND TO THE REST OF MY
CHILDREN'S CHILDREN

CONTENTS

CONTENTS—*Continued*

Part IV
THE MURDERER OF STILICHO

Part V
BEGGAR BEFORE GOD

Part VI
THE RECONCILED

FAREWELL!

HAIL!

PRESENTING ROME AND A ROMAN

I WAS BORN WITH A FUNDAMENTAL CONFIDENCE THAT LIFE IS good; and I have learned by all my life of more than seventy years that the chief operation of a religious heart is to reveal life as a matter of rejoicing. All my learning rises up to this: The single measure of a man's joy in life is his love of God.

Now, before beginning the action of my story at the climax of the reign of the Emperor Theodosius the Great, I ask the pleasure of giving a view at large of my Roman world, and I wish to fulfill the ancient courtesy of introducing myself, a Roman.

ROME

I have always had a vivid sense of the deep, fertile and living space of earth outflung in lovely light, and often see the Empire as it were spread out beneath the vast eye of imagination. A Roman citizen of illustrious family, I, like the Emperor Theodosius (and the Emperors Trajan and Hadrian before him), was born to Roman grandeur in Spanish sunlight, when my father governed there, and I accompanied him to Africa, to Asia, and to Constantinople and Greece; yet most of my early life I grew in the city of Rome. The reading of Tacitus and Plutarch, not to say Virgil, Homer, Herodotus and the older Pliny, gave me a rich dream of the broad reach and color and peopling of the world. From Britain to Persia, from the gross German forests to the swart Libyan sands, from the Armenian mountains and the paths of Xenophon to the sea gates of Hercules and the stormy peaks of Atlas, the earth was my home, and Italy its garden, and Rome its city. And all this bright contiguous Rome-mothered spread of strong and lovely earth was fringed by the strange mystery of man-haunted regions sweeping on to China and to India and to unguessed rims and regions beyond the great Western sea. And still the heart of all the earth was Rome. Indeed, it was incredible that the fabric of so great an Empire, murmuring under God with its multimillioned souls, could crack and the earth itself not fall to pieces.

9

I wonder if there has ever been a time such as ours, when a proud civilization, held inviolate for nearly a thousand years, has had the noble City which gives its Empire name broken into and ravaged by rude new barbarous men? Perhaps when news of the defeat and ruin of their fleet at Syracuse reached Athens the moral shock to the Greeks was as profound. I don't know. But the Athenians, of course, brought ruin on themselves. Thucydides and Plato both make it clear that the Greek populace had a genius for voting in favor of their immediate passions and wants regardless of the most reasonable advice and warning of a few farsighted men. We Romans, with our genius for organization, haven't suffered from that trouble. Among us nobody, not even in the Senate, really votes for anything; the government is organized to do it all, and I remember once spending four days seeing eleven officials to find out who was responsible for a puddle of sewage outside my garden wall, only to find that so far as the government was concerned the offense didn't exist: There was no document to verify it. I had my own slaves clear it up, and then I paid a fine for interfering in public affairs. Often, deciding to send an army here or there, the government would simply impress some into service and tax the rest of us to pay for it. With us there seem to be a thousand officials between any private individual and any primary act of state, with a somewhat divine and quite fallible Emperor at the pinnacle of authority. Naturally nobody you can point out can be held responsible for an act that may reverse the fortunes of your life. And I will say, from personal experience in high office, that our form of imperial paternalism did not realize that money is the sweat of the people. We gathered tax money in by blind squeezing and poured it out like inexhaustible natural water on the army, the unemployed city mobs and public works and games. I suppose even natural water is exhaustible; but surely the sweat of the people has its limits. Whether our way or the Greek way most deserved ruin I don't know, but we both got it.

And of course anybody can attribute to the gods, or to the opposing faction, or to the Barbarians, what he hasn't the heart to blame on himself. My grandfather maintained that if only our recent forebear, the Emperor Julian, had lived long enough to re-establish thoroughly the time-honored worship of the gods, from Jupiter to the lares and penates, Rome would have been better off; and my father always insisted that the removal of the statue and altar of Victory from the Senate House by order of the Emperor Gratian (with Bishop Ambrose for his guide) portended awful rewards; Synesius, in a polished oration, said it was all on account of the Barbarians; and the Christians, from Jerome and Augustine to my wife's mother, claimed Rome had more coming to her for her Pagan idolatry than she had yet got.

In the tribulation of events it finally became obvious to me that on the human scale passion is blind, wisdom is crooked, and I have never met or heard of a man who achieved perfection in the conduct of worldly affairs: Among the philosophers even Socrates had his Xantippe, and among the Emperors even Marcus Aurelius had his weariness. One assumption I live by is that every man of good sense has now and then wanted to kill himself in rage or despair at the sheer incomprehensibility of life and his own doings. And as for the Emperor Honorius, with whom I had much to do, his ineffectual puberty was blinder than passions and his manias were crookeder than wisdom, so that he greatly facilitated the present ruin of the Empire.

When I got to the place where only one murder stood between me and the Emperorship I could see that government by murder is perhaps the lowest and most brutal form of government, but is nothing new; the Egyptians, the Persians and the Greeks did it, and some of our Caesars brought the practice to commonplace.

Perhaps one of the tragedies of human society is this, that no public man is as good as his private self might have been. Or it could be put the other way around, since we are all in part public, that society is composed of the tragedies of people. Once he knows this, a sane and compassionate man will love individuals more and society less. And, of course, a society which promises to achieve spiritual comfort without tragedy at its heart has become crushing and sterile, with a lie in its teeth, and no longer worth the ruin of persons it demands. Presently the people will find this out and will let such a society be torn to pieces by the curs of carrion and the wolves of audacity.

I realize now that I entered and took part in the fatal climax of one of the great dramas of civilization, and across the face of the earth and the years of my life I can still hear the thunder of Rome falling.

A ROMAN

As I have said, I was born with a fundamental confidence that life is good. The fact that I have lived seventy-odd years would not amount to much unless I had been able to retain a respect for life and an affection for people.

Drawn into the Emperor's household as a young man, I was enabled by my opportunities and my passions to participate in dramatic wickedness in high places. I enjoyed it. I do not disdain even my miseries; they were good of their kind, too. Barely able to save my private life from complete ruin, I nevertheless felt quite competent to help bishops, generals and Emperors to run the Empire. Sometimes the wickedness I received and sometimes the wickedness I spread gave a rude shaking-up to my fundamental confidence that life is good. I might have run mad or I might have become a saint; we're all frail, and those two extremes tempt us out of this world. But I just kept on trying to find my place between madness and God. At last age and time have brought out what was basic in my character from the first: the serene and steady pleasure of a smiling mind.

A smiling mind is like a light that plays on moving waters. For the life of a man is a smile of God. And when I say that I don't mean either Jupiter or Jehovah smiling in his beard. I mean the radiant incarnation of being, at mysterious motion, from conception to death, within the confines of each man's tragic mortality.

I've always been able to find a man or a woman who sensed what I felt and understood what I was talking about. I think it's as simple as this, that people know life is at center an almost incredible mystery, and we love to communicate our strangeness to one another. For the true interest of a man's life to himself and to others is not only in what he did in the lusty days of his doing, but this interest resides deeply also in what the man at last thinks about it all when he finally matures, reflects and weighs for value. Then the open heart understands the wordless and the unexplained, and, in my experience, compassion and sympathy are established. This is a delightful thought, for it leads me to hope that between the lines of my story the reader is going to meet and understand the inner man of my heart. For his interior life is the vital part of a man.

And I am glad that there are hosts of people who like to be told in a sound and cheerful manner about the passions, follies, crimes and disasters of youth, for it gives me a sense of warm fellowship to know I am not condemned at the outset. It is not only that many others have either lived or want to dream of living a life more passionate than prudent, more human than holy. It is also a thing I know to my comfort, that though individuals may here and there be harsh in their censure, my brother humanity at large is, like God, wonderful in mercy. We endure much and await more. Moreover, even such a man as Augustine, Bishop of Hippo, according to his own *Confessions*, was human long before he was holy. By a fortunate chance, which I shall tell, this Augustine was for a while my private teacher when I was a boy. . . .

I hope by now I have conveyed in words something of that warm subtle sense of an actual meeting—how it is to feel the presence of a man before you know his name or hear his story.

My name is Gregory Julian, and before I became something of a man in my own right I depended for a sense of security on the illustrious Julian name. The Gregory often embarrassed me; my mother's mother was related to Gregory of Nazianzus, the great Christian philosopher and bishop who was the son of a bishop, who was ordained a priest and made a bishop against his will, who despised bishops in general and hated the Emperor Julian in particular; and our women, though we were Julians and a sound Pagan family, had a weakness for the name. Thus some comedy of marriage a couple of generations back passed on to me two names out of harmony with each other. And also the Gregory doubtless indicates a strain of Greek subtlety in my forthright Roman nature.

Also a saying of this Bishop Gregory fell into my boyhood like an arrow out of heaven; I cherished it with glee for several childhood years. What he said was: "I have not time to offend God." It was my first experience of finding something mystical or magic in a given set of words, so that I could utter them with a sense of hurling magic power out of myself to flash in the world about me. As a boy of five or six I chased peacocks through our gardens with that spiritual arrow, laughed it up at trees and echoed it in palace corridors. Then I forgot all about that spiritual heritage for many years.

When I was more eloquent about grief and suffering and doted on the fiercer aspects of being alive I often thought of and sometimes called myself by grand titles: The Favorite of Venus, The Sinner of Saint Ambrose, the Murderer of General Stilicho, The Outcast of Saint Augustine, or The Betrayer of Rome: Such titles symbolized for me dramatic phases of my life. Perhaps they are still not out of place as provocative headings in this story of my life. But guilt and suffering are honors more passionate than I care to carry to the grave. I earned them, I bore them and I cast them away.

Finally this:

At the heart of any story I could ever tell would always be the tragic wonder of the human spirit and the greatness of its search for God. I have found out that a man's life is a religious experience. Now in my old age I begin to tell my religious story, of passionate action in the world, more for the fellowship of the bewildered than for the delight of the orthodox. God is my perpetual Guest. I still am busy at learning how to be His joyous host.

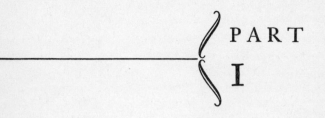

PART
I

THE FAVORITE

OF VENUS

CHAPTER ONE

THE PRIEST AND THE OWL

AT THE AGE OF TWENTY-ONE I HAD MAGNIFICENT NOTIONS of my own future, but just at this time the religious and political passions of society were interfering with my life. I had to do something about it in order to marry Marcia.

I have always been able to distinguish between the pleasure of an afternoon and the happiness of a lifetime. On the day of the priest and the owl I had been disporting myself with my wellborn friends. It was a hot afternoon in Rome in September of the sixteenth year of the reign of the Emperor Theodosius, or, as Christian scholars like to point out, 394 years after the birth of Christ. A number of us were bathing in the palace gardens of Quintus Gaius Tullus.

We met sometimes at one palace, sometimes at another, but most often here where the fountains played into the first pool and the pools emptied one into another over marble spillways, where the gardens had the sweeps and turns of splendor and musicians played soft light tunes in a colonnade behind the cypress hedge. It was a joy (after some hours at my law books) to throw off my clothes, oil my body and work my muscles in trial with some other youth, wrestling him on the lawn under the hot blue sky; or to engage in a vigorous fencing match with short gladiatorial swords; or for a group of us young men and women to run races or play tossing games on the lawn with a large stuffed ball; then, in a healthy sweat and ruddy from hard breathing and laughter, to plunge into a crystal pool, frolic, disport, come out to lie in the sun, play dice on a marble bench or stroll about conversing in fragrant places. To feel the good exertion of my own body and to watch the flash and sport of the free bodies of my friends in the sun at our swimming and playing gave me a lift of delight. Set free from the mask of our clothes and out in the open air, we wore on our bodies God's weaving of light and shadow with a radiant and flowing beauty.

That day, after a lot of this vigorous play and delight, I lay outstretched on the edge of the largest pool, wondering how to overcome a complexity of foolish obstacles so as to marry Marcia at once.

Marcia was a good young girl. I liked her ready laughter and the warmth of her round face. Her face was round, her cheeks were round, and I suspected her body would be round after round in an entirely gleeful fashion. Yet the light of serious love was on her face, the earnest of eternity suffusing her moments of mirth. I had tried to have her join our bathing parties, because I wanted her to know my friends and I was eager to see her body at play in the sun and in the water; but her mother, Calvena, would never let Marcia go to any of the palaces where mixed bathing was the custom. Marcia's mother liked to point out what she called the contrast between Marcia's pure Christian innocence and my sinful Pagan license.

But I considered in my heart that the principle of the female is fertility, not innocence. Moreover, Calvena, being a strong-minded woman with a poor education, did not understand Paganism. Pagans—of the high type—were reserved; it was Christians who knew sin. There was an immense sobriety about Paganism, trying to solve life by reason. We Pagans sought so hard to enjoy the best in the highest way that we lost the faculty of being happy in the trivial. And the wonder of life is composed mostly of trivia.

At any rate, a young man hates to find himself in a ridiculous situation, and for me to be prevented from marrying Marcia was certainly ridiculous.

The deep seeping warmth of the sun had penetrated and relaxed the muscles in my young back, which had become overtense during days of anxiety. I had for a moment forgotten the terrible political situation. My intended marriage might seem a small private affair in comparison with the public disaster threatening so many of us—my father, for example, might be the next governor prefect of Italy or might be condemned as a traitor, according to how the battle came out—but a young man's thoughts return to his own breast, and until the owl came and brought on that day's climax I thought of Marcia and not of the Emperor Theodosius leading his Christian army against our Pagan forces.

Lying with my forehead on the crook of my elbow and my eyes closed in shadow, I played with an absurd hallucination. Marcia's mother wanted me to become a Christian; then she would agree to the marriage at once. I imagined a priest standing above me, ready to convert me, to whom I was saying, "No. Of course not." He wore a soft plain tunic, brown. He was a short man with narrow hands and narrow feet and not much flesh on his bones. He had a long face, further elongated by his high forehead and small brown beard. His hair was short and he wore a drooping mustache. His nose was quite long and thin, but lumped and flared at the nostrils; his lips were thick, and his left eyebrow arched higher than his right, and his eyes were large and seemed even larger because of the stillness in them of steady spiritual light.

As happens in daydreams of this sort, we knew each other perfectly well, and yet I hadn't the faintest notion of who he was. When I said: "No. Of course not. Marcia should become a Pagan. That would settle it," he looked down on me in sorrow, made the Christian sign with his thin graceful hand and said: "Your sin be mine."

"Thank you!"

I must have said "Thank you" aloud, for I felt the bare toes of a young woman touch my shoulder and heard a voice I knew well.

"For what do you thank me? Or are you dreaming of your little Christian?"

I knew Dionie's voice and touch very well, and of course her vital presence dissipated the daydream priest.

I had plenty of reason both to like Dionie and to mistrust her. I sometimes boasted that women were of no use to me except for the joy of their flesh—which to a young man is a lot of use indeed. In the carnal pride of my young manliness my soul, I suppose, was half asleep, or was even unbalanced by the too insolent good health of my masterful body. Perhaps nature retards the spiritual maturing of young men in order to promote the blind business of procreation. Or it may be only this, that young men have not had enough experience to understand a hope of full rich life, but think the vivid things near them—and what is more vivid than a live young woman such as Dionie?—are the ultimates.

Without looking up I grabbed for Dionie's ankle; but her swift cool heel slipped through my hand and she went off laughing.

I lifted my head for a look. I saw the sun shining down along Dionie's lovely young back and saw her motion and life. Then I lowered my head again to try to think about Marcia, "my little Christian." And presently the image of Dionie's supple bright beauty faded into the depths of my mind.

Two years before this, when I was nineteen and she was fifteen, I had been betrothed to Marcia Fabian, who was related both to Ambrose, Bishop of Milan, and to the fabulously wealthy Sextus Petronius Probus; but the marriage was being interminably delayed because of political and religious difficulties.

My father was a zealous Pagan and her mother, Calvena Ambrosia Fabiana, was an extreme Christian, and as power shifted between these

two parties in Rome, now one now the other thought of new demands
by which to delay the marriage.

Old Probus steadily favored the marriage and had brought about the
betrothal in the first place because even in ill-health and approaching his
latter days he liked the idea of an alliance, through Marcia, with the
illustrious Julian family. We Julians were by no means poor, but Probus had drained so many provinces in his amazing sequence of governorships that he was probably the wealthiest man in Rome. He had promised to dower Marcia with estates, slaves and gold enough to turn almost
any young man's head, and I had at that time a robust desire for fortune: I had a career to begin, and wealth would be useful. My father
was prepared to give me almost an equal amount, plus the dignity of a
great name. My father favored the marriage (from time to time),
partly because the wife of Probus was giving money hand over fist to
Christian uses and it would be a victory to get a large share under our
Pagan influence. But I think mainly when he favored the marriage it
was because he had always thought Marcia the loveliest child in Rome.
Her glow and joy infected his heart and reminded him of her father,
who, until his death, had been my father's deepest friend.

The first impediment, which had delayed the betrothal itself, had
been sex. I think Marcia's mother was out of her mind on the subject.
Calvena was a slender woman with intense black eyes and a consuming
tautness of feature who made sudden gestures of ferocity and despair
with her lovely arms. My father said before she became a widow Calvena had been more relaxed and that even her voice had had a haunting loveliness. But when she became a widow her voice went off pitch
and the tension began to draw her face. My father was outspoken and
said: "That woman has set Christianity between herself and a man, and
is going crazy from it." At any rate, she spent most of her time with
devout women such as Marcellina, the dedicated virgin sister of Bishop
Ambrose, whose house in Rome was a veritable nunnery. Both Ambrose
in Milan and Jerome in Bethlehem wrote these ladies book-length epis-
tles in praise of utter chastity for girls and for widows. They held dedicated virgins, male or female, to be higher in the sight of God than
reproducing mortals. They told mothers how to raise daughters in obscure purity, even advising that young girls be kept away from church
(or at least severely chaperoned there) because there was apt to be noise
and drunkenness during service. And Calvena wanted Marcia to follow
the lead of Marcellina and dedicate herself to virginity.

The poor child was nearly persuaded, but actually a passage in one of
the letters of Jerome so horrified her that she took a stand, declared her-

self for humble humanity, and said she would never of her own free will deny the fulfillment of her sex. This passage in Jerome's letter—and I saw a copy of the letter, too, for those things were handed around—was advising a young virgin in the selection of her slaves and her eunuchs, and it read like this: ". . . look rather to their characters than to their good looks; for, whatever their age or sex, and even if mutilation ensures in them a compulsory chastity, you must take account of their dispositions, for these cannot be operated on save by the fear of Christ. . . ."

I was proud when I heard that Marcia had cried out that she knew of no passage in the Gospels where Christ commanded his followers: "Fear thou me!" She said His message was love, and the essence of her life was love, and to love a man and bear and love children would not disable her from following Christ.

In short, it seemed to me, when one way and another I had heard all these things, that Marcia had a good, healthy and lovable acceptance of our human endowment with sex, which is not unlike a lovable acceptance of human life itself. For I may as well remark right here that in my long life I have heard tell of many times and places where sex relations have supposedly been pure, simple and natural, but I never heard of anyone saying that this was true in his own time or place or person; and my conclusion is that sex, like life itself, is of an original and infinite complexity which no man, or woman either, has yet mastered. There was nothing in my Pagan training to make me despise the body and its functions, while certainly from the poets and philosophers I had learned to love also the mind and spirit of man and to conceive of a unity or synthesis of all the gods, including Venus, in the unknowable splendor of deity. But to my story.

Marcia's mother wept, but gave up her attempt to compel Marcia to vows of chastity.

Marcia's cause was greatly helped by the fact that just about this time the monk Jovinian was making a stir in Rome. He had been an ascetic in bare feet and dirty rags in a monastery connected with Ambrose's church in Milan when he decided that self-imposed torments of squalor and poverty were not required by Christ. He deserted the monastery, came to Rome, dressed and ate well, frequented the baths and conversed with ladies. From all I ever heard—and I talked to him and knew those who knew him—Jovinian was neither a voluptuary nor a profligate. He simply held that it was not negative renunciations but rather positive works which were pleasing to God. He further held (which outraged many monks and priests) that the Virgin Mary, though virgin when she conceived, was no longer virgin after having given birth to Christ.

Frankly at the time, being myself a reasonable Pagan, these theological distinctions meant little to me, though they caused spilling of blood among Christians.

At any rate, Jovinian's gossip and finally the little book he wrote and circulated gave relief to many self-compelled celibates. Certain consecrated virgins and monks forgot their vows and married, including not a few who had been living together under the "brother-sister" fiction of tacit fornication, and the Christian lay folk, those to whom religion was a part but not the whole of a sufficiently troubled life, applauded the good sense and bad Latin of Jovinian. It was at this point that old Probus put pressure on Marcia's mother, and my betrothal to the courageous girl took place. Everything was ordered for a quick marriage.

But the ascetic party, led by Senator Pammachius (who used to attend regular meetings of the Senate not in his toga but in the black garb of a monk) denounced Jovinian to Pope Siricius.

Jovinian was excommunicated by Pope Siricius, but everybody knew that the man of real power in the fast-growing Catholic Church was Ambrose of Milan, so Jovinian and his close adherents went to Milan to appeal to Ambrose. Ambrose convoked a small council of bishops of northern Italy and blasted Jovinian into desecrated obscurity, condemning him as a Manichean heretic. To Siricius Ambrose sent a fierce letter of praise, commending the Pope for protecting the Christian fold from this "heretical wolf who showed no reverence for virginity, recognized no order of chastity or degrees of merit, and even dared deny the perpetual virginity of Mary."

To my mind, Jovinian was being unjustly defamed. I thought then, and after a long life still believe, that both sexual asceticism and sexual profligacy have their roots in a contempt for women. And for man to despise woman reveals scorn or fear of the first principles of life. But a low view of the nature of woman was at that time a commonplace of the Christian Church's teaching.

However, Calvena wrote Bishop Ambrose about me, and while his reply did not forbid, it did not advise marriage at all, and certainly not the marriage of a Christian girl to a Pagan. Calvena seized the opportunity to put off the wedding until I should become a Christian. Of course this enraged my father, who said time enough had been wasted, the marriage should take place at once, nothing more being required but that Marcia should renounce Christianity. Her joy, her virtue, he said, made her worthy of the highest Pagan honors. Both families were too stubborn either to end the betrothal or to conclude the marriage. It didn't help matters that our palaces were adjoining and that my father and Calvena had been fighting friends since childhood. Marcia and I were helplessly caught in the religious passion of the age, incarnate in our parents.

I lay by the pool, thinking that if I became a Christian it would be like a betrayal of my father, but it might clear the way to my marriage with Marcia. I was wondering if I could become a Christian without being forced to spoil natural pleasures with a sense of sin and evil. I wanted to be a happy man, and the avowal of shame and the praise of suffering seemed a poor way to begin. But to marry Marcia seemed a good way to begin.

I felt a cool touch of fingers on the warm muscle at my bent elbow. There was Dionie, standing at shoulder depth in the pool beside which I lay, her face on a level with mine, waiting for me to smile.

I always ended by smiling at Dionie, even after one of our fights.

"Let me tell you something, young Julian," she said, and it was as if she had been watching over me while I lay there, reading my thoughts with that predatory intuition of women. "There is no answer to life. You live it. The Christians refuse that way. Their first principle is to despise the life they have and could live for the sake of the life they presume to be coming hereafter."

"You prefer Venus?"

"Venus. Isis. Above all, Cybele, mother of gods, riding her chariot drawn by lions."

She smiled and her finger tips touched lightly again on the muscle of my arm. She had woman-tricks with the tips of her fingers, knowing how to make their slightest touch bear comfort or offer invitation. I liked the way she read my thoughts and touched my arm.

Dionie was just my age, but she had a more penetrating knowledge of the world than I. She had been married to an older man when she was sixteen, and they had lived in Alexandria. About a year before, they had divorced each other so that he could make a marriage closer to the purple. He had gone to Constantinople and she had come to Rome. She was of an old senatorial family and was mistress in her own right of large estates in Africa and in Greece, as well as in Italy and Gaul.

She had let herself get a little plump, which was a pleasure, but I warned her there was a difference between being voluptuously firm and lazily fat. She always laughed at that, saying, "When the political situation clears so that I can make a choice with confidence, I'll trim myself to perfection and select a husband with an interesting future. Until then I'm enjoying my own life." Then to tease me she would add, "At the moment, Gregory, you're too young. If I were to marry you now,

you would always let me dominate you. And I hate dominant females.
Three years from now, perhaps I couldn't hope for a better man. But I
won't wait three years."

Now I felt her hand suddenly clutch my arm, her fingers digging in
with fright.

A large dusky owl flew low over the pool where we were bathing, and
his fatal shadow crossed the heads of some of us. The somber creature
landed on the small Temple of Victory at the end of the palace garden.

There was a scream from the middle of the pool, and Dionie and I
both looked there.

One of the girls, in frantic excitement, thrashed through the water,
climbed out of the pool, and ran along the marble edge, her lovely body
flashing in the sun against a background of cypress hedge. She leaped
over young Flavian, who was leaning on his elbow staring after the owl,
and sprang up the steps of a marble platform, where she poised for a
dive, looking like one about to hurl herself from the Tarpeian Rock to
death. There was silence. Then the wild tension left her figure. She
folded her elbows against her breasts and put her face in her hands, and
while her figure slowly bent and relaxed to a kneeling position she began
to sob, with her wet hair hanging over her fingers. Her elbows were now
pressed into the flesh just above her knees, and I could see her breasts
shudder and her belly contract with her sobs. Then she became very still,
and the sunlight was golden on the arc of her grieving back.

I knew her father was involved, like mine, in the struggle against the
Emperor Theodosius, and the owl had announced disaster to her heart.

Thus the owl, flying over us and roosting on the Temple of Victory,
brought on that day's climax. Our whole group, which through the past
spring and summer had been so sportive and gay—the most delightful
group of young nobles in Rome—was now tense, distracted. Our mood
for several weeks past had itself been a fatal omen.

The ominous suspense of awaiting news from the North of a battle
bound to be fought—a battle which would affect our lives—had finally
sapped the golden joy from all of us. The Pagan army under Flavian,
Arbogast and Eugenius might save us. The Christian army of Theodosius might be our ruin.

I sat up and dangled my feet in the pool, and Dionie, who had been
standing motionless in the water with no heart to swim, reached for me
to pull her out of the water. I caught her under the armpits, gave her
a strong lift, and she sat down dripping beside me. Her hair, which she
dyed red, was still dry; it was frizzed out in bangs over her forehead and
piled high on top.

We watched young Flavian go up onto the platform across the pool to comfort the girl who was sobbing there. But he didn't know what to do. He stood above her, arms hanging, head bent. Together they made a human statuary of prophetic grief, foreshowing, if we had only known it, the sorrow and ruin in store for our generation of wealthy and noble young Romans.

Dionie, beside me, had a supple body, and her skin, deepened to olive richness by daily bathing and sunning, made a soft contrast to mine, which had more of the red of copper in its hue. She had a ready and warm compassion, she loved her friends. Looking now at Flavian standing in grief above the sobbing girl, she said, "How can Flavian comfort anybody? He knows his father is fatally involved, with no choice but to conquer or die."

Then she looked at me. Her eyes widened, so that their greenness flared with excited light. "You, too, Gregory Julian! Your father is in great danger!"

"My father, my marriage—everything!" I gave the last vague word a passionate emphasis, for "everything" was a code word in my mind for my secret—and perhaps vainglorious—desire to become Emperor.

I looked about in the sunlight and languid air. I suppose there were nearly thirty of us there that day, and, except for a few fathers, mothers and little ones, most were in the prime of youth, quick, graceful, limber-bodied. But now we were all caught still with fright.

I was afraid.

Suddenly I stood up. I seized Dionie's arm and pulled her to her feet beside me. Then I shouted, and my voice had the ringing energy of command and anger in it. "Let's drive that damnable owl from the Temple of Victory!"

The effect was marvelous. It was as if my voice broke an enchantment and struck heavy chains from the bodies of us all. I was one of the youngest there, but my bold shout was like a trumpet blast of authority, rousing hearts to action. Men and women sprang up, came to sudden life, left the pool, ran about the lawn and playfield, snatching up any sort of bat or ball or sword. We swarmed yelling down the sweep of gardens, scattering peacocks as we ran, to the lovely Temple of Victory.

That Temple of Victory had special significance to all the Pagans among us—and most of us were either Pagans or only nominal Christians. Ever since the late Emperor Gratian (under the spiritual guidance of the Catholic Bishop Ambrose) had confiscated the revenues of the Pagan temples and ordered the altar and statue of Victory removed from the Senate House the Pagan party had fought hard to get the revenues back and the statue restored. We had almost succeeded when young Valentinian was Emperor of the West (after the murder of Gratian); but Bishop Ambrose exerted his full power and frustrated our success. Then Valentinian was murdered by Arbogast. But at some of the palaces—this one, and my father's, for example—Temples of Victory had been privately built as a sign to the gods of fidelity. For an owl of ill omen to have landed on just such a temple when at any hour we expected news of the crucial battle was a horror.

The ugly hooded fowl crouched in a cornice above the marble columns and scarcely blinked its eyes at our howling approach. We threw a rain of our swords, bats and balls and even stones up at him, but could not dislodge the fatal creature. We again began to feel terrified.

"Flavian!" I shouted. "Come here to the pillar!"

He came. I had him stand against the pillar; then I clambered to his shoulders, stood on them and, being more than usually tall, I grasped the owl.

There was a shout of wild joy from my friends jostling below. The owl sank talons deep into my hand and beat furious great wings in my face, but I got down to the ground, holding him, not doubting that Senator Tullus would want to kill him and examine his entrails for omens of our fate.

At that moment the head eunuch of the Tullus palace, a lean Oriental with cruel eyes and black hair, came striding up to the elder Tullus and said in a voice I thought loud with high-pitched malice: "Arbogast and Eugenius are defeated. The Praetorian Prefect, Virius Nichomachus Flavianus, has died by his own hand in the Julian Alps. *The Emperor Theodosius is victorious!*"

I let the owl go. I wiped my hand across my breast, leaving a smear of blood which ran down my ribs and belly. Young Flavian seized a short gladiatorial sword from the ground and would have plunged it into his heart if Dionie had not been quick enough to lunge against him, deflecting the blow and giving me time to seize the weapon from his suddenly weak hand.

I said to him bitterly, "Your father, yes. Mine, perhaps. But our young fates are not hopeless yet!"

Dionie took my wounded hand in hers and looked at it, though my blood spilled into her palms. "Get this wound cleaned at once!"

Something personal, obscure, but connected with deep instincts, moved me at the sight of my own blood being received into Dionie's hands. It was not a thing I liked. For a moment it made me weak. I tried to free myself. "It's nothing," I said. "I must hurry home before my father kills himself."

She looked up at me with green fire smoldering in her eyes. I was sure she perceived all I felt and knew better than I what it might mean. For a moment her face was cruel and primitive, gloating in triumph. Then she pulled me down to my knees where the overflow from the pools sparkled in a marble trough past the Temple of Victory, and she washed my wounded hand in the flowing water. My blood came off her hands, too.

She looked at me, still with that green deep strangeness in her eyes. Then she said, "You're free. Go!"

I looked back and saw her still kneeling there, gazing at her own wet hands with their fingers spread.

Then she closed her right hand and pressed the knuckles against her lips. I knew—without being able to see, I knew—that some trace of my blood remained between her knuckles and that with her lips and tongue she was sealing it forever invisibly there in some female ritual of primitive delight.

I couldn't waste any more time on the youthful and private matter of Dionie's sensuous enchantment, for deeper passions had to be faced.

I was sickened by the profound shock of knowing that from now on, not I, but the world, would declare my father in treason. My father might, because of his high sense of honor, even now be preparing his own death. For my father always retained to himself the last great freedom of the Stoic, the free and courageous right to die when he might choose, by his own will and hand.

CHAPTER TWO

THE NETS OF PASSION

I MUST SPEAK OF FATHER AND SON, OF EMPEROR JULIAN AND Augustine, of Theodosius and treason and religion, to show at once what nets of passion had caught up my life.

I speak first of a deep and manly love. I honor the name of my father, Marius Cincinnatus Julian, and I cherish the great spiritual gifts that I received from my father.

During the past weeks of tension and peril, before the issue of our disaster was known, my father had shared with me his knowledge, his wisdom and his passion. I grew more deeply familiar with the angles of his face, the timbre of his voice and the resolution of his gestures during these days when he admitted me into his spiritual world of fact, symbol and passion. The old human fire of a man being a man was strong in his breast.

We dined together, just the two of us, or strolled together in our palace garden, or studied pertinent documents in his office and library, or the two of us together, in our finest chariot, drove out to visit and honor the tomb of his wife, my mother. These were days of communion, and possibly of farewell, between father and son.

His speaking was forthright. "I have put your life in hazard, Gregory. You are my only son. I want you to know where you stand and where I stand. Every private life is also partly moved and molded by reverberations of public affairs. Yours and mine are no exceptions. I have committed myself to that which, if it succeeds, may save Rome, and if it fails will be called treason. Although success in this will make me one of the highest officials of Empire, and will put you in line to be Emperor, I have not done it out of ambition or lust for power. I have done it in the name of the gods of Rome."

My father was a man of medium size and of a compressed hard strength; when we walked together I was half a head taller than he, but he was a man of such direct purpose that his stride always equaled that of my longer legs. We walked together in the companionship of an equal stride and in the warmth of compatible harmonized differences of temperament. He loved the secret wildness of my imagination which sometimes brought on my bursts of robust laughter, and I loved his passionate honor. He was a trained orator and often spoke to me in a memorable conversational eloquence.

After we did libations of honor at my mother's tomb he turned to me before we remounted our chariot in the sun. His face had the composed gravity of honor.

"When you were a boy," he said, "and I hired Augustine, that African, to be your tutor, he touched your imagination with the fire of his religious despair. Remember him as an example of what I want to express. Each troubled age has, I feel sure, its own form of public passion which stirs and disturbs a multitude of private hearts. On that subject men may then be roused up to violence, to sacrifice, to base perfidy or sublime heroism, or they can be made sick and helpless by indecision. In our age this passion is religion, Paganism and Christianity being the great opponents, the very life of Rome at forfeit in the struggle, and with fierce and bitter fissures still costing men their lives within the Christian sect. From Rome to Constantinople, and round about our whole blue sea to the fringes of Spain, the Empire smolders with religious passion, so that a cry of propaganda from either side on a crowded street too often leads to riot, arson and atrocity. Add to this the fury of the Christians against the Jews and the intrepid onslaughts of Barbarians from out deep and silent reaches of earth, and you can see how many flamelike tongues there are to the violence that threatens our Roman world."

He paused, bent his head a moment, searched his heart. Then, looking directly into my eyes, his whole face ashine with his whole truth, he declared, "Merely to be ambitious, merely to seek power in such a time would be utterly corrupt. I love Rome, Gregory. Rome is being ruined. Theodosius is not helping matters by relegating powers of the State to the Christian Church. Their Christ persuaded; their church compels: It is a counter-State. Theodosius is not Rome. I am faithful, as I have always been, to Rome. The Rome of my fathers and the Rome of my gods!"

During these days, by such thoughts and such speeches, my father was making his position, regardless of its peril, irrevocable. To be with him, to listen to him in his trouble, sharpened in me new powers of perception. I had to learn to see the general notions of man and society manifested as incarnate, concrete and real in the person of this man I loved. I had to conceive of and deal with the world on more mature terms. I had to realize that a man, by his passions, his actions, his symbols and his very utterances, creates ruling facts in his own life. Once a man by such means makes speculative or even fabulous matter true for the deeps of his own heart, you can no longer say it is not a ruling fact in his life. It would be childish to dismiss it as irrational, or rationalization, or private myth-making. Though it be all these and more, what it is in its fullness is that man living. My father was living intensely in these days of his commitment and peril.

My father was an eminent man, trained in the law. He had served as governor in provinces in Spain, in Africa and in Asia. He had inherited wealth and increased it. If this present usurpation of Eugenius were to succeed, he would certainly rise to the honor of the consulship and would almost certainly follow Flavian as Praetorian Prefect, a position second in power only to that of the Emperor. The quickest way to rise in honors, power and wealth in our time—which is probably true of any time when power is highly centralized—was by favor-seeking, obsequiousness, bribery and the other predatory arts of corrupt politics.

But my father had chosen to base his career on hard work, detailed knowledge and efficient handling of the complex problems of office. You could see it in his eyes, which were clear, candid and fearless; he looked at men and at things to see in truth what ought to be done and was both patient in meditation and swift in decision as to how things ought in truth to be done.

He was a great lawyer, in the classical tradition of Ulpian, Papinian and the Julian of two centuries ago. Our Roman jurisprudence, at its highest flowering, had never been equaled in the world for creative intelligence in the field of humane social relations—including civil, commercial and private affairs—and had not been equaled for constructive freedom of mind, based on a sound and ethical philosophy of human life, working to build an orderly world society. My father knew this golden age of the law had passed and our time was decadent, but in all his official business he held in high regard the noble concepts of Roman legal genius at its best: that law is the art of the equitable and the good; that justice is the constant and increasing will to render each man his right; and that the fundamental precepts of law are to live honestly, not to injure one another, to render each his own. A man shall not promise what he cannot give, nor demand what is not his. My father avoided definitions that were too binding, for the free mind and the free act sustain society; and he repudiated old authority when new fact or plain experience proved it in error.

"Our Roman law, Gregory," he told me, "our vital Roman concept of justice is the great net of equity and good which holds world society together. We must not let its cords and ligaments grow brittle, nor dare any man weave his part of the great fabric falsely. A dishonest or a stupid or an inhumane judgment not only ruins a client; it corrupts society."

My father had his seat in the Senate, but the Senate had lost its function. He served clients in the highest tribunals, but edicts and rescripts of the Emperor could countermand reason and justice. Some awful sickness was corrupting, had corrupted, the old Roman vigor of mind and soul. My father had a clear perception of the profound change that had taken place.

"The creative action of the free Roman is withering. Men want security, not creative action; they seek refuge, not justice. Even our law has changed from a world-building instrument, enabling free men to act creatively in equity and toward good, to a mass of deadening rules which bind each man to a restricted function."

My father was a man who, though others could not see it, knew he had a spear in his breast and lived on under this mortal wound of a society which deadened his high creative functions.

But in spite of all this, if religious passion had not biased his judgment, I think he would never have supported Eugenius. Like most Pagans, my father was tolerant of any form of religion, as such; but he hated the way Christianity was encroaching on and taking over powers of the State. And bitterness was added to his feelings by the fact that whereas he—like so many Pagans—admitted the right of Christians to their beliefs, the Christians considered any religion but their own a base and damned corruption.

"Theodosius," he said, "has given to the Christians what is not his to give, the private consciences of private men. That is a profound offense against justice. These Christians will be our ruin. First they speak of love, then they seek privilege, finally they demand obedience: By these moves they destroy justice and subvert the State. A man like Bishop Ambrose, trained as a lawyer and a governor, must know what he is doing—destroying Rome to build their church."

In the light of these revelations of my father's passionate beliefs I got a frightening sense of the deep and violent cleavages in our society. And I recognized that my father's honor, his intensity and his noble seriousness elevated him morally—whatever might happen in the shallow mischances of politics—far above all taint of treachery or treason. If he failed and was called a traitor, I would still know he had lived and died faithful to Rome and his gods.

I came upon him one morning in the great hall of our palace standing before our larger than life-size bronze statue of the Emperor Julian. My father stood proud and silent there. A shaft of early sunlight was on his head and shoulders and on the head and breast of Julian. The posture of the Emperor was imperial, the bearded head noble, and the sun now like fire on his lips, so that the man himself seemed just to have spoken to my father.

Aware of me at his side but still gazing at the majestic bronze, my father exclaimed, "No man likes to have his gods abhorred!"

Set in the wall beside the bronze of Emperor Julian was a large bronze plaque on which was lettered one of the noblest utterances Roman ever made, and the sun that morning burnished the words with splendor. Both in the words and in the statue we two living Julians felt with us the living presence of the Great Emperor Julian. I also felt the presence there of Augustine.

I was conscious in full of the profound formative significance in my early life of this Emperor Julian, of his words and, by a deep emotional connection personal to me, of Augustine the African. I must tell it here. I am not forgetting my father, no, nor Marcia nor Dionie nor the fatal power over us of Theodosius; but I must gather the might of memory also into the web and tension of my drama and reveal the secret fount and energy of my desire to be Emperor.

After generations of foul and bitter martyrdom the Christians had won an imperial convert: Constantine had established Christianity as the official religion of the Empire. We Pagans did not fail to remark that Constantine, after composing the Arian heresy at the Council of Nicaea in favor of the Catholic doctrine of the Trinity, found occasion to murder his eldest son, suffocate his wife in the steam bath and poison his eleven-year-old nephew, which led us Pagans to doubt the regenerative power of this new religion on the character of a man. Then later the Emperor Julian restored Paganism to its old honor, but died before the position was firm. He was mortally wounded in battle against the Persians, fought on for Rome until loss of blood sank him to the ground, and there in his tent, on the fringe of battle in the fields of Asia, he uttered from his couch his own noble funeral oration to his watching friends.

Among them was Ammianus the historian, who took down the Emperor's words. My father had this whole great utterance cast on a large handsome bronze tablet and set into the wall in our palace, and he made it my first lesson in manhood to get the words by heart, so that I might never forget that I, too, was of the noble Julian strain.

Here, then, are the last words of the Emperor Julian, which became the first great lesson of my life and were of constant force in the molding of my character:

Friends and fellow soldiers, the ripe time of my going hence is here, and I discharge, with the cheerfulness of a ready debtor, the demands of nature. I have learned from philosophy by how much the soul is more excellent than the body; and that the separation of the nobler substance should bring joy, not grief. I have learned from religion that an early death has often been the reward of piety, and I welcome, as a favor of the gods, the mortal stroke that saves me from the danger of disgracing a character until now supported by virtue and courage. I die without remorse, as I have lived without guilt. I am glad to reflect on the innocence of my private life; and I can affirm with confidence that the supreme authority, the emanation of Divine Power, has been preserved in my hands pure and immaculate. Hating the corrupt and destructive maxims of despotism, I have considered the happiness of the people as the end of government. Subjecting my actions to the laws of prudence, of justice and of moderation, I have trusted the outcome to the care of

Providence. Peace was the aim of my counsels, as long as peace was consistent with the public welfare; but when the imperious voice of my country called me to arms I exposed my person to the dangers of war, with the clear foreknowledge (which I had acquired from the art of divination) that I was destined to fall by the sword. I now offer my tribute of gratitude to the Eternal Being, who has not suffered me to perish by the cruelty of a tyrant, by the secret dagger of a conspiracy or by the slow tortures of lingering disease. He has given me, in the midst of an honorable career, a splendid and glorious departure from this world; and I hold it equally absurd, equally base, to seek or to decline the stroke of fate. This much I have tried to say; but my strength fails me and I feel the approach of death. I carefully say no word to influence your votes in the election of a new Emperor. My choice might be imprudent or injudicious; and if it should not be ratified by the consent of the army, it might be fatal to the person whom I should recommend. I shall only, as a good citizen, express my hopes that the Romans may be blessed with a virtuous sovereign.

I could never forget showing this plaque to Augustine, later Bishop of Hippo, who gave me private lessons for a short time when I was a boy. I have always believed it was this Augustine who set up those disturbances in my spirit which led me to suspect and mistrust the apparent explanation of passing events, so that I learned to hold things in watchful memory until later reflection, perhaps after years, gave me a more satisfying insight into the shocks and awakenings of life.

For at first I thought him a swift, marvelous and frightless man; but he showed and told me of a more tragic self, so that I saw him as hard pressed as any man in the natural order.

Augustine was a young man then, not yet a Christian nor famous. He had come to Rome from Africa with his mistress and his son to make his fortune as a teacher. I know now what he called it in his *Confessions:* ". . . Seduced and seducing, deceived and deceiving, in diverse lusts. . . . In those years I taught rhetoric, and, overcome by cupidity, made sale of a loquacity to overcome by. . . ." In short, he was trying to earn his living in desperate spiritual circumstances.

At first in Rome, however, he had been deathly ill with one of our fevers. Then his pupils showed a dishonest cunning in deserting his class just before payment was due. Through my father's friend Symmachus, who was then prefect of Rome, Augustine was applying for a public professorship at assured pay in Milan. Meantime my father employed him to give me a few lessons and paid Augustine in advance because the man needed the money.

I read with him the *Hortensius* of Cicero, which lifts the mind toward divine philosophy, and I was too young to understand what we read or why we read it.

But there was something lean, dark and self-devoured about the man which made him an exciting teacher for a young boy. No matter whether the subject be grammar or rhetoric, a man teaches best what he is; and at that time Augustine was neither a Pagan nor a Christian, and to call him a half-persuaded Manichaean would fall short of his measure. What he was was a man in search of a vision fit to live by, and what his presence taught me was the internal strife and suffering of a distracted soul.

I had begun to trust him as my teacher, and my heart beat more rapidly when he came.

He took me once to his lodgings. It cost me breath to keep up with him; he trod the street with the alacrity of guilt. I expected him to run, but he moved with the restrained violence of insatiable longing. Where he lived was neither base nor elegant, but rather dreary. He showed me the bed on which he had nearly died, and as if to himself he said, "Would it have mattered?"

His son Adeodatus, about my age, was clean and placid, but Augustine's woman, the mother of his son, gave me a fright. I knew how my mother was surrounded with servants, comforts, respected and loved. But this young woman, silent, her hair dank on her hot forehead, her dark eyes wide and still, her mouth composed in the design of enduring pain, was like a reproach to my innocence and good fortune. I saw things then beyond my understanding; they are in my memory still and are now more nearly understood.

It was one of those cases where the man dressed as well as he could on limited means, the child was neat and clean, and the woman was a fatal victim of an unequal love, of inferiority, of poverty, of shame. I think she offered a greater love than the man's torn and troubled heart could receive or return. It can be a terrible thing for a woman when a man cleaves to her in carnal compulsion, but she loves him with all the pain of her wounded spirit.

Augustine took his son and me that day to one of the large public baths. The woman stood still in the shadowed air, looked upon us all, and especially Augustine, with a smile more deep with pain of love than any I ever saw, and let us go.

I have paused on this tragic recollection of a woman's silent pain because this is a story of my spirit, and that was one of the unforeseen lessons of the spirit Augustine taught me.

It was on another day that I took him with pride to where the Julian plaque was imbedded in the wall. He read it aloud swiftly with his African accent. Then he said, "So he dies without remorse, as he lived without guilt, and he neither seeks nor avoids the stroke of fate. You Pagans in your way are as bad as the Christians in theirs, and I doubt if even the Platonists know what life is about."

He glared at me, his eyes ablaze with inner torment. He glared at the statue of the Emperor Julian. To a child of ten or eleven years he was a dark imposing passionate man. He was fighting some Fury to the death in the confines of his own breast, secretly; and I was frightened. I was frightened of what he fought, but never of him; and because I trusted him I had no defense against the words he next spoke in a passionate outburst of his suffering.

"Life, young Julian," he cried out bitterly, "is an inconsolable sorrow. *I cannot see the face of God!*"

With that outcry, he turned on his heel and left me. Any innocent boyish faith I may have had in the kindly presence of the gods guiding and guarding the flow of our lives was shattered then, for he had taught me in one outcry an unforgettable lesson about the tormented heart.

I trembled and could not see. Then I blinked my eyes and slowly read through again the calm last words of the Emperor Julian and regained my pride and composure, more on the surface than in the depth of my soul.

(It was a changed Augustine I had to deal with years later in Africa, just before the sack of Rome by the Barbarians. There was then a dark grandeur about his spiritual confidence, and yet he was still the same passionate soul he had been as a young man. But I'll come to that meeting and struggle between us more fully in its place.)

I even touched the bronze plaque with my fingers for comfort, especially tracing that one sentence: "I die without remorse, as I have lived without guilt." And I said to the air where Augustine had stood, and hoping the great statue would hear me speak, "The Emperor Julian was a noble man!" I had a boy's dream that if I became Emperor I would live up to the great Julian in honor as well as in name.

At our next and last lesson I gave Augustine my own handsome papyrus roll containing two pastoral poems of Virgil as a parting gift of affection. He looked at me, his lips trembling, and said, "You have a clear soul, young Julian!"

Thus both Julian and Augustine became live and powerful forces in my memory.

My father and I, standing before Julian's statue, knew the Christians named this great Emperor "Julian the Apostate," and we considered ourselves honored, even by distant cousinship, to bear his name and their spite.

Julian was succeeded by Jovian, a cheerful young Christian fond of wine, of women and of a moderate amount of war. And truly, during the thirty years since the death of Julian, the Emperors had been nominally Christian, but had as a rule been either young or weak, or both. Theodosius, out of Spain and a confirmed Catholic, now was a great exception: He was definitely a Christian and he was mature and he was able. He had inner force and vehemence.

The only man in the Empire equal to Theodosius in public stature was Ambrose, Bishop of Milan. No other man before Ambrose had dared to say to an Emperor: "Thus far and no farther!" But Ambrose had said it, and Theodosius had bowed the mighty polity of Empire to the mighty polity of God, and had humbled his imperial person to the holy person of the Bishop of Milan.

I think my father never recovered from that blow, and it more than anything led him into the present trap of potential treason.

But before I try to make a clear simple statement of this complex situation of possible treason in which my father was so dangerously caught, I want to say an honest word, if I can, about my feelings on this subject of religion. I think it was the passion of our age because it was the hunger of our hearts. Not even we of the senatorial class, who were wealthy and fortunate and could have at choice the best pleasures and comforts of the time, had true quiet of mind or peace of heart. I wonder if there has ever been a time such as ours, when sheer moral fatigue had drained joy out of so many faces, when many men and women favored by the gods with honor, power, fortune, yet took to drunkenness, adultery, suicide, or to aberrant forms of asceticism? Neither the elaborations of intellect nor the satiations of appetite ended in serenity. There was a sense of ruin in the air we breathed and a sound of violence in the lives we led, through all classes of society from the slaves to the Emperor.

I think there are times when only religion can save society from disaster, and our time was one of those; and sometimes a society is so rotted by its own growth and glory that it cannot be saved even by religion, and our time was one of those. When times are as bad as that it becomes the desperate business of the solitary heart to labor for truth and seek God. At the time, I was young and spoke neither so openly nor so simply about the matter as I felt then and speak now. All about me roared and glittered the increasing semblances of death, and my heart ached to lay aside death and see God. I could say much more about sects and doctrines and dogmas, from Homer to Plato to Plotinus, or from Democritus to Lucretius, or from Isis to Mithra, or from Moses to Christ and from Paul to Ambrose, Augustine and Jerome; but I would get no closer to the central simplicity of my religious life and, I am convinced, of the lives of multitudes of my fellows in our time of trouble. Our hearts ached to lay aside death and see God.

I believe that feeling overpowered the heart of the Emperor Theodosius when he bowed his diadem to the miter of Bishop Ambrose.

Theodosius had done a horrible thing, one of those shocking acts which debases the moral tone of a whole people. After defeating the usurper Maximus and allowing the execution of that tyrant (our age was distressed with usurpations, tyrannies and treasons) Theodosius made a triumphal visit to Rome, then in 390 went to Milan and while there got news of the riots in Thessalonica. In Thessalonica the people had a favorite charioteer who was a brute, and they were also irritated to have a large body of Barbarian troops quartered on the town. Botheric, the Teuton commandant of the troops, put the charioteer in prison for new insolent immorality—popular charioteers were accustomed to grant themselves freedom to the point of rape and murder. The mob rioted, murdered Botheric, and dragged his body through the streets. The news enraged Theodosius in Milan.

Theodosius was a man of vehement temper; he let go his wrath and called for slaughter. Ambrose interceded and got some sort of assurance that atrocity would not be done. But the master of offices, Rufinus (who in due time wanted to murder me), and probably Eutropius, the eunuch chamberlain, reinflamed the Emperor, and an order was sent off. Later Theodosius sent a second order to cancel the first, but it was too late.

The people of Thessalonica were invited to a grand display in the Circus. Thousands came. At a signal, soldiers rushed in and began to kill, making no exception for sex or age, guilt or innocence. In three hours of butchery seven thousand were slain.

Bishop Ambrose retired from Milan and wrote the Emperor a letter which amounted to excommunication: Ambrose would not officiate at the mysteries in the church while the Emperor was so soiled with blood. The thing went on for several months. Theodosius felt sorrow and remorse, and sent Rufinus to Ambrose with private apologies. But Ambrose, in the name of God and the church, held firm until at last the Emperor humiliated himself in public penance for some weeks, laying aside his imperial ornaments and entreating pardon in church with tears. Bishop Ambrose solemnly readmitted him to communion at Christmas.

From then on there was no doubt of Catholic power.

When the news reached us my father cried out, "What has Rome fallen to, when an Emperor bows to a bishop!"

Theodosius saw young Valentinian installed as co-Emperor, then returned to Constantinople. Arbogast, the Barbarian general of the Western armies, dominated Valentinian and within two years reduced the wretched young man to an enraged and trembling impotence. Then Valentinian was "found strangled" in his palace gardens at Vienne, and Arbogast, too wise to elevate himself to the purple, proposed Eugenius for that honor. My father, Symmachus, Flavian and other Pagan Senators knew Eugenius well. He had been a teacher of rhetoric in Rome, had risen to high public office—owing his advancement to the Pagan circle—and was considered a suave scholar and an amenable man of the world. Of course the legions under the command of Arbogast supported their general's choice, and so, too, did my father and his fellow Pagan Senators. Eugenius began to rule (or Arbogast began to rule through him), and one of the first clamors of my father's party was for the restoration of the altar and statue of Victory to the Senate House, together with revenue for the Pagan temples and the Vestal Virgins. Bishop Ambrose opposed such a move, but not with full force before he learned whether or not Theodosius would accept the usurpation. Then (just a year before) Theodosius had announced the elevation of his younger son, the boy Honorius, to the purple as Emperor of the West, and we all knew where we stood. Eugenius restored the altar and statue of Victory and granted to individual Senators, my father among them, large revenues with which to finance religious services in our Pagan temples and to use in behalf of the Vestal Virgins. Now Ambrose let off his full blast, excommunicated Eugenius, and awaited Theodosius.

In Rome it was a year of Pagan revival. My father was in high spirits and saw a return of old glories. He practiced divination and sought opportunities to fulfill priestly functions. By the beginning of this year our festivals were being celebrated with great show and color, those of Isis and Cybele leading on into the Floralia with its raucous and ribald gaieties. Both Flavian and my father, by the arts of divination, foretold the overthrow of Christianity and the victory of Eugenius, and my father even prophesied the death of Theodosius, which was treason. Divination, particularly if it hinted at ill for the Emperor, was punishable by death and confiscation of property.

Theodosius resorted to Christian magic. He sent his eunuch Eutropius into the desert to consult the holy hermit John, who spoke through the window of his otherwise sealed-up stone hut, and the hermit prophesied that Theodosius would win the conflict but would die in Italy.

The morning of the day of the priest and the owl, again in our palace hall, my father said, "When I was a boy, the Emperor Julian held me on his knees. His death was our calamity. Look, as you stand here, you, my son, have his features more than I. Theodosius the Spaniard, too, is a great man, but his extravagant splendor may well destroy us. The meeting of the armies and the fateful clash must come any day. Gregory, I am bound in honor, as your father and as a Julian, to offer you your chance and your choice."

"You mean I shall press north and join the army with Flavian? I could make it in three days and nights by swift relays of horses."

"No. . . . Let's step aside from this statue. I feel the great Julian's presence too strongly here."

We took about ten paces, until we stood beneath an arch where the god Mercury faced across to the goddess Minerva. My father looked into my eyes a moment before he spoke. He was preparing to say something that came hard to utterance.

"The Emperor Julian, you recall, was but a nephew of the Great Constantine. Constantine had sons and closer heirs. Young Julian was sequestered among the philosophers in the academy at Athens. When Constantine died and murder for power began, Julian was thought too insignificant to be murdered. And so he survived to become Emperor. There is time left for you to take ship to Athens. If things fall foul and Theodosius triumphs, you may, like the great Julian, survive for a great destiny. No man who lingers in Athens is thought dangerous. For some strange reason that is the soft deep spot of Empire where a man can ripen without assault. I warn you, most men who go there no longer ripen, but rot. The choice is yours. Will you go?" He stood back a full step and tilted his head, and watched closely, as if he would read my purpose as it formed in my eyes and features before I could utter it.

I said, "I thank you, Father, for honoring me both with chance and with choice. You have wrung it from your heart, against your sense of honor, by the depth of your love. You know as well as I do that it would not be the same with me as it was with the great Julian. The main differences are these: I am not the nephew of Theodosius, as he was of Constantine; and you, the man in most jeopardy, are my father. I stand where you stand. I stay in Rome!"

His arm instantly clapped on my shoulders, and his eyes rejoiced. "You are worthy to be Emperor. May the Gods ordain it!"

My wild and rude young laughter resounded in the halls of our palace.

And eight or ten hours later our fatal news came from the North. Theodosius had gathered his armies, crossed vast stretches, penetrated the Julian Alps, and won the victory. Arbogast, Eugenius, Flavian were dead. A dozen powerful Senators in Rome, including my father, were at the mercy of Theodosius for treason.

And we at the Tullus gardens had fought the ominous owl and had heard the fatal news.

My hand bled from the talons of the owl.

CHAPTER THREE

THE BURNING OF A PALACE

I HAD A SLAVE BIND MY THROBBING HAND WITH A STRIP OF linen, got dressed in two minutes, and summoned my bearers with the litter.

In addition to the bearers I had brought eight other attendants with me because of the tension of the times. I gave them instructions. "We will go home. The livery and litters of the Julians are well known in Rome. We will be recognized by malcontents who will be bold in the knowledge of our disaster. Keep in close formation, but hold to a decorous pace. It shall not be said that a Julian has taken fright and hurries through the streets of Rome."

To get from the Tullus palace to our own meant winding down from one of Rome's noble hills through narrow, tortuous places and up twisting ways to another hill crowned with palaces.

Moving along an eminence outside the Tullus walls, I looked out from my litter at the glorious blaze of Rome in the setting sun. Gold and bronze roofs of palaces, temples and majestic buildings were emblazoned by the sun, and the vast gorgeous city spread out its labyrinthine magnificence, Queen City of the world. Particularly the golden dome of the Temple of Jupiter, crowning the Capitoline Hill, flashed out spokes of radiance like a diadem above the city. The dark conical tops of noble trees stood like spires near mellow marble; I could see down into the vast Forum of Trajan, and I could see dark swaths of tenements where the mob spawned; I could hear the far day-end shout of the mob at the Circus. This was the eternal prolific city of my heart, and now its vast confines, its palpitant glory and its uneasy multitudes were webbed for me with threat and danger.

I wanted to reach my father as soon as possible. I was less distracted now and had begun to reason with myself. I tried to persuade myself that my father would not kill himself at the first stroke of the fatal news (as young Flavian had tried to do and the elder Flavian had done). My father was a practical man and would probably wait for the formal accusation of treason before running on his sword or opening his veins in the bath. But I could not feel sure of anything. I wanted to reach home quickly to add what courage I could offer to his own courage and wisdom, to let my father know he had a faithful son.

I could not relax on the pillows in the litter. I sat upright and tense, watching for the first sign of violence. My mind was like that suck-pool awhirl between Scylla and Charybdis. The shock of the fatal news had destroyed my certainties. I was, for the moment, a young man with no future except appalling danger.

We had not jogged more than halfway down the hill when in a narrow stinking passage between foul tenements of the poor we encountered a band of monks in dirty rags. They recognized our livery and our insignia on the litter and began to yell, shake their fists, and throw stones. "Down with the Julian apostates! Anathema on the antichrist!"

My attendants beat them off with sticks, and we proceeded. I had sat straight, not turning my head even when one of their stones hit me a sore blow on the cheek. Luckily the fracas was too short to develop into one of those riots swollen by the inrush of mobs of the wretched poor.

I had a deep sense of riot. I was with my father at Antioch, as a boy, during the cruel riots there. The beast of the crowd first broke loose, then ravaged and then was abased. And I heard the golden-mouthed John Chrysostom preach to the affrighted. It was there in the East, too, that I got my first alarming sense of how vicious and destructive a frenzied band of monks can be. All such things are spiritual furniture in the room and moment of my life.

My bearers were approaching the end of a narrow street to cross a park when we heard the angry tumult of a gathering mob. The space of the park was swarming with rioters. Already they had torches flaring in the dusk. I quickly learned from their outcries that it was not simply a riot against Pagans. Rome was gorged with several hundred thousand people who did no work, but lived on the free rations of grain, oil, wine and bacon provided by the government. A fleet of grain ships from

Africa was delayed, rations were short, and they were rioting. For generations the moral fiber of the Roman mob had been rotted by this guarantee of free subsistence. They would not work for anything, and when their needs were not met they would riot, burn, and plunder. Many of us had armed our more trustworthy slaves to protect us from this mob. Yet many Senators, including my father, made a good thing of these semifamines—often, I believe, delaying the grain ships on purpose and selling private stores of grain to the imperial treasury at a fat profit so the government could stop the riots by doling out supplies. I knew that right now my father's huge storehouse down on the bank of the Tiber was nearly full of grain.

I saw there was no chance of getting alive across that park, through the rising fury of that mob, and I ordered my bearers to turn back and proceed by another route. It took me half an hour longer to reach home. The sound of increasing violence sent up a roar of throaty terror from the streets below.

The little lamps were burning on our marble steps in honor of our doorway gods. I rushed into the house and cried out, hoping my father was still alive.

My father answered my third call, but before I realized he had answered I called desperately again, and I found him at work in his study.

I embraced my father with such evident joy and relief that he laughed with pleasure. Then, standing back, I told him earnestly, "The mob has seized on the victory of Theodosius and the delay of the grain ships to start rioting. They have already set fire to some buildings. Their anger is swifter than usual. We Julians will be targets of their fury. We should go at once to our villa on the Tiber until the worst violence is over."

The shifts of my father's head were quick and the penetration of his glance deep. His resonant voice was under the control of a steady will, but the blaze of his black eyes indicated inner force. I suppose my brindle hair (which was very nearly red in some lights) and my hazel eyes were midway between his brunette coloring and the blue-eyed, red-haired fairness of my mother. She and a late-born child had died together two years before, and my father and I had but each other.

He answered me with calm gravity. "Some of the Senators have done what you propose. They have left the city. Not I. As the Emperor Julian said, 'I hold it equally absurd, equally base, to seek or to decline the stroke of fate.' I'll live out this crisis here in Rome."

I tried a few arguments to persuade him, until his face turned red and stern.

He spoke with final severity. "We know liberty is dead and the predatory prosper. But we are still free Romans, free to end, if we must end, in unflinching honor."

I was proud of him. I was hearing the voice of an ideal Rome, of a Cato, a Brutus, a sound Julian. "What is your plan?" I asked him.

"To put my affairs in order. To commend you, so far as I may, to as many friends as may survive me. Then to await the word of the Emperor Theodosius. If the word is proscription, I shall not wait for public execution, but shall do the honors of my own death. It shall then be for you to leave Rome, going to such friends as may survive me and shelter you. Petition for the return of my confiscated properties. A few men die, and these storms pass. You have yet a future."

There were tears in my eyes, and I bent my head.

He put a hand of comfort on my shoulder. "Theodosius is a man, and what a man may do is not certain until he does it."

"Marcia—Calvena—through them an appeal to Ambrose, who has influence over Theodosius . . . "

"Shall I beg my life of a Christian? Look at me, son—shall I?"

I looked into his eyes. I stiffened my face. I said it. "You shall beg your life of no man. Neither shall I."

The light in his face was sudden and glorious. He embraced me. He kept himself in good condition; I could feel the hard vigor of his muscles. He said, "I have a son!"

I was embarrassed and changed the subject. "This of course," I said, "ends all thought of my marriage to Marcia. But the immediate problem for tonight is to protect our palace from being broken into and burned down by the mob. You have things to do. I'll arm a troop of fifty slaves and patrol our grounds all night. You may work without fear of interruption."

My father was a practical man. "Pick your fifty," he said, "from our Barbarians. They have more sinew for a night like this than our Greeks or Asians."

I called two of our most dependable freedmen, made them my lieutenants, and we mustered and armed about fifty of our stout Goths. It was not too soon. The sound of the mob was coming on in the dark, and there were already fires splurging red up into the black night above our hill.

I posted small armed groups round about our walled-in palace grounds, and then at the head of the remaining troop made regular rounds. We easily drove away a few first skulking vagabonds, but, though for a while no large force came, the night had in it the uneasy sound and smell of riot.

Before the real outbreak came I had time to reflect on just what it was I was defending, in addition to my father's life. It was not Paganism, nor was it special privilege of Roman nobility. As close as I could come to figuring the thing out, I had in mind an ideal of Roman justice, decency and order under which men could build good lives. I realized this was a vision of old virtues which had made Rome great, and that they were not being notably practiced in my day. Still, I loved them and was that night defending them from the insanity of mob action.

I knew such men as Jerome and the historian Ammianus had satirized the vicious and corrupt life of the people of Rome. Certainly here in the greatest city in the world, teeming with a million swarm of men, those who had scorn in their hearts could find any weakness, folly or vice they desired to prate at, and vice makes livelier news than goodness. But I knew from partaking of it that our circle of patricians, headed by such men as Senators Symmachus, Flavian and my father, neither led nor associated with those who led soft licentious lives. Among us, friends were honored, morals were respected, learning was favored, and Rome was loved. Perhaps these older men in my father's circle were more elegant than able, more conservative than daring, more eager to restore the past than to create the future; but they were what was left of the salt of the old noble Rome that produced its Cincinnatus, its Catos, its Antonines and lately its Emperor Julian.

Each time on my rounds my spirits fell when I took the narrow passage between our walls and those around the Fabian palace, adjacent to ours, where Marcia and her mother lived. I could see from certain lights that they were having some sort of modest dinner in there—perhaps, if I judged Calvena right, with two or three Christian clerics as guests. There seemed to me no hope now of my marriage to Marcia ever taking place.

It made me sad. I was of an age to marry and wanted to marry. But if my father were condemned and ruined, there was no chance of it. And though I felt no deep sentiments toward Marcia herself, I did not look for the future to present me with another bride her equal in dowry and in character. I sorely regretted that we had not married a year ago, and I took it for granted that I would probably never see her again.

I could not quite believe in the final fatality: my father condemned and, as he put it, doing the honors of his own death, our estates confiscated, myself an exile. And yet, without believing it, I carefully went over those probable events, even picturing myself on a ship bound for Africa, where in Carthage or Alexandria or as far off as Antioch in Asia Minor I could perhaps start in as a teacher of grammar or even rhetoric to make my painful and lonely way upward again in the world. Some friend of my father's in some distant province might even have the courage to employ me in legal administration because of my training at law.

I heard shouting at a distance and led my troop at double pace along our dark wall to a far corner, where we found at least a hundred rioters attacking our post there. One of my Goths was down, but two others were flaying about with savage swords. We surged into the mob and beat and slashed and drove it back, at first like a sullen beast. But the insanity that knit it together was shattered by our onslaught, and all its poor wretches became suddenly separate frightened individuals. They scattered yelling in separate ways of desperate flight, leaving behind a dozen or more dead and wounded.

It was at the end of this half hour of street fighting that I realized the sky was lighted behind my back. I thought another mob must have come from elsewhere and set torches to our palace. I gathered my men and led them back on the run.

Soon I saw it was not our palace but Marcia's that was ablaze, and that all the environs were choked with a yelling rioting horde. I had about thirty men. I dispatched one of my lieutenants to bring up the other twenty and, without waiting, formed my men into a phalanx and led them slashing into the mob. We cut our way gradually toward the entrance of the blazing palace.

I saw Marcia, her mother and three men trying to fight their way out of the palace, but the mob was driving them back into the flames with clubs, stones, torches. I recognized some of the Fabian slaves and realized they must have revolted and joined the rioters. I had no doubt there was trouble in many quarters of shadow-vast Rome that night, and I could not count on the prefect of the city getting troops to my aid in time to be of use.

My Goths were gorgeous fellows. I shouted to them: "Freedom to every man of you who comes out of this alive!"

And we thirty fought like a hundred, keeping a solid formation like a great and terrible many-armed beast. The fury of flames lighted our bloody labors. Those in the foreranks of the mob, shoved against us by the insane hordes behind, were in agony at our onslaught, for they didn't really know how to fight and they could not flee. We cut them down without mercy to strike terror into the whole throng and break up its idiot destructive power.

My hand, wounded by the talons of the owl, began bleeding again and streaked my slashing arm with red.

We reached the palace steps. I snatched Marcia in my arms and planted her in the midst of my men, then rescued her mother. Two of the clerics had fallen to their knees and were shouting thanks to God for this their martyrdom. The third was a giant fellow, whom I knew by the name of Pelagius. Some called him Scotus or Britto because he had come to Rome from Britain a dozen or so years earlier. He had been a sort of secretary to Pope Damasus, and made talks and wrote little books in favor of his own doctrine of free will. He thought men ought not to excuse their vices under the pretense that Adam's fall made them perforce sinners, then after a soft and rotten life consider themselves purified and saved by baptism on their deathbed. His teaching appealed to me as a sort of Christianity fit for living with in this world, but doctrinaires like Jerome dismissed him as a "hulking porridge eater."

At the moment, in the midst of our Southern passion and violence his colossal calm struck me as the last outrage of the comic. There he stood, massive, big-faced, with the blazing palace doorway behind him, the furious mob before him, the two priests crazy with lust for martyrdom on their knees beside him; and, turning his great curly head from side to side, he roared at the crowd: "What's all this! What's all this!" He was like some giant, standing arms akimbo, yelling at a horde of idiot pygmy children to stop their foolishness and go home to bed.

I let out one burst of harsh laughter, and yelled back at him, "It's your death, if you don't move!"

His great head stopped still, he glared at me. He shouted, "If I ought, I can!" Then with a swift and smiling calm he stooped down, yanked the two praying clerics to their feet, picked up a club, and came to the forefront of my men with me to help us beat our way back through the mob and away from the flames.

Each place I looked, I saw in the red smoky light a hundred wild and savage faces in which the latent individuality had been brutalized, degenerated, and obscured by the social singleness of mob violence, so that I was forced to think the divinity which irradiates the uplifted face of a free man is corrupted by leveling and absorption into the mass.

We had slashed and battered a path for scarcely a dozen paces before Marcia, squirming under the arms of my Barbarians, was there with us, a sword gripped by both hands and a Bacchanalian glory in her face, whacking away for all she was worth.

The huge Pelagius shouted, "Lay on, child! Deal strokes for Christ and Britain!"

"I fight for Gregory and God!" she yelled back at him, then looked at my face with an expression that was a prayer. Then her eyes flashed and she fought harder.

Such was the time and place and moment, fighting for our lives against a vicious Roman mob, that I received the mortal wound of Eros. Throughout all the troubles of our betrothal it had never occurred to me that I might fall in love with Marcia. But suddenly the tender bright mortality of her flushed, young and vivid face broke into my heart with the irrevocable anguish of human love. I could not speak. I let her see the tears in my eyes. Then I fought like a man gone mad with joy to save her life.

My other twenty men were fighting their way toward us through the smoky emblazoned air, and when our two groups joined, the insanity of the mob broke. Its fury fell, its pressures sank, its cowards fled, and single persons, awakened out of the mad dream of mob violence to their own manhood, turned in charity and grief to their own slain and wounded on the street, while roaring flames gutted the Fabian palace and lighted the wretched scene of our human passion.

I led our bloody and sweaty Goths to our palace, where my father took over the care of the two women and three clerics. Then I led my men back to scatter the remnants of the mob and save what we could from Marcia's home.

It was nearly dawn when I returned. Marcia and her mother were asleep. The two scant clerics had darted off to safety in some church. My father and Pelagius sat eating bread and meat and drinking; my father drank wine and Pelagius drank great quaffs of milk.

Pelagius pointed a sausage at me. "That girl fought like a Briton wench," he said, "and now she lies asleep like a baby, with dew on her lip. Young man, you would be a fool not to marry her!"

"I wish I could."

"Remember my slogan, boy. It's the beginning of a good Christian life. Always say to yourself: 'If I ought, I can!' Then God will be with you."

I looked at my father. His face was noncommittal. He knew our fortunes were at their worst. "You fought well, son."

"Yes. I led our men with skill, and they were brave. I promised them their freedom."

"They shall have it. You deserve food and rest."

"I'll take a plunge first."

I went out to our gardens, stripped off my clothes, and plunged into our bath. I swam about while the stars paled and the sky lightened.

At last I rose up dripping in the dawn and stood on the marble brink of the pool. Gazing straight across the garden where I saw a peacock and silver pheasants strutting around the pedestal of our statue of Venus, I made the first great vow of my life, lifting my arms and saying aloud: "I will have no other woman before Marcia!"

CHAPTER FOUR

THE FEARS OF OLD PROBUS

Neither did my father sleep that night. When i came into the house again I found him busy writing. Pelagius the Christian had retired to a couch in the corner of the room. His sleep was placid, with an occasional snore that was like a rumble of contentment.

Since our society operated on the patron-client system, my father, as one of the chief patrons in Rome, always devoted most of the morning hours to receiving his hosts of clients, hearing their troubles, arranging their difficulties, providing for their advancement, even giving food and money to those who were destitute. I generally helped him in these obligations, so that I would know better how to conduct myself when I became a rising young patron in my own right.

"Not many will come today, Gregory," he prophesied. "They will be afraid of compromising themselves."

"I was surprised to find you talking to Pelagius so long."

"Because he's a Christian cleric?" My father smiled at the huge sleeping figure. "He's an interesting man. I've met Britons before, and they have a deceiving vagueness of doctrine and purpose that conceals great ability for persistent action. He brought up an interesting point. He said it was by now widely known in Rome that I had recently practiced divination and had prophesied the death of Theodosius. He maintained I was in more danger from that than from my support of Arbogast and Eugenius. He said it would be bad politics for the Emperor to kill fifty or a hundred Senators for supporting a revolt, but good religion to dispose of one for practicing magic rites against the Emperor's life."

"What have you done that Holy John did not do? He predicted the Emperor's death in Italy."

"A man has to die somewhere, and this Christian visionary did not say when. Both Flavian and I in our divinations, confirming each other, found but a brief time left to Theodosius. Pelagius also pointed out what Theodosius must believe: that the hermit John speaks for God, while my message comes from what the Christians call devils. He was really warning me that there are fanatics in Rome only too willing to press the charge of treason on the grounds of divination."

There was something about my father's calm that I did not like. I narrowed my eyes for a sharper glance. Had he, perhaps, become somewhat fanatic himself? Had the thought entered his head that there could be Pagan martyrs as well as Christian ones? Being a political martyr would not appeal to him. Politics was a practical matter and might cost him his life only because it engaged his honor. But religious martyrdom might engage his passions and encourage him toward folly.

He was staring at the floor like a man in a dream. Suddenly he lifted his head, gave me a piercing glance, and told me, "Something went wrong at my former rites. Theodosius did win the battle. I am thinking of trying again, to confirm or refute my prediction of his death."

I had to attack that folly at once, before he committed himself to it. I knew warnings of his personal danger would be in vain; his whole manner was that of a man who already considered death as his companion.

I made my attack on grounds for which he was not prepared. "Father, I have vowed to marry Marcia. If anything prevents it—your ruin or her death—I shall never marry."

He was visibly shocked. He took two slow deep breaths while he searched my face. "When did you make such a vow?"

"Half an hour ago, standing on the edge of the pool, gazing directly at our statue of Venus."

He got up and paced the floor. His distress was acute. Finally he stopped before me and spoke in a low rapid voice. "You cannot go back on a vow made to one of the gods. You shall marry Marcia or marry no one. I consider my life forfeit. I shall no longer interfere. You will be able to do nothing with her mother. I know Probus favors the marriage personally, but fears it politically. Go at once to old Probus, make what terms you can, and effect the marriage within three days before word from Theodosius arrives to settle my fate. Once I am proscribed and my property confiscated, you can do nothing with Probus." He clenched his fists. "I only hope you don't have to become a Christian to fulfill your vow."

"I have vowed only that I would have no other woman before Marcia. But I will not buy her by pretending to believe what I do not believe. My love is a clear pain which I shall not soil with perfidy."

"Forget what I said about divination. Go at once to old Probus. I give you freedom to speak for yourself. I don't really know at this late moment of danger what argument you can devise to persuade him. He'll fear all Pagans today."

"I'll take Marcia and Calvena with me."

"And that Briton." My father went over to Pelagius and stirred him awake. "My son will conduct you and the ladies to the palace of Sextus Petronius Probus. They will undoubtedly want to live with him until their palace is restored."

The sleepy giant rose to his feet, rubbed his eyes with his fists, stretched his great arms. He sank to his knees and uttered a morning prayer, then came with me.

We had Marcia and Calvena awakened and presently were on our way, in several litters with bearers and attendants, to wait on Probus. I found that the way Marcia smiled at me in the morning, with her soft and clear and lovely face glowing with pure joy, made my heart desperately merry and seemed to double the flood of light pouring on all the world I saw.

I told Calvena I was going to ask Probus to settle our marriage at once.

Marcia, who did not repress her emotions, shouted like a joyous child, "I knew it had happened! I knew it!"

That I had fallen in love with her, I suppose.

Calvena was in a state of shock from the events of the fire and the attack of the mob. Her hand was cold, her face was drawn, and her black eyes, usually flaming with tensity, looked sick and dazed. She sighed. "I will do what Uncle Probus says."

We went to the enormous and splendid Anician Palace, where Probus, as head of the Anician family, was master.

Probus at first would not see me, but Marcia wheedled consent from him with a story of how I had saved her life and Calvena's. Then he insisted on seeing me alone, for fear others might make twisted accusations out of things we might say. He dismissed his other morning petitioners—and no man in Rome had more favor seekers.

He was old, he was frightened, and he was sick. "What are you trying to do, young Julian? Ruin me on my death bed?"

"Indeed, no, sir. I petition for my speedy marriage with Marcia. What are your terms for that?"

"Terms? Speedy? Your father is ruined, and now you want speedy terms. You want to drag me down in the odium of his ruin. You forget I am a Christian. You forget I am loyal to Theodosius."

"More or less."

"What? You dare?" His old hands trembled. His old face screwed up in a wrinkled stare of monkey fright. "Of course . . . I did aid Eugenius . . . but I kept Ambrose informed. My greater weight was for Theodosius. My wife is a devout Christian. I shall be baptized before I die."

"It is unlikely that Theodosius will call for a general proscription. He is not a man of small terrors, as Valens was. And my marriage to Marcia at this time would be taken as a symbol that the whole Pagan party wants peace. Theodosius has shown you many honors, and he would consider that in this you had repaid him by a brilliant stroke, allying the family of the Julians with your Christian grandniece."

He was impressed. He ceased trembling. The old man loved doing things to please people, only he was subject to hysterical fears for his health and his safety.

"If only your father hadn't practiced divination and prophesied the death of the Emperor! Will you become a Christian to wipe out that crime? Will you?" He sat up and poked his head forward eagerly. That old head had not yet been baptized; he was waiting to get all his sins in first.

I wanted to say no outright, but I knew it would frighten him off. I suggested a compromise. "Here, sir, was my idea. You have promised a splendid dowry to Marcia. It might be said that I was marrying her to gain that Anician wealth for the Pagan party. Let it be given to her under these conditions—and have them noised all over Rome—that I shall have no control or use or advantage of her wealth until such time as I may become a Christian, and that if she should die before I become a Christian, then all those estates of hers shall revert to Bishop Ambrose for him to devote to the use of the Catholic Church."

"Hmm!" He grunted as if I had struck his pudgy body a blow. He squinted his eyes and peered at me. "Did your father suggest that?"

"My father gave me freedom to speak for myself."

"You'll go far. Amazing skill at compromise! I'll tell you something I know. I have swifter means than any other man in Rome of getting news. I know Bishop Ambrose is even now interceding with Theodosius for clemency toward the Pagan party. If the sentence of death doesn't arrive in three days' time, the edict of mercy will come a few days later."

I pressed my advantage. "If you wait for the edict of mercy, you will not gain so great credit for having done a healing stroke between the parties for Theodosius. Ambrose, too, would applaud immediate action."

"Give me a day. Give me a day! This is a frightfully delicate matter for a man on his deathbed. I have chest pains at night. And my legs and feet—oh, how my legs and feet hurt, even in a tub of water! Yesterday my stool had flecks of blood in it. I have five doctors in constant labor to save me. All arrangements have been made for my baptism at a moment's notice. There is nothing that would more delight my dying heart than to witness your marriage to Marcia, but suppose Theodosius should be in a passion? Remember Thessalonica! He's a violent man first and repentant afterward. Give me a day to think it over. Now my heart is palpitating. I need my physicians. Go, before I collapse."

I left the presence of the wealthiest man in the Empire, excepting only the Emperor.

Marcia had persuaded her mother to allow her to wait where she could see me. The two women stood together near a column in a colonnade around a garden where flowers bloomed and a fountain played.

"Will he, Gregory?" Marcia took my hand.

"He's frightened. He wants a day to think. There's hope."

Calvena looked cold and depressed. "You're not married," she said. "Let go his hand."

Marcia blushed.

I bowed formally to each of them in turn, but I winked at Marcia, and as I turned and left, her laughter rang out in merry peals.

CHAPTER FIVE

I MAKE A MOVE TO PROTECT MY FATHER

I WENT STRAIGHTWAY TO HERACLIAN TO DEAL FOR PROTECTION for my father, and found Heraclian stripping jewels from a sobbing girl.

I had found out this about myself and other young men: We did not quite understand the world as our fathers saw it. Between a son and a father there is always the barrier of authority, and I think a youth needs an older man outside his family to help him across the line of dependence to manhood. I know I had been in need of an interpreter of the world of action who was older and more experienced than I, but who did not have parental authority and who was closer to my generation than to my father's. Heraclian was the man I had turned to for this sort of leadership.

Now that my father, in these weeks of crisis, had so fully brought me to himself as his companion and equal, I saw clearly how far Heraclian fell short of my father in nobility, in wisdom and in love.

Heraclian was about ten years older than I. He was one of those men of driving ambition who in time of social strain and trouble use predatory rather than creative powers to advance themselves. Heraclian knew whom to strike, and when, to gain for himself a higher foothold. I never really learned where he came from; to me he was a man with an obscure past and a brilliant future. He had been in Rome some years, using law courts as his means of advancement, with the set aim of rising in public office to senatorial rank. He got most of his money by speculation in building and by exploiting tenement properties. The housing situation in Rome for the majority of the people was abominable, and in any great city a shrewd man can make profit out of abomination. I did not like Heraclian for the predatory strain in his character. I had been young enough and had heretofore been secure enough so that I did not fear it. I liked him for other reasons.

He was a handsome man, dark, saturnine, who kept his body in remarkably hard condition despite more festal living than was common in my father's circle. He was not of our circle, though he had gradually been pressing through me toward my father's patronage. He was what might be called the leader of the young Christian opportunists, those who became Christians for practical and political reasons. I was fascinated by his hard realism, by his thoroughly Roman understanding of the adage that "what works is good." Heraclian's success confirmed my opinion that men who get things done do not bother their heads about the religious truth of what they are doing, especially if their field of action is war, business or politics. They concentrate on the effectiveness rather than on the value of their actions. Heraclian, being such a man, gave me many insights into the operations of power in society.

At the time I had great admiration for his severe skills and was flattered by his readiness to be my tutor. He admitted frankly that I was worth his while. "Every man," he said, "is selfish. You need never doubt a man's motives—just figure out what it's worth to him to do what you want, and if you find the right pressure you can make him do it for you at less than his price."

I also enjoyed and admired what I might call the sporting side of his nature: He knew the horses and charioteers most likely to win; he knew how to give a sumptuous dinner to a group of young men; when a Senator's son was chosen to spend thousands on becoming Praetor and giving the public games Heraclian was an expert adviser on how to get spectacular effects, where to secure animals, gladiators and other elements of planned atrocities that won the support of the Roman public. Finally, he had a passionate interest in the theater and liked training female pantomimists to a high standard of performance.

The girl he was punishing when I came in was a dancer. I found them in his dining room, which had not yet been cleaned up after his last night's dinner. On the tables, the couches and the floor were the scatterings of a festal night. I had never seen the girl before. She crouched and trembled in front of him while he stripped off her bracelets, her anklets, her necklaces and rings and berated her in his sharp resonant voice.

"Most abominable performance! You ruined my dinner last night. That you should slip on the floor where food had been thrown I could forgive. But your gestures! Your timing! Your handling of the veils! Awkward, gross! You forgot everything I have taught you. You're only fit to dance for the lewd rable in some low den."

He saw me standing there and turned some of his vehemence on me. "This Furia has proved herself a stupid little fool. I intend to have her lashed so that the scars and welts on her back will render her unfit to display her body. I'll turn her into a slave of the stewpots."

The girl shuddered and sank wailing against the wall. Heraclian dangled the jewels in his hands—powerful hands with black hair on their backs and broad stubby fingers. He looked at the girl in contempt, and then, cautiously searching my face, asked, "What favor do you seek, young Julian? This is not a pretty time for one in your position to compromise my doorway."

I had expected such frankness; I knew the man well enough not to be offended. "My position is excellent, Heraclian. I may be of use to you."

That startled him. He set the jewels down on a table. "It will take about three days for news to reach Rome that your father is proscribed. If I know him, he will end his own life, and you will be a pauper."

"You and old Probus hold different views of the situation. I have just come from Probus."

To Heraclian the name and wealth of Probus were symbols of his own towering envy and ambition. "He let you in?"

"Certainly. I have persuaded him of the wisdom of letting my marriage to Marcia take place within a few days."

He searched my face to detect a lie, but was evidently uneasy. "Old Probus! If he considers such a step, he must have more news than I know. Come. Tell me the facts." He spurned the girl Furia with his sandal, and said, "Lie there. I'll dispose of you later."

And indeed she was lying now on the floor against the wall, her dark hair disheveled about her narrow strange face. She looked about seventeen years old, was scantily dressed in a few veils, and had dark slim legs and small firm breasts. She was a Greek. She gave me a swift agonized glance from wet eyes, like an animal begging mercy. I saw no immediate way to interfere in her behalf, but while I reclined on a couch with my back to her, talking to Heraclian, I was conscious of her fear-steeped body shuddering on the floor.

I had not been tutored by Heraclian for nothing. I wanted his promise before I gave him my facts. "The point is," I said, "that you will gain nothing now by any attempt to further the ruin of my father. If you hear of any of the Christian party wanting to press charges against my father for divination, you have most to gain by putting a stop to it."

"When a great man is ruined the few small men who tear him down are bound to gain."

"But when those small men try and fail their disaster is certain."

"If Probus favors your marriage to his Marcia, it would be worth my while to stop certain moves against your father. If you can give me facts to demonstrate why Probus would dare such a step, I could hold off those moves temporarily and stop them when and if the marriage takes place."

I took a deep breath; my tension was eased. Pelagius had been right in warning my father against this danger, and I had come to the right man to have it removed.

I gave him a detailed account of the night and the morning. The point he seized on was old Probus' news that Bishop Ambrose was interceding with Emperor Theodosius for clemency toward the Pagan party.

Heraclian was honest about it. "You've done me a favor to come to me direct with that news. I must move at once to stop certain plans afoot here in Rome. Meantime, you do all you can to hasten the marriage. This is the chance I've waited for."

"I knew I could save you from a false step. I'm glad to have done so. But you're too swift for me. Why is it the chance you've been waiting for?"

He laughed and slapped my knee. "You've plenty to learn, young Julian. I'll win the governorship of a province from this, instead of the ruin I might have if you hadn't told me. Stick by me, and we'll go far."

And then, suddenly sober, intense, direct, he delivered me one of those lectures I so much valued and admired as an interpretation of the world of affairs. "Forget Rome the city; consider Rome the Empire. What is going on? By Christ and Jupiter, it is magnificent and terrible! Our Bishop Ambrose is forgetting the Empire and building a church. We Christians don't give a fig for this world, but must establish theocratic dominion over souls. Christ has said our kingdom is not of this world. Once we get the souls, we'll have the world, too. Ambrose and Jerome know that. You Pagans think of Goddess Rome and forget it was not the gods but the legionaries that gave you empire. There stands Theodosius, the single Emperor, bearing more worldly weight than one man can—and who are his soldiers, who are his generals? Stilicho the Vandal, Richomer the German, Alaric the Goth, Gainas, another Barbarian. These Barbarians don't know it yet, but theirs is the fist that holds the Empire together and can rend it apart.

"And who is left after Theodosius? Suppose the prophecy of Holy John of the Wilderness is true, that Theodosius shall die in Italy, and that the treasonable divination of your father is true, that Theodosius shall die soon? His two sons are left, Arcadius, not bearded yet, weak, under the power of Rufinus, who will cut throats to become Emperor himself; and Honorius, still a boy and weak and stupid, with Stilicho right there in Milan, general of the armies. What would happen if Theodosius died? Who would stop the murder of Arcadius and Honorius, leading to the mortal clash between Stilicho and Rufinus? If anybody—if it can be done—only Bishop Ambrose, on the spot in Milan.

"Aside from those dark possibilities, the present real situation is this: Theodosius will make a dozen, a hundred changes in office. New governors for old. The moment word reaches Rome that Theodosius gives amnesty to the Pagan party, a dozen leading men will gallop night and day to Milan to thank the Emperor on their knees and petition for governorships, to bribe and wheedle their way into favor with Stilicho and Rufinus and pray their way with Ambrose. Thanks to your news, I shall leave today and be there ahead of them, and make the advantage of time stand me in stead of rank. I'll have my province before the swarm arrives. The moment you're married to Marcia, you should leave Marcia with her mother and follow me to Milan. I can use your new influence with Ambrose in behalf of both of us. Only fools would stay in Rome at a moment of crisis and opportunity like this!"

"You'll say a word, before you go, in this matter of my father's divination?"

"I'll stop what has been started. Also I'll spread the rumor that immediately after your marriage you are going to Milan to have Bishop Ambrose instruct you in Christianity."

"That would not be true."

"It would be effective. And if you go to Milan, it would also be true, for Ambrose instructs the whole city. Once in Milan, you may not be converted, but you cannot escape the instruction." His eyes flashed with high humor of his certainty and power.

Affection for my father and admiration for Heraclian's skill dazzled my lonely sense of truth. I accepted his offer and stood up to go. I saw Furia lying there on the floor, her face now buried in her arms. "Don't have her whipped. She's a child."

"Do you want her? I'll give her to you."

"Not on the eve of my marriage."

He laughed. 'She's a greedy bitch. A hundred lashes wouldn't hurt her half so much as she suffers from my taking away the jewels I and my guests have given her."

Looking down at her slim long legs and the dirty soles of her bare small feet, I had a sudden desire to see her dance. "Tell her to dance for us, and let me judge if she deserves the punishment."

"Done! Furia!"

She stirred and sat up at the lash of his voice.

"One dance. That in which you ruined my party last night. Your life hangs on your skill."

While she stood, shook her hair, and breathed deeply to still her terror, Heraclian told me it was Alcyone she would dance, Alycone seeing her husband Ceyx drowned at sea and mourning so bitterly that the gods turned her into a kingfisher and Ceyx into another sea bird.

The girl began to move, I thought, still in real terror; but soon I saw she was wrapt in the power of imagination, approaching the stormy sea cliff to behold the drowning of Ceyx. These dancers, when they had native skill and sound training, could fill the imagination of the beholder with the throb of legendary life; and this Furia, knowing she faced the mutilation of her body and the ruin of her hopes if she failed, put on a performance of strange and penetrating beauty, all the more effective for its purity and restraint. I could hear the cry of the desolate sea birds while she mourned her lost lover in flowing attitudes of grief.

When she came to silence of feet and stillness of body in her last motion I blurted out, "Give her the jewels, Heraclian! She's magnificent, and if you taught her—"

"Of course I taught her!"

"—then you're a genius!"

Furia flung herself at my feet and embraced my knees to thank me, and Heraclian, who had a flair both for cruelty and for generosity of gesture, broke out in great laughter and spilled her jewels back over her smoky hair. She instantly let go of me, gathered up her baubles, and fled from the room, her narrow face flashing with greed and joy, her fingers fiercely clutching the jewels.

"Thanks for another service," Heraclian said. "I can make use of that girl in Milan. Stilicho likes praise, Ambrose likes piety—but Rufinus likes flesh!"

CHAPTER SIX

APPARITION OF DIONIE

WHEN I GOT HOME I FOUND MY FATHER HAD BEEN RIGHT in his prediction. There had been a great falling off in the number of clients who had come that day to honor him as their patron and to seek his favors. Not having advance news such as I had passed on to Heraclian, they no doubt felt they would compromise their wretched desires by association with my father. I felt this desertion of him more deeply than I had felt the first efforts of Probus and Heraclian to rebuff me on the same grounds.

But my father was cheerful about it in a new quiet way. He said he was pleased, for it had given him time to write letters in my behalf. He sat at a table, writing with ink on papyrus rolls, and light from a window shone on the bald crown of his head. His motions had a quiet certainty, his voice had a convincing integrity. He said he had decided the wisest thing for me to do was to make ready at once to sail for Antioch in Asia, where an old friend of his was then governor and would surely take me into his service for a new start in life. He pointed to a roll of papyrus already fitted into its little bright leather case. "I have written him at length."

My father seemed to have forgotten that I had been busy on affairs affecting us both. He so fully considered himself a condemned man that it took some time to convince him that my marriage to Marcia was fairly assured. When I finally explained that Bishop Ambrose was pressing to avoid death reprisals against my father and other Pagan leaders he took it not like a reprieve but like a wound. His face paled, his nose seemed to narrow into a deathlike sharpness, his eyes looked stricken. For a moment he could not speak.

Finally he bowed his head and said, "Ambrose the Christian gives me back my life. That is the greatest humiliation of all."

I was too young to have learned what may be a man's most bitter lesson and one which comes more often in middle age than in youth; and that is, for a man to find himself so humiliated and helpless in the ruin of his hopes—hopes not suited to the inexorable onflow of nature and history—that even the gift of survival is more bitter than the invitation of death. I could not understand that my father's heart and will to live were broken—that he saw nothing left for himself but to endure the despair of a frustrated life.

I was bound in honor and filial piety to tell him how I had got Heraclian to stop action against him by the Christian party on grounds of treasonable divination.

"Why did you think I desired to live?" he asked me bitterly.

"I desired you to live, Father."

He put his hands to his face and wept before me, a thing I had never seen in my life till then. Presently he said, "All the gods are one God, and He breaks the human heart."

At that point a secretary came in bearing a wax tablet just received from Sextus Petronius Probus. It was addressed to my father, who opened it and read what old Probus had written on the two surfaces with his own aged and infirm hand.

My father seemed to be reconstructing some scene in his mind, readjusting himself to new fatalities. When he spoke he gave me a paraphrase of Probus' letter, enlarged by his own commentary. "Probus has certain news, Gregory. Paganism is ruined. You will not live to see Rome happy and fortunate again under our gods. One of the old man's swift private messengers has arrived on a lathered and exhausted horse from the North with word that Bishop Ambrose has won a promise from Theodosius that no Senators will be executed. Surely this confirms the fall of the Empire and the rise of the Catholic Church? Only Flavian, who fought and lost and honorably killed himself in defense of our gods, is to have his properties confiscated. I wish I had fought and died beside him. Probus wants your wedding held tomorrow, before this news officially reaches Rome. He sees in that speed the advantage you suggested, that he will gain credit for healing a breach when he might be supposed to fear that move as dangerous." My father laid his hands flat on the table and looked at me severely.

I was unprepared for the bitterness and accusation that flared in his eyes. "What can I do, Father? You feel a personal injury from me in this, and I have not meant it."

He slapped the wax tablet with a vehement hand and declared furiously, "This marriage would now be a monstrous thing. I forbid it!"

At first I froze in fear of his anger and authority. Then I began to tremble as I could feel myself about to defy my father for the first time in my life. "I'm a grown man. You have no right to forbid it."

He talked with the speed of the anger that reddened his face. "It will be said we hastened this marriage to save my life. It is bad enough to be ashamed of Rome without my son shaming me in the sight of Rome. I shall send a message immediately to Probus denouncing the whole affair."

"I shall go there myself and tell him I am ready to marry Marcia tomorrow."

We glared at each other. My fists were clenched and I felt sick, but I summoned all the power of my will to hold my eyes steadily on his. My father opened his mouth to say something, but then, as if his tongue were paralyzed and his throat dry, he said nothing. Neither did his eyes waver from mine. But a change came over his face. He was looking at me as if he had never seen me before, and as if he were amazed, touched to the heart by what he saw.

As if the vision were too much for him, he lowered his head. He spoke softly, almost to himself. "My life is canceled. I want you to marry Marcia."

Then, looking down between the crevices of his fingers as into great depths, he quoted that lovely Greek poem: " 'The times are impious, and new gods flatter inexperienced hearts to seize the world; I shall follow you, O gods of my fathers, into immortal chasms of remembered time.' "

He looked at me gravely, with sorrow and love in his face, and said a strange thing: "Every son must learn to forgive himself for becoming a man by the death in his heart of his father's authority. I did not know until now that it is at that moment when authority is dead and the boy is free that a man most loves his son."

He rose abruptly, stood one moment with his hand on my shoulder, then raised one arm before his face like a shield and walked rapidly from the room. I heard him call out my mother's name in a stricken voice. There was no one left on earth to comfort him.

At the thought of getting married tomorrow I became quite practical for an hour or two. After the wedding, I would bring Marcia here, so first I gave orders concerning the preparations to be made, with special attention to the bridal room. Then I sent slaves to invite my friends to the wedding. I had a light lunch, and should next have looked for my father to help with other details.

Instead, I ordered a litter and had myself carried to see Marcia, which was foolish. She was not allowed to see me. Everybody there was too busy for guests. They didn't want me near the place before tomorrow. These messages were given me, with genial commentary, by the big Pelagius.

"Poor wretch," he said, smiling while he said it. "The groom is a nonentity the day before the wedding. Now, don't go get drunk. Don't kill time in bad company. If you had the sense to be a Christian, you would have plenty of business on your knees between now and the wedding. Hymen, Bacchus and Venus will just get you into trouble if you dote on them. Avoid the baths, avoid the wine cellars. Marcia is a tender and innocent child. You'd better just go home and learn to pray. You ought. You can."

I felt like punching his big stomach. But I liked him, too. "Tell Marcia I love her."

"She knows that. It's the most surprising thing about this wedding. But I'll tell her anyway. When a Roman loves the woman he's going to marry, he's half a Christian already."

I snorted, waved good-by, and had my litter carried toward Dionie's house. She, at least, would let me talk out the tumult in my heart. But then I thought how gossips would make scandal of the appearance of my litter at Dionie's house the day before my wedding. I dismissed my litter and went on afoot.

As I approached Dionie's house I stopped to think again. If she were home, she would certainly let me talk for a while, but while I talked I would be watching her face, her lips, the subtle motions of her body. She had a charming way of loosening a garment. There would come a moment of silence in which I would forget tomorrow in the desire of today. I looked down the street, saw where it led, and, beating my palm with my fist in a kind of irresolute distraction, I turned in my tracks and walked the other way. For some distance I felt like a sore wound the loss of the passionate pleasure I was willfully denying myself, and I was shocked and made heartsick by a new knowledge of the divisions, depths and complexities of my own nature.

I didn't feel like going to any of the temples or to the Forum or places of noble show. I felt lonely and small, and kept to back ways and narrow places. I got clear down to the Tiber, near one of the bridges, and saw a few small boats unloading produce on wharfs. I thought it regrettable that a strong young man of my class couldn't sweat in the sun at honest labor like that. I envied some of the Africans, Greeks and Barbarians I saw carrying loads on their bare shoulders, wiping sweat from their eyes with grimy wrists and lifting their chests with great intakes of breath when they dumped their burdens.

I wandered on. I came to a slave market. The dealer, who looked like a Syrian, caught my eye, noted my dress and that I wore jewels, and at once assumed that I was some patrician's son wanting to buy a girl concubine. He insisted he had a virgin, lovely, beautiful; he had been keeping her hidden in his hovel until just the right purchaser should come along. He didn't dare touch me, but he did all he could to enchant me into his inner precincts. The slaves he had on display in his outer yard were a cheap lot, looking dull and stupid, no doubt destined to be sold at low prices for trivial uses.

"I'll buy the girl," I said suddenly.

"Don't you want to see her first? Come. She will undrape. You will be transported. I'll make a fair price, but first you must see her."

I took off a gold chain. "I'll give this for her. Bring her out."

He seized the chain greedily and felt its weight. His face screwed up with cunning. "Ah, you trust me! You know her worth at my word!" I must have paid him far more than he had hoped to get for the girl.

He brought her out. She was a slim frightened child, and looked hungry. Perhaps she was thirteen years old. She cringed from the slave dealer, and she cringed from me.

I felt her shoulders with my fingers, and said, "Come on, girl. You'll have a good meal and a decent bed tonight."

She started walking along two steps behind me. I told her to come to my side, I wanted to talk to her.

She said her name was Amantha. Her parents lived in a village in the north of Italy. Only a month ago they had sold her as a slave to pay off taxes. "It was me or my brother. He was younger, but he will grow to be stronger and more able to help them. And then he is a boy. The baby was a girl. We put her out on the hillside. After two days she stopped crying, and animals took her away. So they sold me and paid the taxes, and how they'll pay them next year I don't know."

"If I gave you your freedom and sent you back home, what would happen?"

Tears came into her eyes. Her voice trembled, and I was appalled at the child's honesty. "They would sell me again. What else could they do?"

"Listen, Amantha. I am getting married tomorrow. I am going to have you bathed and cleaned and properly dressed. I want you to be maidservant to my wife. She and I will take good and gentle care of you as long as we live."

Without a word she took my hand and clung to it all the way home.

My father had been busy all day and he had an important engagement for dinner that night, but he had taken pains to provide for me. To my surprise, I found he had arranged a fine dinner and had invited a number of my young men friends. He provided us with the best of his wines, and before he went out he started off our feast with a libation: "To Venus, to Marcia, and to my son!"

We had entertainment while we dined and more wine to drink than young men needed. We reclined at the tables while musicians performed, girls danced and singers sang us songs of Hymen. Anacreon and Catullus were our chosen poets that night, and Priapus was the god of our conversation. Of course many of the ribaldries of my friends were directed at me, and I was now and then distressed by an unbalanced and too personal emphasis given to stories of sexual prowess. Ribaldries occasionally became obscenities. But on the whole it was a loud, robust and hilarious young male party, and I was grateful to my father for arranging it.

In the end, in my room alone, I had to face what I had been avoiding, the shock of solitary silence through a lonely hour. The strains of music had died away and the fumes of wine were out of my head. My thoughts in solitude made the wide swing from the sexual and impersonal to the religious and individual aspects of love, and I searched my heart for understanding.

I thought of Marcia. She would not have spent the night at lusty ribaldries. I could imagine her praying, after the fashion of Christians and especially a young Christian girl tutored by the writings of Jerome and Ambrose and nurtured in a circle of devout women. Would she not be on her knees, with her palms together and her eyes lifted in a final appeal to Christ to forgive her frailty and bless our marriage? She would pray for me, too.

I had been deeply impressed by what had happened to my father during these past fateful hours. I could hear his somber voice telling me that Paganism was ruined, that I would not live to see Rome happy and fortunate again under our gods and that the fall of the Empire was being fulfilled by the rise of the Christian Church. Such words would have been but interesting intellectual ideas in themselves, had I not seen their meaning symbolized and made incarnate in the spiritual suffering of my father.

I gave my thanks, indeed, to Venus. But presently I wondered which of the many gods had true concern for my future; and presently I wondered if any of our numerous gods was more than an ineffectual shadow of my own immortal longings. Divinity was like an awesome abyss above my head, and I in the dark sweep of eternity stood naked and alone in my mortal flesh.

I could hear Heraclian speak again. What he had said about this being a moment of crisis and opportunity I now saw in another guise. I almost heard the rending sound of ruin as the strife of forces—Pagan, Christian, Barbarian—wrenched apart our society into fragments of destruction.

Then again I felt the touch of Dionie's fingers on my arm and heard her say: "There is no answer to life, young Julian. You live it!"

It seemed to me that my only hope and beginning had to be found in simple human companionship, communion and comfort at Marcia's side. The core and meaning of human life must be in the union of man and woman in love. As a man and a woman loved and treated each other in their union, so would they build their lives, so would they love and treat living things in the world about them, and if they were good to each other, their goodness would be a radiance that spread. There was, I thought, a little madness in all acts and conceptions of solitaries; only from a union in love of man and woman could human good arise.

Then I was frightened as I began to understand what it really was that I felt toward Marcia. Certainly I loved her—but why did this love come upon me as an irrevocable anguish instead of as a simple and radiant joy? Why had there been so much sorrow in my father's face when he told me the moment had come when he loved me most? Why had the child Amantha, whose parents had sold her into slavery, accepted their betrayal of her life with such clear love and simple tears? Why did the Christians speak of Christ, the epitome of love, as a man of sorrows and acquainted with grief? Was there something perverse, either in human life or unfortunately only in myself, that made love so silent a pain?

I decided it was only myself. Some flaw in my character had deceived me and had shut me off from the simplest purity of perfect joy. How, if I loved Marcia at all, could I feel as I felt, that I cradled her in my grief and sang in the presence of her vulnerable heart the old song of infinite sorrow? In the deep of that lonely night it began to seem to me a monstrous thing that I should marry one so tender and lovely as Marcia only to gather her in to the death she herself had wakened in my heart.

For now I saw death clearly—in my father, in myself, in our Roman world. I saw death as the subtle and monstrous destroyer, not as a part of life but as the paralyzing enemy of life.

Then I thought of Furia.

I remembered Furia, Heraclian's dancing girl, shuddering on the floor against the wall, and the little bare soles of her feet as she had danced before us Alcyone's story of grief, and the faint beat of her bare soles on the cool stone was the startled music of antique pain. Not Furia the girl shuddering on the floor in temporal fear of the lash, not Furia the girl clutching her jewels again, flushed with worldly greed; but Furia the dancer, the mortal for a moment immortal in her dance, revealing everlasting visions of love through the flowing attitudes of grief, lived and moved again in my mind with all the interpretative power of creative imagery and symbolic rhythm.

Furia taught me the meaning of human love by the perfection of her showing of grief.

For was it not this that I felt toward Marcia and that my father felt toward me? That one I loved was mortal? Knowing that, I suddenly knew death at the heart of life, but death as a great intensification of beauty, as a deepening power of tenderness, as a source of compassion, until grief itself became the light my love held up to lead me through the dark windings of human destiny while I gave out of my soul what shelter I could to Marcia, my companion, mortal at my side.

For how could a man who feared death and shunned grief know the meaning of human life at all? The desire for a safe, a secure and a prolonged mortality was a blind, cruel and deceiving passion, and the flight from sorrow was the death of the heart. Love—love of man and love of God—was lighted by grief and made pure by the presence of death, and the very essence of immortality was the utter suffering frailty of my moment of mortal being in the flow of infinite time.

I had worked my way to a vision of human life more penetrating—and more dangerous—than I had as yet the character or the experience to sustain. We sometimes see a truth beyond our strength to bear, when our spirit strains to enlarge our life. I was too young, too weary and yet too vivid in the flesh to fall on my knees, sobered and humbled.

Instead I felt eased and delighted. My conscience was at peace, for this much was now clear to me, that I loved Marcia and was free and eager to make her my wife. I was a happy man! I could feel the joyous grin that must be making my whole face shine.

I loved my father. I loved the whole world. I loved Furia, too, the memory of whose dance had resolved my fright—that wild and pagan child, with her swift slim legs and sudden toss of her enchanted greedy face.

I blew Furia from my mind with a puff of gracious gaiety. Then I sang to my light heart one of Sappho's tender songs:

> " 'Come, Venus, come
> Hither with thy golden cup,
>   Where nectar-floated flowerlets swim.
> Fill, fill the goblet up;
>   These laughing lips shall kiss the brim—
> Come, Venus, come!' "

My conscious mind was brilliant with remembrance of Marcia's gay and radiant warmth. And, as a young man will on the night before his wedding, I made a circle of my arms in the air before me, as if I were clasping Marcia to my breast. I could almost feel the throb of her body in my arms. Then I lay down and slept like a child through the deep hours of the night.

But I was not a child. I had touched and been touched by many lives, and strange forces were at work, and I was aroused by a startling experience.

I was less superstitious than many of my contemporaries, less superstitious even than my father; but I had never conceived of myself as a purely physical entity, a sort of incomprehensible congeries of dancing atoms (after the fashion celebrated by Lucretius) in a vortex of other clashing changing congeries of atoms. That would be strange enough, but mortal life is stranger than that. I do not know if time has folds and windings in eternity beyond our human comprehension, so that sometimes events to come present their apparitions to us beforetime. I don't know.

This is what I saw and heard:

Suddenly Dionie—an older and changed Dionie—stood beside my bed, with her face wounded and her clothes torn, and cried: "Save me! Save me!"

This apparition of things to come frightened me. Why was she older? Why was she ravaged? What was her claim on me? And from what was I to save her?

I started from my bed, flung myself between her and the door to fight off her pursuers and assailants. She wept on my shoulder.

I was wide awake. I knew it was Dionie . . . and yet suddenly I saw it was dawn and I stood in my room alone. . . .

But years later, on a certain night when Ravenna was distressed with murder, this apparition was to be confirmed in reality . . . or in what we mortals naïvely call reality.

CHAPTER SEVEN

THE LAUGHTER AND DANGER OF LOVE

MARCIA WAS LAUGHING AS I CAME TOWARD HER, AND HOW shall I say what wonder of innocence and youth I saw in her face? It was not laughter aloud that I mean, but a lovely laughter of her spirit greeting my soul with love as I reached for the warmth of her hand. Her mouth was serene in the delicate motions of a hovering smile, and her large clear dark eyes were eager with mirth. I thought I had never seen a face so young, so pure, so radiant with simple faith.

I knew Dionie was watching me. I could feel it, though I did not know where she stood, the way you can feel it when a cat watches you from under a chair or from the branch of a tree. Suddenly I was haunted again by the full force of the strange apparition of Dionie crying in the night—some future night yet to be lived—for me to save her, and I suddenly dreaded what Dionie might do to the radiant peace in Marcia's face.

But Marcia, without a word, raised a finger and firmly rubbed the crease from between my eyebrows until I smiled down into her eyes. I was drawn into the charmed and happy realm of her own innocence. I clung tighter than I had expected I would to Marcia's direct warm hand.

Instead of a Pagan marriage, with Marcia in a flame-colored veil and a Pagan priest examining bird entrails for favorable omens, our wedding was a Christian ceremony in which Marcia wore a white veil and the Bishop of Rome, who was not so severe about mixed marriages as Ambrose, was the priest. In other details our marriage festivals, Christian and Pagan, were so much alike that you couldn't tell them apart.

When the sacrament was concluded the massive Pelagius beamed on us and said, "You ought; you did. God bless you, children!"

But then he took one of my hands and one of Marcia's in his big paws and embarrassed us by a loud slow boom of warning: "Avoid—avarice! Avoid—ambition! Avoid—adultery! These three vices cause more divorces in Rome than any others. But what is the slippery sin that leads down and down to perdurable damnation? Convenience! Avoid—*avoid convenience!* Have charity, have faith, have children: Those are the virtues that hold man and woman together within the smile of God!"

Marcia's cheeks had flared crimson, and my mouth had set hard, which made the hearty Briton monk laugh loud. Then he gave us each a kiss of peace and beamed and wheeled away.

I saw Dionie peering at me over her shoulder from within earshot, with a feline insouciance in her water-green eyes. I dreaded the meeting that must surely take place between Dionie and Marcia.

During the first hours of the festival Dionie kept her distance from me, but she cast me swift, intense and intimate glances that made me feel uneasy. I did not know what delicate cruelty might delight her.

Her clothes were of the Alexandrian style, that is of colorful, clinging and filmy material, so that men watched the movements of her body with caught interest. But her highly developed sense of beauty, curbing her motions within the design she meant to offer, left an impression of grace, dusky richness and charm, a sensuous vision of Pagan loveliness to haunt the mind.

Marcia saw me intercept one of Dionie's glances. She turned and looked frankly at Dionie, and then with an intuitive penetration that amazed me said, "Cleopatra has come to Rome again. Only this one is not quite brave enough to be a queen. Take me to meet her, Gregory."

"Later." I drew Marcia away. "The poet is going to recite our wedding ode. Let's get wine and a comfortable place."

We took our golden cups of wine and sat on a marble bench in the garden with many wedding guests crowding about us while the poet stood on a dais with his papyrus scroll, waiting a ready silence.

Our wedding hymn, in the classical style, had been struck off overnight by this young poet newly arrived from Egypt. This was the first time Marcia and I saw the man, who was to become an intimate in the drama of our lives. As he stood on the dais, scroll in hand, the sun sharpened one side of his nose and cast the other side and eye into a pool of dark shadow.

His name was Claudian, and his spirit was dramatically compounded of the subtle Greek and dark Egyptian souls. While he chanted the wedding hymn aloud to the wedding throng in a musical voice (accompanied by a lyrist) and with his dark eyes watchful for effects, I decided I liked him. For the most part this epithalamium was conventional in its evocation of Venus, Eros, Hymen and the other Greek and Roman deities of love and marriage, and conventional, too, in its flattery of the families of the bride and groom, though this flattery was particularly honeyed in the direction of old Probus and his sons Probinus and Olybrius. Claudian was evidently putting his muse to work to further his career.

Neither this excess of flattery nor his skillful use of conventional wedding-hymn patterns caused me to like him. It was the way he stood, lean, limber, short and dark, battling with solitary courage for a footing in this society where he was a stranger, that won my affection. I still remember him as he stood there, spiritually vulnerable as only poets can be and desperately courageous as poets must be; and in spite of certain tragic affairs that later developed between us I say that Claudian became my deepest friend. I do not know what it was in me that drew his soul to mine, even when he most profoundly mistrusted the injuring world; but often in the years to come he restored my common sense with penetrating ironies born of understanding and affection. And once in Milan I saved him from suicide in an hour when his soul was split with despair. I would say that there burned between us a flame in which we found our own lives and each other's purified.

And certainly in that wedding hymn of a hundred and fifty lines, struck off overnight to buy favor with the family of Probus, were here and there flashes of his true genius and outcries of his authentic soul. My heart was stirred by his inborn music, and I was to learn very soon that Marcia had an astonishing memory for some of Claudian's lines.

The feasting, drinking and merry celebration carried on through the day. Among the older people the mere fact of such a wedding being held eased fears and tensions, and the rumor spread that the Emperor Theodosius was not going to take reprisals against dozens of Pagan Senators there, against such men as my father, Symmachus, Lampridius. Finally old Probus, more red with wine than was good for him, confirmed the rumor with his specific news, and so far as I could notice my father was the only man among the endangered Pagans who felt humiliated at having the Christian Bishop Ambrose save his life and property. One Senator began embracing women right and left in joy and relief, and another caught the arm of the Bishop of Rome and declared his intention of becoming a Christian.

While her husband made his announcement of imperial clemency

Anicia Faltonia Proba, she who gave so much money to Christian uses, came to me and Marcia, enfolded us like a mother with great calm and dignity, and said to me, "Gregory, be good to this child." I promised her I would try with all my heart. And yet it was this noble Proba who was destined, on a terrible night in Rome, to witness and in part to cause the deepest tragedy of our marriage.

It was soon after Faltonia Proba left us that I saw Dionie and Claudian coming together toward Marcia and me. They were talking to each other in melodious and fluent Greek, and I suddenly thought there was between them a suave and subtle understanding of darkness.

Marcia and I stood up, and after I presented Dionie to Marcia, Dionie presented Claudian to both of us.

Dionie rested her provocative fingers on my arm. "Gregory, darling," she said, "live your life. Be happy." Then she kissed me and whispered in my ear in a low carrying tone that surely Marcia heard, "I think I've been a fool to let another woman have you."

The thing was strange. Those words did not seem to bother Marcia at all, but she turned half behind my shoulder to shelter herself from the direct presence of Claudian, as if for protection from outreaching tongues of invisible flame.

"You had no choice, Dionie," I said. "Venus determines what mortals fulfill."

She laughed. "Is he not thoroughly Roman, Claudian? Both of them? Open, clear. There are no dark windings of Old Nile in their souls. Happy children! But of course all Roman marriages—as I know from my own experience—come with a divorce attached for use when convenient. That behemoth of a Briton monk was right when he bellowed warning to you against convenience."

Claudian had not said a word. He looked at me gravely and looked away from Marcia as if her presence hurt him.

I thanked him for his poem.

He bowed and asked, "The whole thing?"

"Probus can thank you for most of it. I thank you for certain lines wherein your heart moved."

For a startled moment he looked into my eyes. Then we smiled at each other. Somehow, as if I had given him armor that he needed, he feared Marcia less after that and smiled at her, too. But while he stayed she still took shelter at my shoulder.

"I dreamed of you last night, Gregory," Dionie said. I could feel my hair bristle as she went on. "It was perfectly absurd. I was in some town as full of canals as it was of streets. It was night. There were cries, and murder was being done. Soldiers wounded my face, tore my clothes, and chased me when I fled. I was beating and crying at your door for you to save me, when I woke."

"Gregory! Your face is white!" Marcia cried.

A deep voice boomed at my shoulder, "The hour which frightens grooms draws near!"

It was Heraclian. Never had I been more glad to see him,

He had decided his presence at such a wedding was worth to his career at least one day's delay in his journey to seek favors in Milan. My father had reproved me for letting such a man into our circle. "Ambition stains his face. There are enough like him already in high place, without inviting more."

Heraclian was wearing a toga, with its intricate folds disposed to perfection, although my father doubted Heraclian's right of birth to our noble Roman garment. Of course nowadays to assume the toga was the legal privilege of almost anyone.

I introduced him to Dionie, for he let me understand by a slight gesture that he had interrupted us so as to meet her. Heraclian's strong figure, with its harsh lines, and the hair showing on the backs of his muscular hands in the clear daylight made him appear almost brutal beside the poet Claudian.

Heraclian talked to Dionie with the full brilliance of his willful charm, and I knew her well enough to recognize a calculating interest in the way she studied all evidence of his force, from the masculine vigor of his body to the ambitious hardness of his face, and then let provocation light her eyes and her sensuous smile. I saw them much together the rest of the day, and once, drinking, Heraclian had his arm about Dionie's waist.

But the dominant image of the whole festival for me was the radiance of life in Marcia's smile. Her sparkling eyes, her flushed cheeks and her tender lips flashed a thousand variations of joy and wonder. Her lower lip was full, and her upper lip was infinitely mobile; when her lips parted it was like a new awakening and motion of life. And now and then, when she closed her eyes and the dark lashes were at rest, it was like a pause in music. As dusk drew near I became frightened because I had an increasing sense of drawing near, on an irreversible course of robust masculine desire, to something virginal, tender, divine.

Several times Calvena came to take wine away from Marcia's lips. But I drank more than Marcia and often shared my golden wine cup with her lips. She held my arm and leaned against me and met my eyes over the wine-cup brim with such merry ease that I thought Venus herself had chosen me her favorite and was bestowing on me a demigoddess from her immortal train.

Only I had not counted on the rude old god Silenus, with his laughing belly and wedding rites.

Finally, when dusk filled the garden, we enacted the last scene of the feast. I took Marcia from her mother's embrace and, led by flute players and torchbearers and accompanied by gay crowds of ribald singers, I conducted her home, scattering to children in the streets handfuls of nuts in prophecy of happiness and fertility.

We reached our threshold accompanied by three ushers and three bridesmaids, who followed me as I lifted Marcia across the pure white cloth and green decorations on the threshold.

I offered her water and fire. Then the leading bridesmaid conducted her to the nuptial couch, which was covered with a fragrant thickness of flower petals. There I invited her to recline.

She looked lovely and flushed, her brown eyes sparkling with anxious delight. I removed her outer cloak and begin to untie the double knot in her symbolic woolen girdle of virginity. At this signal the groomsmen and bridesmaids, with a final fling of merry laughter, left us to ourselves, and our marriage night was all our own.

Then, prepared as I was, with a young man's trembling earnestness, for the consummation of our union, things I had not dreamed possible began to happen.

First, some idiot—I blamed Marcia's mother—had secured the knot of Marcia's girdle of virginity with a sharp pin. My wine-tossed fingers, fumbling at the knot, got severely pricked, and I let out a howl and began to suck blood from a finger.

As if this were a signal old Silenus had whispered into Marcia's ear, she let out a whoop of laughter and began to strew flower petals in a little cyclone all about her. The petals fluttered down and clung to her hair and eyelashes, and one caught on her lower lip. She sat on the bed with her legs drawn up and ankles crossed and arms set, exactly in the position of a statue of Buddha, with an Oriental grin on her face. I had bought a figure of this Oriental god one day in a bazaar, and I saw at once that Marcia had assumed his position.

"Stop laughing! Stop grinning! Where did you ever see a Buddha?" I demanded.

She flung her arms wide, sprang from the bed in a whirl of flower petals, and cried, "Buddha! Buddha! Who is he?"

She darted here and there about the room, eluding my reach, until

I cornered her. Then she raised a finger and shook it in my face and quoted me some lines from Claudian's wedding hymn:

> "And thou, young husband, put no trust
>   In rude assault on her virginity;
>   She will love you better, as she knows she must,
>   In gentle motions toward felicity. . . ."

Seeing her leer at me through the toss of her smoky locks and shake her finger like laughter, all the while with a merry grin, so exceeded all my expectations that I danced a patter of ridiculous steps and chanted back at her other lines from Claudian's poem:

> "Use not thy nails, startled bride,
>   Like Scythian women bold,
> But cast your garment soft aside
>   And yield as you are told."

Then we joined arms and pranced about the room, singing these and other ribald verses. Marcia was wonderfully witty with the disport of her young body, and strutted and postured hilarious imitations of some of the guests at our wedding, including a magical satire of Dionie pretending to be Cleopatra. I applauded her refreshing comic gift with tickling, chasing and acrobatics of my own. Finally she purred and smiled and curled on the floor like an unassailable cat, and I became a wolf, guttural on the promontory of the bed above her. We were laughing so hard at our own and each other's antics that tears streamed down our cheeks; and we ended sitting on the bed, arms about each other, and laughed and kissed and kissed and laughed.

It was only then, with all tensions gone and our hearts swept clean by laughter, that we looked at each other in tender silence and wonderful mutual trust, and, bowing our heads with our cheeks pressed warmly together, said each of us a little prayer.

My thanks rose up to Venus, for sweet is the flesh of the young to one another; and Marcia's thanks ascended to God, for great is his gift of man and woman to each other.

While we slept in our new peace together, my father, in his solitude, was making over certain properties to me and was considering in his heart a journey from which there is no return.

CHAPTER EIGHT

IMPERIAL FROWN AND FAVOR

The first embrace of marriage perhaps ought to be recognized as much more than a sexual experience: It celebrates the transition from the grand and dreamy speculations of youth to the hard exigencies of participation in racial life. I had no such conscious thought, but I did have a new feeling about having begun actual operation in the social world. I had studied law, and now that I was married I meant to begin my career. Such a view, putting career in the forefront to engage the mind's eye, is superficial; the cherishing of a woman and the opportunities and joys and responsibilities of fatherhood ought to be envisioned first, for they are primary. But it takes more simplicity of heart than I had—or than our society had—to see first things first.

I would like to sit discussing this matter with Socrates, who had wife and children, and Epictetus, who had neither wife nor child; but they are long since gone. . . . I'll get on with my story.

I am eager to speak at once of Bishop Ambrose of Milan, who for the next few years was the most challenging figure in my life; but a good telling of my story also demands that I speak of the Emperor Theodosius, whose frown or favor, backed by an awful, if not sacred, sense of his supreme worldly power, could shift a man out of his securities, allegiances and hopes.

Late in that year, while the new delights of our marriage were still fresh and Marcia and I made merry in mutual solace of tender pleasure, the Emperor Theodosius came to Rome and dealt Paganism its death blow.

First, weeks ahead of him, had come the detailed news of the miraculous battle of the Frigidus River, in which he had defeated Arbogast, Eugenius and Flavian. Flavian had set up in the hills statues of Jupiter holding golden thunderbolts. These had been overturned and the golden lightnings given as spoils to the soldiers in the Christian army of

Theodosius. Though the Pagan god had failed, the first day of battle was desperate. By nightfall ten thousand of the Empire's Goths lay slain, and their captain, Alaric, cried for more help from Romans. Theodosius was despondent. His generals urged retreat. He said he could not bear that the Cross should give way to images of Jupiter. He knelt in an oratory on a hill behind his camp all night in prayer; about dawn he slept. John the Evangelist and Philip the Apostle came to him in his dream and said they were sent to fight for him. He rose, called on his army to follow the saints without fear, and moved down onto the plain for battle again.

Then, at the crisis of battle, even at the point of a fatal wavering of fortune against Theodosius, the terrible Bora, that fierce and sudden wind of those parts, came roaring out of heaven from behind the army of Theodosius, impelling his men forward with mighty push, boiling a storm of dust into the eyes of the enemy, tossing their arrows back at them and wrenching the very javelins from their hands. Alaric and his reassembled Goths fought mightily for Theodosius.

The victory of Theodosius was complete, and it was said in Rome, when we had the story of these miracles, either that the Pagan gods were impotent against the armies of the Cross, or that our own deities, offended by our many insults, had turned their backs on the name and fortune of Rome.

Marcia was considerate of my father's grief and did not boast her religion either to him or to me. She and I had more intimate and enjoyable concerns. When a world society is changing, breaking up, tormenting lives, it is still—and perhaps fortunately—in the power of nature to hold the interest of young lovers focused on each other.

Marcia would wake up in the morning more suddenly gay than I. She had slender legs and nimble joints, and she would sit on the bed in the position of Buddha, delighted with the morning, while I rubbed sleep from my eyes and tried to see her better.

I could tell from the round of her face and her apple cheeks and her bright good lips that to be slender or fragile was not in her nature. She had just passed out of plump girlhood into a transitional year of growing taller. The pleasures and fertilities of maternity would round her out again, and I looked forward to this increase in the warm and roseate beauty of my already lovely companion.

"You smell better than flowers. You smell better than wine," I assured her.

"Ha! I married a marvelous nose! He scents divinity in this tawdry world. God will find you, Gregory, and snare you by the fragrance of my woman's hair." And she dangled her head and let her hair toss across my nose. "And such a generous mouth, too," she teased. "Not even three of my kisses would cover it."

"Your mother must have been stingy with food, or too Christian to let you enjoy it. With me, every one of your curves will get more round."

She would tousle my hair, tease me with a kiss, and spring from the bed. "In twenty years I'll be your fat wife and mother of your ten children. The pool! The pool!"

She would dash out to the pool, and I would chase after her. The first morning I saw her running like that in the early sun I said at once to myself, She moves with a lovely body. . . . She would always stop short at the edge of the pool, even though the weather and the water were warm. I would dash by her, plunge in, come up turned around and looking at her.

"I don't see how you dare—so suddenly!" She would dip a foot in to the ankle, draw it out, hug her breasts as if she were really cold, then close her eyes tight and jump in with a big splash. She could swim well, but I never could get her to enjoy diving. "It looks nice, but it's no fun, Gregory. When I jump in I wham the water with my bottom and make a splashing great to-do. I love that!"

We would sit on the edge of the pool for a while and talk about the perfection of our marriage. We were amazed at the people we knew who had gone through four or five divorces and marriages in search of the joy so simply ours by loving each other, and we had fun laughing at the preposterous story then current in Rome of the woman who had divorced twenty-two husbands and married a man who had divorced twenty wives, and people wondered what would happen next. The wife died, and the husband went about boasting: "I was her twenty-third, she was my twenty-first. Now that she's dead, give me three years and I'll beat her record!"

Perhaps such stories as this had prompted Jerome to write from Bethlehem to the Christian ladies in Rome that "in marriage there is not so much good to be hoped for as there is evil which may happen and must be feared."

I suppose any of the ascetic Christians would have been horrified to see Marcia and me wrestling on the grass in morning delight, chasing each other around the pool, splashing and disporting in the water. But our play made us happy and openhearted with each other. Little Amantha would come out with a towel and dry Marcia while one of my slaves dried me.

We were both of us fond of Amantha, who said she was happy to be our slave. "It is better than home," she said. "When you have a baby, if it's a girl, you won't have to put it out on the hillside for animals to eat." She wanted a child to love, to cure that remembered pain.

My father sometimes watched us at our dalliance and sport as he went about the garden, pausing in moody silence before a statue of Venus or Mercury, Hercules or Jupiter. He was very fond of Marcia, and she could make him smile when I could not. But even when he smiled it was only a cover for the pain of profound disillusionment.

I thought he had aged greatly in the past six or eight weeks. I suggested to him in the humor of my own good fortune that he was still a man short of fifty and ought to marry again. "Sooner or later my career will take me and Marcia away from Rome. You don't want twenty or thirty years of solitude. It's not good for a man, father."

"I know. I know." He shook his head.

I knew he had several concubines among our slaves, but that unequal association could not give him the solace of mutual understanding and affection. "There are young women in Rome of noble family who would be proud to accept your offer of marriage."

He looked at me in a sad sort of surprise. "What do the young know of despair? How can a woman console a man for the death of his gods?"

I knew he had changed in some deep silent way; I knew it because I felt differently in his presence now from the way I had formerly. Once it had made me feel confident to join my father. Now when I approached him I had a dark sense of unease, of disaster.

When Theodosius reached Rome the priests and priestesses were expelled from the Pagan temples, the temples were closed, and a pall of despair settled on my father's heart. The most fatal thing of all to him was this: that after an unviolated life of eleven hundred years the sacred flame guarded by the Vestal Virgins in the Temple of Vesta, the sacred symbol of the undying light and life of Rome, was extinguished, the Vestals scattered, and the sacred precincts opened to the profanation of the curious. "Rome," my father cried, "shall never emerge from this act of darkness!"

The horrible impiety of Serena crowned for my father this spiritual disgrace. Serena was a handsome imperious young woman who was to become of great importance in my life. She was the niece and adoptive daughter of the Emperor Theodosius, and she was the wife of his favored general, Stilicho the Vandal. Serena entered the condemned and sacred temple of Vesta, went to the shrine of the goddess Rhea, and from the neck of the goddess took a necklace and hung it about her own proud, lovely, young and mortal throat. It was a sacred rope of pearls, a fatal rope of pearls.

An aged Vestal Virgin, one of the last priestesses of the order, saw the profanation, shook her old fists above her head, and predicted that Serena would expiate that crime someday with choking horror in her mortal throat. It was said the old priestess was mad. But I lived to know Serena well—her pride, her courage, her beauty; I lived to choose between her and another in following the lure of power; and I lived to see her strangled.

Theodosius addressed the Senate, which had been predominantly Pagan, and overnight that august body became overwhelmingly Christian. Christian orators proclaimed that the whole city was evangelized and that a new spirit was renewing Rome. But my father said, and I agreed with him, that the ancient and cowardly vice of convenience, the vice that destroys societies, was in full operation. Men afraid of losing office or seeking to gain new office became nominal Christians for worldly benefits. It was a further corruption of the city and the Empire, not a spiritual renaissance.

It was now that my marriage proved a political success. Old Probus got his reward. The Emperor let it be known that for the coming year, 395 (here and hereafter I date my story in the manner of the Christian scholars), the sons of Probus—Probinus and Olybrius—would be the consuls and give their names to the year. The honor might cost them a million in spectacles and doles to the city mob, but it was still the greatest of all ineffectual honors to be had, and when before in the entire history of Rome had two brothers, two sons of one man, been the two consuls of the year! Claudian set to work at once on a panegyric for the occasion.

And the Emperor came, almost like a private person, to the Anician Palace of old Probus. Of course it was not only my marriage to Marcia that brought these honors. I learned that from the curious distinctions made when the Emperor received guests at the Probus mansion. Marcia and I were invited, but my father was not. It was made clear that Marcia would be presented to the Emperor but that I, while allowed to enter the great hall, would not be allowed to approach His Sacredness.

Seated high at an end of the great hall, in purple robe and scarlet slippers, wearing the pearl-studded diadem of the ruler of the whole world, Theodosius was indeed a majestic man. His face was made up of the planes and vectors of vigor, the shadows and curves of passion; in his expression there was a watchful mobility. He would be, I could see, quick to resist, to strike back at the blows of circumstance. He was about fifty years old, weathered and hardened by the storms of Empire, and pierced, too, by private tragedy. Just before he had left Constantinople his young second wife, Galla, had died in childbirth. He buried her, wept, and came to his war. He had two sons by his first wife—Arcadius, a youth of fifteen, and Honorius, a boy of eleven—and by the second wife his only surviving child was a little girl, Galla Placidia, who was there that day holding the hand of Serena. Galla Placidia was a honey-haired child with the flash of imperial temper and intelligence in her eyes. But the boy Honorius—our Augustus—was sullen, with large, dark, dull and downcast eyes.

Standing near the Emperor during the reception were the two next most powerful men in the Empire: Rufinus, the Praetorian Prefect, and Stilicho the general. Rufinus was a lean dark rapacious man whose depredations on private property were infamous. He never let slip a chance to confiscate a property, he sold and resold governorships, he played on the evil impulses of the Emperor; it was Rufinus who had pressed the massacre at Thessalonica. He saw to certain private murders for his own advantage. Bishop Ambrose had called him a dog to his face, but no one less than Ambrose would dare such frankness. For Rufinus murdered men who got in his way.

Stilicho was another sort of man, tall, with a marvelous springy carriage, a proud head and an earnest face. He was about forty years old then, with his hair beginning to turn gray, and he was definitely one of those men who caught the eye and won confidence in any crowd.

There was not much I could do but stir about and observe the noble and powerful from a distance. I saw Marcia bow and kiss the Emperor's hand, and even from a distance I could see his face warm with a smile as he spoke a few words to her. When he finished, suddenly in the pause of silence Marcia laughed out loud. It was a moment of consternation. But evidently the Emperor enjoyed her youth and spontaneous joy, for he tossed both his hands in the air, laughed himself, then patted her shoulder affectionately.

Claudian, beside me, said, "Your wife has made your fortune!"

I was hurt by the whole business. I said, "That's not the way I want it made."

He looked at me with sharp envy. "You already have wealth and position," he said. "I have nothing between myself and death but the gift of words. I have to seek favor."

It was then that I noticed the Augustus, the boy Honorius, standing off to one side with no one near him. No one dared approach him unbidden, and he stood there, lowering and alone, making no sign that he desired anyone to come near. He was isolated by his own sullen majesty.

Suddenly I realized the boy was lonely, tormented and jealous. He was so overshadowed by the grandeur and imperious ease of his father that he wanted to withdraw from humanity.

I took two cups of wine and walked toward him. My sympathy for the wretched boy made me forget the sacredness of the imperial family.

He saw me coming, lifted his head, and scowled.

"Could I serve you wine, Augustus?"

"No."

"May I serve Your Majesty in any way?"

"No." He stuck out his thick underlip and glared at me.

Too late I realized that what I was doing was being observed in all its perilous folly. Silence increased in the great hall. Others stepped back, leaving me more plainly alone with the young Augustus and intruding on him.

I stepped up to his side. "It is good wine."

His mouth relaxed a little, and he took a cup.

"Did you have a good journey from Constantinople?"

"No. I have chickens there. I had to leave them behind."

"Chickens are amusing. Fighting cocks are handsome."

Actually the boy smiled at me. "I like hens better." Then he drank his wine, I drank mine, and his expression changed to dull hatred. He said, "Here comes Rufinus. Don't tell him we talked about chickens."

Rufinus, with two armed guards, came upon me from behind. The guards seized me, and Rufinus dashed the wine cup from the hand of Honorius. "It may be poisoned, Your Majesty!"

General Stilicho had now arrived. He stood in front of me and searched my face. He made his decision. "This young man is not a poisoner, Rufinus."

"He intruded his low person upon the imperial presence."

Rufinus, dark and angry, demanded my name. I knew from the ferocity in his face that I had made a powerful enemy. As a privilege of his office Rufinus wore a purple robe reaching to his knees (only the Emperor could wear a purple robe reaching to the ankles). I saw the glistening of his cropped whiskers among the wrinkles in his lean swart face, and the power of rapacity sharpened his features and gestures. The man was vain and murderous. I thought he smelled of death.

Honorius watched and said nothing to defend me.

For a moment my fate hung between the two men of power, Rufinus and Stilicho.

And then the Emperor left his dais and walked across the hall. Everyone else bowed back from his sacred passage. I saw Marcia's face, round and white with fear.

A mere motion of the Emperor's fingers made the guards release me. Then the Emperor, Honorius, Rufinus, Stilicho and I stood in our separate group while the throng of guests watched the drama of my forfeit life.

"He could have murdered the Augustus, Your Sacredness," Rufinus said. "He is the son of a treasonable Pagan."

Stilicho held silence. Honorius glowered.

Now, close up, I saw the real force in the man Theodosius. There comes to be something more than mortal in a man who rules an Empire, if he be conscious of the weight and force of the thousand powers behind him. What he could not do with his breath or arm merely as a man, he knows he can do with Empire. But I also saw that under the mask of imperial power the human man was sick. There was puffiness around his eyes and a dropsical thickness in his fingers.

Theodosius spoke. "Who are you?"

"Gregory Julian, Your Clemency, son of Marius Cincinnatus Julian."

"The son of a man I have forgiven for the treasonable crime of reading my death in the foul entrails of animals. And you step unbidden into the sacred presence of my son. Speak!" The vehemence of rising fury was in his voice.

I staked my life on the truth. "Your Clemency, I saw a boy standing troubled and alone. Here in this great room, where all was pleasure in your august presense, the boy stood apart, and none had courage to offer him the kindness of friendship. I was so moved by his humanity that I forgot his divinity and came forward to offer my affection."

Theodosius wavered.

Rufinus overreached himself in his efforts to destroy me. "He persuaded the Augustus to drink. It might have been poison. He said something that made the Augustus smile. We'll find out by torture what it was."

"I saw my son smile." A shadow of profound sorrow crossed the Emperor's face as he looked down at his unhappy son. I think he knew that the boy was mentally slow and emotionally turgid. The Emperor asked me, "What did you say that brought a smile to my son's face?"

I caught a low flicker of appeal from the boy's eyes. For some reason, fateful in his own mind, he didn't want it known we had talked about chickens.

"Your Clemency, I think it was some trifle about the ways of nature, but a realization of my present peril has frightened it from my mind."

He looked at me steadily a moment. "Your peril grows less. I like my son to smile." Then he held out his hand for me to kiss, and the tension in the crowd watching us was broken.

When I looked up his eyes were waiting, and I felt the shock of the full force of his penetrating intelligence; but I did not flinch, and he liked that.

"Few men dare hold my gaze. You and your young wife will join our imperial train on our return to Milan. I may wish to know you better, young Julian!"

Honorius still said nothing, but I could see the rigidity of hatred with which Rufinus heard these words.

General Stilicho put a hand on my shoulder. "The Emperor has commanded you. Come to me tomorrow, and I will advise you on details for the journey."

The final parting from my father wrenched my heart.

We stood face to face, man to man. We gripped each other's hands hard. We had things to say that words could not encompass and looked at each other and said nothing. My father let go my hands, took me in the hard seizure of his masculine embrace, kissed me on each cheek, stood back, half averted his face, and said with the vehemence of a troubled heart the last sharp word of parting. "You face a new life. Go!"

I turned toward the outdoors and Marcia and the journey, and felt— for mystic filaments still bound me to him—my father's withdrawal into the silence of an inner room. I did not hear or see, but I felt a door close, and I felt a mystic chord of communion draw taut to the breaking point. I turned to go back—but what could I do? What could I do but part from him again?

For many days I felt the secret silent strain of imminent and everlasting severance from my father.

Thus it came about that by imperial command I abandoned my father and followed fortune to Milan, where I found Heraclian already in residence, married to Dionie and using her wealth and his cunning to further his career. Their villa was next to the villa my father had given me in Milan as one of my properties.

But my going to Milan was a fatal move. I should have stayed in Rome with my father.

PART

2

THE SINNER

OF SAINT AMBROSE

CHAPTER ONE

SERENA: HER POWER AND HER WARNING

It was a gorgeous journey, in crisp and brilliant weather, during which Serena showed me her power and gave me a warning and the Emperor alarmed us all. The Emperor traveled in splendor; the scarlet-plumed praetorian guardsmen carried the sinuous banners of Rome, emblazoned with purple dragons, and a guard of honor bore the ensign of Christ. We thronged the great road in a long parade of majesty, wealth and power.

The Emperor desired that Marcia and I travel with Serena and the imperial children in vehicles close behind his or, on other days, close behind where he rode horseback; and this looked like an honor assuring me a brilliant career. But twice a day Serena made clear that I did not belong where I was. Before starting each day's journey and again when the day's journey was done she would say, "Leave us now, Gregory. It is our Christian time for prayers."

My outcast status was all the more emphasized in that Serena said once, and did not need repeat, "Marcia is a Christian. She of course will join with us while you leave us to our worship."

It was the first time in my life that I had been put in the position of an outcast. I was troubled. I knew it was foolish to try to ally myself in hopes of a prosperous future with a group which considered me alien in so central and vital a matter as religion. But what could I do? The Emperor had ordered me to come and had assigned me my place.

I could feel, too, from hidden alarm in Marcia's manner and from the way she cried some nights while she thought I slept, that this official emphasis on my religious unworthiness was a burden on her heart. I had no doubt that Marcia remembered as well as I did that severe passage from Bishop Ambrose's letter to Marcia's mother which had delayed our marriage.

"The Catholic Church," Ambrose had written, "disallows marriages

85

with Pagan heretics. How can two be united in love if they be divided in faith? Beware, Christian, of giving your daughter to a Pagan or a Jew or a heretic or anyone at all who is not of your own faith. The only unions blessed by God are those between men and women who have received Christian baptism, who hold the same religious beliefs, and who can join together in prayer to the Author of their wedded happiness."

Neither on grounds of my reason nor in my concept of religious charity, neither in my small understanding of Christ's teaching nor in my constant wonder about God could I believe such a doctrine was true. God is not exclusive.

But I saw, in the troubled insufficiency of actual experience, that Serena's pointed discrimination, under the pretense of religion, was in fact casting the first shadow on the happiness of my marriage to Marcia. This, indeed, was the beginning of the deep loneliness of my adult life.

Standing aloof and alien from all of them at their devotions, I would count on my fingers what kinds of Christians there were. Omitting schisms, such as Arianism, and intra-Catholic factions, such as Donatism, I reduced the kinds of Christians to six:

Nominal: Those who called themselves Christians for practical purposes. Heraclian was one of these.

Mistaken: Those who thought they were Christians, while at heart they neither understood Christianity nor practiced it. Many Pagans thought they had become Christians, but merely worshiped old gods under new names. Fanatics, too, were mistaken Christians.

Tentative: Those who became catechumens in a sincere effort to find out if they ought to try to become Christians. This was the only possibility I could envisage for myself.

Now and Then: Those who were moved by Christian thought and worship while at their devotions or while in trouble or while grateful for happiness. Marcia was one of these.

Real: A certain few who devoted the entirety of their lives to following Christ. I thought Pelagius was one of these, and that Bishop Ambrose was another.

Perfect: Was not Christ alone the perfect Christian?

The only category I could see for myself was that of becoming a tentative Christian. There were honorable reasons, such as fidelity to my father, why I should not take such a step. Also, I had a deep fear of Christ and his teachings, for it is a lot easier to praise God in general than to follow Christ in particular.

And who would want to despise more than half of mankind—Pagans,

Jews, heathens, heretics—in order to be accepted by one church as a follower of Christ?

But I liked Serena and, insofar as she allowed personal affections to sway her, Serena liked me. Throwing me twice daily into an odious religious light was with her a matter of political policy. There was no actual Empress, and Serena, niece-daughter of the Emperor and wife of Stilicho the general, was obviously the foremost woman in the Roman world. The nature of her policy and of her ruling passion became clear to me on one of the later days of our journey to Milan.

We were sitting on a rock above a village, from which we could look down and out upon the sea. Seven of the imperial guards stood in an arc on the slope above and behind us, aloof, silent, watchful, with their spear butts planted on stony ground by their feet. Serena had been distracted for several days, and now she really wanted to talk, to regain and reform her inner harmonies by a talk in comfort and pride. She honored me by saying, "After the strain of these past three days your good spirits are refreshing."

She gave my face a cool frank glance and smiled—a smile like her name, serene and secure. I was mature enough to understand what she left unsaid—that, while I obviously admired her, she knew me to be sufficiently dazzled by her superior age and position so that I would not disturb her with an assumption of intimacy. She liked to be called "Your Serenity," and that is how I addressed her.

However, I saw no reason to pretend she was not a woman. "Your Serenity reminds me of Homer's Queen and of Virgil's. I think Helen must have had your charm and Dido your nobility."

Her cheeks flushed faintly, and her mouth relaxed. Then she said with cool amusement, "I am not flattered by your poetic allusions. Helen of Troy committed a monstrous nuisance. I have no sympathy with such a woman."

"But the gods compelled her to it," I argued.

"The gods are nonsense. See, don't I wear, unharmed, this precious necklace snatched from the idolatrous image of your so-called mother-goddess? Helen was simply a vain and beautiful woman with low morals. And Dido was a sentimental fool to kill herself. Instead of flinging her wretched self on the funeral pyre, she should have led Aeneas to Italy and become the first great Roman matron."

She spoke in a cool temperate voice, and her eyes, watching me, shone with a cool brilliance in her bright face. I could not help thinking of Minerva, gray-eyed daughter of Jove, but on a slender, proud and upright scale: Her wisdom was limited, but not her integrity.

She wore the fatal lustrous necklace of pearls which she had seized from the statue of the goddess Rhea in the Temple of the Vestal Virgins, and delicate flushes of color in her throat and cheeks warmed the light of the pearls. She did not in dress or motion put emphasis on any of her possibilities of seductive beauty. At the age of thirty, moral firmness and imperial assurance gave her an arresting quality that would hold its light perhaps for many years. Her nose had the arch of strength and pride, and her lips had the swift intelligent trick of forming unspoken words of reply even while you spoke to her, but she always paused to restudy the matter, with nervous swift flashes of light in her eyes, before she uttered her judgment. If her aims and mine had been the same, I would have trusted her on any occasion with my life. But only one man could be in such a position with Serena, and that man was the Emperor Theodosius, her uncle and (by his act of adoption) her father. His aims were hers—from Spanish vehemence to Oriental splendor.

At that time of year there was snow on the higher Apennine peaks, and when we left Florence the Emperor had decided not to go through the pass to Bologna, but to go down along the coast to take another pass through the mountains toward Milan. Then the Emperor Theodosius felt unwell, and Serena had brought the Roman Empire to a halt at this village by the sea.

I had witnessed the remarkable scene. The Emperor looked puffy and ashen at breakfast and had stumbled as with vertigo on rising. Men surrounded him. Serena turned her head, saw it, then moved with a leap, wild and sudden, piercing her passionate way to his side, brushing off those who would help him, giving him swift support in her own strength. The arm she flung about his shoulders in a warm sudden flash was the arm of love, raised in passion, to ward off death.

The Emperor shook himself a little, irritated, I suppose, by this public show of weakness. He stood on his own feet and said, "I am well enough to go on with the journey."

"Father! We stop here. You go to bed."

"Now, Serena!"

"Be quiet, Father. Rest. The Empire is your business, but you are my business." Then the passion of command made her voice resound. "Stilicho! Order the troops to encamp and the vehicles to be stayed! Rufinus! Summon the physicians! Gregory! You and Marcia watch over the children until you hear from me!"

Serena moved like a sweep of wind, bending forests to her sway. An impassioned wife could not have been more fierce, determined and swift at taking over command of a husband's illness. Within half an hour Serena was undisputed ruler of the Emperor, of his physicians, of the sickroom, and had cast all business and officials of Empire down into second place while she guarded the life of the Emperor. No one could doubt the woman's power when her passion was roused. Authority burned like fire in her face.

I think what surprised me most was to see Stilicho, master general of the armies of the Empire, obedient to his wife, as if he, the Vandal, the Barbarian, could not yet believe after a dozen years of marriage that he was the equal of his imperial wife.

Serena had stayed with Theodosius three days and nights while his physicians labored. He had been purged and bled, and now the swelling in his legs had gone down and pasty puffiness had been reduced from his face. She had come back that day to the children, who had been under my care and Marcia's while she was at the Emperor's sickbed.

Late in the afternoon Serena had wanted me to take her for a walk, out in the open, up on the slope. She left orders to be called instantly if the Emperor needed her. She had chosen this jut of ledge rock, and we sat there in the late mild sunlight of the December afternoon.

She had permitted me to sit, rather than stand. "Three days with five of other people's children would exhaust any man," she said.

"We got on wonderfully. Little Galla Placidia wanted to play running the Empire, with herself as Empress. Honorius, of course, was Emperor of the West. We appointed your son, Eucherius, Emperor of the East, and your two girls, Maria and Thermantia, took the offices of General Stilicho and Rufinus. Marcia was the Senate."

"And what was your position?"

"I was the Barbarians. The armies of Honorius and Eucherius, led by the Empress Galla Placidia, defeated me and reduced me to slavery in a great battle on the banks of Mount Vesuvius. Your Serenity's son Eucherius said it ought to be the banks of some river, but Galla Placidia, as Empress, issued an edict saying the battle would take place 'on the banks of Mount Vesuvius.' Then they cut off a lock of my red hair, and I was led in triumph through the streets of Constantinople, fought two lions and a bear in the arena, and was made Bishop of Antioch and Spain. We went down to the beach for sea shells and brought back a whole basketful to use as money."

She studied my eyes, then my mouth. She said, "It's not a little thing, nor without danger, to win the affections of those children who will one day rule the world."

Serena sat with her hands in her lap and her limber back straight and moved her head in easy calm to take in the whole view. The cool stillness of her gray eyes was emphasized by the length of her straight eyebrows and by the elaborate crown of her strong golden and warm-shining hair.

The village below us was small and appeared gorged with people as on a gala day of feast and fair; this was because of the numerous vehicles and many hundreds of people in the imperial cavalcade. There were many tents set up skirting the town, and of course lots of country people had come in with produce for sale. The little harbor was crowded with fishermen's boats from up and down the coast.

Serena pointed out to me that we could behold the Empire in little there below us with far more clarity than would be possible in a view from one of the great seats of government, such as Rome or Constantinople.

"Here is our land. There is our sea. The Emperor, God's chosen head of the world, rests in what is the palace of the village. The legions of General Stilicho represent Empire-wide command. See the imperial dragons afloat in the breeze above their camp which half rings the town! Those two, my father the Emperor and my husband the general, are the stay and bulwark of human society on earth. I am the one woman they both depend on! Down there on the beach you can see the troop of Goths that arrived this morning under command of their young chieftain Alaric: He, with his chestnut locks and brawny breast and proud blue eyes represents the countless Barbarians federated in faith to the Emperor. Alaric should have waited for us on the plain at Milan—if, indeed, he should not already have returned to the Danube. But he is ambitious to become a general and puts himself forward like this. A little chilling by Stilicho will cool his ambition. And God will fully restore the Emperor's health, for none but Theodosius can hold this complex of forces, stretching from Persia to Britain, together in harmony. I'll never fail him!"

She meditated a moment, or perhaps she prayed.

"Look, Your Serenity!" I pointed toward the beach. "Alaric has come out of his tent and mounted his horse. I had a close view of him this morning, leading his Barbarians. He fascinates me. I never saw a man who more reminded me of Aeneas first appearing before Dido: 'He stood forth, shining in clear light, head and shoulders like a god, radiant in youth, with luster of joyous eyes. . . .' It's as if Alaric had sprung up among us, in a weary age, out of the youth of the world."

She looked down at Alaric galloping along the beach and ruined him with a word. "He rides perhaps too high a dream." It was as if she were knocking a hero from his horse.

She moved her hands, putting them on the stone behind her hips, and leaned back on her arms and took a deep free breath of rich sea-fragrant air. She spoke softly. "It is wonderful to be at the center of Empire like this and see it whole!" Then she gazed in long silence at the blue and gold sun-flecked sea.

I looked at her and wondered how this woman would dispose of me, she who could dispose of Alaric—the radiant young Visigoth, captain of his people, who wanted to be a Roman general—with that deadly condemnation of an old society: "He rides perhaps too high a dream!" I wondered: Can the youth of the world be so easily destroyed by enthroned power?

I heard a small stone rattle and, looking up, saw a peasant coming down a dusty path with a stick in his hand and his back bent under a large burden wrapped in goatskins. He stopped suddenly, like an animal warned of danger. The guards held him in their level stare, and one half raised a spear. He looked at them, he looked at us, then he turned off the path into the bronze-green brush, and I could see the top of his pack move on slowly above the brush, on down the hill. Did he know how close he had been to that one who in all but actual name was the living Empress of Rome? Serena, rapt in her restful vision of Empire from its center, had not noticed him. She gazed out over blue sea.

The much-in-little of the incident gave me a feeling that something terrible was taking place: on the part of Her Serenity, ignorance, and on the part of the lonely peasant a circuitous withdrawal that had in it elements of cunning, mistrust and treachery.

That peasant had startled me with a revelatory warning about the basic insignificance of people of importance. There would be a hundred thousand of him to one important person. There are too many of the lonely and obscure for a name like Emperor and an organization of offices to be sufficient. Those important persons who run governments but forget about the greatness of the lonely people—their simple need for friendship, for love and for religion—are not really governing, but rather losing the faith of men. Friendship, love and religion are basic spiritual needs which no government provides—and so an Empire falls because the lonely people, in their greatness, have found it hollow and turn away into the hillside brush to seek meaning in life elsewhere.

There was also something ominous in the nature of the bronze-green brush on that slope. In a great sweep of land near this village no crops grew. Once it had been a place for vines and grain. The small farmers had been taxed out of production, and the land was going back to brush and waste. Italy grew more and more dependent on Africa and other far places for grain and foodstuffs. When neighbors cannot help one another in hunger, but must cry to government and to far places for the goods of life, that society must rot.

Serena, still gazing out to sea from her high and powerful center of presumed authority to mold the Empire, talked softly of dear things. "He will be well and whole again. The burden of Empire is so great! I remember when I was a child in Spain how I waited for him to come from his estate to visit ours, and I would leap into his arms and call myself his daughter. Then when Gratian appointed him co-Emperor he did indeed take me to Constantinople with him and adopted me, and I alone—not his first wife and not his second, but only I—could calm his distress and ease his sorrows and comfort him in counsel. He trusts me as no other woman has had his trust. He shall be whole again!"

Serena let out a sigh, sat straight, brushed her hands together, and bent her glance on me. "You are a patient young man. What have you thought while I sat here dreaming aloud and regained my peace?"

"Your Serenity has showed me the Empire—but we have no Virgil."

She laughed. "Can you fill that place?"

"I'm better at thought than at song. But if Your Serenity would permit, I could ask a poet I know to come visit me in Milan. I think he's good. If he is good, there is something about a poet that gives clarity to a whole age and preserves it for history."

"Who is this poet? In Constantinople, which is too soft for great poetry, we have heard of no new poet in Rome."

"He has just come from Egypt. He composed the verses for my wedding, and some of the lines had the divine flash. He's a client of old Probus. He's now writing a panegyric on the consulship of the two sons of Probus. But I think he would be honored to visit me in Milan in order to pay his respects to Your Serenity. Claudian is his name."

She thought a moment, not I believe of herself, but of the dynasty of Theodosius. "We are worthy of a poet. Invite him, please."

Once more she gave my face that grave study. "You are clever about others, young Julian. What place have you appointed for yourself?"

I knew it for a treacherous question and that she was putting me in hazard. "I can only guess what my service may be. I have guessed that the Emperor has it under consideration whether or not I am fit to be chosen officially as a friend of our Augustus, young Honorius."

"Honorius is a difficult child, and with him you do remarkably well. The Emperor is impressed. But so long as you are a Pagan I don't see how you can hope for any official acknowledgment."

"Would it not help heal the conflict to have a Pagan in high place as official companion to the Augustus?"

"No. It would be a signal for intrigue, for false hopes and for new difficulties. It is because I like you personally, young Julian, that I have been so frank. It is within your choice whether you remain a Pagan or become a Christian. The Emperor may ask you, once for all, to make such a choice. . . . There is another matter I am reluctant to mention because it concerns a child."

"I am fond of children."

"That is obvious. And they grow fond of you. But imperial children are not like others. In five years Galla Placidia could be betrothed and in seven years she could be married. Frankly, Galla Placidia makes too much of you. I wish, Gregory, that you would be more distant with that little girl."

Serena watched me narrowly as she said this, and I knew she had come at last to the heart of her examination of my character. My immediate political future and perhaps the course of my life could depend on how Serena judged me now.

"Little girls go through their phases." I tried to gain time.

"Not that little girl. She's intensely jealous of me, and she already knows she has twice the mind of Honorius. Soon she will not be satisfied to play at being Empress."

I was frightened at how open Serena had made the implications of corrupt possibilities. There was almost nothing I could say without putting myself at her mercy for uttering treason and harboring treasonable thoughts. For things a man can handle with sanity and normal affection in ordinary life become perilous and corrupt near the apex of power. Imperial children, indeed, are not like other children: Their lives are caught in webs of policy.

I had seen this suspicion growing in secret and had hated it and had hoped that silence would let it die.

During the journey I had got on well with Honorius, though it was a quiet association, he being inclined to a morose boredom. He was too young to be in puberty, so I judged he must have by nature a clouded spirit. But I found I could start games with Galla, a sound, plump and spirited child, and get Honorius to join us. Galla often commanded me to take her on my lap, and she would flash willful defiance when Serena disapproved of our frolic. That child knew the language of power and had the wit and will and temperament to back it up. Serena usually ended by laughing at the way I played with the little girl.

But Serena had begun to give me certain narrow glances and watched my face with silent prophetic speculation until I, too, had begun to peer toward what Serena saw: The man Galla married would be within a stroke of becoming Emperor of Rome. I think at some moments Marcia saw it too, and her smile faded.

For Galla Placidia was something special. She was not only the daughter of an Emperor, but two of her uncles and her grandfather had been Emperors. She inherited force and intelligence not only from Theodosius (how unlike his sons!) but from her grandfather Valentinian, who, though of Barbarian origin, had made himself Emperor, and from her grandmother, the late Empress Justina, that difficult and passionate Sicilian woman who stubbornly remained an Arian heretic till the end.

I was appalled at the revelation of how cunning and corrupt can become the prophecies and pretensions of intellect in the presence of the possibilities of power. Theodosius, a man worn by the weight of Empire, by extravagance of pleasure and vehemence of nature, had begun to show himself an ill man, moved into the insecure neighborhood of death. He would die. A few years of cautious calculation and careful moves on my part—Christianity assumed, Marcia abandoned, Eucherius removed, Honorius dominated, Galla Placidia become my bride . . .

These thoughts had been the more terrible in that to speak of them, even for the sake of denying them, would be treason. Perhaps this enforced concealing in the mind of corrupt thoughts—which others also have to bury—is one of the worst poisons infecting souls near the apex of power.

This very afternoon the child Galla Placidia had herself given me a chance for dangerous relief. She had announced that she was coming on our walk with Serena and me. Serena had said no. Galla seized my hand and cried, "I will! I will! Gregory is mine! He's not yours!"

"Gregory belongs to Marcia," Serena said.

The child's eyes blazed. "I'll marry him when I'm Empress!"

Serena stiffened like a blade of steel. Marcia gasped.

I seized Galla under the arms, lifted her up, and kissed her forehead. "I love you very much, Galla Placidia, but when you're ready to marry I'll be an old man with a laughing belly and ten sons. You can adopt me as your uncle."

"Poof! Such an uncle!" And she, too, laughed and let us go without more than a malicious little smile of triumph at Serena.

But while Serena and I sat on the hillside ledge above the village and Serena waited for my promise to turn my face against the child, the shadows of power and corruption were on me.

While she waited, while I sought a careful way out of hazard before speaking, I saw Alaric return to his camp on the beach. He had set out in proud hope toward Stilicho's headquarters; he returned now somber, proud, defiant, checking the pace of his horse. No doubt some request he had made had been put off or refused by Stilicho. "Chilled" was Serena's word. But so far does reality exceed our dreams and our fears that neither Serena nor I could have guessed that Alaric was destined to be of dramatic importance in Galla Placidia's fate. And so, too, the bold young brother of Alaric's wife, who sat even at that moment down on the beach, in the tent of Alaric, clad in wolfskins, dreaming perhaps of his hunting realms in the forests along the Danube. Still buried in the breasts of those two Barbarians, Alaric and his brother-in-law Ataulphus, were exploits destined to amaze and confound Rome.

The sun was setting in the sea, and its last red light was on Serena's face. Far out, near where the sun seemed to set, was a lone rocky island, like a dark and fateful ship on the heavy breast of ocean.

I hated to promise, for whatever high policy of Empire, to make myself false and odious toward an affectionate child. "It is hardly my nature consciously to wound a child's affections," I said. "But if Your Serenity wishes . . . " I broke off and waited for her to feel the burden.

"You should wish it yourself, Gregory!" Her voice was sharp.

"We will reach Milan in a few days. Then I will be in my own villa, and the children will be with Your Serenity in the palace. Galla Placidia will know the journey is over and will neither be hurt nor surprised if such business as the Emperor gives me keeps me away. And Your Serenity has pointed out that, since I am a Pagan, I may get no appointment at all, but simply be sent back to Rome to obscure private life."

"You're stubborn. And you are fond of the child."

"It's more than that. You're a mother. My wife is pregnant. I'm going to be a father. It would frighten me to be willfully false to any child."

She started to speak, then hesitated. I had touched some chord deep in her heart, and I heard her whisper to herself what I recognized to be one of the sayings of her Christian religion: " 'Suffer little children to come unto me.' "

She stared at the sun until it was gone and dark-blue light swept across the sea and the ship of silent stone held the rim of the world. She sat there, foremost woman of the Empire, lovely in twilight, ignorant of the doom coming out of heaven toward her face—for I beside her was the young man whose averted face would destroy her husband Stilicho, and about her throat glimmered that fatal necklace of her own death.

She felt a chill, squeezed her sides with her arms, put a bright scarf on her shoulders, and after a strange unsatisfied last look into my eyes led the way down the path.

The seven imperial guards flanked and followed us.

CHAPTER TWO

THE EMPEROR'S TRAP

THE SIMPLE THING EACH MAN WANTS IN HIS HEART IS eternal happiness.

Not even the sticks and stones of grandeur, up-piled by pride and prowess, can satisfy or hide this vital desire for eternal happiness. To pretend inwardly or aloud that we want other things instead does not quench our human desire for eternal happiness. Why not cease to be ashamed to admit the truth, and say outright: Each man wants eternal happiness?

Therefore I believe the story of the life of his spirit, seeking its path toward God, is the true story each man should try to learn and ought to tell.

I was shaken to my depths when I met Bishop Ambrose, and exclaimed, as one moved by a revelation: "We have met before!"

The shock of recognition made me realize that the mysterious and incalculable flow of spiritual affairs is the true course of a man's life, and that he deludes himself who thinks the provable, the tangible, the worldly are of first importance. The life of the soul cannot, in our mortal span, be detached from the touch and taste and smell of our worldly doings; but neither can the mansions we build with brick and crime and gold be lived in by anything but the soul. It is the life of the soul that gives us our final astonished measure and meaning.

Milan I remember as a place of radiance, not of moiled magnificence like Rome, nor of dark and watery gloom like Ravenna. First, on a rare bright winter day with wind-cleaned air, the city rested on the plain, while afar the remote and splendid mountains cut the blue sky with sharp gleams of snow. Compared to Rome, the city was clean and small and new. And we could easily go in part of a day to Lake Como among its mountain steeps, where ancient forest rose above shining water. One knew at a glance and breath why Pliny had loved it there.

The Emperors had long since deserted the conglomerate splendor of their massy dwellings on the Palatine Hill in Rome. There was something stubborn and resistant about the republican spirit of Rome that offended the absolutism of Emperors. A hundred years ago the Emperor Maximian had built his palace at Milan, which had been since then the principal seat of imperial government in the West. Thus the Bishop of Milan was, you could say, the Emperor's bishop. In addition to the Imperial Palace, the bishop's dwelling and the governor's headquarters there were a growing number of handsome public buildings, temples, theaters, basilicas, luxurious public baths and—the main joy of the people—a large circus where crowds could watch chariot races, sports, games and exciting atrocities. Along the town streets were many deep shady arcades where, protected from hot sun or biting north wind, citizens could carry on our Roman outdoor life of gossip and business. Many of these arcades were made colorful with mosaics, statues and other works of art. And of course our Roman love of flowing water had seen to it that the city had its full share of fresh sparkling fountains. Around the city proper stood a double range of massive walls, thickened on the inside by dwelling houses and guarded on the outside by a moat. Outside the walls palaces, villas, temples and huts spread far into the country among gardens and orchards and farmsteads. The whole plain was fertile and made lovely by rivers, the blue-flowing Adda, the low-banked Ticino, the rivulet Olona against the walls, and only as far off as Pavia the rapid Po dancing its waters along between rows of poplar trees.

The villa my father had given me was a mile or so outside the walls, and Marcia and I had settled in there with several freedmen to take care of our business and a modest retinue of slaves to take care of our comfort and of all menial work. It was a small estate, with gardens, orchards, a farmyard, pastures for a few sheep, cows and horses, an enclosed bath fed by a clear stream, a good library in the house and room for modest entertaining. It was an unpretentious place, suitable for a young married couple at their start in life, and I could see at once that as my position and wealth improved I could easily enlarge the buildings and buy near-by land.

Adjoining us on the north, toward the mountains, was the much larger and more pretentious estate of Dionie, where she and Heraclian had already established themselves and begun political operations.

Dionie's hair was no longer red; by I know not what Alexandrian arts she had changed it to a delicate pale-golden sheen of straw, and now pearls and rubies were the jewels she wore to warm her beauty. Neither her green eyes nor her seductive mysterious smile had changed. I was glad she was our neighbor, but Marcia was not.

The streets of Milan were particularly colorful at this time, for not only was the Emperor in residence, but, because he had recently won a major victory, there were thousands of legionaries and many federated Barbarians encamped near the city and not a few Goths living in their big wagons within the city itself. At Alaric's camp near the Circus we saw the blond Visigoth women and children at home in hide-covered wagons with their men. Marcia and I, making a tour of the city, saw even a band of Huns, and truly those terrors of the outer fringes of the Empire were frightful little horse-riding men.

Among Alaric's Goths, who a generation ago had been pressed out of their German forests down against and across the Danube by the Hun swarm, there was a legend that these Huns had sprung from an unholy union between unclean spirits wandering the wilderness and certain Gothic women driven from their tribes centuries before for witchcraft. The faces of Huns seemed like lumps of dark dough with fierce black points for eyes. They scarred the faces of their children with iron before the babe sucked the breast, so that a child tasted blood before milk. They were squat men with strong necks, powerful shoulders, narrow waists, and they clamped their bowed legs like iron to the ribs of their horses. A few bands of these flat-faced bestial little men, with the savage stink of the wolf about them, had broken away from the ravaging Hun horde, like sparks shot off from the tail of a comet, and filtered into the Roman armies; but their main hordes still pressed and harried the margins of our world from northern Germany to Antioch in Asia Minor.

But the Goths, the Franks, the Vandals were clean-limbed fine fellows with handsome women and jolly dirty children about them. Especially among the Goths there was a youthful notable vigor, a readiness for new actions and new ways, a heartiness not hidebound by old prides and intrenched privileges. I was impressed by the color of their costumes and the masculine force of their manners. I was too foolish to realize that old Rome had more need of their creative vigor than they had need of Rome's rotting majesty. I think Stilicho, himself a Vandal, had at least a dim sense of ways in which the Barbarians might save Rome, but Serena's dominance emasculated him and betrayed his vision.

Serena had made to me neither threat nor promise, but I was sure that by now she had made some statement, for or against me, to the

Emperor. I fretted for some days, waiting, wondering, not knowing whether appointment or dismissal would be my lot.

About the tenth day an imperial messenger arrived at my villa, requesting that I return with him to the palace.

I hurried to tell Marcia. She was in a portico, sheltered from the wind, enjoying the morning sun. I could see the light of beaming pleasure in her face from a distance before I could make out her features.

"The summons is from the Emperor himself," I told her. "This interview will be decisive."

"You are bound to have good fortune, Gregory. Now that they know you, they cannot help wanting you."

"Even though I'm not a Christian?"

A shadow crossed her face. She bowed her head. When I lifted her face to kiss her lips, her dark eyes were full of tears. I think it was unfair of me, knowing that her thoughts were simple, to use the ironic play of my more subtle mind to provoke her spontaneous tender affections. But I loved her quick warmth of emotion.

I went with the messenger.

At the palace I was taken into a high-ceiled private-audience chamber where the Emperor sat on a divan with Bishop Ambrose as if they were two old friends. I had never before thought of the Emperor, that almost sacred head of the political world, as having a friend.

But it was on looking at Ambrose that I stopped short and cried out, "We have met before!" Then, to cover this impertinence as well as I could, I took two steps, knelt down, bowed my head, and waited for the Emperor to speak.

What I had seen in a flash was the Emperor in his brilliant robe and slippers, a big man, powerful, but with his face now ravaged, pallid and weary. Beside him at ease sat Bishop Ambrose, a smaller man (and, like the Emperor, half a century old) with narrow hands and narrow feet and not much flesh on his bones. He had a long face, further elongated by his high forehead and small brown beard. He kept his hair short and wore a drooping mustache. His nose was quite long and thin, then lumped and flared at the nostrils, his lips were thick, his left eyebrow arched higher than his right, and his eyes were large and seemed even larger because of the stillness in them of a steady spiritual light. His look was grave, something melancholy, as if he longed for his immortal awakening. He wore a plain brown tunic, and I could have mistaken him for a poor plain citizen if I had not so clearly, so vividly, seen him once before as a priest.

I heard the Emperor exchange a few whispered words with Ambrose.

Then Theodosius spoke to me. "Where have you met Bishop Ambrose before, young Julian? You may stand while you tell us."

I stood, looking from one man to the other. Theodosius, despite his illness, was astute and watchful and made me wary; but Ambrose, when I looked at him, made me feel better than myself and prepared for truth.

"I fear to offend Your Clemency and His Eminence the Bishop by what you might call my Pagan superstition; but at Your Clemency's order I must tell the truth. In Rome on a day in September I lay beside a marble bathing pool with my head on my arms, and without lifting my face I nevertheless saw standing above me the perfect semblance of the man I now see seated beside Your Eternity. He asked me to become a Christian, which would facilitate my marriage to Marcia. I said no; rather Marcia should become a Pagan. He then, with sorrow in his face, made the holy Christian sign above me and said, 'Your sin be mine.' I felt I knew who he was, and yet I did not know his name."

I turned to face Ambrose. "Instantly when I saw you here, Your Eminence, with the Emperor, I knew you and now know you for Bishop Ambrose. I know, but I do not understand."

"You distinguish well, young Julian," Theodosius said. "Too many think that to know is to understand. We know that trees blossom in the spring and that stars wheel in the sky and that men and women are swept by love; but these and a thousand other things of wonder that we know, we do not understand. Perhaps the bishop can help us."

Ambrose smiled and then spoke in a voice which, while not musical by nature, was by training pleasant, firm and free, sounding with a kind of purity that belongs only to a voice never used to dissemble. And it was notable that Ambrose spoke to the one in trouble rather than to the one in power, directly addressing me.

"What you say, Gregory Julian, rings true. We have, then, met before, though not in the flesh. But indeed our spirits have met. When my cousin Calvena wrote to me to inquire about your marriage to Marcia I advised against it; but I prayed for you. If we seem to know each other—for when you entered this room my heart knew you—it is because our souls have met before now in the true realm of the unseen. Had your soul not been seeking truth, it would not have met mine praying for you there."

I stood humbled before them. By now I understood how this frail Ambrose could be more powerful than this forceful Theodosius. The Emperor was only master of men's desires, but Ambrose was dedicated to their needs.

The Emperor was thoughtful, for a moment holding his chin in the slightly swollen fingers of his right hand. Then, fixing me with an intense deep-reading glance, he explained, "We are concerned with one of those matters of grave choice. It is weighted with greater perils than the selection of a governor for all Gaul or the appointment of a general. Honorius is only a boy, and yet we know there is something troubled about his spirit, some inward irresolution that shadows his mind. We have seen him, who hides his heart, trust you and respond to your affection. When God calls us home Honorius will be Emperor of the West, and if you are still beside him, your influence will be fateful. You are young and untried, and we know the awful corruptive force of power. Therefore, politically it would seem the safer course to put you beyond the reach of corruption, ordering you to lifelong ease in private life. Our daughter Serena almost favors that, and she has studied you. Rufinus would be even more severe. But we grieve at our son's solitude of spirit. You might be the one who could open his prison. But then again, if we let it be known that a Pagan—and, moreover, a Julian—has been officially chosen as companion and tutor for the young Augustus, seemingly concluded strife may be renewed, wrath arise again. What hope can you see for yourself in all this? . . . We want no ready answer. Take your time, for you are in the presence of one who understands power and of one who is enlightened by God."

I glanced slowly at these two foremost men of the world that I knew. Sunlight from a tall narrow latticed window was on the Emperor's head and made designs as of fire on the threads of gold and crimson in his purple robe. Then the shaft of light made a pool of brilliance on the stone floor at my feet. Ambrose was more in shadow, but shed his own spiritual radiance. The Emperor had spoken with majestic assurance, without any imminent sense of his own death, though some strangeness of the light revealed death residing already, untimely, in his face.

How much had Serena, how much had Rufinus warned the Emperor against me? The way of security for me would be to return to Rome and private ease. Being young and robust, I dismissed the thought almost at once: What did I want with mere security and ease? The boy Honorius needed a companion and tutor. It was quite true that I had established a friendly contact with him that might help him out of his averted solitude. It would be cruel to abandon him. Obviously the way of service would be near the peak of power, at the side of Honorius. There was no practical reason why I should not phrase some promise to be faithful to Honorius, base my hopes on that, and do all I could to get this key position near the top center of imperial power. For I certainly saw that close to this way of service would constantly be the tempting possibility of deviation toward glory and power. It was this invitation toward glory and power that stirred my heart and already alerted me with fear. Were there not untold possibilities, even within the scope of honor, that might lead me in due time to co-Emperorship with Honorius? A man would not have to abandon his wife and marry Galla Placidia to achieve that. Gratian, a young Emperor, far more capable than Honorius, had requested Theodosius to become co-Emperor to help him in the great burden of ruling so vast a world.

I summoned my courage to tempt and trust fortune. I began to say to the Emperor alone that I would be faithful to Honorius.

But the Emperor was not alone. After saying "Your Clemency . . . " my voice stuck. Bishop Ambrose sat there. I could feel his spiritual weight and clairvoyant attention. He had met my soul and would recoil from any sophistry. My throat burned dry. I could not speak at all. The blazing pool of light on the stones at my feet dazzled my eyes, and I seemed ready to pitch headlong into an abyss of light.

I realized that my fists were clenched tight at my sides. I realized my jaw was clamped tight and my neck was corded with tension. Without looking, I felt certain that Bishop Ambrose had stretched out his arm and hand to reach my spirit and help me.

Suddenly I lifted my face to look straight at the Emperor. Because I had been staring into the abyss of light at my feet he appeared to float before me in blazing brilliance, and to this burning vision of power and human glory I uttered words that frightened me as I heard them. "Your Clemency, I would serve Honorius faithfully if I could. But I am a Julian. My heart dreams of glory. There is no hope for me!"

"Ha!" He let out the explosive syllable, straightening and stiffening where he sat as a man will who has been astonished. He leaned forward, brilliant and alert. "Thousands have fawned on me for favor: You dare to tell the truth. Ambrose, the boy is dangerous. We'll put him to work!"

Ambrose spoke quietly, and his three words were devastating: "Christ cures glory."

I saw a smile enlighten the face of Theodosius. "Young Julian, you are not yet chosen for Honorius. You will be told in a day or two of interim duties. But you have earned our friendship, and Bishop Ambrose will light your way to Christianity."

I then came as close as I dared to suicide by an ironical turn of phrase which might sting the Emperor. "I thank Your Clemency for bestowing on me your friendship—and your faith."

His eyes flicked, but the flash of anger did not come. He held my eyes steady. Then the smile came. "How deep is this Paganism of yours?"

"As deep as my love for my father, and as deep as my love for Rome."
He turned to Ambrose. "The boy has courage and a proud spirit,
Bishop; but you know how to bow the spirits of the proud to God."

We knew he was talking about how he had bowed to Ambrose regarding penance for the massacre at Thessalonica.

Ambrose rose and came to my side. "Grace comes as God wills, Your
Excellency. I have prayed for this young man before; I will pray for him
again. Let his sin be mine."

The Emperor relaxed and chuckled. "To be the chosen sinner of our
good Saint Ambrose is a greater honor than any I could bestow. You
have made your fortune with God, young Julian. Stay in His favor and
you need not fear mine."

"Favored by Your Eternity, honored by Bishop Ambrose, I am raised
above fear."

A curious, cunning smile lighted his face. He said with ironic humor:
"Statesmen are astonished, young Julian, when they see a good sound
homely youth like you hold the daughter of the Emperor on his knee.
Statesmen fear the future. But I watch and arrange for it." He chuckled
and held out his hand for me to kiss, saying, "Galla Placidia has ordered
me to like you! That child was born to be Empress!"

I touched his swollen finger tips and kissed the back of his hand. I
said nothing. I did not dare say anything. But I was amazed at this
veiled hint that Theodosius, unlike Serena, unlike Rufinus, might favor
my affection for Galla Placidia. He might definitely plan to rid me of
my wife and marry me to his daughter. Emperors had done the like
before.

He let this ambiguous hint of crowned glory or warning of disaster
sink with terrible force into my mind. Then his final word of dismissal
was like an imperial edict, putting my conscience to torture in the
Emperor's trap: "Our good Ambrose will instruct you. We expect you to
become a Christian catechumen within thirty days! For, as Ambrose
says, Christ cures glory."

I accompanied Ambrose out of the palace to the street. I had learned
by now that those who have close contact with the Emperor are watched
closely, with envy, with malice, with calculation. One tries to hold an
inexpressive face on leaving the Emperor, for each expression will be
probed for meaning—"What favor has he got?" "What policy is being
affected?" "Will this man who has just seen the Emperor be able to aid
or hinder me?" There seems to be something odious and corrupting
about political distinction which makes a man watched and feared, so
that he needs in turn to be fearful and watchful. But, once we left

Theodosius, I realized it was a spiritual honor to accompany Ambrose along the street. Walking with the great priest, who was loved in Milan, I felt no need to harden my face against the expression of my feelings. Those who saluted him included me in the smile of their affection. After the strain of the interview it was restful to share in the peace that Ambrose inspired.

I went with him as far as his church, noting that he walked with graceful quiet as if the soles of his sandals were softer than those of other men.

I spoke to him in a troubled voice. "The Emperor has in effect ordered me to become a Christian. My honor toward my father is involved. I was dazzled in His Clemency's presence, but the more I think of it, the more I realize it would be better for me to return to Rome and private life. I am caught in a religious trap against my will. What shall I do?"

"I have many duties, Gregory," he told me. "And you have a spiritual problem not to be disposed of between this and that. Come to my house this evening. Let us have a long talk in quiet together."

I went home, buffeted by black and by brilliant thoughts.

I had a troubled afternoon with Marcia. She was in that early period of pregnancy when women are apt to be more nervous and even less reasonable than usual, and I, frightened at the trap the Emperor had sprung on me, was sharp with Marcia, who loved me rather than the Emperor who had trapped me.

I began in a gloomy and outraged fashion by saying it was shameful what pressure Christians would use to increase their numbers. By the time I had told Marcia a biased version of the interview I had put her on the defensive as one of the Christians who was trying to trap me. She, on her part, misinterpreted every one of my generalizations as a personal remark passed in judgment on her. I said Christianity would end by destroying the Roman Empire, and Marcia said that if I loved her I wouldn't talk that way. I felt she didn't understand all the ramifications of my problem, and she felt I didn't love her enough. I was ashamed that I did not dare tell her that the Emperor might even have plans for me and Galla Placidia, so I shouted my Paganism louder.

"Epictetus," I stormed at her, "holds as noble a view of God as any man needs. The ethics of Marcus Aurelius are good enough for me. I'll be satisfied with honest philosophy and private life!"

She held her ground with equal fury and lashed back, "If you hate me and want me to stop praying for you, say so!"

"By all the gods! Have you been praying for me?" I shouted in rage.

"I couldn't stand it, the way Serena sent you away from us at morning and evening prayers. So I prayed every time to Christ Jesus to make you a Christian." Then she lifted her face and cried out, "Save him, O Christ, save him!"

"Betrayed by my own wife!"

I stamped up and down the room, beating my palm with my fist, while Marcia, tears streaming down her cheeks, cried out again and again: "Save him, O Christ, save him! Save him, O Christ, save him!"

Finally I seized and shook her, then held her struggling in my arms until she was exhausted and sobbed against my breast while I buried my face in her hair and wept. "Marcia!" I whispered. "Marcia! I would be a Christian if I dared. But I am afraid of Christ."

"Oh, Gregory, I love you. I love you so much!"

"Pray for me, darling."

Sweet and comforting then was the way she cried on my breast. We restored each other to peace.

Marcia, through her mother and through a long acquaintance with Marcellina, Ambrose's sister in Rome, knew far more about Ambrose than I did.

"Tell me all you know about Ambrose," I asked her, "for I must face him tonight."

CHAPTER THREE

AMBROSE

MY EXAMINATION BY AMBROSE WAS NOT WHAT I EXPECTED. Marcia told me all she knew about Ambrose, and I have now, out of memory, much more to add.

Ambrose loved me with deeper charity than any other man, except my father; and I failed the one as greatly as I failed the other. But Ambrose wrought deeply in my life, and I hold it a point of honor and enjoy it as a remembrance of love to present now a full portrait of this great good man of Milan. I want this one man's nobility to rise up memorable above all others in my story as in my life.

His Life

Ambrose had an older sister, Marcellina, and an older brother, Satyrus, and when he was a baby his father was prefect of Gaul—governor, that is, over Spain, Britain, Cis-Alpine Gaul and Trans-Alpine Gaul, residing at Trier.

There one day the child Ambrose slept in a cradle in the open court-yard of the governor's mansion, and his mouth was open as he slept near the fountain among flowers. A swarm of bees suddenly alighted and covered the child's face and lips and kept entering and coming forth from his mouth. The maidservant cried out and would have slapped the bees away with a cloth, but fortunately the child's father was walk-ing near by with his wife and daughter. He caught the arm of the maid-servant and commanded, "Be still! Fright will anger the bees, and they will sting the child to death!"

Happily the infant did not waken or cry or try to beat the bees off with his small arms and fists. And while the elders watched, tense and not daring to interfere, the bees rose and swarmed beyond sight into the lofty air. The father, relaxing from his terror, said, "If this little child shall live, he shall be something great."

After the death of the father, the widowed mother settled in Rome with her children. Marcellina there professed virginity, and the boy Ambrose, accustomed to seeing his female elders kissing the hands of bishops, held out his hand for Marcellina's kiss, saying, "You ought to do it, for I shall be a bishop." And she reproved him for making light of matters beyond his knowledge.

Ambrose and Satyrus, the two brothers, loved each other and rose together. They were like Castor and Pollux, those half-divine brothers, the one not whole without the other and each made whole by the other's love. People did not think of them separately, but thought of them together; and each of them thought of himself first as the other one's brother. After they finished studying law, Probus was their patron, and they followed him to Sirmium to assist him in his work as governor. It was Probus who secured the appointment of Ambrose as governor of Liguria, so that Ambrose went to Milan, with Satyrus to help him, and for several years governed the province. Probus may have been glad to elevate these two good brothers out of his sight, for Probus governed with rapacity, and honorable young men too near at hand would be as bad as a troublesome conscience.

Auxentius, the Bishop of Milan, was an Arian, not a Catholic, and old. When he died the people were divided as to whether to have another Arian or a Catholic for their new bishop. The partisanship rose to the fury of riot, and Ambrose, hoping as governor to stop the thing short of bloodshed on the stone paving of the church with Arian Christians and Catholic Christians breaking one another's heads, went to the church and addressed the angry people. Gradually he calmed them to silence; and in that silence a child cried out: "Ambrose Bishop! Ambrose Bishop!"

The people who had been divided in anger took this as God's sign, became united in desire, and all voices cried: "Ambrose Bishop! Ambrose Bishop!"

But Ambrose did not want to be a bishop. To renounce the world and enter priesthood in response to inward call of God in the soul was one thing; but to be thrust into it by outward clamor of public demand was another.

He turned to his brother Satyrus, saying, "I do not want to be a bishop. What shall I do?"

And Satyrus promised, "Whatever you do, I am with you."

Ambrose was thirty-four years old, with a brilliant course of worldly honor before him. As a governor in the Roman Empire every great city was open to him. He could rise in wealth and honor and settle finally in Rome, if he liked, as one of the great rich men of the world. If made Bishop of Milan, there he must stay.

So much for ambition, which may be conquered.

But what of natural desires?

He was not an Arian, but of the Catholic party. It was becoming a set rule in the Catholic Church that bishops could not marry and ought not to have female consorts. Even those bishops who were already married when consecrated were supposed thereafter to be continent, and, if the wife died, not to marry again.

Ambrose might consider whether he had the strength of character to be thereafter chaste. For what would it profit a man to deny his flesh and then fail to fulfill his spirit?

Ambrose must have known not only some who undertook chastity, were frail, suffered, and were not chaste; but also those others who made of asceticism an idolatry, so that their carnal continence bore the fruit of spiritual insanity.

A reasonable man, who would mean to abide by so grave a decision, would hesitate, at the ripeness of his powers, to cut himself off for the rest of his life from sexual function. To transfer so willful a power of the flesh into spiritual channels could not be an easy choice to make or an easy resolution to maintain.

The repression of desires, with its attendant anger of soul, would be fatal. Only a man who understood the liberation of soul to be found in positive sacrifice, not in repressing, but in renouncing desires, ought to take such a step. Ambrose may have turned about to his soul and said: "Am I such a man?"

So much for carnal vehemence, which may be spiritualized.

But what of the sweet simplicity of a woman at a man's side, and children holding their hands? What of the thousand spiritual consolations in the long daily flowing of years that a woman loved and loving shares with a man? What of the radiance in the face of his child when a father stoops to lift it? Only a man ready to lay down his life forgoes all hope of these most lovely and solacing of all human things.

The people clamored for Ambrose to lay down his natural life and be their bishop; but Ambrose did not want to be a bishop.

Ambrose left the church and in his capacity as governor ordered certain criminals to be put to torture. Such a thing he had not done before; it should have turned the people against him, but they shouted in the market place: "Your sin be upon us!"

Then he went home, saying he would retire from all office to devote his life to philosophy; but the people still clamored: "Ambrose Bishop!"

So then he sent out for and had brought in to him, publicly, through crowds oppressing his house, common painted women who lived by prostitution. Not even this changed the shout: "Your sin be upon us!"

He prepared for flight. He left the city at midnight, thinking to flee to Ticinium; but he got caught and lost in God's mystery of a night of sevenfold darkness and only circled the city of Milan and was seized at the gate of the city by a crowd at dawn. The people held him and sent to the Emperor Valentinian for an order to make Ambrose bishop.

To be baptized in the primal strength of midmanhood and sin no more was frightening enough; but also to be consecrated as a bishop might well appall a serious man and make him turn about to ask his soul: "Am I so good a man?"

Once more Ambrose escaped and hid outside the city on the estate of Leontius. But a public edict of the Emperor warned none to hide this man, and Leontius gave him up.

Then Ambrose bowed to the will of God.

He was baptized, fulfilled the lower ecclesiastical offices, one a day, and on the eighth day was consecrated Bishop of Milan.

From that day forward, because of the nature of this man, the power of the Catholic Church began to modify the power of the Emperor. In certain crucial matters, where he deemed the spirit was on trial, Ambrose told Emperors what they could and could not do.

Too soon his brother Satyrus died in his arms, and he wept. He lived another quarter of a century without the comfort of his brother beside him.

In Milan young Valentinian and his Empress mother Justina (Galla Placidia's fierce grandmother) tried to seize one church for the Arians. Ambrose prevented them. They threatened him with seizure and exile, and he still prevented them. He drove the Arian sect out of the Western Empire.

He, by his preaching, eased Augustine's hard way to God, and he baptized Augustine.

Mothers did not like their daughters to hear his sermons on virginity, lest they renounce marriage. He persuaded Theodosius to act harshly against some Jews in the East whose temple had been destroyed by Christians. But he also persuaded Theodosius to penance for the massacre at Thessalonica and to clemency toward my father and other Pagans after the fall of Eugenius.

He built a great new church in Milan.

When he came to die he stretched out his arms for the last hours in the form of the cross.

His Customs

After he became bishop it was his custom to leave the door of his house always open for any to come who might need him. It was his custom to teach and baptize aspirants and to preach and have singing in church, some of the songs being wrought by him. He was one who prayed many times during the day and rose several times at night to pray. He accustomed himself to one meal a day and did not eat much then. He sat in the portico of his courtyard, reading to himself, and often when he wrote at night he dismissed Paulinus, his secretary, to rest and did the writing himself. He did away in Milan with the custom of feasting and drinking at the tombs of martyrs. He often went to that part of the church where those were sheltered who were insane—possessed by devils —and so laid his hands on them that many were cured. He crossed the Alps twice in behalf of Valentinian, but would not accustom himself to allow the office of bishop to be belittled by Maximus or any other Emperor.

He was accustomed to speak gravely and walk in dignity. And he would weep with the penitent as if their sins were his own. He was accustomed to judge from the way a man stood and moved what the man was, "for," he said, "the condition of the mind is often seen in the attitude of the body. For this reason the hidden man of our heart is considered to be either frivolous, boastful or boisterous, or, on the other hand, steady, firm, pure and dependable. Thus the movement of the body is a sort of voice of the soul." And he was accustomed to listen for the man in his voice. "In speaking of the voice," he said, "I certainly think it ought to be plain and clear. That it should be musical is a gift of nature, and is not to be won by exertion. Let it be distinct in its pronunciation and full of manly vigor, but let it be free from a rough and rustic twang. See, too, that it does not assume a theatrical accent, but rather keeps true to the inner meaning of the words it utters." And he also would say: "It is seldom that anyone is silent when speaking profits him nothing. A man's speech is the beginning of human error. Bind up thy words that they run not riot and grow wanton and gather up sins for themselves in too much talking."

His habits were forms chosen to express or liberate the spirit of Christianity.

He was accustomed to guard against anger, saying it disordered the mind and left no room for reason.

He was accustomed to leaven justice with mercy, "for," he said, "that which holds society together is divided into two parts—justice and good will, which is also called liberality and kindness. Justice seems to me the loftier, liberality the more pleasing, of the two. The one gives judgment, the other shows goodness."

He had a way of being pleasant without jesting; of being firm, not officious; of being simple, not self-righteous.

He rose early; he worked late; he did many things better for God that other men do worse for money.

And many people loved him.

His Appearance

The slight frame; the narrow face; the brown hair and beard and mustache and the long thin nose; the sad clear eyes and slender hands and feet, and perhaps only the lips a little thick: All these harmonized in a spiritual radiance.

He wore ecclesiastical robes only at the altar, dressing otherwise as an ordinary Roman citizen, but plainer than most, making no flair of white or vivid garments, but wearing plain tunics and, when the weather called for it, a soft brown cloak.

He walked without pomp, he sat without show, seeming really to live and move in the patience of a separate quiet.

Beside the Emperor Theodosius, whose face was ravaged with passions and powers, Ambrose looked like a father quiet with wisdom; beside General Stilicho, the deep-breasted leader of legions, Ambrose had the stillness of awaiting peace; beside Rufinus, lean, lusts etched in his face, Ambrose looked like a light that does not fail.

When he rose in the church to preach, suddenly he was tall, as those things are tall which lift the heart to God.

When he sat in the portico of his house, in the sun and shadow, reading, the stillness of his communion with God spread about him, and men waited for him to lift his head before drawing near.

In the midst of many he appeared to be alone.

His Spirit

This man Ambrose had the power of distinction.

In our Roman world we had built ourselves up to the brink of toppling ruin by neglecting to distinguish betwen good and evil, right and wrong, temporal and eternal. Practical Romans wanted to know how to get things done. "Try this and that. What works is right." I suppose we got our word *pragmaticus* from the Greek word of similar sound referring to one skilled in business. We had just forgotten that a busy fellow, successfully doing things, is not necessarily doing good things or right things. We forgot, even, that things apparently useful or expedient today might plant fatalities for tomorrow.

Moral growth, moral stability and finally moral existence itself become impossible when this pragmatic or utilitarian philosophy permeates a society. Surely we Romans proved that this ingenuity, this science, could build a great state. The state is without love, and the stronger the state becomes, the more desolate society must be. Presently a sane man no longer cares to preserve a civilization full of objects and actions but devoid of love.

And spiritually we Romans were dazzled and bewildered by all the weight of all the religions of all the people we had conquered. Our Roman breasts had been invaded by a thousand gods, some lovely, some obscene, some dreary. Augustine, after Varro, pointed out our extravagant specialization in gods, not only for marriage but for all sorts of affairs. A hundred gods accompanied a man on the street, and God had become inaccessibly remote. Our tolerance had weakened our real belief in anything; we gave momentary service to a steady flow of incompatible doctrines. Naturally we were a heartsick people, overstuffed with accomplishments and devoid of clear spiritual purpose.

The greatness of Ambrose in such an age was the clarity of his power of distinction and his spiritual firmness in behalf of principles. He knew the difference between "I want" and "I ought," between "I can" and "I should," between "this is law" and "this is love." He could distinguish between the polity of God and the polity of state, and could fulfill his authority with spiritual firmness. His breast was not invaded by a thousand conflicting gods, nor his will weakened by toleration of every new fashion that came along. He did not need a different specialist, either mortal or immortal, to guide or excuse him in each different act of his life. As he himself said: "So far as I am able, I am accustomed to refer all my acts to the Lord and never to turn away my mind from Him, nor make more of any man than of the Grace of Christ."

THE EXAMINATION

It was precisely such purity of purpose that I feared when I went that evening to confer with Ambrose. I was as sick with worldly expectations as any other young man in our time. With the awful blindness of Caesar (*Veni, vidi, vici*) I wanted to go places and do things. My passions, including no doubt my fears, assented to this, that and the other opportunity of the days and engaged my mind in able support; but as yet my heart assented to nothing single and simple. Who, like Caesar, comes and sees and conquers is drying his soul to a death without love.

Ambrose was seated at a table, writing, when Paulinus his secretary brought me in. He dismissed Paulinus with a kindly blessing for the night, lighted another small lamp, and we conversed in the solace of dim light.

He began by saying this: "Curiosity moves us all, Gregory. A man enters a room, sees another man writing, and cannot but wonder what is being written there. I want to share my thoughts with you. Let me read what I have just written."

"I would be honored to hear it."

He smiled as he picked up his scroll. "Perhaps you will be less frightened of me after you grow accustomed to my voice."

He began to read, with the flicker of lamplight on his narrow face, and read gently, like a man of quiet reason and deep affection, truly not beating me with his words, but sincerely asking me to share them, and seeming also to offer them to a higher judgment than my own.

I had a strong sense of a third Presence abiding with us two, for Ambrose in spirit and manner gave continual honor to that Divine Guest indwelling in the human heart: God was with us.

" 'The enticement of earthly lusts creeps in,' " he read from his writing, " 'and the outflow of vanities takes hold of the mind, so that the very thing which you desire to avoid you think upon and turn over in your mind. It is difficult for a man to guard against this; to escape it altogether is impossible. For our heart is not in our own power, and our thoughts suddenly stream forth and confound our mind and reason, and draw us in directions other than we purposed. Who, indeed, among the many passions of this body, among the many enticements of this world, can walk securely and purely? The eye looks, and the sentiment of the mind is deflected; the ear hears, and the resolution is perverted; the sense of smell acts and hinders thought; we touch and take fire.

" 'But there is not only this corporeal touch of the five senses.

" 'There is also an interior touch, whereby that woman in the Gospel, who had suffered twelve years from a bloody flux and had not been healed by her physicians, touched and received healing from Christ. This touch with which Christ is touched is the touch of faith. The woman was immediately healed because she drew near to Him in faith. Believers are not they who press upon Christ, but they who touch Him. It is by faith that Christ is touched, not by bodily contact. No one touches Christ who does not touch Him by faith. The torrential flow of worldly passions will be dried up by the warmth of the saving Word if you do with interior touch draw near to Him in faith and but touch the hem of His garment. When anyone so touches and believes, the wrath of God departs and life comes.' "

He laid down his scroll and said with a tone of melancholy, "Wrath departs and life comes! Do we not live in an age of wrath, Gregory? This our Empire is no longer—if it ever was—a great society flourishing in the singleness of a radiant faith. What might have become a wonderful variety of persons and nations in living articulation under God has degenerated into an insane wrath of warring cliques: the army, the Barbarians, the officeholders, the city mobs, the patricians, the Jews, the Catholics, the Arians, the Pagans, the slaves—each group out for its own aggrandizement, and confusion confound all the others. And into the midst of that turmoil, with no clear light to lead you, you are now being thrust by desire."

I could feel his sympathy, his compassion; but above all I was moved by the way this great man treated me as his equal, without any remoteness of pride or pressure of arrogance.

"I want light to live by," I admitted. "But Christianity may not be the only light in the world."

"Ah, yes. So it was with Augustine when he was troubled. You wouldn't know the man, but he has just been made Bishop of Hippo in Africa."

"You mean he who taught rhetoric here in Milan?"

"Yes. You do know him?"

"He was my tutor for a while in Rome before he came to Milan."

"I didn't know that. I am glad to hear it. And you were how old?"

"Ten or eleven years."

"He was not a Christian, then. What sort of things did he teach you?"

"Nothing specific that I particularly remember. But one great lesson he taught me indirectly: the torment of trying to see God."

"I suspect great teachers seldom teach specific facts, but rather waken in our hearts the mood of understanding. I daresay he frightened you?"

"He did. I was frightened by the torment with which he burned. The more so because I trusted him and liked him."

"I think he wanted to see God with the eyes of the flesh and to confirm the vision by reason; but God is seen by the inner eye of the heart, and the vision is confirmed by faith." He looked at me thoughtfully. "I know Senator Symmachus well and have heard your father spoken of with respect. I know the Paganism of Symmachus is more a literary and philosophical sentiment than a religion. Is it like that with your father?"

"Until the recent political strife got his passions involved, perhaps it was. Until the recent crisis he was more a man of affairs than of religion. Now I believe he would die for his faith in our traditional gods."

"And you believe in those gods, too?"

"I honor my father. I love him. I have heard that your father died when you were very young, and thus you missed, perhaps, what I value so highly: the firm guidance of a mature masculine affection. He taught me to trust him and allowed me not to fear him. The feeling grows on me that I should return to his side in Rome. But I have had letters from him bidding me stay in Milan, forget not honor, and revere the gods."

"And you believe in these gods?" He returned to the question I had not answered.

"I don't know. I can honestly say I have enjoyed the thought of many of them. Do they not symbolize the flow and variety of life? Belief per-

haps in the end has to be single. I believe in a Supreme Deity. I want
to lead an effective life in this world."

"You honor your father. You believe in God. Then why do you fear
Christ?"

"If Christ conquers, Rome must die, and I love Rome."

"You interest me. I wish you would think a moment and say more
fully what you mean by that."

I sat in the dim light assembling my thoughts. I made the matter as
clear as I was able.

"I am but a scant reader of Christian scriptures, but I think I have
learned this much, that to become a Christian is to cease to be a Roman.
An old civilization like ours is a large and long accumulation of the
things men are able to do; but just because they could be done—have
been done—does not mean they were all worth doing or now harmonize
with one another. Yet to be a faithful Roman, to try to uphold and prolong the vast and intricate web of good and evil that is our Empire is to
have worldly things set in the heart, and is to serve Caesar before God,
however the heart may yearn for God. And whatever may be conceived
concerning our own gods and those we adopted from Greece and Asia,
it is surely clear that Christ did not propound empire. No. To become
a Christian is to cease to strive for the comforts, dominions, powers and
achievements of this world. If I turned toward Christ, Rome would die
in my heart. I love Rome, the Empire, this vast mortal complex of vice
and glory, of fallible ever-changing onflowing human good and evil. . . .
And may I go further, at hazard of offending you?"

His smile was delightful as he said, "You listened to my sermon first!"

"I can readily see, then, that to become a Christian a man must cease
to be a Roman. But this I wonder: By the way men are now building
the dogma and powers of the Christian Church, is there not danger that
to join the Church one must cease to be a Christian? I can see the possibility of a new sort of thing, politico-religious, not quite Roman and
not quite Christian. You could call it Roman-Catholic, a sort of semi-
spiritual form of empire and perhaps good to save a crumbling society
from ruin. But I suppose Christianity—true Christ-following—will always be a solitary thing, found here and there in separate saints shining
apart like stars in heaven."

Bishop Ambrose did not take offense. Neither did he enter into argument. He tilted his head to one side and said with soft irony, "The
Emperor has not commanded me to make you a saint."

Then he rose and came toward me, and I, too, rose.

He placed his hands on my shoulders. "Although you are a young man of large frame," he said, "and of good homely features and even of red hair, all unlike my brother Satyrus, who much resembled me; yet my heart is astonished at how like him you are. So you hold your head as he did, the strong sound of your voice is like his. My heart is refreshed as if he had returned to comfort my age. I cannot but love you as if you were the son of my brother Satyrus!"

Then he kissed me on each cheek and stood back and wept, saying, "Forgive an old man's tears. I dearly loved, I still love dearly my brother Satyrus."

"And what shall I do about the Emperor's order to become a Christian catechumen?"

"Theodosius has given an order to both of us. Let us obey him in so far as God allows. By such light as I have I shall guide you and instruct you. Do not harden your heart, but open it. The Emperor has given us thirty days. Sometimes he is impatient. If that is not time enough, I will intercede with him for more time."

"Still—I must become a Christian?"

"Not against your will. If God does not turn your will toward Christ, I will be your advocate before the Emperor to have you released from his order."

Then I knew I had been found and taken hold of by a spiritual father. But I did not know my own father was on the verge of death.

CHAPTER FOUR

THE STROKE OF THE TIGER

THE ONSLAUGHT OF DISASTER, LIKE A STORM OF BLACKNESS, struck in mid-January; it shocked my soul and made my mind reel.

The prelude was pleasure and excitement. The Emperor, who enjoyed display, had decided to give a day of games in the Circus in honor of young Honorius. Heraclian, who had not yet secured a governorship, was put in charge of all arrangements, and the Emperor made me Heraclian's assistant. We had less than a month in which to secure the gladiators, the wild animals, the charioteers and all the other necessaries for a daylong entertainment of sport, spectacle and atrocity. We had a whole caravan brought up from Rome, and we scoured northern Italy from one sea to the other for whatever might add dramatic splendor to the event. I enormously enjoyed the whole business, which went on through all the hours of daylight and late into many a night. Heraclian was a passionate showman and wanted to be certain not only of prize charioteers, deadly gladiators and excellent wild beasts, but of every detail of decoration, from the Emperor's box at the Circus down to the costumes of interlude dancers and athletes. From the claw of the lion to the petal of the rose, we worked for dramatic effects.

We had our headquarters set up in the palace. Heraclian, with his square fists and hard jaw, was a good executive. His analysis of the job was this: "We can order what we want, young Julian. We have the Emperor behind us. He loves splendor and won't care how much we spend. Theodosius knows how to bleed a thousand with taxes to please ten thousand with gift and show."

Indeed, it was evident in his palace at Milan that Theodosius enjoyed magnificent living—silk, gold, jewels, feasts and entertainment, with bonuses for the army and extra free rations for the city mob. I enjoyed this glitter. I was not one who disdained the achievements of human-kind. There were muttering priests, philosophers and reformers who would level things down to plain gray subsistence for one and all. But it seemed to me that the desire to enjoy the fine fruits of industry wakened the ambitions and efforts of men who might otherwise still squat in some squalid cave, eating raw beasts.

We didn't dare speak openly of the Emperor's health, but Heraclian saw as well as I did that Theodosius was walking with death as his companion. Heraclian revealed this by saying: "Now that I've calculated chances, I lean more toward Stilicho than toward Rufinus. I don't want to move to Constantinople, and Stilicho is going to be the man of power in Rome and Milan. I shall make Rufinus a present of that dancing girl Furia just in case, but we must have one of our best gladiator combats fought in honor of Stilicho."

Not even Serena could stop the Emperor from overworking, overeating and other excesses. Theodosius enjoyed young women about him with rich flesh and poor minds. Persons of importance came daily from all quarters of the Empire, and I suppose a thousand lamps burned in the palace by night. Theodosius did not subdue his life to prudence. I became convinced that older people, like Theodosius and my father, die usually of the effects of their own characters. It is not really disease, but the operation of their spiritual natures that brings on their end; so that any of us who is not stricken in youth or later by unexpected disease or violence may be sure that his own qualities, by which he accepts life and lives it, include his own acceptance of and invitation to death. This thought by no means appalls me, for to die of those same qualities and values of your own moral nature by which you choose to live ennobles the opportunities of life by adding choice, dignity, honor and welcome to death. Theodosius, it seemed to me, was welcoming death with a last flare of splendor.

I had scarcely any time to see Ambrose in those busy days. I did go to church with Marcia, which pleased her. After the sermon she and Heraclian would stay for the celebration of the mysteries, and Dionie and I, with a crowd of non-Christians, would go outside to wait. Ambrose was the builder of this church, and it was a noble work, especially with sunlight warm on its stones. We would stroll about in the forecourt, under its colonnades or near its fountain.

I told Dionie I was rather shocked at the first few sermons I heard Ambrose deliver, against greed, against adultery and in favor of virginity. He made it seem that all people of wealth were out to wound and cheat their fellows; greed, adultery and drunkenness were the diseases of society.

"He seems offended at the vigor of life. And yet I can't really believe that, for he is a man of great courage."

Dionie and I strolled arm in arm in the sunshine near the fountain in the courtyard. Her hair was piled high and beaded with jewels.

She squeezed my arm against her warm side. "Adultery is a cold-hearted word for the pleasures of love. Have you forgotten we were night fellows in Rome in my bed of delight and laughter?"

"Neither of us was married then," I pointed out.

"Watch out the man Ambrose doesn't enchant you, Gregory, or you'll end up a bishop!"

A strange shock passed between us. I felt it, and I am sure she did, too. It was a swift, silent and deep recognition that she and I still held pleasures of love in store for each other and meant to revive them. We exchanged a glance and knew we had made an appointment, vague, indefinite, for some future occasion. Our former embraces had been delightfully free of those moral considerations involved in marriage. Now adultery was our desire, our intention.

Meantime, in answer to my invitation the poet Claudian had come up from Rome, and he helped keep Marcia entertained while arrangements for the imperial games devoured my time. Marcia was never really gay with Claudian, the way she was with me; her eyes became dark and still as she watched him. And he seemed to make a point of extra courtesy toward her.

Claudian brought letters with him and much news from Rome. First, old Probus had finally confirmed the fears of his hypochondria: He had died. He had been baptized on his deathbed. Marcia would receive some of his vast wealth.

Then there was delightful news from Marcia's mother. Calvena, finding herself intolerably lonely without Marcia, had suddenly married an older Senator who wanted companionship, and they had retired from the noise of Rome to a lovely estate on Capri.

The brevity of the letter from my father made me uneasy. "Since we parted," he wrote, "I have had heavy dreams and dark admonishments in the night. But I fear not to do what the gods command. It is not only these new Christians who are chosen as spokesmen for prophetic realities." But Claudian said my father's color was high and that his health seemed good, only his eye and his thoughts were turned inward.

I noticed that Marcia looked strained sometimes when I came home; I blamed it on the nervousness of her pregnancy. But then she was relieved and happy when Claudian left us to live at the palace. It had worked out wonderfully. I was able to arrange for him to read some of his poems before the Emperor and the imperial circle. Claudian, lean, alert and dark, knew this was his great chance; he struck off and read effectively a poem in towering praise of the exploits of Theodosius. The Emperor listened, I thought, with the tired patience of a sick man. But Serena was greatly moved. She got for Claudian a minor appointment on General Stilicho's staff so that he might live at the palace and fulfill the major function of court poet. Claudian promised he would never forget what I had done for him.

Marcia said, after Claudian left us: "Home is sweeter with just you and me together."

We had much bad weather—mist, rain, wind and even snow. For days at a time you couldn't see the far-off mountains. Then on a gloomy evening of dark dank fog we felt the tremors of an earthquake. All this violence and gloom of nature depressed Theodosius. He began to hold imminent the realization of that prophecy of Holy John of Lycopolis, uttered through a window of a stone hut, that he, Theodosius, would die in Italy. He overworked himself with great affairs, formalizing an edict of amnesty for all who, like my father, had wrought against him; devising means to assure the safety of his sons in their coming rule of the

Empire; laboring with Ambrose on behalf of the Church. He looked forward to the games as a day of pleasure and rest.

Then the air dried, the sun came, and the day of the games was warm and bright. I was overjoyed when Marcia and I walked out in that morning's wonderful sunlight.

"It will be a success!" I hugged her and danced about with her in my arms. "Glory for Gregory!"

"Be careful! The baby!"

I let her stand, and pranced alone. Then I placed my two hands on her belly to feel the presence of our child and began to say something wonderful about myself as a father. But suddenly, like a man hit between the eyes, I stopped. My hands fell to my sides.

"Gregory! What happened!"

"My father! I don't know . . . an awful sense . . . Something snapped in my brain. . . ." I raised my forearm to cover my eyes, and for a moment felt dizzy.

"He'll be all right. Claudian told you his health is really perfect."

"He and I had a bond between us. Something is broken. Marcia! I have to go to Rome. Something fatal is happening to my father. I know it. I must go immediately after the games, tomorrow morning."

I should have known by the force and finality of that snap in my brain that the mystic cord binding me to my father was sharply broken, which could mean only that my father was dead.

Heraclian and Dionie arrived with their retinue, and Marcia and I went along with them to the games.

Dionie noticed the change in me. She squeezed my arm with sympathy and affection. "Some blow has fallen, Gregory. Can I help you?"

"I don't know what it is. I am filled with dread for my father."

"You are subject to these insights. Perhaps he has had only some minor accident."

"I must leave for Rome tomorrow."

Her fingers dug into my arm in a swift spasm of terror, as if some intimation of death had come between us to ruin all promise of pleasure. I think what she feared most of all was death. She tried to live in the illusion that she would be young in the midst of sensuous delights forever. She recovered quickly, boldly, slid her fingers down my arm to squeeze my hand, and said, "Your premonitions are false. I feel it."

The performances of the morning, some lesser gladiatorial combats and minor chariot races, built up the feeling of excitement. The stadium was jammed full of people. Though it was small compared to such things at Rome, it was a joy to the people of Milan, and eight

or ten thousand packed together in such a place can shake the air with
the reverberant noise of man.

Marcia and I, as well as Heraclian and Dionie, were allowed the honor
of sitting in the imperial box with the Emperor, his family and the highest officials. Over our heads was a purple awning upheld by spears of
gold. Being familiar with the vast Circus Maximus and the huge Colosseum at Rome, I wondered if the Emperor's box wasn't too close to
the level of the arena. I worried a little that some miscast javelin might
fly over the parapet into our midst.

Toward the dinner hour the arena was cleared of broken chariots and
dead bodies, and the heralds, after a blare of trumpets, announced: "The
March of Elephants, in honor of the most noble Rufinus, Praetorian
Prefect!"

This was Heraclian's great bid for favor with Rufinus. He knew
Rufinus liked to confirm his power by acquiring females. Nine trained
elephants came in their grand slow-paced massive march around the
arena, each holding in its trunk the tail of the one ahead. On each elephant's back sat a naked black African with a gilded pronged rod to man-
age the beast. On each elephant's head stood a lovely young slave girl,
each from a different part of the Empire. Wearing bangles on their
arms and flowers in their hair, these girls displayed their warm and lovely
torsos nude; from waist to ankles each wore a sort of Oriental pantaloon
garment of filmy brightness, each a different rich color. They carried
tambourines which they beat in rhythm as the great beasts marched,
eyes ablink and tusks flashing in the sun.

In front of the imperial box the elephants broke their head-to-tail line.
Eight of them lined up side by side, the ninth and largest came forward,
raising and lowering his great lazy ears. On his head stood Furia, the
dancing girl owned by Heraclian. Scarcely moving her feet, but beating
on her tambourine, she did on the magnificent tower of the elephant's
lifted head an amazingly realistic dance of offering and submission to
Rufinus, offering all the seductions of her body and the breath and
bodies of the eight slave girls on the other elephants to the pleasure and
desire of Rufinus. Then she stood still. The elephant blinked his eyes
with primeval cunning. The shiny black man reached forward and
touched the elephant's trunk with his gilded rod, and the elephant
curled back his trunk, easily lifted Furia off his head, stepped forward
and deposited her, standing, on the parapet directly before Rufinus.
There was a superb animal splendor in the ease with which the great
beast offered the body of the young woman.

A roar of delight thundered out in the stadium from the crowd. It thrilled me, too, but also impressed me that the parapet of the Emperor's box was too low for imperial safety. Some other elephant, some other time, might lash a fatal proboscis around an imperial person and dash him to death.

I could see the heaving of Furia's ribs and belly from the strain and effort of her dance, and her eyes, brilliant with pride of her performance and greed for rewards, were fixed on Rufinus. He took a jewel from his ear, put it in her hand, and accepted her and the other eight as his slaves. He bowed his glorious acknowledgment to Heraclian, then pulled Furia down to sit beside him in the box. So confident was he of his power that he refused Serena's offer of a scarf to cover Furia's breasts.

Heraclian's audacity had won a success. Rufinus obviously had had his lust aroused and could satisfy it. The Emperor really enjoyed the spectacular manner in which Heraclian had made this scandalous gift. Emperor Theodosius turned to Heraclian and me, his sick tired face warming with a smile. "Well done! Masterly showmanship! Heraclian, I want you to try your hand on a really lavish scale in our magnificent hippodrome at Constantinople. Remember that!"

Then he looked at me. Galla Placidia had squirmed away from Serena to squeeze herself in between me and Marcia. On great occasions such as this I always wore a certain large jeweled emblem of honor inherited in our family from the Emperor Julian. Little Galla had wheedled me into taking this from my toga and affixing it on top of her hair to simulate the diadem of an Empress. Its emeralds and pearls shone cool and splendid on top of her golden hair.

"And you, young Julian," the Emperor said slowly, with all the weight of his power behind his words, "continue to show yourself worthy of any honor. Even the highest you may dream could yet be fulfilled." His voice sharpened. "Come to me soon a confessed Christian, and I will be as your father." He paused, and a strange light of warning, such as the light you sometimes see flash across the face of a black and violent storm, flashed across his countenance. In tones of unearthly majesty he said, "These things are spoken in the wisdom of encroaching death!"

It made me feel on the verge, not only of glory, but of catastrophe.

A moment later Marcia whispered to me, "Gregory, I have a chill. Take me home."

"We can't leave without the Emperor's permission. There's another event before dinner."

It was the Emperor's words which had chilled her. She picked Galla Placidia up from between us, and herself moved next to me, setting that child of fortune and potential power on her other side. Marcia pressed her breast against me and pleaded with me in a whisper again. "Don't become a Christian, Gregory. We're happy as it is."

With the elephants gone, the last action of the morning's performance was ready. Heraclian had decided it would be more exciting to pause for the dinner hour on a climax of fight and death.

A criminal was led out and left standing alone in the sun-swept arena to await a tiger. He was a Macedonian who had done murder, a powerful black-haired fellow with a lot of hair on his naked breast. He looked about in uneasy alarm for the coming of the animal meant to mangle and devour him. The sunlight of heaven was on his forehead, and the saliva of his fear was on his lips.

Just as the trap door opened and the tiger entered the arena, lashing its tail and swaying its head, the Emperor Theodosius rose, with Serena and Stilicho helping him. His face had a green and deathly look. One of the imperial guards set his shield and spear down at my feet and went to help the Emperor.

No one can explain these things. They started to bring the Emperor past where Marcia and I sat with Galla Placidia and Serena's children, and the tiger, inspired by who knows what fell gods or demons, raced across the arena, in utter disregard of the Macedonian criminal, straight toward the imperial box.

I didn't stop to think things out. I seized the shield which the guard had set at my feet and sprang between the Emperor and the parapet just as the swift tiger bounded in a magnificent arc and would have cleared the parapet and struck the Emperor if I had not met the impact of the beast with the massive shield. I was flung back whirling on top of Marcia, my weight knocking her down and the heavy shield striking her a terrible blow on the head. The tiger clawed at the parapet, slipped, and fell back into the arena.

The Emperor, mortally ill with his heart affliction, ordered Honorius to stay and the games to go on. He ordered me to watch over the children.

Dionie dared speak up. "Gregory's wife is badly injured, Your Eternity."

"Then let him care for his wife. You and Heraclian watch the children. Stilicho and Serena will return."

They took the Emperor to the palace, put him to bed, summoned physicians. Ambrose was notified to come.

Meantime, I got Claudian to help me with Marcia. At first he was more unstrung than I, but I was glad to have a friend at my side. Marcia was unconscious; I feared she might be dead. I sent slaves for a litter and had her carried to the nearest place I could think of—Ambrose's house.

Ambrose was hurrying to go to the Emperor as we arrived. He turned to his secretary. "Paulinus, take care of these children. Find a doctor." We put Marcia to bed in a small room. Her breathing was low. Judging from how shocked and sick Claudian looked, I must have looked pale and dreadful.

Paulinus brought in two Greek physicians, a master and his student. I had no confidence in them. They looked hungry. They drove us out and closed themselves in Marcia's room.

I sank to my knees in the portico and tried to say a prayer. I didn't really know how the Christians prayed, but for Marcia, a Christian, it ought to be a Christian prayer.

This made Claudian furious. He seized my arm and tried to pull me to my feet. "You fool! Mice build their nests in the head of God!"

I remembered the story he had told me of his shocking disillusionment. Until several years ago he had been one who wrote poems and oracles in verse for the priests in the great Temple of Serapis in Alexandria. Imperial orders came to destroy the temple and the huge image of the god. When in a moment of terror this great image was toppled over, the god's head split open on the stone floor and a huge nest of mice scattered and the animals scurried across the stones. Seeing these mice come out of the head of the god had shocked Claudian into leaving Alexandria and coming to Rome to make his fortune.

I cried out, "In Christ's name let me go!" Then I shrugged my arm loose, and, instead of praying, I wept.

Claudian shook me. "You would do better to get those idiot doctors out of there and bring in some old woman who knows how to take care of sick bodies. I'll do it myself." He rushed off.

In half an hour the doctors came out.

"She's dying," the master said.

"She will die," the apprentice added.

I clapped for the slave who carried my purse and paid their greedy hands. They left.

I stood by the bed, looking down at my tender, young and lovely wife, amazed at the purity of her quiet face. I had neither inward nor spoken thoughts at that moment but felt an almost unbearable pressure of silent love.

Claudian returned with a fat old woman who at least was clean, though she did have a strong personal female odor. Her name was Crassa, and she had a dingy fame in Milan as a procuress and healer.

She felt Marcia's breast and head with her broad quick soft hands. She felt down under the covers.

"Now," Crassa said, "this is a lucky thing. A child in the belly, but all quiet there. She won't lose the child. All that matters is the blow on the head. Did you beat your wife with a club, young noble? I've seen worse come out of it only a little crazy."

She called for a dozen bricks to be warmed, and laid them along Marcia's sides and legs. She placed an emblem of fertility on Marcia's navel to save the child, demanded my ring and set it between Marcia's breasts —"as if you lay there, young husband: She will cling to life"—and put a little bag of scented herbs on Marcia's forehead.

By nightfall Marcia's breathing and heartbeat had improved, though she remained unconscious and had sinking spells. Claudian had left. Ambrose had not returned. A messenger came, summoning me to the palace. The massive Crassa said there was nothing I could do. She sat fat and stolid in the doorway of Marcia's room. "Death can't come in past me," she promised.

Seeing her massive body there in the doorway reassured me, for Crassa had the strange power of inspiring confidence in both good and evil. Blind and primitive forces seemed bound to harmonize with destiny in her presence.

But at the palace conditions were shocking. Ambrose met me and led me to where the great Theodosius lay on his couch of gold and purple. "He wants to touch your hand in gratitude for leaping between him and the tiger."

I knelt at the couch. The great weary dying man asked, "How is the child, your wife?"

"She lives, Your Eternity."

He touched my head. "I die. I trust you. Be faithful to my son Honorius."

"I shall be faithful to Honorius."

It was a vow made to a dying man. Ambrose, Serena, Stilicho and others heard it.

I stood back. It was an awful scene. It lasted hours. This Spaniard had lived hard and died hard. His face was puffed, his limbs were swollen, his breathing rasped noisily. During this last battle of mortality the great Theodosius did not renounce the world; he clung to his majesty with a fierce strain of spirit and disposed of the world before he left it.

Stilicho and Rufinus, mistrusting and hating each other, watched at the left-hand side of the couch, catching and clinging to every whisper of the Emperor's that might give one power against the other. Serena, torchlight flickering on her impassioned face, sat at the right of the couch, often holding the Emperor's hand.

Ambrose administered final religious rites. The Emperor was propped up on pillows to ease his breathing. Oddly, in the puffiness of the rest of his face his nose stood out sharp and thin; and his eyes alternately went dead and flashed fire.

At a gesture of his weak hand, yet a gesture still imperious, I brought his two children to the foot of the couch. Honorius was trembling and let me hold his arm to steady him. Little Galla Placidia, with a glitter in her eye, clung to my hand fiercely as she watched without flinching the monstrous process of death in her father.

During past weeks Theodosius, knowing his death to be at hand, had written out his will in part; but now he grappled with dissolution while, between heaving throes, he made final disposition. Honorius would be Emperor of the West, a boy of eleven years. Arcadius, the fifteen-year-old lad in Constantinople, would be Emperor of the East. General Stilicho was appointed Regent in the West and Rufinus Regent in the East. Serena was to be as a mother to the Emperor's children. Her place would be here with Honorius and Galla Placidia, but let her not forget Arcadius. Honorius could in due time be betrothed and married to Maria, the elder daughter of Serena and Stilicho. Let it be well known that Ambrose was spiritual guardian of Honorius. Theodosius pointed at me as the chosen companion and tutor for the boy Emperor, under the guidance of Ambrose. He warned that Alaric was ambitious and discontented, and that the rising power of the Goths must be watched. Let those in political power aid those in spiritual place to strengthen the Church and eradicate Paganism and heresy.

The dying of this man was a rending of the Empire in twain, under boy Emperors, with the Regent of the East and the Regent of the West as mortal enemies.

The torches held their angry blaze in the great chamber.

For a moment the astonished look of a small boy who has been accosted by a great stranger lighted up the Emperor's ravaged face. It was a beautiful expression of human wonder. Then Theodosius shuddered and died.

Serena squeezed her arms against her belly and groaned like an animal thrust through with a mortal spear. It was a sound of ravage and grief that sobbed out in the great hollows of the death chamber and re-echoed down the hallways of my mind at night long thereafter.

Galla Placidia tugged at my hand until I lifted her, warm, solid, heavy, in my arm. "Gregory, am I Empress now?" she asked.

"No, darling. Not yet."

She buried her face against my neck and sobbed.

I took the children to a nurse in a far part of the room. A messenger went to announce to the legions that the Emperor was dead and Honorius was Emperor. I was awed by the death of Theodosius, but I was in a torment of anxiety about Marcia.

I could not leave without permission of someone in authority. Bishop Ambrose was deeply engaged in giving spiritual comfort to Serena. I turned to General Stilicho and asked leave to depart. Rufinus stood beside him.

"You have been a help with the children," Stilicho granted. "I see no need for you to stay longer."

"And no need for you to return hereafter." Rufinus added a sharp and permanent dismissal from service.

Stilicho would not accept this intrusion on his new authority. "Hold!" he said to me. Then he faced Rufinus. Stilicho, the deep-breasted stalwart Vandal, risen to the peak of Roman military power and now Regent of the West, faced the lean, dark and sinister man of political might. "I have been appointed guardian of the Emperor Honorius, and Regent here."

"I am still Praetorian Prefect!"

"I am still General of the Armies!"

The two men glared at each other in hard hostility. This was the first outbreak of the new order, of the split of Empire, of that cold and competitive hatred between the East and the West that was to be so fatal in the years ahead.

Stilicho turned back to me. "The Emperor bade you be faithful to Honorius. Go to your wife now. An official place will be made for you here later."

Rufinus gave me his look of death, and the smile I returned only enraged him further. I thought in my pride: What can he do to me now? I have the upper hand on the dark scoundrel! But even at that moment one of his secret agents had left Rome and was well on his way to Milan with news for Rufinus that would enable him to destroy me.

"Until I leave for Constantinople," Rufinus warned Stilicho, "I'll set extra guards to watch over Honorius."

"It would be well if I could do the same for Arcadius!" Stilicho countered.

The two enraged men were thus accusing each other of the hidden desire to murder the young Emperors Honorius and Arcadius. I could see that what comes through as government has little to do with reason, for it is the result of the interaction between persons in power. Those men of power, in their two antagonistic persons, opened a deplorable fissure in our world society. They couldn't have done it without power. And I wondered: Could they have done it in a sound and sane society?

I left the palace and hurried through the deep silence of dark star-glittering night to Ambrose's house.

Crassa, the massive, lewd and benevolent old woman, still sat in Marcia's doorway, dreamily watchful, darkly alert, primitive and knowing. "Death came, snuffing and stinking. I refused to give way. Death went elsewhere," she said.

"The Emperor has died."

"The one or the other. I could have saved him had they summoned me there; but here was my place." She rose up, massive and sound, struck me a robust blow on the chest with her fist. "So, young husband! We have lost an Emperor but saved a young wife. She will be good for many love nights yet. You can thank Crassa."

She laughed, then went in to look at Marcia by the light of a little terra-cotta oil lamp. Marcia's face was pale and still. "Two lives," the gross Crassa said. "Mother and child both saved. A good night's work." A leer of lewdness and joy lighted her dark heavy face.

She took her amulet and gave me my ring. "One more setting of warm bricks along her tender flanks and she'll wake up and groan. Let her lie quiet two days, or if she babbles with a thick tongue, four days. You and she will be making one joy with two backs before the week's out."

When I paid Crassa an extra amount she thumped my chest again with her solid fist. "Good, young noble! Good. I've got a red-haired wretched daughter. She'll starve if I don't do something to save her. This will pay for a few days while I think, while I plan."

Marcia regained consciousness toward evening of the next day, but she did not babble.

Indeed, she could not talk.

She made an effort. She strained her throat, twisted her mouth and moved her tongue, but could not form words or make any except odd whimpering sounds. She was frightened. I comforted her until her tears dried. She took broth and slept, clinging to my hand.

For two days and nights it was the same. She listened and heard me and responded with tears or with smiles or by lifting her hand and touching my lips. But she could not utter a word.

Toward evening of the third day I was snatched from her side by news of dark things done at Rome.

CHAPTER FIVE

CAESAR AND CHRIST

MY FATHER AND I OWNED CONSIDERABLE PROPERTY. THERE were the mansion and warehouses in Rome, villas near by in the Alban Hills and down on the seacoast, various farms and vineyards in Italy, the villa at Milan, another on Lake Como, cattle ranges in Spain, plantations in Sicily, grain estates in Africa. My mother had left me properties in Greece and in Gaul. I suppose here and there we had thousands of horses, tens of thousands of sheep and fives of thousands of cattle and certainly a multitude of slaves, besides various manufactories, warehouses and tenement properties. I never had bothered our freedmen in charge of these things for an accurate list of all our holdings.

The deed done at Rome enabled Rufinus, as Praetorian Prefect, to confiscate all this wealth; but this was trifling compared with my father's life and my liberty.

Formerly our Caesars had been cremated; then the man's effigy was installed in state on a gold-and-purple couch in the handsomest room of the palace. For weeks, as if he were still alive, the daily routine of imperial power was carried out in the presence of the ashes and image of the dead Caesar. Finally ashes and image were conveyed in splendor and pomp to the tomb, and statues of the deified Emperor began to appear.

But with Christian Emperors it was different.

The body of Theodosius was embalmed. It was placed on a splendid catafalque below the altar in Ambrose's basilica on the third day. The Egyptians who embalmed the body had been delayed while they searched nearby markets for some of their potent mysterious fluids. The funeral rites were to be held the next morning. After that the body would rest in state in the palace for forty days, at the conclusion of which time Ambrose would deliver the funeral oration. Later, when the roads were open and the tomb ready, the corpse would be conveyed to Constantinople.

Ambrose, who had been at the palace on this third day, came home hurriedly and strode into the room where I sat beside Marcia in her muteness and fear. "Come speak to me in my study, Gregory."

I squeezed Marcia's hand. "Try to sleep, darling. I'll be right back." She looked alarmed. She tried to say something, but could not. She placed a hand over her lips to hide the futile distortion of her gentle mouth. Then she turned her whole face away from us to hide her anguish. Perhaps somehow she knew sooner than I did that there was real danger that she might never see me again.

Ambrose walked rapidly ahead of me. I faced him in his study. I had never seen his features and his whole bearing so alert, so grave. "Gregory, your life is in danger. Fatal news has come from Rome to Rufinus. I was at the palace when the news came, and that has given me time to warn you."

I realized in a flood of shame that I had forgotten the premonition of disaster to my father. It came back with dark force. "My father!"

"You know?" Ambrose watched my eyes sharply.

"Nothing. I have had forebodings . . . vague, dreadful. . . . What has happened to my father?"

"Then you are, as I thought, innocent of complicity in his crime. He must have been possessed and driven to madness by demons. He practiced divination again. On the morning before the Emperor's death he rose in the Senate and announced that steaming entrails of animals had shown him for certain that Theodosius was dying even as he spoke. The Senate was aghast at such treason."

"I should never have left him. My father needed me in Rome."

"His madness drove him further. He said his divination had shown him that Rome was doomed unless a new Julian Emperor rose to restore the old gods. Then he went home and opened his veins in the bath."

I remembered my father's strength of body and warm good face. I felt suddenly pale and sick, standing before Ambrose.

"That prophesy of a Julian Emperor fatally marks you, his son."

I didn't understand what Bishop Ambrose was saying. I groaned, "O Father! With no one who loved you there!" I turned away and hid my face in my hands.

"Rufinus claims you are the Julian usurper named in your father's prophecy. Rufinus claims you poisoned the Emperor in a plot with your father. Rufinus is now making out orders to confiscate your father's property and yours, and for your seizure and execution. My only chance to save you from the vengeance and rapacity of Rufinus is to get you at once to the church for sanctuary."

I looked at Bishop Ambrose in dull incomprehension. "Why should I be saved? I am guilty of deserting my father."

His voice sharpened with authority. "Act now. Grieve later!"

He took my arm to urge me into motion, and from his slender fingers, clasping my tense muscle above the elbow, I felt an unaccustomed flow of spiritual forces. He so looked into my eyes with a penetrating radiance of charity that I felt that he not only could save my life but also had the power to heal my grief.

Not waiting for other company, the two of us went out onto the street and started for the basilica.

We were a hundred yards from the beggar-clotted entry to its colonnaded forecourt when I saw the praetorian guardsmen coming at a brisk march down the street. I never doubted they were on the mission of my death. Their spears glinted, and their scarlet-plumed helmets gleamed with my death. The tramp of their feet roused the beat of my heart to wildness, and my fear severed me from the divine shelter of Ambrose.

They had come around a corner at the other side of the basilica into a blaze of sunset light. There was no reason for them to recognize me as quickly as I did them. I bolted from Ambrose's side and ran full speed for the portal of the church. My sudden dash revealed to the guards who I was, and they broke into a run. I was twenty paces nearer the portal than they as we converged. The clot of beggars saw danger coming. They leaped and scattered. One of the praetorians hurled a spear. It came plunging in low, shot between my legs, and tripped me up. I hit the stone paving hard, scrambled up, scraped and dazed, and ran stumbling down the middle of the court, past the fountain, and entered the door of the church only a breath and a stride ahead of two soldiers. Dozens of people in the courtyard started aback, gaping at us. I got not quite to the altar but as far as the catafalque on which rested the body of the Emperor Theodosius. There I stood at bay with my back against this imperial couch of death.

The two soldiers, moist with anger, drew up short and stood glaring at me and panting for breath. Actually I think they were more in awe of the imperial corse than they might have been of the sacred altar. The rest of the squad had not dared enter the church on an errand of violence.

In a moment Bishop Ambrose came. He stood between me and the praetorians. "This is holy ground and not a place of violence," he said.

"The man is guilty of treason."

"God is judge in this place, not Rufinus."

The guards breathed hard and looked at me savagely. They estimated the strength and loyalty to Ambrose of a group of priests and other Christians who had gathered about us; then they turned on their heels and marched out of the church.

"Rufinus will order me to give you up," Ambrose prophesied. "That was a bold dash you made. We will have time to appeal to Stilicho."

"I came with you without thinking. Then I ran here without thinking. What right have I to Christian sanctuary!"

"You knocked, and it was opened unto you."

I hung my head in a wave and weight of grief and despair. "I am innocent. But I loved my father. I honor him. I am no more afraid to face my doom than he was. I, too, shall go home and open my veins. If you love me, be kind to Marcia."

Bishop Ambrose put a hand on my shoulder. "Gregory, it is more craven to despair than to seek justice. It is more craven to despair than to seek mercy. Wait here. Christ be with you and comfort you!"

I swung to the opposite extreme. "I'll have my revenge on Rufinus! That dark scoundrel is going to be murdered!"

Ambrose shook his head in sorrow. "Vengeance is a denial of God. Your mind is shaken by the shocks of grief. I say again, Christ be with you!"

I felt insulted in my wounded fury, and cried out, "Christ taught that even self-defense is a denial of God. Will Christ restore the life of my father? Will Christ cut out the heart of Rufinus?"

I saw I had wounded Ambrose. He made the Christian sign before me and said, "Your sin be mine!"

I wished he had not said it. I did not like that "Your sin be mine!" saying. It lessened the feeling I had had of being sheltered and healed by his active love. There was about it an air of negative intrusive self-martyrdom. "I'll bear my own sins," I said at last in a sullen but calmer voice.

I saw there were tears in the man's eyes as he watched my face. I realized that Ambrose was a subtle and aloof man in whom flashes of direct, vigorous and active love might be followed by pieties and shadows of his own lonely necessity. His soul had never forgotten the death of his brother Satyrus. I felt the shame of wounding a man who understood grief and was protecting my life. I clasped his hand with my full young strength, not realizing that I probably hurt his slender fingers. I said, "Your love has done me good!"

His eyes widened with a positive flash. "For all your rude young strength and boiling up, how like Satyrus you are in the end!" he exclaimed. "You will be saved by love, young Julian. All men fear so strange a thing. Fear itself is afraid of love. But Satyrus was not afraid of love."

Then he left me in the care of Simplician, an elderly priest with dry hands and a very large nose. This man assured me that I was on doubly sacred ground, being near the altar and beside the body of the great Theodosius. Moreover, the sacred remains of two holy martyrs were interred there and wrought miracles.

"Violence," Simplician concluded, "does not penetrate the basilica of our holy Bishop Ambrose. He has upheld the temple of our Lord Christ against Emperors before now, and this Rufinus is no Emperor."

I watched Bishop Ambrose walk all the way down the long floor of the church to the door. I had a forlorn sense that I was losing something vital, and when his figure vanished I bent my head and sighed and felt drained empty of all good cheer.

Several priests had already begun to stretch across the nave of the basilica a heavy rope of purple cord to keep people from pressing too close to the Emperor's bier. They fastened it to waist-high movable posts about four paces from the catafalque. The elderly Simplician, with graceful motion of his dry hands, drew for me an imaginary line just behind the catafalque. "Stay behind the purple rope," he said, "but since you are not a Christian, please go no closer to the altar than this line imagined here, nor grieve the holy martyrs with tread of Pagan feet."

There, in a space twelve or fifteen feet wide, stretching across the basilica, with the Emperor's couch of death like an island in its center, was my space of sanctuary. I did not mind honoring old Simplician's imaginary line which kept me—a Pagan—from intruding on a too sacrosanct Christian spot. I thought, He's an old man, but a good one. . . . (And, indeed, with words very like that, Ambrose, on his deathbed, was to appoint Simplician as his successor to the Bishopric of Milan.) The altar, a rather plain wooden affair with a few objects on it which I did not understand, had no religious meaning to me. I was more superstitious about treading over the bones of the martyrs, Gervasius and Protasius, for they might well have miraculous powers and use them against me if offended. I would knowingly step on no man's grave.

But also, that figure on a cross, which stood near the altar, caused me alarm, a slow, a deep, an increasing alarm.

I think almost any man has had experience fighting for his life and knows the joyous invigoration, roused up by courage, of fighting a good fight. It was a very different and strangely interesting experience to be compelled to passive waiting while another man—Bishop Ambrose—fought for my life out of my sight, beyond my hearing; I could do nothing, outwardly, but wait. What happened in the inward man, then, was new and different. While Ambrose fought to save my life I carried on an inward struggle to evaluate it. Was it worth living? Was it worth saving? I felt my grief, my despair, my solitude and my helplessness.

And I stood between Caesar and Christ.

Caesar on his bier was a familiar presence. His head and shoulders were slightly elevated, and his whole figure lay just above the level of my eyes. He wore a splendid robe and jewels and scarlet slippers and a diadem. So I had seen him in life. He seemed almost to breathe. His bold and waxen Spanish nose still seemed to smell the smoldering of Empire and the sparks of power. What is life? What is death? Even the body of this man made me tremble. He it was who might have favored, in some dim time to come, my marriage to his daughter Galla Placidia, my succession to his power. What now of power and glory? I am sure I made a deep silent symbolic identification between my father, dead in Rome, and Theodosius, dead there before me. And my grief was sharpened, my fidelity to my sense of sonhood was deepened.

But off to one side of the altar, raised on a low pedestal and lighted by oil lamps, was a dreadful image of Christ that I looked at once and tried not to look at again. It was a figure of Christ crucified, a little larger than life size, carved out of wood and painted in colors of human flesh. It was hard to believe he was not a real man, hung there on nails. He was naked. He wore a crown of thorns. His head hung. His muscles were pulled. His wounds bled. His mouth was open to inbreathe agony. Compared with the serene dead reclining corpse of Theodosius, gowned and jeweled in worldly splendor, an august father in final sleep—compared with Caesar the naked Christ was a terrible presence of agony.

I turned my back on Christ's passion and, like a condemned man, stood guard beside the corpse of the Emperor. But still the cruel image of the crucified Christ haunted me and more than once compelled my stiff resistant glance. We Romans were not supreme artists, like the Greeks. The Greeks had given us images of our gods in serene and radiant beauty. The whole dream of Paganism was to turn away from suffering toward beauty, composure and peace. This realistic image of man in the agony of death offended and frightened me. It brought to consciousness a new dimension—suffering accepted, suffering sought—and that was a revolutionary deepening of conscious thought from which I desired to flee. But stiffen my back as I would, Christ in agony watched me and haunted me.

For simple human comfort and to escape from Christ and Caesar, I fixed my eyes on a woman on the other side of the purple rope. She was one of those interested women who stand, fist on hip, watching what goes on. Not young, not old, but interested. She watched me, she watched the priests, she watched the people. She would shift her weight from one leg to the other, fold her arms across her breast, and still watch what was going on. She would turn her head at a sound, raise her eyebrows, smile. And all the time her face was eager and her eyes alight with intelligent interest. She would go home to tell her family all about it.

I felt a sudden flash of anger against my father. He might have been driven by dreams and passions to practice divination, prophesy Theodosius' death and destroy himself. I had seen the groundwork of that madness laid when I was with him in Rome. But why that dreadful prophecy of a Julian Emperor? He must have known that would destroy me. This anger burned out in one hot flash. For what can those marked down by the gods do? Had not I myself been marked by the gods to strike Marcia down with a violent blow on the head from the shield on my arm? I loved her no less than my father loved me.

So at last it really came, like blackness from without, like tides from within. I suffered all the dull nudgings and beatings and blindings of grief. Without making a sound I yet cried in my heart for my father. My whole breast ached, and I was dazed at the calamity which had befallen Marcia. Perhaps she would never speak again. Perhaps her apparent partial recovery was only an illusion and she, too, would die, as the Emperor had died, as my father had died . . . as my mother had died. For now I remembered how as a small boy I had gone secretly with offerings to fertility shrines, begging the gods to send me a brother; and finally, when I had almost forgotten those boyish prayers and was almost a man, my brother was born dead and my mother died with him.

The bitter phrase of Claudian's disillusion, like a bell of despair, rang over and over again in my skull: "Mice build their nests in the head of God!"

And I heard again that terrible groan, as of a stricken animal, that Serena had made when Theodosius died.

Why had a man so sane, so good, so reasonable as my father been ruined by political and religious passions?

Why had my instinctive effort to save the Emperor from the tiger resulted in such brutal damage to Marcia, who was innocent?

Gregory the Emperor. *Gregory Imperator!*

The words came like a flash and a shout in my mind.

Suddenly the hot focus of my passions blazed up in a fierce acknowledged desire to be the foremost man in the world, robed in power and glory, feared, obeyed, seated on the throne of untouchable grandeur.

My father had prophesied no less. I looked at the face of the dead Theodosius and muttered savagely, "Your daughter and your crown!" Then in this fury of pride I turned to face Christ, hanging naked and bleeding on his cross, as if I were above the need of being saved by agony, above the need of being saved at all. I thought his body moved. The knees straightened. The belly contracted. The shoulders heaved. His head lifted to gaze at me. I began to tremble in hysterical tension. I had an impulse beyond reason to go fling myself at his feet and cry, "Mercy!" It was my lonely human need of love, grown infinitely profound.

The mind is a wild thing. All this time I had not moved much or appeared, I am sure, outwardly strange. I was not really crazy. It was simply that in those hours of uncommon strain I was more intensely, more consciously aware than a man usually is of the deep stress and swift strife in those unfathomable depths of the psyche where dreams, passions and images brew.

What happened next astonished me for years.

I did not fling myself at Christ's feet.

I conquered the impulse of subjective self-abandon, the wild desire to throw away my life in one outcry of faith. I became logical, rational, reasonable. I viewed the image objectively. Christ, my father had often said, was an obscure man who went about preaching against the stable order, urging the poor and discontented to follow him in destroying the old and taking over the new, until finally his fellow Jews, alarmed at his subversive teaching and following, got the Roman authorities to crucify him. Even that much was less a matter of historical record than of hearsay evidence. Pliny and Tacitus, for example, had reported only what was being said long after the event. And in a dozen or more generations since then—as my father analyzed it—the Christians, in order to build a Church, increase their numbers and magnify their power, had developed, revised and canonized an accumulation of fiction, legend and dogma centering around this radical teacher. The human Jesus, my father had pointed out, was an obscure man who got into tragic difficulties as a result of his subversive teaching, while the supernatural Christ worshiped by the Christians was the fabrication of a thousand minds.

Such an analysis was supposed to prove that the worship of Christ was absurd.

But the absurd, the unreasonable, is a vital part of human life. My very position there in sanctuary between Christ and Caesar was absurd. I was not able to dismiss Jesus for being obscure, nor the Christ for being imagined. For whether or not I could believe we are all to be saved by the slaying of a God, that image of Crucifixion made me know in my heart forever that he whom they called the Christ was bitterly tortured by my fellow men for his love of man. And he had said, "Forgive them, Father, for they know not what they do!" It was greater love than I had courage to accept.

Thus, while I believed in Christ's suffering, I did not like it, I did not want to participate in it. Reason takes offense at suffering, but faith does not. I was reasonable. I understood with clear sorrow that reason judges and decides by concept and without the fertile sympathies of love: And nothing more surely destroys the happiness of men than an absence of love in their doings. But I could not accept the absolute humility and utter sacrifice of crucified love.

I said courteously to Christ, "I cannot accept your way."

I turned to Caesar, letting my mind soar in a dreamy dishonest imagery of temptation: Gregory Julian the Emperor! Marcia, the invalid, would be tenderly hidden away and cared for by Gregory the Emperor and Galla Placidia, his Empress bride. But the bold waxen Spanish nose of Theodosius, cold and dead (as my father was cold and dead), cut the fumes of dreams like a sword. I loved Marcia. I had a real affection for Galla Placidia as she was, a child, but no insane desire to prey upon and abuse her as a means to power.

I said courteously to Caesar (and to my father also): "You cannot help me now."

I had forgotten Ambrose, and Marcia was stricken mute. I felt separated from everybody, deprived of fellowship, utterly alone, and without any core of faith to hold my life together.

And then, at deep levels, my life broke up in sorry fragments. It was as if I had dropped a lovely vase on the stone floor and the shards lay scattered round and round my feet. It was a quiet, clear and irrevocable sense of disaster. I knew, I knew profoundly, that I had no other task in the world but to try to mend my own shattered soul; and, flooded with the wisdom of a broken heart, I knew I had the courage and the patience to keep on working at the job until I died.

I closed my eyes a moment, thought of Marcia, and said, "The spiritual forces of nature heal and defend you!"

It was like a death and farewell.

Then, standing upright in the body, my spirit stooped down to begin the infinite work of gathering and mending.

I wonder how many of us are not at all what we seem. I believe it is a common tragedy of youth to diverge in outward action from our inward need, doing trivial things well (such as rising in place and power) to make up for and hide (and alas, only increase!) the vital spiritual failure.

For years to come I was to lead an apparently proud, active and vivid life in the world; but all the time I was in truth a lonely spirit stooped down to earth trying to mend the intangible, mystic and painful fragments of my crumbled and fallen life.

CHAPTER SIX

THE EMPEROR'S MIRACLE

I SAW THEIR DAGGERS. THREE YOUNG RUFFIANS FROM THE street stood close to the purple rope and growled at me:

"Coward!"

"Eunuch!"

"Slave!"

Their faces were hard with malice and hatred. I don't think they hated me in particular; they were just the sort of brutal young killers and destroyers that cities breed, vicious young bloods who love to stir up riot.

"Come from behind this purple rope," they taunted me. "We have gifts for your guts!" They slashed the air before them with their dagger blades.

They kept up such vituperation for ten minutes, until two monks came and shamed them away. They made me cutthroat signs of death with their daggers as they left, then broke into harsh and contemptuous laughter.

Actually these insulting fellows did me the good of restoring some of my common sense and robust love of the villainous ways of men. With human vitality so vigorously expressed by such careless young brutes, I could well believe in the long strife and continuance of human affairs. A lot of Christians had the fanciful notion that the world was about to end with Christ's second coming and the day of judgment. The way they calculated was this: Since the year of the Crucifixion there had now been just about as many years as there are days in a year—therefore the end was at hand.

The wealthy Paulinus of Aquitaine, later to become Bishop of Nola, and his wealthy wife Therasia were such believers. Only a few months ago this Paulinus, a Roman of our class, well known in my father's circle, a former consul and governor, had shocked us by throwing over Rome, fame and fortune to go off from his rich estates into a monastery, while his wife retired to a convent. They both had been guests in our house; I knew their looks and the sound of their voices. And what was his motive? Well, Paulinus himself put it like this: "Against Christ's coming my heart quakes and trembles to its inmost fibers, my soul has terrible foreboding of the future, lest, bound fast by weak fleshly cares and loaded with the weight of worldly things, when through the opened heaven the awful trumpet sounds I may not be able to lift myself on light pinions to meet the coming of the Lord. . . ."

Ambrose had preached a joyous sermon on this conversion of Paulinus and Therasia. But the three villainous young men with their noisy daggers made me think that the grand and terrible comedy of Rome and the world would wag on a long time yet. And I didn't want to be shut out from it.

When the inward mind is sick and the soul despairs and the shock of disaster repeats its weary beating against the brain, a man still sees, as in a dreary pageant, what goes on around him. So it was with me.

Torches were lighted around about the Emperor's couch of death and lamps were lighted on pillars. The church that evening and night was like a great whispering gallery where all the gossip and rising excitement of Milan came flowing past me. People thronged in to behold and pray for the Emperor and to see, in sanctuary, Gregory Julian, the pariah, the criminal, the doomed man.

The handsome sturdy young Barbarian, Captain Alaric, came in with five of his chief men. He paid no attention to me. But after a brief prayer for the Emperor he said to his men, not caring who heard him, "We Goths fought bravely for this man Theodosius. We snatched him victory from defeat. Thousands of our brothers died to save his Empire. He is gone, and we have not had our reward. Neither Stilicho nor Rufinus will hear our just demands. We fought, we bled, we have been dismissed. Let us return to our home below the Danube. Let us remember this insult."

There was anger afire in their fresh and vigorous faces. Alaric, with his glistening locks and fine impassioned blue eyes, was like a proud and outraged young hero ablaze with ambition. I admired his powerful legs and brawny shoulders and the kingly courage of his voice.

People who came in later spoke of the Gothic troops and wagons leaving Milan. I heard one man, looking at the dead face of Theodosius, dare to say, "Our extravagant Spaniard there, who bled us dry with taxes, had plenty of money for splendor, but none for the Barbarians who fought at his side."

Ambrose was a long time returning. By this I knew he had not won anything like a pardon for me.

Rufinus himself came before Ambrose did. He had with him a small band of his notable sycophants. They came like a gorgeous troop of the mighty, and the humble slunk aside to make them way. I was startled to see among them Heraclian and Dionie. Heraclian looked more brutal in that company, but Dionie looked chilled, hardened and cold. I waited for her to see me; then her face would, I was certain, light up.

Rufinus took note of me. It was his reason for coming. While this mortal enemy was there I stood straight and motionless, too proud to show fear. He had not come to pray before the Emperor, but to foment trouble. He let a crowd draw about him. His lean corrupt presence brought out the evil in their faces. He harangued them with a sneer in his voice: "There lies the great Emperor Theodosius, slain. There stands the foul murderer who poisoned him. How long shall this crime be hid by the stubborn blindness of Bishop Ambrose? Is this sacred place of Christ to be sanctuary for a vile murderous polluted heathen!"

There was a stir and mutter in the crowd. A woman stepped forward and spat on me.

Among all those hostile faces I could count alone on Dionie to look on me with love. I stood straight and proud and watched for Dionie to smile, to make one of her deep-reaching glances or gestures of love.

Dionie made no sign.

I was not too shocked to see Heraclian, the opportunist, fawning on Rufinus. But I was deeply wounded by Dionie, standing there as if she were blind and could not see me, as if she had never known me.

The simple need of love roused me and I called her name: "Dionie!"

I saw her moisten her lips and turn her face away. However false and treacherous her heart, her profile was beautiful in torchlight. Her cowardly denial of my need for love enraged me. I clenched my fists and glared at her in lustful fury. Though she stood beyond my physical reach, my angered desire seized her and ravaged her in the outraged violence of my heart. She was too close and often bound to my life not to feel now my inward storm of passion. Out of the subtle green corners of her eyes she must have caught a glimpse of my flashing lust and anger, for she stepped quickly into hiding behind Heraclian's hard solid figure. And so I turned my baleful gaze direct upon Rufinus.

He made a contemptuous toss of his fingers, saying, "Gregory Julian is marked for death!" Then he led his party of Empire scavengers out through the crowd.

An uneasy air of violence remained in the church after Rufinus took his party out. I could smell the sweat of anger increased among the people, and this tone of violence gathered as the hours passed. Six or seven monks moved about in their robes like spiritual soldiers, keeping a fragile hold on order, and boys swinging pots of incense spread a sacred fragrance among the bitter profane odors of hatred. There began to appear on the floor about my feet small and nasty objects, most of which had hit me before they fell to the stone.

Then Simplician, the good old priest with the dry hands and the big nose, came to me with shy sweetness and put into my hands a scroll.

"What is this?"

"I have taught some children to write. Jesus loved children, and children love to copy down his sayings. This is his Sermon on the Mount, copied by a boy of twelve with pudgy hands, from the Gospel according to Matthew. You should have seen him wipe back his forelock from his brow and make his letters neat. Look!" He opened the scroll so that I must see. "Are not those good square letters done by a clear-eyed boy? How easily you can read them!"

Caught unaware, I read aloud: " 'And seeing the multitudes, he went up into a mountain: and when he was set, his disciples came unto him. . . .' Yes, it is handsome writing for a boy of twelve."

"His father is a mule driver, working between here and the seaport. The boy worked his square little fist five weeks, getting this as perfect a copy as he could. Then he said, 'Father, it is for you. Now let me make another for myself.' . . . Please read more to me. I like your voice."

I spread the scroll and read the simple lettering:

" 'And he opened his mouth and taught them, saying,

" 'Blessed are the poor in spirit; for theirs is the kingdom of heaven.

" 'Blessed are they that mourn, for they shall be comforted. . . .' "

I stopped. I looked at the priest. He spread out his hands and smiled at me in that pure kindness which says: I have given you the best gift my heart knew how to give. Then quietly he left me. I held the scroll tight in my hand, stubbornly fighting to keep back tears.

" 'Blessed are they that mourn . . .' "

Actually, with the awful figure of Christ on his cross so near me, so real, I could not find the courage to open the scroll to read any more. I had only a vague recollection of having read that part of the Christian Scriptures before; and yet, without really knowing what the little volume

contained, I clung to it because my heart was touched by the way and
the moment of the gift. And oddly enough—I don't know why—people
stopped throwing bits of filth at me while I stood there holding that
boy's copy of Christ's sermon.

Finally Ambrose came, and while he was there an uneasy quiet was
restored.

He told me how matters stood. Rufinus had set guards at every exit
to seize me the moment I dared emerge. There was no question about
my property. That, Rufinus had confiscated. I was a pauper. It was a
question only of my life. Obviously I could not live in sanctuary in-
definitely, and Ambrose was trying to win surety for my life, on condition that I would accept exile. Rufinus had exiled men before now and
sent assassins after them. However, Stilicho, backed by Serena, had
adopted a position of adamant neutrality, saying, Let Ambrose and
Rufinus fight this out. It was easy for me to understand from this that
Stilicho, prompted by Serena, did not want me to fulfill the command
of Theodosius to become the tutor and companion of Honorius, in
which place I might threaten their power by gaining influence with
Honorius and, as she grew older, with Galla Placidia. It was more
politic for them to abandon me. Rufinus was determined to make an
issue of it: Ambrose must give me up for execution in Milan. Rufinus
would delay his return to Constantinople until he had seized and executed me. He would stir up the populace, foment riots. "We will see,"
he had told Ambrose, "how much blood in the streets of Milan—nay, in
the very church—you can stand in behalf of that foul murderer who
plotted to seize the Empire." He was already sending his agents into
wine stews and brothels to get trouble going.

Ambrose proposed to spend the night on a sermon which he would
deliver in the morning, upholding my right to sanctuary, to mercy and
to justice. He would scotch the lies of Rufinus, win the people and
ward off violence. "He is challenging the sacred rights of the Catholic
Church," Ambrose said. "I will not fail Christ's Holy Church!"

Bishop Ambrose looked toward the figure of the Crucified Christ and
made the Christian sign. He treated me impersonally. I could feel it.
I could feel a change in him now, an edge, a willfulness, a quiet of inner
calculation: He was hardening to fight for principles and powers of his
Catholic Church, and I was less a man loved than an impersonal factor
in that struggle for the Church.

I had felt when he brought me in to sanctuary that he loved me and
had power to heal me. But now I felt that he had lost the power to
heal me, for he was using me as a stone to build his Church. He must

have had a hard time with Serena, Rufinus and Stilicho. The brutal weight of political action had seemingly despiritualized him for this hour.

"How is Marcia?" I asked him.

"She whimpers, but cannot speak."

Then he gave me a final stern scrutiny, estimating my stability for use as a pediment or key in some arch of power—it was as if patches of stone had entered his spiritual face—and, compared to the open depth of his former love, he left me like a stranger.

After Ambrose departed I felt my profound loneliness and began to have more faith in evil than in good, more faith in the victory of Rufinus than in the victory of Ambrose. Even suppose Ambrose won a complete victory for the Church: I would go into exile with an unhealed heart. Aboard ship for Africa some agent of Rufinus would knock me on the head and throw me into the sea.

I felt that the only person to whom I could have communicated my real feelings and from whom I could have found understanding and help in my real needs was my father. I had begun to realize that I loved Marcia tenderly with a youthful and natural goodness, but we were not bound together by the mature strength of tragic insight. I was left alone in the world without my father. Our love for each other had been greater than I had known until I was bereft of him.

I had been shaming my father's honor by standing there in Christian sanctuary. I realized that in a deep sense Paganism was a man's real faith in his own human integrity. At the heart of Paganism shone a noble light which for a thousand years had lit the moral course of great and noble souls. Neither my father nor the Emperor Julian would have been so afraid to die as to permit riots to be stirred up in his behalf. So good a man as Plutarch, so great a man as Marcus Aurelius, so honorable a man and Pagan as my father would not disavow personal integrity for either longer or greater ease on earth. But, above all, my father would not have stood where I stood, waiting for Bishop Ambrose to determine his fate, even to use him as an instrument of Church policy.

I decided that, as a self-respecting Roman and Pagan, I must leave that Christian sanctuary and meet my fate with my own resources.

I made a careful attempt to ease my way under the purple rope. Instantly people began to mutter, crowd and press toward me. I could see at once they had accepted the purple rope as a line of sanctuary, and if I got beyond it I would cause an outbreak of violence then and there.

I did not desire willfully to profane Bishop Ambrose's church, for even if he had now transferred his energy to the struggle for a principle of power, he had begun in love and had often showed me love.

I thought that waiting deeper into the night, until the crowd thinned perhaps, would give me a better chance to escape from the church and to make my stand and fight on good profane ground.

I was physically nervous by now from natural causes. Behind the purple rope I paced from one side of the basilica to the other, looking for a drain or other convenience provided for a call of nature. But there was no such convenience in that part of the church. I could not commit a nuisance in a holy temple and keep my self-respect as a Roman of the patrician class. I realized how we are a thousand times bound by emotional training, and that there are many instances in which a man would rather die than do a rational act which would make him comfortable. My discomfort increased.

Riot or no riot, I began to calculate, I'm going to get out of this cowardly and tormenting situation!

I still held the boy's copy, on a little papyrus roll, of Christ's sermon. I decided to keep it. As I looked at it, without opening it to read, an interesting thought came to me, clarifying a distinction between Paganism and Christianity. Paganism in its best form was based on reason, and a man judging with reason would not know until the last event of his life whether or not his life had, all in all, been worth living. Christianity was based on faith, and precisely on the faith that a man's life was divinely worth living, regardless of temporal events, past or future. In a way there was only one event in a Christian's life; that event was faith; it was eternal. I thought it would be interesting to discuss this with Bishop Ambrose, if I lived to see him again. And I thought I would like to show Galla Placidia the boy's scroll, if I lived to see her again. Perhaps the one child made me think of the other. Also, I had given her help at forming letters.

Or was there a permanent connection being made, deep in my mind, between my father's fatal ambiguous prophecy of a new Julian Emperor and my interest in Galla Placidia?

My muscles were jumpy, my belly was tight with discomfort, my mind was in turmoil. I began to feel hardening purposes of hatred. Only two people had really betrayed me. I wanted to escape with my life so as to get my revenge on Rufinus. And I would make Dionie pay with passion and tears for the wound she had given me. Rufinus must pay, and Dionie must suffer!

Then Crassa, the dark and massive old enchantress who had driven death from Marcia's couch, came to my aid, not by intention.

Crassa came thrusting into the church and battered her colossal way through the knots of people to the purple rope. Following behind, in the swath she forced open, were two lean beggars carrying a stretcher heaped over with a vile and verminous robe of sheepskins. They set the stretcher down, and Crassa, addressing the crowd, cried out, "My daughter! My dead daughter! We have come to the Emperor while she is still warm in death!"

Then she turned to the Emperor and shrieked, "Oh, Mighty Serenity, intercede where you are now with Christ and angels and all the gods for a poor woman's daughter!"

From my side of the purple rope I saw a wonderful thing. An edge of the sheepskin robe was folded aside, and I saw a woman's scrawny hand scratch a bulge of hip. But to other eyes, a corpse lay there, covered in the vile robe from head to foot.

"O Emperor! Hear, O Emperor! A miracle! Hear!" Crassa shouted and flung out her arms.

Nothing happened.

Her face darkened with rage. She yelled again. "A miracle for your people, O Mighty One! A miracle!" But this time she gave the pseudo corpse under the stinking robe of sheepskin a violent kick in the side.

There was action.

The figure on the litter sat up with a shriek and flung the sheepskin robe aside with such violence that it landed at my feet. For good measure, a crutch clattered out onto the stones. The woman had lank red hair and a ghastly sunken face and bony white arms with red freckles on them.

Crassa screamed, "The Emperor has heard! The Emperor has answered! My daughter is restored to life. The Emperor's miracle! The Emperor's miracle!" She yanked the scrawny wretch up onto bony legs. Crassa wasn't going to have her effects questioned or lose time. "To the streets! To the streets! Take my restored child to the streets. Proclaim the Emperor's miracle!"

The astonished and superstitious crowd surrounded the haggard red-headed wench and began to push with her down the nave.

All backs were turned to me.

I seized the vile sheepskin robe, wrapped myself in it. A dirty rag from the stretcher served to cover my head and face, leaving opening only for one eye. I took up the crutch and hobbled after the crowd. I caught Crassa's powerful arm. "Help me out of here, Mother."

"You're no son of mine."

"That was no miracle."

She recognized my voice. "Ha! The young husband. Cling to me. I'll get you out."

On the way out she explained in crafty whispers. "My poor daughter. What could I do? She's been a prostitute a dozen years, and she's grown too scrawny for that trade. All that's left is to be a beggar. But a beggar starves, without a reputation. Now I've made her fortune in Milan as the beggar wench raised from the dead by the Emperor!"

I clung to her arm, and she let me hobble at her side out of the church, past the praetorian guards, across the forecourt and clear to the street.

CHAPTER SEVEN

THE GOOD FATHER

I KNEW I COULD NOT STAY IN MILAN, WITH MY LIFE FORfeit, feared, avoided by friends, hiding like a rat in dark and foul places, to be hunted down and murdered by secret agents of Rufinus.

I stayed with the crowd while I tried to improvise some plan. We surged down the street, proclaiming the miracle, dancing and shouting around the now famous beggar wench. It was hard going, for a long line of lumbering Gothic wagons came against us from the opposite way. Horses drew some, mules others and oxen others. The Goths lived in these great wagons with their women and children, and were now on their long way back to their Danube forests. I supposed they would move a few miles out of town to congregate with hundreds of others for a few hours rest and then make a multitudinous noisy start onward at dawn.

I thought I would be safer among the Goths than with the city rabble, so I went the way the Goths were going. As soon as I decently could I found a wall and relieved myself, letting out a great and grateful sigh as the pressure relaxed. Then I felt free, courageous and ready to hazard action for my life.

I saw two praetorians, on patrol, coming from the basilica entry toward me. They were not yet suspicious, but if they got near and examined me, I might be lost. I left my crutch on the ground at the base of the wall, strode out into the road, still obscured by that stinking robe of lice-infested sheepskin, still with the foul bandage around my head. I simply began walking alongside a Goth who was driving a team of dark-red oxen with a big skin-covered wagon lumbering behind.

I kept on walking with the Gothic wagons, out of the city, eastward on the plain.

I was delighted with my courage and skill and even proud, now, for noble reasons I could think of as having inspired my escape. I had spared Ambrose trouble. I had saved the church from becoming a scene of violence. I had not betrayed my father by seeking refuge in Christ. But I had to laugh at myself, too. I would have dared twice as much to answer so acute a call of nature as had tormented me.

The train of Gothic wagons stretched out ghostly and creaking in the dim winter moonlight, and there was a faint shine on the horns and sides of animals and a live gleam in their eyes. Near any stream, where mist had frozen and fallen, patches of hoarfrost spread out on the ground. The rude-limbed Gothic driver spoke to his oxen beside him, and his oxen responded with a movement of their whole horned heads and steaming nostrils. I could see for myself that the living together of animals and people is a lovely thing on an earth of wondrous beauty.

But under the surface, deep down where the man dwells in his lonely heart, I was sick, desolate and broken with grief. And what I saw, as clearly as if I stood at her bedside, was Marcia, frightened, unable to speak, not knowing why I failed to return to her side. And all the while my steps in the darkness led me on and on away from her.

When my life was at helpless hazard in the church, I had not thought of Marcia as one who could heal me; but now that I was free and had my courage back, a fierce desire to shield and comfort Marcia surged in my heart. It was one of those swift clear absolutes of emotion that determine for a young man his course of action.

The wagons slowed down, joined others, and congregated in a dim multitude on the plain to rest out the four or five hours of darkness.

I moved fast, and planned as I moved.

It was only half a mile to my villa. I went there, drew near, crept carefully. Rufinus must have concentrated on holding me in the church and left actual seizure of my property by his agents for the morrow. There were no praetorians about.

I went to my steward's quarters, wakened him, identified myself by removing the bandage from my head, swore him to secrecy, and got his help. From the house I brought out jewels, money, warm fur robes, weapons

and cheeses and meats. We hitched a team of strong blue-gray mules
to a stout two-wheeled farm cart, loaded in my supplies, covered them
with hay, stretched some mottled red and white cowhides, fur side out,
over hoops to make a shelter of the cart, then loaded in two hams and
a jug of wine. I still wore the old sheepskin robe and put the vile bandage back on my head.

I paused. I felt at a loss, as if something vital were missing. At first
I didn't know what it was. Then I realized it was the scroll containing
Christ's Sermon. I had laid it down somewhere. I looked around in the
shed and stable, but I couldn't find it. I suppose a little thing like that
sometimes symbolizes a great deal. This seemed to symbolize all the
losses I had had in my life. It was as if I had lost a deeply needed spiritual gift, as if I had lost—almost as if I had rejected—a seed of light
given me to plant in my heart. But I couldn't bring myself either to
give up my plans or to increase my hazard by hunting around longer in
the dark.

I shook my head vigorously to get rid of the sensation of having made
some deep and silent error.

I mounted the cart and drove back toward the city, thinking of a boy
with a steady fist and clear eyes and a lock of hair he often brushed back
from his forehead, a boy whose father worked a string of delicate-
stepping sober-faced little Gallic mules between Milan and the sea. The
boy had copied out Christ's Sermon, and the priest in the basilica had
given me the little volume with tender grace when I was being reviled.
I felt it base of me not to have taken better care of that symbol of human goodness.

But as I drew near the city wall I got my mind back onto worldly
matters, the risk I was taking and how to meet it.

At the gate I was stopped by soldiers.

"I'm bringing in some hams and wine for good Bishop Ambrose," I
explained. "He will bless the wine and use it in sacraments."

"Pass!"

I stopped on a side street and carried the two hams and the jug of
wine around the corner afoot.

Not even at night did Ambrose shut his door. But a praetorian stood
guard there, no doubt posted by Rufinus. It was most unusual. He
let me in, however, with the hams and the wine.

Moving quietly, I set the hams and the wine down in the courtyard.
I could see a light still burning in Ambrose's study. He was probably at
work on his sermon in behalf of the right of the church to give sanctuary.

Marcia's room was dark.

I stood there a full two minutes, breathing slowly, thinking hard. What if Marcia, wakened and frightened, made an outcry? I did not think Ambrose would let himself be an accomplice in my escape, and certainly not in what I intended to do to the praetorian on guard outside. I was going to hit that man on the back of the head, fatally if need be.

Carefully I slipped off my sandals to be the more quiet on my bare feet.

A chair scraped on the stone floor in Ambrose's study. I froze stiff and still behind one of the pillars of the portico. Ambrose came to his door, with lamplight behind him. "Gregory? . . ." he questioned the air softly. "Gregory? . . ."

Could he not hear my heart beating?

"Surely I feel his presence . . . " he said to himself. He stood there looking about in the dim light. He did not see me. And yet, from what he said next in his soft carrying voice, he must have believed I was near. "God be with you, Gregory!"

His blessing, like a return of love, made me feel good.

He looked around for another moment, sighed, and went back in to his writing.

I crept silently into Marcia's room and stood very still until I could see the dim patch of her face. Then, as gently as I could but swiftly and firmly, I clapped my hand over her mouth so that she could not cry out, and whispered, "Not a sound, darling! Not a sound!"

At first she struggled. But then she recognized my voice and gripped my arm in a confident way.

I whispered close to her ear, "We must leave silently. No matter what I do, don't cry out. Follow me." I removed my hand from her mouth.

"I'll follow you, Gregory," Marcia said.

She stood up. It was only then, after a moment, that we recognized the miracle. Her power of speech had returned. She had said clearly: "*I'll follow you, Gregory!*"

I embraced her in hard swift silence and held her trembling against my body. Then I threw a robe from the bed over her shoulders and led her out.

We caught a glimpse of Ambrose through his lighted doorway. He was not writing. He was on his knees, praying.

I picked up one of the hams to use as a club. It was heavy and cured hard. In the corridor to the street I touched Marcia on the shoulder to

make her pause. Then I went out and with a single blow, swinging the
hard heavy ham against the side of the praetorian's head, felled the man.
He reeled against the wall and sank to the ground. His helmet rolled a
few feet away. The street was silent, empty. I felt his pulse. He was
not dead. But his mouth gaped, and a gleam of the moon shone on his
teeth.

I strode into the corridor, caught up Marcia in my arms, and carried
her around the corner. When we reached the wagon I set her in its
shelter, covered her with hay, and said, "Lie still, darling, until we are
well out of the city gates. I'll tell you when."

She caught my neck and kissed me and whispered my name with joy.
"Gregory! Gregory! I'm so glad you came for me!"

I did not want the praetorian to be certain it was the man with the
hams who had stunned him. I went back, put the ham in the courtyard
with the other one and the wine, and made a final check of the praetorian's regular breathing. Then I returned to the cart and drove out of the
city gate.

There the soldiers scarcely shifted their spears.

"Did you see the bishop?" one asked.

"He was on his knees, praying, in his study. I left the hams and wine
by his door."

"He prays for all of us. Even for wretches in stinking sheepskin like
you."

"He's the good man of Milan," I said. "We are all his sinners."

I drove on about half a mile, then stopped to tear the malodorous
sheepskin robe from my body and snatch the foul bandage from my
head. These I hid behind some bushes. I took off my own cloak and
tunic and, standing naked in the pearly moonlight, shook the clothes
violently to free them from lice. My flesh tingled in the cold, but the
freshness of night air was clean and wonderfully tingling against my
body; I could feel surfaces of my torso and limbs contract and stir in
refreshed reaction. Reluctantly I put my garments on again, then got
Marcia out from under the hay. Holding her close in my arms, I asked
her how she felt. Was her head all right? Did she feel sick or weak in
any way?

She had one reply to all such questions: "I feel restored, completely
restored."

I kissed her soundly for our young love's sake and because we both
felt like it.

I wrapped her in a fur robe and myself in another, both to keep us
warm and to make us appear less Roman. Then I got some wine and

cheese from the back of the cart. We sat together on the seat eating and drinking as I drove the alert-eared blue-gray mules.

Marcia was bewildered at my strange way of seizing her from the house of Bishop Ambrose. "Why were you so long in coming for me, and why didn't you just come with some of our slaves and a litter and let them carry us home?"

I realized Ambrose had told her nothing. "We can't go home . . . we have no home. Rufinus . . ."

I gave her a swift outline of the events of my ruin. I think it was hard for her to believe in so much malice and perfidy. But she believed in my father's death.

"I liked him so much. And I know he loved me. He was so lonely. He . . . he . . ." She broke off, cried, and wiped tears from her eyes with the back of her hand.

I put one arm around her shoulders, holding her warmly to my side as I drove. Her bodily presence relieved me of the last traces of those philosophical and religious anxieties with which I had struggled earlier that evening. My head was clear for practical problems. "If Rufinus traces me, anything could happen."

"I was frightened. I needed you. You came for me. My joy was so great that I could talk again." She repeated: "You came for me! Nothing else matters now."

It was good of her to say that nothing mattered since I had come for her. She did not seem to realize that we faced exile or hiding in one form or another, that I had snatched her from the shelter and safety of Ambrose's house to share my ruin and jeopardy. She was not putting her mind to the facts of Empire and power politics in which I was embroiled. We would be lucky to get out of Italy alive, and after that how would I regain favor so as to get back to Milan and resume a hopeful future? I was irritated by Marcia's failure to grasp the realities of the situation, and yet, because of her recent illness and because of her pregnancy, I didn't want to frighten her.

A pregnant woman was certainly going to be a handicap. Looked at with masculine detachment, it appeared almost like a mistake on Marcia's part to be pregnant at such a crucial time. Her pregnancy emphasized the quality in a woman which thwarts the clear use of a man's reason in a critical situation. I felt the necessity of impressing Marcia with a more realistic view of what we faced.

Well, now! I had studied rhetoric and law, had prepared myself for some great initial speech in the Senate, the Forum or before the Emperor on some crisis of Empire. It might have been said, then, that

Gregory Julian's first oration changed the trend of events! Now disaster had robbed me of opportunity, perhaps forever, to make that first oration. Why shouldn't a young man, so unfortunately ruined, avail himself, to stir up his courage, of the only consolation left, and deliver to his wife, to the night, and to the gods the rhetoric stifled in his breast?

I removed my arm from her shoulders so as to be more free to think and gesture. With glances into the dim night ahead and up at the stars and at Marcia's warm round contented face I gave her what I could only consider an impressive, a masterly summation. I felt the increasing glow of my own genius for politics and amazed even myself by my penetrating insights.

I explained the inner workings and coming events of Empire, revealed the most secret impulses of Stilicho, of Serena, of Rufinus. I confessed that I was a dangerous man because of my father's prophecy that I should be Emperor. I outlined a plan to make Claudian my secret agent in Milan. And finally I revealed the path I would follow to success: "I shall present Stilicho with a great and accomplished political favor. And I know what it's going to be. It's going to be the Goths, who are now disgruntled and in a mood to make trouble.

"The Goths are a serious problem, but a lucky one for me. We've had Gothic slaves since I was a child. I know their ways and their language. I like them. I'll be able to get on good terms with Captain Alaric. I can persuade him he will do best to favor Stilicho, and then I shall let Stilicho know I have won Alaric's sizable force to his side. Of course it will take time, but I grasp the whole situation so clearly that I see real hope of success. Eventually I'll be back in Milan, close to Honorius, and with my wealth restored. It can't be done in a day or in a month. We may have a hard life for a long time among the Goths."

I finished in the orator's quiet final flush and waited for Marcia's answer of pride, understanding and confidence. She looked at me gravely, then bent her head, thinking, while a beautiful inward smile hovered about her lips. On the ecstasy of my own rhetoric I rode high, among the glittering grandeurs of Empire. I realized I might have said a brilliant word about Gildo the Moor, who was growing dangerously powerful in Africa. But it would be better to leave that for a later talk, because Marcia had thoroughly a woman's mind which would not grasp the total design of political reality in one lesson.

Marcia spoke, and her answer staggered me.

She was not worrying about my political ruin or about my brilliant analysis and plan of action, and she had no grasp of Empire at all;

but she was facing, on the simplest terms, the intensely personal problem of her own pregnancy. She said: "Gothic women have their babies. There must be midwives among the Goths who know how to help. I'll be all right, Gregory, even if we don't get back to Milan before June."

Her realistic concern with the basic processes of life brought me tumbling down from the abstract grandeurs of Empire to the prime simplicity of my real human situation: I was a young man taking care of the young woman who was carrying my unborn child.

The shock of falling from abstract speculation to the real ground of life, from ambiguous prophecies of Emperorship to actual realization of fatherhood, was so outrageous that I roared with laughter, which startled the mules into a rapid run.

And when my laughter ended and I reined the mules down to an easy pace I had a deeper sense of life, with Marcia warm beside me. Until now I had counted our mutual pleasures of the flesh as a fine accomplishment of my virility and had thought of those gales of delight as sufficient unto themselves. But now I got my first true sense of something more living and lasting, like sacred fire, at the heart of the sensuous storms of sexual union. The profound onflow of primal life had been the true burden of those ecstacies. I had for the first time a clear sense of the interflow of living process which binds together father, mother and child in community of life. The realization flooded through me in a spiritual tide of warmth and wonder. I gave Marcia a jolly hug and said, "Let the Empire fall as it may. I'll take care of the three of us!"

I slowed the blue-gray mules down to a quiet-footed walk, and we wound our way into the midst of the silent swarm of Gothic wagons. We lay on the hay in the cart, twined our fingers together, and talked in soft words and warm comfort until Marcia fell asleep, and a child within her.

I, Gregory Julian, the father, lay awake alone, watching, thinking, considering what it was to be a father.

I thought how easy it was for a man to get interested in all sorts of games and problems, from rhetoric to Empire, from philosophy to war, displaying the marvels of human intelligence and the purity of reason on atoms and armies, on religions and stars, while all the time avoiding that one near problem which demands the fullest development of a man's intelligence and the most profound use of his reason: how to be a good father. It was easier to be an Emperor or a saint, a general or a priest, an architect, a lawyer, a poet, a teacher, a master, a slave, than it was to be a good father. It was easier to be a son, a brother, a husband than to be a good father. This common mature role of fatherhood, assigned by nature to most men, was the hardest of all to fulfill as it deserved. What could be a higher ideal or a greater achievement?

As I realized that this problem alone—how to be a good father—was the supreme problem of maturity and called for the highest conceivable moral, intellectual and spiritual development in a man, I said to myself in astonishment: "God is the only adequate father!"

I felt the goodness of a smile on my face and, being young, I then fell asleep.

And we were of the Gothic multitude when dawn came and our journey began.

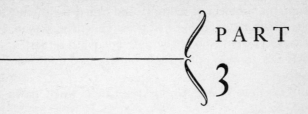

PART
3

THE ADULTERER

THE CHILD AND THE KING

ALARIC LED US A RUDE CIRCUITOUS JOURNEY OF PERHAPS a thousand miles, through Illyricum, past Thessaly and north of Thrace, finally out of gorges and forests onto the great pastures of Moesia, where in the full flood of springtime radiance the wild and nameless flowers bloomed as high as the horses' knees all down sunny slopes to the shining flow of Danube's waters.

We camped by river and crag and startled many a village in our passing. We wound by the cool green forested base of cold high mountains and crossed frothy rivers with tumult and shouting.

I was wakened to fresh wonder at men and earth.

A Roman and a lover of our mistress city of the world, a believer in our imperial power, I was almost an intellectual, nearly ready to mistake ideas for men and things. It was a good shock to my mind and emotions to move among the original stuffs of nature—ice and stone and turbulent water, avalanche and crag and star-sweeping wind. And men, too, were more themselves and less their pomp and vanity. Among the Barbarians life was so direct and simple that I readily smiled at anyone I met and spoke to any man. In Milan and Rome this had not been true; in cities, among the cultivated, it is against custom to carry a ready smile for strangers, so that the heart cools and the face grows stiff.

Instead of comparing, judging and playing proud with the reported thoughts of other men, I got a few original thoughts of my own. It was one thing to have culled a superior and satiric notion of these Barbarians out of Plutarch (when he spoke of their ancestral cousins, the Cimbrians):

"Now, these barbarous people had such a glory in themselves and disdained their enemies so much that, more to show their force and boldness than of any necessity that compelled them or for any benefit they got by it, they suffered it to snow upon them being stark-naked, and did climb up to the top of the mountains through great heaps of ice and snow. And when they were at the very top of all, they laid down their long broad shields under their bodies and lay all along upon them, sliding down the steep high rocks that had certain hangings over of an infinite height. . . ."

It was quite another thing, once we had reached a high mountain pass on our way out of Italy, to be dared by young Ataulphus, the brother of Alaric's wife, and a dozen of his friends to prowl naked up the snow field in the sting of glittering wind and come sliding on a shield down in precipitous lurches, edging a dizzy cliff. I did it because I was dared in the name of the courage of Rome; they did it in robust hilarity of dangerous play and, I think, to celebrate racial memories of Northern origin. I got going too fast toward a precipice, flung myself from the shield and brought up skinned, bruised and dazed against a tree, but the shield went on over and fell too far to be heard when it hit. The ribald lads went jeering by, and I stumbled on down, blue and chattering with cold, until I came upon one who had crashed against a rock and broken his leg. He laughed at the painful comedy of his own mishap, and because I dragged him on his shield down to the wagons he accepted me as his brother and a Goth.

But the point was that I lost my intellectual concept of being superior to such idiot play, and a dozen more times before we got out of the high snowy passes I clambered heights with the naked young men, viewed a world of massy peaks, and plunged headlong and yelling down on the belly-thumping shield. I liked the zest and hilarity of the Goths better every time I did it. And I liked myself better, too, for breaking Roman patterns of prudence and profit, for playing at direct hazard with nature in pure joy and boldness of youth. On my shield I streaked down icy steeps at hissing speed, naked man at play on mighty mountain. I still have scars on my ribs and back where falls and slides on snow and ice seared off my skin. They remind me that among the Barbarians there is a robust hilarity that we Romans lack, but that once in the flush of youth I rejoiced my heart in such boldness and laughing folly.

Marcia thought many a day of rude weather and hard going would displace our child, and I was particularly anxious lest some of the more violent river crossings might bring on a miscarriage. I felt my fatherhood strongly at each new hazard to Marcia. When a stream was not too deep I carried her across in my arms rather than have her jolt across in a wagon. She said: "When he gets born at last, I'm going to name him the child of a thousand bumps. Whoever did this to women? All a man has to grow is a beard."

A woman would scarcely know how a father carries his unborn child in his mind and heart and yet is torn and tormented too by the child's implicit threat to the mother's life.

In some sort of obscure recognition of my father's death I let my beard grow. It turned out to be a sturdy bronzelike beard, glinting red, and I flattered myself that it made me look like some of the portrait busts of the Emperor Julian.

I became well known as Alaric's Roman. Apparently his guest, I was actually his captive. At any point on the journey Alaric could have sent me under guard to the nearest Roman official as a man wanted for execution by Rufinus. But, fortunately for me, Alaric had an unappeased longing for the warm bloom of the South. The ice of ages was in the blue of his eyes, but they sparkled with the sun and fire of racial dreams older perhaps than even the snow and ice that had nurtured his ancestors. There was a radiant beauty of Athens and a burning power of Rome which his heart longed to know, and these Goths had faith in bards and teachers who could web for them a dream out of the flowing of words. He wanted me to bring him closer to the warm word of the South. But he did not want to be openly tutored by a man younger than himself. He used a naïve device to save his pride. He appointed me tutor to his wife's young brother Ataulphus, and then attended our lessons as often as he could "to see that I was teaching the lad properly."

Even before we got out of Italy I said I could do better teaching if we had books. Alaric settled that problem in masterly fashion. He sent out Ataulphus one night with a squad of valiants; they broke into the sequestered villa of one of our retired Roman dilettantes and plundered his library. They brought back a dreadful collection, overloaded with erotica and with voluminous letters of mutual praise written to one another by noble contemporary Romans who felt certain posterity would cherish their elegant style. Beautiful papyrus scrolls in finely wrought tubes of ivory or cedar or leather contained only corrupt or vapid matter: The poorer the mind of the writer, the better the lettering and case of the volume. I dumped batches of such stuff into the first river we crossed, saving out a motley remnant of Greek and Roman works by men of good heart and sound mind. My farm cart was converted into a traveling library, with a wild and gay twelve-year-old boy driving the pert mules; and Alaric set Marcia and me up in one of his big skin-covered wagons with an old man to drive for us and an old woman to cook for us. I was grateful that this provided Marcia with care and rest.

Ataulphus was a resentful pupil. He hated Rome bitterly. He was a handsome youth, aware of his Gothic nobility, with a flash of blue eyes and a toss of yellow hair. He was beginning to form powerful shoulder, leg and back muscles, such as Alaric already had, and he liked hurling a spear at a target from a galloping horse. Alaric knew some Greek and had me read the whole of Xenophon's *Anabasis* aloud, although Ataulphus could scarcely catch a word. Ataulphus refused to learn Greek. Greeks, he said, were too soft for him. Well, the Greeks had softened since Xenophon's day.

I fell at first into the sophisticated man's error of mistaking customs for intelligence, enjoying a civilized disdain for what I considered the inferior intelligence of these princely Barbarians. They smelled more meaty than we Romans, they ate grossly, they laughed rudely, they jested with physical vulgarity and had foolish faith in primitive customs. It seemed obvious to me that, being the rich heir to a thousand years of Graeco-Roman culture, I had the better brain. I forgot I wasn't the one who wrote Homer, neither was I Marcus Aurelius, nor any great truth seeker in between. But I soon began to suspect that Alaric was working at a bold design with daring intelligence and that Ataulphus had a good mind when he wanted to use it. Teaching Ataulphus was fighting him, and he proved formidable.

I remember once in Dalmatia we sat on a fallen log with breeze on our necks. Ataulphus held a spear across his massy knees and was sharpening the head with a stone. Alaric had been on one of his side missions to confer with scattered Goths and had just come to stand over us, a ruddy and noble captain. I complimented Ataulphus on his remarkable improvement in Latin.

"I learn it the better to know my enemy."

"Are you going to overthrow Rome?" I asked him.

He darted a quick glance up at Alaric, then said: "Yes!" He turned the spear on his knees and began to sharpen the other edges.

I laughed at the preposterous idea of Rome being overthrown by Goths. I made the joke grotesque: "All right. Rome is in ruin. Then what are you going to do?"

My question startled him. I think for a moment he saw the vastness of Empire and the horrors that would ensue if it fell into chaos. I seized the chance to speak of the productive and stabilizing power of peace, justice and law. A youth named Wallia, then others, came up as

I spoke. It was hard for me to make clear to Ataulphus—and Alaric—the blessings of Roman peace, for they were descendants of deposed kings and recipients of the Roman yoke.

Ataulphus seized up his spear and plunged it into the log between us. The shaft vibrated in sunset light. "Thirty years ago," he said, "our Gothic nation was oppressed by the Huns, debouching in their beast swarm out of the bowels of Scythia and driving us down against the Danube. We appealed to Roman mercy, and your Emperor Valens let us, a million strong, cross the Danube into Moesia. That was great mercy. But you took our arms, which to warriors was disgrace, and you watched us hunger. Then you sold back to our humiliated and starving fathers arms for honor and dogs and dead swine to eat in exchange for our wives and daughters for slavery and prostitution. You sent our young men as hostages into Asian cities and on an appointed day massacred them. You let us roam the lands south of the Danube, but no province was ours. We've scattered a few log-hut villages in wild places. We can wear gold collars as federated troops of your Empire and win the battles of Theodosius, but you forbade us ever to elect ourselves a new king. And neither Stilicho nor Rufinus pays what Theodosius owed. Your mercy was treacherous, your justice was vengeful, your law is for Romans first, and your peace is our shame and death."

I could see the fire of stern agreement in Alaric's face as the boy spoke, and other gathered chiefs clamored praise of these bitter sayings.

Then Alaric looked down at me with a poise of indecision that not only did me great honor but that I felt was of grave political importance. He was a man who generally took counsel of majesty in his own breast. But at this moment I could see he was waiting for me to speak for Rome. The mind of the Goths had spoken, and I was to answer for the mind of Rome. He looked tremendous standing above me, waiting to judge—tall, deep-chested, broad-shouldered, carrying his fine blond head as proudly as Stilicho or Theodosius, his large flowing mustache half hiding his great mouth, his wide-apart large intense blue eyes watching for the quality of my expression. His ears were hidden by locks of his shining hair, and gold hair glinted on the massive molding of his bare arms. He rested his fist mightily on the hilt of his sword, and his other hand just flicked at the gold collar of Roman federation that he wore around his strong ruddy neck.

With all the restraint I could summon I rose slowly to my feet so as not to be so overtowered by this man. Tall for a Roman, I was not by half a head so tall as Alaric and was no where near so solid or strong.

I addressed Alaric. "You wiped out most of those grievances at the

battle of Hadrianople. After you defeated Valentinian, Rome was still
in power, and you made your treaties with Theodosius. But now, if
you want to go back across the Danube, elect a king, and drive the Huns
from your old homeland into unknown regions from which they came,
Rufinus can't stop you, and Stilicho will praise you."

Alaric's muscles tightened at my implication that the Goths did not
have the power—perhaps not the courage—to recapture their homeland
from the Huns. "We like it here," he said. "We are a great and growing
people. We have been moving toward lands of more sun for ten
generations. Perhaps we will never return to the ice and forests of our
original North. We need space to live."

"Rome has more space for friends and allies than for enemies.
Rufinus is a low-grade Roman. Stilicho is a princely Barbarian. You
will flourish best if you keep faith with Stilicho and fill an honored
place in upholding Roman peace. Our ideal of Roman peace is still the
great principle of order in world society. And you ought not to excuse
yourself from the challenge of a great principle because in weakness this
or that man has failed to live up to it."

I saw a sardonic turn to his lips. "The weakness of this or that
Roman seems to have spread to Rome itself. Have I not seen in Milan
your soft men and lush women? You have rich who cannot fight and
poor who will not fight. The sun ripens; the sun also rots."

"Rome doesn't fall in a day. Brennus and his Gauls found that out
eight hundred years ago. Hannibal and his Carthaginians found that
out six hundred years ago. Next your cousins the Cimbrians were
shattered on the plain near Milan, they and their ten thousand
wagons. Rome breeds men for crisis. It is foolish to throw your
shoulder against the gods."

I had cast the best seed I could, but I didn't know how it was received,
for our debate was broken up by the wretched outcries of a woman. She
had been stripped of all her clothes and shorn of all her hair. She came
running, stumbling and crying past us, driven by an angry Goth who
flogged her shoulders with a heavy strap.

I tried to leap between the savage man and the tormented woman,
but Alaric's massive arm, hard and powerful, pushed me back. "He is
her husband. He caught her in adultery. That is her punishment."

The man drove the woman in cruel shame past wagon after wagon,
to be seen and scorned by hundreds of men and women and children.
That night she drowned herself.

Marcia, trembling beside me in the dark, asked, "What happens to
the man with whom she committed adultery? He is an adulterer, too."

I couldn't answer, neither could I sleep.

I thought about Gothic morals. The Goths would drink hard, fight hard, gamble passionately, betray their foes, but demand good faith between man and woman. They had not acquired our sophisticated notion of equality or competition between the sexes, which leads to the corruption of adultery, to infertile perversions or to the revulsion of chastity. Among the Goths a man and a woman were as the completion of each other and lived together in faithful monogamy. It was an honor to overcome a man in physical prowess, but dishonor to overcome a woman by seductive art, nor did the women think it anything but disgrace to conquer a man by passion or charm. The Goths seemed to think about other things and were not obsessed with sex as we civilized Romans were. In war, in civil economy and in personal relations the Goths had a rather small set of ideals and fairly well lived up to them, while we Romans, with our great civilization and rich cultural heritage, knew almost all the ideals mankind could think of and readily canceled one with another as convenience prompted.

Many a night I worried over the problem of what Alaric was doing. When occasion demanded he flaunted and insulted Roman authority and plundered farms and villages to provide for his people. He made side trips with groups of chiefs and held conclaves in our camps. He sent off messengers ahead, north, south. Our numbers were increased by newcomers. Once, far along on our journey, I rode with him and a group of his chiefs into a deep forest where the Goths (despite their Christianity) had a shrine to some elder prophetic god.

It was alarming.

The early Eastern bishop, Ulfilas, who had converted the Goths to Arian Christianity, had translated the Bible into their language, but had omitted many of the old books telling about violent warrior kings. "The Goths," he said, "had better not read of battles. They love war too much already."

Here in the primitive forest, where the great trees seemed as old as time, with bulky trunks that could hide a horseman, any Christianity the Goths had was left behind them. Alaric had that day a taut alert radiance, a bright burning of life new to me. I can express it only by saying he was closer to the presence of the gods, nearer them in greater simplicity, than any Roman would know how to be: And they were not gods of mercy but of battle and dominion. He left us watching in the resonant hush of the dim great forest and went forward to the shrine, where lank-haired sybils greeted him with unearthly paean. Three of their sacred white horses browsed near and lifted their heads to watch

Alaric. He did his oblations with sword and shield and spear coming to life in threatening ritual, then stood with arms upraised, a giant heroic man, while a stormy murmur swept the boughs of the age-ennobled trees.

He returned, stride by stride along the lofty forest aisle, a man enlarged for destiny. His face was ablaze with power and confidence. He told his companions—and wanted me, the Roman, to hear: "The gods have bespoken me, prophesying: 'King you shall be, and penetrate the City!' " And, of course, "the City" was Rome.

As we rode our horses out of the forest a large wolf bitch crossed our path. She was indolent, dull-eyed and had a sticky snout, as if she had just left off gross feeding. Alaric hurled his spear before the rest of us could breathe twice. The spear pierced into the lungs of the beast, and when she tried to twist her head to bite the shaft her gaping mouth foamed with blood and she fell, threshed the soil with her legs, and died. I did not need the exultant cries of the Goths to remind me that a she-wolf had nursed Romulus and Remus, founders of Rome; and this symbolic slaying made dramatic confirmation in the telling in camp of the prophecy of the gods about Alaric.

This prophecy became a belief of terrible power among the Goths. It became the faith of the people. It was the seed of havoc for years to come. Events soon convinced me that it was at least a half truth.

Marcia didn't worry about such things. Marcia had a strong sense of wealth and comfort and was often pained by the rude and even squalid manner of our life among the Barbarians. None of this bothered me. On the other hand, she got more direct and simple pleasure out of any sort of individual than I did. While I worried over "the significance of the Barbarians" or "the tension between Rome and Constantinople," Marcia enjoyed individuals, scenes and weather as she found them. It was comical. I didn't much care how I lived, and I brooded over abstractions of Empire; she hated living as rude people lived, but enjoyed those people. Sometimes her complaints were angry, sometimes they were humorous; but she never lost courage. She worked with constant vigor to keep a clean and orderly space about her. She kept her hair clean and fresh, sponged her body daily, even if she could get only one bowl of cold water, cared for the few clothes she had, and kept the inside of our wagon clean and freshened with balsam boughs. She was a real fighter to uphold the immediate decency of our living place. I made occasional spurts of effort to help her.

But the vicissitudes of our camp life and the rudeness of long journey brought on Marcia's labor ahead of her time, in the seventh month so far as we could figure. This was in April as we poured out from the limestone crags and came down on the great pastures of Moesia and saw outspread, waiting there for this dramatic arrival of Alaric's cavalcade, a multitudinous all-gathering of the Gothic nation. It seemed there must be a thousand camps of a hundred wagons each mottling the rolling contours and vales and sweeps of grassy land, and the lazy drift of multitudinous campfire smoke hazed the air until at times the sun seemed milky.

As soon as we could stop our wagon I ran ahead to Alaric's wife, and she came herself with a midwife to where Marcia groaned. The lore of midwives exceeds my knowledge. I held onto Marcia's hand during several spasms of her pain. Then I was chased out of the wagon and told by that shrewd strong woman: "The signs are for a long hard labor. Keep out of the way. This is woman's business."

Alaric's wife softened the dismissal. She left, saying, "Why don't you take a horse and go see how we Goths make a king? You can see our nation gathered. Alaric will be made king today. Others wish for the honor, but of Alaric alone have the gods prophesied it."

Serena herself could not have spoken, and moved on, with more pride.

So the Goths were indeed defying Rome, breaking their treaty and electing a king in open rebellion! Their multitude before me was too great to take lightly. But who could stop them now? Rufinus, back in Constantinople, had few troops; Stilicho had most of the Eastern as well as the Western legions with him in Italy. And we had news of Asia Minor being harassed, almost to the gates of Antioch, by fresh hordes of Huns. I began to see the bold grandeur of Alaric's design.

The midwife had frightened me, and my confidence was undermined by remembering that my mother had died in childbirth. There is something terrible about the helplessness of a man when his wife is caught up in the hard wrench of the natal process. I would stay by the wagon for an hour, then go off on a horse, presently to come back at full gallop in alarm. Once when I intruded into the wagon itself to ask anxious questions, the midwife threw a bowl of water in my face to drive me off.

The Gothic chiefs were holding loud council in a big tent. They were armed and drinking and shouting. They considered that a few heavy drinks brought forth more loudly a man's true opinions. After thirty years without a king many Goths besides Alaric were eager to contend for the honor of leading the Gothic nation in rebellion against Rome. Crowds of warriors had gathered near the tent. There in the sun a dozen or twenty naked young men kept up a wild and ceaseless dance among outthrust swords and spears. Now and then as **outcry** or rumor burst from the tent some bull-chested Goth would bellow against the hollow of his shield, and a dozen, a hundred, others would take up the roar.

Horsemen would come in driving cattle and sheep they had plundered from remote farms. Young Goths would swarm out to slaughter the bleating or bellowing beasts with spear and sword; then skin them with bloody hands and toss the hides to women to clean and cure; then carry whole sheep or legs and sides of beef across blood-splotched grass to brawny women at firesides, who spitted and roasted the meat. At fire after fire the great hunks of bloody meat were being seared and smoked and sizzled till the odor was wonderful. Half-naked children grubbed about in glee, seizing for gobbets and dodging blows. I saw a bearded father and his naked boy lying on the grass, propped up on their elbows, each grasping and gnawing at a rib of raw steamy beef and grimacing toward the fire through tangles of tallow-colored hair. I greased my own beard, gnawing a foreleg of lamb.

Finally with a roar and clashing of sword and shield the council ended in the tent. The chieftains strode out tumultuous. Deep-breasted men blew loud blasts on great long oxen horns, and six powerful fellows raised Alaric above their shoulders on a heavy brilliantly painted shield. The crowds roared.

"Alaric Baltha!"

"Alaric the Bold!"

"Alaric King!"

He stood there splendid, prime, stately, above the people, above the fires, holding a hard bright shield, wearing a golden helmet with scarlet plumes, and he spoke of their great nation, united again, in defiance of Rome, under a king whose ancestors had been kings.

Thus, borne aloft by the stalwart shield-bearers and accompanied by armed chieftains, priests and sybils, Alaric went in procession from camp to camp as the sun set and night came and the fires blazed up. I could tell where he was, a mile or two off in the dark, as a new roar of acclaim came from a newly reached tribe. Drunkenness and disorderly joy increased through the night. I galloped out across the dark resounding ground to witness several of Alaric's receptions in the night. His powerful voice had begun to rasp with much speaking. He would recount the miseries and the sufferings of the Goths, which he had shared from childhood up; the softness, the villainy and corruption of Rome; the courage, the numbers and the power of the Goths: "We will take what we want and use what we need. The god has spoken. I am destined to penetrate into the City!"

I know not what elder god of primeval forest had assailed the ear of his inner heart, saying "Penetrate into the City!" But I had been in the forest that day and had seen its effect on him, and now, by their roars of joy, I knew the prophecy was taking root among the people. I had an inborn confidence in the unassailable authority of Rome, and I thought what folly for these folk of wilderness to dream Alaric could lead them into the labyrinthine might of Rome, city of stone and gold and men and gods!

But gathered about Alaric, focusing in him, were strange powers, something more than brawny-armed chieftains. There were Arian Christian priests blessing his kinghood. Arians and Catholics had risen to the pitch of bloody massacre in the very churches of Rome not long ago when Damasus, the Catholic, struck hardest and killed most and became Bishop of Rome. There were Gothic sybils and priests voicing ancient beliefs from forest and ice. The Bull, the Sun, the Moon; God, Christ, the Virgin; even Mithra and Mercury and Hercules were there. I got an alarming sense of a great people at a moment of onward motion; they were impelled by forces beyond their comprehension, yet for vital action wanted word from the source of truth. I saw and heard Alaric convince them not only of his kinghood, but of his God-relationship. I saw a people swayed by this man who left them in no doubt that he spoke out of close communion with the source of truth: Man of Godhead.

Centuries of rule by Caesars, corrupting and corrupted by power, had taught us Romans that no one ruled our Empire by a true God-relationship; it was money and legions that counted. We believed in policy, not in truth. As an educated Roman, self-conscious of Rome's eternity and grandeur, I thought these Goths were making a mistake in policy and were being misled by a fragmentary truth. But I could not deny what I saw and heard and felt: There was a sounder moral tone, a more free and effective vitality among a people seeking truth than among a people calculating policy. To see a feasting tumultuous people, joyous and wild by the great night fires, roaring and raging their vital belief in the true God-relationship of Alaric their king, made the hair prickle on the nape of my neck. No one of them feared Alaric; they loved him. Having seen what faith was among a people, I turned away sick at heart for Rome's great loss of faith.

It would no longer do for Rome to take pragmatic action in vanity and conceit. Our "eternity" of Empire faced a situation too big for political shoulders. We had lost our God-relationship; we had corrupted our God-relationship through centuries of growing power and for practical purposes. Romans as Romans no longer believed in God or in man. We had become a contemptuous people. We needed a giant soul to restore us to our birthright.

Toward dawn, after sixteen hours of labor, Marcia gave birth to our son and lay exhausted. The child, prematurely born, was frail, with thin shanks and pale ribs and wobbly head. My heart was pierced with profound compassion for his fragile life when I saw him, and I held him in my cupped hands like a divine but unfinished token of human pain and courage and beauty.

CHAPTER TWO

THE SWORD OF STILICHO

THE CELEBRATION OF ALARIC'S KINGHOOD WENT ON FIVE more days and nights, and I suppose several thousand acres of grass were trampled down in games, dances, contests, brawls. During those five days Marcia was feverish and sick, and I had to appeal to Alaric's wife to find me a wet nurse for my son. She got me a placid sturdy girl with full young breasts whose own baby could by no means suckle her dry. I would see her sit in the sun with her large voracious baby and my frail weak son, one child at each breast, and on her face a placid thoughtless expression.

I got clean soft lambskin to wrap my boy, and in the cold of night I would sleep with him against my body to keep him warm.

Marcia's fever went down, she regained strength and presently was able to nourish our child at her own breast. His pale arms and fists would lie limp against her breast while his chin or nose pressed against her nipple. I would part his blue lips with my little finger and set his mouth where it belonged, and he would suckle weakly, pause to breathe and rest, then suckle again. When he opened his eyes for a moment he looked wounded in spirit by his too-soon struggle to breach the womb, but after he had fed he would smile, as if healed, and sleep.

I named him Marcus.

"Poor thing!" Marcia said, folding him in the lamb's wool to keep him warm. "I wanted to do better than that for you, Gregory!"

"My misfortunes brought you to premature childbed. What you have done is wonderful. He will grow. He was hard born. He has earned the wisdom of undeserved pain. He will be one who heals his brothers."

Marcia's face got very pink, and her dark eyes seemed to fire up larger and rounder. She poked out a merry finger and twiddled it in my beard, chanting gleefully, "You love him! You love me! You love us! Ha, my Gregory, we love you!"

It was one of the moments when I saw Marcia best, in the beautiful and candid glow of her vulnerable innocence. My heart turned over in a surge of wonder, for I saw an immortal soul rejoicing in its mortal form. One of the vital secrets a man bears in his heart and cannot express is that in some high moment he has loved a woman and seen her thus. It is the seeing of God that lovers know.

Also, during these days of rebellious Gothic festival I had time to weigh and plan my own future. In the early days of our journey I had been able to send off several letters to Milan. The only answer I got was a letter from Claudian, addressed (to conceal my identity) to "Alaric's Roman."

"To Alaric's Roman, greeting from Claudian Claudianus the poet. It is cold in Milan. You would freeze here. Only a child princess has warmth for your name. Cytherea likes you better absent. The Shepherd may pray for his lost sheep; I don't know; I keep away from his subtle influence. Mars is off on a bold venture to the Rhine. He would let you prove your worth, especially now the dark scoundrel is far off east. I have won small leverage, but use it as I dare. Wait. Watch. Place hope in Mars. Dionie fears your name, but wakes at night and hears your step. Tell Marcia Milan has lost its lovely violet till she return. . . ."

It was easy to read that Galla Placidia remembered me; Serena was glad I was gone; Ambrose might be praying for me; and Stilicho, who was on a military mission to the Rhine, would give me a chance to prove myself, especially with Rufinus back in Constantinople.

I would have to wait, perhaps until the end of summer, until our fragile Marcus was stronger, and then consider the risk of escaping from Alaric and hazarding a return to Milan. Nevertheless, as if I were already back in Milan, close to and influencing Honorius, I worked out what I called "The Julian Policy." I had promised Theodosius on his deathbed to be faithful to Honorius, and I meant to fulfill that promise. My policy was a four-point program:

I. Uphold Honorius
II. Unify the Empire
    a. Depose Rufinus
    b. A single strong Regent—probably Stilicho
III. Restore religious tolerance—that is, let Pagans as well as Christians enjoy freedom of religion.
IV. Assimilate Barbarians—for example, stop a rebellion such as Alaric's by making Alaric a general, and give the Goths not a whole province but stated parts of various provinces to separate and settle them.

I thought also I ought to persuade Honorius to return the seat of Empire from Milan to Rome so as to revive some old and valuable principles and powers of the Senate.

Working at such political designs bolstered my hopes; it gave me at least a dream of the future. It was no God-relationship, such as Alaric had, restoring vision and might to a people. It was not even truth seeking. Actually, policy making (in contrast to truth seeking) is one of the flowers of despair and disposes a man toward evil—but I did not know that then.

I was able, by devious means, to get off a letter to Stilicho, to inform him of the incipient rebellion of the Goths, the elevation of Alaric as king and the danger to peace. I estimated the number of Gothic warriors and prophesied that Alaric would play the East against the West for his own aggrandizement. I assured Stilicho of my fidelity to Honorius, to himself and to Rome.

Then Alaric the king, with a large army picked from the great gathering of Goths, led us up through some blue limestone crags and on southeastward to affright Rufinus in Constantinople.

At one of our stops I rode my horse up to the cavernous open back of our wagon, dismounted, and stood there talking to Marcia, who with quick flicks of her hand was keeping springtime insects away from our baby's face.

Marcia's warm round face was flushed with emotion, and her brown eyes glowed with an earnest light. I was very conscious of her vivid intensity and felt like taking her in my arms.

Marcia was determined that our son should be baptized a Christian. It frightened her that among the Goths there were only Arian priests. An Arian baptism, she said, would be more likely to damn than to save the child. Because Marcus was frail and his survival still in doubt, her heart yearned for a way to bring him speedily to a Catholic bishop for this sacrament.

I was at first amused by her superstition and tried to tease her out of it. "Your mother and other pious but silly women have filled your mind with fables. When a man has been injured and soiled by much living, some rite of purification will do him good. But an innocent child needs no such thing."

"Bishop Ambrose is not a silly woman. He knows and says that hell is real, and that's where the unbaptized go."

She talked vividly of hell. I watched color come and go in her face. I was astounded at the sincerity and depth of her emotional belief in the hideous certainty of hell, and of hell yawning for the unbaptized. I tried to show her by concrete example the cruel heartlessness of such a belief, comparing our new frail child with the seasoned, vile and defiled Rufinus. For Rufinus had finished building a splendid church in Constantinople—out of the blood and wealth of his victims. He had called together the bishops of the East to consecrate the church, and at its consecration he was baptized.

"So this corrupt man of murder, greed and lechery shall attain to heaven, and our innocent child, who does not yet know how to make any choice, shall be given to the gnawing of the ceaseless worm and the scorching of quenchless fire! How can you believe such a bitter doctrine?"

"Comparisons with Rufinus mean nothing. Salvation is not comparative, Gregory; it's individual. We are each one of us born in sin and must come to Christ or go to hell. I love Marcus. I'm frightened for him."

"Our friend Pelagius doesn't say we're born in sin. He's a good Christian, close to the Pope of Rome and admired for the goodness of his life. He says infants are as free of sin as Adam before he sinned, and are not damned."

Marcia was suffering. Her voice had a vibration of pain in it. "I've heard Ambrose preach. I've read letters from Jerome. Mother read me a copy of one of Augustine's sermons. They all say Adam sinned, and because of that, lust began, and so now there cannot be a child without some lust, and every child is born with sin."

"Your love is like pure and fresh warm wind in springtime, darling. You don't know what lust is!"

"When I lie in your arms I do!" She blushed at what she said. It made her radiant.

"Lust, nonsense! It's not your nature. Your whole being gives sex a good and fruitful name. It is easy for the forlorn and injured to call sex bad names, for it is so near the vital center of our mortal being. I think a man has to respect himself, cherish a woman, and be devoted to life before he can give sex a good name. I don't know about Ambrose or Jerome, but I think Augustine never loved the woman who suffered at his side and bore his son. I think that hurt his soul, for he saw the woman's pain. I saw it myself. Now he hates all motions of sex. But we have rejoiced in our love and in giving ourselves to the flow of life. That is not sin. We are not Augustine. We do not need to cast his shadow of hateful pain over all children in the world and taint all love between man and woman."

Marcia was still afraid. "Please, Gregory! There may have been sin, and Marcus might die. We must each come to Christ or go to hell. It is our duty to save our child who is too tiny to save himself."

"It is our nature to love our child. We will do all we can to nurture his life and comfort his spirit. We will not begin by considering him to be a creature of hell."

I would not assent to this doctrine that when a man and a woman devoted their bodies to each other in the normal urgency of human life there had to be a taint of sin about it, so deep a taint that it must even spoil any child conceived. It seemed to me to be a pronouncement of anger against life itself. Marcia was so often inspired by lovely and healing insights that I grieved to have her wounded by this anger spread about the world by troubled ascetic minds. I thought the earth was good and the people on it were good, and our human sin was to despoil the one or injure the other. I thought it was a sin to teach people to hate life.

"You don't even believe in hell!" Marcia said, bewildered.

I loved what I can only call our divine power to conceive ideals and harmonies of beauty, of love and of perfect peace. I admired the courage with which we strive. I could never hate our frail mortality, which suffuses all our acts and yearnings with a tragic love. "I believe in sorrow and in love and in God. The pulse of joy and the smile of peace are in these three. I do not believe the mystery is known, either of beginnings or of endings."

I took Marcus in my arms and bowed my head to look at his frail, pure and tender face. His eyes were open, and he looked up into mine. I could see that he trusted me and was not afraid: I loved him, and it was the strong will of my body and my life to shield him.

Then I felt a great loneliness on the earth, together with my wife and my son. Marcia had a lovely, spontaneous and vulnerable nature, now hemmed and hedged and terrified by hard doctrine devised by suffering men. How could I guess what spiritual wisdom our child had won in his birth struggle, the harder in that it came upon him before he was matured to meet it? And I, alive with a persistent sense of God, had to grope as best I could beyond my understanding. I thought how our great hunger for love and for truth and our great passions for mating and for survival rise so powerfully out of the primal mystery of life that our reason is shocked and staggers; yet still must our reason labor to save our lives from mere brute being. If our Pagan concept—a little life, worthy of courage, and then a little life in the memory of those who utter our dead names, and then nothing known—was pathetically inadequate to fulfill the heart, then also this Christian concept of eternal tortured damnation even for a child was so terrible that it must break the heart. I thought: What terrible symbols, leading to what tragic acts, our need of truth can devise to answer the impenetrable mystery of our human life! Holding my child, compassionate for my wife, I could not assent in my inner heart to the worm and fire of hell for a babe in arms.

I think Marcia was startled by the depth of emotion with which I spoke. "My heart would sicken and my love of children would die, leaving me only in terror at the horror of creation, if I could believe that little children like this—how many millions I know not, before, now, and to come—were intrinsically damned to torments of hell. I will allow him to be made a catechumen by Ambrose, if we ever get back to Milan; and when he is old enough to choose his own answer to his own deep mystery I will allow him to be baptized, if that is what he wants. With all the love we can give him, let him grow and answer out of his own breast to his own mystery."

Marcia turned her face away from me and wept, saying, "I pray for you both."

Then she took Marcus out of my arms, loosened her garment, and gave him her breast. Pure light of the sky sparkled in tears on her cheeks and shone on the warm full tenderness of her breast and on the cheek and closed eyelids of the suckling child. It was a mystery of nurture, binding mother and child together, very beautiful to behold, and leaving me, the father, profoundly alone and apart.

I went to see Alaric, to try once more to persuade him to send me to Milan as his ambassador with overtures to Stilicho.

"You see my power," Alaric said, "and as a Roman you are wise to want it for Stilicho. But you forget my pride. When I was in Milan, after the battle of the Frigidus, captain of so many Goths slain to win that battle for Theodosius, I made overtures to Stilicho, and he, with Serena behind him, chilled me. Now Stilicho shall make overtures to me. And Rufinus, too, for Constantinople is overripe."

Indeed, we had plenty of news of the ripe rottenness of the affairs of Rufinus at the crown of his life.

News had just reached us of the marriage of the Emperor Arcadius. Rufinus had matured plans for the marriage of his daughter to Arcadius. Arcadius apparently did not care much for the girl, but he was only about sixteen years old, insipid and easy for Rufinus to dominate. Then Rufinus learned of trouble down in Antioch. A man by the name of Lucian had bought the high office of Count of the East from Rufinus at a great price. But now this Lucian, administering his wealthy province from Antioch, was disgracing Rufinus by good and just administration. Rufinus wanted no officials who did not govern as he did—by rapine, spoilage and extortion. He went down to Antioch as prosecutor, judge and executioner, and relieved Lucian of office by having the man beaten to death with lead-tipped leather thongs.

While he was away on this business Eutropius, the eunuch chamberlain of the palace, inflamed the young Arcadius with desire for a beautiful Barbarian girl. Her name was Eudoxia. She was the daughter of Bauto, the Frank, a general in Rome's armies, and she lived with the family of Promotus, who had been one of Rufinus' victims. Eutropius worked with fine secrecy, so far as the palace and the people were concerned, and with ravishing effect on Arcadius.

Rufinus came back from Antioch, more accursed by the people, and Constantinople was made ready for the imperial marriage. Rufinus saw himself almost secure, as father-in-law of the Emperor. The wedding procession set out from the palace. Eutropius halted it at the house of Promotus, entered, invested Eudoxia with the royal robes and jewels, and took her—not the daughter of Rufinus—back to the bed of Arcadius. This superb treachery injured Rufinus with ridicule throughout the East.

But Rufinus was still Praetorian Prefect, with two ways open to his monstrous ambition: He could murder Arcadius and seize power or he could force himself upon the boy as co-Emperor. He would have done one of these things, no doubt, if Stilicho had not had the bulk of the Eastern army with him in Italy. The best he could do was to have Arcadius send a sharp order to Stilicho and Honorius to send back the Eastern legions. Stilicho himself led the whole Roman army east from Milan.

Alaric and his powerful army of Goths now reached the plain outside the walls of Constantinople. We could see the walls in the sun and people on the walls.

As a Roman I was ashamed of what then took place. Rumor said that Eudoxia, the bright-cheeked young Empress, had spirit and wanted to fight. The Emperor hid in the depths of the palace. Eutropius made preparations for a royal flight. The people now rioted, now trembled, in the streets. A number of Gothic slaves broke out of the city, came to our camp, and rejoiced in their freedom.

Rufinus, casting aside his official Roman dress and putting on Barbarian garments of animal skin to flatter Alaric, came out with an embassy, sat in Alaric's tent, and bought his own safety with the property and peril of others. He told Alaric in effect, "Retire from Constantinople, and I give you leave to plunder Macedonia, Thrace, Thessaly and Greece. Only be kind enough to spare several extensive properties in those parts which belong to me personally." All this Alaric won without siege or threat, simply by appearing before the city with his Goths. Rufinus went back into the city, proclaimed himself its deliverer, and celebrated by squeezing more taxes out of the people.

Alaric led us on a route of pillage through Thrace toward Thessaly. It was peculiar business, haphazard, chaotic and hard to define. We were not an army but a conglomeration, a tide and throng of robust humans rolling across the countryside. We would pass by a town and burn a village, or skirt a village and plunder a town. A band of young Goths, with cruel joy in their battle-axes, might one day murder the people on an estate they wanted to ravage, and the next day, at another estate, trade gifts and hold a barbecue. Sometimes a family or three or four families of Goths, with their wagons and cattle and dogs, dropped out to settle on a group of farms that took their fancy, while at other places settled Goths pulled up their roots and joined us. Some shrines were plundered, others passed by. Romans were made slaves, and slaves were made free. In some towns women were raped and children butchered, and in others they were put in a church and protected while the town was ravaged. And yet there was a primitive barbarous design: Alaric grew stronger, his forces grew larger, and his people's wagons grew heavier with looted wealth, while fear of the Goths spread onward ahead of us.

I had to think with chagrin: What had Roman government come to? None of these people was too remote or hidden to be found and oppressed by our Roman taxgatherers, but now when the Goths came to injure them Rome did not defend them. It was disillusioning to see so vividly that our great imperial government was better able to crush than to defend the people. And I also saw how dangerous these Goths were. They had great power to destroy, but they did not know how to govern. Roman weakness and Barbarian force co-operated to produce chaos.

Then in Thessaly, as we rolled westward, we came upon Stilicho's army rolling eastward. There was a sudden stillness, as if before a mighty clash.

Here I saw that Alaric was a good general He commanded his stirring people without confusion. The place was a grassy plain with a few small trees scattered in the heat of the sun. Alaric gathered his folk in a great circle and had the men dig round about the camp a double trench to kill off flames, should the Romans set fire to the sun-browned grass. Then he arranged double rows of great oxhide-covered wagons, like a double wall about a city. The Goths could fight a strong defensive battle with slings, arrows and javelins from within this fortification and still be ready, if any Roman weak point developed, to lunge out in roaring cavalry attack.

Half a mile away the gorgeous purple dragons of the Roman army were afloat in the air, and Stilicho's forces in great strength poised astrain for battle. Why did not Stilicho, whose force was the greater, attack?

Alaric called me to his tent on the afternoon of the second day. "I am sending ambassadors to Stilicho. I want you to be their interpreter. Take your wife and child and go with them. Stilicho thinks he can hem us here until we hunger for food and thirst for water, then strike us in our desperate weakness. Tell him for me—he may believe you more than he will believe my chiefs—what a large pool of fresh water bubbles with springs in the midst of our camp and that we have meat and grain for weeks. He wastes good fighting time."

"Thank you. I am glad to go. If that is all I have to tell him, you waste good time for making peace."

"Tell Stilicho he can make peace with me now if he will appoint me general of the Roman armies of Thessaly and Greece. Otherwise I will make my peace with him on stricter terms after I defeat his army. My chiefs will bring back his answer. I have treated you as a free man. When I recapture you after my victory I shall count you among my slaves."

I could see no sign of fear, of weakness or of worry in his big, intent and eager face.

Young Ataulphus stood beside him, armed for battle. "I'll capture you myself, Gregory," Ataulphus said.

"I'm not a trained soldier," I answered him. "But you'll find a sword in my hand when you come for me. I rather think I will come for you, here among your own wagons."

Both Alaric and Ataulphus liked my answer, greeted it with a robust yawp, and we parted with mutual respect. There was a final flash between Alaric and me of something extraordinary and prophetic. Our hands clasped, our eyes meeting, there passed between us a knowledge that we two were fashioned by the gods for other meetings, and at last in some moment of terrible and tragic destiny a final meeting.

Stilicho, his General Gainas and other officers received us in his tent. Claudian was there. Claudian and I met with sudden gladness and embraced each other. He embraced Marcia, too, in his poetic enthusiasm. Then he sat apart with Marcia, and Marcia held our child. Claudian had been appointed a tribune and notary on Stilicho's staff, but his real business was to record and later set to verses Stilicho's heroic actions.

General Gainas was a heavy-set Goth with round jowls and small brutal eyes.

Stilicho had changed, I thought. There was more iron-gray in his hair. His stature and breadth had seemingly increased. There was a steadier consciousness of great military power in his eyes. But I could think of him only as the foremost of generals, not as a man of imperial majesty. He did not seem to have acquired yet that extra sense of absolute civil power which had made Theodosius so formidable. He greeted me with a stern simplicity, neither offering nor denying a later warmth.

I said I had come to interpret for Alaric's chiefs, but then to stay to fight for Rome, for which I would need armor and a sword. At that a warm smile touched his broad lips.

The conference lasted two hours, until the thickening of darkness on the plain, and then Alaric's chieftains rode back to their camp carrying torches aflame above their heads.

Stilicho's answer to Alaric was: "You have broken your treaty with Rome and ravaged Roman places. I'll strike when I'm ready and make peace as I please." It was spoken like a Roman.

Gainas urged, "Strike at dawn!"

"You're a Goth yourself," Stilicho told him. "You can't bear not fighting. A few more days of this waiting strain and the Goths will be wild to show their courage in disorderly onslaught. We'll have them the easier."

I said, "Rufinus has disgraced the Empire. Arcadius is in danger of being murdered. After you defeat Alaric you ought to remove Rufinus and hold both East and West together under your Regency."

Stilicho looked at me sharply. "Many fear I may do what you say I ought to do."

Claudian found a tent where Marcia and the child and I could pass the night. There was a kind of happiness and eagerness in Claudian's face and bearing. He was proud of his position and vividly interested in the life of the army.

"Stilicho is a great general. Wherever he pitches his tent, there is the fatherland of his soldiers. They're high-strung to win him victory."

We heard deep song at the break of day. Marcia recognized it at once. "It is early service. A group of Christians. They are singing Ambrose's hymns!"

She was up in a moment, carrying Marcus, and I reached her only after she had got a dozen yards from our tent. We went together through dew and dawnlight. We found a priest leading a group of several hundred legionaries in outdoor morning worship. As the sun came up and lighted their faces they sang one of the hymns Ambrose had written and set to music for his churches in Milan. Marcia joined in at once, and presently I, though not a Christian, felt the lift of so many voices in worship and also sang. These hymns of Ambrose were wonderful for their simple clarity, for their clear acknowledgment of the deep needs of the human heart and for their unmistakable naming of God.

I could see how this morning worship refreshed Marcia's soul, restored and renewed inward beauties which now shone outward again from her warm delightful face. I had now and then attended Arian services among the Goths to see what they were like, but Marcia would not approach their form of Christianity and had grown spiritually hungry for open worship with fellow Catholics. Now with the legions of Rome she joined the devout in worship, morning and evening of every day, and always took Marcus with her. She asked me again to let her have the Catholic priest baptize our child. It was hard for me to deny her request; and when I denied it she looked up into my eyes a long moment with a smile lovely and sad, then went off, rocking Marcus in her arms and singing softly to the child and herself some snatch of song. I stood there feeling the sadness a man feels when he knows the woman he loves has closed off part of her heart in secret from him.

Claudian had been watching us from a place apart; he saw us separate; he intently watched Marcia walk in the sun; then suddenly he turned away from all warmth and light back into the dark cleft of his tent. I think Claudian retained some wounds of dominance inflicted on him in childhood by his mother and suffered dearth, rebuff and self-denial in his relationships with women. This must have been the harder because his poet's soul would more intensely know its longings than would our easier souls. I know he once wrote some verses about what pain love was to a man so poor.

The movement of armies is slow, but of messengers, swift.

Messengers came that morning with imperial orders to Stilicho. He was shocked by what he read. His face paled, and anger made him tremble. Both the hand of Rufinus and the hand of Serena reached out to stay him at the moment of action. Arcadius, Emperor of the East, commanded his brother Honorius, Emperor of the West, to deliver at once to Constantinople the legions of the East and the due share of gold and jewels and portable wealth of their divine father Theodosius. And he enjoined him not to molest the forces of Alaric on the way, for what was done from Greece and Thessaly to Thrace was no concern of the Western Empire. This was the hand of Rufinus at work.

The imperial order from the boy Honorius to General Stilicho amounted to this: "Obey my brother's command!" It was backed up by a letter from Serena to her husband in which she assumed and asserted that fatal dominance she had always held over Stilicho: "I am the true heir of Theodosius; you are not quite a Roman and not quite a Theodosian." She had a dangerous power to emasculate Stilicho in moments of crisis. She bade him, for the sake of peace between the two halves of the Empire, to divide his army, send half of it off to Constantinople, and return to Milan with the other half.

A kind of desperate fury spread through the Roman camp as rumor of this dreadful shameful news got about. What, let Alaric go! What, sunder our army in half!

I went in rage and folly to Stilicho. "This is monstrous! This is the death of Rome. Give me leave to go out of this tent and speak to the legions, and I promise you they will acclaim you Emperor on the spot. Even as Theodosius was the mature and able Emperor for young Gratian and his younger brother, so you can bind the Empire together again and rule it as it ought to be ruled!"

Stilicho sat at his table with his fists clenched together, his arms tense and his jaws tight. He looked right through me. Gainas stood beside him, his brutal little eyes alert and shifting.

Finally Stilicho opened his mouth and uttered a groan from his chest. He said, "Serena doesn't see what this means. She . . . or yet my honor . . . holds me bound to obey.'

He was silent. He turned and stared up at Gainas. Then he stood and drew his sword, which had a jeweled golden hilt. He was tense with fury. His voice was terrible. "Gainas, take the legions of Arcadius to Constantinople. Carry my sword with you. Plunge it into the bowels of Rufinus. Gregory!" He turned on me. "Go with Gainas. Bring my sword back to Milan when its work is done."

There was noisy grief among the legions at the sundering of the army. All the days and years of Theodosius these men had been brothers in war. The horde in Alaric's camp was amazed to see our threatening Roman host part and one half turn back westward while the other skirted round the Gothic camp and passed on toward the east.

Claudian and I parted, conscious of Roman shame.

I said, "Serena will ruin Stilicho and Rome."

"No. It is the greatness of his honor. He helped Theodosius put down two usurpers of Empire, Maximus and Eugenius. He will not stoop to be a third."

"Why murder Rufinus, and yet not rule?"

Claudian looked at the ground. I saw his lips curl. "Rufinus," he said, "is scum of the Furies."

I took Marcia and my son on with General Gainas and that half of the army toward Constantinople.

General Gainas would tell me nothing of his plans. Brutal, cunning and physically powerful, he told me with frank sarcasm, "This is a military matter. Stilicho and I and a few other Barbarian generals are running this Empire. When I need a young Roman noble as a messenger to Stilicho I'll let you know."

"Stilicho appointed me to bring his sword back to Milan."

"If and when I am ready to return it."

I was shocked by the picture of Barbarian power Gainas presented. It was dreadfully true. Stilicho the Vandal controlled the armies of Rome and Italy; Alaric the Goth held sway from Greece to Macedonia; Gainas, a Goth, could dictate to Constantinople; Tribigild, another Goth, had large forces in the Near East; and Gildo the Moor held Africa. The Roman world, in an atmosphere of fatally increasing tension, was at the mercy of these Barbarian generals. The death of Theodosius had ended Roman control of the Roman world.

And I got the impression that if Rufinus were not too arrogant, General Gainas was ready to make a deal with him against Stilicho.

Early in November Gainas brought the legions to a halt on the plain outside but close to the walls of Constantinople. This place, the Hebdomen, was what you might call the counterpart of the Field of Mars at Rome. Here the legions were accustomed to drill and maneuver and on special occasions be reviewed by the Emperor. There was a handsome marble platform, bright in the sun, decorated with statues and flags, where the Emperor, elevated above the crowd, was accustomed to receive homage and bestow honors.

During a couple of days ambassadors went back and forth between

General Gainas and Rufinus to settle the terms for presenting the legions to the Emperor. Gainas knew he had the power to bargain for a good bonus and other conditions suiting his ambition. The camp was full of rumors. It was said that for a large sum of money and appointment as master general, Gainas had offered to betray Stilicho and help Rufinus shatter the Empire. Others said Gainas was going to assassinate Rufinus and declare himself Emperor.

Gainas summoned me. He was in a mood of fierce energy and anger. He glared at me a moment, then said in his harsh strong voice, "Tomorrow I present the legions to Emperor Arcadius. This evening Rufinus is sending ambassadors to dictate to me the terms. *Dictate!*" He made an obscenity of the word. "I want you here as Stilicho's witness."

Three noble sycophants of Rufinus, more notable for their exquisitely clipped and perfumed beards than for their intelligence, came to our camp that night, and by torchlight in the tent of General Gainas gave the orders of procedure dictated by Rufinus.

Arcadius, on his pedestal, would welcome the troops, Rufinus, standing below him, would be asked by the boy Emperor to step up onto the royal eminence and accept the honor of elevation to co-Emperorship. At this point General Gainas would be required to declare the loyalty of the legions to Rufinus, and Rufinus would offer a bonus to the army.

On one side of a table stood General Gainas and his top officers, on the other the three ambassadors of Rufinus. I stood behind the general, looking over his shoulder. One of the ambassadors set a heavy bronze box, which a slave had been carrying for him, on the table and opened the lid. It was full of new gold pieces.

"Look at one, General. The thing is already accomplished!"

General Gainas clutched a fistful of coins out of the box, spilled some on the table, then looked at the heap of them left in the palm of his square hand. He gave a coin to each of his officers and one to me, commanding, "Look at them, and see what is done!"

The coin I held up between my thumb and forefinger was heavy and seemed hot to me when I saw that it was stamped with the portrait of Rufinus and the words: RUFINUS EMPEROR.

General Gainas reached to me for Stilicho's sword, which I had been holding at his request. He banged it down on the table beside the casket of gold, making coins rattle. Its steel blade and bejeweled golden hilt glittered in the torchlight. "This is the sword of Stilicho, master general of all the armies of Rome. I shall present it to Rufinus tomorrow!"

"Keep the gold!" The ambassadors were delighted with their success. They departed. The scent of their perfume lingered in the tent.

Gainas turned to the massive Barbarian captain on his left. The man's lank hair was greased with butter, and his powerful arms were tattooed in blue and green. "Captain Herulian, you will present Stilicho's sword to Rufinus. Take it."

Herulian picked up the sword in a huge hand and held it out above the table like an oversized dagger, pointed at where the ambassadors of Rufinus had stood. His eyes glittered, and he laughed harshly. "Ha! Rufinus!"

The next day, while a strong sun burned away a soft mist and smell of the sea was in the air, the imperial cavalcade came out of the city to the Hebdomen with chariots of gold and banners of purple. They were followed by a multitude. The royal party, accompanied by officials, guards and slaves, went to the marble tribune. Arcadius, the young Emperor, took his lofty stand on the imperial podium among statues and flags and under a canopy of purple silk. Rufinus stood two steps below him. The army was ready. The Emperor was ready. Trumpets blared.

Arcadius welcomed the troops, the foot soldiers with their shields and swords and spears, the armor-clad cavalry on armor-clad horses, many a plumed helmet, and, stirring above all, the sinuous dragons afloat in brilliant air.

Crowds come out from the city cheered. The face of Eudoxia, the young Empress, flashed bright with hope and pride. Rufinus greeted many a soldier by name and smiled and pranced in readiness for glory. It could be seen that he was already Emperor in his heart. I sat on horseback beside General Gainas, and Rufinus, recognizing me with a start, gave me one moment's piercing glance which certified that my death would be one of his first imperial acts.

Formations of soldiers, commanded by the stertorian shouts of Captain Herulian, wheeled from left and right and closed in on Rufinus. Rufinus thought they were getting too close and stretched up the flat of his hand to command them back. They came on. Rufinus reached up and twitched the garment of Arcadius, who stood trembling above him. It was the signal for the boy to ask this man he feared to step up and tower over him as co-Emperor. But Arcadius had turned pale with terror. The assassination of weak Emperors by strong generals was an old and hideous Roman story. For all he knew, the oncoming wave of soldiers was the breaking of his doom. He opened his mouth, rather to cry out than to speak, but no sound came.

The soldiers now hemmed in Rufinus against the imperial podium, shield to shield and with threatening spears. The anguished man flung both of his arms in the air and cried out: "Soldiers of Rome! Today I am to be made your Emperor! Gold! Gold!" Then, turning his frightened face, he screamed upward, "Arcadius! Act!"

Captain Herulian strode forward, flashing Stilicho's sword in the sun, and, mighty of voice, roared doom: "Death to Rufinus, tyrant!" Then he plunged the sword of Stilicho into the lean vitals of the astonished Rufinus and roared aloud: "The sword of Stilicho smites you!"

Rufinus heard even as yellow fear glassed his eyes and he fell.

Then insane savagery broke loose. The body of Rufinus was hacked and torn and trampled. The head was carried on a spear above the crowd, and someone of macabre mind took up the severed right arm of Rufinus, manipulated the tendons so that the fingers grasped, and went crying through the crowd and later through the streets of the city, "Give! Give!" as if even in death the insatiate rapacity of Rufinus could not be stilled.

CHAPTER THREE

THE BODY AND THE WAVE

IT WAS A NIGHT OF CARNIVAL IN CONSTANTINOPLE. MARCIA was shocked by the brutalities and retired with our baby to the apartment provided for me in the palace. I should have been shocked, but I had a robust young appetite to stomach such villainy; I felt a sort of vicious exhilaration. He who had sought my life and stolen my wealth was dead. Now I would regain both property and position.

Eutropius, the eunuch chamberlain, gave a feast in the palace that night in honor of the assassination. He was now the man of power. I studied his face, and I regretted that Stilicho had not met the challenge of opportunity, had not at the ripe moment made himself Emperor.

Eutropius, this yellow eunuch, yellow with misery or with jaundice, or with both! His life had been seared along the pathways of baseness. The glory of Empire had given someone the power to seize him as an infant from his mother's breast, castrate him, and enter him on all vileness of servitude. He had been forced into every degradation of sexual impotence, from bathing and anointing voluptuous mistresses to servicing perverted masters. His heart was eaten out with tragic knowledge of human degradation. In his dark envenomed breast there was only one tender human light. Eutropius had a sister; he loved her; for none but her could he ever dream of goodness.

This man was now ascendant over Arcadius, the sixteen-year-old Emperor. Bright young Empress Eudoxia, although Eutropius had brought about her marriage, had the spirit to fight against him. Eutropius held the young Emperor in grip by the only methods he knew, by devising for Arcadius lascivious pomp and lecherous pleasure, including sexual perversions and drowsy syrops of the East. Arcadius so lacked intensity of life that in him these vices were like a slow-wasting languid fever.

Where Honorius Emperor of the West was torpid, Arcadius Emperor of the East was timid. The mother of these boys—the first wife of Theodosius—must have been a sheepish stupid woman. Arcadius, with his timorous and muted nature, was not fit for the vehemence and intrigue of his imperial palace. He would have made a sweet and gentle acolyte in the service of some shrine, or he could happily have been the slave of some strong kind master. What he liked to do was to dismiss Eudoxia's handmaidens and wait on her himself. This soon made her impatient. Although he had got her with child, it was a palace jest that Eudoxia had greater longing for love than Arcadius could satisfy. It was predicted that not all her children would have the same father.

When I got to know the boy better I decided that what would have suited him best of all would be to go back to Spain, where he was born, and there tend a flock of sheep on hillsides sloping up from the River Ebro. He could have fulfilled such a life with lovely grace. But he was so fatally crowned with power that he could not find the simple life his soul required.

I was reminded of the interest Honorius had in chickens. The two Emperors of the world were better fitted to look after chickens and sheep than to try to rule the brawling affairs of man.

At the feast Eutropius gave to celebrate the murder of Rufinus there were a thousand beautiful things. Flaring torches lighted the great chamber, subtle and exquisite perfumes scented the air; the long tables were laden with glowing fruits and gorgeous flowers; the silks and fabrics and jewels worn by the guests were astonishing for their variety and richness; a constant sound of music haunted the high hall, rare fragrant food was brought in on wrought-gold platters, and sweet wine was served in lovely Grecian cups. Jugglers performed, a panegyric on Arcadius was declaimed by a poet, smooth-limbed boys and girls danced and sang, and actors performed tableaux of the loves and delights of the gods. I saw countless separate things that revealed a sudden beauty.

And yet it was a hideous feast, corrupted and perverted at its heart by our common knowledge that we were celebrating a murder. Sensate delights, crowded upon one another to the point of orgy, still were not enough to undo murder or to make murder a good thing. It was rather as if the feast indeed made murderers of us all, so that what in itself was sensuous and lovely was by abuse made sensual and brutal. Our laughter was shrill and vicious, our wit lascivious and cruel. As the throbbing sensations increased I felt blackness of hatred gather in my head. I thought it was the accumulation of all my sufferings rising to the point of catharsis.

I was so crazy that I seized and shook my neighbor and shouted, "This party is doing me good!"

He leered at me. "It's not my first murder," he said.

Our eyes met, and we shared evil.

I let myself go, seeking other glances with other men and women. It was an obscene communion and exploration of human vice, in which we did not courageously show ourselves to one another for what we were—tragic, mortal and desiring eternal happiness—but rather bound ourselves together in a cowardly vaunting of our worst wounds of death, such as lust, perjury, murder and despair. Each one awakened the falseness of his life and openly nurtured the worm of death in his heart.

For me the climax of this mass hysteria was brought on by the actions of Furia the dancing girl. Heraclian had presented her to Rufinus on the head of an elephant. Rufinus dead, Eutropius put her on display as part of his spoils. I saw Furia pass beside a fountain with roses in her arms and remembered vividly how I had first met her in Rome cringing on the floor at Heraclian's feet. Then I had intervened to save her from Heraclian's brutality; now the sight of her aroused my lust.

The corrupted motions of this beautiful young woman caught instant attention. She sprang up like a sin-bearing daughter of Circe, with sinuous lust sheathing the motions of her body, and placed a crown of golden roses on the head of Eutropius, the yellow eunuch. Her fingernails glittered with green-gold lacquer as her voluptuous arms brushed the eunuch's shoulders. Her lips twisted, and over the head of the eunuch she so falsely caressed her eyes met mine in a glance blazing with a cruel flash of depravity, while stark misery seared the yellow face of Eutropius, the ruined slave of imperial grandeur, freshly crowned with golden roses.

Then the musicians began to play, and Furia danced barefoot on a broad sheen of black marble that was scattered with rose petals of as delicate a pink as a virgin's most tender flesh.

Her dance was an exquisite allegory of the death of a chaste maiden, but like everything else that night its values were perverted, and she won a roar of lewd applause.

When Furia finished dancing I left the feast and followed her along corridors to a dim chamber.

Lust, like a fire, quickened my drunken legs.

There was a table there holding a bowl of fruit and a vase of flowers, glowing in the dim light and fragrant. Furia turned to face me and then cowered back and back, step by step, as if in dread of rape, while saffron veils parted and fell to the floor from her warm body. It was a provocative dance of practiced harlotry. I took off a jewel and tied it in a strand of her dusky hair. Her teeth flashed in a greedy smile, and we sought our fierce enjoyment.

We suited each other in that climax of depravity, for Furia drew blood from my lip and it was my first sexual experience in which a will to destroy dominated and perverted the procreative urge of the body. Instead of being caught up in the radiant energy of the young husbandman sowing divine seed of life, a wave, as of death in my mind—like some momentous black wave that overthrows a ship in a storm—gave me as it were a murderous desire to sow the pains of death in the body of the woman in my arms. She drew blood from my lips, and I made her cry out like one wounded.

When I left Furia I went striding down one corridor and another, beating my palm with my fist, and gloating aloud: "That did me good! That did me good! Rufinus is dead; I've taken his woman. That did me good!"

I found a room far from Marcia's and plunged into a kind of dead sleep.

In the morning I wakened desiring Furia, my body, my senses and my mind still in the roaring onrush of some vast wave of death.

Marcia had begun to worry when she wakened and did not find me. I came about noon and found her sitting still and frightened with Marcus in her arms. When I leaned down to caress my son, the little child, who had never before been frightened of me, looked frightened, as if he sensed the dark wave of death tossing my soul. I stiffened back before he began to cry, and he smiled, as if some fatal danger had passed and not caught him yet, like a storm wave on the violent sea that hurls but does not quite founder a delicate and lovely ship.

Marcia, too, felt a shudder of premonitive peril. "Where were you all night, Gregory? How did your lip get torn and swollen?"

"Wine," I lied to her. "I don't remember."

She knew it for a lie. She stopped looking at my face. Lowering her eyes, she stared for one moment at my groin, and some dreadful intuition cut across her face with pain. "This place is horrid. I hope we can leave for Italy soon."

"I'll inquire about ships. We ought to sail before the winter storms."

"Please, Gregory, let me have Marcus baptized before we sail. No sea voyage is safe."

"I forbid you to bring up that subject again."

"We are not safe, we are not with Christ!"

This enabled me to feel justified in anger at Marcia.

I did not inquire about a ship. For days the wave held me, and my body surged and my mind raged with a new swollen willfulness. I rejoined Furia many times, both of us tossed in a moil of dark splendor.

Our lust was real and of great force. But what is lust? Are not all the strong simple words for intense human emotions but end names we give to complex intimate human relations? I think our deep joys and our deep sorrows are rooted in our intimate relations with those we have wanted to love and trust. The lust of today may be the outbreak of some failure in love long ago.

At any rate what was going on was of profound human interest and extremely mysterious. For Furia and I were celebrating one of the oldest of human tragedies.

I think there could be no human fellowship if we did not touch one another. Those few who set themselves apart, their flesh never comforted by any touch of other human flesh, become forlorn and crazy. The body also has its truth to give and receive; there is something lonely about the body, longing for handclasp, for caress, for surrender and embrace. And the flesh is a richer medium than the mind perceives or than the spirit tolerates. The flesh in its occasions is constantly breeding new dreams of life, and any man who remembers the warmth of a woman in his arms must know that goodness and healing were present. Furia and I, in the awakened living of our flesh, enjoyed our fornications. For the flesh is too rich a medium to be entirely the slave of a troubled spirit.

But the mystery was harder than this. The proud mind and the aspiring spirit do not always know how to accept the humble gifts of the flesh. Sometimes the body demands what disturbs the mind and offends the spirit; or the mind decrees what injures the body and darkens the spirit; and often the spirit yearns to soar free of the heavy body and the bewildered mind: And dissonance among these three is pain. Who cannot remember a moment of love, of harmony, like an attainment of eternal happiness, when a doing of the body was understood by the mind and rejoiced in by the spirit—some moment of love or adventure or of prayer?

But as Furia and I celebrated the old tragedy, its mystery was deeper than this. Furia's soul had been insulted by her life of servitude and harlotry, and I felt myself outraged by the cruel death of my father and the base persecutions of Rufinus. Also I was being hurt by the silent religious strain between Marcia and myself. Neither Furia nor I had learned to accept our suffering or to forgive our enemies or to be ourselves; and so, not loving but abusing each other, we sought (each alone, though toiling together) to assuage the pain of spiritual failure in the intensities of carnal vehemence. Intensity, without love, is inward dying. But I thought then that I was proving in myself an increased masculine power, for this particular form of intense dying in the depths of the heart—sexual passion without love—has, certainly for the lusty young, all the appearance of intense living. Now I believe we failed. Furia made herself a deeper harlot. I made myself a crueler man. Such was our tragic attainment, lighted by our bodies' pleasure.

And so it was that while I carried off to sea a new brutal manliness, a more arrogant will and a more demanding spirit—like a rooted rage of death in the heart—my flesh had also won another dream of the warmth of life; but the old pain was not assuaged, and all my enjoyment had seated a new pain.

I think now in my warm old age I have almost learned to reconcile my heart to the mystery of this pain of our human imperfection, which occurs so many times, in so many forms, by means of so many acts, all the days of our life. Is this not the oldest of human tragedies, that we must touch one another to live, but we do not know how to bring peace?

It was Marcia who got us out of Constantinople.

She watched my expression day after day. She had her own thoughts. She made no open accusation. But finally one day she said, "I've waited. You've done nothing. This palace is rotten with vice. Are we going to stay here forever, until you and I and our child are corrupted and damned to hell? Gregory, I won't stand it any longer. I've made arrangements myself for our passage. Our ship sails for Italy day after tomorrow."

I was amazed at her audacity in taking so serious an action upon herself. And yet I was relieved, too. The wave of deathliness which had surged across my soul for weeks had begun to seem, like a tidal wave, to pass roaring on beyond some rim of consciousness into dark night.

Marcia waited for some angry response I might make.

I said, "Thank you, darling. We'll go!"

I carried onto the ship Stilicho's sword, with its jewel-studded gold hilt. I also had on deck a big wooden chicken coop with a solid bottom of slabs of wood, for I was of my own accord bringing back to Honorius his beloved flock of chickens. I had added to them a very special golden pullet which I had bought in Constantinople. I was sure Honorius would like this little hen and give her a special name.

For days our voyaging was fair and sure. I loved to take my son Marcus to the prow of the ship, hold him there and watch the wonder of the tremendous sea. Marcia sometimes stood with us, her face lovely in the wind. I wondered how much she knew about my adulteries with Furia. I adopted the view so common in our time, that wives have to get used to the ways and needs of men. To hold such a view in security and self-esteem a man must often harden his heart and repel the tenderness of his wife.

Marcus had gained strength and laughter and was growing well. His arms were active, his legs were strong, his eyes were quick and deep with spiritual light.

Our ship anchored for two days in the harbor at the Piraeus, and I took Marcia and Marcus up to Athens because I wanted my wife and son to see the crowning beauties wrought by the hands of men. In one of the smaller temples we stood before a large statue of Poseidon. His great figure in marble was painted dark blue, like the wine-dark sea, and this old god of our sea looked powerful and grim. With golden reins he drove a team of leaping dolphins, done in black marble, leaping out of cruel waves. I set Marcus on the back of the leading dolphin. His little pink and tender human legs shone radiant as he bestrode the dolphin of the god, and he clapped his hands. His face was bright with glee.

"Please take him off," Marcia begged. "It's idolatry!"

"Poseidon is our guardian on the voyage. We must not insult him."

But I lifted the child off in my arms.

We went up onto the Acropolis, and it was in the majestic hall of the Parthenon, while we gazed at the magnificent statue of Athena the Virgin wrought in huge splendor by Phidias, that Marcia suddenly threw her arm up before her eyes and ran. I hurried after her, carrying Marcus with his cheek warm against mine. I found Marcia out in the sun, crouched down on the top step against one of the great pillars of the Parthenon, sobbing into her hands. I lifted her up. She clutched both me and Marcus and cried in anguish against my breast, "I am afraid of all the gods while we are not safe with Christ! I want my child baptized before we sail again!"

I neither reasoned nor argued with her hysteria, but ordered our litter and had us carried down into the city, then got a carriage to drive us back to our ship at the Piraeus. Marcia stopped trembling when she got away from the mighty enchantment of the most beautiful Pagan city in the world.

We sailed.

We rounded Greece into unquiet waters. All one morning the great gulf of the Ionian Sea vibrated with the tremendous silent forces of changing light, the quartering of the sky by towers of cloud and the heaving of ocean under the onslaught of wind. Black dolphins leaped out of the wave crests before the ship, and Marcus, as if he remembered bestriding the dolphin of grim Poseidon, reached out his hands toward those dark spirits of the sea-god's world. Marcia trembled at the danger of the sky and the leaping water, and I know she prayed.

Then the violence of light and wind centered in a roar of darkness. Black storm overwhelmed us. The sailors labored and yelled, the passengers played. I got Stilicho's sword from the cabin and held it in my hand and held Marcus close in my arm while the ship tossed and the wind screamed.

The ship heeled, recovered, shuddered, and rode six sickening waves of death. The seventh assault of sea doom foundered the ship, and we were cast into the sea. Holding Marcus in one arm, I had just time to hurl Stilicho's sword in a savage glittering arc over into the sea and clutch Marcia in the other arm thus freed, before the deck turned out from under us and we plunged into the black race of ocean.

The chicken coop floated like a raft. I pulled Marcia and Marcus to it, and there we clung one moment before a smashing wave tore Marcus from between us. I swam madly after him, unable to equal the black race of waters. His swaddling clothes had been torn from his body; I caught those, then let them go.

The heaving ocean sent up lacings of blue fire from the bottom deeps. I saw the lovely body of my son troughed and tossed among running veins of this blue phosphor fire that laced the overturning deep; there was yellow seaweed in his outreaching hands, and his face was under water looking down the dark hollows of death. Then his exquisite soul foundered in the surge, and the whole vast and heavy-swinging sea became the everlasting cradle of my son.

I cried into the wind a loud cry of grief, for it is a hard thing for a man to yield his son back to the gods. . . .

Marcia and I reached Milan in the bright harsh cold of winter, with chickens for Honorius, but without the sword of Stilicho, lost in the sea, and bereft of our son. Marcia had a spiritual wound that neither lonely grieving nor shrill excitement nor the drinking of much wine could mask or heal. And she was afraid of her religion now, for would not Ambrose have to tell her she must believe that our child, unbaptized, suffered in eternal hell?

In my heart there was no peace.

CHAPTER FOUR

MY FATHER'S WORDS

ACTIVITY AND SUCCESS ARE GOOD CONCEALERS OF GRIEF. I WAS a long way from knowing that grief ought not to be concealed, but should rather, by an enlargement of love, be set as a new light in the soul.

My year's absence was rewarded, I think, with more success than I could have won by staying in Milan.

I gave Stilicho a grim detailed account of the murder of Rufinus, a report on the state of affairs in the East and a long report on the ravaging of Thessaly and Greece by Alaric and his Goths. He forgave me the loss of his sword and regretted my loss of my son. "You have made yourself valuable," he told me.

When I presented the chickens to Honorius the dull boy's heavy face showed a little light. Receiving back his chickens was to him, in his torpor, what restoring a province to the Empire would have been to his father Theodosius. And he especially was moved by my gift of the new golden pullet, which he at once baptized a Christian and named Roma, and which he kept and personally cared for in his bedchamber. This little hen was destined for a long life and great fame as the favorite of the Emperor Honorius.

Honorius asserted himself. I was not only to be his tutor and companion—to which Stilicho readily and Serena reluctantly agreed—but he insisted I be made a Count of the first rank so that I might aid and support him in the Imperial Council, that cabinet of leading men which exercised the power long since lost by the Roman Senate.

Serena did not like this, but Stilicho insisted I was quite useful to him on the Council. "Gregory has special knowledge of the Goths, and Alaric is becoming a major problem. He also has made valuable contacts through which he is able to keep me informed about what goes on in Constantinople."

Marcia and I moved into handsome apartments in the palace, and I gave lessons to Honorius. We were frequently joined by Galla Placidia and the three children of Stilicho and Serena. Galla Placidia, who was growing fast, was the most intelligent of them all. She was glad to have me back and hugged me as her own. She had a question to ask me in secret. "When am I going to be Empress, Gregory?"

"Perhaps when you marry."

"I don't want to marry. I want to be Empress. I know more than Honorius already."

"He's a boy, darling. That's the way things are."

She looked at me, her cheeks flushed, stubborn, angry, her eyes aflash. "I'm mad at God. He could have made me a boy, and then I'd be an Emperor, too." She thought a moment. Her chin stiffened. "I'm going to be Empress. I'm glad you're back, because you're going to help me."

It took months of legal and personal effort on my part to get back properties Rufinus had taken from me and from my father's estate. Over in Constantinople Eutropius simply took over (on behalf of Arcadius) the spoils of Rufinus, even cleaving the Empire more deeply by confiscating some of Stilicho's wealth. I never did get back my Eastern properties, but managed instead to get hold of some estates in Gaul and Britain and a good villa on Lake Como from the plunder of Rufinus. I re-established myself in an effective position of wealth, and I had enough zest and confidence to know I could get more if I needed it. I discovered also that a man of wealth faces decisions and responsibilities that take time, judgment and moral consideration. Those who act as if wealth gave them unlicensed power are apt to get murdered, as happened to Rufinus.

I gave Claudian many specific details he was able to use in his political poem, the great invective against Rufinus, which it was his job to write. This poem—recited by Claudian at court, then spread abroad— amounted to a state paper, justifying the murder of Rufinus and praising the name of Stilicho.

My friendship with Claudian developed in warmth. We often sought each other out to sit an hour or two in a quiet place with wine, discussing the outer world and the inward man. It was a relief to tell him all about Marcus and to say: "I will never love another child the way I loved my son. I go down in the waves night after night in my dreams, but I cannot reach him again." And it was a relief to Claudian to let me know the loneliness a poet feels in a world going crazy with political and religious passions. "In both Church and State every act and word is a play for power. All they want of me is that I should pervert my song into propaganda. In an age of hate like ours it is better not to be born a poet." We often enjoyed together satirical chuckles and bursts of laughter upon perceiving and revealing to each other new idiocies and villainies of the world.

I pushed all my advantages, making light of that hard question in an active man's life: How shall he both do his work and serve truth? I was active in the Council, discussing policy, writing memorandums and directives, going on special missions to Rome for Stilicho. Stilicho was able to use me to establish better relations with the Senate. I was certainly young for this, but I had audacity and a real faculty for interpreting opposing factions to each other in such a way that we could find common ground on which to get things done.

I entered full swing on a brilliant career of honors. A good measure of my rising position was the fact that a man named Florentinus, a Pagan and a high official, tried to block my progress because it threatened his power. I fought him back to hold my gains and get more. He continued my enemy.

Openly busy and elated, I was in secret frightened and unhappy. My grief for the death of my son took deep roots in my heart, although I covered over the showing of it with all this new activity. And our son's death was a central unresolved misfortune between Marcia and me. The things we did not say to each other were a silent sickness between us.

I had begun to feel in my own life a thickening, a growing density of interweaving power beyond the knowledge or hope or will of an individual man. There was a superhuman grandeur of forces, present, stealthy, blind and terrible of stroke, threatening a man's frail life. Suddenly I knew Aeschylus better than I had ever known him before, and I kept asking myself with silent inner amazement that dread question at the close of his *Choephori:* "How can the wind of doom be lulled to sleep and stilled?" And in the hollows of my life I heard the dark wind on the roaring water that engulfed my son.

It was no use to try to comfort Marcia with rational arguments or Stoic philosophy; she believed what she believed and suffered accordingly. She did not conceive again, and said her fertility was blighted. Once when I came home, found her drunk, and took the wine away from her, she said, "I gave up heaven to be with you and our son in hell."

I began to realize the time must surely come when in the last desperation of self-defense she would blame me for all she suffered and for all she imagined our child now to be suffering in hell.

Claudian, too, was deeply affected by our trouble and tried to help me pull Marcia out of her despondency. He went with us to the theater or to the games, and at parties helped me guard her from drinking too much. Her smile was no longer spontaneous and warm, but was wounded, and her eyes no longer glowed with lights of candid affection, but were evasive and haunted by a tormenting sense of guilt. She had nothing outward to do and was left all day long a prey to this inward destruction.

I think this tragedy, with its implications of more pain to come, deepened my insight into my father's heart.

On my first mission to Rome I did, with sorrow and regret that I had not been able to do them sooner, the burial honors a son owes to his father. One of my father's concubines—her name was Liris—had loved him; she had preserved his ashes in the hope that I might return to raise his monument. After the list of his honors on his stone I wanted something of his own voice and spirit. I thought of the little Greek poem he had sometimes quoted: "The times are impious, and new gods flatter inexperienced hearts to seize the world; I shall follow you, O gods of my fathers, into immortal chasms of remembered time." But then I remembered a cry more purely from his own deep breast, wherein I heard his own voice, his own courage and his own tragic fate. So it was that I put these words of my father on his memorial stone:

ALL THE GODS ARE ONE GOD AND HE BREAKS THE HUMAN HEART

Then I held the urn containing my father's ashes in my two hands and reheard the vital sound of his voice in my head. It was deeply strange. I found it an utterly sad thing to hold the ashes of my father in my two hands, and strange and sad to bury them.

When I got back to Milan and told Marcia she said I had put a dreadful legend on my father's tomb. "It's a curse! It's a curse! First your son, now your father. Damned. Why do you hate me so!"

I was troubled, but I had chosen the words in faith and love, thinking my father had the right to his own tragic courage. And after days of searching my heart for my father's presence there, I knew at last he was a great soul and not afraid of his own deep words. Surely so long as I or any man beheld tragedy in human life my father, so speaking for himself, would not be forgotten. And deep in my soul a subtle consonance was established between my father's outcry of mortality and the terrible cry of Christ on the Cross:

"My God, my God, why hast Thou forsaken me?"

But Marcia brooded and accused, "You are destroying us, Gregory, with your sin and despair."

Her heartsick voice and miserable eyes faced me with one of the profound difficulties of a man's spiritual life. This was my dilemma: I had no formulated concepts about immortality or a future life, but Marcia held the Christian concepts of heaven, sin and hell. I saw for myself, in Pagan terms, that the gods were by means just; that calamity and good fortune both were blind as to how they struck and where they fell; and I couldn't see that events were any different under the Christian God. I felt a normal man's urge to do something about so cruel and stupid an arrangement. But what could I do? I had enough humor to refrain from taking hold of the universe, shaking it up, and making it over to my own improved pattern. Still, I could see how man's spirit, offended by the pains and vagaries of misfortune in the days of his life, could posit a future life and a day of judgment to turn the scales and balance the rewards. Being a reasonable man, I did not believe that positing a thing made it true. I did not believe in the Christian's heaven or hell. But I was also an unreasonable man, emotionally responsive to my human associations, and I did associate with Christians who believed all this. Their strange ideal of immortality, heaven and hell, was a positive emotional force I had to deal with in my personal life among them and particularly with Marcia.

It's as simple as this: When you eat breakfast with a woman, what she believes colors her conversation with you and affects your day, and you and your beliefs affect her day. Socrates said, Know thyself, and Christ said, The truth shall make you free. Divinely speaking, yes. But I was a married man, leading an active life, all of which was very human and intricate beyond knowing. The concepts influencing the lives of other people, whether true or false, were part of the reality of my life, for I lived my life with people, not all alone with truth. Any truth I could find and spread about among my fellows would be good for all of us; but while at that labor we had also better recognize we had one another's passionate errors to deal with, too.

I had to get help somewhere to ease my deepening sense of guilt and to bring healing to Marcia's mind.

On my next mission to Rome for Stilicho I hunted up Pelagius the Christian, for I believed Marcia would listen to direct word brought back from him.

Big Pelagius was a happy Christian, and I had not encountered many

of those. Fierceness, sadness, inwardness, abasement more often sig-
naled out the Christian than did happiness. I offered to have milk and
cheese brought in, but Pelagius refused. "I'm fasting."

"By way of penance?"

He laughed and patted his belly with a great hand. "Heavens, no! By
way of common sense. We have more of that commodity in Britain than
you do in Rome. I dwell in a huge body, and I have learned that occasional fasting keeps it in better health. And I feel a better Christian for
a good night's sleep than I do for crying my sins on my knees all night.
My idea of penance is not self-punishment. First I look around for the
true cause of the sin in some slip or falseness of my own will; then I try
to do better next time."

He gave me a warm confidential smile. "Sometimes, Gregory, I can't
find the reason why I failed or sinned. Would you believe it? I am not
perfect. I am not superior either to mortal limitations or to cosmic laws.
That's salutary knowledge. So I pray God to forgive me, I forgive my
foolish self, and try again to do good." He leaned forward. "Why so sad
an eye, young Julian? You've been whipped till it hurts."

I told him about Marcus. His big ruddy face got ruddier with out-
going warmth of affection. "Now that's sad," he said. "Did you cry?"

"My heart cried out. I held my tears."

"In the Stoic tradition. Like your father. Are you trying to drive yourself mad? It's a sad thing when a son dies. A father ought to cry. A
mother ought to cry. That beautiful child, lost on the dark wave. Hold
your tears, and you'll hate his death. Unuttered love turns to self-hate
and sickness. We cannot change the awful and mysterious wonder of
life, but when we ought to weep, we can weep. Cry, man, and you'll
know you loved your son!"

It was very strange how right he was and how deeply his direct, humane and simple words thawed some of my icy fear. I was not ashamed,
but rather comforted, to have him see my tears for my son come forth in
a flood. They left me like an untying and pouring out of knots of blackness, and let in light. I felt not less, but more free and manly through
weeping.

"His spirit was lovely," I said, "and he had learned to laugh."

"We have our life a shorter or longer while. Each of us can work while
it lasts to make it good."

"And a man like you can help one like me who hasn't the sense to
know why he is sick. Thanks, Pelagius."

Then I asked him—no longer for my own sake, because I was no longer
afraid, but for Marcia's sake—if he thought our child was damned.

He sat up, alert, like a lion shaking its shoulders and lifting its head. "No! Infants are as free of sin as Adam was before he fell." He raised his huge hand and large forefinger. "And how has that infant lifted its finger against God? In what sin? What rebellion? What blasphemy? The thing is absurd!" He shook his good and honorable head. "There are a lot of monks who deny the flesh, despise man, and hate the world. All their arguments are from injury toward suffering. I believe in the love of God and the aspiration of man. Our original potential is to be good, and we ought to labor to become so. Our greatest need and joy is to fulfill each man his own goodness. It's a hard work. We must try to see ourselves as we are. We must help each other, which is love. So you come to me for help. I do what I can. But no greater help has been offered to man for fulfilling in joy his own goodness than is offered by Christ. Seek Him."

"I wish Marcia could talk to you."

Pelagius looked me over with one of those penetrating flashes of vision that plunge deep, then fly off. "She drinks, you say? She gets shrill? Watch out, boy. Watch out! Marcia's a good little wench, but she's a woman. Their souls are different from our men's souls. Haven't you learned that, with such a female, what God may do hereafter is not so worrisome as what the man is doing right now? Have you crossed her will? Have you given her cause to doubt you love her?"

"I'm sure it's the religion, the child's death and her fear of his damnation. So is she. She has told me so."

"You may both be sure and both be wrong. The leaning toward self-destruction—from what you tell me, that is what the poor girl is doing— is itself a great lie, and the reasons she makes apparent are probably false ones. Watch out, boy. I warn you. She's a good wench, but a child still and more female than most."

Pelagius also said he had studied the words I had had cut into my father's memorial. He repeated them now. " 'All the gods are one God, and He breaks the human heart!' You are a son of good faith to let your father so truly speak for himself. There he has uttered the final great and tragic words of Paganism. 'All the gods are one God, and He breaks the human heart!' That is the fullness of mortal wisdom. But no man's words are so full of grace as the words of Christ."

" 'My God, my God, why hast Thou forsaken me?' "

He shook his shaggy Briton head vigorously. "No, boy, no! He also said, even after that cry and yet on the Cross, 'Father, into Thy hands I commend my spirit.' But as the risen Christ, the Son of God, our divine Mediator and Saviour, he further spoke, and for eternity speaks, saying,

'Follow thou me'; and yet again, 'I am with you all the days, even to the end of the world.' And all the words of Christ are first words and last words, linked each to each in harmony of heaven, for Christ is eternal." He shook his finger at me. "Gregory, I warn you, I tell you, I pray for you: Hear but one of his sayings with your whole heart, and you shall not rest until you seek him utterly."

I was happy that night. I experienced in my room alone one of those moments when peace, like a serene light, clears and relaxes the mind. I thought Marcia would be glad to hear most of what Pelagius had said. But surely he was mistaken about her having a hidden cause for her trouble. I needn't bother her with mention of that. I thought of my father and of my son with a silent deepening of love in their remembrance, then slept in peace.

CHAPTER FIVE

DIONIE

Dionie was in Rome at this time, using her influence with Laeta, widow of the Emperor Gratian, to carry through some intrigue for Heraclian, and it happened that we started back for Milan on the same day. I had the advantage of imperial privilege in the use of the road and of government facilities. With a boastful gesture I invited her to leave her slower and more difficult private conveyance and join me, an important person favored by the government. She accepted the challenge.

If Heraclian had not been in Gaul, Dionie would not have gone to Rome alone; and I was later accused of having planned the whole thing. I don't believe I was that predatory. This is what I had done:

Stilicho disliked and mistrusted Heraclian. But Heraclian had got hold, one way or another, over various men of power and could not simply be rejected. Stilicho wanted him out of Milan, but certainly didn't want to honor the man with a governorship. I knew Heraclian's greed and solved the problem for Stilicho by suggesting that Heraclian be given a five-year appointment as defensor in one of the troubled parts of Gaul. This officer—defender of citizens—was supposed to relieve the citizens from the overweening pressure of governors, judges and taxgatherers. Our Theodosian Code put it this way:

Thou, Defensor, must in the first place exhibit the character of a father to the commonalty; thou must not suffer either the rustics or the city dwellers to be vexed with inordinate assessments. Meet the insolence of office and the arrogance of the judge with proper firmness, yet always preserving the reverence which is due to the magistrate. Claim thy right of freely entering into the judge's presence when thou shalt desire to do so. Exclude all unjust claims and attempts at spoliation of those whom it is thy duty to cherish as thy children, and do not suffer anything beyond the accustomed imposts to be demanded of these men who certainly can be guarded by no arm but thine."

This pathetic law, creating this treacherous office, revealed the futility of piling law upon law and office upon office to amend corrupt government.

Heraclian saw the point at once; it gave him a five-year sinecure in which he could practice two-way demands for bribery and later return to Milan a wealthy man. Dionie was furious with me because she did not want to leave the court society for some provincial far-off place. In the end she refused to go; she stayed in Milan, and Heraclian went up into Gaul. He actually preferred leaving her as agent of his affairs at court. And I was ashamed of myself for foisting a man like Heraclian on an already oppressed province. But anyone who—as I did in my position —adjusts himself to the opportunities of government becomes corrupt.

Thus there was nothing either maliciously preplanned or remarkable in my meeting Dionie by herself as we both prepared to leave Rome for Milan.

Wary and suspicious, she accepted my challenge and got into my carriage. We were strained and unfriendly at first; she kept searching my face out of the green corners of her cat's eyes. She assumed—rightly— that I had not forgiven her for her rejection and denial of me that night in the church when she was of the party of Rufinus; and she assumed— wrongly—that it had been part of my revenge to have Heraclian sent off from Milan to Gaul. I no longer felt afraid of her superior worldly knowledge, but felt my knowledge at least equal to hers and my position even more powerful than hers. I let her feel that the youth she had toyed with in Rome was now Count Julian, a high member of the Imperial Council.

She made herself vivacious and charming to hide her fear. For two or three hours we had quite an entertaining duel there in the carriage, fighting each other with refined weapons of silence, of irony, of wit. Finally Dionie thought up a master stroke. "I dare you," she said, "to join with me in saying not a single word until we reach the next milestone."

"Agreed."

I sat looking straight ahead. She leaned warmly against me and laid her cheek on my shoulder. When we reached the milestone she said softly what only a woman could dare to say: "You know I'm a coward."

I said nothing. I held my stiff straight position. I had an inordinate desire to burst out laughing, and it took great effort of will to suppress all sound. Dionie raised her head from my shoulder in alarm. She studied my face, which I held as stiff and stony as I could. I could hear the horses and the wheels on the good hard road. Dionie's breathing became rapid. "You *are* a beast!" she exclaimed.

Then I let go, breaking forth in a gale of laughter. I seized her by the shoulders and gave her a good shaking while I laughed. She responded with peals of laughter as ready as my own.

After that my pretensions and her fears were gone. We neither of us had either the desire or the will to deny pleasure. We agreed it would be a shameful waste of our delightful youth to be enemies. We remembered that we had always enjoyed each other, regardless of treachery and mistrust.

Dionie was witty about love. When I entered her room where we happened to pass a night—at Bolsena or Clusium or Florence—she met me with happy eyes and open arms, and we entered on our pleasure as a thing of freedom and laughter.

When I left her room at dawn in Florence I paused at the door to bow my delight and to leave a smile. Dionie sat up in bed. Her fragrant hair, which she still dyed like silken gold, tumbled with a shake of her head about her shoulders, and light from the window spread a cool radiance over the deep flushed warmth of her lovely arms and breasts. It was a moment of such clear and happy affection between us that we laughed at each other in lyric joy.

We went on by way of Pavia.

Paulinus, Bishop Ambrose's secretary, was in Pavia on Church business, and there he saw Dionie and me leaning against each other in the warmth of chuckling pleasure as we walked out on the street in the evening to enjoy the people.

Back in Milan I found Marcia in one of her shrill moods of distracted chatter and shallow laughter. She fell from this into grief within an hour because she wanted comfort. I gave her all the reassurances I had brought back from Pelagius—as a Christian she did not need to believe our child was damned. But she had reached that depth where suffering feeds on itself. "Pelagius," she said, "is no bishop."

"Pelagius is a good man and a good Christian."

"You're not a Christian, Gregory. You can't understand. Why are you so happy and I so miserable!"

Then she gave me a strange glance which, had I not known her essential innocence, I would have considered lewd and depraved. "Teach me the pleasure of sin, Gregory. You know it!"

I found out she had gone to the fat old Crassa, that massive woman who had guarded death away from her door, for love potions and fertility amulets so that she might conceive another child.

I heard her moan in her sleep at night without waking. It hurt me to overhear her grief in her sleep and to know I had helped cause it.

But I was extremely busy with the imperial children and the Imperial Council. In order to help run the Empire properly, did I not have both to consolidate my position and increase my power? A man whose busy day is fragmented by the kaleidoscopic shifts, challenges and opportunities of immediate action on the worldly and political level is too tired at night to labor with spiritual problems.

Marcia's nerve-wracked condition offended me. I wanted mirth and sensuous delight. A morose and moody young wife is a disappointing bedfellow, especially when the husband feels he has caused her sorrow. Now and then I turned to Dionie for this pleasure I desired. I could laugh in bed with Dionie, whereas Marcia sometimes cringed and wept or sometimes overstrained to grasp at passion. I began to feel anxious and divided, myself. I began to find more pleasure in the business of Empire than in the strain of intimacy with a troubled wife and a troubled conscience.

I realized with a shock how bad things were with the inward spiritual foundation of my outwardly brilliant successful life when I returned to our apartment in the palace after an exhausting session of the Council. Alaric, freed from defeat by the splitting and recall of Stilicho's army, had plundered Macedonia, ravaged upper Greece, entered Athens and got tribute in place of sacking the city, and was now despoiling his way toward Corinth. I received and passed on to the Council a private report of what Alaric had boasted in Athens. "Athens," he said, "is the citadel of beauty. I enter it softly to receive its pleasure. When I go to Rome, which is the seat of power, I shall smash down its gates and take what I want. The gods have said I shall penetrate the City!"

The impossibility of Alaric and his Goths smashing the gates of our Eternal City was obvious to any good Roman, but the insult in the boast was also obvious. I supported Stilicho in his assertion that he must take an army to Greece and put a stop to Alaric's rising insolence and power. We had to beat down the timidities of some, the parsimony of others and the very difficult supporters of Serena, who took the view that Alaric was Constantinople's problem and that nothing should be done to cause dissension between Honorius and Arcadius, the two sons of Theodosius. It always seemed, at the crucial point, that Serena could not bear to have Stilicho completely inherit the power of Theodosius; under the fiction of its belonging to the two boys, she had the illusion that she had inherited this power herself.

I asserted that if we did not stop Alaric now in Greece we would have to stop him later, when he was stronger, in Italy.

And finally Stilicho broke up the meeting with his fiat of authority. "It has to be done. I'll take my army to Greece and do it!"

I came back to my apartment tired and yet elated. I felt myself on the side of real power in the Empire and doing good work to support that power. I knew my opponents—in the zest of youth I was pleased to consider them my enemies—were already whispering: "See how arrogant he acts. This young Julian must think he really will fulfill his father's prophecy and become Emperor!" It was a dangerous whisper, but flattering, too. An anonymous enemy had gone so far as to scratch on a wall: "Honorius, beware of Julian." I was brooding with inward vision on premonitions of glory.

I found Marcia vomiting into a basin and our slave girl Amantha holding her shoulders in her spasms. Marcia, in a fit of despair, had taken poison to kill herself. Amantha had caught her at it, and poor Marcia, already not wanting to die, had stuck her finger down her throat to induce vomiting. I called in one of the palace physicians. Marcia was not even critically ill, but she was miserable. I sat on a couch and held her in my arms for hours that night while broken sorrows came from her breast, now in weeping, now in pitiful questions, now in little cries of deep hurt. The inner spiritual life of our marriage was close to ruin. Once she left off accusing herself and beat my breast with her fists and cried, "You damned adulterer! Oh, you damned adulterer!"

I didn't know whether she was referring to Furia or whether she had found out I was taking pleasure with Dionie.

But I still thought the deepest thing was her heartsick longing for and fear of her religion. Again and again she trembled in my arms, whispering with real pain, "I have lost Christ. I have lost God. Oh, Gregory, my soul is sick! Why can't you help me? Why won't you love me and help me!"

"We need greater help than there is in ourselves, Marcia darling. The only place I know to turn for help is Ambrose. Let us go to him."

"He will only tell us we have damned our child to eternal hell. And you are damned. And now I have damned myself to be with you and our child."

I made the decision a firm one. "We will go to Ambrose."

My positive declaration did comfort her. Something like confidence, like a sense of direction and purpose, began to animate her sick body. She stood up alone, looking frail but courageous. "Thank you, Gregory. I still feel tainted. Let me sleep alone tonight."

I watched until she fell asleep, then had Amantha bring me some bread, cheese and wine.

I was fond of Amantha, who was a plain good little slave and growing up. I put my arm around her shoulders and gave her a squeeze of affection and comfort for the trouble and fright she had had with Marcia. The girl winced and shrank within my arm. I was surprised. I had to question her sternly before she would confess that her back pained her. She blushed when I took off her garment to see what was wrong. There were sore stripes on her back where Marcia had whipped her that morning in a fit of cruelty. I got some ointment and rubbed it on her back gently. It was a well-formed back, and her breasts were maturing. She gave me a shy smile of gratitude as she put her clothes on again, and I sent her off to bed.

I ate the food she had brought me, then slept on the couch.

CHAPTER SIX

A WOMAN'S GLANCE

WHILE WE WAITED FOR AMBROSE TO RECEIVE US IN HIS study the next evening Marcia trembled and wanted to turn back, but Ambrose kept us waiting only a moment. Just to see the man renewed

Marcia's faith in him. She at once kissed his hand, found relief in tears, and took immediate shelter in his outreaching love. Although he held out his hand to me I did not move to kiss it, because my reaction was opposite to Marcia's. I felt myself endangered; I had a sharp premonition that Ambrose was not going to be entirely gentle. I stiffened in an effort to keep a clear hold on my power to reason and to focus my intelligence in defense of my position.

His smile showed he was not offended. He was too seasoned in dealing with people to be offended by a young man's fright. "The male is proud," he said.

His sandals were laid aside, he was barefoot, and a basin of water stood near by. I realized we had come just as he was about to rest and wash his feet after a long day. It was a curious thing to notice, but I must say that his narrow bony feet with prominent anklebones looked pale and tired of mortality and yet, by their very suffering, looked pure, strong and beautiful on some pathway toward God. I had a strange sense that when he moved he walked on light. Something in the man's character gave my eyes a more poetic light to see by. His presence always changed me to something better than my accustomed self.

He had aged a lot since the death of Theodosius. I judged from some new ease of the wrists and relaxation of the fingers that his hands were tired of holding onto this world and were preparing to let it go. But the silent, deep and radiant inwardness of the man now shone with increased clarity. I could not help knowing that my crude spirit, troubled, darkened and unrefined, was in the presence of a great purging power. If I was not careful, I would be toppled over like a child by a wave or like an unsteady barque by a wind out of heaven.

I began my offensive at once. "The Church," I said, "has certain doctrines that bring more pain than peace. I have brought Marcia here to you because of one of them. She is in deep trouble."

Ambrose looked from one of us to the other, his mouth nearly hidden under his long mustache, his large eyes, under the uneven eyebrows, alight with silent melancholy. He said, "I can see she is in trouble. Her chin trembles, and your lips are stiff. Sit down, my children. We will talk at ease and at length, and I promise you we shall find out which one of you two needs me most."

He began to search our hearts by revealing himself, which is the way of love.

He began by telling us that Queen Frigitil of the Marcomani had sent envoys from 'way up in Germany with gifts to the church of Milan, asking that Ambrose send her a writing on the Christian faith, for, though many Germans were Pagans and many others were Arians, she sought to learn the true Catholic faith from him.

"I write such things more slowly now than I used to do, for there are very many things which are beyond the reach of our intelligence. When I first became bishop I began to teach what I had not yet learned myself. I had to be learning and teaching at the same time, since I had no leisure to learn before; and I fear I wrote too much, too rapidly, out of my intelligence, rather than very little, very slowly, out of faith. God is beyond the reach of words."

He paused, and in the silence one remembered, as it were reheard, the good, plain and pure resonance of his voice which, because he spoke from his heart, had no false notes in it. Then, looking at Marcia and at me with deep intimacy, he confessed, "How little the sorrow of man can say to the glory of God!" It was not an exclamation of rhetoric, but a quiet saying out of deep places of the heart.

And during another moment of silence I was certain that he prayed. Marcia looked at me with a mute appeal to do something or to be something that I did not know how to do or be.

He then told us that the church at Vercelli was having an internal factional dispute over the election of a new bishop. He smiled. "You know. how strangely I became a bishop. And now I have to write a veritable treatise on episcopal elections. I may even have to go to Vercelli to compose their troubles. I long only for silence in which to seek Christ, but many other duties are given me. I have helped you two before, I have prayed for you often, and now it is my duty to help you again. But somehow it gives me deep comfort to have you come here to sit with me like this. What is your trouble, Marcia?"

Her face turned a warm red the way it did sometimes when, having four or five things she wanted to say at once, she couldn't get any of them out and had to wait for the bursting through of something from deeper within. When it came it surprised me, for I had never thought of this particular way of expressing her trouble.

"I can't pray!"

Ambrose studied her a moment, then turned to me.

"And what is your trouble, Gregory?"

"I want to help Marcia get back her happiness."

"That's not a trouble, but a good wish of love. Please, children, tell me what is going on. When did it begin, where has it led?"

He had won our trust so fully and so simply that it was an easy outpouring to tell him of our life among the Goths, of the birth of our child, of our disagreement and strain over the question of baptism and of our son's death in the sea.

"Is my child burning in hell?" Marcia asked Bishop Ambrose.

His long narrow face, with its especially long nose, was grave and sad. For a moment he put his hand over his eyes as if to shut off outward sight, the better to meditate the sorrow and sin of human life.

"No," he said, "no. But a great harm has been done. These innocent infants are not damned and cast into the lake of fire. And yet they are lost, for without the sacrament of baptism they cannot attain to heaven."

I was about to argue, but Ambrose raised a thin impressive hand to silence me. "I know all the arguments, Gregory. Do not forget that I was a lawyer, a political man and a governor before God called me to Christ's service. We are not talking philosophy or political or social matters, but the mystery of divine truth. We are bidden to believe rather than to inquire. It is good that faith should go before reason, lest we seem to exact reason from our Lord God as from a man. Let God Himself, the Creator, teach me the mystery of heaven—not man, who has not the knowledge even of himself. Whom should I believe about God rather than God himself? It is necessary to believe that God's oracles in the Scriptures are true. Faith is the beginning of a Christian man."

I was surprised to see that Marcia, instead of being appalled, was comforted by his words. The tears had dried on her face, and her round cheeks had better color. Her smile was extremely sad, but not tormented, and her eyes seemed for a moment free of those evasive flicks of guilt. She looked at me steadily to see how I would answer.

I gave the direct answer. "I am not a Christian. I am no more nor less than a man in this world, facing its misfortunes and seeking its joys. God has given me more of reason than of revelation. I have to use my reason to bring light into my life. And what I like about reason is that it does not solve mysteries by edicts of pain or by abdication."

All this while Marcia had said nothing; she still said nothing. The shift of the pattern was obvious. I had brought Marcia to Ambrose for spiritual help. At their first contact she had been fully flooded with faith in his spirit. Now, from within the faith which she shared with him, she simply watched while he brought me to judgment.

Ambrose made one of the most difficult of Christian statements. "God calls those whom He deigns to call, and whom He wills He makes religious."

He was enough of a lawyer to know that this was a law without
mercy, a predestinate damnation of multitudes, regardless of the good
they might strive for and fulfill. It left no ground on which a man could
try to exert his will for good and no impetus to stir his heart toward
faith. Ambrose was only superficially dogmatic. What he revealed in
his next words was the mystic passion which was the real depth of his
lonely nature.

"You have seen the rebellion and threat of the Goths. I have seen
and heard more than you know or dream. The Empire is indeed breaking up. The end of the world is coming upon us; we are in the waning
age. We are very near the second coming of our true Lord Christ and
the judgment. Yes. Time falters. Eternity is at hand. We are witness-
ing the end of the world. I grant you that there is nothing in which a
man more excels other living creatures than in the fact that he has reason, inquires into the causes of things, and holds that the author of his
being should be searched out. But now there is no more time for lifelong speculation and deathbed repentance. I say again, we are witness-
ing the end of the world, and the time of judgment is near. Now must
the ardent soul long for many kisses of the Word and be consumed
with desire for union with her Divine Lover. Every soul is called to the
grace of Christ. He wishes no one to be condemned, but all to be absolved. Every creature may be redeemed by the price of the Lord's
blood. They who perish, perish by their own negligence. Do not flee
and hide thyself from Christ! Where Christ is, there are all things."

Ambrose was exalted. I was astonished how in this man the mute desire of the flesh for carnal union and the articulate desire of the mind
for worldly union with power and knowledge had been transfigured into
a mystical desire for the union of the soul with Christ. I had never before seen any man, let alone a man such as Ambrose, of true depth and
great development, seized up in a spiritual transport. This was a prelude
to that strange act I have mentioned before: how Ambrose, when he
came to die, lay for hours with his arms outstretched in the form of the
Cross, as if receiving the bliss of Christ in the agony of death.

He closed his eyes, folded his hands, bowed his head and cried out in
prayer, "Come, Lord Jesus, seek thy servant, seek thy weary sheep!
Seek me, find me, take me, carry me! Come, for thou alone canst recall
the wanderer. Come and seek thy sheep, not now through servants and
hirelings, but in thine own person. Take me in the flesh in which Adam
fell. Carry me in the Cross, which brings salvation to those that err,
which alone gives rest to the weary, in which alone whosoever dies shall
live."

While he spoke, calling from his heart for Christ, I heard the cry of my son, deep lost in ocean's old eternal roar. No one knows the noises in another man's head; but, having heard my own resound, I was willing to guess at both wild dissonance and sweet harmony in Ambrose or any other man. Perhaps Ambrose heard the song of his lost brother Satyrus while I heard the sorrow of my child.

There was a long silence when Ambrose finished. Both he and Marcia, by their silence, threw the burden on me. Ambrose had uttered faith and passion and mystery for both of them. It was left to me to join them or be abandoned by them and go my way alone.

I tried once more to define my way. "If we are not to reason," I said, "what is left but assertion? Each man asserts his own truth. I am a Pagan——"

Ambrose, once more alert, broke in. "Yes, go on. What truth do you assert? Now that death is an end. Now that there may be a shadowy limbo for disembodied spirits. Now, simply, that you are bewildered and do not know. It's no use, Gregory. You have failed to see the great distinction. Each Pagan asserts his own truth, which changes with his mood. No Christian asserts his own truth, but a Christian bears witness to Christ's truth. There is much goodness in you. You have brought Marcia to me for help because your love cannot bear to see her suffer. But you, Gregory, are in the deeper trouble, for you are the injuring party, and I truly believe your heart secretly knows this."

I rose to my feet. My face was probably flushed with anger. "Not I, but a pernicious superstition has injured Marcia and is spoiling our marriage, our love, our lives."

Ambrose joined battle in earnest now. "The wife of a Christian man would still be able to say her prayers. The wife of a Christian man would find comfort for her grief in the fellowship of Christ's Church and would find forgiveness of her sin in contrition and tears and penance." His voice sharpened. He, too, stood up. "You are depriving Marcia of the truth of Christ. Have you a greater truth to offer her than the truth of Christ? If so, speak it out and heal the pain in her soul."

For a moment we looked into each other's eyes. I had never seen wrath in this man before, wrath like a flame and a sword. The wrath of a spiritual man is somehow more terrible than brutal anger.

I looked at Marcia, and her silent eyes were pleading with me. What truth indeed shall a man offer to his wife to comfort her in despair? Plato on ideal essences? Lucretius on atoms? Cicero on old age? Plutarch on morals? Epictetus on suffering? Marcus Aurelius on stoic nobility of soul? The woman was alive. I knew her breathing. My ear against her breast had listened to the beating of her heart. What could I do for the pain spread in the mysterious depths of her being?

Philosophers offer ideas to the mind, which is a pleasure and good but is something less than offering truth to the person. This saying of things to absent persons is a poor shadow of communication, for vital communication requires the presence of the person and love. And a man and wife, aware of each other with the penetrating intelligence of love, communicate by means of a full intensity of their beings and say more in a motion than the mind can know. To communicate a healing truth to Marcia I would need to be living by that truth myself. I was certainly not living by Christ's truth, of which Ambrose said I had deprived her, nor by any clear truth I could name or reveal. I was myself groping.

How can we once for all make up our minds about eternal truth when we don't even know the motions in the air behind us?

I turned away. Ambrose kept after me with the lash of a terrible insight. I bowed my head and stooped my shoulders to the storm of his words.

"What is really going on is more fatal than you think, Gregory. You are stronger than Marcia, and she loves you, and the assertion of your will is seducing her from her faith. What have you given her to cling to? You have embroiled yourself in the affairs of Empire with a force and zest that I fear has somewhere in it a lust for power. Neither are your other lusts hid nor your adulteries unknown. It was a great misfortune for you the day demons prompted your father to prophesy you might be Emperor. Who will say what odious dreams the evil spirits have set in your heart? They are implanted there with so subtle a malice that you, meant to be and meaning to be good, do not know them for what they are and do not know how they poisonously flourish. Did you not take joy in the murder of Rufinus? Have you not sent a man into Gaul to fulfill your lust after his wife? Who is betraying this marriage? The Christian wife or the Pagan husband? What are her crimes and treacheries and adulteries? Only Christ can purge you of such secret poison, and until you are purged Marcia's suffering must increase."

I took two steps away from him, trembling, sick, frightened. I heard a peculiar splashing sound. I turned and saw Marcia kneeling on the floor with the basin, washing Ambrose's feet.

I was aghast, shocked and humiliated to see my wife reduced to so servile an action. She, the daughter of a great and ancient family, the wife of a man of illustrious name, debasing herself to perform the duty of a slave! No blow I had ever received more bitterly injured my pride.

I lifted my eyes from that stooping woman to look at the face of Ambrose, ready in my mounting rage to destroy whatever smile of triumph there might be on that terrible man's face. My heart turned over at what I saw, turned over in a kind of death that did not kill. All the wrath had gone out of Ambrose's face. There were tears in his dark sad eyes. His whole face was transfigured with what I can only call a divine pain, like a vision of supernatural humility.

I heard Ambrose, Bishop of Milan, the greatest prelate in the Roman world, whisper to one I did not see, in tones of ecstasy not meant for mortal ears: "Thy handmaid, O Christ, has humbled me!"

And then I saw that the way Marcia washed his feet was strangely beautiful. In the beauty of her act and in the transfiguration of his face and the unearthly joy of Ambrose's response I witnessed a complete subversion of all our Roman values: not who could wield the greater power, but who could render the purer service of love.

Moments like this of high tension and spiritual insight are wonderful—wonderfully purging and refreshing—if you don't have them so often that they convert you into a poet or mystic and set you constantly seeking them as a kind of self-intoxicating irritant of the soul. My perceptions could lead me into considerable stress, and my temperament could endure considerable stress. I could apprehend possibilities of a different life, but it was not my nature to suffer a radical conversion. I was a child of this world in my daily living, and, both wanting and seeking light, I yet was not one to reject this world radically so as to become a child of light. Men like me are lucky to have poets and mystics around; their choice suffering and vision enlighten us. We ought to be more gracious toward them than we are, not only to ease their burden but also to fructify our own lives. For example, a man who fails to love Christ on this count alone shows himself a dullard.

For a moment, then, with this vision before me of enacted Christian charity in a little room at the heart of the Roman Empire I felt an almost unbearable loneliness, like a tension of the spirit to the point of bursting. I was not ready to give up Rome for the Church, nor ready to deny my father and my son for a mystic union with Christ. If Ambrose was right in believing the world was ending and the judgment at hand, I had to face out the last days alone, equipped only with the sufficing of robust senses and the wisdom of common desires. It seemed that I could not follow Ambrose and that I had lost Marcia.

I made my concession to this enormous spiritual pressure with a heavy heart. "Marcia need not turn away from Christ. I am willing to search for the truth of my own spirit and offer it as it is to those I love and to the world. I'll turn my face toward Christ. I'll find out how far I can go."

Then Marcia gave me a glance.

One of the things I profoundly enjoy about life is the astounding fertility of human relationships, so that no moment of high emotion and intense spiritual insight is safe from the comic shock of devastating change.

Marcia's upward glance at me from her washing of Ambrose's feet was not religious: It was primitive and female.

Ambrose had been dealing with our marriage problem in the abstract terms of a religious intelligence, but something more primitive than that keeps going on between a man and his wife. Really, God-hunting men are dangerous to women, and women know it. A wife feels safer if she can get her man to accept conventional religion, stop chasing after God, stay at home, and belong to her. Marcia called it "being loved"; I rather think it was an indirect form of domination.

At any rate, the primitive, cunning and fiercely triumphant little glance Marcia dared dart up at me shattered the ideal purity of the moment as a symbol of supernatural charity, subverting the whole of Rome in Christ's name. Instead it rendered the moment very human, warm and revealing in another way. I saw in a flash to the heart of our marriage problem. It was a spiritual struggle, all right, and Marcia had been injured and tormented by a spiritual insecurity, but it was not a matter of the Christian religion. It was the old man-and-wife problem; Ulysses, I think, solved it fairly well with Penelope, but Jason made a mess of it with Medea, Agamemnon made a ruin of it with Clytemnestra, Adam defaulted fatally on it with Eve, Augustine failed with his woman, and Stilicho was making a bad solution of it with Serena. Ambrose had not solved but had avoided this problem by not having woman or wife. Marcia's soul had the deep dreamy unrelenting woman's will to dominate her man and keep him adoring and contented at her side, and my man's soul had its equal desire to go off God-hunting where and when I would throughout the bright actions of this world: And yet we wanted to live in creative human union together.

Once I saw this revelation in Marcia's vivid glance, I broke out in a roar of rude and robust young manly laughter. Ambrose started back, Marcia stood, the wet rag in her hand.

"Marcia," I said, "will not want me to become so intense a Christian that I abandon her to follow Christ."

She was thoroughly feminine and did not like my irony. She threw at my face the wet cloth with which she had been washing the saint's feet. I caught it with a quick hand so that I got only a trifling splash on the cheek. I finished in direct simplicity what I had begun in irony. "We love each other in the deep old human way."

The delightful child sprang across the room, flung herself into my arms, beat my breast, and ended by kissing me.

Ambrose had the swift spiritual insight to sanctify our return of love. He blessed us in Christ's name.

CHAPTER SEVEN

NOCTURNAL VENUS

MY ADULTERY AND MY AMBITION WERE THE TWO THINGS Bishop Ambrose had most condemned in me. I looked on him as my spiritual father, as the only man I now knew who wanted to help me find God and live in goodness. His criticism of my ambition seemed excessive, but his condemnation of my adultery worried me. I made all the allowances I could for his own celibate life and for Christian doctrine—and still was not free of anxiety.

I rehearsed in my mind many arguments in favor of adultery, and I suppose the most forceful was also the most simple: that I enjoyed it. For a vigorous young male there is a rising run of pleasure from the first glance of provocative interest to the climactic embrace in the rush of blood. Having experienced this pleasure a few times, a young man is confident it will be pleasure again. There may be some men who are never roused or pleased in this way except by the one woman they have chanced to marry. I was not such a man. And it is hard to convince young people, in the rout of their pleasure, that adulteries divide and despoil the heart and choke up the spirit with emphasis of flesh. I was not the first man to insist I loved my wife and still wanted to enjoy my adulteries. Perhaps on profound analysis it might be found that such men neither loved nor enjoyed, but only suffered the vivid excitement of sense distraction. Even so, adultery affords its illusion of pleasure and peace to a divided and distracted mind.

Such generalizations did not quiet my anxiety, for I was not young men in general, but Gregory Julian in particular. And Marcia said: "I know about you and Dionie. Bishop Ambrose didn't have to tell me."

How, exactly, was it with me?

I had not pursued or assailed Dionie with any immoderate passion. Derogatory words like "lust" and "concupiscence" seemed to me wrong words to describe our interest in each other. When Dionie chuckled in her throat and opened her arms in warm delightful welcome, "play," "pleasure," "refreshment" seemed the appropriate words. We frequently were content to spend a few hours together in comfortable conversation and laughter, during which the charm and wit of her temperament would relax the strains I was under; and if at other times our mutual desire for intimacy brought us to embrace, it certainly seemed to me that we brought one another human and healing solace and a quiet peace. I know a man's tendency to idealize what he does or wants to do, until an idealization of adultery looks almost like a picture of love. But it wasn't love, a light at the core of life; it was casual and peripheral. I knew that I was not Dionie's only "lover," and I appreciated that as one cause of her cheerful ease, her amorous warmth, then her serene detachment. I also knew she would be treacherous and destructive if the subtle center of her security were endangered. But it was precisely ease with men, on the basis of present pleasure, that was her mode of security. Was she not beautiful and skilled both in enjoying and in pleasing men? She would toss her hands and laugh at "adultery, that dreary word invented by those sour ones who never learned how our bodies love to play. Ah, Gregory, the flesh is sweet, and I will not spoil its innocence by any deep exclusive attachments!" I considered that Dionie, with her green-eyed smile and her subtle charming touch, had, without laying any permanent claim on my life, helped me stay for the most part sane and cheerful through Marcia's crisis. And why should a wife be so greedy of a man's person as to deny him his pleasure?

It is quite probable, I consoled myself, that, if I had not had the healing pleasure of adultery with Dionie, I would have been driven to divorce Marcia. Was any more proof needed that in my case adultery was a good thing? Good for me, good for our marriage, and so—good for Marcia.

Thus I was less distressed in this matter at that time by the Christian sense of sin than by the Pagan sense of honor. I remembered too well the biting condemnation by Epictetus of a literary man—at least, one who passed for a man of letters—who was guilty of adultery. "If," said Epictetus, "laying aside that fidelity for which we were born, we form designs against the wife of our neighbor, what do we do? What else but destroy and ruin—what? Fidelity, honor and sanctity of manners. Only these? And do we not ruin neighborhood? Friendship? Our country?" And so on. Who can trust us? What place can we find in society if we cannot even be a friend? Are we not wicked and of no use and fit for the dung heap? But Heraclian was such a man and Dionie such a woman that I could console myself against this Stoic doctrine. I did not pretend to the high virtue of friendship with Heraclian. Heraclian had told Dionie that her adulteries might be to his political advantage, and she had assured him that she would not neglect his advantage after first considering her pleasure. Their marriage was an affair of convenience in which they understood each other. I did not feel honor-bound to respect any convention of fidelity between those two.

I scolded Marcia for having stooped to wash the feet of Bishop Ambrose. I ordered her to remember that she was the wife of a Count of the Palace and companion of the Emperor, and also the daughter of an illustrious family. She was pleased that I scolded her, for it was evidence of my emotional concern in her personal conduct.

"I saw by your glance," I concluded, "that you didn't do it out of religious piety so much as to shock me. What does Christianity mean to you, anyway? I really want to understand."

As nearly as she could explain her Christianity to me, it was an amazing, illogical phantasmagoria of superstitions, fears and authoritative dogma, lighted up and redeemed by a strong tender yearning of her own spirit to be good. Her Christianity was not her real religion. Her real religion was more simple, and she explained it in these few words: "If you love me, I'll be all right."

"I do love you."

Her chin trembled. "You love Dionie."

So there it was: Ambrose would like me to give up everything for Christ, and Marcia would like me to give up everything for her, and I wanted to love women and fulfill a brilliant career, all in the name of utmost happiness.

I had made no promise, except that one—that I would turn my face toward Christ to find out how far I could go toward Christianity.

I began going to church regularly with Marcia, although I was of course excluded—and for my sake Marcia generally stayed away—from the mysteries open only to the baptized communicants. This standing of the Church between man and God I did not like. But I found the ritual and singing in Ambrose's church of great interest and deep emotional appeal.

Claudian often came with us for precisely this reason. As Claudian said, "Man always requires and always creates for himself ritual forms to harmonize and renew his spirit. You go dead inside without the mystery of some ritual."

I thought what he said was true. But solitary rituals are a little mad. A man needs to practice ritual in common with other humans, for then there is a deep joining and celebration of human solidarity underneath the level of irritating and lonely self-consciousness.

And because I liked Ambrose I was pleased to hear Claudian say further: "I don't remember how many varieties of ritual I've participated in, from the obscene to the ascetic, but I tell you, Ambrose is a genius. With his simple heart-striking hymns and noble antiphonal pacing of music he has created something here in Milan that our darkening age desperately needs. This is the only open communication I get with great poetry in our time. When will men learn that shared beauty is more necessary than imposed law for holding society together? This ritual created by Ambrose will bring and hold men together when Rome's laws have decayed." Claudian's religion was not Christianity, but something else, rare and interesting, which I surely want to speak of later.

The effect of Ambrose's preaching was cumulative. He praised chastity, faith and charity; he condemned adultery, greed and pride. But something else, out of the depth of the man, came through. It was what I can only call the image of his life, that secret and yet unconcealable assumption of his own meaning that a man makes in his own soul. With Alaric I had seen it shine forth as the assumption of a high historic destiny he was to fulfill—no less than the ruining of Rome promised him by the oracle in the forest. With Theodosius it had been the assumption of majestic power. With Ambrose it was the assumption of conscience enlightened by love. My need of Ambrose increased every time I heard him preach and felt increasingly the force of this conscience enlightened by love. I remember on one occasion, while he preached, saying to myself with a tingle of astonishment chilling my neck and scalp: Ambrose is the conscience of the Roman world! Then I was appalled at the thought: When that man dies the Roman world will have lost its conscience!

My political enemy Florentinus, who had fought me ever since my success with Stilicho began, made political use and abuse of my frequenting the church. Florentinus was an able man, an ambitious man, one of those men with a pink placid face and tireless energy. He was several ranks above me and in closer favor with Stilicho than I. Claudian was working on a long poem about the Rape of Proserpina which he was dedicating to Florentinus. Florentinus thought he saw my design to use my direct influence with Honorius and (as she grew older) with Galla Placidia to overleap a dozen ranks to high and sudden power. He started the rumor going that I was attending church as a first step to gain control of Marcia's wealth under the terms of our marriage contract, for I was to have control of her wealth if and when I became a Christian. Also, he said, I was taking the step to consolidate my position with cool-eyed Serena and the imperial children. Finally he warned the Pagan party, of mild strength in Milan and great strength in Rome: "Watch Gregory Julian. He is going to betray you!" I realized I was going to have to stop the man sooner or later, or he would ruin me.

However, I did not decide to reject my search for spiritual truth on so short a trial as the easiest way to stop his rumors. For I realized in a dim troubled way that my personal spiritual matters were more important to me than the affairs of Empire. I had to start with my own spirit; I wanted it to be sound and sweet and whole. I doubted if the outward world could either mend or destroy the inner man of my heart, and at the same time I knew I was not so solitary that the outward world was not part of my inward living. This attack by Florentinus made me quite aware that inwardly I was anxious, divided and confused. A man is not self-derived, self-explanatory or self-fulfilling—still he is a man. "For I am not eternity," said Epictetus, "but a man." The Pagan man was a temporal unity, but an eternal fragment. Some intimation or some intonation of Ambrose, preaching, made me suspect—I may even say, made me hope—that Christ taught otherwise: that a man was an eternal unity and but a temporal fragment. But when these thoughts, or ideas *felt*, bordered on mysticism, I let them go. I couldn't understand them, they were not reasonable.

I kept my villa outside the city open, staffed and ready for use or entertainment. Now I remembered how on the dangerous night of my escape from Milan I had lost or mislaid the scroll, copied out by a boy and given to me by the good old priest Simplician, which contained Christ's Sermon on the Mount. I remembered the acute sense of loss, as of losing the seed of light, I had felt then. The next time I went to the villa I looked for the scroll. I found it on a beam in the stable, where I must have reached up to place it while I had made ready the cart and team of mules to go after Marcia. The scroll was covered with dust, which I blew off.

I sat down on the lintel of an open door into the cool stable, in a warm flood of springtime sunlight, enjoying the odors of hay, animals, leather, manure, and read the sermon through, relieved of some obscure anxiety just to have found it again. I was wearing sandals, and I was amused that my bare toes had picked up a couple of straws. Comfortably I scratched my back against the frame of the doorway. I felt the warmth of the sun come clear through my beard to my cheek and through my tunic to my ribs and legs. It was a peaceful and receptive hour I spent there, reading and reflecting on what a man named Matthew had set down, more or less aright, years later and by hearsay, about the teaching of Jesus the Nazarene. Jesus had presumably spoken in Aramaic, and probably two or more generations later Matthew had written in Greek, and what I had in my hands was someone's Latin translation.

Finally I sighed and slowly shook my head in the sunlight. I was disappointed. I did not see how these peculiar teachings could be applied to my life. At this time I was extremely busy helping Stilicho ready his army for an attack on Alaric in Greece. I did not see how a man helping to prepare for a battle, fighting pressures and intrigues at court, dealing for equipment and supplies with hard rapacious men, aware of enemies like Florentinus who desired to defame and displace him—in short, I did not see how an official in the Roman Empire could follow this Nazarene and still remain an official in the Empire. I rolled up the scroll with a kind of haunting sadness. For, in addition to much comment on the Jewish law and prophets which was of scant interest to a young man trained in the splendor of Roman law, and in addition to an impractical ethic of nonresistance, there were melodies and beauties and spiritual lights too fragile for this harsh world and yet too lovely to let go: They passed the mind and reached the heart. "Blessed are they that mourn: for they shall be comforted. . . . Ye are the light of the world. . . . For where your treasure is, there will your heart be also. . . . If therefore thine eye be single, thy whole body shall be full of light. . . ."

I took the scroll back with me to the palace. I told Marcia: "I have decided to stop seeing Dionie, except as it may happen on public occasions."

Marcia blushed, suddenly became very shy, and looked down at her hands. I felt quite foolish and awkward and almost certainly had a silly grin on my face. I had not known, not until the moment I greeted Marcia and told her, that I had reached any such decision. For a moment we both felt extremely young, like two little children who do not quite know how to start playing together. Marcia took a lock of her hair and brought it across her cheek and mouth and looked up at me with a sweet quiet expression in her eyes. Then my silly grin changed form into the sound feeling of a true smile, and I was glad this silent change of will—perhaps even change of heart—had come over me.

I procured as full a set as I could find, in the Greek, of the Christian Scriptures, and I advanced the time of my rising in the morning an hour so as to study these matters an hour each day.

I know better now than I did then that there is a superrational harmony and, as it were, a divine essence about even the inadequate human hearsay report of this Nazarene's teaching that will not let go the heart of a man who, in a moment of wanting to be good, receives any part of the message once. So far as I know, Jesus alone, among all the great spiritual men risen from our human moil and suffering to teach us, treats a man as not a mortal but as an eternal being. This teaching, once heard, so deeply penetrates the heart that to reject it is to reject also anything less that any other has taught, while to accept it is to abide with hope. Until all a man's courage is shattered, the remembrance of Jesus remains. Despair alone is able to reject Christ.

It is therefore a terrible thing to reflect that a man can, and most of us actually do, live out our lives by the counsel of despair. We may live and act with honor, with courage, with charm, with moral decency and civil rectitude, and still do it at bottom in despair. It is noble to achieve so much; it is tragic to have done it without hope.

I discussed these matters with Ambrose in his garden. I said I realized, as one trained in the law, that a sense of immortality underlies the very concept of justice. I told him I knew of no other teacher except Christ through whom a man could find his eternal being, and that, so far as I could see, the only point in time where the trap of mortality was breached was the moment of Christ's passion, crucifixion and resurrection. "And still, I do not believe. It is a dream of the heart that will never leave me, and a scandal against reason that I cannot accept."

"I like your heart, Gregory, and your mind, too. You have a searching spirit. The binding that binds you is an almost incredible pride. In a sense what you really believe is this: The Roman Empire is the greatest achievement in the universe, in spite of God, and you suspect you might yourself be the highest achievement of the Roman Empire."

Walking and talking, we passed beside a certain rosebush. I watched Ambrose turn back a leaf and bend a stem. Then one by one he plucked off four or five small bugs or lice that were eating the leaves and a worm that gnawed entrance into a bud. These little creatures he absent-mindedly crushed in his slender fingers and dropped to the ground while he told me that, since the omnipotent, omniscient and omnipresent God was good and just and the God of love, a man ought in faith to abandon his will to the will of God, finding love, salvation and life everlasting through Jesus Christ, within the Church, by grace of the Holy Ghost; for outside the Church there could only be sin and death.

The creative results of meeting and associating with other people are incalculable; for when two of us come together it is not only what we say, but how we move, how we look and sound, what we are and what we do that awakens, each in the other, new possibilities of vision, of thought, of action and of desire. I have always felt that the most powerful force in my life was another person, man or woman, hand to hand beside me. And so it was now with Ambrose.

Ambrose never knew that the terrible sermon of his slender absent-minded fingers, plucking and killing bugs, chilled my heart because I, not he, made it the analogue of the words of faith he was uttering with his voice. Were all of us outside the Church, then, like bugs or worms on the tree of life to be wantonly crushed by the Gardener's fingers and dropped to the ground?

I think this was a climax in the process of probing and speculation I was carrying on. I know I gradually felt a revulsion in my morning studies and began to retrace some old passages of my education among the great Pagan philosophers. Soon I tired of them, too. I reached the bursting point and let out a wild young yell, a splendid Dionysian shout that brought Marcia bounding out of bed and running to my side with her feet bare and her garment half fallen from her breasts. I snatched her off her feet and sat her on my lap and delivered a joyous tirade toward my table, which was littered with papyrus volumes.

"Plato, Plotinus, Ambrose; Pythagoras, Augustine, Jerome; Epicurus, Epictetus, Marcus Aurelius: What's the matter with you noble old men! Not a one of you believes it's a good life for a man to love women and do the work of the world. You addle my young male brain. So!" I squeezed Marcia's warm delightful body against my ribs. "So! The real is unreal, and the unreal is real. By your wisdoms, either life is unfit for human beings, or human beings are unfit for God. Still, in my robust and vulgar youth I am haunted, as always, by a sense of God. Look you, sirs, God is perpetually the Guest of my heart. You advise me to sit on my backside, without woman on my lap, close my eyes to the world, and contemplate the ineffable. I cannot do it. Certainly not now. Here are Marcia's good warm real buttocks planted on my good strong real legs, with her breast at my rib and her cheek at my chin. Venus roars in my blood, and Rome cries out work to be done and honors earned. If Your Nine Venerable Excellencies will pardon my robust cheerful youth and folly, I must be off now to love woman and fulfill a brilliant career, all with the blessing of God. Truly I must go about hunting heaven within the world and God on the steps of the morning waiting to greet me!"

I gave Marcia a sound kiss, and while I kissed her she, with a sweep of her arm, swept a dozen scrolls of divine philosophy off the table onto the floor. "Como!" I shouted. "Como!"

But Marcia was sobbing, with her eyes pressed and concealed against the base of my throat. I felt her hot tears on my startled skin.

For weeks Marcia had been making a courageous effort to get hold of herself. By an effort of will—it was not quite a change of heart—I had stopped philandering with Dionie, and Marcia had tried hard to become all the woman I needed. But I had been much away from her in the final tasks connected with Stilicho's departure across the Adriatic with his legions (and Claudian went with him) to tear Alaric's army to bits in Greece. What happened in Greece that summer was bitter, insulting and preposterous. However, Marcia was too much alone. She dreaded my ambition and still ached in remembrance of my adulteries. I did not like the strain she was under; it showed in a settling of pain about her mouth.

The way some men read the meaning of the world for them in the sweep and scope of nature, as lonely Lucretius did, or in the rich interweaving of books, as Cicero did, or perhaps in the imaginative flow and harmony of ideal concepts, as Plato and Augustine did—so I most often read my world in the intensity of expression in the faces, bodies, speech and gestures of persons. I have heard it said that only through reverence and awe can a man find the unity of his life, and I confess frankly that for me there was in my perception of persons an awakening of reverence, of awe, sometimes almost of terror, so that I wanted to veil my seeing from a mystery too great to be borne. And I was the more deeply moved by these revelations of life in one I knew intimately, as I knew Marcia. Thus for me this pain settling about her young courageous mouth was pain at the heart of the world.

"Stilicho's gone. I've time to relax. I'm going to take you on vacation."

I told Ambrose I was going. It was hard to do that man any favors. The Church, you might say, provided him with a fine house, good robes and priests to assist him. The articles he needed for personal use were few and simple. I had produce brought in from my farm for his monks and their poor, and I gave sums of money to his church. But I wanted to make him personal gifts. Finally I hit on the plan, which proved pleasing to him, of making the effort to greet him at least once each day, as a son would greet a father, simply to find him out, face him, and offer a word of greeting and affection, with no business to be done or favors to be asked. Therefore I always let him know when I would be away from Milan for a few days, so that he would know I was neither neglecting nor forgetting my daily expression of what was to me a deep affection for a wonderful man. Since a sort of Divine Presence was always with Ambrose, he had the insight and spiritual firmness to keep my relationship to him always simple, human and free of idolatry.

I think I stirred him to more sudden little smiles than did anyone else who knew him during this last year of his life. His wit and grace were indeed equal to any of my occasions. This time he smiled and said, "For a man to give comfort and rest to his wife is a good form of prayer. Do this for me, Gregory. Pick up a warm small stone at the edge of the lake, hold it in your hand, and, looking about you, consider Who made the earth and the heaven and all that is in them. That I shall count as your prayer for me." He smiled, then chuckled. "That takes care of Marcia and of me, but leaves you out. Since you are still too ignorant to know how to pray for yourself, the old Bishop of Milan will pray for you, his special sinner."

In golden weather of splendid sunlight on the green trees and white roads I took Marcia to my villa at Lake Como. As we drove northward across the great Ligurian plain toward the grassy swells and forested mountains and wondrous sky-flung snow-steepled Alps, I said, "Marcia, darling, let us forget all religions in the world, except one. Let us make our sacrifices to laughter-loving Venus."

Marcia did not answer at once. She held my hand. Tears came to her eyes. Then she spoke. "I am bewildered, Gregory. What *is* love?"

Our age was deeply divided on the question of love. It seems that an age of deep social change and of passionate religious strife, involving the clash of ideas, must inevitably labor to interpret this word love. The word was used and abused all along the line from abomination to glory, from corruption to blessedness. The young must live and mature by the word: What shall it mean to them? We humans are procreative beings, and I know not how any man can utter the word love without the resonant vitalities of sex suffusing the very sound. Some Egyptian and Oriental cults in Rome brought forward sex as the entire meaning of the word; and on the far other hand even Ambrose, seeking to express the blessed love of God, spoke of "kisses of the Word" and "the union of the soul with the Spouse of Heaven." We are men, and not other than men, in the subtlest vibration of our deepest words.

How can I, speaking for the kind of person I am, speak for all men? For me at that period—I'll speak out for myself—the problem of love, enriched by all the connotations of sex, was the primary problem to be dealt with on the threshold of a good life and on the threshold of religion, if it be possible to separate these two. Quite naturally in my robust youth the ardor of my life was centered in my will rather than in my imagination, and I was more prone to learn by experience than to know by intuition. But I had the humor to grant that I need not mistake myself for a turbulent monster of the senses who had to experience everything before knowing anything. I had some imagination and intuition and also some respect for the moral values in my training and education. I was willing to have learned from Hippolytus that Artemis is not enough and from Odysseus that Circe is too much.

Having grown up in Rome, I was aware of the astonishingly fecund variables of Venus. There were plenty of people who lived in a kind of wasteland with no moral or spiritual horizons, to whom such words as faith and love and God had no particular meaning. These weary sensationalists were like ghosts, sapped of vitality by the distress and breakup of the age. I did not look for enlightenment among these who had ceased or had never begun to struggle for God. But I knew of no religion and no social code which did not find sexual love one of its main problems, a problem connected with good and evil, matter and spirit, life and death. Some gods demanded eunuchs, some called for harlots, some clamored for virgins. The Galli of the Magna Mater sacrificed their male potency, castrating themselves as the greatest good they could sacrifice to that Mother God, while in the cults of Mani, of Mithra and of Christ, often men and women renounced sex as the greatest evil they could deny in love of God. Such extreme appeals did not waken my affections. Neither was I allured to practices of love between men, my desire being toward woman.

I scarcely indicate the possibilities involved. But with all these passions, prejudices and pressures in his environment a young man had to wonder what he himself was doing: what he wanted to do, what he ought to do, and what love meant to him. It does not take much thinking to realize that in the problem of love man has a vital connection with his fellows, with the universe and with any finding he may find of God. Even Lucretius, that lonely man who loved the hills and the sea and thought he ought to destroy religion, opened his great poem with a hymn to Venus and later tried to scorn love in a hundred or so love-hungering lines; also he prayed devoutly to imitate his Greek master with the same sort of religious fervor with which an ardent Christian prays to imitate Christ.

I said to Marcia quite honestly, but with my arm around her shoulders when I said it, "I don't know, darling, what love really is. But I think golden Venus waits on tiptoe to come to our aid."

We found that this rich-crowned goddess comes swiftly to the aid of the married young who appeal to her to restore their mirth. Laughter-loving Venus returned to us with golden daylong charm and sweet nocturnal warmth.

Marcia's finger tips were rosy, and the backs of her hands were warm. Once again we rejoiced in young mirth together. Our thoughts were vivid, our laughter ready, and tenderness returned. When we lay all along each other's responsive length, quickened by mutual rhythms of love, we experienced spiritual renewal. Her eyes were clear. Her smile evoked mine. And my outright laughter made her heart dance. We climbed steep trails in forests, expanding our nostrils for deep intake of redolent odors, and bent back our heads to gaze up through tracery of evergreen boughs at the intense radiant blue beyond and beyond. Up and up we climbed to the edge of fields of snow. We gobbled our food. We sailed daylong in a little boat on the lake, where the sparkle of water and the rise of mountains revealed the sweep and brilliant flow of sun. At the edge of the lake we found warm coves of sunlight where we could take off our clothes, lie on the warm earth, and steep our bodies in the sun until the fogs and knots of winter dissolved out of us. I never tired of watching the supple beauty of Marcia's form either in repose or in motion. I thought perhaps there was implanted in the Greek strain of my nature that Hellenic love of the beauty of the human form, for I felt a desire, perhaps when I saw her sitting on rocks by the blue shining water, radiant, alive and young, a desire to capture that vision of immortal beauty intimated in some of the lovely and serene works of Greek art.

I asked Marcia if she ever felt a similar tense expectation, pressing like a promise up from below the level of consciousness.

She laughed, bent down to touch her toes with her fingers, then straightened full upward in sunlight, stretching her arms above her head while the breeze toyed with her hair. "What you see, Gregory, is all woman, from tip to toe!"

And yet I trembled at what I saw, a work, a growth, an incredible presence of Being. I rose to my feet with a deeply religious thought in my mind. At the edge of the water I picked up a small warm stone and held it in my hand. I looked at the lake, at the mountains, at the sky. Then I looked again at Marcia, the curve of whose shoulders was more warm and lovely than the warmth and beautiful curve of the little stone in my hand.

"Am I terribly proud, Marcia? Ambrose thinks my pride is monstrous."

"I love you the way you are, Gregory."

It was a woman's answer. But the stone in my hand said: "Yes, you are proud." I clutched it tightly.

We took late nocturnal strolls to a jut of rock from which we could look down and see the stars of heaven shining in the deep silence of the lake, while some night bird called out for its mate over the water. And through the lazy play and ardent solace of these days and nights our hearts were purified and we found each other's goodness again.

In the villa our large bedroom had a hearth where we could build a fire. The chimney was imperfect, and often the room was suffused with a rich tang of wood smoke. We liked to spread fur robes on the floor near the hearth and play in the play of firelight.

For truly, now, all is not rare sentiment or exquisite ecstasy between a man and woman any more than it is all secrecy and lust. Often there is delightful play, witty, comic, even ribald. It has been my experience that a man and woman engaged in private rites of love do often provoke each other to a hearty cleansing laughter that heals the soul of many wounds which neither ecstasy nor passion can touch. There have been nights when the smothered laughter of intimate ribaldry has washed out cankers from my heart and restored sweet breathing to my soul. I have praised God for the mirth and comfort of His gift to men and women— their warm bodies for one another suffused with the humor of life as well as with its ecstasy and its tragedy.

There by the fire, deep in a night when our mutual laughter had deeply sweetened and harmonized our love, I woke from subsequent profound slumber. The fire had settled to a hot pile of embers. For a moment that connected me with other times in my life and other places in the world, I thought I was waking in the night beside one of our fires far off in Moesia, among Alaric and his Goths. Feeling the soft red glow on my closed eyelids, I felt the earth at my shoulders, the forest about me and the stars above. I waited for a dog to bark or for some Barbarian to utter deep-throated laughter at a distant fire. The silence moved me to open my eyes, to sit up.

I saw where I was.

Marcia slept in the serene and easy flow of ruddy light from the pile of embers; it was as if the only source of light in the world shed its warm, benign and softly undulant rays on the only woman in the world; and tremendous beyond the hope of apprehension was the infinite sweep of dark and silence all around. The first moment of this experience as I gazed on her was dreadful. I saw our human body bare, under the aspect of eternity. How shall our fragile form endure the tides and torrents of infinity? I had an impulse to toss my arm before my eyes as one who hides from a blast of light. Then I almost moved to cover Marcia with my own outflung sacrificial form, across her breast with outstretched arms, as if that could have saved our frail and lovely human body from being beaten down, as against a rock, by the downpour of shattering arrows of eternity.

I held my heart against the wild beat of these fears.

Yet I trembled as in a sense I beheld our bare human body under the terrible light of eternity, which makes us all one, which makes us all equal and—lost? Are we lost? The infinity of the universe is outward, and our infinity is inward: What can we do? Neither can we draw all outward infinity within us, nor pour forth all our inward infinity out of us: What can we do? Yet I could not conceive more maddening torment for any man than to become abandoned alone to his own infinity: What shall we try to do? Hide? Cover the frail, the lovely body, and hide?

The dogs were barking in the far woods, and the Gothic stalwarts were laughing at their firesides. And I was there, and in Rome, and upon the dark wave with my lost son in my bare arm. I must hide and hide from too much knowledge of the good and evil of space and time. The Emperor Honorius, poor stupid boy, had a magnificent garment embroidered with gems and golden and scarlet thread that his imperial body might be hid. So it is this to see our nakedness in eternal light that we cannot endure the manifest and tragic radiance of our own being? Frightened, we hide within clothes our own prime evidence of God. As with Adam and Eve, "the eyes of them both were opened, and they knew that they were naked; and they sewed fig leaves together, and made themselves aprons." Our silly clothes are meant to shelter us not only from weather, but, if we have not love, our masking clothes shelter us also from the devastating knowledge that all men are brothers; and our clothes, giving us the illusion of temporal identity—the slave, the priest, the soldier, the prince!—shelter us from the awful knowledge of eternity and from the certain knowledge that Inconceivable Power created us. So Adam and Eve did not love each other and were afraid and contracted into painful hiding from the shock of sin, and the sin was to fear, not love, each other.

I did not cover Marcia's nakedness, neither did I conceal my own.

Gradually I felt a profound tranquillity, as if peace had been reached through sorrow and through beauty by love. Religious fears of the infinite and the eternal dropped from me like a withered shroud. My arms relaxed in my lap. Marcia's quiet little face, her relaxed body in the repose of sleep, with the glow of ember light on her from her instep to her brow, on her serene closed eyelids and tender smiling lips, composed all the slumbering beauty of eternal things.

I looked with a gaze of surpassing tenderness on this woman I loved and saw the vital wonder of our bare human body as the revelation of pure eternal being. The mortal body and tragic life of man is radiant evidence of God, and should not be hid. I thought no man could experience or perceive this in himself, but only by love, through another. I thought, with tears in my eyes and a smile born at the heart of my life, "This is love. It can never come again. It can never go away. . . ."

There was now a deep sense in which no other woman but Marcia could ever be my wife.

For some time as I experienced the rise and flow and deep inward enlightenment of these things, Marcia had been awake, wide awake and aware of me. She did not open her eyes, but I knew her breathing had changed, I could see a different stir in the satin warm hollow below her ribs. Her heart, changing its beat, translated a new subtle motion to the curve of her breast, and a pulse appeared high on the side of her throat near the vital and tender hinge of her head. Her lips moved in tenuous motion from smile to smile, and above all I could feel her consciousness with me like a presence. Some deep divine intuition held her at peace in our profound communion, in an aura of warmth, in a glow of embers.

If I could put it into words I would have to say my experience was this: that eternity does not slumber and life does not cease and no man need hide and no man is alone and to love a woman is the depth of life. But I'm an old man now. Tears fill my eyes. More than fifty years have passed. We suffered much. Marcia died long ago. My words are inadequate. I cannot say what I have to say, yet I know what I know. What was then is now and was and is forever. . . .

There was a sense—a deepest sense of heart and soul—in which no other woman but Marcia could ever be my wife. This was love. It could never come again. It could never go away. I reached out. I clasped Marcia's warm waiting hand and said, "Dawn is near. Heaven is within the world. And God stands on the steps of the morning waiting to greet us!"

For about a year, until after the death of Ambrose, Marcia and I enjoyed our interlude of most intense lyric happiness. She entered into her period of supreme youthful bloom. She had a way of telling me with spiritual clarity little things about herself and her life and her meetings with people, and much lore of my mind and heart was the pure gift of her spiritual perception. But our nature is deep, is strange. Beyond the room of our shelter is the city, is the empire, is the world, and the wandering of abyss among the sun and the moon and the multitudinous stars. And beyond the room of our shelter is also that terrible and shining City of God that the old men know. And some Hunter, some Slayer, is also abroad, invisible, with arrows that wound, that wound unto death and nearly unto death.

CHAPTER EIGHT

THE DEATH OF AMBROSE

THE DEATH OF AMBROSE IN THE YEAR 397 WAS A CATASTROphe in our Roman world. Stilicho, knowing of my affection for the great bishop, sent me as his personal ambassador to Ambrose to do all I could, in the name of Empire, to prevent or delay Ambrose's death.

Stilicho, of course, would not entrust so great a mission solely to so young a man. He persuaded six others, old and noble citizens of Milan and long-time intimates of Ambrose to go with me. They were all devout Christians, and Stilicho had a hard time persuading them to go, for, they said, "This is an unseemly thing you ask us to do, to interpose the fear and fright of human desires in the working of the will of God." Finally it was agreed that they would go to lend human maturity and solemnity to the mission, while in the presence of Ambrose they would say to him only that they had come to him in the hope of his recovery, and then in unison they would repeat the Lord's Prayer. "To do more than this belongs not to us, but either to priests or to God."

Stilicho, worried, in awe of the event, troubled by the weight of Empire, was not satisfied. There was great appealing goodness in his face and deep concern in his voice as he said, "It is not enough. The death of so great a man at a time like this will be the ruin of Italy. We have been betrayed and undermined by the court at Constantinople. I don't mean only that they have sent assassins here secretly to murder me—I can take care of such treachery—but they have empowered and fattened Alaric on our borders. They are supporting Gildo in his revolt in Africa. African grain is going to Constantinople, and famine is threatened in Rome. Disunity between Pagans and Christians is on the increase. Ambrose is the great figure of justice in our world, and everybody knows his power to intercede with God by his prayers is greater than that of any other living man. Our world will darken if Ambrose dies. Fear will spread. What I implore is only this, that he, who is known to have restored the blind to sight, the crippled to wholeness, and even the dead to life by the exceeding purity and power of his prayer—that he should now pray God to prolong his own life. If he would, he could."

The six elder men were silent, stubborn, unwilling to go so far as to intrude on the spiritual wisdom of Ambrose. One of them finally said, "Ambrose is a saint. We are sinners. He alone knows when and how he ought to pray. For many years, for a whole generation, he has been our guide; are we now to presume to lead him?"

I put myself forward. "He knows I love him, and he is fond of me, General. Let these men give weight and honor to the mission, and I will be spokesman."

Stilicho's native force came through. A smile lighted his tired strong face. It was always a relief to him when he could make a decision against that paralyzing inner sense he had of being a Barbarian and inferior to the noble-born Roman. "I accept your audacity. Go, and Gregory speak."

I with my red-gold beard and the six graybeards went to wait upon Bishop Ambrose.

Our mission took place late in March. In February Ambrose had gone to Pavia to install and consecrate a new bishop there, and on the way back, in one of our foul Ligurian storms which come down off the winter mountains in a gusty dark turmoil of sleet and fog and bone-searching cold, he had taken ill in the chest, having fever and weakness. Being too ill to follow his custom of doing his own writing, he had begun dictating to his secretary Paulinus an exposition of the Forty-fourth Psalm. A little by day and a little by day he had explained the text as far as the twenty-fourth verse: "Wherefore hidest thou thy face, and forgettest our misery and trouble?"

At this point Paulinus the secretary suddenly saw a flame, shaped like a shield, come down and cover Ambrose's head and gradually enter Ambrose's mouth. The face of Ambrose whitened like snow, then became of mortal color again. Paulinus could not write until the vision passed, and when the story was told it was proved from the Acts of the Apostles that Paulinus had witnessed the descent upon Ambrose of the Holy Ghost.

Without dictating more words, Ambrose's narrow-bearded head, with its great sad spiritual eyes, hung far to one side, too heavy for his heart, and he never finished his exposition, although there were only these two verses left of the Psalm:

For our soul is bowed down to the dust: our belly cleaveth unto the earth.
Arise for our help, and redeem us for thy mercies' sake.

Soon he went to bed. His dying was steady and slow.

We came into his presence where he lay. His long thin hands were quiet on the brown wool cover over his slender frail body, and his feet, so narrow and so long for his slight stature, poked up the cover as it were in a miniature volcano. His head, slightly propped up on a simple pillow, made a slow turn to greet and attend us. With his skin so frail, the redness of his broad lips was more noticeable among the soft graying hairs of his mustache, and the unequal arching of his eyebrows, the left higher than the right, the more stood out.

The six elders knelt before him, they muttered a desire for his return to health, and with unequal voices and tears they repeated, not in harmony, but brokenly, the Pater Noster. Ambrose said it with them. His voice was clear, as if there alone he still retained vigor. After the solemn "Amen!" he looked at me. "And why do you stand, Gregory, when others all are kneeling?"

"They have come to accept God's will and ought to kneel. I have come as a man to make a request of you as a man. They come in truth, even also in sorrow, to pray for your rise into heaven. I come only to ask, in Stilicho's name, in Rome's name, and because I love you, that you rise to your feet."

"And by what means am I to cease dying and rise to my feet?"

"The power of your faith in prayer is great; if you would, you could."

"You believe that?"

"Yes."

"Then your faith exceeds that of these Christians on their knees. Why are you not a Christian? The addition of your prayer to mine might indeed work a miracle."

"What I believe of you is greater than what I believe of myself."

He looked at me steadily, deeper into my soul than any other man ever looked. His eyes filled with tears. He reached out a weak hand, palm up, offering me something unseen. He said, "Your sin be mine."

It was then at last that I understood what this man Ambrose meant when he said those words to me, electing me as his sinner. It was no cheap piety. It was not self-indulgence in self-sought martyrdom. It was what the Christian apostle Paul meant by charity. It was the fulfillment of the second of Christ's two laws: "Thou shalt love thy neighbor as thyself." Here this man, purified and on the brink of eternity, thus opened to me the cupboard of his soul and made me the equal sharer of all the bread of his life, even though I came with tainted mouth.

The elders had risen. They stood about with their arms heavy. They were ashamed of me. My arms, too, were heavy, and my hands like lead. I was ashamed of myself.

Ambrose watched me, and a faint smile softened the sorrow in his eyes. "A spirit," he said, "so like that of my brother Satyrus cannot be lost. Christ be with you, Gregory!"

He took several slow breaths, waiting for strength to return. Then he said, "Thank Stilicho for his so great concern. I thank each of you for your love. But neither a man, nor a ruler, nor an Empire ought to lean on me, for God is their strength. I have not so lived among you as to be ashamed to live on; but I am not afraid to die, for our Lord is good."

I could not but remember in a flash the similar yet profoundly different words of my great Pagan forebear, the Emperor Julian, on his deathbed: "I discharge, with the cheerfulness of a ready debtor, the demands of nature. . . . I die without remorse, as I have lived without guilt. . . . I have trusted the outcome to the care of Providence. . . . I now offer my tribute of gratitude to the Eternal Being. . . . I hold it equally absurd, equally base, to seek or to decline the stroke of fate. . . ." In the illumination of this flash I could not fail to apprehend that, while both Julian and Ambrose were great men in their living as in their dying, the ultimate vision of Ambrose was more simple, pure and clear and deep than that of Julian. For while the words of Julian showed worthy pride, courage and piety intermixed, yet not perfectly fused, the words of Ambrose showed all of these things, and also love, fused in pure faith.

We departed with our sad news for Stilicho.

I myself continued my custom of going to see Ambrose each day, if only to smile at him. Bishops and priests came from various cities to pray with him, and often I could get no farther into the room than to let him see my face over their heads and shoulders. I knew he was glad I came.

The last time he spoke to me was strange and something to remember. He smiled at me across the ranks of priests, I think in a confused moment of dying, and called me by his brother's name, "Satyrus! I am glad you have come for me, Satyrus!"

I asked old friends of Ambrose, who had known his brother also, if I was like to Satyrus. They said no, but quickly glanced at me again, and one said my voice was like that of Satyrus, a deep masculine voice which, without being raised, could yet be heard in the next room. Another said perhaps there was a quality in the way I moved that was like a memory of Satyrus. But those who heard Ambrose's clear words had no thought that they were addressed to me; they said the holy spirit of Satyrus had come to lead back his beloved brother to heaven.

Then on the last day, which was Good Friday, Ambrose lay in prayer for hours with his arms outstretched in the form of a cross, and though his lips moved no one heard a sound, and he died early in the morning of Easter Eve.

The body was placed in state in the cathedral, and during the night-long Easter vigil many of the devout saw him arise, walk about, and sit in his episcopal throne in the apse, and saw, too, a form like a star hovering over his body. But, though I was there, sad and quiet, with Marcia holding my arm, I did not see such things, nor did she, our eyes not being in that way cleansed. After Mass on Easter day the corpse was removed to Ambrose's basilica and buried near the relics of the Saints Gervasius and Protasius. The throng was the great human stream of Milan and all places near by, pressing body to body until the pillars and walls were warmed with human warmth, and those possessed of demons cried out that Ambrose the Saint was tormenting them.

I cried inwardly for the loss of my spiritual father, but did not scream aloud, being perhaps not possessed by a demon of that sort. The worm in my heart was more of sorrow and despair than of outcrying; for my natural father, and Theodosius my father in power, and Ambrose my spiritual father, now all three were dead, and I was sick at heart with the heartsickness of a lost child. Marcia, among others, threw her scarf on the bier of Ambrose, hoping it would achieve miraculous virtue by touching the saint's remains. But then she herself was afraid to touch it and had me carry it home, and I dreaded that it should ever be worn again. We put it away in a box of sandalwood and lost it somewhere later in the ruin of our lives.

I had not thought the death of Ambrose, which was so deep a blow to the slowly emergent maturing of my soul, could mean much to Claudian. When I did see what it meant to him—what burden it laid upon him that he did not know how to escape—I was astonished.

The death of Ambrose was the close of an age. Unified civil majesty had come to an end in the Roman world with the death of Theodosius, but while Ambrose lived our Roman world still had a great voice of conscience. Jerome, long noisy, and Augustine, beginning to be heard, were not spokesmen of the Empire, but of the Church apart from the Empire. But a great society will speak, will find in one man or a few men its voice. When Ambrose died the burden of speaking for the Empire was thrust upon Claudian, and broke him, for he was summoned by a power beyond his lone resistance to tell the world lie after lie in the name of Rome. His large poems are a boasting of the pride of Rome during nine years, and writing them ruined him. So it was that he, in his tense lone person, enacted the final tragedy of Rome's creative gift. That which had its robust prosaic youth culminating in the urbane intelligence of Cicero, which then flowered in the poetic radiance of Virgil, which later bore the vast and somber fruit of Tacitus, which came to melancholy autumn in the resigned patience of Marcus Aurelius—all that long resounding vision and voice of Rome flared up in a last outcry for rebirth, even as it died its painful death, in Claudian.

When I reflect on the matter in this way I realize we Romans had work to do, but never had a great message for mankind to live by. We said less well what the Greeks had already said, unless perhaps Lucretius was part of the Great Voice speaking out to and for man. If I may go to Democritus and Lucretius, I would say the atom contains the principle of life; and if I may go to Aeschylus and Christ, I would say the Word contains the principle of love: The harmony of these two is the goodness of life, their perversion is death. If Virgil had not been seduced on the one hand by Homer and on the other by Augustus, he might have spoken out more fully as a man to mankind. Cicero would never quite give his own life for his own word. Marcus Aurelius gave up mankind and spoke in sad piety to his own heart and to God. It surprises me to find that I do believe that he who most nearly found in the terrible and tragic heart of Roman action a word for mankind to hear and better know our life was Tacitus. With Tacitus it is not exactly what he says, but how he saw: He saw Rome alive, powerful, terrible, a profound and splendid tragedy.

But Tacitus was gone. Ambrose was gone. Claudian was the voice of Rome. Claudian, the dark and lonely one.

I owe a compassionate memorial to my friend Claudian. We all helped bring tragedy one upon another—that's just common humanity —but what happened to Claudian turned out to be deeply and dramatically integrated with the toils and perils of my own soul. If I move the focus of my story over toward Claudian for a while, it is because he in his disaster planted strange and wonderful fruit for my soul to nurture.

CHAPTER NINE

CLAUDIAN THE POET

CLAUDIAN WAS A WONDERFUL TALKER, EITHER IN THE FLASH of a searching remark or in the poetic richness of a voluble mood; he knew more than any man I ever met about the dark and nether majesty of the soul. He knew because he loved it. I think Augustine might have known this dark deep of our nature, but hated it. What to Augustine was a source of evil and deserving of punishment was to Claudian a deep place of inspired generation, of harmonies, visions and beauties to be sought, loved, and won.

I always thought Claudian was in love with cool-eyed Serena. He was about thirty years old and she only a few years older. When he read one of his long effective poems to a brilliant assembly in the palace Serena was always the first to applaud. His poems never failed to praise Theodosius and Stilicho and sometimes openly praised Serena, and Serena never failed to order many copies to be made and sent out through the Empire like manifestoes of Theodosian grandeur. There was a lingering tension of desire in the way Claudian watched Serena, he with his lean figure, black hair and hot dark eyes, she so stately, with snowy throat and golden hair and cool gray eyes; and there was something splendid in the way she gave him her hand to kiss, after one of his recitals, as if Minerva offered a hand to Orpheus come out from the caves of hell. But what man could really win that woman's heart from a dead Emperor, the great Theodosius?

It made Marcia shudder. "No one can love Claudian. Why does he break his heart with hope?"

"Why do you say such a terrible thing, darling?"

"It's true. He's not like us. Any woman would know he's like fire from the underworld."

"He's a great soul. He's the loneliest man I know. He's the deepest friend I have."

Occasionally there were rumors that Claudian and Serena were lovers in fact, but these rumors always died out before they went far, and the actual impressions given off by the living presence of Claudian and Serena among us killed the rumors. It was even hard to believe that Serena was Stilicho's wife and the mother of his three children. She was that strange anomaly, a chaste wife and mother. But it never seemed to me she was either cold or sexless. I had heard her cry out at the deathbed of Theodosius. And Claudian stood apart, clear, brilliant, passionate, in some strange sense neither touched nor to be touched. Perhaps Marcia was right, there was something of the nether world about Claudian, as if his soul had ranged vast precincts of generative darkness and loved a knowledge we all would fear. I believe he had a great message for the Roman world; I believe we needed to hear it; but we corrupted him and made him sing our song instead of his.

It was almost impossible for a man in my position, high in the ambitious ranks of those competing for power, to have a friend. We had partisans and enemies, not friends. Actually, with women coming more and more into the competitive field of political action, love, too, was at hazard, for there were many women at court who increased their power and position by use of their seductive charms rather than by aptitude for public affairs. It was my good fortune that Claudian was not a competitive soul. His struggle was a poet's problem of inward song. Simple sinecure was all he needed to wrest from power, and Serena had given him that, a place on Stilicho's staff, a generous allowance and quarters in the palace. And Claudian didn't care whether I lost my position or rose to be Emperor. "That," he would say, "is your folly. I don't believe it is worth the energy you waste on it." I felt he was my friend; I thought I was his friend. But there is a constant change of relationships under pressure of living.

We of the high imperial group were all bound up in the history of the times as well as being interbound with one another in an intricate complex of personal relationships. The history of those years was quite interesting and formed the background of what was going on desperately in Claudian's heart. First, in 396, was the insulting affair of Alaric in Greece; in the next year came the death of Ambrose; that was followed by the revolt of Gildo (causing famine in Rome) and the war against Gildo in Africa, and then came the marriage of Honorius. Each of these things in its way, because of his peculiar position and because of his original and lonely insights, piled up havoc in Claudian's soul. I was infuriated by the affair in Greece, but the wound it gave Claudian was deeper.

Stilicho had taken his army there and had opened his campaign against Alaric with instant success. Alaric's host had plundered cities and shrines, and the Gothic wagons were crammed with spoils. Stilicho hounded them back without a pitched battle, then hemmed them all around in a rugged place where there was little water and less food. There he besieged the Goths, intending to starve them into destruction. While the Roman legions sat there, confident of victory, their days became relaxed and their nights became wanton with the soft pleasures of the decadent Greek world. Claudian was shocked at the fornications of Stilicho. I think it was not that fornication shocked him so much as that he was distracted to see Serena's husband take Greek dancing girls into his bed. It raised one of those double-edged questions of a removed soul: "Why does he do this to Serena?" and "If he does this to Serena, why can't I have Serena myself?" It may even have occurred to Claudian—for his perceptions of the dark inward world of the spirit were acute—that Serena had done dreadful things, spiritually, to Stilicho's manhood.

At any rate, Greek pleasures and Alaric's desperate cunning foiled Stilicho's plan of campaign. All at once—no one quite knew how— Alaric had pulled his host out of Stilicho's trap and was in flight northward. Stilicho, with forces sufficient for the purpose, stirred to pursue and destroy Alaric in one blow. But then, as once before, came the crowning insult, out of the East and supported from Milan by orders of Serena, who dominated Honorius. Arcadius, Emperor of the East, or Eutropius through him, ordered Stilicho to leave Alaric alone; Serena confirmed the order, through Honorius: "Do not divide the sons of Theodosius!" Stilicho was emasculate again. He brought his army back to Italy in frustrate rage.

Constantinople gave all of Illyricum and Greece to Alaric, making him master general for the Eastern Empire in those parts, with complete charge of the armies, the arsenals and the wealth of this crucial dividing territory between the now more deeply divided Western and Eastern halves of the Roman world.

Claudian came back to Milan sick at heart. His hero Stilicho was tainted, and Serena, when he approached her, by an instant physical gesture, a thrusting of her hand, a firming of her chin, a stretching of her lips, declined Claudian's unspoken advance; but still she held him inbound to her by the tone of her voice and by some slow blaze of light in her cool gray eyes, which acknowledged his need. For perhaps Serena, too, wanted to break the toils that bound her, and could not let Claudian go because he was her obscure hope. As high priestess of the Theodosian dynasty she was too remote for the touch of a poet, but within the consecrated form of the priestess, like a bound captive, was the body and life of a woman. There can be recognition on deep levels of vital human need and response, though formal action denies them.

There was another catastrophe in the affair for Claudian. He had been at work for months on a long poem of his own choosing, *The Rape of Proserpina*. He was dedicating it to my enemy Florentinus. It was not a political poem, such as Serena and Stilicho required him to write, but a real searching for his own genius, a celebration of the generative forces of the deep underworld. Stilicho wanted a scapegoat for the betrayal he had suffered in Greece, and I was able to give him evidence that Florentinus was heading the Pagan party in secret moves to undercut Stilicho's power. Stilicho removed Florentinus from office and disgraced him. Claudian could not finish and give out a major poem dedicated to a disgraced man and still retain his place as court poet.

"Finish it if it means so much to you," I advised him, "but don't let anyone know."

"Sing, but be not heard!" His response was bitter.

He knew, of course, that the ruin of Florentinus improved my position.

He never finished the poem. He finished and recited at court the second part of his harsh invective against Rufinus, with its great praise of Stilicho and its dreadful final picture of hell, almost terrible enough to have been the work of a Christian. It was as if the love in Claudian's soul for the richness of all darkness, his love for the splendor of that vast underlying subconscious realm that generates a thousand wonders of the soul of man, had turned to hate under the cramped and bitter pressures of power. We greatly praised the poet who gave voice to our pride and our hatred at the cost of his own soul.

And he suffered our praise like a slave's brand burned into his soul. Perhaps he was not a divine enough poet to stand out alone—in an age when he was the only poet—against the blind demands of Empire, or perhaps he was not a whole enough man to free Serena from the tyranny of her fateful obsession. Those inward strains which form the soul of a poet to bring his fellow men new gifts of vision and harmony often also render him unfit to cope with the brutal exigencies of social power and with the unpredictable absolutes of personal passion. Two who, like

Serena and Claudian, knew their need and could not meet it were tragic; and a society like ours, which corrupted its poet, was far gone in ruin. But there we all were, passionate workers in the moving living web of our time and place, neither knowing what we wrought nor able to cease our complex creations of vital, wonderful and tragic things to come.

Following hard upon the death of Ambrose, which clearly left Claudian to speak for Rome, the affair in Africa once more put his soul on trial between power and truth.

The revolt of Gildo in Africa was serious. Gildo the Moor was a powerful and vicious man, one who slew his blood relatives, who perverted virtue and refined ferocity, who got Africa under his governance and shut off the grain supplies of Rome and Italy. Stilicho, recovering from his disgrace in the affair with Alaric in Greece, won favor by close consultation with the Senate in Rome. Claudian wrote letters and speeches for him. Fear of famine had begun to set in, and actual famine threatened. The Senate declared war against Gildo; Stilicho began to make ready an army for the African campaign. Claudian worked day and night as his secretary.

Things got so bad in Rome, which had already felt scarcity because of two years of drought, that the Senate, defying the Christians, called for the enactment of an ancient Pagan rite, the barefoot rite, which amounted to a prayer for rain and food. Senate, magistrates and people gathered on the Tarpeian Hill in great dolor, like a multitude dying. The magistrates were without their purple, the lictors carried the fasces in reverse, noble women in sad garments and with hair disordered marched in barefoot ranks. This cavalcade of despair moved to the Capitoline Hill with priests calling on all the gods aloud. It was a scandal among Christians, a relief to the Pagans, and brought no food to Rome. Neither did prayers by the Pope and by bishops in Christian churches feed the hungering city.

Stilicho was too busy reorganizing the army to do much else. I used my special influence with Honorius to rouse his stubborn insistence that I be given new authority. "It is like feeding chickens," I explained to him. "First you have to get the grain." I worked out and administered a plan to scour the granaries of Gaul and Spain to feed Rome. It was emergency labor under high pressure. Knowing Heraclian's ability to get things done, I put him in charge of a central bureau in Gaul to collect and forward foodstuffs. I knew he would make a lot of money out of it and increase his political power; but he did gather and send commodities in quantity by land and by sea, and we did feed Rome before famine and riot and pestilence got out of hand.

My part in public affairs of this kind was gratifying. I woke in the morning conscious of many and important things to be done and confident that I could do them or get them done by others. In Milan, in Marsalia, in Rome I appeared as a man of importance with the weight of imperial authority behind me. I spoke in the Senate, heads of cities and governors of provinces acted on my decisions, and I had a real zest for what I was doing—that is, marshaling food supplies to protect the health and welfare of the greatest city in the world.

When I personally came up to the Tiber wharves with the first flotilla of grain boats brought down from Marsalia I was received by a riot of joy in the city. A general's military triumph could not have won more heartfelt praise. Even a band of Christian monks shouted as I passed along the street in my chariot: "They hungered, and he fed them!"

I made some mistakes and distressed a few touchy persons, but in general it was said that I had done a good job. A number of Senators who had been friends of my father wrote me personal letters commending my energy, my over-all justice and my success. Then modesty was exceeded; by order of the Emperor Honorius and the Senate a statue of me was placed in the Forum at Rome, and the inscription called me "Julian the Provider." I myself, one early morning, saw poor people lay roses before it.

I was pleased with the praise, but I honestly believe what I enjoyed most was the development and use of my skill for affairs in a public crisis of real proportions.

But Gildo was still brute master of Africa.

Gildo had a brother, a barbaric handsome dark fellow named Mascezel, and his sons had been murdered by Gildo. There were many delays, but when the army was at last ready Stilicho put Mascezel in command. Stilicho remained in Italy. Mascezel sailed for Africa. There were storms and hindrances, and when Mascezel finally landed on the African coast he was timid of the weakness of his army and the power of Gildo. But Bishop Ambrose came to him at night in a dream and three times struck the ground with his bishop's staff, saying, "Here!"—meaning that Mascezel should fight where he was. When the forces of Gildo lunged forward on the day of battle Gildo's standard-bearer stumbled and the banner fell down. Those behind thought it the signal to surrender. Many surrendered, many turned in flight. Gildo fled, was caught, and was murdered. It was a victory with scarce a battle. I think Gildo's enslaved and brutalized forces simply hated his tyranny and turned on him and got rid of him.

Mascezel came back to Rome and then to Milan a hero, gorgeous in pride and apparel. Claudian swiftly wrote the first part of his poem on *The War Against Gildo*. It was a strong political poem, restating the great Theodosian theme, praising Stilicho, praising Serena, admonishing Arcadius and the East to desist from treacherous support of enemies of Rome, such as Gildo and Alaric. There was a bold hint that both boy Emperors ought to realize that Stilicho was the true single ruler of the total Empire: "East and West live in amity and concord beneath the sway of one ruler." This was a desire, not a fact. The hatreds and treacheries between East and West were increasing. Claudian put all this political matter in, including a picture of the famine at Rome, Stilicho's gathering of the army, the alleged nobility and boldness of Honorius, who had married Stilicho's daughter Maria in the course of these events. Claudian in Part One of his poem carried the ships of Mascezel with the army through storm to the coast of Africa and to the eve of battle.

He never wrote Part Two, in which he meant to celebrate the battle and the victory with a closing eulogy of Stilicho, the great leader and savior of Rome. For this is what happened: The victorious Mascezel, after reaching Milan, was one day riding horseback across a bridge over a deep torrent with Stilicho and other military notables; and Mascezel, heavy with armor and gold, was pitched by his horse, or thrown by arrangement, from the bridge into the river; and Stilicho laughed and detained the others, and they all watched Mascezel drown. A victorious general and possible rival was no longer in Stilicho's way.

Claudian couldn't finish his poem. He dared not praise Mascezel for victory, and he could not bear to vomit up another line of gaudy praise for Stilicho in this particular victory. For Claudian had been on the bridge and had seen all that happened, until a live struggling man became a wet bulk of death rolled over stones by a torrent.

"Stilicho is the greatest man we have. I still love him. But what men sometimes do is horrible," Claudian told me. "The poet I was meant to be is dying and rotting in my soul!"

Claudian had already been sick at heart for months over his part in the marriage of Honorius and Maria.

In various poems for recitation at court and for circulation throughout the political high society of the Empire, Claudian had drawn—and continued to draw—a noble portrait of an ideal prince, handsome, beloved, intelligent, at once docile and courageous, wise and humble. To this portrait of a remarkable young Emperor he attached the name of Honorius. We all knew as well as Claudian that Honorius was not such a prince. Honorius was a well-grown youth, almost handsome, almost strong; he wore magnificent regal garments well. He was a fairly good horseman, although he did not like to ride or hunt. He was a dull student. He had a slow voice and a dull eye. He liked to be let alone to administer the affairs of his chickens and other domesticated fowl. He was fond of his chickens and good to them. He was particularly fond of the now fine golden hen Roma, which I had brought him as a pullet from Constantinople.

Ambrose, so long as he lived, had restrained Serena and urged delay in the marriage of Honorius, but Serena began pressing for it as soon as Ambrose died. She said the marriage of Honorius and Maria had been ordered by Theodosius on his deathbed, and it was her business to see the sacred orders of Theodosius fulfilled. Stilicho kept resisting and putting off this marriage, and Serena kept pressing for it even as she was already beginning to press for a betrothal between Galla Placidia and her son Eucherius.

Maria was a sweet gay soft young girl with very rosy cheeks. She had played with dolls and had thought of herself in terms of motherhood all the years I had known her. Just as Galla Placidia was always prophesying, "When I'm Empress I'm going to do this and that," so Maria was always saying, "When I have babies I'm going to . . ." She was Stilicho's favorite child; he played with the curl of hair by her temple and liked the flash of her eye and command in her voice when she said, "You've got to be a good grandpa to my babies!"

Stilicho knew perfectly well that Honorius, Emperor of Rome, was torpid if not degenerate. He called me in for a personal conference and asked me frankly for my opinion. "What is the boy, really? Is he perverted? Is he mad? Or is he just stupid? You're his companion and tutor, Gregory. You know him as well as anyone does. Tell me. No matter what Serena's ambition demands, I don't want to sacrifice my daughter to a monster."

These are sad things to tell about, on the dark borders of human tragedy, but I want to make them clear, for none of us lived uninfluenced by one another, and this trouble was one more phase in the critical life of the Empire. Among other things, some seeds of Stilicho's murder were in it.

"Honorius is not a monster, General. He is stupid. He is secretive. His mind is never going to be of high quality. I have watched out for signs of developing cruelty, and I am glad to say I have seen none."

Stilicho was angry, not at me, but at the whole situation. He demanded an answer to his real question. "What will he do to my girl?"

I was surprised at how certainly I answered. "Nothing."

"You mean, no harm?"

"Perhaps great harm to one so eager for love and children of her own as Maria. I mean nothing. Honorius, so far as I can make out, is almost devoid of sexual desire. I thought to help him in the matter, and on advice of the court physician I introduced a skilled young concubine into his bedchamber. She came to me in tears the next day. She could do nothing with him. She was humiliated."

"I didn't know such a thing was possible!"

"The physician says it is rare, but he has known one or two like cases. He calls it chastity through lack of interest, a matter of nature and not of virtue. Once in a while, but not often, Honorius will kiss Galla Placidia and look at her in a way I do not like. But that is all."

"His brother Arcadius has children."

"With a faint heart, General. And they say in Constantinople that Arcadius is not the father of all the children of Eudoxia."

"I can't see how Serena, a mother——" He broke off, looked at me, and sighed. "Thanks, Gregory. I'm glad for your reassurance that the boy is not vicious. The actual presence of a wife in bed, after marriage, will no doubt change conditions. I pity my daughter."

Serena continued her pressure. She even had Claudian write verses in which Honorius addressed pleas of passion to Stilicho to grant his daughter as an Emperor's bride. She circulated copies of these verses. When the matter became almost a scandal Stilicho finally gave in to Serena.

It was a magnificent wedding, thronged with nobles from Italy, Gaul and Spain and princes and ambassadors from far places. Claudian wrote and recited a set of Fescennine songs and an epithalamium, full of the customary prophecies of sexual prowess, favors of Venus and assurance of offspring. Venus, for example, begins her address to the child bride: "All hail, revered daughter of divine Serena, scion of great kings and destined to be the mother of kings! . . ." Maria's cheeks and wide-spaced eyes and golden hair shone bright, and often an exalted breath drawn in through parted lips lifted her swelling young breasts. After the recitation Claudian left for his room with sickness at the stomach and a splitting headache. "Why didn't I kill Maria?" he said to me. "It would have been kinder." Maria was decked and dowered with an enormous gift of imperial jewels. The marriage bed was adorned with gems and royal purple and exquisite flowers.

As months passed, a curious pall of fright settled on the face of the new young Empress, like frost that kills too early blossoms. She had been elevated even higher than her mother; Maria was the only woman in the

Western Empire—the only Augusta—privileged to have fire carried before her when she came and went.

I knew her well, as I knew all the imperial children well. She came to me and cried and beat my breast and said, "Do something for me, Gregory. Do something for me!" She assumed that I knew what was crushing her heart.

I had a long talk with Honorius. He sat with his head bowed and shaking slowly as I talked. He answered, "I told Aunt Serena not to make me marry. But Maria and I had to do what Aunt Serena commanded. I can't do anything. Maria has quit asking me. She has quit crying about it. Now she shrinks from me and has bad dreams and moans, disturbing my sleep. Still nothing happens. I don't want to do anything."

I could tell from an odd vibration in his voice that he was deeply hurt.

Galla Placidia, with a growing girl's suspicion of what was going on, said, "Maria's a fool, Gregory. She ought to be proud and happy. She's Empress, isn't she? That's more than I would be if I married Eucherius. I hate him, and I hate Serena."

Rumor had it that Serena, jealous of her position, was administering strange potions to Maria and Honorius to prevent them from having offspring. For who, outside a circle of intimates in the palace, could believe that the Emperor and Empress of Rome, although married for nearly a year, both remained virgin simply because the Emperor lacked desire?

The whole business was dreadful, and Claudian suffered both for his part in it and for the streak of blindness or coldness in Serena that had brought it about. "The gods made me a poet," he said, "and I have corrupted the gift into a curse." His agony deepened.

My participation in all these affairs had not rewarded me with peace of soul. There was a gradual steady increase and consolidation of my place in power, it is true; it would have taken a greater than Florentinus to unseat me now. Like all the men around me in high place, I accumulated more wealth, more authority and more opportunities. I valued these things and took care to defend and improve them.

But there began to be an increasing difference in emotional quality between my public and my private life. Will, zest and intelligence are needful in public affairs, and as I prospered I gained in a sense of being useful, even important. I had a very real place and function in the society of power, and my will and zest for participating in central political and social problems of Empire increased. More and more of my time was devoted to these things, and more and more of my day-in and day-out enjoyment of life was founded on public activity. I earned a reputation as a man who was able, was willing to work hard, and who worked on terms of confidence and good cheer with other men. A saying I often used in imperial conferences was this: "It's got to be done; let's figure out how we can do it." And I was always ready to take responsibility. For days at a time, when affairs were most pressing, I almost forgot that I had a private life.

There was less seasoning of good spirits in my private life. Marcia bore me a daughter, a sound and cheerful child, and Marcia doted on the little girl. I let her have this child baptized, as she desired. But somehow this baby, called Livia, did not waken a deep response in my heart such as had been evoked by my lost son Marcus. Under the comfortable conditions of life in the palace the child had no direct need of my attention and protection. I was so busy I scarcely saw her for weeks at a time. Then I might take her up for half an hour to toss and tousle her, like an animal plaything.

Amantha, the good slave girl, also bore me a child, a son—but of course a child by a slave concubine is never quite the same as a legitimate son. Amantha was profoundly grateful to have a child; to her it was like a life restored in return for the baby exposed by her parents to weather and beasts on the hill. But Amantha bearing me a child reawakened that streak of cruelty in Marcia, and I finally had to separate Amantha from our personal service to protect her. I kept her at the villa in the country, out of Marcia's reach. It seemed that the time of lyric love between Marcia and me had passed; we considered ourselves as well suited to each other as husband and wife could expect to be.

I had not seen Dionie in private for an amazingly long time. She had disdained to make any effort to regain my interest. However, during the Emperor's wedding festivities she was making something of a fool of herself with a black-bearded ambassador from Persia. He used too much perfume in his beard to suit me. I rebuked her. Then she came with this Persian to a large dinner I gave at my villa. Dionie had once more changed the color of her hair, wearing it now that rich deep-toned color of a polished chestnut. She was acknowledged to be the most beautiful woman at court. But she came to my party, with this Persian, in a scandalous garment. It was, I believe, exactly such a garment as Pliny had in mind when he said of the courtesan Pamphilia: "This woman ought not to be deprived of the glory which is due to her, that of having invented a dress which exhibits a woman perfectly naked." And that night Dionie used the wretched Persian as a mirror in which to rouse and show me my own desires. In the end I took her home, and there she got her revenge by assailing me in bed with such a stream of witty talk and jest and laughter that I was as impotent as a frightened boy until finally I cupped my hand over her treacherous mouth. She had planned the whole thing with full knowledge that bed is an ideal place for a witty woman's revenge. We laughed at it together before morning. I promised to be rough as a soldier if she tried that again. "Darling," she said, "you were as rough as a soldier!"

Marcia no longer appeared to suffer when I resumed fairly open relations with Dionie. And Dionie was quite treacherous and made skillful efforts to get me involved with her in one of those destructive passions where the woman feeds on the increasingly weakening will of the man. For a curious reason she was not able to catch me in this way. I was profoundly hurt by, and could not and did not want to escape from, my final love for Marcia. The full revelation of this love had come upon me during that night of vision and vigil at Como. Marcia had never followed me to such heights or depths. I was alone.

Marcia knew that I loved her in this way, which was like a depth of longing for something more than human, and it made her uneasy. It was not a new way, but rather a confirmation and deepening of what I had first felt for her on that night in Rome long ago when I rescued her from the mob that set fire to her palace. I suppose the two central facts in an ordinary man's inward life—his love for one woman and his search for God—are the hardest of all to explain. Perhaps in those years in Milan Marcia would have preferred to have me show more obvious fidelity and more noticeable dedication to her wishes, instead of a silent consecration to some mystery of her being. I could be irritated by her habits and decline her wishes; I could expend my distractions on other women; I was capable of simple affection for Amantha and an oblique passion for Dionie. With other women I expressed various degrees of desire to forget myself, to shut off the suffering of deep experience with the curtain of sensuous and sentimental irresponsibilities; but with Marcia I was moved by a desire to know and to become myself. With other women I was chasing after thin images and deadening sensations, sometimes achieving momentary warmth of comfort, good for my anxious heart like warmed wine on a chill day; but they could never for me make all the seas laugh and the earth bear fruit and the sky glow radiant. Still I was always conscious, as one is conscious of being alive, that if I were ever to find such peace with God, this peace would be illuminated for me by my love for Marcia.

Sometimes with grieving candor I would say to myself that a life such as mine, without inward form, was sick and sorrowful; that I did not love Marcia, but only knew I could love no one else and could not find the inner whole of my life so long as I failed to love her. Still, inescapably, my spiritual attachment was to her.

I wonder if women do not love, and want to be loved, in some other way.

I was able sometimes to talk to Claudian about these things, which was a good companionship that I needed.

"When will you learn, Gregory, that women are mothers of spiritual death so as to assure the continuance of bodily life?"

"You argue from Serena, not from Marcia."

He cocked his head and moistened his lips, then shrugged his shoulders in his odd Egyptian fashion. "Perhaps you're right. No two women are the same. Serena is a distorted shadow of Athena, and Marcia is a lovely echo of Proserpina. But a woman with a child is always something else than the woman a man loves. Marcia's fingers move differently in the air now that she has a child again."

I never did understand the relationship between Claudian and Marcia. When they met I was aware of a very real and vital response of persons between them. Often it was like a shock and made me suspect it might be deep and dangerous. I was also aware that they did not understand it; and they treated it like a dark thing, a fated thing, to be avoided as long as they could avoid it.

Claudian was smiling with a new gnomic insight. "In a way, Gregory," he said, "you cheer me up. You are certainly the rising young man of Empire if ever there was one, and your position is envied by a thousand hopeful little greedy men with a third of your intelligence. Your young beard sparkles with the favor of the gods. But I see you're a man like any man. Your soul burns with the pain of woman and the pain of God. You restore my faith in the unknowable and tragic necessity of suffering."

I laughed. "You draw your dark sayings up from the oozy bottoms of the Nile."

"Yes. Egypt is too old to have given birth to a happy man."

"It's not Egypt. I am almost certain that Pluto was your father and that you will greet me with a banquet of great splendor someday down in the underworld."

Fiery spokes of delight lit his black eyes. "You know my parentage and the gorgeous world from which I truly come!" Then, as swiftly as one of those blazing stars that fall down across the sky, his mood changed, and he cried out, "Why have I betrayed my father Pluto and all the rich radiant wonder of my fatherland, the nether world, to sing the rotten lies of Rome!"

Only a few nights later I came into Claudian's room. I found he had cut open veins in his wrists and was bleeding to death. He was seated on a stool with his arms hanging down between his legs, and his lifeblood was flowing into a large bronze basin. I startled him so that he jerked one hand, and a ring on his finger struck the rim of the basin, giving out a deep rich-toned reverberation.

"Go away," he said.

"Strike the basin again. That's a wonderful sound."

I stood there, he sat there. We stared at each other for a long moment of intense unspoken struggle while his blood dripping into the basin made a faint, delicate and pleasant sound.

Finally I sighed, relaxed, and shook my head. "The choice, of course, is yours. I don't understand why you need to do it."

He was quite pale. There was a glitter in his dark eyes. "The choice and the reasons are both mine."

"I'm leaving for Constantinople in the morning. I came to say my temporary farewell. If it is to be final, I would like more time. We could talk of last things, as friends ought."

His pallor made his hair and eyebrows look extraordinarily black and his nose very thin and his lips quite sad. "The poet is dead. I am disposing of the man that is left. There are no other last things, neither friends nor demons."

I stepped forward and with a ring of my own struck the bronze basin sharply once and in a moment again. The deep notes filled the room with resonant sound, then died away. "The bell is not cracked. It can be sounded again."

He looked up at me. Tears were forming in his black eyes. He lifted up and stretched out his arms and bleeding wrists, but turned his face away. I tore strips from my tunic and bound his wrists so as to stop the bleeding.

"I will never forgive you for this, Gregory."

He was weak. I helped him to his feet and aided him across the room to a couch.

"You'll be all right, Claudian. Those incisions will heal in a few days. I'll sit here and talk with you until you fall asleep. I expect I'll be in Constantinople three or four months. Stilicho wants me to make a real effort to get them to stop their infringements on the West. I'll have to do all I can to undermine Eutropius. If I can work out a power alliance between the Empress Eudoxia and Bishop John Chrysostom, there ought to be hope."

Claudian's face, now that he was lying down, had lost its pallor and was becoming flushed. People react differently to loss of blood. His reaction was that his cheeks flushed, his eyes became very bright, and he began talking. He talked fluently, rapidly, often not making sense, but often in the flash of a phrase or a stroke of ironical comment giving me new and deeper insights into his troubles and his spirit.

In one angry outburst he roared at me: "Go, like a hound of death, on your mission of Empire and bring back new vile matter for me to corrupt into imperial poems! Rome has almost unfailingly devastated the souls of her great ones, forcing them to lie or keep silent. Hers was never Athena's dream of wisdom. Roman peace! She is the red slut, Power. She has sprawled with her thousand lovers and devoured them and spawned a million cruelties of law and lust and violence. See how she bestrides the world with the torch of war! She has gutted the earth for the jewels in her head; her vast breasts give suck of blood to all sons of power; and her hot thighs and prolific loins are terrible in birth of atrocities. If there were a God, there could not be a Rome!"

Marcia was shocked when I told her about Claudian. She had an attitude of refusal that she took when something greatly distressed her. I always thought she had learned this attitude as a small child in defiance of her mother. She took it now. She clasped her hands behind her back, looked down at the floor, and shook her head sharply in denial, saying over and over again, "No ... no ... no!"

She finally accepted the facts. She sat down, her arms limp and tears enlarging her eyes. "I wish he hadn't done it. I wish you hadn't told me." Then she looked up at me strangely, the color chilled out of her round young face. "It would have been better if you hadn't stopped him."

"What a thing to say!"

"I'm sorry. I'm so frightened. Gregory ... take me to Constantinople. Take me with you, please. Please!"

I took her in my arms. I did all I could to comfort her. She was now in the full bloom of her young physical maturity, with a firmness and roundness of flesh and a glowing warmth of bodily vitality that was a joy to hold in my arms. I wished I could take her to Constantinople with me. At that moment I wanted either to take her or to resign my mission. We had previously decided on practical grounds against Marcia's going. Our little girl Livia was cutting some teeth, she was apt to be fretful and feverish, and Marcia had said she couldn't bear to leave the child behind in that condition. Both of us had such a deep sense of the tragic loss of our son that we would not for a moment consider hazarding the life of our new child on a sea voyage.

We clung to each other that night in tenderness and anxiety. I think married couples remember certain nights when their love-making has had an intense silent profundity, as if they were joined in a supreme effort to seal their union forever against ultimate peril. So it was between Marcia and me that night. Our communion exceeded all words of love and was a sacred seal upon our living together; we imparted to each other and shared with each other our deepest blessing.

At the break of day, in the first light of morning, we looked at each other, quiet, smiling, tender and at peace. Marcia relaxed on her pillow. In a moment when her eyes were closed and her lips were parted I placed a kiss on each of her eyelids to guard her from harm.

Yet, because we were mortal, all this could not absolve us from mortal peril.

CHAPTER TEN

A VISION OF DARK AGES

I. The Rock of God

There is purification of a man in a sea voyage. As we sailed down the Adriatic and around Greece and into the Aegean Sea lovely with islands, a great serenity suffused my heart and sweet calm settled on my mind. It was as if I drowsed in radiance and was being borne along in peace somewhere between time and time. I had left time hard at work wearing out lives and souls in Milan and would find time all too soon again wearing down lives and souls in Constantinople; but this interim at sea was a spiritual interlude of healing and refreshment not squeezed and gnawed by time. And the ease of my memory, remembering good things, was full of light and wonderful.

My heart laughed and rejoiced when the spiritual personality of Marcia, created of a thousand unforgotten aspects, visited the measureless fields of my inner mind. She was brisk, sudden and merry, making the space where we lived a shelter and a home. How her eyes were round at the theater, how she clutched my hand at the games! Then also, when I stood apart, I saw her in public, among personages at court, or in church, or in the market-place arcades of Milan: direct, spontaneous, with energy and courage and ready affection. And her fingers, as Claudian had said, moved differently in the air now that she had a child again.

Remembering these and so many other things, I realized that a husband forgets that his wife is much more of a person than shows in her habitual relationship to him. In direct contact with Marcia I subdued much of her positive strength and joyful variety; we fell into patterns and attitudes with each other which concealed much rich variety and many potential developments. It was very good to be away from her and to summon from deep affection free and delightful images of her character, to restore from the deeps of my memory to the conscious play and flow of my mind a Marcia more completely a woman, a person, an individual: And thus I found out more surely who this woman was that I loved. She awakened my wonder and deserved my admiration and astonished me by each time exceeding my most creative expectations of just what she was like.

I began to realize that through our years together of tenderness and tragedy, of anxiety and tribulation and solace, I had lived more richly and fully than I knew with a woman at once visible and invisible, easy to describe and surpassing description: a lock of her hair blown across her lips, her laughter heard in another room, her weeping in the dark or her thoughtful consideration of a child on a muddy street; her quick glance at Serena, her earnest persuasion with Galla Placidia, her cool smile for Dionie; her chin lifted and her throat full as she sang in church, or the way of her hands with cloth and needle and thread: All these things, and more than all such things, was the glowing and flowing life, the being and the mystery, of my best companion in the world.

There also came, or dwelt in my mind, another spiritual companion, Ambrose. I was not surprised at this. It is common experience to remember the absent and recall the dead. Their lives have been created in our memory, I know not how; but they do return in spiritual reality. Ambrose was in this way as real now as ever he had been to my mind on any day in Milan just after I had left his house or the church in which he had preached. But I was alone and meditative on the ship; I had time to think about the spiritual reality of the return of Ambrose to the fields of my memory. I realized how much of our human communion is made up not of direct contact but of inner awareness of one another's spiritual reality. I put my thought down as best I could in words. Another might have made a poem of it or a discourse or a Socratic dialogue. But I knew what I meant when I wrote it in a plain sentence:

Each one of us is lonely in his own mortality; but the essential of the soul cannot be lonely, for all of us are part of one another's immortality.

I wrote it down and kept the writing, for somehow this thought seemed to me a growth and maturing of my own spirit; it gave me a larger and better space of love to live in; and I confess I made the writing and kept it in the same sort of childlike pleasure I had had years before, as a little boy, backing up against a doorframe and making a mark over the top of my head to show myself I had grown a fingerbreadth in stature.

That night I dreamed of Ambrose, which was something stranger even than his companionship in wakeful memory. He looked himself and his voice was his own and his narrow right hand reached out gently toward me. "Come, Gregory," he said. "I am waiting for you at the Rock of God."

It was a happy dream, although I did not understand it. What it seemed to say was that the serenity of profound loneliness, on this sea voyage that seemed to be between time and time, or outside the scope of time, and my grateful acceptance of this mortal loneliness had set me free to participate in an immortal fellowship and peace. I had been very tired in my soul, and now I let myself rest.

We had only golden weather, with soft winds and sparkling seas. Our pilot grew bored with the monotony of so easy a voyage and began to exercise his skill and court his own excitement by sweeping close to little islands in the Aegean Sea. On a fair midmorning, with a soft following breeze, he toyed too close to a spine of rocks extending out from the cliff of a small island. The waves rose over these rocks and burst and foamed. A slow strong wave tossed our stern very easily a few extra feet aside, and the rudder struck rock and splintered and floated bobbing on the sea. There was way enough on the ship for the pilot to slacken sail and drift into the island's neat harbor. Anchor was dropped.

The carpenters studied the damage, said they could put in a new rudder by nightfall. We would sail again in the morning.

This was one of those stone-built islands, with a few green patches and some olive trees, a little harbor, a little village of fishermen who sold their catch in Athens, a church on a hill, neither as beautiful nor as large as the several shining temples on another hill, and three small mountains in the blue sky beyond. The merchants on our ship went into the village to try to do some business. Two young men we had picked up in Athens—they had attended the academies there and now hoped to make their fortunes in Constantinople as teachers of rhetoric—invited me to go to a wineshop to drink with them and discuss philosophy, but I felt like stretching my legs alone and started off to climb the hill where the lovely Pagan temples shone in the sun.

I could hear the mallets of our ship's carpenters striking pegs of wood. The pathway parted, one fork going up the hill to the temples and the other fork going up the other stony hill to the modest Christian church. I can't remember that I gave it a thought. I took the left-hand fork, toward the south, and climbed a steep narrow path to the church. It was built of unpolished limestone, showing quite warm in the sun and quite cool in the shadow. I looked down at the village, the harbor and at our ship and clearly heard again the carpenter's mallets striking wood. Then I turned into the silence of the church.

It was fragrant and cool inside. The priest or bishop of the place stood with a young man beside the baptismal font. He was shaking his head in an unhappy negative, and the young man, smaller than I but of agile and wonderfully proportioned physique, had his head bowed down and tears were on his cheeks. They were not talking.

My sandals on the stone floor made the only sound in the little church, and it was not much of a sound, for my step has always been soft and wary. I thought, after a glance, that baptism in this church would be done by complete submersion, for the font by which the two men stood in trouble was an octagonal stone affair, partly sunk and partly raised above the floor, large enough to hold several men at once and containing now two or more feet of water. The water was very still and caught a reflection of light from a high window. Probably women from the village carried jars of water on their heads up the steep hill to keep it full. I asked the priest and the youth in Greek what was the trouble.

"His brother desired to be baptized, but yesterday was drowned at sea, and now this boy wants baptism for his brother in his brother's name. What shall I do? I do not know if it is right, I do not know if it is wrong, and the matter is sacred."

I liked the priest for his simplicity and the boy for his emotion.

"Please," the boy said. "I saw you come off the ship. Perhaps you are a scholar and can help me save my brother's soul."

The priest and the lad stood there, looking up into my face, waiting for me to speak. The matter was quite simple. I said, "I am one who was a good friend of Bishop Ambrose of Milan, and it happens I have talked with him about baptismal matters."

"The great Ambrose!" The priest actually bowed to me, then crossed himself. He was a thin hard-muscled little man of middle years with sea music in his voice.

"If your brother," I reassured the boy, "had a pure wish to be baptized but death prevented him, it is almost certainly accounted as done. So Ambrose preached concerning the young Emperor Valentinian, who desired baptism but died too soon."

The boy lifted his head, alert, persuasive, wakened to hope. Something glittered in his black hair. "He had a wish! It was most pure!" The boy showed his teeth in a smile, while yet his dark eyes had tears in them. "While we clung to broken pieces of timber in the water he said to me: 'In Christ's name, Miletus, I wish to be baptized and saved.' And I said, 'So, too, do I, brother Timotheus.' And we clasped hands and agreed that if either of us lived, that one would ask our priest to baptize him for both of us. Timotheus had not my strength. He drowned. I am come."

I realized the specks of glitter in his black hair were brine of the sea.

I turned to the priest. "I know of this thing happening in Milan, not often, but now and then, when one died in desire of baptism, but too soon, a brother or a parent was baptized in the name of the desiring one. And Ambrose said the apostle Paul had allowed similar rites at Corinth."

The priest's face lighted with joy. "If it was done under Paul in Corinth and under Ambrose in Milan, I will do it here! May Bishop Ambrose—who is a saint, and his miracles are known in all churches, even here—may he watch over us!"

The movement of these events was all so simple, so pure, and seemed so right, that I now with the utmost readiness and pure intention asked the priest: "Will you baptize me, please, along with Miletus and his drowned brother Timotheus?"

And it was done.

Miletus and I stripped off our clothes and sat in the tank of chill water. I felt the coldness tighten the skin around my legs and loins. Then the priest submerged us in turn, in the name of the Father, the Son and the Holy Ghost. During submersion my eyelids and neck especially felt the coldness. I held my son Marcus in the secret arms of my memory while it was being done, and around the space of my heart there seemed a good warmth. Miletus was baptized first for his brother, then again for himself.

We stood a moment in the cool air of the little church before we put on our garments. The priest told us Saint Ambrose had stood at his shoulder and guided his hand and spoke all the words to his heart. He said that because of Ambrose helping him he considered it the purest baptism he had ever performed. Instead of doubting him I accepted the love in the man's heart.

But how shall I express one of the most complex mysteries of my own heart and mind? In a sense of gratefulness and peace I felt that Ambrose, a spiritual reality present in my memory, had heard me confess Christ and was glad; and yet also I felt a poignant thorn crease my heart because the bodily Ambrose was not there and I had spoken too late for him who had loved me to hear me with the ears of the flesh. I can only say that this was another of those riches of love that surpass my understanding.

When we came out into the sun, the three of us, I felt water drying on my hair and beard and down along my body under my clothes. Down in the harbor the mallets of the carpenters were silent; they were fitting the finished rudder to the ship. The resting of sunlight on the water—which was red in the reflection of the ship and green in the harbor, purple at the cliff and tawny foam at the rock spine—spread shining from island to island and on outward on vast blue surrounding sea, where there was enormous space for winds to wander.

We looked across the steep ravine to where the Pagan temples shone so lovely in the sun.

"We call that," said the priest, "our Acropolis, after the way they do in Athens, and no one seems to know how ancient the temples are or who built them." He turned. "This church has a fortunate history. It, too, is very old, though not so old as the temples. Some of our fishermen were at Athens and heard the apostle Paul and were converted. When they came home here they built this church. And later the holy apostle Paul paused once at this island on his way to Ephesus—perhaps even as you, on account of a broken rudder on a ship—and he entered this church and blessed it and baptized nine souls in that very font where I, with the aid of Saint Ambrose, baptized you, Gregory and Miletus, and, in your sponsorship but in his own name, the drowned Timotheus. And when the people asked Holy Paul what they should call this church of ours he looked about him and saw where it was built and how it stood, and he said: 'Call it the Rock of God.' And so it is we call it to this day, the Rock of God."

II. "I AM GREATER THAN GOD!"

The corruption of Constantinople in this year 399 was deep and terrible; and I arrived there to do, for the good of Empire, a secret corrupt thing.

I was deeply stirred at Constantinople by what I can call only a vision of dark ages. Far off from home and rested after the detachment of my sea voyage, I saw beyond the opportune affairs of the day. I saw the Empire broken up within a shell of seeming Empire; I saw a flight of great intelligences out of the Roman civil world; and I saw women in a new and frightening role. These were elements, energies, of a profound and tragic disorder breeding in the Roman world. And the great of the earth were destroying themselves.

Stilicho had sent me to Constantinople for one clear and secret purpose: to unseat Eutropius the eunuch from his tyrannical throne of power.

There were four great ones at Constantinople—Eutropius, General Gainas, Bishop John Chrysostom and the young Empress Eudoxia. The four of them were embroiled in a bitter struggle for power, and each of them was engaged in a personal tragedy of ruin.

What was going on was a fourfold revelation of the awful majesty of what the Greeks call "Moira," what the Romans call "Fate," what the Jews call "the wrath of the Righteous Almighty" and what the Christians call "the justice of God." The great old Greeks—Homer, Aeschylus, Sophocles—perceived in what they called "hubris" the seed of a man's ruin. How can I express it better than to say the man of hubris feels himself greater than God? When a man dreams in his heart, I am greater than God! then this hubris, pride, insolence, arrogance, unrighteousness comes forth in the acts of his life and prepares him for ruin. The old Greeks admonished men to seek wisdom as a shield against hubris; the mighty prophets of the Jews cried out, "Walk softly in righteousness before the face of the righteous Lord"; the Romans of old said, "Hold to honor and justice against arrogance"; and the Christians were saying, "Pride is the sin of death; be humble in Christ." It seems that all peoples know that the madness of doom rises in this dream of the heart: I am greater than God! It is the dream of death for a man or for a nation.

Within six or seven years of my visit there the four great ones of Constantinople had all been encompassed by ruin. I want to focus what light of compassion I can on the tragedy of Eutropius, the first of the four to fall. Let me frame his ruin in three flashes of the ruin of the others, taking Eudoxia, who was the last to fall, first, as one approaches the heart of a catastrophe from its outer fringes, coming by steps of lesser agony to the terrible center.

To start with Eudoxia—six or seven years later than our ruin of Eutropius—after she had encompassed the exile and death of Bishop John

Chrysostom, the still young and sensual Empress Eudoxia, enjoying her single supremacy in the East, with her husband cowed and her lover ardent, was destroyed by a miscarriage; and the Christians said, some that God thus avenged the exiling of Chrysostom, and others that the wages of adultery is death.

Before that, when Eudoxia and Chrysostom combined to ruin General Gainas and got his head on a spear, Eudoxia had her statues carried through the East and set a huge silver statue of herself on a lofty pillar before Chrysostom's very Church of Holy Wisdom, and people worshiped it, and Bishop Chrysostom unleashed his tongue against the rich, against rich and powerful females, against Eudoxia, Empress. She had him exiled into Asia Minor, thinking he would die on the harsh journey; but he lived, and after several years she ordered his removal toward the desert, on which journey he died. Also, the great church of St. Sophia was burned and ruined in the course of these affairs. And Pagans said, "So it is, even when a bishop exults over men."

Earlier, when Eudoxia, Chrysostom and Gainas had conspired to ruin Eutropius, General Gainas thought he could be at last in the East what Stilicho was in the West. He insulted Count John, Eudoxia's lover; he brought his soldiers rioting into the city; he took over for his Arian Goths a church in Chrysostom's Catholic city of Constantinople. In the fighting and riots seven thousand Goths were slain, during which time a swarm of Catholic Christians climbed onto the roof of the Arianized church, cut holes, and threw down burning brands to roast alive the Arian Christians trapped inside. Gainas harassed the city from outside the walls until his army disintegrated; then he fled toward the Danube, tried to raise a new army, and was trapped by Uldin the Hun. Uldin, who wanted to buy favor with the Eastern Emperor, murdered Gainas and sent his head solidly fixed on a spear back to Constantinople. "Behold," people said, "the vainglory of a Barbarian come to naught."

And Eutropius was the first of the four to summon his own death, while I was in Constantinople doing my treacherous little to speed his ruin.

When a flash of light singled out the face of Eutropius under the imperial awning at the Hippodrome, during the pomp and splendor and yelling hysteria of the chariot races, I could see that he used a lot of paint, like a woman, to conceal the actual color and creases of his face. Soon several thousand of us, crowded into the great confines of St. Sophia church, were to see the wretched man unadorned, the stringy-haired yellow eunuch, his teeth chattering, his skinny arms atremble, crying for God's mercy.

Eutropius had sent assassins to Italy to murder Stilicho—we had foiled that; he had fomented and supported Gildo's revolt in Africa, trying to starve Rome—we had foiled that; he was continually helping Alaric to build up power against us on our border—we feared that; he was deepening and hardening the break between the two halves of the Empire—and we deplored that. Stilicho saw that Eutropius had to be removed.

Then to our astounded ears in Italy came the announcement that Eutropius was appointing himself consul for the year 399. This is best described as a religious outrage against the thousand-year-old dignity, grandeur and honor of Rome. There were two consuls for the year, giving their name to the year, one under each Emperor. I do not exaggerate our emotional view of this honorary symbolic office if I say the consuls were the annual gods of all Rome stood for and hoped for; they were, for their year, patricians, the symbolic fathers of the people and of the Emperors. To have one of these a eunuch was an unbearable blasphemy.

The whole East, being more accustomed to depravity, took it with a kind of obscene ridicule, but Italy and the West were unified in rage. How could a year under the symbolic auspices of a eunuch be anything but degrading, obscene and barren, with fertility polluted and shame adored? What could be expected but plagues, famines, earthquakes and other monstrosities? The Senate sent delegates to Stilicho urging outright war. But Alaric as master general of Illyricum had so far built up his strength on our border that Stilicho dared not leave Italy exposed while he took an army to Constantinople to unseat Eutropius, and assassins we sent to cut the man down had failed.

I had persuaded Stilicho I might be able to do something by intrigue. Several provinces in the East, suffering invasion by the Huns, had appealed to Stilicho for military aid, and the ostensible purpose of my mission was to offer the Emperor Arcadius several legions from his brother Honorius. But when I got to Constantinople I found conditions were even worse. Tribigild, a Gothic warrior, was ravaging Asia Minor. He had a fierce ambitious wife. She had goaded him on to do in those parts what Alaric had done, and shown could be done, in Greece and Illyricum. The first expedition against Tribigild had failed; Eutropius had been forced now to send Gainas out as general. It was Gainas the Goth against Tribigild the Goth. Actually the two men were cousins of some sort, secretly united in a conspiracy of their own against Eutropius.

What was going on in the East had ceased to be merely political or military. Basic moral values were subverted and despised. Law and integrity were in ridicule. Individuals were setting themselves up as greater than one another and as greater than God. I was reminded of what

Odysseus said to King Alcinous: ". . . For a jealous race on earth are we, the tribes of men."

I thought at the time that I did an excellent job, worthy of a chapter in history. I realize now that the forces of corruption and distintegration had so deeply set in that it would have been harder to save Eutropius than to overthrow him.

What little I did was not worthy of a Christian. The curious, almost accidental fact of my baptism had not had any appreciable impact on my daily life. It seemed to me a dreamlike thing, done between time and time and not of this world. I kept it secret. I did not want anyone to know I was a Christian now. I was not one to whom naming myself a Christian brought either ecstasy or peace; rather, my inward life became a harder toil, for I knew I was not what my baptism gave me a technical right to call myself. I did not even like to think about it myself. It was as if I had planted—or allowed to be planted—a secret and dangerous seed in my soul, and now wanted to forget it was there, for perhaps it would grow and by some incalculable mightiness rob me of my ordinary life. I really believe I was profoundly frightened by this strange thing I had done, and tried to conceal it from my own awareness by resolute worldly action.

I was not received as an ambassador. I was insulted and ignored. Weeks passed without my being able to get an audience with either Arcadius or Eutropius. I was given such a preposterous message as this: "Eutropius the Chamberlain, to Count Gregory Julian, the spy of Stilicho: You may stand on the street this afternoon and see the Emperor pass in his chariot." Drawn by spotless white mules with golden harness, the chariot of Arcadius flashed with plates of gold, and in the shadow of purple and gold I could just see the dim insipid face of the oppressed young Emperor. The young Empress Eudoxia, whose second daughter, Pulcheria, had recently been born, was secluded like a prisoner in the palace. It was said that Count John of the guard was Eudoxia's lover and sweetened her seclusion.

The government of Eutropius was really a scandal, even by Eastern standards. The Emperor Julian in his short reign had cleared out Oriental excesses of vice and luxury, restoring Constantinople to a Pagan decency; Theodosius had brought in pride, vigor and splendor; but Eutropius had brought back in double measure a glut of voluptuous extravagance and sensual turmoil. From Greece and Constantinople down into Egypt he had raised the miserable and treacherous class of eunuchs to new insolence and power. By their gaudy dress you knew them. For example, one formerly a cook in the palace kitchen was now master of offices, wearing jewels and embroidered silk and conducting large public affairs with the mind of a kitchen tyrant.

Eutropius had set up a regular and exorbitant schedule of prices for the sale of governorships and other lucrative offices. He had sent off into exile favorites of Theodosius, some to the roots of the Caucasus Mountains, others to the burning Libyan desert. He kept up a continual soft riot for Arcadius, with fleets of barges and ships always ready to sail across the Bosporus to Ancyra, and when the bejeweled Emperor and his concourse of tribunes, domestics and generals returned to the city from days and nights of debauchery the troops, the banners, the trumpets would meet him as one returning to celebrate a military triumph. You might say Eutropius was murdering the young man with corruption. And in so far as I could understand it all, the single desperate ideal in the wretched yellow eunuch's heart was his unceasing effort to elevate his sister to a position of wealth, dignity and respect in the world. She was a good simple woman. He made her wealthy. But his own indignity, the base crime of castration perpetrated on him in his infancy, reflected back on her, and she was ridiculed by those fatal voices on the street, the market place and the corridors of palaces: "The eunuch's woman! The eunuch's woman!"

I established correspondence with General Gainas, I communicated directly with Bishop John Chrysostom, and through three Christian women, Castricia, Eugraphia and Marsa—they were greedy women and weavers of death who had formed a cabal with Eudoxia—I was put in touch with the Empress. The only function I fulfilled was to co-ordinate to a slight extent these three forces against Eutropius. Eudoxia hated him; Bishop Chrysostom hated the corruption of morals he was spreading; and General Gainas, pressing for power, watched from his small brutal eyes for his moment to spring to murder, and to rule.

Bishop Chrysostom was the greatest orator in the Church, East or West. I had heard him when I was a boy, during the riots at Antioch. I heard him now. He was older, skinnier, parched and bald, but still deserved his name, "Golden Mouth." Actually he had suffered a great misfortune when he had been seized at Antioch on the order of Eutropius, concealed in a vehicle, and brought to Constantinople to be made bishop against his own desire and against that of ruling Churchmen. He was a man born to utter splendor from a humble place; he was too fierce to remain safe on an episcopal throne of vast temporal power.

I think it is healthier for all concerned when any great human organization, Empire or Church, is ruled by law and that law administered by average reasonable men of common sense. Geniuses, however superb in their own dominant gift, are apt to make a painful mess for everybody of ordinary bumbling affairs. The commonplace work of the world calls for humor, humility, common sense and even, I dare say, now and then a little stupidity.

Chrysostom distressed the clergy by driving them toward celibacy and ascetic living, depriving them of their "sisters" who by custom kept house and bed for them, and of glitter and gluttony—that is, of pleasant living and good eating. His ideal was a stick of dry fish and a glass of water in a bare room. He sold gorgeous plate and ornaments of the Church to establish hospitals for the poor. Eudoxia won his favor by large gifts for his charitable works. He loved the poor and hated the rich and roused up the people of the city against monstrosities of vice and greed. The poor love to be roused up to hate and to destroy even needful things they know not how to replace. I reflected that it was easy for a bishop, assured of his food, his shelter and his comfort by a wealthy church, to preach the virtue and blessings of poverty. But Chrysostom carried things too far. He even cut out formal dinners, eating spare meals alone, which offended custom.

Of the four contenders for power in the Eastern half of the Roman world Chrysostom was by far the noblest and most intelligent, but even he was fighting for certain rectitudes and repentances with a ferocity that was neither merciful nor humble.

But then I always preferred freedom, with its searching creative power, to authority, with its death mold of obedience.

Arcadius hid as well as he could behind his own timidities. Eudoxia still had power to frighten him into action. I finally got into the palace for a secret interview with Eudoxia. Like most Barbarians from the North, she had yellow hair, a fair complexion and blue eyes. She was larger than our Italian women. She was energetic, vain, ambitious and a little stupid, and had that sensual talent some women are born with of compelling a man to be aware of her body.

I persuaded her that she should not disdain Arcadius simply because he was abject rather than passionate toward her. "Wait," I advised her, "until Gainas has a victory and, with that power behind him, demands the removal of Eutropius. Then go to Arcadius and tell him Eutropius has insulted you and thereby outraged him. You will see his abject sentiment for you converted into destructive fury against Eutropius."

She looked me over the way a woman looks over a man who might be of private interest to her. Then she shrugged not just her shoulders but her whole torso and said, "I'll try anything against that foul eunuch.

But don't think that when I'm in power I mean to share it with Stilicho." Her eyes narrowed, and she reached inside her garment to ease the pull of some ribbon on one of her firm breasts. "Nor share it with you, Count Julian!"

I could see how an unreflective energetic sort of male would be attracted by such a woman; she had a warm bright bloom of youth and an inborn sensual power. She took in a slow breath through parted lips, and color mounted up her throat to her cheeks. Then I could even see how such a fine young female creature would appeal to herself and would desire to have her body figured forth in statues to be carried throughout her Empire and placed on columns, even before the Church of Holy Wisdom. Startled by the shadow of our mortality, we humans are beautiful creatures.

General Gainas did not win a victory over Tribigild. The two simply conspired and drew near the Bosporus together, and Gainas sent over a letter to Arcadius demanding the dismissal of Eutropius. It amounted to this: "Give me Eutropius, or I'll bring over my army and take your city!"

Arcadius was frightened. Eutropius, roused to rage and fear, skittered along the corridors of the palace, with jewels in his sandals and jewels in his hair, and each of his footfalls made a nervous slap on the polished stone. He broke in on Eudoxia the Empress, scattered her women, and shrilled at her: "This is your work. Stop it at once. It was I who foisted you upon Arcadius in place of the daughter of Rufinus. I made you. I can ruin you!"

At that moment Eudoxia began to rule the Empire of the East. She slapped Eutropius on each cheek with a fierce strength of passionate anger, and those two deadly blows cast the miserable eunuch back into the deep hell of degradation, servility and torment that had been his tragic lot almost from birth.

Then Eudoxia disheveled her hair, snatched up her two children, and ran in real or simulated hysterics to Arcadius, screaming that Eutropius had threatened frightful outrages against the Emperor's wife and children. Arcadius, with the aid of Eudoxia's lover, Count John, and the palace guard, haled in Eutropius to his presence and, before the Empress, stripped him of his powers, his jewels, his insignia and his hopes, and ordered him, scarce better than naked, out of the palace on pain of death.

Eutropius, with the pitiful cunning of animal fear, knew the palace had risen against him, the army was coming to destroy him, and the city mob hated his yellow image of corruption. He fled to Bishop Chrysostom, to the very altar in St. Sophia church, and fell down, embracing a pillar of the altar and crying for mercy. This was ironical. Eutropius, to get at his enemies, had passed laws denying sanctuary of the Church to men he had wanted to destroy. But Chrysostom, disdaining these laws of Eutropius, now defied the soldiery of Gainas and the agents of Eudoxia and protected the man. He gave Eutropius sanctuary in the church all night.

I don't know how many more than a thousand or two thousand of us crowded into the church of St. Sophia in the morning. But Chrysostom was ready for the throng. He mounted the platform that served him for a pulpit and raised his tense hand in a commanding salute for silence. When the crowd was still he gave a signal. Curtains were drawn aside from the altar, and there we saw the ravaged old eunuch crouched in chattering fear under the altar table.

Chrysostom preached a massive sermon on vanity, corruption, pride and ruin. Surely it is a terrible thing when any man speaks to thousands pressed shoulder to shoulder, with faces lifted to him, and he begins to play on their mob passion, and *it* begins to sway and provoke him, until a mutual bond of hysteria endangers love and truth in any soul there; for how often is a crowd a gathering of the bitter together in one society of violence! Certainly the church stank now with the sweat of thousands desiring vengeance. I could feel my heart grasped in the horror of mob passion. I got my back against a stone pillar to be in a better position if violence broke. The whole aim of Chrysostom was to convert violence to repentance. Unfortunately he could only do it by being himself the whiplash of the mob of us, by inflicting on Eutropius the final cruel indignities of triumphant words.

"Behold vanity of vanities! Behold the enemy of the Church, fallen to ruin and being protected now by the mercy of the Church! Where now is the splendor of the consul, the lascivious dancing girls and feasts, the blazing torches and lamps of magnificence? Where is the flattery of the city, the acclaim of the Hippodrome, the shouts of thousands? Where are the jewels and magnificent garments? He who was furious against the Church has fallen headlong from the sparkling of power to the darkness of ruin. His night and dream of the world show bare as death in the light of day and truth. See how he crouches and trembles and his teeth click together; his tongue chokes his throat with fear of death. . . ."

Being among the taller persons there, I could see, over the tense and jerking heads of the crowd, the desolate, knotty and shrunken figure of the yellow eunuch, lashed by the tongue of Chrysostom, excoriated by the hateful thousands of glances licking over his body like worms of evil desire.

Then Chrysostom addressed that victim of all the world, saying he did not come to insult the poor ruined wretch crouching there, but to show us all that this was the proof and reward of corruption of vanity. He had warned Eutropius before—why had not Eutropius heard? "If you had wisely accepted my strictures, the caresses of the world would not have ruined you. My wounds would have brought you health; the kisses of the world have brought you immedicable death."

What strange abuse was this! I thought, even as Chrysostom said it, he had waxed grandiloquent. He was mistaking his eloquent ego for God. For what right has one man to wound another, dreaming that good will come of it; or what right to expose a man's wound to edify a mob? Not by Chrysostom's wounding, but by God's wounding, might Eutropius have been healed.

And then I sickened, even as I thought that, and I looked into a most awful blackness of darkness: For, in God's name, had not Eutropius— snatched from his mother's breast, castrated, debased, enslaved, defiled, polluted, tormented—had not Eutropius suffered wounds enough from God and man to hush in shame and pity and fear the tongues of all men so that none would ever speak against so profoundly crucified a soul? While yet Chrysostom fulminated against vanity, riches, pride and disobedience to the Church I turned my face hard against the stone pillar, and with tears streaming down over my cheeks I prayed God to give eternal peace to the heart and soul of Eutropius.

Chrysostom won the promise of life for the man, and Eutropius accepted from the Emperor the gift of exile to Cyprus. Eudoxia in her barbarous vehemence had him pursued, taken off his ship and brought to trial. As happens when anger insults justice, he was not tried for his real crimes, but was condemned and executed for a trifling villainy. It was alleged he had once harnessed to his chariot a pair of sacred animals of a breed and color reserved for the Emperor alone, and for this treason he was killed.

Really, the old Greek ideal "to take possession of the beautiful" seemed, in the midst of these bitter affairs, a remote philosopher's dream, and the Roman ideal of justice under law was travestied by our passions and powers.

But the tragic and ruined world of Eutropius contained also the sublime awakening of Augustine. While the one died dark death in the East, the other sang a new song out of Africa.

III. Augustine.

Embroiled as I was in such events, it is no wonder that I had a vision of the ruin of Empire and felt an encroachment of dark ages to come. And it was dramatically heightened for me by my chance turning from the debased and ruined manhood of Eutropius to the spiritualized manhood of Augustine.

Whether with my aid or simply out of the forces intrinsic to the situation, the purposes of my mission had been fulfilled, and my time was my own. While I waited several weeks for a ship to sail home for Italy I was at my ease in a handsome villa overlooking the splendid golden waters of the city, seeing sails and sky and the work of gentle winds. I was refreshing my spirit with a few days of reflection on the world in general and on the conditions, ways and possibilities of my own life. My reflections were greatly stimulated by a new book I was reading. This was the *Confessions* of my onetime tutor Augustine, now Bishop of Hippo in Africa, in which he related much about his life and his religious conversion. The book was not yet to be had from a bookseller; all the first copies had gone to bishops and priests. Bishop Chrysostom allowed me to borrow his copy, and I at once hired scriveners, three of them, to apportion the manuscript among them for copying. Thus I secured a copy of my own. I believe it was fairly accurate, for I hired able scriveners to do the job.

The shock of Augustine's *Confessions* came upon me slowly, penetrating into my sense of world disorder and reaching my sense of personal disorder.

What I perceived as the three major energies of tragic disorder in the Roman world were, first, the breakup of Empire within a shell of seeming Empire, then the flight of great intelligences out of the Roman civil world, and, last, the frightening new role being played by women.

There was, of course, the fatal major fissure between East and West. Britain was uneasy, Persia threatened, Egypt arrogant, Africa unstable, Spain lethargic, Gaul self-centered, and the peoples along the Rhine were in ferment. Huns and other such brutes ravaged the fringes of Empire and sent more decent Barbarians—displaced Goths, Vandals, Franks—into flight, unrest and revolt toward Roman centers. I had had firsthand experience both of Alaric's power to destroy and inability to rule and of our Roman inability to protect the people we taxed from the destruction of Goths, of Vandals, of Scythians or of Huns. Rome was a great name for a great space of earth, but the spirit and vitality of the name no longer filled the space. I saw all this more clearly in Constantinople, away from my familiar surroundings and more immediate tasks to be done. Seeing it, I appreciated for the first time the true greatness of Stilicho. He had ruled in a disintegrating world for nearly five years now, from the death of Theodosius in 395 far on into this closing year of the century.

There was no one in Constantinople, there was no one else in the West, who was trying to hold the actual Empire together. Eudoxia was simply going to enjoy her pinnacle of opportunity to fulfill sensate desires and female vanities. Serena was trying to prolong what was already dead, the rule of Theodosius. But Stilicho was trying to mend and build with what we actually had. I began to realize why the gray thickened in his hair and why the lines deepened in his large good face.

Stilicho, a Barbarian, was the last of the Romans.

And why did he stand, so stalwart, alone?

It was reading Augustine's *Confessions* that revealed to me, with a slow deep shock, the answer to that question.

Of course I remembered Augustine from nearly twenty years before, lean, dark, tense, passionate, restless. As I read his book I heard his voice, with its African accent, and saw his gestures, and his swift sharp eyes flashed in my memory.

At first I found his theologizing rather tedious, often like a recitation by rote. But the form of the book shocked me. I had never read anything like it. Men write books to one another, not to God, although the good book is always one in which a man tells other men what he knows about God or how he has been seeking God. But here was a man telling his story to God direct. There seemed to me an impiety in this self-election of a man for so long a gossip with God. God, it seemed to me, might in His infinite wisdom be bored by so long a personal prattle, with its esoteric and even feverish passages. I, in my mortal limitations, was fascinated. I read by the hour. I rather suspected Augustine of using a literary device, that is, of addressing his confessions to God so as the better to be heard by men. It was a bold outrageous break with all the traditions of elegance.

Then, in addition, I soon found that Augustine was, like Petronius and Apuleius, a good storyteller; and it was exciting to read a good story about persons and places of my own time and known to me. There were Rome and Carthage and Milan, Ambrose, old Simplician and Augustine himself, so vivid in memory: above all, Augustine, the passionate one, telling God, Whom he had found ("late have I loved Thee!"), of his tormenting search for God.

"Ha!" I said to myself. "Here is a great Roman writer to stand beside Claudian! One good poet and one good prose writer could revive Latin letters and give the Roman world its voice and vision again!" I was really excited. I planned to write Augustine a letter.

Often a man reads a book not for what is in it, but for what he is seeking or would like to say or promote himself; and so I read Augustine's *Confessions*, seeking signs of a Roman renascence. But for all his vigorous inelegancies of style, Augustine is a dangerous man to read for your own purposes rather than for his. Soon I realized he was not telling his story with the charming salaciousness of Petronius or with the ribald aesthetic delight of Apuleius. This man was not making a joke of himself to entertain the public, nor, like Claudian, Cicero or Virgil, pleasing empires or republics. This man had staked his life on what he wrote, and that was another matter.

It takes a great accumulation of suffering to write a good book, and all a man's suffering must be enlightened by the spiritual sanity of a sense of God before he writes his good book. Those who deny their suffering or throw it away or utter it rude without the sanity of spiritual enlightenment can tell us nothing. Augustine had gathered all his suffering into the mighty struggle of his own spirit, had achieved the enlightenment of an irrevocable sense of God and the warmth of human compassion; then he wrote his book. Inasmuch as a book is only great in so far as it deals with God, I began to realize that this was the greatest personal book I had ever read. I knew then the smallness of Claudian, and knew then of myself what it was to be a little man of scant account.

It was my misfortune that I began to judge the book before I was matured in spirit, but it was my fortune to love it. It became my book for years, and the growth began of an indomitable desire to see Augustine himself face to face again—but this is by way of things to come. There in Constantinople, not having yet dared let it be known in public that I had had myself baptized on an island in the Aegean Sea, I began to realize that, despite the surface crudities of overstated sentiment, here at the core of this book, confessing God to the world, at the core of the man Augustine, was a great intelligence at work. And it was God, not Christ, he had found.

I began writing my letter to Augustine, aglow to praise his book. After greeting him and reminding him that he had been my tutor a short while when I was a boy, arousing a personal affection that I still felt for him, I stopped. I couldn't write any more. For I saw now how he had set up the great weight of his intellect and the deep passion of his heart against the ways and continuance of our Roman world. Had he not made it vivid that he thought to hold official position as a master of rhetoric was to be worse off than a drunken beggar on the streets of Milan? It was a profoundly subversive book, as bad for the Empire as an army of Barbarians in the heart of Italy.

It was all the more powerful and persuasive for being not a logical work of reason, but a passionate, sensuous re-creation of deeply experienced joys and anxieties of life, illuminated in the focus of a brilliant imagination. Though written in prose, its essence was poetry, intense and disturbing. For it cried out, as in a great song, directly to the emotions: "Behold, Romans! I have lived your life and found it rotten almost to the very death of my soul!" Like all great art, it spoke directly to the individual man: "Behold, Gregory! I lived the very life you are trying to live and found it rotten almost to the death of my soul!" Again, as great poetry, it was one of those books which, once read, can never be extirpated from the fabric of your life, because of its impassioned appeal to the whole emotional man. When a fellow man cries out from his heart, we never forget him.

To respond to Augustine's book and also love Rome was to be a divided soul. I don't know how long I had been such a divided soul, but the *Confessions* of Augustine made me shockingly conscious of my own inward schism. Being unable to write him a simple letter, I took refuge and comfort in looking forward to a long discussion with Claudian of Augustine's new and vivid estimate of the lives we led. Claudian, with his dark ironic genius, would help me hold my own against the subversive power of Augustine's passion and intelligence.

But how could Claudian's poems, perverted to voice the pride of the Roman world, stand up against this new great voice of the Catholic world? Our perversion of Claudian made him now seem all the more the dying-away sound of a ruined age. Augustine was the great new voice and spokesman for living men, and Rome was not his theme.

This is but a frail glance of my lesser mind toward the deeps of so great a book, a book which speaks for itself with wonderful intelligence of a man's whole heart and world and hope of heaven.

But even by this glance I saw what had happened and why Stilicho stood alone, the last Roman administrator, and why Claudian stood alone, the last Roman poet.

The great intelligences had abandoned Rome and fled into the Church: Ambrose, Jerome, Augustine, Chrysostom, even the less notable Paulus of Nola; and before them men like Origen and my distant Greek relative, Gregory of Nanzianzus. All of them might, as it were, have looked at Rome's proffered honors, shaken their heads, and used the words of Bishop Gregory: "No, thanks. We have not time to offend God!" This was indeed a calamity. Any age which has four or five truly great intelligences has the creative potential of being a great age, an age of restoration and rebirth. Why had they fled? Why had they abandoned Rome?

I came upon the dreadful thought that no great intelligence can flourish except upon a sound moral base of resolute faith. Men like me, of minor intelligence, could still retain a sufficient faith in Rome to act and, in our small way of day-to-day half solutions of increasing problems, somewhat flourish, even though secretly anxious and sick at heart. But Augustine, Ambrose, Gregory of Nanzianzus, with their more penetrating minds, saw the rotten sand beneath the apparent stone. To stay there, for them, would be to go mad or to resign themselves to a ruined silence or—as Claudian was doing—to accept and participate in corruption. For great intelligences the past is not enough, neither is the present; they are bound up in the process of reality leading on into the future, and some sense of eternity in them seeks eternal value in all trivia of time. More terrible than the inroads of Barbarians, more terrible than internal political particularism, was this obvious flight of our great intelligences out of the Roman civil world. When the few truly great minds of the time reject the common principles accepted as a basis for action by the common people of that time, I think that age is drawing to a dark end.

I made a distinction, too, between great intelligences and those bitter minds which hate a society and try to destroy it, using any base or violent means. They are of the brood of destroyers and tyrants, moved, by hatred, toward dark fellowship with anger. Great minds are always illuminated and moved by the intelligence of love.

Stilicho—whose love of Rome was great, but whose spirit was injured by the domination of Serena and whose mind was only practical, not creative—stood alone against massive and treacherous disintegration of the Empire. There had been a sense in which Ambrose, from his bishop's throne, had held the civil world together, but Ambrose was dead.

In Augustine's book I also saw in a new way what women were doing. I was astonished in the *Confessions* by the revelation of the guiding prominence in his life of his mother Monica. I had met his mistress and his son when he tutored me in Rome; I had not met his mother, and he had not even mentioned her to me. Now it was clear, on his own evidence, that she was the ruling spirit in his life. Of course there had before now been men dominated by their mothers; once in a while such a man rose to prominence. For nearly a thousand years the strong Roman mother had taught her son the path of honor, courage and public service, and for a thousand years the Roman father had been the true father and master of the family. Now here was Monica teaching her son to despise the world, to avoid any career of public honor, and to despise his own father in favor of God. I got an impression that somehow or other Augustine's mother had made him ashamed of himself—I mean, ashamed of his actual being—from his childhood on. She had imputed dishonor

to the early motions of his soul, especially any least motion toward freedom from her—and what more painful torment could a mother possibly
lay on the soul of her son? His sexual distress, I thought, was the symbol
rather than the heart and reality of his torn spirit's strife to overcome
this maternal denigration and to achieve the freedom of an integrated
manhood.

But lest I probe, with crude assertions, beyond my depth, let me warn
myself in Augustine's own words: "Man is a great deep, Lord. You number his very hairs, and they are not lost in Your sight: but the hairs of his
head are easier to number than his affections and the movements of his
heart"—or, as Paul before him spoke, "No man knows the things of a
man, save the spirit of man that is in him."

How dangerous it is for a mother to intrude upon the soul of her son!
Women were assuming a new role. Monica was one, Serena was another, Marcellina the sister of Ambrose a third, Eudoxia, Galla Placidia,
that good old Christian woman Faltonia Proba, and soon—when she
grew older—Pulcheria, daughter of Eudoxia: These women were making
it their business to help the Empire down to death.

I saw the dark age coming—the Empire broken in fragments, culture
sinking to brutishness, vast order converted to a disorder of violence and
rapine. And it seemed to be the new business of women to help the Empire down to this death. For there is a sense in which men create an
empire and women bring it to a close. Perhaps women have a stronger
faith than men in the dark inner mystery of gestation and are less afraid
to face a new dark age. I did not know the answer to such a question,
but this was my conjecture: When women step forward out of their role
of fertility to compete with men in worldly affairs, to seize dominant positions or (like Monica) to turn men aside from the world's work, they
have sensed both that men have lost faith and that the form of society
has grown sterile and destructive. They come forward to finish that society off, for when men have lost faith and a society is destructive, the
meaning of gestation is threatened, and a dark age fertile with possibilities of regeneration is better than bringing children into a way of life
that has lost faith and lost meaning.

I never met an intelligent active woman who said things like this; they
usually flared up in resentment when I said them. But why was it that
in our time so many and many of our finest women rejected motherhood
as their primary role, competed with men, sought position and power
and offered themselves at their infertile periods for adultery (correcting
their errors by miscarriage or abortion) or, conversely, as Christians, as
Manicheans or in some other sect, consigned themselves to outright vir-

ginity, urging men to do the same? Why? I myself was persuaded that there must have been a deep powerful urge in the women of our time to bring the Roman Empire to an end. They certainly acted as if they were sick of it.

This general vision right or wrong, of the ruin we faced, of the crumbling within the shell of Empire, of the flight of great intelligences out of the Roman civil world, and of the new mortal ministrations of women, was my own, and it shocked me profoundly. I was a lover of the world, of Rome, and did not rejoice in adumbrations of its death. It gave me a sense of unreality, of being ineffectual, as if there were a dark void both in the Empire and in myself, a void surrounded by a shell of such tension that it seemed impossible to avert a shambles of disintegration, violence and ruin. The whole bright Roman world would become a thousand dark and broken disparate pieces, with no center of aspiration, no place of order and no society for civilization, with every private life rendered greedy like the blind mouth of a suckling pig.

Stilicho, I said to myself, is our last hope. Stilicho must make himself the true Emperor of the whole Empire. I am going to help Stilicho hold together what we have, through this crisis, as long as we can hold it! I thought the year 400 should be the beginning of Stilicho's reign as Emperor.

I sailed from Constantinople in a stern and resolute spirit. I thought I might return to the East, not as a mistrusted and insulted ambassador, but as Stilicho's proconsul, or even, so that my father's prophecy might be fulfilled, as Stilicho's co-Emperor in the East. On this sailing I grieved again for the death of my son, and I longed for my warm return to Marcia's side. It was the first time since our marriage nearly seven years ago that I had been so long away from her. It had stretched into an absence of seven months, and I missed her good laughter and tender dark eyes. So it was that I sailed with resolution and hopes toward home.

But on the voyage home, instead of that serene sense of poise between time and time which on the voyage out had so purified and rested me that I had asked for and received Christian baptism, I fought a heart-searching struggle brought on by my spiritual re-encounter with Augustine. For the deepest and most lasting shock of Augustine's *Confessions*, which I read again and savored slowly during the voyage, was the clarity with which it revealed to me my own spiritual condition. I always had a tough, a tenacious temperament. I always clung fiercely to what I was, in spite of the powerful draw of what I was becoming, and clung to each new thing I became even as this newness labored to displace the old. Sometimes I thought my spirit was like a big ball of fighting dogs rolling down a hill, snapping at one another's bellies and throats and legs as they rolled in tumultuous tumble, and all of them good dogs, too. Sometimes I really had to laugh to endure myself.

At any rate, I clung to what I loved in Paganism, I clung to my love of Rome, and I clung to my baptism. I decided I would tell no one in Milan that I had been baptized a Christian, not because I was ashamed of that act—I held it to be one of the good acts of my life—but because Augustine's book showed me so clearly that I was too far away from seeing God to set myself up publicly as one who had found God. I wanted passionately to lay aside death and see God; but in the great cadences of Augustine's spiritual book it was made clear to me that I did not yet know how to say what he said: "Let me not be my own life: of myself I lived evilly, and to myself I was death." Nor was I able to say to the Divine Guest, "Grant what you command, command what you will."

However much I might regret some of my doings and try to improve them, however much I was misled by my reason and tried to reason better, however much I was blinded by my will and tried to enlighten that will, I just did not find it in my nature to despise my life, reject my reason, or abandon my will. Perhaps I was one who would always know that God was near, who would always seek Him, but I would never cry out: "I have found Thee!" Somehow, to my mind, the teachings of Christ were so lovely and his agony (like that of Eutropius) was so great that I felt it would be a deep impiety in me, as I was, to go about saying: "I am a Christian." Not even when I became a bishop in Spain were these problems solved for me.

Then on a day, suddenly, I saw that Augustine was a child, and that cheered me. The book lay on my lap, and my mind had been ranging over his wonderful discussions of time and of memory. The powerful purity of his intelligence enabled me to perceive what I had never even guessed before, that time was relative to space and motion. He would discuss such a problem with the scientific acumen of an Aristotle and then convert mere knowing into pure wonder. How he did this with his study of memory was even more remarkable; he studied the deeps of the mind, not for operational knowledge, but to find the filaments of a man with eternity.

My musing must have made some sort of intuitive leap, for suddenly I said: At last the child in his heart found his father, and in that his manhood, and became whole.

Once, as a small boy, when I came with my father from Spain back to Rome, I was taken with earache. Now, all at once, that scene was present in my memory. I lay on a couch in a room where the bull of Mithra was painted on the wall—in Marsalia—and my father himself stooped over and dropped three drops of warm olive oil into my ear and eased the pain. As I saw myself there and my father bending over me I could see I lay on my right side, so it was my left ear which received the drops of soothing oil, and the pain was in my left ear, and I like Augustine was at heart a child. The very fact that I could remember on which side I lay and which ear suffered revealed to me how the original child dwells and persists throughout life in the man; the whole of life is added to the original child and nothing is absolutely lost to the wondrous accumulating memory. But by immense labor of his spirit the child in Augustine's heart had recovered from the dishonor imputed to him by his mother. I was not yet free of—I knew not what. But I was convinced that a man remains a child in the deep and striving places of his soul, and there he is a child of God, Who is the only adequate Father of so pure and radiant a wonder.

I wanted very much to go to Africa to see Augustine again, face to face. I might well persuade Stilicho to send me to Africa for one purpose or another. I would take Marcia with me. I wanted to ask Augustine questions, I wanted to toil with him, face to face and mind to mind, and out of that toil come perhaps nearer to my seeking and my need.

Thus, physically rested, perhaps more mature and spiritually somewhat changed, but with inner tension and stress, I reached Milan. The desire of a husband, after long absence from his wife, was strong in me.

I found Marcia piling up her hair and singing softly to herself before a mirror. When she saw me reflected in the mirror she turned abruptly, and her lips parted in a cry that was not of joy. She was afraid of my coming and avoided my embrace. At first she showed an assertive new defiance, as if she, too, had changed during seven months, becoming more positive and daring in her own right. She clasped her hands behind her back, lifted her chin, and defied me.

I closed the door of our private room, stood with my arms open, and said, "Come. I want to kiss you."

After a moment her chin began to tremble; she turned her face away from me and wept. She said she was not well and could not share my bed, and she watched me with fright. So great a disappointment roused my anger, and I demanded a reasonable explanation. Marcia stood before me, her face red and swollen with anguish she could not utter. She looked at me with that terrible dark-eyed sorrow of an animal about to be slaughtered. She laid one open hand three times against the garment over her belly in a slow frightened little gesture.

That gesture set off a blaze of revelation in my mind; in the stunning flash of it I saw standing like a dark figure of bitter fate the only one who could have been there. I cried out his name: "Claudian!"

Marcia buried her face in her hands and sobbed. She was with child by Claudian.

Claudian had cried out in the night of the world, and Marcia had heard his cry of horror in the dark. And she had tried to comfort him on the space of her breast with the warmth of her heart.

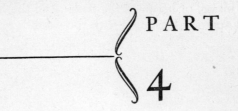

PART

4

THE MURDERER

OF STILICHO

CHAPTER ONE

WAR IN ITALY

SERENA SUMMONED ME. HER USUALLY COOL GRAY EYES HAD
an icy coldness. She did not offer her hand for me to kiss. She let me
linger down on my knee before her a long time while she imposed on
me an imperious gaze of repressed anger. She held her lips pinched; the
planes and angles showing in her face reminded me of the great Theodosius. But, unlike him, she looked tragic rather than splendid. Beside
her stood Olympius, who was an officer in the army but conducted himself as if he were some sacrosanct priest.

Olympius smiled at me and was the first to speak. "We have heard,
Count Julian, that you have had yourself baptized a Christian. This is
high good news." His voice was gracious, soothing.

I knew the pious Olympius, but I was surprised to find that during
my absence he had made enough progress to be, as it were, an unofficial
minister to Serena. This man, in time so fatal to her husband, now
seemed to have her confidence. Olympius was a man whose buttocks
jounced as he walked; at the public baths you would never find him near
the cold plunge but always at the hot pool or in the steam room. He was
very publicly a Christian. In his carefully built reputation for piety he
was as near to being a monk as a layman could come. But his aims were
political. He was the soft insinuant counterpart to Heraclian's hard
practical opportunism, and while Heraclian was still in Gaul, Olympius
had been working upward toward leadership of the Christian party. Good
old Simplician, the new bishop, trusted him in political matters. He was
fat about the eyes and fat about the mouth, but his nose was sharp, and
he had a sharp knob of a chin. His hair was remarkably black and glistened
like an oily shield on his head. He would never have fooled Ambrose;
Ambrose would have read the inner man of Olympius' heart from his
waddle, his voice and the pseudo-pious play of his hands.

Olympius had beautiful hands and kept them very clean and made
lovely practiced gestures with them, but if you watched him a long time

275

you realized he almost never touched another human being with those beautifully formed immaculate hands. It was as if he adored the purity of his own hands and would not defile them by touching brother humanity. Indeed, men are strange in their personal rites and symbols and peculiar necessities. I knew for a fact that Olympius had had a sculptor take a mold of his remarkable hands and then cast them in gold, and he kept these gold replicas on an ebony table in his house, like divine golden birds come to rest on a mirror-black pool.

I was not going to deny what I had done. I answered him. "I have made no announcement of my baptism. That is my private affair."

"You are too modest about such a good deed. Hide not your light under a bushel. Luckily the Church takes care of her own. Our bishops correspond with one another, you know. The baptism of a Count by a small priest is worth writing to Milan about, especially when Saint Ambrose himself miraculously helped in the sacrament. And many private matters—" he paused, looked at Serena—"become public knowledge."

Serena spoke now. "You may stand, Count Julian."

It was cold; for years she had addressed me as Gregory.

"I thank Your Serenity."

She spoke with a clipped severity. "It is good you have become a Christian. It is a pity you waited so long. It is quite proper for a Christian to put his wife away for adultery."

Olympius interrupted. "I have persuaded Her Serenity that a man of your ability, newly converted to our faith, need not be lost to great work through the sin of another."

I was still in a state of moral shock, verging, I think, on insanity of the temporary raging sort. If I had not been in the imperial presence of Serena, I would have struck Olympius down with my fist. It took the utmost coldness I could summon to stifle my fury.

"The matter is not simple," Serena said. "At our request the poet Claudian is leaving Milan to take up residence at Rome. An adulterous woman is not fit company for the Emperor and Empress, nor for us, nor for our children. She must leave the palace. Your public usefulness may not have come to an end, providing you divorce her. You need no more time than today, Count Julian, to move from here to your villa. But perhaps you have sins of your own to confess and atone for; you may need a week or two to decide on your future. Communicate with Olympius."

She was deadly. Her cold repressed anger was deadly. I stood there, looking directly into her eyes. She fought me off with the full force of her will so that I could not, or would not dare, penetrate to the real depth of her suffering. She had not hesitated to probe my wound and to deal the blow before Olympius; but she was using all the majesty of her Theodosian grandeur to shield herself from my perceptions. There were other adulterous women at court besides Marcia. It was Claudian —Her Serenity's poet Claudian—who had betrayed her, as Marcia had betrayed me.

It would have been the part of political wisdom for me to accept her dismissal, bow, and leave at once. But I had already looked too deeply into her eyes. I had seen, and she knew I had seen, the anguish of her heart. Actually my awareness of her pain comforted my rage. I had the audacity to speak to her in language she would understand but Olympius would not.

"Your Serenity may remember how once on some rocks above a village by the sea we discussed Helen and Dido and the vision of poets. I always believed in the depth of Dido's heart, and I am reminded now of how Aeneas met her in the underworld, fresh from her death wound, and how her burning and fierce-eyed spirit turned away from his pleading of love and regret."

Serena had risen. There seemed to be both fire and tears in her gray eyes now. She parted her lips as if to speak to me, then gave me a wild, a frightened look, and yet a look strangely lighted with gratitude, the look not of a queen but of a woman whose heart was touched and who wanted to cry out.

She did cry out. "Go, Gregory. And God forgive us both!" Then she swept from the room before I could move.

Olympius stood there in astonishment. He raised his hands in pious amazement, bringing them almost together as for prayer. I reached out swiftly, seized both his hands in mine, and, squeezing them as hard as I could, smiled wickedly and thanked him for favoring me. With my considerable strength I continued to crush those precious hands of his until his cheeks paled and tears came into his eyes. It was one of the few times I had ever acted with direct malicious physical cruelty toward a fellow human being. I certainly was not sane while I administered torture to his adored hands. I gave him intense physical pain, but also, I am sure, spiritual pain even more wounding.

I was insane for months, really. A certain dangerous brilliance and rapidity of public affairs gave me plenty to do with the outward appearance of sanity; but underneath my superficial show of practical skill I was a man in spiritual collapse, rent by jealousy, wrath, despair, dreaming of murder, dreaming of suicide or steeped through, during long sleepness nights, by paralyzing misery. I did not report back to Olympius about what I was doing or intended to do. I worked out my political fate by other means, directly with Stilicho. I also warned Stilicho that I thought Olympius was treacherous.

"I need treacherous men, too, to run an Empire," Stilicho said.

I removed Marcia at once from the palace to my villa outside the city. I told her with bitter eloquence what ruin she had brought upon me, shattering my love, betraying my honor, and ruining my career. She was hurt, she was frightened, and she wept.

"This is no new thing," I accused her. "It happens you got pregnant at last. It may have been going on for years. How long have you loved Claudian?"

"I didn't love him. And it is your adulteries that have gone on for years, not mine."

"I suppose Livia is Claudian's child, too, not mine?"

"She's not his. Livia is your child. I never loved Claudian."

I found out that jealousy, like lust, fills a man's mind with vivid carnal images. But I had always been the hero of my images of lust, and now I was the betrayed and outraged fool of these odious images of jealousy in which not I but another man closed with my wife.

There would be little spiritual enlightenment in describing the degrading sullen scenes between us. Marcia insisted her adultery was no worse than mine. Adultery was adultery. She refused to see that her bearing another man's child was a worse insult to my honor than Amantha's bearing me a child was to her honor. Amantha, I pointed out, was a slave. I didn't really believe Livia was Claudian's child, but I kept demanding that Marcia tell me how long she had loved Claudian.

"I don't love him. I never loved him. I love you."

"What do you call it, then? You're not cheap. You're not common. But you did sleep with him. God knows how many times. You love him."

"It came like death. Like madness. For both of us it was an evil fate."

She refused to confess that she loved Claudian. On this point her whole character asserted itself. She turned on me, she defied me. "He and I were meant to destroy each other. All right, we've destroyed each other. But I never loved him."

Finally I asserted the authority of a Roman husband. I arranged for Marcia's sequestration in a private part of my house. I gave her my ultimatum. "You will stay secluded here until you are ready to confess that you love Claudian."

"Then what will you do, murder me?"

"You admit it?"

"It's a lie. I don't love him. I don't even hate him. He's a stranger. We were snatched down to hell."

"I'll keep you shut up in here until you confess everything."

She stood with her hands behind her back and her chin lifted. "Divorce me if you want to. Kill me if you want to. I'll never tell that lie. I never loved any man but you."

I kept her in seclusion. Some evenings I tormented her there; sometimes for a week I did not go near her. She continued to defy me.

In public matters I several times warned Stilicho against Olympius.

"I don't trust Olympius," he said, "but I have to use him, favor him. We're on the edge of a religious civil war."

The situation was tense and extremely dangerous. Since the death of Theodosius, Stilicho had tried to put into effect a policy of toleration. Pagans had not been proscribed, their property had not been confiscated. They had regained first hope, then courage, then belligerence. The Catholic party wanted them wiped out. In the main there were the two parties. The Liberals clamored for religious tolerance, reopening of the Pagan temples and a ceasing of legal, political and financial favors to Christians. The Catholics demanded renewed laws against all forms of Pagan worship. Either party was ready to plunge Italy and all the West into civil war on behalf of its own high principles.

"I need you, and I need Claudian," Stilicho told me. "Serena irritates me by messing up important political affairs with moral prejudices concerning private sexual matters. Claudian, however, will be of great service in Rome. He's there now working on a panegyric on my consulship. His poems have effect, and he knows how to strike the note of unity. I want to send you on a mission to Alaric."

Stilicho's consulship in the year 400 was an important matter. By contrast with the Eutropian blasphemy of the year before it would restore a sense of dignity and glory to Rome. And with a good dramatic sense, Stilicho was putting on a double ceremony, first in Milan, where the Catholics predominated, then in Rome, where the Pagans had more power. Milan was already filling up with patricians from Rome and all Italy, come to celebrate Stilicho's opening of the year. Then they and half of Milan would go back to Rome to repeat the affair on a more splendid scale.

Stilicho asked me a direct question. "We have the news of your baptism. Now you are a Christian. How is that going to affect your politics?"

"You are my politics, General."

"Good! That's what I need, a few sound men to help me hold this thing together. Heraclian is back."

"He's capable and not to be trusted."

"I'll watch him. You go deal with Alaric for me."

Heraclian was back from Gaul, working with Olympius, building for trouble. As soon as he came back Dionie divorced him. I saw her, and she told me about it. Knowing the character of their marriage and her character, I understood as quite sufficient the reason she gave as the true one for the divorce.

"Why, Gregory? It's very simple. I no longer like the black hair on the back of his hands."

She suggested that I had more than sufficient cause to divorce Marcia. "She needn't have let it go so far. An abortion would have been quite simple in the early stages. The longer you keep her, the more fool you make of yourself."

I was in no state of mind to be told by anyone what to do about Marcia. I kept her in enforced seclusion.

It was a rude and difficult journey at that time of year over through the Julian Alps into Illyricum, and I took only a small retinue with me because of the hard going.

Alaric, on a man-to-man basis, was glad to see me. He was splendid in the flush of power. As master general of Illyricum he had cowed all the officials sent out from Constantinople and was the real ruler of a great province. But he was a Barbarian and a warrior. He had greatly increased the military power of the Goths, but with the help of several bad seasons, he had brought the province to the verge of famine. The Goths ate a lot more food than they raised. There had been a late summer drought. The coming spring and summer looked bad.

"You keep too big an army together," I said. "Spread your Goths out on the land, planting crops and raising pigs."

Politically Alaric was not so glad to see me. "Stilicho," he said, "would love to see my army weakened."

"You're a better man than Gainas. Why don't you move back toward Moesia and Constantinople? There's food there, and it will relieve the famine pressure here."

"There's food in Italy."

"Also, Stilicho is in Italy."

We watched each other.

"You talk common sense, Gregory, like some of my older chiefs. You forget, I am an uncommon man."

"A man of great intelligence, of great audacity, of great vigor. Still, all men are fated; and only Stilicho is fated to have the impregnable might of Rome behind him."

Alaric in part saw reason. He planned an expedition into Moesia. "Once my food supply is improved," he said, "I'll be all the more able to share Stilicho's power with him."

There was a magic in the name of Rome. Master general though he was in a great province of the Eastern Empire, Alaric had never yet satisfied or outgrown his ambition to be one of the top generals of Rome. And he was still haunted by the prophecy in the forest, that he should be king of the Goths and penetrate into the City. Alaric was not a man of cunning and deceit. His blue eyes had the blaze of honest force. "Tell Stilicho that the time will come for him to share power with me, or, as the gods have ordained, I shall take it."

"The first noise of your wagons in Italy will unify the whole of the West against you."

I returned to Milan too late to go to Rome for the celebration there of Stilicho's consulship. And I returned to an empty house. That is, Marcia and Livia had gone. She had left a letter, saying:

Do not blame any of the slaves. They could not stop me. I am taking Livia to Rome. I will no longer embarrass you. You are jealous and stupid and stubborn. I still love you and hate the injury I have done you and will never love any other man.

What everybody in Milan was thinking was obvious: Marcia had run off to Rome to be with Claudian, her lover. I had a climactic storm of my insanity at this new defiance and insult, and while it was boiling up my mind I fulfilled the formalities of sending messengers to Marcia in Rome announcing to her that our marriage was over, we were now divorced, and neither of us had any further claim on the other's person or property.

She sent back word, still defiant:

I accept your divorce, as I must. Marry whom you please. I have married once and will have no other husband. But I don't want you back, either.

The blow that began really to tell was this: Marcia, scarcely more than a child when I had married her, had somehow developed a will and integrity of her own, had defied my wrath and my punishment, and of her own free will and on her own terms had left me. The frenetic fever of my jealousy and self-torment subsided, and I went running about on my lean legs in a state of burning inner sorrow. The depth of my sadness exceeded expression; it was not reasonable and it was not sane. Still, I lived with it.

In desperation I had secret inquiries made in Rome, and I was informed beyond doubt that Marcia never saw Claudian. She lived in the Probus—or Anician—Palace with good old Faltonia Proba. If she had carried on her affair with Claudian, I might have taken refuge in anger. But there was no refuge from the clarity of this rejection. I made ready to go to Rome to talk to her; but, having already divorced her, I was at the last too proud to make such a fool of myself. She is dead, I told myself.

I might have taken legal steps to force her to restore Livia to me, but I didn't want a child, and I didn't want revenge. It never occurred to me that our young daughter Livia might be the real tragic victim of our anger and our failure.

Surely the worm of death was in my heart. Whatever my life was, I was not contented. I woke in the morning hating and fearing the day. What shall a man do, once he knows the worm is in his heart? And what is this worm in the heart but lust for the majestic power of death? During those years I lived by persistence rather than by hope and by patience rather than in pleasure. I was a stranger among people, because I lived a stranger to myself. I lived by one lie and another from one day to another, working at my own slow self-destruction. I went to the monastery Ambrose had established just outside Milan and spent a week there, toying with the notion of renouncing the world and becoming a monk. The place was physically clean, morally ascetic and intellectually squalid. I got some rest and saw I was ridiculously unfitted for such a life. I took Dionie to Lake Como for a week, but would not take her near the villa where Marcia and I had been so deeply moved by love. Such a trip with Dionie, skilled at pleasure, was physically refreshing, intellectually stimulating and morally squalid. I came back realizing that I did not want to marry Dionie, but pleased with my ability to interest and enjoy such a woman. Even so, when I had to be alone in my villa I would fall into the dark house of my own soul and would cry in my spirit: What is the use of living?

I would say now that a man's God-relationship is his primary or only native wealth, and I was then trading mine off as fast as I could for despair.

Despair may wear the crown of success; despair is a hard driver of an active man and makes him get a lot done to forget himself.

It is rarely that other men are interested in the state of your soul: They want to know which side you are on. I've seen men tried, condemned, and executed for seeking truth instead of taking sides. This human practice is older than Christ or Socrates, and still goes on. As for me, my truth seeking was at a low ebb, and taking sides in public affairs is always an easy way of seeming to avoid the grave and painful problem of enlightening the soul. To avoid dwelling on my intolerable private uncertainties, darkness and lack of truth to live by, I worked out the side-taking matter with Stilicho; and to be of the most possible apparent use to the endangered Empire, I became active in the Catholic party, but counter to Heraclian and Olympius. I set up what I called the Liberal Catholics. The word "liberal" in politics is generally a lie, for power and power seeking are not by nature liberal. A few creative natures, those who give, those who are humble, those who love, are liberal. They form no party. On the larger scale, looking beyond Italy, it was becoming obvious that the real leader of Catholic policy, since the death of Ambrose, was going to be Augustine of Hippo. Olympius corresponded with him. I loved Augustine, the God-seeking poet of the *Confessions*, and I could not bear to seek out the lower man of politics.

At the moment he was engaged in a bitter struggle in Africa against the Donatists. It was a fight not over doctrine so much as over political control of the Catholic Church in Africa. In certain realms of the spirit Augustine had creative liberality, but in the politics of the world and the Church he set a tone of tyrannical authority. His slogan was: Unity in matters of importance, tolerance on minor matters and charity in all affairs. But he meant it to be understood that the Catholic Church alone had divine inspiration sufficient to decide which matters demanded the obedience of unity, which could bear toleration of differences and what was meant by charity. In the matter of the Donatists, for example, he called conclave after conclave of bishops until it was settled beyond doubt that the Catholic Church demanded unity against the Donatists, that no Donatists or their works would be tolerated and that it was the office of charity to send them off as quickly as possible to perpetual sojourn in hell. Further, though he denied the imperial power any right to interfere in affairs and decisions of the Catholic Church, he claimed it was the duty of the government to help effectuate Church decisions and, in this case, to issue edicts and employ civil powers against the damned Donatists.

The man knew what he was doing; he was building the Catholic Church up to pre-eminence, and he was a master builder. In my miserable eyes this was neither God seeking nor an imitation of Christ, but was serious and bitter human politics. Augustine's tone and influence reached Milan; it was felt in laws promulgated and edicts issued in the name of Emperor Honorius. I wrote some of them myself, denying here, granting there, trying to stave off the religious civil war which had already reached the pitch of riot in some less guarded communities. In one province the Liberals would seize and beat priests; in another the Catholics would pillage and burn a temple. As we temporized with this law, then with that law, the one party or the other would howl that Stilicho had betrayed them. My old enemy Florentinus was one of the leaders of the Liberal, or Pagan, party. He had my name down on his list for murder when the time came, and in like manner Heraclian and Olympius had the name of Florentinus along with mine on their list of death.

Nobody wanted justice; all just wanted power. And unfortunately the people of Italy were getting poorer and more dependent all the time. Powerful governments or churches or parties need a lot of money to feed their strength, and they end by taking away from the people their money and means of independence. Nobody wanted independence or integrity; all just wanted power.

Then Alaric came to our rescue.

Alaric's venture into Moesia had failed. There he had meant to join up with Gainas, but he was too late. Gainas was murdered before Alaric could reach him. Alaric picked up new contingents of Goths and came rumbling back toward Italy. He made a small foray over into Venetia to see if Italy would shudder. Italy, rent by party strife, was so busy asserting the political rights of conflicting religious passions that it was like a crazy dog which furiously bites itself and neither sees nor smells the approach of the lion. Alaric withdrew to prepare a more massive return and onslaught.

Stilicho thought of recalling some legions from Britain and Gaul. But it was dangerous, for those men up there loved power, too.

I suggested, "We know Alaric. The people don't and won't believe it. All they want is to break heads over religion. They need the thing dramatized. Let's start to raise an army. Conscription makes a loud noise that will wake Italy up."

Under Stilicho's guidance I worked out a set of orders for levying troops. We canceled all kinds of long-standing exemptions from military service, taking into the army even undertakers and minor clergy. The Christians complained the loudest, but in no time at all Italy became aware of the giant menace of Alaric on the border. And to make this awareness hold fast we instituted a program which forced all important cities, from Ravenna and Aquileia to Rome, to set to work repairing old walls and building new ones. Wall building would keep the threat of war and invasion dramatized for a couple of years, if need be.

The internal threat of religious civil war seemed to die down, and Italy appeared at last superficially unified. Appearances are wonderful. At the public baths in Milan one day, as I came from the cold plunge toward the warm pool, I saw Olympius and Heraclian together with Florentinus and another leader of the Pagan Liberals, and I joined them as a fifth member, "Stilicho's man, Count Julian!" We sat there, fresh and naked, at the warm pool, then in the steam room. We laughed and talked together like a group of friends and even scratched one another's backs for the good feel of it. Being notables, we were noted, and the news spread through Milan and beyond of an amicable coalition of all parties against Alaric. We didn't mention politics, but the rumor spread of our "Conference at the Baths," and within two weeks as far off as Rome people were repeating "the very words of the Bath Agreement." Pagan met Christian in the Forum and shook hands on it: "Italy against Alaric! Unite!"

Such affairs have convinced me it is silly to complain that the world is deceived by appearances; we have nothing else to go by but appearances. No matter how far you refine your analysis, even down to the atom of an atom (like Democritus and Lucretius), the most minute premise you have left is still an appearance. In the end and in the beginning a man acts on his intuitive belief in what he deems to be the truth in appearance. Thus when we and the world are deceived it is not the appearance but our own inadequate intuition of truth that deceives us. All the truth is there all the time, if only we could see it. All I have to do at any time or any place or in my relations with any other human being is to ask myself Pilate's question: "What is truth?"—and then, not wash my hands, but stake my life and my soul on my own answer.

Because this is so simple and so perfect, and I and other men are so frail and so self-deceiving, the best we can say is, "God is truth," and the best we can do is to seek Him. In most of the business of my life, which is a good example of energy and fortune and folly, I have been, like Pilate, asking "What is truth?"—then washing my hands and following the most comfortable self-deception I could devise. It has been different— richer, deeper, maturing and creative—those too few times when I have stood fast and labored, knowing I was seeking God—even though I did not find Him. For some strange reason the mistakes a man makes in a sincere search for God do not sicken his soul, but strengthen it with hope for new seeking; while the errors of indifference, like the errors of arrogance, corrupt his soul. And from beginning to end the sum of all appearance is the circumstantial evidence of God.

Winter came on again. In Stilicho's behalf I had agents working for me in Alaric's camp. They brought me news that Alaric had sent troublemakers into Germany to rouse the Gothic peoples there. We could see the unfolding of a large plan: The two great columns of Barbarians would debouch upon Italy, one from the North, the other, under Alaric, from the East.

"I must pacify the Rhine," Stilicho said. "That is our real frontier."

We could also have agreed that our frontier was off in the heart of Asia, where the Huns initiated pressure that set up waves of violence against Rome. There is a kind of terrible comedy when an Empire hollow at heart worries about its remote frontiers. This was late winter of 402; within eight years we would worry about the very walls of Rome.

Alaric made his first move sooner than we expected. Coming up over the Pear Tree Pass in the Julian Alps, his wagons and horsemen blotted out the stars. They came down and gathered like doom in those eastern hollows on the fringe of Italy. This time Italy shuddered, and the dark reverberation of fear crossed the plain toward Milan and rumbled down the Apennines to Rome. Terror began in the palace. Olympius instilled fear into Honorius. The Emperor wanted to flee. Stilicho would not hear of such a disgrace to Italy and the great name of Rome. Despite Serena, he summoned Claudian to Milan.

"Gregory, I have to go to the Rhine and stop that revolt and get back here before Alaric strikes. He will have to wait till after the spring floods. I count on you to hold Milan. It's a matter of moral courage. You will have to forget your personal feelings and work with Claudian. He fears nothing on this earth and can write announcements to the people of clarion courage."

Stilicho left with a small band, traversing frozen lakes, threading Alpine gorges in the monstrous grip of winter, and we did not know if we would see him again. Claudian came. Our friendship lay like a dead cold body on the floor between us. We worked together in a sort of fierce and bitter endeavor. In all that had to be done I never misunderstood him and he never failed me. I was, for some dangerous weeks, political master of Milan, was in effect Emperor pro tem. For the first time in about two years I returned to live in the palace. What surprised me most was that Serena trusted me and counted on me. We both knew that if Alaric struck before Stilicho returned, Milan would be in mortal danger.

Every Council meeting was a demand to remove the court to Genoa, to Sicily or up to Arles in Gaul. The fear had thickened as far as Rome, where many who could fled to Corsica, to Sardinia, to Sicily and even to Africa. The great turgid generality, who end by facing and enduring what comes, were of two minds: The Pagan group put hope in walls, in Stilicho's return, in sheer brute resistance, while most of the Christians thought, apparently, it was about time for the world to end, and put their faith in God—but if they had any gold they buried it. And of course all this was accompanied by the usual real or imagined prodigies: Storms of unnatural violence struck, wolves abounded, monsters were born, stars fell, and the earth shook.

At every meeting of the Council I roared and beat the table and shouted down every form of cowardice that came up: "We stay in Milan! We stay in Milan!"

And after every meeting Serena encouraged me and thanked me. Once she clasped my hand and paid me the highest compliment (except for the final tragic one yet to come) I ever received from her. "Gregory, I was wrong to mistrust you. Theodosius was right to trust you."

Then, dropping my hand and looking thoughtfully down at her own hands, she said: "I love Stilicho. My heart is with him where perhaps he sleeps in some ice cave in the bitter mountains. My life has been strange. I love him; he is heroic; but I could never bear to let him take the place of Theodosius. I stopped him in Thessaly, again in Greece. Either time he could have destroyed Alaric and made himself Emperor along with the two boys. If he had, we wouldn't be in this trouble now. . . . Gregory, a thing you dared to say to me when no one else would have dared—about Dido . . ." She stopped. She thought a moment. "I love Stilicho the way Marcia always loved you. No woman loves Claudian, for his is a soul hurt in his childhood beyond a woman's healing."

It was a moment of candor, of confession, of honor between us. She was a great woman, though dark doom was her lot.

Alaric did not wait for Stilicho to return nor for the floods of spring to subside. He came on like a noise of disaster across the plain toward Milan, crossing the torrents and ravaging the land. I reinforced the gates, organized the food supply, and pressed citizens into volunteer troops to guard the walls. I put Heraclian in charge of the soldiers. It was his first taste of military power, and he liked it.

Alaric seized the bridge and both banks of the Adda.

He sent in his message. All he wanted of Honorius was to be made a Roman general, equal in rank to Stilicho, and to be given northern Italy, or perhaps Gaul, as a suitable place for his people, and then he would help Rome fight her enemies. Otherwise he would sack Milan and take Honorius hostage.

I answered him: "You know me. I know the impregnable might of Rome. Go back to Illyricum before we destroy you."

I know it was like telling a lion you would wring his neck if he didn't go away from your frail tent. But still I shouted in Council: "We stay in Milan!"

For the purposes of this and that decision I was not only master of the city, I was Emperor of Rome, and once I sat an hour thinking of the forlorn Honorius and of decisions I had to make in his name and of the greatness and complexity of Empire. I realized how frail a margin my intelligence had over his stupidity when it came to choosing what right thing to do and how to do it. But there was a margin. And I realized that without that margin of intelligence which enables a few men to make fewer or less fatal mistakes there would be no broad human society and no civilization. A few years later I found out that this margin of intelligence, if it be without moral soundness, is more cruel and corrupt than stupidity.

Someone started the rumor that Stilicho was dead, bringing new terror and demands for surrender into the city. I thought Olympius had done this, but could not prove it. I had two men executed for trying to set fire to the gates in the city wall. I made a speech to several thousand soldiers and people in the main square. My voice can be heard from a balcony and out over a square and carries a man in its tones, but it took me half an hour of dynamic self-projection to win the confidence of the crowd. Then I began to see my force take hold here and there and draw in larger groups; it was vital, like the spreading of blood in a field of cloth. At last I began to feel this mob response and the exhilarating enlargement—or, rather, inflation—of myself by the crowd's emotion. It was a good deep draught of the wine of power. It went right to my head, and I liked it.

For the better part of an hour what I told them with loud hypnotic insistence amounted to this: "We stay in Milan! If we give Alaric the city, it will shatter the courage of Italy and he'll take Rome, too. If we make him pay for every stone with blood, Milan will save Rome, and Rome will stand and destroy Alaric in the end. Let the cowards hide in their houses behind the shelter of their women. Let all true Romans stand ready to fight on the walls and in the streets. *We stay in Milan!*"

I was able to give new heart to the timid, but had not stopped the treacherous.

CHAPTER TWO

TRIUMPH AT ROME

MANY BELIEVED STILICHO WAS DEAD, FOR HE HAD UNDER-taken a stroke of peril and audacity, going with only a handful of followers into the midst of an angry rebellion, where the least slip was immediate death. It would have taken a bigger army than we could spare to quell the threatening Germans. To do nothing would certainly have brought them down upon us along with Alaric. If they hadn't murdered Stilicho outright, perhaps by policy, bribery, prestige and threat, he had pacified the angers there. We had no news, one way or the other, and fear darkened our confidence. I had already stopped two attempts by traitors to open the gates to Alaric. Heraclian wanted to betray the city and make a deal with Alaric.

Claudian was bitter about this. "I know Stilicho. He does not fail."

"All right," I said. "Prepare an announcement. Have copies made. Post it in the city. Name the day of Stilicho's return."

We glared at each other. Claudian sat at a table and made calculations. "It would require two more weeks for any lucky man. Stilicho is better than that. He'll be here in two days."

"I wish I could believe you, Claudian. There are a hundred treacherous ones willing to open the gates to Alaric. If they believe Stilicho is coming, they won't dare risk it. Two days is two days. Post the notice."

"It has to be worthy of Stilicho and carry a signature of authority. Will you risk your name and fate?"

"And if he doesn't come?"

"There will be a riot. The mob will murder you, and Heraclian will open the gates."

"Sign my name to it."

"Roman!"

"Poet!"

Our eyes met and there was a flash between us, a wonderful flash of our lost friendship, like lightning that flares beyond the rim of the world. It was a profound thing between us, manly, honorable, verifying that what had been good had indeed been good.

He wrote rapidly, crossed out, wrote again. This was his final version:

CITIZENS!
STILICHO, SAVIOR OF MILAN AND ITALY,
WILL BE HERE IN TWO DAYS.
—*Count Julian, Prefect of the City.*

We put copyists to work all night and before dawn had several hundred of these notices posted about the city. Daybreak brought on a clamor of new courage. Hundreds of people rushed to the walls. They expected Stilicho at once. If there was to be such a miracle, why wait two days for it?

Heraclian shook his head at me with a wicked smile of pleasure. "You have ruined yourself by prophecy. You've cast your last die in this fatal gamble. On the third day I take over the city. All the odds say Stilicho is dead."

I knew he could do it if Stilicho failed to come. And we both knew that Heraclian's first step in taking over the city would be to murder me.

But Stilicho didn't even wait for the second day.

We saw him from the walls, riding hard with his small troop. He avoided the bridge held by Alaric's men, swam the torrent, galloped to the gate, and removed his helmet. His prematurely white hair shone in the sun. The shout of glory from the walls was tremendous, and I opened the gates of Milan to Stilicho. By the power of his fame and character he had quelled passion along the Rhine: Alaric would have no allies.

The Goths, who could be deadly in open-field battle, were never so good at besieging and storming cities; and now that Stilicho was there in command, Alaric knew the difference and moved off his sullen horde, pillaging farms and villages as he went.

Now that the battle of moral courage had been won and I had not let the Emperor flee from Milan under Alaric's threat, I had no objection when it was decided to move the court out of Milan. I urged the restoration of the center of power to Rome, claiming nothing could do more to dramatize the unity among Emperor, Senate and people.

Stilicho had a more realistic sense of affairs. "Honorius is a Christian Emperor," he said, "and Rome is not yet by any means a Christian city. It's still Pagan and republican at the roots. If we concentrate both powers in one city, we'll have political and religious civil war in six months."

I saw his point and regretted that it was probably true. It was decided in Council to move the court to Ravenna, which had marshes to defend it and access to the sea where ships could be kept always ready to carry the divine Emperor off to safety if peril became so great.

I had no objection to Ravenna, except on grounds of taste. I did not like Ravenna. It seemed to me a run-down, moldy little city in a swamp. If a man neglected a pair of shoes for a week, they turned green with mold. But Stilicho felt that, with Honorius safe in Ravenna, he would have more freedom to maneuver against Alaric.

We crowded in upon the city, with its dismal ditches and turgid estuary, and, among other things, I started a great deal of public work on new buildings, improved water supply, paving of streets and general rehabilitation. If you took a drink of water, you could taste it for two hours. I brought in enormous stocks of wine. Dionie came over with the crowd of us, I suppose as much on my account as any other, although as usual I was not her only lover, nor she the only woman of my pleasure.

I personally supervised the building for Honorius, using the finest marble and bronze, of quarters for his chickens and other birds. The golden pullet he had christened Roma was now a fine plump hen and his favorite among all his chickens. He intended to care for her so well that she would become famous for her age. At bottom Honorius remained always grateful to me for understanding him and his chickens. Empress Maria, poor child, had lost her verve and color; she was slowly dying of virginal humiliation, and the miasmatic air of Ravenna was not good for her. A lot of us had slight or severe attacks of dysentery on first settling there. Some died, but on the whole we got used to it. There was a sort of peninsula or island out in the estuary on which grew a lot of pine trees; these pines were about the only attractive feature at Ravenna.

In profile, from the left side, Dionie was still the most beautiful woman at court. I had a sculptor make me a bas-relief of her head from this view, and she was quite pleased that I gave it a prominent place in my house. She would look at it and chuckle: "Still fit for love, eh, Gregory? How much flesh does a man like? I mustn't let myself get too fat!"

Galla Placidia once came in and looked at the bas-relief. She shook her head. "You would be foolish to marry her, Gregory."

Galla Placidia was a full-blown lovely young girl now, old enough for betrothal, even for marriage, and Serena was increasing pressure for Galla's betrothal to her son Eucherius. Galla Placidia had never, like the unfortunate little Empress Maria, looked forward to being married and becoming a mother. Her swift bright eyes were still on the one goal: to become Empress.

She liked Ravenna. "It's small and dirty," she said. "When my time comes as Empress I can build great palaces and churches here and be remembered for a thousand years. Honorius hasn't enough sense to do anything like that. But you have."

Claudian had written a fine poem in praise of Serena, but he did not come to Ravenna with us. Serena sent him a formal note of thanks and wished him a safe return to Rome.

The state of military affairs was perilous and abominable. Not only was Alaric on the Ligurian plain with his massive force and fierce ambition, but our legions were a strange mixture of incompetent recruits, disgruntled Roman veterans and Barbarian auxiliaries. Romans had long since got in the way of thinking that the army was a place for political action, in which a man took sides to get the best bonus offered. The Barbarian auxiliaries were the best fighters. Stilicho really had to depend on his Vandals and Franks, his Huns and Alemans and Goths to fight Alaric's Goths. And certain officers were under suspicion of dealing with Alaric. One of these was our Gothic general, Saul. He was said to be ready to go over to Alaric with all his cavalry. It was a lie, started in malice, by someone who wanted trouble and disorder.

This Saul was an unusual Goth, being short, thin, intense and wiry, whereas most Goths were broad big-boned muscular giants. He felt the suspicion that was on him, and his bottled-up fierceness became more intense. Some people claimed he was a Hun, because his nose had been flattened by a club and his eyes were black. He could have been a Hun by rape and yet a Goth by birth and training, for many Gothic women had been caught and bred by Huns and then rescued again by their own people.

Stilicho, without giving battle, had gradually pressed Alaric westward toward Pollentia. Alaric was by no means afraid to fight. He was skillfully drawing back to a place where, when he won, he could cross the pass to Genoa and march down the coast to Rome. He was being urged on by his wife, who had grown magnificent. She was tired of Greek treasures and slaves and wanted imperial jewels for her hair and Roman girls for her handmaids.

On Easter Sunday at Pollentia the Goths, being good Arian Christians, were celebrating the holy day. Thousands and thousands of them had already been marked on the forehead by priests with a smudgy cross made of dampened charcoal and ashes. They were celebrating the resurrection of Christ, Son of God. The furies of courage, of being suspected of dishonor and of battle lust broke loose in the lean tight breast of that hard little man, General Saul. Whether at Stilicho's nod, or out of his own uncontrollable ferocity, he suddenly gathered up his cavalry and fell upon Alaric's camp in a thunder of horses and a thousand-throated fury. Later a lot of Catholics set up an awful howl about attacking even Arians on Easter Sunday, but Stilicho said, "War is not Christianity."

It was seesaw carnage all day long. Alaric, with sacrificial boldness, pulled back all the men he could to draw them up in battle order, exposing his massy conglomeration of wagons, loaded with the plunder of Thessaly and Greece. Stilicho backed up the onslaught of Saul. In the shamble of wagons the Gothic women were heroic in a way long since lost to memory of Roman matrons. They bared their breasts and loosened their hair and fought the cavalry barehanded, screaming. They worked wiles, too, hauling out from the wagons the spoils and treasures to tempt the Roman forces to stay for rape and plunder while Alaric reorganized his forces. The sons of such women are not defeated in a single battle; they live to breed and fight again. And the Gothic women were notably fertile. Alaric came back in great might and began cutting the Romans down. Saul charged again and was killed, and his leaderless cavalry broke, but Stilicho came up behind them with foot soldiers. In the end Alaric had to choose either to surrender or to abandon his wagons and women and children in order to draw his fighting remnants out of reach.

He withdrew. Many enslaved Romans were released, much plunder was taken, and Alaric's own wife and children were among the hostages. It was for Stilicho one of those victories so near to a defeat that he simply had not power enough left to pursue and destroy Alaric.

He made an offer. Alaric was to move out of Italy, back to Illyricum. We Romans would keep as hostages a great many Gothic women and children. Alaric recovered his wife, but we kept his children. Then Stilicho, slowly rebuilding his forces, edged and nudged Alaric back and

back. Near Verona Alaric turned like a wounded lion for one more leap
and stroke, but Stilicho decimated the Goths, and Alaric barely escaped
through the mountains.

For a month or two Stilicho was shouted up as the savior of Italy.
But soon Olympius, working on the theme of the blasphemy of the
Easter Day attack, began to whisper to death Stilicho's glory, and other
discontented souls asked, "Why does he always let Alaric go?"

I myself had the temerity to ask Stilicho that question. I had never
before made him so angry. His broad face got bright red under his
white hair. "Even you can't forget that I'm a Barbarian! There has
never been a man more faithful to Rome than I!"

I saw I had hurt him deeply. "My thought was to fight the rumors
set up against you. I fight better when I know reasons."

He calmed down. He looked weary and he looked sad. "What have
I got to work with, Gregory? An Empire crumbling in my hands. The
Christians, setting their hearts on heaven, or at least on the glory of
their Church, have sapped the patriotism out of Italy. Gaul is restless,
Spain is remote, Britain is touch-and-go. Africa, our grain supply, is
Augustine's hotbed of strife with the Donatists. And Germany—I kept
them quiet there long enough to stave off Alaric, but Germany is a
storm center and will go on breeding storms, especially with the Huns
pressing and pressing from the East. There are only two men holding
Rome together. I am one, and Alaric is the other. I could have captured and killed Alaric, left Illyricum a vacuum and our border exposed. Eliminate Alaric and his Goths, and Germany will debouch
upon us, Gaul will move into Spain, Britain will move into Gaul. If I
could whip out of Alaric his insane desire to be glorious in Italy, I
couldn't ask for a better man to help me hold this whole thing from
cracking apart. I'm a Vandal, I'm a Barbarian. All right. Where are
the Roman statesmen and generals? You, Gregory, are the only man
who has come out of Rome in my time who sees beyond party to the
greatness and the peril of Empire. All the rest are dividers and spoilers,
or have fled into the Church. The other man who sees is Claudian,
and he's a poet and an Egyptian. Can you and Claudian hold the North
against Huns and Germans while I hold Italy, Africa, Spain and Gaul?"

"No. We can't. That takes a man with an army behind him."

"Then there you have it, Gregory. I need Alaric. *Kill Alaric, and
Rome falls!*"

There I had it indeed: Kill Alaric, and Rome falls; or kill Stilicho, and
Rome falls.

Claudian did a great service by producing one of his grandest poems, a celebration of Stilicho's war and victory over the Goths. He recited it to a crowd of patricians in the Temple of Apollo in Rome that summer. This was the poem in which the name of Stilicho was linked with that of Marius, who centuries before had defeated the Cimbrians on the Ligurian plain and saved Italy. The Emperor and the Senate honored Claudian with a statue in the Forum.

This was the inscription beneath the statue:

To Claudius Claudianus, *vir clarissimus*, son of Claudius Claudianus; tribune and notary, master of the ennobling arts, but above all a poet and most famous of poets. Though his own poems are enough to insure his immortality, yet, in thankful memory of his discretion and loyalty, Their Serene and Learned Majesties, the Emperors Arcadius and Honorius, have, at the instance of the Senate, bidden this statue to be raised and set up in the Forum of the Emperor Trajan of blessed memory.

Then, in Greek, the lines:

"Rome and her kings—to one who has combined
A Homer's music with a Virgil's mind."

I never told Claudian that, working through Symmachus and other friends of mine in the Senate, I originated this honor for him and that I myself wrote the inscription. When I had done this I ceased hating Marcia and ceased thinking of her as dead.

But more was needed than Claudian's poem.

We planned, for the opening of the year 404, to make Honorius consul for the sixth time and to have him go to Rome both to open the year and to celebrate his triumph over Alaric. Claudian set to work on a panegyric for the great occasion. This was only the third time in about a hundred years that an Emperor's triumph was to be celebrated in our eternal city. The preparations were tremendous and the expectations glorious. For some days before it began Rome had one of those spells of foul wet winter weather. Really, it did us a good service, for it washed a thousand cartloads of filth out of the streets, made the roofs shine, washed down the massive marble buildings, and cleaned the air from earth to sky. The sun came out in golden brilliance, and the banners were gorgeous.

On his triumphal march Honorius, who was handsome to look at, had Stilicho at his side. No one could miss the point, thus dramatized and at once restated in Claudian's panegyric, that Stilicho was the real man of triumph and the true great one of Rome. Nor was another point missed. Eucherius, the son of Stilicho and Serena, moved side by side with Galla Placidia, sister of the Emperor: In the presence of Honorius they kissed in public, and the Roman world knew that this was a betrothal. Eucherius, who had spent much time in Rome and often exercised his horse on the Field of Mars, was something of a favorite, being handsome, steady and of good carriage. This betrothal was Serena's triumph. Now she saw herself finally secure. If anything happened to Honorius, her son would be Emperor, and if nothing happened to Honorius, her son would most likely be co-Emperor before he was twenty.

The celebration went on for days. Among other things of note was a dreadful scene one day in the Colosseum. We were putting on, as a matter of course, combats of gladiators, and the stout fellows were mauling and butchering each other to the delight of thousands. When decadence has set in, people love to mass together in crowds to participate as spectators in violence and bloodletting. But this day a monk by the name of Telemachus, either mad or inspired, leaped down into the arena and screamed for this carnage to be put to an end. There was a minor riot. People hurled stones at the monk. Even the gladiators turned on him. He was beaten, hacked, and trampled to death. But as a result a group of powerful Christian leaders waited on Stilicho and demanded an edict against the brutal gladiatorial combats. Stilicho called me in for my opinion.

I said, "Julius Caesar began this sort of thing—bread and circuses—to debauch the people and increase his power. I think it would be a good thing now for Honorius to end it."

The edict was issued in the name of Honorius, and was an honor to the Christians and to the wisdom of Stilicho. Telemachus deserved and achieved the name of a martyr. Death combats of gladiators ceased in Rome from that day, and other cities began to abandon them.

I was under a secret emotional stress all this time, waiting for a private message from Ravenna. Dionie had become a deathbed Christian just before we others left Ravenna for Rome. She had caught one of the several severe illnesses too common at Ravenna—perhaps because the place was so dank and dirty—and neither she nor the physician I brought in had any hope of her recovery. She was very frightened of her death. When faced with the stupefying blank mystery of coming to an absolute end she could not bear it. She wanted some sort of postmortal existence. She begged me to bring in a priest and had herself baptized a Christian. Then she wanted to make a will, leaving her considerable wealth to the Church. I prepared the document for her. The physician warned me not to be too much in her presence, but I was not particularly happy about living and thought it would be no great matter if I had the same illness and died of it, too.

Then Dionie, in a spasm of utter fright, cried and begged me to marry her. "I should have married you in Rome before you married Marcia. I was a coward then. I still am a coward, Gregory. I want, once in my life, to be the wife of a good man."

"I am no such man."

"Good or bad, don't let me die except as your wife. It's too lonely. I am terrified."

I think at that moment she was not delirious or feverish, but rather the opposite. I put my hand on her forehead and felt it cold; her lips were cold and blue-looking. For Dionie and me to marry seemed a travesty. By all the standards of adultery, a man and woman in our situation have no responsibility toward each other. A man takes care of his concubines, and ought to; but my relationship with Dionie, which was only a selective kind of whoring, was an irresponsible form of polygamy. We adulterers think highly of action without responsibility. And it is an interesting arrangement of nature that to take action without responsibility degenerates a man. And now Dionie wanted me, somehow or other, in the great action of her death, to share a responsibility by marrying her. Why me instead of one of her other lovers? And what had I to gain by marrying her on her deathbed? She had signed a will leaving all her money to the Church.

I did it because her lips were blue, her forehead was cold, and her eyes were frightened. I did not do it as a formal assumption or recognition of moral responsibility. The woman was wretched and frightened and cried for help, and I was moved by her cry and did what I could to help her. I might as well confess the truth: After years of association based on the premise of pleasure without responsibility Dionie and I were committing, in the presence of death, a single act of love.

The priest was uncertain whether it was proper to marry two such persons in such circumstances, but the clergy in Ravenna were rather simple and were overawed by the influx of the Emperor and his court. At that time I was, among other things, prefect of the city, and my authority could set aside his doctrine. He married us, and that same night, when Dionie fell into a coma, he gave her extreme unction. In the morning I left for Rome. I kept the marriage a secret.

I could not understand why word had not yet reached me of Dionie's death. I did not regret the pathetic gesture of marrying her as a final comfort, and I was sorry she had to die. It made all our pleasures seem to have been so fruitless, so weary, and life seemed like a long gray ache in the breast.

I had not opened my palace in Rome. I was staying with the Emperor and the imperial group on the Palatine Hill in that vast conglomerate, the work of centuries of wealth and power and splendor, the Palace of the Caesars. A thousand purple awnings were on the building now, and from cells for slaves underground to airy balconies with golden roofs it was like a city, teeming with slaves, officials, nobles. I never knew a tenth of the people I met in corridors, arcades, baths, gardens. We had a number of social affairs in the huge throne room of Domitian to which came a stream of princes, kings and patricians from all over the Empire. The Emperor Honorius sat on a dais; the Empress Maria, being wan and sick, was seldom there. And everyone knew that Stilicho and Serena, mature, proud, able, were the pair that ruled. I got Honorius to send Marcia an invitation—that is, an order—to come to one such party.

I had tried to see Marcia. Of course I was admitted into the Anician Palace by the Probus family, but Marcia would not appear while I was there.

Faltonia Proba, the widow of old Probus, scolded me. "You married a lovely young girl. You seemed like a good young man. Somehow or other you ruined her life. She should have married a Christian, or, better, become a consecrated virgin."

"I am a Christian."

"So I have heard. In name, at least."

The handsome old lady was a Christian both in name and in works. I respected her. I confessed. "Once a man is baptized, it gets known, and he passes for a Christian whether he deserves to or not. I do what I can to help Stilicho hold things together, but my own life, inside me, is rotting away."

"At least you are honest. I advise you to go to Pelagius for help."

I was afraid to go to Pelagius.

At any rate, Marcia had to come in answer to the Emperor's invitation. She brought Pelagius to protect her.

Sorrow is well wrought into the design of the world. Marcia was no longer lovely in the bloom of youth; her expression was disharmonized, and her eyes were frantic with spiritual injury. I managed to draw her and Pelagius aside into one of the alcoves where the black marble wall had gold panels polished like mirrors. Shocked by the destruction I saw in Marcia's face, I was better able to see my own face reflected in the polished gold, and in myself I saw the tormented lines and shadows of spiritual failure. My smile was false, I was getting too heavy, the flesh was puffy around the eyes, and the expression of the eyes was without trust and without hope. Seeing myself thus in one stunning glance, I found I had nothing to say. Nor did Marcia want to talk to me. "You've forced me to come," she said.

"I'm sorry. How is the child?"

"Livia? She's all right. You never loved her, and she knows it. So she comforts herself by pretending you did love her and I took her away from you."

"I mean the baby."

That was the only time she looked at me, sharpened by surprise.

"Claudian's?"

"Yes. The ba—Claudian's!"

"He's all right, too. Please go away."

Pelagius, standing there, massive, solemn, not liking what I had done, took Marcia's arm. "We have heard of your marriage to Dionie," he said. "I have made it part of my business, on Marcia's behalf, to keep track of what you do. That you destroy your own soul is bad enough, Gregory. But why do you wish to be cruel, too, to this woman who in the sight of God is your only wife?"

"When Dionie dies . . ." I don't know what I was going to say, but Pelagius stopped me.

"It has nothing to do with Dionie. I had hope for you when I thought you might become a Christian. Now you have confessed Christ and betrayed him."

I was angry. "Church! Church! Church! I expected better of you than this, Pelagius. Are there none of you good official Catholics who can forget your rules long enough to see a man as a man is? Can't a man seek God, even through the rite of baptism, and not find Him? Can't a man desire the peace of Christ until his soul is sick, and still find no peace? Your Church rule is so simple: Confess Christ and sin no more. But a man who really seeks truth may find out he is a complex horror to himself."

"You'll never love your neighbor if you never love yourself."

It was hopeless; it was miserable. I turned on my heel and left them. Then I turned back abruptly, seized Marcia's shoulder, and demanded, "What do you call him?"

"Who?"

"Claudian's boy!"

She was frightened. Pelagius pushed my gripping hand away from her shoulder. She looked right at me. "I call him Gregory."

"That's what I heard. I wanted to make you tell me yourself."

"I had him christened Gregory in memory of my husband, who is dead."

We glared at each other for a moment, then Pelagius put his arm about her shoulders and took her away.

I went out of the palace and down the hill into the Forum. The moon was bright and the air mild. I had of course not forgotten the statue erected to me in the Forum on the occasion when I brought grain into the starving city: Julian the Provider. I remembered that poor people used to come and lay flowers before it. A man likes to walk by, with an air of not too much concern, to see his own statue in the Roman Forum. Mine was neglected now, just another one of the swarm of statues. But, without being surprised, almost feeling that it was fated and natural, I saw Claudian not far off, standing still in the moonlight, looking at the bronze statue of himself.

I knew he was married and on the point of leaving Rome. He had become interested in the daughter of a wealthy couple from Africa. They had refused to let him marry the girl, for he was a poet and poor. Then he made his last appeal to Serena, and she wrote him a letter, offering the continuance of her favor if he married and settled in Africa. With this the parents accepted him, and he had been married several weeks.

Neither was he surprised to see me. As I approached he remarked, "I'm saying good-by to myself."

"We both got our statues in the Forum."

"They're bronze. They're hollow. Poets are God's men. That was my birthright. I traded that off to become a pimp of the court and won a hollow statue in the Forum. Now I've married for money. It is my last mistake."

"Perhaps in Africa . . ."

"Perhaps I shall not reach Africa. Perhaps sometimes in Rome you will remember me and forgive Marcia and be kind to my son. Whom have you loved in this world, Gregory, more than you loved Marcus, your son who was drowned? I think I go to greet your son in the deep singing halls of Neptune. I shall tell him you and I were friends and hurt each other deeply, but spoke a good farewell by moonlight in the Forum at Rome."

Claudian was always nimble and swift afoot. He darted away from me and dwindled in moonlight among columns and monuments. I think he heard me call out: "Friend, farewell!"

A few days later I bought an exquisite golden cup and had it sent to Marcia at the Probus Palace. On it I had had engraved: "To Gregory, son of Claudian, from Marcus, son of Gregory: Live, Brother."

None of us ever heard from Claudian again after he sailed from Ostia with his wife. Whether he reached Africa or whether he drowned himself in the sea on the way I do not know. For nine years, yielding to our pressure, he had corrupted the gift of his soul to serve the arrogance of Empire, and that destroyed him.

I was more stupid than Claudian, less gifted and of tougher fiber. In the public eye I was considered the great Count Julian, in power second only to Stilicho, and a man who could be Emperor. I had moods and miseries in which I wished a tile would fall on my head and kill me, and not infrequently I muttered in my heart, Someday I'll kill myself. But I managed most of the time to keep myself very busy from early morning till late at night with official affairs.

It is really amazing how much of the day-to-day business of human political, social and even religious affairs is carried on by men who, whether they know it or not, are in an appalling spiritual condition. I do not think men commit base acts on the spur of the moment, delivering an immediate evil response to the stimulus of some new situation or opportunity. I believe a man prepares himself for base actions, and later it may or may not turn out that he commits them.

I had at last received word from Ravenna. It was a letter, and Dionie herself had written it. She simply had not died of the illness we expected would kill her. All I felt, I think, was an increased sense of futility. She will live. I will live with her. We are both depraved and deserve each other. We are incapable of love. Love, I thought, is an infinite readiness for revelation and change. A good life would be a continuous present, so lived as not to destroy but to fulfill all that love had built in the past, and still grow in motion toward the prophetic ideal; while always the perfection of choice and the intensity of being should irradiate the vital moment at hand. When you use a moment merely to wipe out the past, or to secure the future, you desecrate your life. I had been doing this too often, and also, like so many of us, I had blotted out the rich possibilities of my day-to-day present with those distractions copiously offered by a society of loose morals and decadent pleasures.

And Pelagius was right, you can never love your neighbor if you do not love yourself. Love has an inward beginning in a man's own soul; love, in the inward man, of his own true being, heaps the spirit full and overflowing with creative good. I did not love myself. I had come about as close as a man can come to conducting an outward life on an inward void. It is, I believe, the gradual effectuation in himself of that absence of love which prepares a man for base acts and the inrush of evil.

I was prepared for evil, and the murder of Stilicho was a great opportunity for evil.

CHAPTER THREE

THE MURDER OF
STILICHO: I

THE MURDER OF STILICHO HAD ALREADY BEGUN, AND IT RE-
quired about four more years. He was a great man, a good man, and not
an easy man to kill.

Prior to the triumph at Rome I was not one of his murderers, but one
who stood by Stilicho and tried to stave off his murder. Olympius, the
pious meddler, had long since begun to whisper Stilicho to death, and
Heraclian was steadily building his own power on the premise of Stilicho's death. I call those two the first murderer and the second murderer. Serena did her share, and Galla Placidia and Honorius did theirs. I
joined in late, but not without effect. It was not any schematic plot for
assassination; it was rather a deadly state of mind, spreading its evil, gathering more and more blind souls into its grip, until finally the man was
surrounded by an inescapable web of human desire for his death. Stilicho himself played a fatal part, almost like one under divine inevitable
impulse to make himself a sacrifice.

We killed him, Rome killed him, he designed his own death: However
you put it, it was the last great wickedness of the Roman Empire, done
in the name of the Catholic Church, the Pagan party and the general welfare.

Galla Placidia was sitting on a marble bench by a fountain in one of
the courtyards in the Palace of the Caesars a few days before we took
Honorius back to Ravenna. She was doing some needlework, and she
looked so lovely, so radiant and so young there in the sun that I stopped
short. I was on my way to notify the Senate of some new taxes we required to increase the strength of the army. During these past four years
and for four years to come—the period of my greatest public success—I
had an oppressive sense of hurry and a ceaseless sense of tedium; there
never seemed time enough to do what needed to be done, and in all my
doings I never seemed to settle any problem once for all. It was rarely

that I allowed the sight of something beautiful to stop me in my tracks and break this persistent pressure of the sense of my own importance in the rushing affairs of the world. But now I simply let my arms fall relaxed to my sides and strolled into the sunny courtyard and stood smiling down at Galla Placidia.

One did not surprise Galla Placidia or come upon her unaware. Her deep-blue eyes were quick, and their intensity was like that in the eyes of her father the great Theodosius when she glanced from under bronze-colored eyebrows as swift to move as birds in flight. Her sense of smell was remarkably accurate—I had often played a game with the imperial children in which I would blindfold them one at a time and ask them to identify objects, such as a vase, a basket, a vegetable, a piece of bronze, and so on, held near the nose, and Galla Placidia almost never failed to identify an article by its odor. She could distinguish the variations in the fragrances of persons, too. We would whirl her around, then all stand very still, and she would identify us: "I smell Gregory . . . Thermantia . . . Eucherius. . . ." And her sense of hearing was acute. Today, without bothering to look up from her needlework, she had heard and identified my stride in the arcade; she had heard my pace change, break short, and knew as soon as I did that I was coming out to talk to her. Then her swift eyes, under those swift eyebrows, caught in one glance my mood of affection.

She was ready for my smile when I said, "Good morning, goddess of spring! You are spun gold and sunshine."

"Needlework! Serena thinks I am still a child."

I sat down beside her and took the cloth in my hand. "You do your needlework well."

"You taught me to do all my lessons well, Gregory. When I'm Empress I'll rule the Empire well."

This girl had a curious effect on me. All that nature and normal growing had done delighted me; she was radiant, lovely, fresh as a blossom—and then I was always shocked by the force, the fierceness and the unforgiving certainty of her ambition.

I said, "What's left of it, you may rule well."

"Why do you say that?"

"I'm gloomy today. We're taxing people into poverty to save them from ruin. Now the Empire you covet to rule can do for three or for five coins what it used to do for one and what, under the Republic, people had the independence to do for themselves. I am sorry for you, Galla darling, but we are spending so much for so many nonproductive purposes that there won't be any Empire left for you to rule."

"Don't be silly, Gregory. There will always be an Empire. And I'll be an Empress."

"Then Eucherius is going to be Emperor."

She looked at me earnestly and shook her head. "No, he's not. Do you want to know something? Serena won't let anyone be Emperor so long as she lives. Stilicho could be, but she won't let him. All she lets Honorius have is the name."

"Columns have ears."

She looked around at the columned arcade and smiled. "So have I. Since you came, two barefoot slaves passed along that side behind our backs and went in the third door. No one else. I'm not going to marry Eucherius."

"Now you're being silly. You're betrothed to Eucherius. These things are arranged."

"By Serena. But Serena is not going to arrange me. And it was stupid of you to marry Dionie. I told you not to do it. But when the time comes to choose the man who actually can make me Empress I won't let Dionie stand in my way if I decide you are the man."

I was only partly amused and partly shocked. There was a long-rooted notion deep in my mind that exactly such a thing was possible. Serena and Rufinus had envisioned it years ago, and Theodosius himself had made both a threat and a promise of it. And I had not forgotten my father's prophecy that a Julian Emperor would save Rome.

"I am going to take more exercise," I told Galla. "I'm getting soft and puffy. You deserve a man in more handsome condition—when the time comes."

"Yes, you'd better" was her cool reply.

I stood. I bowed. "First to the Senate to raise the taxes. Then I'm going to the Field of Mars for an hour or two on horseback."

She picked up her needlework, took a stitch, then warned me: "Just don't mistake me, as Serena does, for a child."

I exercised vigorously on a horse that day in the Field of Mars, then went to one of the vast public baths near by for a good steaming and rubdown by slaves. I heard a paunchy Senator, lolling naked in the steam room, remark to a younger lean hard man: "We've spent a fortune on the army and rebuilding walls, and we've driven Alaric out of Italy. That ought to warn off all Barbarians for a century. I tell you, the power and wealth of Rome are inexhaustible!"

The younger man, whose eyes were black, direct and alight with intelligence, replied: "I'm not a noble or a general or even a public official.

I'm only a businessman. Every time we get in a war and build walls and supply an army to fight a big battle, we defeat business, and every time we defeat business we come closer to ruin."

"That is a plebeian attitude."

"Exactly."

"You don't appreciate the grandeur."

"No. I pay the taxes."

The man was right. Senators had many sorts of exemptions, and the proletariat had many sorts of benefits; it was the dwindling middle class —farmer, artisan, merchant—that produced the goods on which we all subsisted and also paid the increasing costs. I began to suspect that every new increase in the power and function of government drained more lifeblood out of society.

After the grandeur of Rome, with its seven immortal hills and its swarm of people gathered from all the world, and remembering the clean and busy splendor of Milan with those lyric shining vistas of far-off snow-clad Alps, residence in Ravenna was like doing penance. We had built up and increased mud dikes outside the city so that considerable water flowed around the walls, but half the river went in turgid course through the town, where there were extra canals and lagoons. There was a perpetual reek of mud, garbage, sewage and whatever breeds and rots in slow dark water. The frogs were fat, large, numerous and noisy, and the mosquitoes were constantly whining about our ears and bloating on our blood—a man got tired of slapping them and just let them feed. The water seemed to rot the foundations of buildings, and it was common to see a dead body of a man or lesser animal afloat in the oily water. Bargemen with their poles only stirred up more mud and filth from the bottom. The water outside the walls and toward the sea was somewhat cleaner, and ships with sails seemed to squat on it like silent waterfowl caught still in the gloomy enchantment of thickened air and strange haunting light.

It seemed to me that it was never warm and mild in Ravenna; either there was a raw bone-chilling cold, or else a sullen heavy depressing heat. It was hard to raise children beyond infancy in that town; they were born, smiled a few times, whimpered in fever, and died. And among adults fevers, headaches and diseases of the lungs and bowels were distressingly common. However, despite the quips of visitors from Rome, I always insisted that the odor of Ravenna was not of death and decay, but a fecund smell of life generated by swamps, bogs and sea-margin ooze. That men should by choice build such a city in such a place and persist in living there seemed to me strange and wonderful, the revelation of a new mood and depth in the human heart—new to me, I mean, for of course it was primitive.

When we got back to Ravenna I found that Dionie's appearance was shocking. A great deal of her hair had fallen out, and of what was left some, near the roots where there was no dye, was coming in gray. Severe illness is said often to spiritualize the face. It had not done so with Dionie. She had lost a great deal of weight, she was very thin, and now the bone structure of her face was quite apparent and was indeed exquisite in form and balance, a structure of great beauty. But her mouth was frightened, and her green eyes were dull and brutal. She was profoundly offended that she, the delightful one, lover and giver of pleasure, should have been ravaged by disease. She dreaded the moment when I first saw her, I think because she was so frightened at her own ruin that she believed I was going to abandon her and no one else would have her now.

She began her pathetic self-defense by criticizing me. "You certainly look smug and soft, like a well-fed bishop."

"I thought you were a Christian now."

"And you're so infernally big and insolently healthful. I forbid you to look at me like that. I won't have pity."

She was weak and distracted and began to cry. I had never before seen Dionie cry. Gaiety, wit, laughter had been the essence of her charm. "Put poison in my food someday. Please. Please! I haven't the courage to do it for myself."

I took her into my house. I had a house set in the city wall—one side of it was built right up out of the water of the estuary—and there I had a large room with a covered balcony out over the water. I made this our private bedroom, and Dionie spent most of her time secluded there. From the balcony we could look across the estuary toward the pine trees at the other side, or down toward the sea where ships were always ready to take the Emperor on a flight to safety. In the heat of summer there was sometimes a breeze there, either heavy with vegetable odors from the swampy land or with a clean tang if it came from the sea, and sometimes the sunset, with a thousand iridescent lights suffusing water and sky, was beautiful. Dionie brought into the room that bas-relief of her profile and often gazed at it in a kind of moody angry dreaming.

In the course of a few months she regained much of her lost weight and some of her charm, but the flash of her beauty never came back. I think this flash of her beauty had been generated by faith in the pleasure of life, and now she no longer trusted life to be either pleasant or good.

That strange moody brutal spark of resentment always lurked in her eyes. She began to have more confidence in me and to depend on me for shelter and comfort. During those months we came as near to loving each other as we were able, but we never laughed together. Love without laughter is a form of sickness. Sometimes we seemed to slough off our mortal distraction in each other's arms. We were both coming to the end of that period when our religion, if we had any, was sex; a celebration of sex is a rather simple natural religion, with a commonplace repetitive rite, and it either stultifies the mind or becomes so boring that you wish to find some way out to a richer and more spiritual devotion. I think the human mind constantly gropes for a good life, but to seek rest for the heart in a pretension is a mad affair. And for Dionie and me to think we could find ultimate peace in the warm pleasures of the flesh was by now a pretension.

I had begun to feel a deep fidelity to Dionie's sorrow, and there was a kind of healing grace in the way we would sometimes sit almost a whole night through, side by side on the balcony, while the waters stirred in the night and nightfowl cried; now and then we moved a hand to touch each other; we scarcely talked, and we felt each other's sadness and the slow still weight of time. Such nights, in the creative rearrangements of memory, came to seem like slow healing years for two outcast souls.

I myself did laugh when I was alone, a grim sort of snort and chuckle, which is a distracted man's way of snorting at the devil. I take such snorting as a good sign that the stubborn soul has not given up hope and will yet fight onward along its way between madness and God.

I was too busy to be religious.

I went to church frequently now and resumed a practice I had dropped some years ago, of rising early to add an hour to my day in which I could read and meditate divine things, whether in poetry or philosophy or Christian Scriptures. This would pass in our society for being quite religious. But, to my way of thinking, being religious is not a matter of acting this way or that an hour here and there in the day. As I was to find out later, when I was a bishop in Spain, it is not even serving all day long in and for the Church that is religious. I would rather say that a religious man is one who keeps a constant appointment with God. I was far too busy keeping an incessant stream of appointments with the affairs of Empire to be religious. In fact, I began to apprehend not only my own spiritual poverty but the appalling spiritual poverty of Italy.

Here at Ravenna, where I did not remember Ambrose at every turn of the street as I had in Milan, the spiritual decadence of Italy was more apparent. Our bishop was a dull fellow—a lean stringy Syrian named

Peter, emaciated by malaria and wearing a bushy beard—who waited to hear from Pope Innocent in Rome or Bishop Augustine in Africa before he dared say what was what between man and God. And he was brilliant compared to most of the clergy. There was, indeed, not a single man in Ravenna, in or out of the Church, so far as I was able to find out, who was doing creative thinking in morals or philosophy or religion. The most you could expect was a weakening, a dilution or some pathetic perversion of the great original thoughts of men far away or long dead. Everybody's mind was applied to "the facts of the case," the day-to-day pragmatism of getting things done with a kind of arm's-length vision.

Nor was Ravenna singular in this. Because of certain fateful events I traveled a good deal in all of Italy from Rome north. In these travels I enjoyed the scenery, especially mountains and rough rock margins of the sea, but above all I liked going around looking at shapes and faces of people in busy towns. But take half a dozen cities—Ravenna, Rome, Verona, Milan, Genoa, Bologna—and the cumulative sense of anxiety one felt from looking at the faces of people was shocking. It was as if Italy hated and feared all sorts of nameless shapeless possibilities, did its daily work with a dogged misery, and believed in nothing. Passion was not for good, not even for evil; passion was only for party. All fierceness burned for partisan affairs—in the main for the Pagan party or for the Christian party. Each side most loudly spoke out what it was *against*. A man *for* anything was a rarity.

I tried to get away. Out of the busy nothingness of my life I generated a desire to break off from spiritual weariness and pains of failure. I had lost my father and Ambrose, my son Marcus and, though she still lived, Marcia. And Claudian was gone. Who knit my heart to Italy with any promise of joy? I could take Dionie out of Ravenna, go far to a new scene, and perhaps she and I could somehow rest. It was a dream of escape. I was willing to work hard to make it come true. I talked it over with Dionie, and something like a faint light of hope enlightened her green eyes, for a moment erasing that dull brutal look that had for months tarnished them.

I went with a new joyous spring in my step to Stilicho and proposed myself as governor for Africa. I had a good argument. "The North is getting more and more cut off. The poverty of Italy is increasing. We'll never be able to feed Rome again out of Spain and Gaul, the way I managed it when Gildo cut off our African grain. I could hold Africa for you and feed Italy. Also, I want to deal directly with Augustine. He is the great man of the Church, and I want to try to win his co-operation for a better politico-religious spirit in Italy. As it is now, men like Olympius and Heraclian by sending him false information get him to exert pressures that only increase our internal strife."

I never saw a man look so tired. General Stilicho, with his broad shoulders, his fine carriage, his big good face and now nearly white hair—he had just celebrated his fifty-first birthday—had hands that seemed heavy when he moved them, and he looked out of eyes that were slow with the weariness of facing crises that never ended.

He sat there a moment after I spoke, resting his chin on his thumb, and whistled a few tuneless meditative notes. Then he took a deep breath and sighed. "Gregory, Gregory! Everything you say is true. You are exactly the man I need as governor in Africa. I'm going to send you there." He shook his head. "But not yet. You are also exactly the man I need here. Radagaisus is one of those German kings with the fury and ferocity of a wolf of the North. He has gathered a horde of Sueves, Vandals, Burgundians, Alani and God knows what other tribes. He's already brought them south of the Danube into Rhaetia and Noricum. I had to give Alaric such a severe beating to get the man out of Italy that he hasn't army enough left to stop Radagaisus. When winter is over, Radagaisus will invade Italy. His swarm outnumbers my Barbarian auxiliaries ten to one, and they are the only good fighters Rome has left. I have to call in legions from Gaul, even Spain. I have to levy new troops. In the days before Caesar, when men had a real spirit of independence, the Senate could raise such a volunteer army as I need in a few months' time. Romans then would fight for their country. Now we have to force them and buy them. For the first time in eight centuries it will be necessary to arm slaves if we are to save Rome."

He appointed Count Bathanarius, the husband of his sister, governor of Africa; and after the death of Stilicho, Heraclian, on reaching Africa, murdered Bathanarius.

It was indeed a miserable business that I plunged into, trying to gather for Stilicho out of the rotted fabric of a decadent society enough spirited men to defend Italy. To think of the government as providence—the father, guardian and provider—was by now so imbued in the blood of the people that no one wanted to do anything for the country because the government was supposed to do everything for everybody. And of course each man ought to take all he could get for himself while he could.

Outside the walled cities the country was full of brigands and bandits. Alaric's invasion had displaced thousands of people from farms and villages, so that even bands of ten and twelve-year-old boys lurked in the hills as murderers and thieves. The great road systems were falling into disrepair; government officials underfed the horses and mules so they might sell grain on their own account, or sold the animals secretly and made all sorts of deals with bandits. Money saved up in the cities to repair public works was dissipated down the runnels of bribery and corruption. Thousands of deserters from the army infested the back country or lurked in city slums. More and more weary despairing people crowded into cities to live on the public dole. Our secret-police agents, who were supposed to guard public property and prevent maltreatment of persons, had devised a thousand new forms of corruption. We kept hundreds of clerks busy writing out new edicts, rules and regulations, trying to bolster with legal rhetoric in the Theodosian Code the moral rot in countless individuals.

The ruin of individual persons comes before social calamity; and when there is public ruin, then slowly the moral mending of person by person is the way to a new and good society. But nobody wanted to begin the responsibility in himself. The general sense was that the government ought to straighten things out, and if it didn't do so right away, then he who headed the government—Stilicho—ought to be killed.

I found I could accomplish more in these evil days of crisis and limited time by direct order backed by force than by persuasion, and I found that to employ reason wasted time. It got nothing done, if anything could be done, to tell the mentally immature and childishly emotional leaders of the cities of Italy, who wanted the "government" to do everything, that government is nothing but a name for the wasteful doing by and large of those things which individuals no longer have the character, courage, insight and determination to do for themselves. And every new task assumed by government further debilitates the character of the people and will itself be less well done, for the primary purpose of government officials is not to achieve wonders of creative intelligence but to hold onto their jobs by political connivance.

Every time I got something done I gave a dozen officials nervous headaches, and priests and bishops were appalled at my interference with the will of God. For Christians were prone to take an easy way out, saying it was the will of God—let it happen, and leave it to the Church to arrange matters better in the world to come. It was a natural shift of emotional dependence from considering the government providence to considering the Church as providence. I was reminded of that sharp saying of Herodotus: "Of all the sorrows which afflict mankind, the bitterest is this, that a man should have consciousness of much but control over nothing." I could almost accept the Lucretian doctrine of a lot of mindless atoms dancing and colliding in a silly void. The zest of hope was almost utterly drained out of my blood.

But I went at the work with a last grim fiat of faith. I devised new edicts and regulations, I went to the major cities and threatened, cajoled and harassed officials into brief flashes of honor and integrity. Now and then I had to contend with a wife or daughter who offered me her warmest favors to make up for her husband's or her father's incompetence. Here and there, like jewels in rubbish, I found vigorous men who thought something could be done and would take responsibility to do it. I was hated by those I stirred out of lethargy. I made many new enemies both for myself and for Stilicho in the Pagan and in the Christian parties. The great slogan of the people was "Give us everything we want and let us alone!" and I went about saying, "All is lost. Wake up and fight for yourselves!" I threw literally dozens of corrupt officials out of the obesity of their office and replaced them with new men at least frightened enough to work honestly for a while. I had to insist on executions of deserters, armed forays against bandits, and flogging and hand amputations of some of those corrupt scoundrels who were stealing or debouching army supplies. Somehow or other I began to gather and to supply an army for Stilicho.

He complimented me with a plain truth:

"What you have done is half of what we need, and I don't know any other man who could have done half of what you have done."

I gave him plain truth in return: "Italy will thank the two of us by demanding our murder. The Pagans are saying that Radagaisus is a good worshiper of Jupiter and ought to be let into the country to liberate us from the intolerable autocracy of the Catholics; you and I are ruining Italy's last hope of religious freedom by preparing against Radagaisus. The Catholics are saying that Stilicho and Julian have invited Radagaisus to invade Italy to destroy religion and seize absolute power. Take your choice, we're scoundrels either way. Only, at bottom they're all scared. They won't murder us until after we've saved their lives."

Stilicho smiled. "When this is over, Gregory, you can have your choice: Praetorian Prefect or governor of Africa."

"If you will do what your ability and our calamity demands and institute yourself outright as Emperor, I'll be your Praetorian Prefect. Otherwise—Africa."

He looked at me thoughtfully for a moment. "In the end that may have to be done. Even Serena begins to see that Theodosius is really dead and no one has filled his place. She deterred me twice at the outset, when it would have been easier. Perhaps at bottom I'm a general who wants to defend Rome, not rule it. If you and I were one man instead of two, that would be the Emperor we need. At any rate, Gregory, right now I count on you to watch over public affairs while I do what I can with the army. There is bound to be an uproar. If I met Radagaisus on the plain, he would cut me to pieces. I'll have to expose half of Italy before I can trap him. And I've had to strip the frontiers of Gaul while you drained the dregs of cities for such an army as I have. Do you know what this miserable chaotic semitrained force of mine is? It's *the last army of Rome!*"

Stilicho, our last general, in command of our last army: We were facing the crisis of our last hope.

CHAPTER FOUR

THE MURDER OF STILICHO: II

I WAS IN FLORENCE DURING THE WORST OF IT. THE PEOPLE of Florence were a tough and stubborn lot. They had not contributed many recruits to our tatterdemalion army. "We'll man our own walls and fight for ourselves" was their argument. The city contained a great many artisans and traders. These artisans were the sort who took care to do good honest work and usually extra care to make it beautiful. You could probably find a better chair, piece of silverwork or other article of use and beauty in Florence than in any other city in Italy. And their traders or businessmen were independent fellows who drove hard bargains but delivered the goods in full measure and of high quality.

The city also had a religious fervor less related to politics than in other cities, and more related to worship. Ambrose was now their favorite saint. During his life he had often come to Florence, had raised the infant Pansophinus from the dead and done other miracles there, and, since his own death, was known to come and pray in holy radiance in the basilica where once he had preached. Florence was a city where men believed in God and honest work. Spiritually it was the richest city in Italy. It may be that with cities spiritual poverty and great size go together; the immediate opportunities of vice flourish better in the larger conglomerate. Florence was a small city on the Arno, with the hill Faesulae rising behind it, and higher hills and mountains behind that. The man of Florence had a quick step, a sharp eye and a very good laugh. I say again that Florence was spiritually the richest city in Italy.

The laugh had an edge of grimness to it when I got there. The master of the city greeted me: "Welcome, Count Julian, into our trap. Stilicho must mean business if he sends his chief minister to enjoy our hospitality at the present time."

"Stilicho does mean business. I came of my own accord."

"Your presence will be a good omen. We Florentines appreciate the courtesy of courage. I hope you ate well on your way from Ravenna, for men are soon going to be hungry here."

King Radagaisus of the Germans had come down into Italy near Verona. He and his horde had mauled a dozen small cities and ravaged the Ligurian plain. Stilicho, not having a good enough army to meet him in open battle, had retreated to Pavia, where overnight he was trying to make veterans out of incompetents. He had some good Huns and Vandals and Goths as the core of his army, and then a flabby mass of irresolutes. Radagaisus built up fear by atrocity as he moved. On altars of his gods he made human sacrifices of captives. Pagans who thought he worshiped Jupiter began to wake up. Thor and Wotan were not the sort of gods we had in Greece and Rome. Radagaisus had vowed to burn Rome and sacrifice the leading Senators on his altars. A good many of our stout Pagans began to suspect that Christianity would be better than this Northern form of Paganism, and they cried out against Stilicho for not having a bigger army and stopping Radagaisus at once. "And look at this monster," said the Christians, "that Stilicho and you Pagans have invited into the country!"

Radagaisus left Ravenna to the frogs and mosquitoes. He disdained the timid Emperor and headed for Rome, pausing to wipe out Florence on his way. I got through his lines and into the city, almost unattended, by night.

Unfortunately I had to leave Ravenna in charge of Heraclian. Stilicho wouldn't have Heraclian in charge of troops for battle, but he was the only man available to take charge of the palace guard. I say this was unfortunate because in the swift tragedy of later events Heraclian held onto this office with fatal purpose.

When I left Ravenna for Florence I sent Stilicho a message: "Florence has the heart to fight for its life. I'm going there as your hostage to show them we know their courage. Come."

Nobody seemed to understand what Stilicho did. Why didn't he come? They began to think he was a coward or that he had made some traitorous deal with Radagaisus. Hunger makes courageous men angry before it gets so extreme that it makes them too weak for anger. I was treated to hard looks. The master of the city offered me a bodyguard of a dozen armed men.

I told him in front of the city council: "I'll go about your city like any other man. I'll live with you, endure with you, and fight with you. What you must understand is this: Stilicho right now at Pavia is fighting his major battle against Radagaisus. He is driving fear out of his own army before he comes to the relief of Florence. The courage of Florence must be the courage of Italy for some days yet."

Radagaisus had surrounded Florence and cut off all supplies to the city.

Dogs and cats and rats and mice make an ugly diet, and moldy grain is like paste in the mouth.

Pansophia, mother of the child Ambrose had raised from the dead, made public announcement that Saint Ambrose had come to her in a dream and assured her he himself had joined in the defense of the city. The people believed her and believed in Saint Ambrose.

I felt better than I had felt in years. I got lean again, I was constantly hungry, I worked extremely long hours with the city officials wherever I could help at the thousand tasks of rationing supplies, and fighting disease, while laughing at death. I had not ghostly visitations from Ambrose, neither by daylight nor in dreams, but something free and creative was released again in my spirit so that the reality of Ambrose in my memory was very much with me and for the first time since my baptism I found in church the mood, the sweetness and the calm of religion. It seemed to me that I lived in tranquil light. If the siege had gone on to its fatal end I believe I would have died at Florence a Christian in faith as well as in name. At any rate, the good was retained at least by my body for many years; I didn't have time to get soft and paunchy again until I was a bishop in Spain, and by then I had other good reasons not to indulge my flesh.

While Radagaisus oppressed our walls and waited for our surrender and death Stilicho won his battle against fear in a wretched army. Somehow, by the greatness of his person and through his talent as a general, he drove despair out of those wretched ranks, left Pavia, and marched on Florence. I was on the walls when he came up along the edge of the hills and the skirts of the valley. We shouted from the walls, and at our signal all the noise and bells of joy began to resound through the streets. The hordes of Radagaisus were so scattered round about the city in their gloating positions that the king could not gather them for a descent on Stilicho; instead he drew them back up the slopes of Faesulae. Stilicho caught four or five groups west of the city and cut them to pieces. At this point I had the west gate opened and went out with a group of stout young men I had held ready for the purpose. We paused but a moment to greet Stilicho, then rushed back to his baggage train, assembled wagonloads of food, and brought them straightway into the city.

When this was done I went to the church which, because he had dedicated it during his lifetime, was known as the Basilica of Ambrose. There on my knees I thanked God, and this time I am not sure Ambrose the Saint was absent, for I apprehended a ghostly figure standing there, outside my mind, in all the semblance of Ambrose as I knew him, and he made the sign of the cross before my face and said, "Your sins be mine, my poor lost Gregory!"

I wept. I stayed there on my knees. I was faint with hunger and exhaustion. Ambrose faded away. Marcia came, stood there looking at me, and her eyes were luminous with the dark gravity of love that has been injured. There were by now plenty of real people crowded about me, offering their thanks for the delivery of the city. Some of them must have carried me into the bishop's house, where I regained my senses and was given wine and food.

Stilicho achieved an act of military genius, accomplishing against Radagaisus what he had not quite succeeded in doing to Alaric some years ago in Greece. That is, he pressed the Barbarian horde up onto the waterless heights of Faesulae and beyond, surrounded them, made his own unseasoned troops throw up earthworks and dig trenches, and day upon aching day starved the Barbarian invaders into submission. Stilicho kept his better troops ready and mobile, day and night, to meet any efforts Radagaisus might make to break his way out. There was no singing, dancing or feasting in the Roman lines; there was grueling watchful discipline. We could see the enemy's fires on the mountain at night. Sometimes a thousand of the Barbarians, whirling firebrands, would come yelling and swarming down the slope; there would be a bitter hand-to-hand battle, and our line would hold. By such blood and by more insidious starvation Rome's last army won Rome's last victory. Radagaisus surrendered, and Stilicho executed him.

But still I did not know how to reconcile brute actions and spiritual ideals. When I saw the thousands and thousands of the men of Radagaisus come stumbling down off the stubborn mountain, gray as deathly figures of dawn, hungered, festered, harried, to chains of slavery and death by disease and starvation, I realized that these great victories also debase the society that wins them. To start to war is to have lost some goodness. For there is no cause so great that men may destroy other men in its name without being defiled. A man may give his life without spiritual loss, but cannot destroy another man without some measure of disaster to his own soul. What shall we do? Let brutes who don't care about spiritual quandaries enslave and destroy us? Is it better to fight Radagaisus or let him cut your throat on the altar to his brute gods?

I began to suspect that I would never know a man who lived out a man's life with an immaculate soul—no, not even Ambrose, for, with a spirit more radiant than most, even he helped persecute Jews and sought harsh laws against Pagans in behalf of the Catholic Church. I confess that, old as I am, I haven't worked out or had revealed to me an ultimate answer to this fundamental human problem. Why, indeed, should even Christ have blasted the innocent fig tree for not bearing fruit out of season? Passion is in us.

Perhaps it is the function of the spirit to bear witness to what passion is and does: true witness being rich life, and false witness being true death.

I am not certain. But the same old pattern of passion, of gratitude followed by anger, waited on Stilicho with the crown of honor and the sword of death. I couldn't keep up with the treachery of events. I had to hurry back and forth between Ravenna and Rome and Rome and Milan. I had to go on a mission to Alaric; travel was slow, people were stubborn, and, on Stilicho's behalf as well as for the safety of the Empire, I just couldn't keep up with the treachery of events.

Stilicho needed a Claudian now as never before. He needed another three men like me. He needed solid support in the Council in Ravenna and in the Senate at Rome. He needed more money and a better army. He did not have these things he needed. Above all, he needed unity of purpose in the imperial family, and did not have that, either. His murder was afoot.

The first results of the victory were paeans of praise in Florence, Ravenna, Rome and throughout Italy for Stilicho the Savior. Claudian could have formalized this in a memorable poem and, by putting it in words, could have prolonged its effectiveness. But now there was no Claudian. The poet was dead and, so far as we knew, the man also was dead. Four or five piddling panegyrists did the best they could, and were forgotten in a week.

The poisonous whispering began. The Pagan and Catholic parties hacked at each other and tore at Stilicho between them. Why had he not let Radagaisus restore Paganism? Why, since obviously God and not Stilicho had given the victory, did Stilicho claim the honor? Was he preparing to usurp the throne for his son Eucherius and a Pagan dynasty? Falseness and foulness set the themes and played the tunes. Our social life in Ravenna, Rome or Milan, among the supposedly intelligent leaders of affairs, was a getting together to slay the characters of persons not there. We were brilliant. We discussed the weaknesses of people with acumen and disparaged them without charity. Then, when enough wine had done its work, we would attack one another with innuendo, satire and sarcasm. Finally, at most of these parties, the drunken man and the drunken woman would paw at each other in a fumbling of inconclusive lust. Every gathering had this sour and degrading quality of death about it, and I often came away from a brilliant party feeling irritated and unclean.

I was irritated by the odium hurled at me, and I felt unclean because of the base witticisms I had myself contributed to the general corruption. I had considerable skill, too, at defending both Stilicho and myself with venomous irony. But a man, unlike a snake, is poisoned by his own venom, whether he stores it up or spews it out: better not to generate venom at all. I doubt if even the morally refined, humanely sweetened and intellectually enlightened irony of Socrates would stand a man in as good stead before death and eternity as the straightforward religious plain speaking of Christ. "Know thyself," with its ironic and subtle impossibilities, comes not so near the heart of our necessity as "Love God and love one another," in which both forgiveness and aspiration are implicit.

Italy had been saved at the cost of calamity beyond the borders of Italy. Remnants of the horde of Radagaisus retired across the Alps into the Danube basin, joined there with large forces of Sueves, Vandals, Burgundians, Visigoths, Ostrogoths and others left behind, and all these swarmed up the Rhine and over into Gaul. They destroyed for good and all the Rhine frontier, a work of centuries to wall off savagery from civilization, ravaged Gaul with vigorous brutality and even went into Spain, leaving the murdered, the raped, the homeless and the desolate behind them.

We heard the voices of Roman citizens crying from this savage North, "Save us! Come and save us!" Cities were burned and people massacred. A delegation from central Gaul came to us, typical of many, and told us how priests and worshipers had been murdered in their churches, women raped, children slain, prominent men sacrificed on the altars of ugly gods, and those fleeing from their homes butchered by Barbarians on horseback for the sport of it. I noticed the faces of these delegates had a sickness of the soul in the eyes and a grayness of despair under the angry flush of the cheeks. We were being accused of and hated for all their sufferings. It wasn't a singular story, but the same story came from place after place, ending always with that terrible cry: "Save us! Come and save us!" Rome had no manhood left to go to save them; and what had Rome done to the manhood of Gaul that it—outnumbering the Barbarians ten or a hundred to one—could not save itself? I do not know. But I was heartsick when I had to tell these people, "Rome can do nothing."

Honorius met some of these delegations in the Palace of the Caesars in Rome; Stilicho listened to them, and then I spent hours with them denying their requests. We couldn't keep Honorius in Rome, because he kept his chickens in Ravenna and insisted on spending more time there. Olympius and Heraclian, I think, were better able to rule Honorius in Ravenna than they could in Rome. Between them they controlled the imperial guard in Ravenna, while in Rome there were plenty of forces larger than theirs and not under their control. No one quite knew which place would be the center of government next month. Perhaps on the whole Ravenna was the safer as the religious strife grew more bitter.

For now the Christians spread the rumor that Count Julian wanted to see the ruin of the Church in Gaul and Stilicho approved, although both of them pretended to be Christians; and the Pagans were equally angry at us for having given so much wealth and privilege to the Catholic Church that the angered gods were punishing Rome with ruin. Then Serena offended the Pagans by wearing at a large reception that fatal necklace of pearls she had seized years before from the statue of the Goddess Rhea when the Temple of the Vestal Virgins was destroyed. All the old anger against her and Stilicho for having destroyed the Temple of the Vestal Virgins, stolen the necklace, burned the Sibylline Books and melted down gold plate of the gods, boiled up with new hatred. Old friends of my father ceased to speak to me, and once when I made an effort to see Marcia I found the Probus Palace, which was dominated by Christians, closed against me. I don't think a week passed in any city without some sort of fight between Pagan and Catholic, and many of these ended in one or more deaths. It became normal to expect violence.

At this point, seeing the ruin of Gaul, our Roman army in Britain followed an old pattern: They revolted and—having superstitions about his name—raised one of their private soldiers named Constantine to the position of Usurper, or Emperor. I doubt that he was a descendant of the great Constantine—which would have made him some sort of distant relative of mine, for of course the Emperor Julian was a nephew of the great Constantine—but this new tyrant had energy if not genius. He brought his army over into Gaul and obtained an unstable mastery there, then went to take Spain. Honorius had Theodosian cousins in Spain, four Theodosian brothers who gathered what army they could and tried to stop Constantine in the Pyrenees. They were defeated. Two escaped to the east, and two were captured and later executed at Arles.

This slaying of Theodosians was really too much. If Honorius didn't care, Serena did, and Stilicho was forced into the mistake of trying to render punishment with insufficient force. He sent General Sarus into Gaul to destroy the usurper Constantine. Sarus was a gigantic Goth, one of those big red Goths, even bigger and redder than Alaric, but by no means so intelligent. He was brute force enlightened by animal cunning. It was a wasteful foray, ending in defeat and return, and left a picture that a child could understand. Everything north of the Alps was lost to Rome and uneasily held by Constantine; all Illyricum was held by Alaric; Italy, weakened, sick, corrupted by politico-religious hatreds, was held in the name of Honorius by Stilicho with a divided and disintegrating army. If Alaric and Constantine agreed, they could take over Italy; if Alaric and Stilicho agreed, they could hold off and perhaps overthrow Constantine. It was a holiday for fools who solved the whole problem by the proud assertion that Rome, our Eternal City, was too glorious to come to harm.

Stilicho was not a fool. He sent me into Illyricum to negotiate with Alaric while he himself, using all his power, negotiated with the Senate.

Stilicho told me flatly, "Either I buy Alaric or he takes Rome."

Alaric saw the matter clearly, too. "Why should I help Stilicho defend Rome? In another year I can have Italy for myself."

There was something new about Alaric. With increasing age and travail the bone structure of his great face had become more prominent. It gave his appearance a severe new majesty. In the battle of Pollentia, he had got a gash under the left eye and down across the cheek, and the scar was like a stroke of anger. He had always been a man who radiated vigor and confidence, molded on a large scale of forthright integrity. But the defeat at Pollentia had put a touch of gloomy anger in his soul; there was a grimmer colder flash in his intense blue eyes.

"I don't take you for a fool," I said. "Obviously you have been negotiating with Constantine. He can offer you a chance to take Italy, and then you must turn and fight him to hold it. Stilicho can and will do better."

Young Ataulphus was there, no longer a youth, but a grown man. He now was doubly bound to Alaric: Being by birth the brother of Alaric's wife, he was now also the husband of Alaric's sister. Strangely his bitterness against Rome was less than it had been when I was his tutor. Age, marriage and experience had done him good. He watched me thoughtfully. "I remember, Gregory," he said, "how you used to tell me that force of arms alone does not take the place of civil order. I have been into Gaul on mission to Constantine. What he holds by force of arms is a shambles of a ruined civil order." He turned to his kingly brother-in-law. "Alaric, I'm not so sure the ruin of Rome is the best hope of the Goths."

"What is your offer?" Alaric asked me.

"Stilicho will appoint you master general of the army, second only to himself. Rome will pay you a large bonus, release Gothic hostages, and we can work out other details down to swords, horses, cloth and grain."

"And what is my first move?"

"Go down into Epirus, take over all Illyricum and Greece for Honorius. We will cut the province off from Constantinople. With Italy, Illyricum and Greece secure for Rome we can regain Gaul and Spain. Let Britain go. It's nothing but an island breeding trouble."

"If Stilicho will join me in Epirus to prove his good faith."

"And leave Italy exposed?"

"I'll leave half my army here to hold what I have; he can leave half of his there to hold what he has. Our other halves joined, we can fulfill the bargain. It will also cost you four thousand pounds of gold."

We agreed, and Alaric's last word was: "Rome had better keep Stilicho's bargain with me!"

Stilicho placed this necessitous bargain before the Senate. The Senate mistook itself for the Senate of old, when Rome was strong and men defended their liberties. We will not disgrace Rome, they said, by bargaining with Barbarians and appeasing enemies. They stated the proper moral sentiments. However, when I rose and asked a question the noble Senators were silent.

"All right," I said. "How many of you will, as used to be done in the days of the Republic to back such moral sentiments, rise here and now and vow to sacrifice your own property, your own dependents and your own lives in immediate defense of Italy? If any other Senator will stand up, I will be the first to make such a vow."

No one stood up. I heard a loud whisper: "This is Julian's move to make himself Emperor!"

I stood there, and I was hissed by the august Senators.

They accepted Stilicho's deal with Alaric, but Lampridius rose and shouted, "This is not peace we are buying, but servitude!" Then he fled from the Senate and took sanctuary in a church.

A long history of buying comfort at the cost of independence had not really emboldened the Senate. The words of freedom were sound without meaning in that aged corpus.

Alaric started down into Epirus, and Stilicho gave orders to ready part of his army.

At Ravenna, Olympius, Heraclian and Serena were at work on Honorius. Orders came to Stilicho from Honorius not to leave Italy, and with them one more of those fatal letters from Serena to her husband, crying in God's name not to start a civil war between the sons of Theodosius.

Stilicho and I, a couple of tired sick men, left Rome for Ravenna.

By now things were so disastrously complicated that every shade of political opinion could blame something or other on Stilicho or me. Now of course the Catholics, who had condemned Stilicho for attacking Alaric on Easter Sunday at Pollentia, declared bitterly against making a bargain with those Arian heretics; and the Pagans cried, "Look at this new coalition of Christians to drain the last blood out of Rome!" We sometimes relaxed in our strenuous labors at holding the crumbling ruins together to laugh grimly at our personal situation.

And then in this appalling web and weary disaster the one event happened which I thought might save not only Stilicho but the whole Empire.

Arcadius, Emperor of the East, died. Perhaps it is worth recording as a reminder of our natural mortality that Arcadius was not stabbed, poisoned or strangled, but simply died in accordance with his temperament and physique. His life came to its own end without the help of human violence.

The news was brought to me by one of my private agents. I was the first in Ravenna to know of it, and for one night I kept it to myself. It was wonderful how the death of that ineffectual, if followed by the right bold strokes, might save the Empire. I saw the pattern of the major moves in a single brilliant flash. I stayed up all night, one of those interminable yet instantaneous nights when the brain is ablaze with creative vision and a man works out the structure of a plan to crown ruin with shining accomplishment. What I had to understand and work with to build my structure was the deadly state of affairs in the imperial family.

I think societies rise and fall not in geographical spaces nor in citizen multitudes, but in the inner heartbeats of individual breasts. I believe the secrets of society and of history lie hid in persons, wrought by God and not yet understood by man; for if we do not understand the real working of our own life and the lives of our wife and our friend, how shall we boast we know the meaning of the world and the purpose and reasons of society and history? When I start interpreting this crucial palace situation—the purposes and relationships of complex persons—I know I am in the presence of wonders. I had to consider the secrets of hearts, judge for myself, and hazard my life on my judgment. I was neither the first nor the last man who would fall short of prophesying reality: No man yet has fully foreseen the measure of a single moment or of a single action. Thank God we are not bound to the faulty scope of our own passionate minds; it is a great gift to live in a world that surpasses our plans and our desires. It is also a gift to plan and to desire.

First and most simple in my night's work of projecting reality, there was the necrology. The Empress Eudoxia, for several years real ruler of the East, had died in Constantinople in childbirth, leaving Arcadius a widower with four or five young children, of some of whom he was the father, all girls except for the heir to the throne, the son Theodosius. Our Empress, too, had ceased living—it was more like a heartbroken cessation than a dying. During our last sojourn in Rome poor little Empress Maria, once so gay, so confident that life was good and so certain that her womb would be fruitful, stopped breathing with her lips parted and her eyes wide open. We buried her in purple splendor, a betrayed and humiliated virgin whose good dream of being a wife in fact and a mother of children had been shattered by the ambition of Serena and the impotence of Honorius. Serena, with her unflagging Theodosian ambition, had persuaded Honorius to marry her second daughter, Thermantia. And now Arcadius had died, and his son Theodosius was about eight years old. The heir to the throne of the East was too young to rule, and Honorius, Emperor of the West, was evidently not going to have an heir, for Thermantia, like Maria, continued a virgin.

Far more difficult was the situation in regard to Honorius, Serena and Galla Placidia.

Honorius should have liked Thermantia, his new Empress. She had very large protuberant eyes with spacious upper eyelids. She was a big girl with a thin, kindly and foolish smile. She was garrulous, and her laughter was like the cackling of a hen. She would have made no more demands on Honorius than one of his cackling chickens. But Serena had forced the girl on him, and Honorius resented it. Since he never entered her bedchamber nor allowed her in his, it was obvious that Honorius was not going to leave an heir. Unlike Maria, Thermantia was not humiliated; she took things as they were and went on talking a lot and stretching her neck and laughing. She was goodhearted and stupid, and she and Honorius would have made a suitable couple on a small farm.

But people with perverse designs had been working on Honorius, so manly a young Emperor in outward figure and form, so turgid, unendowed and undeveloped within. Chief among these were Galla Placidia and Olympius. Olympius the pious—who in spite of his military office always reminded me of a political-minded priest, with his oily black hair, that sharp nose and chin in a fat face, and those precious immaculate hands he worshiped—had taken over my place of nearness to Honorius. As I had been called on more and more to help Stilicho batter away at the ceaseless problems of a crumbling society, I had found less and less time to help Honorius. I had always tried to bring him into those small parts of imperial duty where he could function without misery or shame. He bestowed honors nicely and received delegations of a certain mild sort with grace and dignity; he carried himself well in opening a year as consul or during his Triumph celebrated at Rome. But his slow mind and ingrown character were not suited for serious affairs.

Olympius, insinuating himself into the place I had been forced by larger affairs to abandon, kept working on Honorius to mistake himself for the actual Emperor. Prompted by Olympius, Honorius began now and then to negate some careful plan Stilicho and I had worked out. He had nothing to offer in its place, for Olympius—like Heraclian, who aided him—was one of those men who worked for power by disintegration. The method of Olympius, which amounted to "Trust me and hate all others," had a hypnotic effect on the ingrown young man of limited intelligence. And Honorius, with his oxlike physical vitality, his sexual lethargy and his slow wits, could develop an almost incredible stubbornness. He could say "No," then glare in silence for two days at all persuasion.

Galla Placidia worked on his emotions. I think having such a brother was one of her misfortunes. It had been obvious to her, since I first met her at the age of five, that she was better fitted to rule than he. She was now a splendid young woman, eighteen years old, tainted by the one cold ambition to be Empress. She thought if she married Eucherius she would never become Empress. Serena steadily increased the pressure for the marriage. Galla Placidia refused and might have held out on her own strength, but she was able to add the refusal of Honorius. Galla Placidia, joining with Olympius, saw to it that Honorius would not consent; the betrothal could go on and on, but the marriage must not take place.

What dim, immature and slowly developing sexual potentialities Honorius possessed had from his early boyhood shown most of their energy toward this young sister of his. Galla Placidia knew this perfectly well and played on it in behalf of her ambition. She encouraged him to fondle and kiss her, developing a relationship between them that was more than that of brother and sister, but less than incest. She was a wonderful study in female intricacy. The darling of the Catholic party, she knew and adhered to the technicalities of virtue and virginity—and she never forgot that she meant to be Empress. She promised Honorius that she would never leave him, never deprive him of her voluptuous affection, if he did not force her to marry Eucherius. Years later, after becoming more of a woman and having been seasoned by personal tragedies, Galla Placidia regretted this early abuse of her sex as an instrument of ambition, and when Honorius at that late date tried to force this old false toying into actual incest she revolted and fled from the palace until after his death. But that was years later, and I only learned of it by hearsay, for by then I had lost my bishopric in Spain and was an excommunicated outcast, far from Italy.

At this early critical time I saw what she was doing to Honorius and tried to stop her, telling her that these perverse and truncated emotions degraded her and were a real danger to Honorius.

She was furious. "How dare you say I'm degraded!"

At this moment I for the first time really saw her as a vital young woman and not as the child I had teased, played with and tutored. Since her recent actions had emphasized her seductive flowering, my response was not one of respect for innocence. I took her in my arms and kissed her on the mouth.

For the first moment she was like a large sleepy child in my arms. My pressure and lust wakened her. Her lips parted, I felt her tongue and felt the surge of her body against mine. Then she slapped my face, broke loose, and ran. This kiss was the open manifestation of another complexity in the murder of Stilicho.

To Galla Placidia's low-grade seductive practices against Honorius, Olympius added a nice touch, assuring the young man, "All Serena wants is for you to give in to this marriage. Then she will have you murdered and make her son Eucherius Emperor. Depend on me to advise you and Heraclian to guard you!"

Now and then, for brief periods, I was able to restore the young man's confidence in me, perhaps by spending an hour with him praising and discussing his chickens, and he would say, "I'm confused, Gregory. I don't want to do all these things I am doing."

"Why don't you do one thing and save yourself further trouble? Make Stilicho your fellow Emperor. That will set you free."

"Serena won't let me."

Serena had raised him. She still, although he resented it, had domination over him. That he could hold out against the marriage of Galla Placidia and Eucherius and occasionally interfere in state policy were his only victories.

I thought a lot about Serena. When I realized what went on at Constantinople, at Rome, and in Milan and Ravenna outside the palace I could not but give tribute to the tone of moral decency imposed by Serena. And yet it was tone rather than reality. What could have been more profoundly immoral than enforcing the marriage of her daughters to Honorius? In a peculiar sense I finally realized that Serena did not live there with us, that she had no real connection with living persons. Serena, I think, was the most tragic of women: Stricken in her gay bright girlhood with a profoundly barren love for her uncle, Theodosius, never to be free of that unsexing idolatry, she quickened the destruction of the Empire and brought to death her husband, her children and herself. What had appeared to be the joy of her girlhood was rather the disaster of her life, only it was many years before the agony became apparent.

Stilicho was a great man and a good man who until now had been robbed of his ultimate faith in himself and made a servant by his wife. He did many hard things with courage and skill beyond other men, he did good deep things with wisdom and foresight, he did cruel base things in frustrate anger; but the shadow of Serena had fallen chill on his soul and forbade his doing the one great thing he alone could have done. He alone among us all was, like Theodosius before him, great enough to be Emperor, holding East and West together in one society.

Now, at last, I was determined that Stilicho should be equal to what the occasion demanded.

Early in the morning I went to wait on him. I managed to see him before the other courtiers arrived. A slave had just finished clipping his beard. I told him I had vital news requiring a major decision. "It concerns you and Serena and me. We must have a private conference at once."

We sent a slave to ask Serena to favor us with an immediate audience. I didn't like going to Serena instead of summoning her to us. It was one of those touches by which Stilicho showed that he still suffered a feeling of difference between himself, a Barbarian general, and Serena, a Theodosian princess.

Serena allowed us in at once, although a slave girl had been combing her hair. The slaves were dismissed. She picked up her gold-and-ivory comb and continued combing her long shining hair. "Well?" She looked at me, and Stilicho waited.

I put it in one sentence: "Arcadius has died, and now Stilicho must be Emperor."

There was a dead silence. The man and his wife looked at each other. Perhaps my presence steeled Stilicho's will, for it was Serena who first turned her head aside. "It is not possible," she said.

I waited a moment for Stilicho to speak. I could sense that Serena's negative was chilling his courage. I had to keep the pressure up. "It *is* possible. It is necessary! It has to be and shall be done."

Serena jerked up her head, her eyes flashed, and she turned her attack on me. "I am the guardian of the heritage of Theodosius. You shall not tell me what is or is not necessary!"

"I tell Your Serenity that this thing must be done. So far as I personally am concerned, you have the simple choice of doing what I say or ordering my death. So far as the Empire is concerned, you have the choice of saving the Empire with Stilicho at last filling the void left by Theodosius, or of seeing the ruin of Italy and the fall of Rome. Alaric, already betrayed by your stopping the general from joining him in Epirus, is marching north, is again dealing with Constantine, and will invade Italy. This time neither Stilicho's army nor your dream that Theodosius still rules can stop Alaric."

"Be quiet!" she commanded.

"What Gregory says is true," Stilicho told her.

She looked at him again, and once more he met her gaze without flinching. But his hold on this first effort at supremacy against Serena was fragile. I could see that his legs trembled. And her face was hot with anger.

I broke in. "I propose a triumvirate!"

That startled them. They both looked at me.

"Honorius is Emperor here." I gave them the bold structure of my plan. "Eucherius, your son, shall marry Galla Placidia and go to Constantinople as Emperor there. With the certainty of being Empress, Galla will no longer refuse the marriage. And the apex and master of the triumvirate shall be Stilicho, true Emperor of both East and West. You will make me Praetorian Prefect. We will oust Olympius and Heraclian. We will gain the powerful aid of Alaric by making him master general in Stilicho's place. Let Alaric take over command of all the Barbarian auxiliaries. Stilicho can win back the support of the Roman legions by taking direct command of them and giving them a bonus on taking the purple. The Christians have been muttering, however falsely, that Eucherius is a Pagan, but when Galla Placidia, the favorite of the Catholic party, marries him, that breach will be healed. Give me a free hand as Stilicho's Praetorian Prefect for the whole Empire and, because I have a talent for human adjustments, I will be able to soften the religious strife, turning at least some of the force of religious passion back into temples and churches where it belongs and getting it out of political action, which only corrupts religion and blinds politics."

"Gregory is right, Serena. He shows us the choice between Empire and ruin."

She stood up, fierce, proud, and shook her golden hair streaming down her shoulders and back. "Do you know what you are really asking?" she demanded of Stilicho.

He knew. He wouldn't say it. I had to say it for him. "We are asking Your Serenity to abdicate. Since the death of Theodosius, at every crisis of fatal intensity you have assumed rule of the Empire. But unlike Theodosius, whose power you dream you perpetuate, you have ruled by negation, and now almost all the great Theodosius built up is at the point of final disaster. Your Serenity also has a fateful choice to make, a profound choice of a woman's soul. Be the wife of Stilicho and save the Empire; remain the captive of Theodosius and ruin it."

Horror sickened her face as I spoke. She put her hands over her eyes and stood there swaying back and forth with her feet flat on the floor.

Stilicho was pale. He raised his arm and made a move toward her. It was a move of humiliation and surrender, and I could stop it only by stepping in front of him and saying to Serena, "We have your consent. We go to finish our plans and act."

She took her wet hands from her wet face and screamed at us. "Go! Go!"

It was painful and terrible. I took Stilicho's arm and got him out of the room.

It was a tentative victory, unsteady ground for an unsteady hope.

CHAPTER FIVE

THE MURDER OF STILICHO: III

Now WICKEDNESS BEGAN TO STEW AND SEEP. I WISH FOR a moment to forgo the comfort of attributing to demons and devils the supernatural power of snatching men down to hell; I wish also to avoid that other doctrine of pathetic comfort, that men are destined to do what they do; and I wish to reject also the amoral ease of saying we did what we did because of obscure character-forming misfortunes in the lost majestic realms of childhood. For if there are demons, there are also angels; if we are predestined to tragedy we are also predestined to God; and in the meadows and chasms of childhood there are seeds of glory as well as seeds of death. What our age least cared to look at or acknowledge was wickedness. I want now, for as long a moment as I dare, to look it right in the face: the reality of wickedness as an operating force in morally responsible adults. It was not for nothing that Athena placed an image of the terrible head of the slain Medusa in the center of her shield of wisdom.

I think it is just to say that there is a sense in which contempt for wickedness was destroying our society. First, the so-called large view, which claims that if you understand why this or that is being done you will broaden your tolerance, can be dangerous, sapping courage and establishing those forms of tolerance which amount to moral indifference. With my talent for getting people to compromise I had a tendency to fall into this error of disregarding a little wickedness here and a little wickedness there so as to smooth things out.

The Pagan stoicism which admonished a man not to worry about matters beyond his control offered the melancholy escape of diminishing a man's field of moral choice until all he had to do was endure and die— this being only the reverse of that other Pagan doctrine, enjoy and die. Platonism, overripening into the mystical doctrines of Neoplatonism, had begun to contemplate transcendent good, to the utter neglect of plain vital human relationships. And, to my way of thinking, the Catholic theologians and molders of doctrine were giving wickedness to the devil and the void, goodness to God, and to man nothing but obedience to what the Church taught.

It seemed to me that the great negative of the Church was its unwillingness to forgive men for being human. To perfect their concept of God, these thinkers were destroying the vitality of man. Christ dealt directly and simply with wickedness, saying, "Take up your cross and follow me," and saying, "Love ye one another." Even Gregory of Nazianzus handled the matter in a forthright way when he said, "I have not the time to offend God, to Whom I render account for every thought and action." And good Pelagius, voicing his favorite slogan, "If you ought, you can," was standing for the responsible mature man making his moral choice between good and evil. But Augustine, rejecting as vile all of man's voluntary life because part of his had been wicked, was bringing to high development in the Church the doctrine which says man is evil by Adam's sin and good only by grace of God, thus making it too easy for ordinary humans to take comfort in their wickedness until such time as God granted them the grace to be good. I as a member of the Church but not yet a follower of Christ had some leaning toward this escape into a moral void. I still had dread of Christ's forgiveness of all men for being human, because to accept that love would be to know wickedness for what it is and become morally responsible for every choice between good and evil.

But perhaps most operative of all in contempt of wickedness was the broad social doctrine that it was society which did things—Empire, government, the people, call it what you will—and not individual persons in intimate relationship with one another. How could there be any wickedness in what was done for the good of the Empire or the good of the people or the good of the Church or the good of the city? We simply refused to place the image of Medusa's head in the center of our shield of wisdom, saying: "Here it is. Let each man know wickedness is real and draw the line at each moment of moral choice, saying of this, it is good, I will do it, and of that, it is wicked, I will not do it."

But we went on holding wickedness in contempt, as if it were an unreality not to be considered, or in this instance or that such a trivial wickedness that it counted for nothing in relation to the great good to be had by doing it. "What! Such a little wickedness to settle so great a matter? Why not?" We might at least have been honest and said to ourselves, "We are corrupt. It is time to mend, each man himself, in relation to one another." However, we went on in our perfidy, arranging the murder of Stilicho for the good of the Empire, for the good of the Church, for the comfort of living out our passions in contempt of wickedness.

Finally—not at that time, but some years later, with Marcia's full sorrow brought home to my heart—I reached this conclusion for myself: that there is a wonderful desire in the human heart for life to be only sweet, that we will devise a thousand doctrines to make seem true, or at least possible, either here or hereafter, an illusion of serene sweetness that is not true. I believe it more nearly true that a man has a right to tragedy and sorrow in error, and that designs of the intellect to eradicate these things are dehumanizing. Each man is responsible to himself, to his fellows and to God for his own suffering. I decided, out of my own experience and quite sufficiently for myself, this: Life is agony. If it be suffused by love, the agony of life is wonderful in its radiance and creative pulsation. It is a stalwart and vibrant agony, with the flare of the spirit and the divine burning-up of the heart that generates this mysterious wonderful light that is a man's life and God's smile. Designs of intellect

for eradicating agony seemed to me dehumanizing mechanics, and obedience to doctrine of comfort or to dogma of salvation put out the light;
it was the ceaseless searching love of God, the bright agony of creative
fire, that renewed a man to brighter flame.

This, I say, I found out years later, when Marcia also honored my sorrow, and the confidence that life is agony was a divine illumination to
me. All doctrines of mere comfort or escape fell like a burden of suffo-
cating ashes out of my breast.

But back to the murder of Stilicho.

My moral position at this crisis of affairs was much weaker than I realized, and my point of greatest weakness was in my personal relationship
with Galla Placidia.

Since that moment when in a flash of masculine arrogance I had seized
her in my arms and kissed her on the mouth, she had changed as much
toward me as I had toward her. I had a comfortable room in the palace
where I often worked late at night without the aid of secretaries. Galla
Placidia took it on herself to come there frequently toward midnight
with a delightful supper of wine, cheese, cold meats and fruit. She would
share it with me and get me to relax and talk. She was quite proper about
it. She always came accompanied by two eunuchs who would remain
standing silently at the doorway, and of course the actual bearing in and
serving of the food was done by her personal slaves. But what she was
actually doing and I permitting to be done was only technically gracious
and delightful. Under the surface it was provocative, distracting and corrupt.

She was a lovely young woman to see, and she dressed beautifully for
these visits. I could tell by the eagerness of her face and the spring of her
step that she came bearing her body toward pleasure. She was in love
with me—the whole man knows such a thing when the whole woman
comes, like a singing, toward him. But she never quite reached me before
ambition, cold as a blue shadow on her rose-and-gold youth, cast its impotence on love; and not a radiant young woman for a man to love, but
she-who-would-be-Empress was there again. For a man's whole body also
knows when a woman comes buying out his soul.

Often during these intimate suppers there would be moments when I
thought I ought somehow to break through that chill guard of ambition
and rouse the dominance of love; I can only say I never made the move,
it did not happen, I was always baffled by the dual forces of offer and denial. Probably if she had not been both a princess and one whom I had
often protected through her childhood, I would have broken the tension
by violence. I did not believe Galla Placidia was either malicious enough

or calculating enough to have planned these effects. Somehow or other I had actually awakened the woman's love in her, and it was at strife with the cruel asceticism of her ambition. There were moments when I saw that she was suffering. What she wanted me to talk about most was the affairs of the Empire, and she showed an increasingly good grasp of the principles of administration.

She would say, "You are going to be at least my Praetorian Prefect when I am Empress."

"At least?"

"There is that about you that could be Emperor."

And there it was, in one sentence, a coalescence of passion and ambition. I think we both knew it was an evil sentence, perhaps one containing murder, for we both knew I would not become Emperor so long as Stilicho and Serena had power. Without Stilicho and Serena in the way, Galla Placidia and I could soon enough persuade Honorius to share the power with us.

I really think that Galla Placidia and I, in our mutual interactions of passion and character during those late evenings when, so to speak, "nothing happened," enacted the moral turning point in the murder of Stilicho. For the repeated tension of offer and denial had its effect. My old and deep affection for Galla Placidia turned to mordant lust, and the desire to have her grew, and her obsessive ambition to be Empress perceived this power gained over me by her seductive beauty.

Even Dionie, reading my moods and remarks when I came home, perceived what must be going on. She was bitter about it. She said, "I never cheated a man that way. When I provoked I responded. I prefer a straightforward harlot to these good girls who play at lust with technical virtue."

"She's bewildered."

"Men are fools."

Dionie had her own room now, because I so often came home late, and if I woke her she could not get to sleep again the rest of the night.

I was interested to discover on the morning of the crisis that Galla Placidia had her own informants in the palace. When Stilicho and I, leaving Serena, returned to Stilicho's private chamber we found Galla Placidia waiting for us there. She looked young, fresh, earnest and alert with positive intentions.

She greeted us with a bold stroke. "I have heard that Arcadius is dead. I think you are going to need my help."

"You must have spies in Serena's quarters."

"That's beside the point, Gregory." She smiled and raised a fresh young arm, offering me her hand to kiss. I kissed it and, while doing so, looked into her large intelligent blue eyes. She conveyed a message of desire and ambition. I resisted it.

"General," I advised Stilicho, "you must take over the palace guard at once, seize the palace, and remove Olympius and Heraclian. With that accomplished we will have a free hand in persuading Honorius to all the rest."

Stilicho was in acute distress. The intense emotion displayed by Serena when I had asked for her abdication of power had shocked him deeply. She had once again weakened his will for decisive action. He said now, "Twice I helped Theodosius unseat usurpers. To seize the palace and force Honorius would be to usurp the throne. Let us do this thing, which I agree with you needs to be done, honorably and peacefully."

"It includes my marriage to Eucherius, does it not?" Galla Placidia asked us.

"It does," I told her. "You shall be Empress of the East."

She rose, looked steadily into my eyes, and smiled. "I would rather be Empress of Rome than of Constantinople."

"The choice is limited. We have a narrow margin of time. Stilicho, you must act before Olympius knows what has happened and gets Honorius stubbornly set against us. Take over the palace at once and do this thing by clean strokes."

Unfortunately at that point Serena came in, her face sharpened by distress and bitterness. Her first words were, "I forbid violence! There shall be no violence among the members of the family of Theodosius!"

"That," Stilicho said, "is what I have been telling Gregory. I am not a usurper."

I knew then that so long as Serena lived, Stilicho would never be Emperor.

Galla Placidia took my arm and pressed her warm side against me so that I could feel her breast and her hip. She whispered, "You see what I mean, Gregory. It was bound to happen."

There was a sense in which Galla Placidia and I at that moment murdered Stilicho. I did only two things. Very briefly, and I thought unobtrusively, I moved my arm across Galla Placidia's back and pressed her side with my hand; she knew it for an acceptance of an erotic compact and blushed faintly. The other thing I did was to say, "All right, General. No violence."

Galla Placidia had eased away from my side. Serena was staring at the proud young woman's face. Then Serena looked at me. She looked sick and frightened. She knew that she had been betrayed and that Stilicho had been betrayed. She knew Galla Placidia and I had done it. But she didn't know how.

Stilicho was standing in moody indecision, saddened by the whole business and not quite knowing what he could or ought to do. He repeated my phrase, "No violence."

Serena, suspicious, wary, said to Galla Placidia, "The time has come for you and Eucherius to marry. You must at last give your consent."

"My brother Arcadius has just died. It would be indecent to marry so soon. I think Honorius should go to Constantinople as uncle and guardian of the child Theodosius and install him on the throne. When Honorius returns it will be time enough for me to marry Eucherius."

Stilicho was startled and looked to me for an objection to such a radical contradiction of my plan for a triumvirate of Honorius, Eucherius and himself. But Serena relaxed with a sudden light of pleasure on her face, for what Galla suggested would still leave Serena final arbiter of Theodosian power.

She spoke at once. "It is better than Gregory's plan, Stilicho. We don't need to upset the whole order of Empire with risk of violence, even civil war."

I put my objection in a negative form.

"I think, General, I could serve you best as governor of Africa, if you will do me the honor of granting that appointment."

He was tired, bewildered and angry. "You mean because I won't this day usurp the purple by violence you no longer desire to support me." He turned to Serena. "And for Honorius to go to Constantinople would be an absurdity. I would have to take the best part of my army along to protect him, thus exposing Italy. Alaric is ready to invade Italy again because I made a bargain with him for Rome and we broke it."

So we arrived at a paralysis of indecision.

Galla Placidia and I went out of the room and down a corridor together. I pulled her into a recessed doorway and kissed her with a flare of passion. Her lips and body promised much. I said, "When?"

She understood and replied, "When we're married."

I straightened myself out of the embrace.

She saw I was angry. "You did well to side with me, Gregory. Now stay in the background. Assume a neutral position. This crisis will end the power of Stilicho and Serena. Don't even divorce Dionie until after Stilicho falls. Then——" She squeezed my arm, lifted her face as if for another kiss, but smiled and moved off rapidly.

I called after her the ironic watchword of all this treachery, "No violence!"

The lies I then told myself in the secrecy of lust and ambition were not even subtle. Galla Placidia was astute. She understood that the antipathy between me and Olympius was so profound that I would never trust him, and she kept the two of us apart in most of the subsequent intrigue. On the other hand she knew of my long association with Heraclian and bolstered my vanity when I asserted that I understood and could control Heraclian's treachery. I would allow Heraclian to be a key figure in making me Emperor, then deal with him as occasion might demand. The whole affair, with the fate of Empire at stake, became a macabre idiot series of actions, a veritable dance of death, with Stilicho as the grave, noble and sad puppet of disaster.

Dionie, watching me like a cat out of her green eyes, smiled and said, "Well, my Emperor! So at last you are going to get what you have always wanted—and Galla Placidia with her fresh young body in the bargain!"

"You're a devil."

"I am the one woman who has read your heart from the beginning. I could still destroy you." She came to me, stroked my forehead with her wonderful soothing hand, and astounded me by saying, "Gregory darling, in spite of all your rotten desires, you are the only good man I have known. No one else would have saved me from despair after my illness ruined my beauty. I have had only two good things in this world—my beauty and your tenderness. I count it greater in you when I know that the only woman you ever loved or ever will love is Marcia. She will suffer more than I when you and Galla Placidia appease your lust and rule the Empire. Will you never forget Marcia?"

I squeezed Dionie's hand. She had brought tears to my eyes. I said nothing.

It was the most sullen, hot, humid and depressing month I ever endured, at Ravenna or anywhere else. The sun never really shone, it glared through the thick humid air, and there was always a kind of sticky moisture on our faces, as if the outward oppressive heat were squeezing forth our venom to show us for what we were. There would be beads of moisture beneath Galla Placidia's eyes and on her upper lip; drops of sweat forming and trickling down from the base of the Emperor Honorius' ears; little designs of sweat formed among the black hairs on the backs of Heraclian's hands and wrists; the throat of Olympius, the few times I saw him in Council, gleamed with perspiration; and my beard always felt dank, my lips parched, and my forehead at once ached as if caught in an iron band and oozed an evil trickle against my heavy eyebrows and down my pulsing temples.

With the aid of my alleged neutrality and Stilicho's paralysis of indecision Honorius, with the sly tongue of Olympius in his ear, came forward as the stubborn, outright and active Emperor. He assigned the feeding of his chickens to a eunuch, kept us in his presence for hours at a time, and ordered this and ordered that. Galla Placidia and Olympius prepared him for these meetings and counseled him afterward. The only point on which Stilicho held out, with no support from me and no opposition from Serena, was the matter of Honorius going in person to Constantinople. What finally won the argument for him was that such an imperial journey would cost a fortune; we did not have the money in the treasury, and to try to squeeze Italy now for a special donation to the Emperor would probably bring on violence, riots, even rebellion. Honorius was fundamentally timid, and nothing scared him more than the thought of violence in his presence.

The plan decided on was like a dream you might have on a hot night of fever and headache. Olympius prepared and Honorius signed two imperial documents for Stilicho to deliver, the one to Alaric, the other to the child Theodosius in Constantinople. Alaric, reinforced by some of Stilicho's Barbarian troops and generals, was to invade Gaul, destroy the usurper Constantine, and then, presumably, settle his Gothic nation in that province. We did not even raise the question whether or not Alaric, angry at our recent betrayal of him, would agree to this. Stilicho was to take Roman legions with him to Constantinople, install the child Theodosius as Emperor, and—also presumably, for in these plans nothing was envisioned beyond first moves—return to his old place in Ravenna. There was obviously no money for these moves, either; they would strip the defenses of Italy, and they would cause serious trouble in the army. This last point was fatal.

Stilicho for many years had been the friend and beloved general of the Barbarian auxiliaries; they were our best fighting men, he had depended on them, and they had not failed him. He had shown them many favors and rewarded them for many victories. The tired, incompetent and second-rate Roman legions hated him for this. Now he was supposed to turn his Barbarians over to Alaric and lead the Romans to the East. To start the whole affair with the completest folly, Honorius insisted on going to the camp of the Roman legions at Pavia to review the troops before Stilicho marched them away. Honorius, who had always hid in Milan or Ravenna from the smell of battle, was an object of jest and contempt to the soldiers.

My heart was sufficiently blackened and spongy for me to accept Galla Placidia's interpretation of this plan.

"After Honorius reviews the troops," she assured me, "Stilicho will take Serena and Eucherius with him. While he is in the East and the Barbarian auxiliaries are fighting in Gaul with Alaric, you will divorce Dionie, marry me, and Honorius will elevate us to help him rule. When Stilicho comes back I shall be Empress and you and Honorius Emperors. And all done without violence."

The corrupt insanity in which we all were webbed had almost a mystic force, as if our wills had been taken over by demons and dedicated to doom.

I put my arm on Galla's shoulder and said, "I look forward to my marriage night and my morning's crown!"

She lifted her face. I took her in my arms and kissed her. There was something triumphant and horrible about that kiss, not as if we were two human lovers, but as if two demons kissed and clung and burned each other on the mouth.

Galla, still in my arms, her breast heaving against me as she caught her breath, whispered, "You're powerful! Alive! You will be a great Emperor, like my father!"

I had been making ready to leave with the official party the next morning and had a few last things to do. It was after midnight when I finished in my office, too late to go home. I often spent a night at the palace, where I had private rooms. With a small lamp in my hand I went along a corridor and across a court toward my bedchamber.

As I turned right into the next corridor and drew near to Stilicho's private chamber he stepped out of his doorway with a small lamp like mine in his hand.

Both of us instinctively raised our lamps so that the light was on our faces. We searched each other's faces for a long moment of silence, like conspirators who could not possibly trust each other but had to come to agreement on a mutual deed. Finally Stilicho whispered, "It is well. If I cannot be Emperor, you must."

Then he said, "Come in."

I entered his room. We set our little lamps down on a table and sat facing each other across their small smoky flames.

"I was waiting for you, Gregory. This may be the last time that I give you an order. I am still Regent of the Empire. You must obey me." I could see him search my eyes, then look for the exact expression of my mouth in the midst of my beard. "Do not come with us tomorrow. Stay here in Ravenna. Rule the city. If I am murdered, then marry Galla Placidia and rule the Empire."

I looked at his big tired face, his white hair, his thick strong neck. He was noble. "There is no thought of murdering you."

"These days of evil have us all confused. There is no thought at all in anything we plan or do—only this dark depth of evil. We both feel it. We both are bound to it. We both obey it. If I cannot be Emperor, you must."

"I will make no move to betray you."

"We are all betrayed. By the gods, by the times, by each other. It is too late."

For one instant, seeing his strong shoulders and noble head in the ruddy waver of light from our little lamps, I felt detached and free from the evil in which we were embroiled, and I felt bound by deep affection to Stilicho.

I suggested the last way out. "Let us go to Honorius now, at once, shake him up out of sleep, cancel this trip, demand the purple for you. I will back you up, and you will be Emperor by dawn."

He took out his dagger and laid it on the table between the two lamps. "Serena is asleep. I stood looking down at her face. Are you ready to pick up that dagger and plunge it into Serena's heart?"

I stared at the dagger. I looked up at Stilicho and shook my head.

He let out a sharp breath and leaned toward me. "Neither would I do such a thing. So I shall never be Emperor. You and I, Gregory, are steeped in evil, but neither of us is monstrous. Neither of us can take rule by violence. The doom of Rome is occurring. There is nothing to do but for me to go on this fatal journey, for you to stay here, and for both of us to wait for events that befall us. I am being destroyed. You cannot save me. Only if you do nothing, but simply wait for Galla's ambition to make you Emperor, you might yet save Rome. *Do nothing! Save Rome!*"

I looked straight into his eyes and let out a deep breath that I must have been holding tensely and long.

I picked up my lamp and started out his door.

He picked up his lamp and followed me to the door. "I have ordered you to stay in Ravenna. When the crisis comes, do nothing to save me. It is a command."

"You are trying to compel me to be your murderer."

"I am my own murderer," he said. He blew out his lamp and let his hand dangle. Oil spilled from his lamp onto the floor. In a last command of anguish he appealed, "When the crisis comes, do nothing. *Nothing!*

They will make you Emperor." He clasped my hand and said, "This evil is almost finished. God approaches. Farewell!"

He turned into his room. I went to my quarters, bearing the small smoky flame, knowing I had made a profound and strange agreement of despair with Stilicho, and asking myself if this wretched flutter of light from my little lamp was all that the next Emperor of Rome had with which to light his way through the darkness and evil to come.

I let that lamp burn all night.

Honorius, Olympius, Stilicho and most of the notables left about dawn on the journey to Pavia to review the troops. I stayed in Ravenna.

I had sense enough not to trust Heraclian, who stayed in Ravenna in charge of the palace guard. I prepared carriages and a heavily armed escort and kept them in readiness for flight, and I set dependable agents in the palace ready the moment I gave the signal to seize Serena and Galla Placidia as my hostages. I kept a good ship tied up in the harbor several miles below the city, manned, provisioned and ready for any voyage. Eucherius went with his father, and Honorius, on a whim, took the Empress Thermantia with him.

I suppose I had in principle foreseen but refused to acknowledge more or less what actually happened.

The pious Olympius had his own plan. For several years he had been working on the general problem of the ruin of Stilicho. He had made full use of the Catholic party; he had used money and pious shows of sympathy to gain several hundred key conspirators in the army; and he had tightened his almost hypnotic control over Honorius.

At Bologna Olympius circulated the story among Stilicho's Barbarian auxiliaries that they were to be severed from their beloved general and sent to Alaric to fight in the North. The troops mutinied, and Stilicho had to stay behind with these Barbarian contingents to restore them to order. The Emperor and Olympius and most of the high officials who had served Stilicho for a dozen years went on to Pavia. At Pavia Olympius informed the legions, by the murmur and gossip of his key men, that Stilicho, who hated them and whom they hated for favoring the Barbarians, was going to detach them from Italy; they would go to Constantinople and never see their homes again. There in Pavia, as Honorius began to review the legions, there was not a mere mutiny, but a riotous rebellion. Every high official there thought to be an adherent of Stilicho was murdered by the soldiers, and the same was done to a number of governors and officials who had come to Pavia from the North for refuge from Constantine. Olympius snatched Honorius out of the mob, conveyed him to the palace, and concealed him in the dress of a slave. The riot, plunder, murder and pillage continued three days. Of course, at the first moment, a messenger was sent to Stilicho.

Stilicho, in Bologna, was sickened by the news. Sarus, his giant Gothic general, and others, urged him to march at once on Pavia, quell the revolt, and seat himself as Emperor. He could not endure the thought of starting civil war in Italy. He temporized and delayed, and yet he halfheartedly made ready to go in order to save the Emperor.

But before he marched from Bologna news came that Olympius had finally calmed the troops and saved the Emperor Honorius.

Stilicho canceled the order to march on Pavia. General Sarus threatened mutiny, but Stilicho refused to start civil war so long as the Emperor's person was safe. That night, as Stilicho slept in his tent under the guard of his faithful personal troop of Huns, Sarus roused his Goths in revolt, stormed through the camp, and all but laid his hands on Stilicho. Stilicho and his small troop of Huns set out for Ravenna, riding hard. At every town on the way he warned the people to close their gates and guard especially all Gothic hostages they held.

In Pavia, Olympius had by now persuaded Honorius that Stilicho had caused the riot there as part of a deep plan. "His whole aim in going to Constantinople is to strangle your nephew Theodosius and seat his son Eucherius on the throne. He meant to have you murdered here, so as to be Emperor of the West himself. I and the Christian party have saved you."

The Roman legions clamored: "Death to Stilicho!"

Honorius signed two letters Olympius had ready, and Olympius dispatched them at once on swift order to Ravenna. The messenger had exact instructions. He was to deal with Heraclian, not with me.

During the Emperor's absence I held the highest civil authority in Ravenna and Heraclian was in control of the troops. The first thing Heraclian did was to place and keep Serena virtually under palace arrest. He intercepted messages she sent to Stilicho. As news began to reach us we expected Stilicho's return. Heraclian kept the gates closed and armed forces ready to prevent him from bringing any large force into the city.

I did nothing for perfidy or against perfidy, but simply awaited the rewards of general treachery. I watched Galla Placidia with desire and paused in the throne room with expectation.

Stilicho reached Ravenna about dusk. He was accompanied only by his personal bodyguard of Huns. Heraclian, waiting with a large body of troops, opened the gate. Stilicho rode through the gate at the head of his handful of loyal Huns. Heraclian's soldiers surrounded Stilicho and his men. It was all done and understood without words. Heraclian led the march toward the palace, where he meant to hold Stilicho under arrest.

Stilicho realized he had power only to start a bloody futile riot, for his Huns were outnumbered more than twenty to one. He made the one simple move not expected. As they rode past the church he suddenly galloped his horse right up to the door, leaped off, and went in.

Even Heraclian realized that, because he and Olympius counted for heaviest support from the Christian party, he dared not violate the sanctuary of the church. Stilicho's Huns took up a menacing position of guard at the church door, and Heraclian disposed a large body of troops all around them and the church. Heraclian asked the bishop to give Stilicho up peacefully, and the bishop refused.

Before dawn the messenger arrived from Pavia with two imperial orders signed by Honorius. Heraclian showed me one, calling for the arrest of Stilicho. It ordered him to be held for trial until the return of the Emperor. Heraclian did not show me the second order, and I did not know of it.

I went back to the church with Heraclian, who showed the bishop the order for Stilicho's arrest.

The bishop, tall and lean, shook his scraggly beard. "I will not let soldiers enter to take him. But I will show him the Emperor's order. He has been praying."

The bishop took the document into the church. Heraclian and I waited on horseback. Stilicho came back with the bishop. Heraclian demanded his sword. Stilicho gave Heraclian a contemptuous glance, then unbuckled his sword and held it up to me, saying clearly, "After Stilicho, Julian!"

I refused the sword. "Keep your sword, Stilicho. This is only an arrest."

He buckled it in place again.

Then Heraclian drew his second imperial document from his breastplate and read it in his loud hard voice. The light of dawn had spread over the pavement, and warm morning mist was rising above the top of the church.

Stilicho's face was weary, and the flesh was slack. He looked like an old lion sick of life. This second letter from Honorius, which Heraclian read distinctly, pronounced Stilicho a brigand and a public enemy of the Emperor and the Empire, and ordered his immediate execution for his crimes.

"That is a forgery!" I shouted, and wheeled my horse to seize the scroll from Heraclian.

Stilicho seized it before I could, looked right up into my face, and commanded, "Do nothing!"

Stilicho bowed his head to read the scroll. His Huns drew their swords and crowded close about him. He read slowly, as if he could not believe what he read. To be sentenced to death, yes. But to be called the enemy of Rome was utter grief. Then he straightened, raised his hand in the warm damp light of dawn, and issued his last command: "Romans! Obey your Emperor!"

Heraclian dismounted. Stilicho knelt on the stones. Before he bent his head he looked up at me. He said nothing, but he conveyed a message. I do not know why he conveyed it to me. It was a strange and to me a terrible message: "This is God."

It was a clear statement of his soul to mine. I wondered if he understood what his soul was asserting. I did not—or did not dare to—understand, and yet I clung to the message as if to save my own soul.

"This is God."

He looked at me a long moment. And as soundlessly as he had conveyed his message I answered. It frightened me, for my soul conveyed a message to his as surely as his had conveyed one to mine: "God is here."

Then Stilicho bowed a serene and noble face, and Heraclian of the hairy hands with one sweep of a great sword cut off Stilicho's head.

All the evil in my nature set up a sudden violent struggle to take refuge in details, striving to compose an aesthetic and dramatic picture of a physical action out of the sensuous details—the flash of the sword, the thud and roll of the head, the shock and sprawl of the body. But I could not achieve that refuge, for Stilicho had said, "This is God," and I had replied, "God is here." No detail can either conceal or reveal God; He remains, no matter what befalls one's body or whither goes one's soul, inescapable. The presence of God is beyond killing.

The first day's rioting began at once between Stilicho's Huns and Heraclian's troops. But I couldn't take refuge from God in that either. I felt a white light blazing throughout me from which I could not take refuge in any thought or act.

I went to the palace to tell Galla Placidia what was happening. My appearance shocked her.

I said, "Nothing I saw, nothing I can remember and tell you, was the actual death of Stilicho. His head came to rest on one side, with the eyes open and the lips parted. The helmet made a clear true ring as it bounced off on the stones. There was his body, there had been his soul; God was there and is here, and nothing has diminished Him. All the details are fruitless, and death is an impossibility. Stilicho is dead."

She brought me a jug of strong wine, a golden cup and a bowl of olives.

I drank a cup of wine and began eating olives. I looked at that beautiful young woman. I took hold of her hand, I felt the warm flesh of her arm. I said, "God is here, too. Life is no longer possible for me. I must go on living."

She was frightened. "It's a shock, Gregory. It will pass."

I put my arm around her shoulders and leaned my cheek against the side of her forehead. I needed her support to stand. "You're young. You're going to be Empress. You can still believe in details. I no longer know how to do anything either to deny or conceal the mystery of God. To see Stilicho's head fall to the ground was not a thing I could either understand or believe. I had preparations all made to seize you and Serena and take you to Rome as my hostages. What a silly idea! I'll never marry you."

"Of course you'll marry me. All our plans will succeed now."

She helped me to sit down. I picked up another handful of olives and began to eat them.

She leaned down, kissed my forehead, then rubbed my temples with her young woman fingers. "Also, I do love you," she said.

Heraclian came in. I had never before seen him so excited, so enthusiastic, so confident, so proud. He danced about, swishing and playing in the air with his red-stained sword, and cried out joyously, "Ha, Barbarian! Done for, Barbarian! I rolled your head on the stones, old boy!"

He tossed his sword on the table, seized Galla Placidia, whirled her about, singing, "Dance, my Empress, dance!"

Then he looked at me, with his fists on his hips, and laughed in my face. "Why so glum, Gregory? Where's your stomach for power? Don't you know the first law of the Empire? First you kill, then you rule, and to be sure you keep on ruling you kill and kill. Great God, I feel good!"

I never saw a man enjoy a murder so much.

Galla Placidia was shocked by the contrast between Heraclian's reaction and mine. She was too young to conceal this emotion, and I could see reflected on her face her swift and cunning effort to find a secure place between Heraclian's joy in the murder and my stunned consciousness that no man can diminish God.

She achieved an amazing moral perversion of words for her own peace of mind. "Stilicho has been removed from office. That had to be. But others remain who endanger us."

Her color was high, her flashing blue eyes were excited, and her lovely figure and golden hair should have roused me to a new pitch of desire by her proffered beauty. My eyes followed the lines of her figure from head to foot and back up again. I said, "Venus on the throne."

She reached for my hand, pleased by my remark. "You feel better now, Gregory."

She gave a little tug, and I stood up. "I see better, darling." I asked Heraclian, "What of the Huns?"

Stilicho's Huns had all been either killed or imprisoned. Friends of Stilicho were trying to get out of the city. Heraclian, Galla Placidia and I formed an uneasy degenerate cabal all that long day, judging and passing sentence on persons not there: those to have their property confiscated, those to be exiled, those to be killed. Nothing we did seemed real to me, but it was all quite horrible.

Once Galla Placidia said, "Gregory! Stop eating so many olives. You'll make yourself sick."

I put the olive pits in rows on the table and counted them. I had eaten nearly two hundred olives. For a while I stopped eating them, but then I began again and for some reason placed the pits in orderly rows on the table.

I said, "I am sick. Death is impossible, for you can't diminish God. Stilicho is dead. We have words for all the details, but no words for the meaning."

"Pull yourself together," Heraclian warned me. "We have serious work to do."

The thought that we three dark little mortals had anything serious to do in the great white light of God struck me as very funny. I restrained my laughter and only chuckled. "I nearly forgot the chickens! I promised Honorius to watch over them."

I summoned a young secretary and sent him to make sure all was well with the Emperor's chickens. This indeed was serious work. Galla Placidia and Heraclian knew as well as I did that Honorius would settle into a rage against us if he came home and found any of his chickens harmed or neglected. We waited anxiously until the secretary reported that the chickens were all right.

We sent eunuchs to inform Serena of events, but none of us would go near her. Heraclian and I took a ride through the city in the afternoon to show the people we were confident and in command. Heraclian, through his various captains, managed all the arrests. I did a reasonable amount of ordinary civic and imperial business—I remember sending an order to the prefect in Rome, warning him that disturbances were likely and he had better bring in an extra supply of grain for emergencies—but no detail of occupation or motion gave me refuge from the white light that was exhausting me. Heraclian went out at night for a tour of the city. For half an hour Galla Placidia and I were alone.

"You must divorce Dionie before Honorius returns."

"There's no hurry."

"If you delay the thing, she'll make trouble."

"I suppose so. She depends on me."

"Well, then?"

"I'm exhausted. Morally exhausted."

I rose to my feet, went to where she sat, stooped down, and kissed her on the forehead. Then I stood there a moment with my hand resting on her shoulder. "I've known you since you were five years old. Even then you wanted to be Empress."

"Yes."

"You will be."

"I know I will."

"Good night."

"Is that all you have to say, Gregory?"

"That's all, darling."

She stood up. We looked at each other. She put her arms around me and kissed me on the mouth. She pressed against me for a moment, then she began to tremble, then she shuddered and stood back. Her face flushed red, her eyes were hot and flashing, her voice was angry. "You're like a dead man!"

"Yes. A dead man, exhausted by God's white light. Stilicho was better than any man who is left. I'm going now. You and Heraclian talk it over after I am gone. You may think many stand in your way and ought to be killed. Perhaps you will decide now that I am one of those you fear and ought to kill. But I'll tell you what I learned today. The deepest motive of fear is the desire to diminish God. And so we murdered Stilicho." I shook my head. I placed my sick heavy hand on her warm young shoulder. "No man's death diminishes God. No man's death can diminish God. Nothing a man can think or dream or do can diminish God."

"You are betraying me, Gregory. I need your help to hold my balance of power against Heraclian and Olympius. I'll never forgive you if you desert me now. Your only choice is to marry me and be Emperor with Honorius. Why else have we removed Stilicho from power, except for this?"

"Gregory Julian was never chosen by God to be Emperor."

"My arms and the throne are open to you. You can have them on your own choice."

"I chose the murder of Stilicho and killed my own desire."

Her smile hardened. Her eyes flashed. "I shall be Empress. With you—or alone!"

I went home. The streets were in uneasy quiet. One or two fires burned in the city, but Heraclian's horsemen, swordsmen and archers were patrolling the streets and breaking up groups of citizens. I knew that here and there, in select houses, arrest and murder were going on. My house was quiet. Dionie must have passed a hard day, expecting any moment to hear from me that I was going to cast her off, or even fearing that she might be one of those chosen for seizure and death. I found she had fallen asleep crouched on the floor in a corner of her own bedroom. My moral exhaustion was so great that I made no move to waken her. I stared at her for a moment and wondered why on earth I had ever lived at all.

Then I saw a small golden wine cup on Dionie's table. Beside it was a little phial of Egyptian glass. My first thought was that Dionie had taken poison. But when I picked up the wine cup I saw it was still full to the brim. She had prepared the potion, then could not take it. I looked down where she crouched in sleep, and saw the gentle stir of her body in even breathing.

I had then one glimmer of moral response. I said to myself, Poor woman. How she fears death! Tomorrow, perhaps, I will try to save her life. Tonight, nothing!

She moaned faintly in her sleep, I supposed in some dream of lost pleasure, but she did not waken. One of her sandals had come off, and her small warm foot looked much younger, much less abused, much more ready for new paths of delight than did her wan, silent and despair-sick face. I saw a tear form and glisten in that little hollow between the corner of her eye and the bridge of her nose. She was weeping, even in sleep.

I simply had no moral strength left, except to say, Perhaps . . . tomorrow . . .

I went into my bedroom, where lamps were burning. I looked at each of the lamps in turn and wondered what the flame was. For a moment Ambrose, as I had always known him, stood there looking at me. I started repeating the Lord's Prayer, but broke off and covered my eyes with my arm. I flung myself on the bed face down, and the voice of Ambrose, speaking above and behind me, intoned the Lord's Prayer with slow nobility.

I slept. I don't know how long I slept.

And then I heard Dionie beating on my door and crying out, "Save me, Gregory! Save me!"

I seized open the door, and she stumbled in, her clothes torn, her hair streaming and a gash bleeding on her cheek. There were yells and strides in the corridor.

I caught Dionie in my arms, carried her out to the balcony and dropped her over the railing into the water. Then I vaulted over myself, plunging 'way under the tepid surface and coming up with a shake of my head. There was an orange swollen moon in the humid sky and a shimmer of orange light on the slow black water. We heard the soldiers shouting on the balcony, and a spear struck the water between us as we swam.

Dionie was a strong swimmer, but the splash of that spear broke her nerve. She seized hold of me in terror, climbed on my back with her arms around my neck, and began to choke off my breath.

Now a shower of arrows splashed around us. One grazed my arm as I tried to reach back to break Dionie's strangle hold. Her weight and her strength in her terror pushed me under water. I had to struggle with a last exertion of will and breath to come up again. Almost instantly there came another shower of arrows from the archers on the balcony. But fortunately Dionie now began to relax the strangling pressure of her arms around my throat. I could hear her sobbing and could feel her body shake along my back like that of a sobbing child; but I was now able to swim freely and rapidly out of range of the archers. Then I felt her body slip from me. I seized her under the arms and swam on my side, using one arm for my stroke and the other to pull Dionie with me. She had stopped sobbing.

A low sudden black rain squall blew in between the water and the moon. I swam steadily toward the shore where the pine trees grew. In the increasing black of rain I could hear the wind-blown pines before I saw them. I could smell them before I saw them.

I carried Dionie up onto the bank, and in the darkness I felt rather than saw the arrow that had pierced her back.

I carried her into the pine woods and sat on the ground and held her in my arms below a tree. Earth-rich and primeval was the smell of the dark deep woods all around us, and all the forest stirred with sound of wind and rain. My dark fingers, sorrowful and gentle, touched Dionie's lips. I begged God to let her smell the earth and hear the rain. But Dionie was silent, with rain on her quiet face, and never spoke or moved again.

PART 5

BEGGAR

BEFORE GOD

CHAPTER ONE

PILGRIM TO AUGUSTINE

HERACLIAN DID NOT HAVE ENOUGH TROOPS TO MAKE PUR-
suits and captures beyond the walls of Ravenna. By noon the next day
I was aboard my ship, putting out to sea beyond the immediate reach of
political treachery. I gave my shipmaster orders to sail for Hippo Regius
in Africa.

I knew where I was going, but I did not know what I would do when
I got there.

I knew I faced the naked and terrible problem of moral survival. I was
too wretched to know how to love God; and without a love of God moral
survival is impossible. I felt with unquestioning certainty that I must go
to Augustine. It was a compulsion, perhaps insane or perhaps divine, but
a compulsion such as a wounded animal might have to crawl back to its
lair. This compulsive desire to see Augustine was the last finger of desperation with which I held off shattering moral collapse.

The voyage of the ship was fair and fortunate, but my days were a
painful long twisting in despair, and my nights were a hideous turmoil
of dreams. In these dreams I sought passionately, desperately, to find
my fathers, and lost all my fathers over and over again. I was, in my
dreams, never in time to save my natural father from his suicide; he
would die with me beating on the door. And the great Theodosius
would reach out his hand, but before I could touch it he would lie
stricken on his splendid couch of death. And when I came running
down dark desperate ways to Ambrose, I would find him with arms outstretched in the form of a cross, beyond my crying reach. And of Stilicho,
again and again, I could not find the body, but only the severed head
with the eyes open and the lips parted. From these dreams I woke
crying, "Augustine! Augustine!"

My dull and wounded mind twisted and turned in frantic desire for
the healing magic of a father's voice which would give me the word and
symbol to relieve me of my burden and of all my pain; and I knew of

349

no such possible father, except only Augustine. He already had a triple hold on me. First, as my tutor when I was a boy; though the time had been short, the penetration of his temperament into the coloring of my life had been deep; I had trusted him, and the vehemence of his suffering, startling my soul, had given a potential scope, depth and peril to my life, which is perhaps most fatefully learned in boyhood and which no other teacher had imparted to me. Would not any man in the deathly struggle for moral survival turn if he could to the teacher who had touched his soul in boyhood?

His second hold on me was through his *Confessions*. I had dwelt many years in the haunting desire to lay aside death and see God; and did not Augustine understand this profoundly when he said, "I am conscious of something within me that plays before my soul and is as a light dancing in front of it; were this brought to steadiness and perfection in me it would surely be eternal life"? I had read his *Confessions* once, twice, thrice, and parts of it many times; but in these last years of political disintegration and my own moral collapse I had been a bad reader of that good book, for I would take the suffering and insight of his passages as my own unction, healing surfaces for an hour because I had not courage to cure wounds to their depth. Often I wore his vision as a mask, much as I had used the mask of power to hide my emptiness of purpose, or as a man might cloak himself with too much wine so as to seem happy. Still the intimacy of his *Confessions* was a hold he had on me; the darkness was coming down on my soul, and this man with a large light was alive in the world: "There is but a dim light in men; let them walk, let them walk, lest darkness overtake them."

And by my prophetic imagination Augustine had a third, a compulsive hold on me. Imagination of this sort, fed more largely on phantoms of despair than on sound realities, bodes forth heroic flashes, notable more for their phantasmal glory and grandeur than for their tried simplicity and tested truth. I said to myself: "The well of my poison will be burst and drained, and swift shall be the sweep of healing when I cry out before his heart and he lifts me up!"

I also knew Augustine in three ways. There was the passionate young soul in torment I had met in the light of day in my boyhood in Rome. There was the God-suffused poet of the *Confessions*, dwelling at large in my imagination like a priest apart and a voice of things to come. I have spoken much before now of these two knowings of Augustine, and only can say again that they were knowings of a high, poetic, passionate and vital soul. The third was the knowing by report, document and hearsay of Augustine the bishop, at work in the world.

As it was with Ambrose and many another in our time—even as it later befell me—Augustine was made a bishop against his desire. Converted by the persistent passion of his own necessity ("For Thou hast made us toward Thyself, and our heart is without rest until it rest in Thee"), baptized by Ambrose, severed from his mother Monica by her death, and returned to Africa, Augustine desired the life of a monk, to study in quiet and to bear serene high witness to God.

He stayed a short while in Carthage, which still dazzled with splendor and vice and, like any city, tried to shout the heart away from God. There he did not dream of miters or of bishops' thrones. He went through the wheat and the vines and the olives inland to Tagaste, the small town of his birth, with sun on its face among the hills. There, with his eyes narrowing to the brilliant light, he sold the remnants of his father's estate and gave the money to the poor. He kept a house not as his own but for the small monastic community he established with his friends Alypius and Evodius and his son Adeodatus. It interests me how the work of one man goes on into the life of another; and so it was here that what Ambrose had worked out in the way of communal monastic life for monks about him in Milan became the guiding form of what Augustine established first at Tagaste and later at Hippo. Augustine was never a solitary; the fanatical ideal of the desert monks did not appeal to him; he lived best among men seeking together what was best. He carried on what Ambrose had begun, a conversion of the old Greek form of the philosophical academy into a religious community. In this community life were manual work, prayer and scholarship, for Augustine deemed it fruitful to be a good scholar in the service of Christ.

In this period he became irrevocably a Catholic, concluding: "Neither in the confession of the Pagans, nor in the sweepings of the Heretics, nor in the feebleness of the Schismatics, nor in the blindness of the Jews, is religion to be sought, but only among those who are called Catholic Christians, or orthodox—that is, keepers and right followers of the whole truth."

He had about three years of confident and fruitful peace in this life at Tagaste. His son Adeodatus, who was said to have a lovely spiritual light shining in his face, died. Then a government official at Hippo Regius, who was weary at heart and sick of soul, wrote Augustine to come in God's name and teach him how to give up the world. Augustine thought the man would make a good monk; and, since Hippo had a bishop, he felt safe to get on a mule and ride over there through hills flooded with sunlight. Augustine gave the yearning official instructions, but the poor good bewildered man could not take the final step. "Once

I become a monk, I can no longer be a Roman official!"—or some such fear stopped him.

But in Hippo Augustine, with his reputation for learning, made the error one day of going to church to hear the old bishop, Valerius, preach. Valerius was a Greek, poor in Latin and scarcely able to speak Punic at all, which was the common language of the town. The old bishop—perhaps with the desperate intent of a tired old man to gain relief at any cost—that day told his congregation that he needed a vigorous young priest to help him, one who knew Latin and Greek and Punic and God. He insisted that they choose a candidate and bring him forward to be ordained. Suddenly, startled, Augustine saw eyes upon him, then felt hands. The people of Hippo were of a kind to seize what they wanted. Augustine struggled, protested, and wept. The people held him and shouted, "This is the man we want!" Four or five men, with others crowding, lugged Augustine forward, and Bishop Valerius there and then ordained him a priest and then—and often thereafter—told the congregation "that it was providential such a man as Augustine had been granted him to build up the Church by the word of God and by his invigorating teaching."

Augustine took over more and more of the old bishop's work. And there was plenty. Hippo Regius was a seaport. Perhaps thirty thousand souls lived there, with thirty thousand energies, stemming from every race you could count and representing every religion you could think of: The Catholics were a small passionate minority. Anger between one race and another was negligible, but anger between one religion and another was sharp, and between the two factions of Christians—the Donatists and the Catholics—it was bitter.

The Donatists and the Catholics each considered themselves the true Christians and the other party false. It had all begun several generations back, I believe in Carthage, over a bitter struggle concerning which faction of two in the church there had the right to choose and ordain a bishop. Both factions chose and ordained bishops, and by now practically every city in Africa had both a Donatist and a Catholic bishop. And of course by now, after so long a schism, doctrinal differences had developed. I had myself in Ravenna helped write imperial edicts in favor of Catholics against Donatists, not on religious but on political grounds. It was made illegal to be a Donatist; Donatists were forbidden to have churches or hold meetings; if they did so, their churches could be confiscated and the individuals could be denied the civil rights to own or will property and could be exiled. However, laws made in Ravenna may forbid and the things forbidden may still go on in Africa.

Government as ordained in the statutes and what men do are never quite the same. Donatists and Catholics continued fighting each other in Africa; they fought in councils of bishops with rhetoric and in back alleys with clubs and stones.

The Donatists were strong in Hippo when Augustine was forcibly made a priest there by the Catholics; they were so strong indeed that they were able to forbid the baking of bread for Catholics in the public ovens. The Catholics of Hippo hung onto their new priest. It was not safe for an educated priest to turn up in a town that lacked a bishop if he didn't want to be seized and ordained. For a few years, until Augustine was actually ordained as a second Bishop of Hippo by old Valerius, he was kept fairly close to Hippo. Once he became bishop and secure to Hippo, he fought Donatists from Carthage to Caesarea. He never let go of the central principle: "Let Catholic worship be one; let its salvation be one."

Of course, it had long since been declared doctrine in the Catholic Church that no one church could have two bishops at one time. Augustine's ordination was improper—he said years later that he didn't realize it at the time; and this again shows that in the Church, as in the state, things declared illegal do not therefore cease to be actual. Augustine was second bishop. He fought a hard fight. He was the prime belligerent of Catholic Africa.

He was more than that, for there in Hippo, bishop of only a small city on the African shore, he became the great publicist of the Catholic Church, a voice rising and ringing throughout the world, until he made it clear to the minds of men for how many ages I know not that there are two Cities, the one sullen and turgid City of Man or of Earth, where passions spin and no heart rests, and the one City of God, where the heart finds home and the soul finds rest.

He must have kept several secretaries and many scriveners busy, for his sermons, long letters, little treatises and massive books came out of Hippo in a ceaseless dynamic flood. His mind was a great community, uttering its multitudinous cry of "God! God! God!" Let who would assail him, he had still the tremendous tongue of spiritual speaking, and never doubted that the Catholic Church, which he loved, wherein he labored, was the only tower of truth whereon to stand and speak for God. He uttered a thousand magnificent things; so great was the vigor of his mind, the splendor of his heart and the intensity of his life that he found out and said anew almost every good and lovely thing so far learned by the seeking and suffering of man; and always at the core, as hard and clear as a gem, was the mighty foundation of his doctrine:

Authority belongs to God and utters through the Catholic Church; Obedience belongs to man:

For the Catholic Church, vigorously spreading far and wide throughout the whole world, uses all who are in error to her own adornment, and to their amendment, when they shall wish to awake from their error. She uses the heathen as material on which to work, heretics as a test of her teaching, schismatics as a proof of her stability, Jews as a comparison to show her beauty. Hence she invites some, thrusts out others, leaves others alone, and of others she takes the lead. To all, however, she gives the opportunity of participating in God's grace, whether it be that they have to be formed, or to be reformed, or to be brought back to the fold, or to be admitted to it.

As he saw and knew and said that each lovely thing is its own confession, and by it evanescent beauty confesses Beauty immutable, so his great voice pronounced that the rising sacred power of the Catholic Church was its own confession of the Authority of God.

The last night of voyage I compared Augustine in my mind with Ambrose. Ambrose was born to the manner of Roman rule, while Augustine fought his way from obscurity to power. From childhood up Ambrose loved Christ and believed in God, while Augustine, wracked by passion, fled God in search of God. Ambrose was a mature spirit of deep calm, but Augustine was a vehement youth even into his old age. Ambrose sought to imitate Christ, and Augustine spoke for God. Ambrose sought to work by love, and Augustine wrought by authority.

My heart ached, and I wept because Ambrose was dead.

I looked backward across the dark sea, as it were toward Milan, trying to peer through the shrouds of blackness of my years for Ambrose like a light that was lost. It was very dark. I could not see.

We sailed past Carthage and skirted the coast westward toward Hippo Regius. My imagination drew large designs of solace soon to come. And my wounded spirit prophesied unreal events it desired in dreamy symbols, saying, Now within the dark hands of my dreary soul Augustine shall set a cup of light and let me rest. . . .

We anchored early in the hot morning in the harbor at Hippo among a number of ships, and I could already see, above other buildings, the forms of several large churches. I wondered which would be the Basilica of Peace, which the Leontian, and which the Church of the Eight Martyrs built under Augustine's own direction. What I really wondered was where I would find Augustine and how I would speak to him.

My shipmaster was a sensible man and wanted to know for practical reasons how long I expected to stay in Hippo.

"Many months. It will depend on Bishop Augustine whether I remain here permanently."

"What am I to do with the ship, Count Julian?"

I, too, out of old habit, could be practical. "Look about for a cargo. You will have time to find one, load, and sail for Ostia or Rome before violent autumn weather makes it too dangerous. Get grain if you can, for Rome always needs grain and pays well for it. But I'll see you in a week or two before you sail."

I went ashore.

It was a hot bright morning with gusts of wind blowing up sharp dust in the streets. The air was thin and dry and the light brilliant—so brilliant that I sneezed twice in the glare. It was a great contrast to the thick damp atmosphere of Ravenna, and instead of the fecund smell of that marshland there was a dry tang here of sun-baked earth.

For years I had entered any city I chose as a foremost official of the Empire, expecting and receiving homage. Before the murder of Stilicho I would have sent a messenger to Augustine to notify him of my arrival and ask him to expect my visit. "Count Julian, Friend of the Emperor, and Imperial Ambassador, requests the pleasure . . ." and so on. Now, however, I took neither litter nor slaves with me, but walked up the street alone, incognito, my semblance noble, my secret miserable. I was wearing my customary clothes, and people on the street noticed at once, not my moral solitude, but the stripes of purple indicating a noble personage of social and political eminence.

When I asked a stranger where I might find Bishop Augustine he said, "At the Basilica of Peace, Your Excellency—and I assure you there is plenty of trouble with the damned Donatists."

I dilated my nostrils. After the clean sea air of the voyage the man had a strong acrid smell; and I soon noticed that these people of Africa had a bitter and vigorous odor, dry and sharp, quite other than the moist smell of people in the evil heat of Ravenna.

"And which is the Basilica of Peace?"

"Allow me to show you the way." The man was lean, very dark, and wore part of his white garment slung over his head to shield his forehead and eyes from the sun. "Perhaps you came from Italy?"

I made no answer to his prying question.

"We have exciting news from Ravenna and Rome, come but three days ago. Stilicho has been executed for his crimes, and Count Julian, Stilicho's chief scoundrel, trying to escape, was shot by archers and

drowned in the river at Ravenna. Perhaps Your Excellency has more
to add?"

"Nothing of consequence."

"Well. I'm satisfied. Whatever news you bring privately to Bishop
Augustine, the rest of us will learn in time, if he considers we are meant
to know it. But it is good to know for certain that both Stilicho and
Julian are dead and gone to hell. For God would not suffer those two
enemies of Christ to persecute the Church any longer. The priest
Orosius, Augustine's aid, gave us a fine hot sermon on the fortunate
delivery of all Christians from the villainy of those two devils. As I tell
my daughter—my wife's dead—you can count on God; He's a good
Catholic."

It was curious and shocking to hear that I was dead and, even in this
unreality of my supposed death, hated by people a thousand miles or
more away who had never seen me. I wondered if Heraclian and Galla
Placidia really believed their bowmen had shot me to death in the dark
water. The soldiers may well have made such a report to avoid punishment for letting me escape. Or perhaps the soldiers believed I had never
got out of the water alive. And of course the report, sent by rapid post
to Rome and Ostia, thence by ship to Africa, would have reached Hippo
sooner than I could arrive by slow voyage all down the Adriatic and
then westward.

I took a kind of rest in the security of this false belief that I was dead.
It was as if I had escaped from the contentions of men, slipping for a
moment out of the multifold strife like a man who gets out of a mob
rioting in the street for a moment of rest in a black doorway.

We turned a corner and saw a crowd assembling in front of the Basilica
of Peace.

"Because of the Donatists, as I told you," my guide and gossip informed me. "Those damned scoundrels, with a horde of savage beasts
they call Circumcellions, fell upon a village near here last night. They
burned Christian homes, broke up sacred vessels in the church, and threw
lime and vinegar in the faces of the priests. One priest is probably
blinded. You will see him with a bandage around his eyes. Then all
night long the scoundrels brought in true Christians and gave them
their choice, either to have their homes burned or be rebaptized as
Donatists. A delegation has appealed to Augustine. He is sure to demand—yes! there, see the soldiers!—Augustine has demanded civil authority to go settle with the fiends of the Antichrist!"

Indeed, a company of Roman foot soldiers stood in order before the
church. There was quite a crowd of ordinary citizens. Then, assembling

in a small group as they came out of the church, were twelve or fifteen clerics. One of them, being led by another, had a bandage around his eyes and proved to be the priest who had had lime dashed in his face. The bandage happened to be a bit of ruby-colored silk scarf which shone in the sun as his head trembled. It was obvious that he suffered and should have been in a dark room in bed, but I heard him say, with great force of will to keep his voice from shaking, "I must return to my church!"

Then a Roman official arrived, driving in his chariot and followed by a dozen armed horsemen. He spoke to the captain of the foot soldiers.

Among three or four elderly priests I did not easily decide which one was Augustine. It was twenty years since I as a boy in Rome had been his pupil and he had been my lean, young, dark and passionate tutor. One of the clerics was too fat to agree with my mental image of how Augustine would now look, another was much too old, but a third one— tall, vigorous, yet rather mild in the face—was, I decided, the man Augustine. Identifying this man as Augustine disappointed me, as if I had looked for a blazing torch and had found only a feeble rushlight. I studied the man's face and thought it too bad that age and authority and security had so dampened down the inward fire.

I also certainly recognized one man there whom I had not seen in ten years, and that was Paulinus, the former private secretary of Bishop Ambrose. He had been some years with Augustine, and it was he who, at Augustine's request, wrote a simple pious brief life of Saint Ambrose. Fortunately Paulinus was too excited to recognize or take note of me in the crowd. He had never liked me; Ambrose's patient love for me had always bewildered and distressed Paulinus, and from the time when he suspected my adultery with Dionie and reported it to Ambrose he had never wanted me to have either the affection of Ambrose or any other good thing. He was a timid simple man, and his feeling toward me was less one of active hatred than of passive dread: I seemed to him a disturbing example of wickedness rewarded. I looked back at the tall man I had identified as Augustine, and I felt profoundly discouraged. Is this all life comes to? I thought.

There was a stir through all the crowd as a small frail man with a grizzle of gray beard came out from the church. I felt a wave of relief, of gratitude, for I had been mistaken in the tall vigorous but mild priest; this late newcomer, with the sharp quick stride of spiritual certainty, was Augustine himself. I had forgotten that I would now be taller than he was. And neither age nor authority had dampened this man's inner fire; there was lightning in the flash of his cheek and splendor in the blaze of his eye. Although he was lean, no more than medium tall, and frail physically, he made all the others appear simple and commonplace. He carried manhood like a flashing sword and wore authority like a blazing crown.

He got onto a white mule which had a green sunshade fastened by a pole to the saddle. He raised a commanding hand. Everybody, even the Roman official in the chariot, fell silent, waiting for his orders. I noticed the stillness of his brow, the intensity of his eyes and the stillness of his upper face, then the extreme mobility of the lower face, mouth, even throat. There was almost a sense of duality of nature, of profound spiritual certainty coupled with great and changeable worldly skill. He had a fringe of silver hair, that scrubby short gray-and-white beard, a prominent nose, a wide mouth with the lips thinner now than in youth, as if the juice of their wild young passion had been distilled into the terrible stillness of the forehead.

He said he wanted no riots. All the townspeople must stay in Hippo. The group of priests and the soldiers would proceed to the village where the Donatists had committed these outrages. Augustine and the clergy would pause at the edge of the village while the soldiers arrested the Donatist and Circumcellion criminals. Then he would restore the priests to the Church and the villagers to the freedom of true Christianity. He gave the commander the order, and the soldiers and all the priests, except Paulinus and three or four others, moved off. Paulinus and the others went back into the bishop's house near the church.

It never occurred to me that I had any choice, any necessity, except to follow Augustine. I don't suppose it took me very much time to find and hire a chariot and be on my way after Augustine, the clerics and the soldiers. Out of Hippo, turning west along the coast, I saw their mass and dust moving in the bright sun ahead of me. To stand in a chariot driving a pair of lively horses stirs a man and straightens his shoulders. I recaptured for a while the illusion of being a man of eminence and honor. The hills were on my left, the sea was on my right. The wind was hot and more steady now. The froth of the sea was brilliant, and the sand glittered. The sound of the sea was wonderful in the sharp clear air. I kept half a mile behind the cavalcade of priests and soldiers, like an outcast or an alien watcher. I kept saying to myself, This is Augustine at work. Now we will see!

Who were "we"? What would "we" see? It was absurd. But the thing gradually became more real. I began to respond more and more to the sharp brilliant impressions of actual events instead of to the inward phantasies of a wounded spirit and a sick imagination. The horses were real, and I drove them in earnest, and the reins tugged at my hands. The wind and the sea and the earth were real. And Bishop Augustine, up there ahead on his white mule and under his green sunshade, was no one remembered or imagined, but the man himself. An astonishing man.

"Augustine is a spiritual Caesar!" I exclaimed aloud as I drove my chariot in sun and dust.

After about an hour the priests stopped, and the soldiers went on.

My compulsion had its own audacity. I drove my chariot steadily forward until I arrived where the priests had come to a halt. I stopped beside Augustine on his mule.

He looked at me, waiting for me to speak, and I looked at him, waiting for him to recognize me. He did not know me; and my stare of habitual aristocracy was in rude conflict with his gaze of ecclesiastical authority.

"I wished to watch this business," I said.

"You are perhaps from the ship that anchored this morning?"

"Yes."

"On official business?"

"No."

He looked at me curiously. He had not recognized either my person or my voice. Well, of course—from a growing boy with treble tones to a bearded man with a deep bass voice was a great change. Also, according to the news that had reached Hippo, I was dead. Why should he recognize me? But he did recognize and mistrust something of my purpose. It was obvious that he had no personal fear of me, but I could almost see written out the question in his mind: Does this man in any way threaten the Catholic Church?

He asked another question. "You come from Rome?"

I gave him a curious answer, as if compelled both to reveal and to conceal the truth. "Is there a place from which the dead set sail?"

Augustine had been a bishop for some years, and he was deeply versed in the spiritual seeking of troubled souls. An answer such as mine could not mystify him. He gave a quick nod of understanding and said flatly, "You came to Hippo to see me."

My visit to Augustine was becoming more and more real and was, both in detail and in spirit, totally unlike my prophetic imagining. It was obvious that he had no need of finding a son in me and that our temperaments so radically conflicted that I would discover no father in him to relieve me of the burden of living my own life. But I was only half sane; as if my brain were split, I was also half crazy. I clung with the ferocity of my desperate fright to the illusion that Augustine had not yet revealed himself. Concealed behind this realistic appearance would be the true miraculous father who would ease me of burden and pain by word and symbol.

He waited for me to acknowledge that I had come to Hippo to see him, but I said nothing. This very act of not speaking did something to that peculiar division in my mind. I felt I had nothing to say to this real man. The Augustine meant to redeem me retreated, as it were, to some corner of my mind to be faced and dealt with in some more desperate moment.

I looked down toward the village. It was on sloping land that rose from the sea to the hills, and the church overlooked the village. Several houses still smoldered and sent up pale smoke in the brilliant sunlight. The soldiers marched upon the church. In a moment there would be fighting.

Augustine asked me one more question. "Are you a Christian?"

I can only say that by now some profound and rapid change had taken place in my spiritual depths, something like a silent unmasking of the soul. I might say it was as if I had recovered the pristine honesty of my early boyhood, and had found again that arrow of truth so strangely implanted there by Bishop Gregory of Nazianzus. For what he had said had been repeated in our family when I was a child: "I have not time to offend God." These words had fallen out of heaven into the midst of my childhood, and, as I remarked at the beginning of this story, I as a child had treasured the saying with delight, as if it were an arrow of jewels and gold, and my own to keep forever. I would say with glee to myself, "I have not time to offend God!" and it would make my heart merry. I had found plenty of time in the years since to offend God plentifully, but this arrow of heaven had not left my soul.

But now in the presence of Augustine, asking if I were a Christian, matters were very different and devoid of glee or delight. This shining and beautiful image of heaven, this bright metaphor of spiritual integrity I now held in a weary, corrupt and tarnished hand. I knew of no falseness left worth living for. Why should I lie to Augustine or continue to offend God with spiritual pretensions? I took Augustine's question in its deepest meaning; not, was I baptized? not, did I pass for a Christian? not, was I a Catholic? but in truth, did I follow Christ?

"No."

He flicked me a sharp glance, then slowly brought his gaze back and studied my face. I believe he had not taken my answer on its deepest level. I was thinking of the strange and haunting beauty of Christ, and it gave me a sad firm quiet not to offend God by a false claim that my wretched spiritual failures deserved the name of Christian. But I believe Augustine was thinking of the Church. My answer meant to him simply that I was not a Catholic. Augustine was a spiritual Caesar of tense and tough fiber. He fought his fight in clear terms: A man was a Catholic or an enemy. Some enemies could be persuaded to become Catholics, some could be compelled to enter the Catholic Church; the rest were damned and had to be thwarted. There was more antipathy than understanding between us.

He shrugged his shoulders and looked toward the village, impatient of my rude intrusion upon his own vital diocesan affairs.

Bitter things were going on. The soldiers had assailed the church. A few of the Donatist clergy and their ruffian Circumcellions were seen fleeing back into the hills. But at least eight of the Donatists, with a fanatic desire to win martyrdom, threw themselves barehanded on the soldiers and were killed. I counted their sprawled bodies later when we went down there. Three Donatist priests and about thirty Circumcellions were captured alive and taken off under guard to Hippo for trial and punishment. As I watched the violence I realized I was tired to death of wrath and contention, of dominion and power.

But I also realized that Augustine had that same rare quality I had noticed in Theodosius: Stern though the matter was, he enjoyed what he was doing. He knew he was right and had zest for the day.

Augustine led the clergy down to the village and into the church. I went along. The people of the village came into the church. Augustine helped the blinded priest with the ruby silk bandage over his eyes to stand before the congregation. The man could not see where he was and turned facing directly toward the side wall, and cried out to the stones before his face, "I have returned to my flock!"

People groaned, seeing him address the wall in his blind anguish.

Then he collapsed in Augustine's arms, and two priests helped him to a bench.

Augustine spoke for half an hour. I was definitely frightened. I stood far back in the church with my hands behind me, open, my palms pressed against the wall. I rocked a little on my feet, and sometimes my arms trembled; then I would bring my hands forward, brush them together, and put them behind me again. It was not Augustine himself nor the sermon he preached that frightened me; I was frightened as any man is when he feels himself being irrevocably deprived of an illusion. I believed Augustine was the greatest living man I knew. I had met in my life four men of surpassing human endowment: the great Caesar of the

Roman world, Theodosius; the great good man, Ambrose; the great but ruined poet, Claudian; and this great spiritual Caesar, Augustine. He alone was now alive, and he stood there in the church before me saying things that gave me no comfort. The illusion of which I was being deprived was the common one that somewhere, somehow, at some time you will meet the person who will relieve you of the burden of living your own life.

Augustine's theme was the Catholic Church. He spoke with authority and as one who expected obedience. He said there could be no salvation outside the one Catholic Church; no one could love Christ except in and through the Catholic Church; no one could find God except within the Catholic Church—for the Divine Truth was revealed by the Holy Spirit to and through the Catholic Church.

"Those who speak against us have not faith," he said; "therefore we ought not listen to what they say."

It was clear to me that a church could absorb the interests of a man— of a great man, for here was Augustine with all his intellectual splendor faithfully devoted to the Catholic Church. But I did not believe a specific church could monopolize God; I thought God might exceed the bonds or bounds of any church. I had no illusion left that Augustine was the miraculous father of my desolate life. Not as he stood real before me, and not anywhere off behind my head, either, in that detached limbo of the cloven mind where fear and desire weave illusions to deny reality. This Augustine was a great soul, the greatest, I think, of our age; still, he was not mankind, and he was not God. Not in Augustine, not in Africa, not in any specific church, but in the deep strange regions of Gregory Julian I had to find my way—or die, perhaps, before I ever found it.

I brought my hands forth and brushed them together a final time. "There is no such thing, I said to myself, as another man who can ease me of living my own life.

Turning thus away from Augustine, in the symbolic sense of turning away from that compulsive hope which had impelled me to Africa, was like accepting death.

I accepted death.

I turned quickly out of the church ahead of the others and drove my chariot rapidly back to Hippo. It was late afternoon when I got aboard my ship. I called the captain of my vessel. "We sail at once for Italy."

"Most of the crew is ashore. Half of them are drunk or with women, or both. I won't be able to gather them before dark."

"Gather them. We'll sail at dawn."

I sat on the deck and stared at the city, at the harbor, at the hills, until twilight, then until darkness came over the sea and the land. I had a sick feeling that I had one more thing to do. This act of turning away from Augustine, as if accepting death, was an insufficient negative. If I really accepted death I would have no need to pretend I had negated Augustine. A man cannot negate another man. Really there was a great lie operative there in Hippo that night: the lie that I could negate Augustine and, bound in with it, the lie that I, Count Julian, was an enemy of God and Christ and the Catholic Church who lay dead and drowned in the rotten waters of Ravenna. Augustine was the man who should know that I lived and that Stilicho had been, not politically executed, but passionately murdered; and I was the man who ought not to leave Africa under any pretense that I had negated Augustine.

We meet one another, we fulfill one another, we complement one another, we are members of one another; but we cannot negate one another.

Before midnight I slapped my hand sharply on the ship's rail and exclaimed, "I have not time to offend God!"

I summoned four slaves and had them carry me in my litter into the town to Bishop Augustine's residence.

The man who came to the door, sleepy and irritated, was Paulinus, Ambrose's former secretary. The light was poor. He did not recognize me.

"I want to speak to Bishop Augustine."

"Come tomorrow. The bishop is asleep. He has been ill lately and needs his sleep."

I seized a lantern from the wall and held it close to my face.

Paulinus stared, crossed himself, and gulped the air of surprise down his throat. "Count Julian! You're not dead!"

"No. I am not dead. I must see the bishop. Let me tell him myself who I am."

Paulinus led the way. There was no door to Augustine's bedroom. He was perhaps a light sleeper, for he woke before we said a word, and asked, "What is it?"

He was a good and resolute warrior; he woke from sleep with extreme rapidity and was fully alert on the instant. He was in command of himself, of his house, of his bishopric the moment he raised his head and spoke.

Once again I held the lantern close to my face and spoke my name: "Gregory Julian."

He said nothing, but got out of bed, put on a robe and sandals, and led me into a larger room which I believe was his study.

Paulinus lighted several lamps. Augustine asked Paulinus, "You knew him quite well in Milan?"

"Yes. This is Count Julian. I never understood why Ambrose forgave him so much."

It was the poor man's warning to Augustine to watch me closely and forgive nothing.

"I haven't come to murder your bishop. I'm a dead man, you know."

"Thank you, Paulinus. You did right to waken me," Augustine dismissed him kindly.

Then Augustine came close to me and in what was fairly good light searched my face. "I can scarcely see any traces of the boy in the ruins of the man. Why do you come to me? For several years past I have received letters from Olympius naming you as a dangerous enemy of the Church."

"I could write you a letter saying Olympius is an honorable man."

"You have come to vindicate yourself?"

"No."

"What, then?"

"I came to Africa under the illusion that I had need of you to relieve me of the burden of living my own life. That would have been a miracle. Seeing you has dispelled the illusion, and I sail for Italy at dawn. But I felt a falseness in not first revealing to you who I am, why I came, and why I go."

"You thought you had to come to me for help, but now you think you only had to see me again so as to be free of me. Is that it?"

"That was the beginning. That much happened this afternoon. But I found I was not quite so dead. I am now sufficiently myself—whatever freedom that may be—to wish to acknowledge that I know you."

"Free to know me? You make an interesting point. The desire to be free of other men is a sort of wish for death. But to become yourself and know your fellows is another matter. I remember when you were a boy I told you you had a clear spirit. I take it the vigor of seeking is still in you. Sit down, Gregory."

"Thank you."

We both sat. We were now not unfriendly, but neither were we intimate. There was a distinct and respectful independence of persons. I gave him a detached and factual account of recent events at Ravenna, including Stilicho's murder and my escape.

Augustine objected: "The man was executed by order of the Emperor. Yet you insist on calling it murder."

"Honorius was frightened into signing orders drawn up by Olympius.

A few of us, with our passions to guide us and the political passions of the Catholic party behind us, contrived to murder Stilicho."

"I don't like that imputation made against the Catholic party." He watched me closely a moment while he drummed his fingers on the table. His hands were lean and quick.

I tried to phrase my reply with exactness. "Sermons against Stilicho, speaking of his death as a relief from oppression, are being delivered in praise of his murder. For myself, I am tired of abusing words in behalf of power. It was murder."

"Murder is evil."

"It was evil."

"You must understand that there may be men known as Catholic Christians who may do evil, but the Church itself cannot do evil. The Church is the Body of which Christ is the Head."

"I trust the Catholic party will not rejoice too much in the evil done by evil men when we murdered Stilicho."

"This is really what you came here tonight to tell me."

"Yes."

He looked at his hands—could he have been looking for some shadow of Stilicho's blood? I don't know—and he nodded his head. He said, with a profound gravity that made the words of the apostle his own words, "We are all members one of another."

I don't know whether or not Augustine accepted my judgment in the matter. At least he took it into consideration. I know that later the priest named Orosius, who was close to him, wrote a history against Rome in which Stilicho was defamed and portrayed as deserving execution, but the Catholic party did not do murder. And later Augustine, in his tremendous portrayal of the City of God, saw evil intrinsic in the world but extrinsic to the Church.

"If you sail for Italy now, Gregory, you will of course be seized and probably executed."

"That is what I believe."

"You invite death?"

"I am indifferent to it. The murder of Stilicho taught me that no man's death can diminish God. You may remember that my father owned—I now own—a large estate and villa quite far south of Rome, among the mountains back of Salernum. I am going there. It is a lonely place."

"You think the Emperor will not have confiscated it by now?"

"Honorius might even protect me. I took good care of his chickens. Olympius and Heraclian will be busy at first seizing what is close at hand.

And since they believe me dead, they won't hurry." I caught myself short and stared at Augustine.

"You see some ghost!"

"Not a ghost, but a giant out of earth. How insane we were to murder Stilicho! Now there is not a general left who can stay Alaric from striding the length of Italy. No one left at Ravenna will have sense enough to make him master general and so save Rome from destruction."

"You believe he has so much power?"

"He is an Arian Christian, but old forest gods rule depths in his heart, and they have promised him Rome. All the power and prophecy of his race are with him. Alaric is their destiny. When we murdered Stilicho we betrayed Rome."

"God's designs are larger than man's errors."

I rose and bowed. "I can do nothing. I seek nothing. Farewell."

Augustine detained me with a gesture. "One thing. When I did not know who you were in the chariot today I asked you if you were a Christian. You said no. You have been baptized and for some years known as a Catholic. Have you renounced the Church?"

"I have been baptized. I have been known as a member of the Church. But there is very little spiritual evidence in my life that I have in any depth followed Christ. I no longer want to live under names that do not name my inward being."

"Paulinus has often told me that Bishop Ambrose loved you. It always bewilders Paulinus. Was it true?"

"Yes. Ambrose loved me. He was a great good man. I loved him."

"If Ambrose loved you, then I know for certain that you are one who seeks God. You will not find Him except as a true Christian within the Catholic Church."

"I am not subtle enough for theology nor enthusiastic enough for absolute religious certainty."

"Nor humble enough to obey God!" His exclamation was a challenge to do battle. The reverberance of all his power was in his voice, and his eyes flashed back at me. The man's power had an outrush about it like the stroke of a lion. It was a fighting power. It was by no means the simple power of love which Ambrose had sometimes revealed. It was a power of righteousness, with the great forces of custom and obedience and authority behind it.

I bent aside from his challenge, saying, "Power is the master which seizes at the world, and obedience is the slave eager to share it. I have found that all the world without was not sufficient substitute for peace within myself."

"You have such peace?" He was not asking me, he was challenging me again.

"No. I am without peace. I have reached, bare and unmasked, the place of pause and silence. The rest will be as it may be, between me and God."

"The rest is the choice between damnation and obedience; and grace comes at God's will, not yours."

"I am not the obedient man but the seeking man."

"Stained still with original sin."

"Or haunted still by original divinity."

I believe the phrase shocked him. He shook his head like a man stung by a worm. "There could never be a Church of men like you."

I smiled. "But there will be a Church, Bishop. I have seen today how greatly you exceed all I expected. I believe you are the only master builder left in the Roman world. An Empire crumbles, and I see you, as a spiritual Caesar, raising up the Church where the Empire fell."

"God alone is the true Builder of the City of God, which shall abide when all cities of this world fail."

I sighed. I was profoundly weary. I had no heart to contend with this great belligerent, this man of insistent and positive power. "Certainly I am an outcast of Rome. Quite probably I am also an alien walled out of this new Empire you celebrate, the City of God. And so, farewell."

He rose. He looked steadily into my eyes. He took a long time to say the one word. I think there was a struggle in his heart between the man who might have loved me and the builder of the temple rejecting a building stone. The word, when he said it, half turning his face away, was rejection. "Farewell!"

Then he caught himself, wheeled upon me suddenly, and issued his final challenge. "You are a powerful-looking man, Gregory, in the prime of your physical life. I noticed the great force of your shoulders and back in the chariot today. I see now your arms are strong, your hands are big, your legs are mighty, and you have a king's voice. A frail old man admires such things. And I can see how in the eyes of Galla Placidia you would have made a splendid Emperor. But I wonder what strength there is left in your soul. Judging from your eyes, your soul is sick unto death."

I fell into a great silence at his words, listening in my heart to the dooms of love. I wonder what other men have had a like moment, in the deep of night, in a quiet room, when what a man says to you opens the heart simply to the deep and tragic reverberation of the dooms of love. I know of no other so profound resonance, within or without the sentient man. I heard the sound and shall never forget it. And everything in the room took on new depth, intense reality; the pens, the scrolls, the furniture, the lamps, suddenly were clear and real and vibrant and seemed to teach me by their human implications how great and sad is the beauty of the world.

I could hear the slow deep resonance of my own voice as I spoke. I think its resonance was purified by the absolute certainty that I was in spiritual communion with a fellow man, for I beheld Augustine as there and then my counterpart in God. "Yea, Augustine, my soul is sick unto death. I had a son I loved who was drowned in the sea. I had a wife I loved, and I drove her from me in jealous wrath. I go to Italy to welcome death."

I looked at him as I spoke and saw him change, or, it would be better to say, I saw him revealed in all his human splendor, a great spirit standing in the full grandeur of tragic light. I had never expected any words of mine to have so profound an evocative power over this spiritual Caesar. But when he answered, speaking as slowly as I had spoken, I knew this was a deep meeting of two men under our common tragic light. "I loved a woman and broke her heart. I loved my son, and he is dead. Yea, man, yea, you and I are brothers. Our two hearts know the hurt of this world. Stay here with me and find God!"

As I looked at him I was amazed that I had never seen a man so clearly before, so absolutely a creation of God. The temptation to resign myself to the shelter of his sorrow and his power were great.

It took me a while to find my answer. "Your wisdom is deep, your goodness is profound, your authority is great; I could not hold my freedom against you. I must go. You have given me in sorrow a brother in this world and saved me from living and dying alone. But I must go to Italy for my final pause and wait."

"Sin is in the will. All happy men obey God. Surrender yourself to peace, Gregory."

I was tired and sad. I looked at the great man with gratitude and affection. "A man, as I am, Augustine, broken by false living down to spiritual beggary, can still see this: There is a difference between surrendering our manhood in obedience to doctrine, or moving by love toward free consonance with God. If I never win near, by love, to that free consonance with God, my soul will yet have had its pure sorrow of knowing what it sought and could not find. And so, farewell."

This time he did not avert his face or say farewell. He signed my forehead with the sign of the cross and said, "God help you!"

I returned to my ship.

I saw my fate, and it was simple. Neither the attainments of power nor the securities of obedience can give that inward peace which is the outflowing of love. No living under any mask—either of power or of obedience—and no ceaseless grasping for the world without would ever again conceal my unrequited need for inward peace.

CHAPTER TWO

THE VIRGIN

WHEN MARCIA HEARD OF MY SUPPOSED DEATH SHE MADE preparations to leave Rome.

Pelagius was making ready to sail for Carthage; thence he meant to travel on to Bethlehem. The news of my death was not only a deep personal shock to Marcia, but it brought on a crisis between Marcia and our daughter Livia. The passion of a child can be quite terrible to the heart of a mother, and Livia had one of those repressed hysterical temperaments that make some young girls strange and untouchable and then, when puberty sets in, gives them the white fierceness of an avenging angel. The false news of my death brought on the first crisis, but I did not know, until I myself appeared later in Rome, that I was the one who, by driving Marcia from me, had done Livia a profound spiritual injury when she was a child only about four years old. Marcia, having heard of my death, forced by the cruel persecution of Livia, and trying to save her own heart and soul, decided at last to go with Pelagius to Bethlehem, taking Livia and the young Gregory with her. She herself, to quiet the fierce hatred with which Livia threatened her, let it be known that she was not just a widow, but one of those Christian widows almost as separated from all touch of this world as a consecrated virgin.

I do not want to relate these coming events, which were dreadful and which struck into Marcia's heart the deepest wound of sorrow; but God's smile has also its deep revelation of sorrow. I can but summon what tragic compassion I have learned and try to tell tenderly, the way the heart does when it sings its song of tears, of my wife tragically wounded, of my daughter tragically slain, and of Rome, the Eternal City, broken by God. I know my mortal heart is not, by itself, great enough to encompass the Divine reason of these profound tragedies; I hope the compassion and the prayers of my fellow men will help me out where my heart fails, and that—by understanding in the words of a man more than a man knows how to speak—the vision may still be wrought between spirit and spirit, and love be felt, be known, be cherished even at the core of disaster. I tell these things to confess what I love: No woman was ever more beautiful than Marcia with our slain child in the humble holding of her arms, and no young girl was ever more tragically slain than Livia, our child. In them I saw an immortal light haunting the death of Rome.

I remember Ambrose telling me once: "How little the sorrow of man can say to the glory of God."

It was not surprising that Marcia herself should have become more devout. The deep desire of goodness had been always in her heart. But everything she did during those sequestered years at Rome was done under the strain of a profound, unceasing and secret anxiety; there was a lie, feeding like the worm of death, at the bottom of her heart. In that faulty form of self-defense which a lie in the heart breeds, she kept her conscious emphasis on the obvious wrong I had done her, and she meant her own good living to appease that injury. She lived those years among a group of noble and pious women, and she chose to save my soul by prayer and by charity. She lived in the Anician Palace with old Faltonia Proba and half a dozen other female relatives who very little partook of the worldly affairs in which their menfolk were active. Pelagius was their religious mentor in Rome, but they were also in correspondence with Jerome and Paula in Bethlehem, and the young girls in the group looked forward to becoming consecrated virgins and going to Paula's convent in Bethlehem, where Jerome himself might be their spiritual father.

Marcia was esteemed by these women, and by the clergy associated with them, for her resolute insistence that no other man than I could ever be her husband. There were sad speculations on the scant possibility of her ever encountering me in immortal life. Perhaps by prayer, by goodness, by sacrifice she could earn Christ's mercy in my behalf and greet me one day with radiant forgiveness in heaven. But Marcia had a great deal of spontaneous energy, so that such piety alone was not enough for her. She established a large hospital in Rome for orphaned young girls, girls of sorrows and troubles, and she did so much good and sensible work among them that they loved her and watched her come and go and wondered why one so good to them yet seemed herself lonely and afraid.

Her dark eyes had that wandering gleam of inward pain—for is it not the most desperate of all spiritual labors to try to build with goodness on a lie? For the lie continually eats out the heart and, like a worm, excretes its poison as it turns, and no good thing attempted gets faithfully done. I had tried to build on lies: I knew how the eye glances fearfully inward toward the absence of joy.

Her position was anomalous. No one could call her a Christian widow, for I, her husband, had divorced her, setting her aside because of adultery. And the growing boy Gregory, Claudian's son, was like her visible cross and ineradicable sin. My name was prominent, my doings were known, and I had occasionally appeared in Rome to address the Senate before we murdered Stilicho, and all this renewed and kept alive the consciousness that she was a woman divorced for adultery.

Where, then, was the lie?

She knew.

Young Gregory was a witty, grave and charming boy, and she longed desperately to love him with a free and whole heart, because he loved her, forgave her everything, and trusted her completely. She could not love him freely because of the lie she concealed; but he, with an intuition equal to his father's, perceived that where the lie began was her pain, and that behind the lie was the truth which he could trust. Had it not been for Livia, I believe the child Gregory could have healed her with her own truth.

But Livia hated her mother.

Livia, I believe, had set up a fierce phantasy to protect her child's heart from the harsh wounds of reality Marcia and I had imposed on her. She created this bright phantasy of a potent and magical love for me, counterpoised by an equally illusory hatred of Marcia. Marcia had deprived her of the father she loved, the father who needed her, the father who could be saved only by her. For of course by the time she was nine or ten years old Livia was steeped through and through with the language of piety customary among that group of Christian women. Not a false wife, but a pure, devoted and fearless daughter could by utter sacrifice save the soul of a beloved father. Proud, fierce, inflamed with such phantasies, she would look at Marcia and ask, "Why did you ruin my father's life? You have no right to pray for him. That is for me."

All this praying and piety among women, like too much theology among men, thwarts the fertile and flowing business of nature and is apt to evoke cruelty and death.

This child had my toughness of fiber, but not my resilience; like her mother, she could be stubborn, yet lacked Marcia's spontaneous warmth; but she had from her grandmother Calvena that dark fanatic streak of hysteria. She nurtured and handled her own hysteria like some child Medea training dragons. She learned all the words and attitudes of the Christian virgin. She had or invented visions, she fasted until she alarmed Marcia, she prayed at all hours of the night. She earned herself the name of one especially marked for sanctity. The slaves in the Probus Palace considered her a saint elect. More than one of them claimed her touch had healed their sickness. She was not crazy; she was terrible. She had the power of enchantment and used it. The slaves would do anything for her. Old Proba and Proba's daughters and granddaughters thoroughly believed that Livia was a child already chosen by Christ as his own.

When she was eleven Livia said she wanted to be consecrated as a Christian virgin. Marcia refused to allow it.

The other women and Pelagius and several priests who were consulted favored it. Many noble young girls were betrothed at as young an age and married a year or two later. Betrothal to Christ, being spiritual, need not wait the full flowering of the flesh. Other girls as young had been consecrated. To wait for the actual disturbances of puberty might endanger the child's soul. Marcia did not try to answer these arguments. She simply said, "Livia is not moved by love. What she is doing is a lie."

They wondered how Marcia could say such a preposterous thing about a child so obviously inspired by religious passion. Livia proved her passion by ascetic practices. She ate one light meal a day and nothing on Sunday. She slept on a bare board. She spent hours on her knees. She let herself be seen in the garden standing rigid against a stone wall with her arms outstretched like one transfixed to a cross.

Old Faltonia Proba said, "Marcia, you are killing the child."

"She hates me. She is punishing me and herself and all of us because she hates me. I can't believe in consecration that has so much self-punishment in it. Ambrose preached that true consecration to virginity was to transcend nature in a sacrifice of divine love. Livia is seeking vengeance for all the wrongs I have done her. I can't talk to her. She hates me with her eyes whenever I come near her."

Other people in the household began to hate Marcia with their eyes when she came near. She would hold the child Gregory on her lap and cling to his love as the only love left to her.

At this time the false news of my death reached Rome. It was a great shock to Marcia. Now she admitted to herself that what she really wanted was not to save my soul but to have me back as her mate. Now indeed she felt herself a widow, and she regretted bitterly the lie she had tried to bury in her heart even from her own consciousness. She said to herself in real despair, It is too late. I can never confess it to him.

But to Livia, who had fought the wounds of reality with phantasy so long, the story of my death brought a fierce joy. "I shall be the sacrifice for my father's soul!"

She lay in her room and refused to eat, saying the time had come for Marcia to relinquish her to Christ or to death. She became weak and pallid and thin; she assumed the awful and patient silence of a child being murdered by her mother. The whole weight of the palace and of the clergy who visited there turned against Marcia. When Livia got too weak to clamp her jaw shut, Marcia tried to feed the child forcibly, but Livia, with a will steeled by hysteria, vomited up the food forced into her mouth.

Marcia threw her arms around the child and sobbed, "Forgive me! Forgive me!"

"I will pray for you and for my father," Livia whispered.

Within a week, eating carefully, Livia regained her strength. She was consecrated a Virgin of Christ at a formal ceremony conducted by Innocent, who was then Pope. She told Marcia, "You must take me to Bethlehem, to Paula and Jerome. You can be a Christian widow now. Gregory will become a priest. I gave my life to Christ for your sins and to save my beloved father's soul."

Marcia began arrangements to go with Pelagius and her two children to Bethlehem. Marcia herself took no vows, but she did accept the status of a Christian widow who would spend the remainder of her life in chastity, worship and good works. She adopted the customary dark, almost nunlike habit of such women. A kind of emotional calm came to her, a humble and lonely sense of hope, for now she felt that if she could live out the rest of her life in simplicities of devotion she might in the end be forgiven for having loved two men. Demetrias, Faltonia Proba's granddaughter, although she was formally betrothed and had expected to marry, was also on the verge of deciding to go with them, renounce the world, and become a consecrated virgin.

The huge and cheerful Pelagius admitted to Marcia, "I'm human. I take comfort in all this. By our chastity we help bring forth new spiritual children. If we ought, we can!"

The ship was made ready for them at Ostia.

It was Alaric, with doom in his deep intense blue eyes, caught in the compulsions of his own tragic grandeur, who delayed that journey.

I myself came to Rome weeks later, on the eve of Galla Placidia's basest crime, when disease and famine were already ravaging the city and bands of children fought dogs for putrid offal in the streets. Perhaps the greatest sin of all of us was the profound evil we brought upon the children of our generation.

I had waited for death at my villa in the bold and somber hills back of Salernum and within sight of the smoldering majesty of Vesuvius, where often I saw red fire in the sky at night and smoke rise up splendid in the sun of day.

This villa, which had been in our family for seven generations and was not new when we got it, was one of those places of old Roman magnificence that seem to partake of the age of the hills and the forests around them, as if they had always been there and would always remain. Remoteness and wildness as well as grandeur were wrought upon it. The view of Vesuvius through a gap in the hills was proper to its nature.

After my mother's death my father and I had gone there each year for hunting, but I had been there only two or three times for a pause and a look since my father's death. I kept several freedmen overseers and a small contingent of slaves to care for the woods and see to the farming. It was a vast, lonely and melancholy place when I got there, with September weather thickening toward autumn, and I was well suited by the somber mood of the place. I lived alone, making no effort to open social relations with other noble Romans in their villas a dozen miles this way or that. I hunted alone. I dined alone. I bathed alone. There was a fine library, but I was sick of words and did not read. I heard my lonely footfall on the mosaics paving the arcades, but was not fleeing from myself.

All I wanted was a few weeks in which to reflect on the weariness and spiritual failure of my life. I wrote a letter to the Emperor Honorius, telling him I had promised his father, the great Theodosius, that I would be faithful to Honorius, and therefore wished to inform his August Majesty that I was not dead, but awaited his pleasure. I heard that all northern Italy was in turmoil, but I believed the man to whom I entrusted the letter could slip through to Ravenna and would deliver it to Honorius in person. I did not know whether the answer would be soldiers coming to take me or a death sentence preceding the soldiers so that I could do the honors of my own death.

I looked in the mirror and saw the face of a sick man, one almost too weary to be frightened; but I suppose no one who is, as I was, morally exhausted is without some terror in his soul. Actually I must have been suffering more than a little, for what I was trying to do was not to know I was alive. Some days I liked to think that perhaps no man solves the problem of life, but each man concludes the problem, and I could conclude it by opening my veins or taking a draught of poison. I had by now lived through so many spiritual failures that even to kill myself seemed only another tedious folly. Privately I was convinced that no one had need of me either for support or for love, and I had no public function.

I had nothing to do and saw no reason either to live or to die. I had lost all ambition to change or influence other people at their being or doing, and I had lived so long under the pressure of a mistaken identity—call it the Mask-of-the-man-who-ought-to-be-Emperor—that now with that mask torn off I did not know who or what I was. I simply had a sense that somehow, somewhere, I had long ago lost contact with my true being, that I had existed for many years with some outward success in a false position and by vain pretensions; and that now it was too late to find or to live my proper, my native life. In a way it was restful to be such a lost soul, alone and astir in that great old stone edifice, for it did not seem that any more would or could happen to me.

I have been told by those who have had the experience—Marcia told me so after the grueling labor in which she brought forth our son Marcus—that intense physical pain reaches a point of saturation where a kind of numb mute endurance sets in and seems to last forever. In like manner, saturated with the hollow pains of spiritual failure and reduced to moral exhaustion, I found these days of my solitude, drained of meaning, seeming longer than all my life. I seldom slept and yet was never fully awake, and neither day nor night made any difference to me. Each hour was too long to be borne, and I endured each hour.

I turned over in my mind, like a man merely confirming the proofs of despair, such news of ruin as reached my remote seclusion. It came like dying sounds of thunder from over the mountains, and with my personal knowledge of far-off things I was able to picture the rage of the storm.

Honorius could not have been expected to do well as unguided Emperor. And Olympius and Heraclian did everything wrong.

To begin with, Galla Placidia had a real sense of wanting to preserve what she governed, while Heraclian and Olympius only wanted to despoil it. Perhaps if I had stomached the murder of Stilicho and stayed in Ravenna, Galla Placidia and I could have withstood those two; but she alone could not withstand them. They sent her to Rome under the care of Serena, which outraged her. The Empress Thermantia, rejected by Honorius, went with them. Serena's boy Eucherius, after accidents and near escapes, was murdered. Heraclian was a man of greed, and Olympius was a man of vengeance; the one counted up property, and the other counted up deaths. Vengeful laws were put through to persecute not only former friends of Stilicho, but also all non-Catholics. The penalty of proscription and death was finally legalized for all "followers of heretical superstitions" who "ventured to meet in public in their criminal audacity."

But a more immediate dreadful error was perpetrated through Honorius by these morally blind ministers. All non-Catholics were at once excluded from public office. The sick civil government lost good men, and the army lost its better officers, who were Goths and Arians. Some thirty thousand of Stilicho's best soldiers were Goths; their wives and children lived in the cities of Italy under rules of gentle hostage. Now, on signal worked out by Olympius and Heraclian, these cities were entered, and the wives and children of the Goths were massacred. The thirty thousand soldiers, who had been faithful to Stilicho and a bulwark to Rome, now, inspired by grief and rage, streamed north to Alaric and cried out for vengeance.

Even against so cruel a pressure of destiny as this—for had not his gods said he would "penetrate the City?"—Alaric held to the course of honor, saying he had made a treaty with Stilicho and Rome; if Rome would pay its promised stipend of four thousand pounds of gold, so long owing, Alaric would retire with his nation back to the Danube and in good faith would exchange noble hostages. Alaric sent ambassadors to Ravenna with these offers.

With Italy exposed, the Roman army ungeneraled and debased, the government in partisan confusion, the greedy Heraclian, the vainglorious Olympius and the pathetically stupid Emperor Honorius insulted Alaric's ambassadors. Heraclian was rewarded for his crime against Stilicho by being sent to Africa as governor (where, on arrival, he executed the then governor, Stilicho's brother-in-law) and Olympius was made master of offices, or first minister. Honorius fed his chickens.

Alaric, his honor insulted by these fatuous men, lifted his dark intense blue eyes to the terrible blaze of destiny. He erupted out of the Julian Alps with his mighty nation and their hungering souls, wounded by generations of Roman insult, inspired by prophecies of their gods. He crossed the plain and the Po and started in somber anger at Ravenna and its marshes. He ravaged his way down the Adriatic coast and crossed the Apennines, came down the Tiber from the north and sat terrible before the walls of Rome, also seizing Ostia and cutting off the city's food supply.

Alaric shut the twelve gates of Rome from the outside and bestowed on the teeming swarm of the earth's greatest city the companionship of famine and plague, so that in time it was whispered in dark places by the mouths of agony, "Children are edible!"

Of course the people of Rome simply did not believe for a long time that what was happening to them was really happening to them. It was simply preposterous that a Barbarian should have the effrontery to besiege this Eternal City and center of the world. The gods would not allow it, and God would not allow it. Alaric was some sort of vile phantasm that must with all his hordes fade away. No one could harm Rome. It was not in the order of nature that a Barbarian king could harm Rome. Seven centuries ago, when the city was small and comparatively weak, Brennus and his Gauls could strike their blow; but now look at the great Forum, the great palaces, the great walls and the two million citizens. Alaric could not do this thing.

Down at my villa I received a letter from the Emperor Honorius. My messenger had reached him in person and he had answered with his own hand:

The Emperor Honorius to Count Gregory Julian, greetings:
Heraclian wants your property. Olympius wants your death. I forbid them both. Retain your property. Continue to live. But I exile you from Ravenna, for I do not want to see you again, and I forbid you to hold public office. Roma, the golden hen you brought me long ago from Constantinople, is doing well; she is the handsomest of my chickens, and my favorite. I take great care that she may live long.

I had been awaiting my death sentence. This was not at all what I had expected. And yet reading it over I could see it was a profoundly true letter from Honorius. He would no longer consider me his friend, but he was rewarding me for having understood, during his many lonely years, his true affection for his chickens.

I felt deprived of a release I had counted on. It was shocking to be faced with an indeterminate length of life. My sense was that I had nothing to hope for and only failures to remember, so that I was without zest for the future and could not rejoice in the past: It was dreadful thus to come to life to live on and on in a meaningless present. I carried that letter from Honorius around with me for several days, looking at it often, trying to imagine how I would endure this prolonged sickness of an unwanted existence. The somber emptiness of my vast old villa mocked me wherever I moved; I was wandering, purposeless, in my own tomb, a wretched man condemned to live.

Then it was my lost son Marcus who turned me toward the rest of my life. He came up as it were out of his eternal cradle of ocean deeps to smile on his lost father and tell me in simple truth who I was.

There was a conservatory full of plants where the lights were blue and green, from the glass and the foliage, much like the lights of the glassy translucent sea. It was a room which many years ago my mother had taken care of and loved. I went in there one day at a still hour. The slaves had kept things growing. The smell of vegetation was strong and sweet, and I was more aware of the sealike greens and blues than of the few year-end blossoms. In one place a glossy vine had been trained to grow up a square stone column, and looking out from among its leaves, like a tender face parting the breeze-winnowed leafage of a soft sea wave, I saw my lost son Marcus smiling down at me.

Aloud I said, "Hello, son. Thank God, you're well!" The words came from as deep in my heart as my son was deep in the eternal music of the flowing sea.

I held my step and stood amazed, both at what I saw and at what I had said from my heart aloud; for how could I so truly see my son and so speak with a sudden outflowing love that had no fear of any death? Tears came to my eyes. I squeezed the lids to clear them, and still I could see my beloved child smiling at me out of his shimmery blue-green sea enchantment. Softly step by step I tiptoed toward him, then again stood poised and still and knew that all I saw was both a profound illusion and profoundly true. Perceiving the profound truth of a profound illusion was a mystic experience revealing a new vision of the world. I had an overwhelming illuminating sense that truth was all about me where I stood. When I was a very small child my father had had a clay portrait or image made of my face and glazed and colored to the life as a gift for my mother. My mother had placed it here on the stone pillar among vines in this sunroom where she loved to work among her plants and flowers. I now had met and saw and knew my lost son in my lost self, and my lost self in my lost son.

A silent prayer of inexpressible love and thanks is a better acknowledgment of what I now stumble to express in words.

This revelation of identity between my lost son and my lost self was to me a sacred experience, and I stood there silent and glad in the radiance of a holy moment. My thought was more like harmonious understanding than like thought, so I perceived the ultimate use of reason is not to acquire knowledge but to approach consonance with God, and in this true purpose of the searching mind love is a swifter guide than logic, and love, which works by acceptance, achieves a larger harmony than logic, which works by exclusion. My harmonious understanding made two serene movements, first up into a cool consoling light, then upward farther into a warm and healing light.

The cool consoling light was of that realm where religion is for lonely persons; God, or Christ, or Name, is their sole companion; and the religious lonely man does not struggle with other persons, but goes separately direct toward God. There I rested in the peace of one who could forgive himself for being all alone, for even the most lonely man, while yet on his way toward God, is not lost. For the desire of the lonely for God is pure.

And then by serene motion my harmonious understanding rose into the warm and healing light, and it was this: I had found my lost self in my love for my son, and now understood that we seek in love of others our own lost or unfulfilled self. Truly, to be whole a man must love every person and every wonder of earth he meets, for the whole of creation, the entirety of being, the continual evidence of God, loved by the soul, is the true fulfillment of a man. And so wise men say simply: Love God. And one in this warm healing light of love can never be alone, for he has found and so loves the divine core of his own being that his life gives itself overflowing outward in love toward all the world.

This final illumination was the special wonder of my experience. In this it was revealed to me that a man to be free and whole needs to discover and love the divine original child that is himself, and his free consonance with God will be the loss of any fear for that sacred child. My son had led me to discover, and my love for my son had revealed to me, my love for the divine original child that was myself; and there in love for this essential child of my being fear was cast out. It seemed certain to me that when a man no longer fears for the divine original child of his being, then his life may be lived in the constant creative acceptance of love.

Faith, I thought, grows bound to what has been, and logic excludes the inexplicable yeast of life; but love, by all its acceptances, is ripeness of the soul for intensity of being, and overflows outward continually.

I was myself by no means perfect when I was lifted by serene motion to harmonious understanding of these perfect things; but surely that moment is sacred in his life when an imperfect man begins to understand perfect things. These immortal lights that are kindled in a man's life never go out, even though in his own frailty, in the crusty habits of old and ignorant dread, he may yet lift the dark arm of fear before the eyes of his soul to hide in darkness from the radiance of his own original divinity. Although a man does not instantly rise from the old tenacities, I, certainly, had eased down that tense dark arm of fear for this time and place in my life.

Quietly, happily and with a swift sureness I made my preparations and left that afternoon for Rome. My fundamental purpose was quite simple: I wanted to join Marcia and my daughter and Claudian's boy. Marcia, of course, might refuse to live with me, but I was happy in the clear faith that I could offer her and the two children love and protection. I could stay in Rome near them. An outflowing of love such as I had begun to feel has a vitalizing freshness like a spring flowing out of the deep earth, and such love knows for certain that there is thirst in the world which will be glad to receive it.

I took the letter of Honorius with me, like a passport to show to the prefect of the city, because I did not expect to be received with pleasure by any of the present officials. I thought it might be possible for a single man to pass through Alaric's lines and get somehow into the city, but during the few days it took me to travel up to Rome I determined on a more interesting plan.

I presented myself to the first Gothic warriors I met and asked to be taken under their guard to Alaric's tent. They saw no reason to do me that honor, but I persuaded them that if Alaric did not know me well, then they could keep me as their prisoner for ransom. They agreed.

Alaric was not in a tent. He had taken over one of the lovely great villas on the ridge of hills north of the city. The place was tossed full of rich stuffs he had plundered from the cities of Italy. It was late afternoon, and he was feasting with several of his chief men from a large outlay of roast meats and other plentiful food.

He was surprised to see me. "Not dead?"

"Not yet."

"Then you come to wheedle me out of some advantage I have won. Gregory, it's too late for that."

The great Goth struck me as being uneasy. His huge frame was restless, his eyes were troubled. His kingliness had hardened into a stern and watchful anger. He was like a bold heroic hunter, alert, aroused, but not quite ready to start killing. With a large leg of goose he had been eating he gestured at the rich spread of food. "Who eats like this in Rome today?"

I told him I came from outside the city and knew only by rumor how it was within Rome.

"Starving. Sit down. I'll let one Roman eat."

It was getting dusk and chill when we went out to a broad terrace lined with dark tall cypress trees. We had a view of the mass of Rome down across the Tiber, shut within its walls. Below the city, toward Ostia, no ships were on the water. Where we could see here and there a stretch of one of the great roads leading into the city, that road was empty. And all down along the hills and around outside the walls we saw the campfires of Goths. There was something dreadful in seeing this greatest city in the world shut within its walls, cut off from the flow of life and food along the river and the roads which had been its arteries of growth for a thousand years. The march of the aqueducts across the ground below us and into the city gave a sense of water flowing in to the million or two besieged people of Rome. But water was all. No fuel, no food, none of the thousand other articles of commerce that hold a city in health even approached the walls.

Alaric raised his great hand and flexed his fingers before me. "Mine is the grasp that holds Rome now. They are starving, and they don't yet believe it."

"What good is a city of death and disease to you?"

"The prophecy. The gods have said I shall enter the city."

"For plunder and revenge would be one thing. To enter Rome as one deserving to be master general of the armies and virtual ruler of Italy would be another."

I saw I had startled him, and pressed on to say, "I think you would do well to send me into the city to open negotiations for raising the siege. My letter from Honorius forbids me any public office, but I can carry your word to the right man."

"They are starving in Rome. I have all Italy at my disposal and feel no need of hurry. Ataulphus is on his way to join me with large reinforcements. When he arrives I can take Rome at my will. Let them open negotiations."

"It would be worth something even to tell them that."

Somehow my offer seemed to relieve him of an anxiety. His blue eyes flashed with a pleased light, and a faint smile touched his broad mouth. It was as if he were not yet ready in his heart for the grim destiny of actually taking the city, and would be relieved if instead he could accept ransom for lifting the siege. His respect for the ancient grandeur of Rome was still profound. He seemed to know that to violate Rome, and so end the dream of her everlasting greatness, would indeed let chaos loose from Africa to Britain.

"I'll send you to the gate in the morning."

The next morning I rode with a group of Alaric's horsemen to the Flaminian Gate. We stopped a hundred paces from the gate, and the Goth captain ordered me to dismount.

"I prefer to ride my horse into Rome."

"They have begun eating horses in Rome. We send no food into the city."

I dismounted and walked toward the gate, watched by archers on the tower and wall. I stood before the gate until the Goths wheeled and galloped off. Then I was let in through a small door in the massy gate. Immediately I was put under guard. I showed the centurion my letter from Honorius, which was sufficient identification so that he marched me off toward the Palace of the Caesars to be interviewed by the prefect of the city.

I had never before been so aware of the strong smell of Rome. ·It always had its sufficient pungent odor, especially on hot summer days, but on a crisp day of early winter such as this the smell was not usually so strong. I began to realize the odor had a putrid tinge, as of decomposing flesh. I pinched my nose and snorted to get rid of the smell, but the smell persisted.

The centurion laughed grimly. "We're getting behind on the collection and disposal of bodies. They stink."

And I saw a thing that astonished me. A boy about ten years old, with a small fawn-colored dog in his arms, was running along the street. A band of a dozen or so ragged scrawny children were chasing him. They caught him and began to beat him. One of them snatched the dog, hit it on the head with a stone, and ran off with the body. The other children screamed and began to throw stones at and run after the one who had seized the dog.

I was badly received by the prefect of the city. His name was Attalus. He was a handsome man, almost as tall as I was, of noted elegance and with a reputation for learning. I had dealt with him before and thought he was at bottom a snob. His vanity, weakness and limited intelligence showed clearly in his strange interlude (yet to come) as Emperor.

"You were close to Stilicho," he accused me. "All who were close to him are treacherous. His widow Serena, from here in the city, was carrying on secret correspondence with Alaric. We set her aside in prison. You are probably their messenger. But you are too late. Only that letter you have from Honorius saves you from my wrath."

"I am not in communication with Serena. I don't believe she has anything to do with Alaric. I have seen Alaric. He says it is for Rome to ask for terms, not for him to offer them."

"Rome never asks for terms."

"Once Alaric is joined by Ataulphus with new forces and begins to attack, it will be too late to negotiate. I smelled death in the streets and saw children beating one another to snatch a dog to eat."

"Take care, Count Julian. I am master here in Rome. Only that letter from the Emperor saves you. But mark, the Emperor forbids you public office. Rome is through with you, Count Julian. We want no more of your traitorous meddling in public affairs. You will do well to seclude yourself from the anger of the people and from my personal censure!"

He dismissed me.

I went to my own palace, where, after they got over the first glad shock of seeing me alive, my people soon provided me with a bath, fresh clothes and a litter. I was going to have myself carried to the Probus Palace to see Marcia. I noticed my litter-bearers looked rather lean and strained.

My freedman said, "Hunger has reached the palaces, Count Julian. Our slaves are on short rations."

"I'll go afoot. Send one slave ahead to announce that I am coming."

When I reached the Anician Palace old Faltonia Proba herself stood at the door to meet me. Her hair was white now, the skin was loose on her face, but for all her years she was erect and noble. I bowed and greeted her.

She searched my face before she spoke. "So you really are alive."

"Yes."

"God's mercy exceeds my understanding. I haven't told Marcia. I wanted to see you first. What do you bring, Gregory? More torture for that poor girl?"

"I wish to offer her whatever peace, whatever comfort she is able to receive from me."

"And suppose she were fool enough to forgive you—tomorrow or next week you'll be seized and executed and so break her heart all over again."

"I have direct word from the Emperor. He has forbidden me public office and exiled me from Ravenna, but he bade me retain my property and my life."

Her stiff old shoulders relaxed a little. She took me to a small secluded room. "Wait here. She had better see you privately. I'll bring her to the door."

I stood there alone for about five minutes. Sunlight from a window threw my shadow across the floor and onto a couch ornamented with gold and covered with russet-colored silk. But I did not sit down. The room was empty. Then suddenly Marcia took three quick steps into the room and stood still, clasping her hands behind her back. Like Christian widows I had seen before, she wore a black garment and a gray veil over her head. She seemed to me at first glance a larger, stronger and better-developed woman than I remembered. Her head tilted a little, her eyes were quite steady, and her lips parted, but she did not smile.

I walked forward and reached out for her hand. I could see the throb of deep excitement at the base of her throat. Her hands were still clasped behind her back.

"Please do not be afraid of me, Marcia."

"You may not want to touch me after I tell you the truth."

Her chin began to tremble. I could see her making a great effort of will. I could tell from the tension of her shoulders that she was squeezing her hands together hard behind her back. Her eyes did not waver from mine as she spoke. "Gregory . . ." She paused, moistened her lips, then went on. "I loved Claudian. He came as in his own darkness, seeking my comfort. He did not know how to receive my love, but I gave it to him. I lied to you when I said I did not love him. But I told the truth when I said I loved you." Her face flushed red. "I have to tell it all, Gregory, the whole truth. Forgive me if you can. I have never believed in my heart that it was a sin to love him and bear him a son. He was strange. I could never reach him or comfort him with all my love. His need was inconsolable. I am glad you're alive, Gregory, and have let me put that lie out of my heart."

She loosed her hands from behind her back and let her arms hang at her sides. She bowed her head and spoke slowly. "Claudian left me, as strange as he came. I loved him, but never knew him. I've tried to be a Christian and hate it as a sin. But he was not of our Christian world. He wore a hood of darkness that haunted my love; I could not reach him there or save him from it. The beauty of life is greater than we are. To call it a sin is an abominable lie. . . . Now I've told you the truth, Gregory."

I suffered as she told me these things, but it was a new and bewildering sort of pain that I did not yet understand. There was no anger in it, no impulse of fear to strike out against it. It was as if I suffered Marcia's pain and not my own, and she appeared more lovely because her suffering was mine.

"I have lived with many lies deeper than yours, Marcia. Let us be at peace."

She looked at me a moment, tears formed in her eyes, and then she was in my arms.

Soon we sat on the couch together, and in a quiet voice she told me many things. Her deepest worry, which I began to understand and share with her, was how the knowledge of my being alive and returned would affect our daughter Livia.

"I resisted as long as I could, Gregory, but finally I had to choose between letting her be consecrated a virgin or letting her die. She could and would starve herself to death. No one else in the palace seems to believe me, but my mother's heart knows that Livia is in hysterical tension. I don't know how the shock of your return will affect her. But we must not injure her more deeply if we can avoid it. She thinks now she has sacrificed herself in supreme love to save your soul because she thought you died without love. Give me time to prepare her. Come again tomorrow."

"I'll come tomorrow. We'll use all love and patience to ease the child."

"Will you go to the Senate now? Anything you could do to help Serena would be good. There's been too much tragedy already."

The Probus men were active in Rome's affairs, and Marcia now told me the story of what was going on in the Senate.

The Senate, in its proud refusal to face the desperate military weakness of Rome, the certainty that no help would come from Ravenna, and the actual power and purpose of Alaric, meant to defend the Eternal City by murdering a woman. There had already been introduced in the Senate a proposal to destroy Serena on the ground that she was the real instigator of Alaric's siege and that, once Alaric knew she was dead, he would withdraw his armies and in some dreamlike fashion vanish out of Italy. The Pagans, who could never forget that Serena had snatched the sacred pearl necklace from the mother goddess in the Temple of the Vestal Virgins, favored this odious crime, and the Catholic party favored it because, as they said, "she is betraying us to Arian Barbarians."

The thing had gone fatally far. However, the Senate really knew it was a futile and cowardly crime they intended, and they were about to seek at least a semblance of imperial command to commit it. A delegation was being formed to go to Galla Placidia, sister of the Emperor, for her imperial approval of this atrocity.

The Senate was not solely responsible. The people of Rome were frightened and angry and wanted revenge. It never entered their heads that man for man they must have outnumbered Alaric's forces ten to one and that a free and resolute populace could swarm out through the twelve gates with any weapons at hand and scour the hills until the Goths were shattered and fled. Someone wasn't taking care of them. Someone had betrayed them. Someone had let them grow hungry and sick. Someone had failed to provide a great army. Someone ought to be killed! The city was feverish with rumors. It was even said that Stilicho was still alive and stood shoulder to shoulder with Alaric besieging Rome. All the more reason to destroy Serena, who must be plotting with Stilicho and Alaric. Serena was already named in the streets as the betrayer of Rome and was being held a prisoner in one of the dingy rooms in the vast Palace of the Caesars where before now victims of popular or imperial anger had awaited death.

"I've talked with the prefect of the city. You know Attalus, with his high-bridged nose and high majestical voice. 'Beware of my wrath, Count Julian!' The idiot! He made it clear that I am considered a traitor, and if I appeared now in the Senate in favor of Serena, this hatred of me would only certify their hatred of her. And the people demand blood. The only chance I have of stopping this thing is through Galla Placidia. She'll probably refuse to see me, but I'll try."

"Do, Gregory. Do what you can. And I'll prepare Livia for your return tomorrow."

I went to the Palace of the Caesars and asked for audience with Galla Placidia. I waited an hour, and word came back that the princess would receive me some hours later in the evening. I did not like being put off for hours more, but it was better than being refused audience at all. Yet I dreaded she might be putting me off until it would be too late for me to interfere. The best I could do was to send back a message thanking her for the appointment and asking her to delay decision about Serena until she could talk to me. To this I got no answer.

I then went to Serena's prison quarters and there was admitted.

Serena greeted me with a cool irony. "So the dead come back to greet the dead."

"We both still live."

"It is but a dream. We live from betrayal to betrayal, and then we die."

She was a gray woman now. That phrase of Claudian's, "her snowy throat and golden hair," no longer applied. Her hair was gray, and the pale gray cast of shattered life lay like ash in the color of all her skin. The woman's bones were still regal, and her spirit held them erect, but the flesh had shrunk, and I could see the hollows between the tendons on the backs of her hands. She wore that fatal necklace of the mother goddess and touched its pearls from time to time with her fingers. Her throat looked fragile now, which had once been superb.

"We met long ago, Gregory," she said. "At first I didn't trust you. At some moments I weakened and trusted you. I still don't know whether or not you are a good man. But I will say I never knew a man so able as you to seem to be seeking good by devious pathways of evil. You always sided with Galla Placidia against me. You chose between security under my power and the hazard of making yourself Emperor through Galla Placidia."

"I never quite chose anything. I never was quite anything."

She looked around the large dingy room, which was dirty and smelled like a melancholy place where fabrics had dry-rotted and rats had died. With a gesture of her hand she indicated the baseness and squalor of her position. "Now at the end have you come to grieve with me or to make your final bid to become Caesar?"

"I am to see Galla Placidia tonight. I shall do what I can to avert this crime."

"Which comes of other crimes you did not avert."

"That is true."

She turned away from me and sat on a bare bench. "Then why not cease seeking this inside mastery of Empire? I know even better than you to what it leads. Stilicho is dead. My daughter Maria, my son Eucherius, they are dead. Thermantia, dismissed by the Emperor, has no purpose left to live. And I am ready for death. It is as I said—we live from betrayal to betrayal, and then we die."

I approached her and waited until she looked up at my face, then I spoke. "I believe I never hated you. I usually admired, yet sometimes pitied you. But now I feel a much simpler emotion than any of those. You and I are equal, Serena, souls of God; we could not be more, we are not less. I came here to tell you that because I wanted you to know you are not alone. I remember Ambrose comforted you when Theodosius died. I wish I could do as much now when no one like him is near."

She watched me a moment, and tears formed in the corners of her cool gray eyes. "Love sounds strangely in your voice. I'll remember it, Gregory." She looked at me with a surprised clarity. "Ambrose always said you would find your way. I believe you owe much to that saint's prayers."

"He loved me and took my sins upon himself. I've begun to learn to bear what is my own."

"I am glad you have brought Ambrose back to my memory. I have been alone in misery too many years. But I can see him now, as if he stood here immortal beside you, and he reaches out his hand shining in pure charity and offers me the healing of Christ's peace. Please go, Gregory. I am in need of solitude and prayer."

"We all need one another's compassion and one another's prayers. Also, I will do what I can to save your life. Farewell."

I went to the door. There I was stopped by four soldiers and a fifth grim man. Two of the soldiers with swords drawn menaced any move I might have made.

Serena rose. One handed her a document. As she read it a flush and a light came into her face. Her head lifted. Her shoulders straightened.

The commander of the little group said, "Take Count Julian away from here. Close the door."

"No!" Serena's voice rang out with her old authority. "Stay, Gregory. I want one who has known me well to see me die."

"This can't be done!" I ordered. "In the name of Serena I appeal to the Emperor!"

"No, Gregory. It is ordered by the Senate. It is signed by Galla Placidia. And I am ready."

The two soldiers held me, one with a sword at my breast, one with a sword at my throat, and my back was against the wall. The other two soldiers stood one at each side of Serena, and the fifth grim man went behind her, a long strong cord of purple silk dangling from his massy hand.

I would like to say that I was helpless, pinioned against the stone wall by two armed men, one with a sword at my throat and the other with a sword at my breast. There was no effective move I could make now to save Serena's life, and that should have absolved me from guilt, from complicity in her murder, from responsibility and from judgment. But I learned in the next moment an inexorable truth about life and a sickening truth about myself.

The truth about life was this: The way a man bears witness to his own actions or inactions both expresses and further determines the quality of his soul. Any man reviewing a long life may well say he did this by choice, that by compulsion, one thing on spontaneous impulse, another in the throes of disaster. But no man can escape from showing forth the quality of his life and of his soul by how he bears witness to what he does and to what is done to him. This truth was greatly shown by Jesus in the garden when Judas betrayed him with a kiss, for then one of his disciples seized a sword and smote off the right ear of a servant of the high priest. Jesus first reproved the disciple, saying, "Put up again thy sword into his place: for all they that take the sword shall perish by the sword." Then, turning to the servant of the high priest, whose face streamed with blood and twisted with pain, Jesus said, "Suffer ye thus far," and he touched the servant's ear and healed him.

The truth I saw of my own soul's sickness was this: I had not the spiritual power to behold and accept and resist not evil, so that clearly I was not a saint, able to accept Serena's death with an immortal compassion. Neither was I so inspired by the violent passion of earthly courage as to leap against the swords and so slay myself in Serena's behalf before they slew her. I stood there paralyzed in the anguished cowardice of clinging to my own life and yet not forgiving her murderers for her death.

That was the first motion, a moment long, but profound in its searching of my heart.

Serena rescued me from its utter ruin. She commanded, "Put down your swords. Count Julian will offer no violence. Let this be decent!"

Their arms relaxed a little, and they turned their face toward their leader for his command. In that moment, released from the self-preserving paralysis of my cowardice, I kicked at the stomach of the man whose sword was near my throat, and I lunged my body at the other one, trying to seize his sword. I showed myself no follower of Christ in this attempt to resist evil, and I showed myself a fool to try to effect anything against those men and their weapons. I made a mortal's try to ward off another mortal's tragic doom, which is neither divine nor prudent, but is what a man does. Yet even this in my wretched and divided soul was not a pure act of courage toward Serena, for I was trying also to redeem myself from cowardice, and that, too, a man sometimes does.

My lunge at the second man deflected his sword from my heart, but he gave me a deep wound in the chest. I found myself, sickened from the shock, thrown back against the wall, with the two men holding my arms pinioned there. It took all the will power I had to hold my head up and to keep from fainting.

I fixed my eyes on Serena's face. For a moment she watched the stain of blood broaden on my tunic and seep down toward my knees. Then for one instant her eyes met mine. They were profoundly meditative and without fear. Perhaps she saw the overwhelming presence of God in things as they are, being, becoming, flowing, and at every moment of motion this pulsation of infinity through forms and acts exceeds our human comprehension in wonderful vitality and terrible beauty.

Serena closed her eyes, lifted her face, and spoke with intense clarity. "I forgive my enemies. I confess my love to thee, sweet Christ. Almighty God, Thy will be done."

The executioner at her back made a swift and terrible action with his powerful hands and the silken cord. He was an expert at his business, for, though Serena's eyelids flashed open at the sudden shock of strangulation, revealing the fullness of her eyes, the light and life died out of them before terror and anger could flare up. I don't know what may have gone on behind her eyes, in her outraged brain, at that supreme climax of life.

I thought it was the most fundamental of all violations of our human nature when a man kills a woman. In the face of this crime I resented Serena's death, out of pride of spirit resenting the very basis of spirit, which is the flux of matter. For (I learned later) it is only by renouncing our own life that we can accept the death of another. Short of that we always feel a resentment, as if their dying has insulted us. But when we renounce our own life, death is not an insult, but a natural motion in the normal tragedy of being, and its vivid mystery enlarges our compassion and deepens our love. Perhaps love is the means by which the soul, set free of the illusion of durable forms, is reconciled to the continuous pulse and flow and wonder of change. And of all we humans may behold of change, death is the most startling, vivid and dramatic display of that primary mystery of our lives.

They allowed me to lift Serena from the floor and lay her on the couch. Some pearls of the necklace of the mother goddess were embedded in her throat. She seemed to me very light, and I was surprised that a body could be so tender yet and still so warm, though life had fled. For the first time in all the years I had known her I noticed the faint haze of hair on her cheek, close to her ear. This amazed me. Then I didn't see her face at all.

I turned to say something, I don't know what, to the blurred faces of the soldiers, but the whole room blackened, and when I recovered consciousness I was on a bed in another part of the palace with a surgeon in attendance.

I asked them to send for Marcia. I wanted to see her before I died.

I think during some days of fever and delirium it was the consciousness of Marcia sitting by my bed that held my thread of life from letting go. For not only was the wound sufficient to have been mortal, but the destruction of Serena had profoundly ruined my confidence in the possible values of life. The deeper vision of love revealed to me at the villa when I had perceived the divine child at the core of my being was like an eternal truth transcending the gross and comic villainies of daily living, and in my nearness to death this vision seemed one thing, and good, but life another. Life, in general, seemed simply not worth the treachery and pain and shock involved in hanging onto it. But the consciousness of Marcia's presence, like a touch of beneficent healing, was not life in general, but was personal particular immediate living, and was worth the last strain of the soul to live it well and find it good.

What is real and what is unreal during days of delirium on the fringes of death? Both Marcia and the physician were certain I did not get out of my bed, but it was painfully real to me that again and again I rose in my last strength and went out toward the great Basilica of Constantine to weep and pray for Serena. But I could not enter the basilica to pray for her, for was it not the Christian party that had ordered her death? Then I would struggle toward the pillars and great dome of the Pantheon to do some Pagan sacrifice in her memory, but could not enter there, for was it not also the Pagan party that had ordered her death? Then I would loiter in the crowded streets of Rome, among the swarms of people, who were frightened, hungry, angry—the people who had demanded Serena's death—seeing not the vague innumerable face and body of man, but each particular body and face, a man, a woman, a child, one by one terribly clear, each one under a pall of despair and caught in a twist of anguish. This vision of unceasing human pain was the reality of my delirium, and death promised to darken it out. Then there was the noise. I found that despair has a great and hollow resounding noise, a continuous nerve-wracking rumble of dissonance that oppresses a man until he thinks he is screaming, and death promises to silence that low insistent ravaging sound.

But gradually I came out of the dark and silent invitation of that death, drawn by a thread woven and strengthened by Marcia's love. Life in general, with its aggregate tragedy, treachery, terror and pain, was not worth living, but every moment of individual life evokes the utmost of the soul to live it intensely and find it good: The marvelous beauty of individual being surpasses any abstractions that may be made about life in general or life to come.

Such, at least, was my return from the fringes of death.

But come, I say to myself, old man with aged bones, how can you dispose of this primary matter, a return from death's edge, with a few pretty abstractions? Come, now, tell the tale over in sensuous terms, the way you felt it. That would be interesting.

It is indeed a sensuous story, a humorous and passionate personal story within, and yet counter to, the agony of Rome, where the oppressive weight of history was on the side of death and ruin.

I had felt myself burning up dry from inside. My fever went down, and I began to feel, as from outside my body, the temperature of the room and the changes of weather in the day. My wound, as it began to heal, began to feel tight, sore and more localized. I could lie with my eyes closed and smell my own freshness when Marcia washed me, and I could smell the flowers she brought into the room. I could now distinguish with my fingers whether I was touching my body or touching the bed. I could look in restful silence at the soothing purity of a white flower in a shadowed corner. I could see Marcia as a full-length woman pausing for a look and a thought as she came toward my bed. I could hear her step and hear her dark garments rustle.

I began to have lucid moments. I came, lured by specific sensations, out from the dark pall of too vast and general a sense of the tragic strife and fatal issue of bewildered mankind. I lay, feeling each breath, like a spent man cast out of a wild sea onto a warm beach. I saw and reached for and held Marcia's warm hand, then separated her fingers and put my fingers between them and grew in hope of personal life. I wanted to tell her how it had been, but could not use words, and so pressed her hand and told her that way. I became irritated by anyone else and clung at first to Marcia's single companionship, refusing to be washed or moved in bed or talked to by slaves, saying that only Marcia's touch and voice comforted me.

Then I began to taste what I ate and even tasted the metal of the utensils with which I ate it—the taste and odor of silver or gold on the tongue, of ivory on the tongue—until soon I wanted to eat and to recover strength, and asked for food that was not available in famine-stricken Rome. I had a few days of real irritation when I felt the dampness of a pillow, discomfort of a cover, resented the smell of certain flowers, preferred the taste of certain foods, and told Marcia please to wear a less widowlike garment. "I want you out of that black, in wine-colored silk with embroidery on it. Wear bracelets again; they chime when you move your arms." I began to speak out in a louder voice.

Then my sexual impulse reawakened and responded with growing desire to the mature and graceful motions of Marcia as she tended my needs and often added an instinctive caress of the hand. When Marcia came back wearing, not wine-colored silk, but a garment blue as Homer's wine-dark sea, which clung to her as she moved and set off the smooth cool freshness of her bare arms and throat, like a sea nymph in a soft blue wave, the eager laughter of Venus in my heart made me a little crazy, especially when she stooped over me and her breasts were not hidden. Although the time and place and my actual condition were not proper to it, I urged Marcia to get into bed with me. She, with startled eyes and full color in her lips, said I was being silly and outrageous, but I insisted, and she said we were divorced and she was at least informally committed to chastity for the rest of her life. And I said not in that blue dress, that loose and lovely gown from the wardrobe of Venus, and I taxed her with having freshly bathed and put perfume between her breasts in expectation of my embrace. And she blushed all up her throat and cheeks to the roots of her dark hair, and her eyes flashed with that light of expectant alarm of a woman who is not going to run away.

She cried, "Your wound, Gregory, your wound, darling?"

Then I felt verily a man and said, "Damn my wound! Get into this bed!"

"But Rome is starving. People are dying!"

"Then we'll breed new Romans!"

I caught her hand to pull and persuade her, but already she had loosed a girdle and tossed her shoulders to let her garment fall like blue sea water rippling down off her body. She stepped out of the sea-blue pool of her garment with a bright flash of her knees and sounded one clear chime of singing laughter which had the joyous sound of letting all death go; and we celebrated an incautious performance of our natural reunion. Once we were in each other's arms, we both made little sounds of delight at the mirth and solace of our refound warmth and folly, and then Marcia proved herself as lovelorn for our reunion as I was.

(Eheu, Venus! The old man who writes these lines still remembers that hour! For all my body felt the smooth, warm and vital body of Marcia in my arms again, and told my soul, "She is here! She is here!" Some trace of prime manhood not yet died out of my aged loins and heart remembers, and my old bones remember the stretch and clasp of our love and tell my soul, "She was there . . . was there! . . ." But I am not such a green old man as to dream of a third marriage to Marcia in heaven, for I who have aged saw Marcia age and die: Alas, Venus!)

And, back to that hour all those years ago, by both the pleasure and pain of our accomplishment (for while it refreshed our spirits, it distressed my wound) I knew myself recovered for the further joys, follies and hopes of a man's living; and then in the drowsy peace of that little sleep that comes, I was happy with Marcia adrowse in my arms, we happy two reconciled in our happy peace in the heart of the beleaguered city of hunger and agony.

And I thought or dreamed that all the path of my return from death was my natural obedience to God, and I agreed with Augustine that he is happy who obeys God, but all the rules are not writ in a book, and I was grateful I had not stayed in Africa with Augustine to obey Him.

And after that, in the next few days, I began to judge and choose and plan for our two lives in the hazard of the world and in the tragedy of being. It was a coming forth from death into a new and deepened and matured return to love.

And I'm glad now I've told it in sensuous as well as in abstract terms, for the recovery of love has its feeling as well as its philosophy. And I feel my life before I value it.

Neither the Senate nor Galla Placidia nor the demoralized people of Rome found in the death of Serena the reward they sought. Alaric only tightened his siege. Plague and starvation increased. Galla Placidia never came in to see me. She sent me a curious note:

Galla Placidia, Sister of the Emperor Honorius, waited to offer you your last chance to be Caesar. You chose Serena, and perhaps death, instead. Whether you live or die, she who shall be Empress now bids Count Julian a permanent farewell.

She had the audacity to sign it "Galla Placidia Augusta." I had Marcia burn it, for in the wrong hands it would condemn the girl for treason.

The Senate had finally to send a delegation to Alaric to ask for his terms for lifting the siege. He asked quite simply for all the wealth of Rome, from pepper and silk to silver and gold, and for the freeing of all Gothic slaves.

The shocked emissaries asked, "What do you leave us?"

"Your lives," Alaric told them.

"Rome is a vast and teeming city. We shall defend ourselves!"

"Thick grass makes easy mowing."

Wealthy people, particularly wealthy women like Laeta, widow of the Emperor Gratian, Faltonia Proba, and, on her more modest scale, Marcia, had been giving all the money and plate and jewels they could to purchase food for the poor; but by now even the stocks of the most rapacious hoarders were exhausted. Whatever bitter tales had come down from cities of old under the throes of famine and of plague were true and actual stories now day by day in Rome. Death, viciousness and social distintegration had begun to rule the city which had lost its daily bread.

This crisis of affairs was in December. I was well enough now to see my daughter. Marcia warned me that Livia would see me only under compulsion.

"The child has to meet life, Marcia. You and I are going to live together again."

"She distorts everything. She hated me for years for depriving her of her father. Now she hates you for not having died. It is as if you, personally and on purpose, were invalidating her vows of virginity, which she made to save your soul."

"Perhaps when she sees me she will begin to respond to what is true."

"We must be patient, Gregory. The child is obsessed."

Marcia did not tell me until later that during my illness Livia had prayed for my death so that she could go on, as a sacrificial virgin, praying for my lost soul.

The plans were made, and I went to the Probus Palace.

I received a warning signal from Marcia the moment I came into the room where they waited for me. Livia was clinging to her mother like a passionately fond child. Her red hair was like a fling of flames about her white face, and her intense eyes glowed from green tones to bronze. She was limber, swift and nearly as tall as Marcia. She sprang forward.

not to embrace me, the beloved father, but as if to save her mother from the touch of a beast. She had the strange beauty of those who have been spiritually injured and out of their injury have evolved a protective hysteria. Her voice vibrated with the intensity of one who has been profoundly betrayed and cries out passionately in a sudden and complete reversal, a reversal of the direction of the hungering and frightened soul's flight from reality, from love, from sorrow, flight from the creative radiance of God in things as they are. For now I was the one she hysterically loathed and Marcia the one she hysterically loved.

"Beast! Beast!" she screamed. "Don't touch my mother! Don't **you** dare touch my mother ever again!"

And there she stood between us, like a child of flame, ready to avenge the wrong we had done her, flinging her life at hazard to keep us apart.

CHAPTER THREE

GOD ON THE STEPS OF NIGHT

THE CRIMES OF CHILDREN STEADILY INCREASED DURING THE next year and a half. Children under fifteen years of age did not often go beyond stealing, arson and the torturing of animals and smaller children, but those between fifteen and twenty years old went in for perversion and libertinage, and they accomplished rapes and murders and riots. Every region of the city developed its vicious gangs which fought within the region or prowled to fight gangs in other regions. Some of the boys earned themselves fame as ruthless and rapacious leaders, and orgiastic and blasphemous rites were celebrated by these ensavaged boys and girls in abandoned cellars and other dark dead ends of the labyrinthine city.

Teachers and priests and parents were shocked and bewildered; but they had lost the confidence of these vigorous embruted young. For what, indeed, were the children doing, in direct, naked and amoral viciousness, but imitating the demoralized practices of the society in which they lived? Of what use is it for a corrupt generation to preach moral precepts to its children? When the Senate orders strangulation of Serena for alleged conspiracy, it will enter the heads of the young to see what it is like to strangle a traitor among themselves. When the Catholic Church strips a Pagan temple of its gold and treasures, children will go thieving down the street of the silver workers. When the state dishonors its obligations, soldiers desert, slaves revolt, parents redouble their adulteries, bands of religious fanatics beat up citizens in the streets, bishops are elected by sticks and stones, justice is sold, hatred is preached and finally the great city of the world is besieged and reduced to starvation and ravaged by plague, children can see for themselves that treacherousness, viciousness and brutality mold the life around them, and that they are free to go to do likewise. For have not adults set before them these examples of how life is lived?

It had taken a long accumulation of perfidy and fear and disintegrating disaster to shatter the natural goodness and pristine innocence of the child heart; but finally we were converting our own children to our own corruption.

Strangely enough, Alaric, the enemy, was the only great figure left of honor and integrity at a peak of power. The Emperor was pusillanimous, his ministers were corrupt, the Senate was fatuous, the Church was partisan, the people were demoralized; but Alaric's word was still good, and he tried to save Rome, tried to save the symbol of Rome as the heart of impregnable world order, before he destroyed it.

To begin with, Alaric softened his demands. Instead of requiring all the public and private wealth of the city, he let Rome buy off the siege for five thousand pounds of gold, thirty thousand pounds of silver, four thousand robes of silk, three thousand pieces of fine scarlet cloth and three thousand pounds of pepper. The desire for silver and gold was as common to the Barbarians as to the Romans, but the manners of the Goths were changing now that their women yearned for silks and fine cloth and the Gothic palate wanted pepper in its food.

The price was paid. Upon fearfully opening one or two gates of the city, it was found that Alaric meant to abide by his treaty. No assault was made. Food could be brought in, and commerce on the river and the roads was resumed. Alaric kept a strict discipline among his people and severely punished any Goths who assaulted or insulted Romans. He gradually withdrew his army from the neighborhood of Rome, setting up his winter camp in Tuscany, where he was joined by Ataulphus, who came down from the Danube country with large reinforcements. And many thousand Gothic slaves escaped from Rome and joined Alaric.

Alaric had shown that Rome was his for the taking. His power now increased by the new forces of Ataulphus, it was obvious that he was military master of Italy. The Emperor, sequestered in the marshes of Ravenna with an army no more than large enough for that city and stripped of all except Catholic officers, could neither restore power to Rome nor drive Alaric out of Italy. And since all provinces north of the Alps were in an internecine revolt against Rome and against one another, there was no one except Alaric strong enough to protect the northern borders of Italy from any new assault. As I remarked to the Probus men in the Anician Palace, "If the Emperor would now appoint Alaric master general of the armies, we could have a generation of peace in which to recover."

"What of laws forbidding non-Catholics to hold public office?"

"That's not religion. That's the political folly of Olympius. Why legislate Rome to death?"

There was a strong sense in Rome that this was a practical solution, and Alaric himself thought so, too. Alaric sent a delegation of Senators to Honorius in Ravenna, asking to be made master general of the armies of the West, requesting a reasonable annual subsidy of corn and money for his army, and requiring the provinces of Venetia, Dalmatia and Noricum in which to settle his people. Such an offer from the man who in fact had all the corn, all the wealth and all the land of Italy at his disposal and at his mercy was not rapacious. Olympius began Ravenna's year of incredible folly by refusing to hear these ambassadors from Alaric and the Senate.

Alaric renewed his proposals for peace, sending a new delegation from the Senate to Ravenna, this time including Pope Innocent in its membership. Even this did no good.

It would take many thousands of words to recount all the details of what went on, but the principles can be stated in a paragraph. Certain eunuchs of the palace had murdered Stilicho's son Eucherius for the Emperor and were now in great favor with Honorius. By intrigue they overthrew Olympius, who, in the course of further vicissitudes, first had his ears cut off and finally was flogged to death. Jovius, who was facile, impressionable and not sure enough of anything to have a policy, replaced Olympius. The laws against non-Catholics were relaxed to win back a few so-called generals. And the real business of Ravenna became, not the saving of Rome or Italy, but palace intrigue. Personal animosity became public policy. So, in a sentence, the grandeur of Rome's world had come to this: Pompous officials and incompetent generals, impelled to treachery by eunuch ministers, made policy for the confused and torpid Emperor.

Alaric no longer saw any hope of dealing with Honorius. He seized the great grain port of Ostia, threatened Rome with famine, and at once secured a response from the city. At Alaric's command the Senate raised the prefect of the city, Attalus, to the purple, crowned him with the diadem, and pronounced him Emperor. Alaric was made master general, Ataulphus was raised to the rank of Count. Alaric's Gothic soldiers conducted the new Emperor Attalus to the imperial palace.

Catholics were shocked, for Attalus had had a Pagan education and had later been baptized by an Arian bishop. But the weight of favor was shifted toward Attalus by Galla Placidia. Since the death of Serena, Galla Placidia was considered the true representative of the Theodosian dynasty in Rome. The rejected, disgraced and pathetic Thermantia (still a virgin and soon to die and be buried in purple alongside her sister Maria) was disregarded. Galla Placidia, assuming all the pomp of an Augusta, received Attalus and supported his elevation. It was quite expected that she would marry him and become Empress. I have no doubt that she considered the step. But Galla Placidia was a shrewd young woman, and she would not fail to see that, beside Alaric and Ataulphus, men of vigor, courage and intelligence, Attalus, with his high whine of voice and high-bridged nose, had better be tried in a crisis before accepted as an imperial spouse. Ataulphus, whose wife had died, said publicly in Rome that Galla Placidia, with her fine figure and golden hair and flashing blue eyes, was as beautiful as any highborn woman of the Barbarians. And presently Galla Placidia held what might be called a tacit leverage of power between Attalus and the Senate on one side and Alaric and Ataulphus on the other.

Now this tragicomedy of Rome's death became grotesque. Heraclian, governor of Africa, shut off all shipping to Italy and began to starve Rome from a distance. Alaric wanted to take an army to Africa and deal with Heraclian but the new proud Attalus and the old proud Senate wouldn't trust Alaric, and sent a weak flotilla under a poor Roman general to do a large job. Alaric with a large army conducted Attalus north to within sight of Ravenna. Honorius was on the point of flight. His ministers came to Alaric's camp and were on the point of accepting, in the name of Honorius, the co-Emperorship of Attalus. Attalus then disdained to share honors and offered Honorius the right to abdicate the purple peacefully and retire to island exile. At this point Jovius and the other top ministers deserted Honorius and joined Attalus. Now news came that the force sent to Africa was destroyed by Heraclian, and at the same time four thousand Roman veterans landed in Ravenna to support Honorius. Attalus began carrying on intrigues behind Alaric's back.

But Galla Placidia was there in the great encampment, both Alaric's hostage and imperial princess. She had personal influence with Ataulphus, and at least her Theodosian name had influence with Alaric. Alaric's next step certainly sounds like Galla Placidia's policy.

Suddenly, there on the field, in front of the army, he stripped Attalus of the diadem and the purple and sent these emblems of usurped power into Ravenna as a gift to Honorius, with a letter from Galla Placidia to her brother meant to establish her as Empress and to bring Alaric and Honorius together.

It was a move so peculiar that it might have worked.

But Sarus, that giant brute Gothic general who had betrayed Stilicho and hated Alaric, erupted from Ravenna with a wild detachment of cavalry and caused a small battle at such a moment as to make it a great insult. Then Honorius pronounced Alaric forever Rome's enemy.

Alaric was finished now with everything except the doom the gods had laid on his head.

He went down and once more shut the twelve gates of Rome from the outside. Once more, this time in the putrid heat of summer, agony woke again, and the fourteen regions of Rome were ruled by hunger and plague. All of us in Rome knew, as you know an avalanche is coming down the mountain and won't be turned away, that this time Alaric would make no terms, but came to destroy forever the dream that Rome was impregnable. He came now to pronounce upon the Empire of the West the dark night of political chaos. The myth of Roman peace and Roman order, which had had a large and effective reality for a thousand years in the affairs of men, was to be shattered at the heart and would lie broken from Alexandria to Britain and from Spain to Greece.

I can't say that during this same period of fantastic political folly and collapse my private life moved on in happy ease. My personal problems, as well as Rome's public ones, seemed insoluble except by disaster.

Livia.

I write the name of my daughter, and my heart aches.

If you had a daughter who was visibly afflicted, paralyzed or blind, she would evoke a deep tenderness and a constant thoughtful effort to help her. Livia was swift and vital, with a wild young flare of nostrils and toss of head. She was cunning, antagonistic and willful. She was beautiful. She was a favorite of all the Probus family in the Anician Palace, and many of the slaves thought of her as already a saint and expected the moment when she would begin to work miracles of the major sort, such as restoring sight to the blind and raising the dead. Having won her primary struggle with Marcia, she knew the pattern of victory. It was hard to realize that such a child might have been so mortally wounded in the mind that she needed more tenderness, patience and healing than a blind girl or a crippled girl.

I never knew a more courageous child than Livia, for she did face and try to solve a spiritual dilemma of the first magnitude.

I had hoped young Gregory was going to help. He was a heart-warming child, with hair as black as Claudian's, quick and sweet and mirthful in converse, daylong happy in his heart and seemingly born to love and comfort people. He still had and cherished the golden cup I had sent him on which I had had engraved: "To Gregory, son of Claudian, from Marcus, son of Gregory: Live, Brother." He liked to stand between my knees when I sat, with one of his hands on each of my legs, and have me tell him about his brother Marcus and about his father Claudian. He said, "I'm glad Claudian was my father, and I am glad you are my father now."

He was really delighted at Marcia's reunion with me and more than made up to the two of us for the doctrinal censures of some older people who tried to find sin in a man and woman returning to marriage after adultery, divorce and separate living.

I did not want to get involved in any such doctrinal disputes before the fact, and so arranged for our remarriage in a small church in a modest district of the city. Once we had married and were living together in my palace, tongues wagged, but Bishop Innocent made no issue of the matter. I legally adopted Gregory as my son. Alaric had not yet accepted ransom for the city, the first siege was still on, we were all underfed and half hungry and by no means sure of escaping the plague. Yet it was quite sound and reasonable to go on with these personal affairs of private life. You don't stop being a person with intensely important private relationships just because a city, an empire, a civilization faces disaster. You still do what you can with the yield of the day. I spent very good hours every day teaching young Gregory Greek and introducing him to the Greek and Latin poets, including the work of his father Claudian.

Livia profoundly resented our remarriage and left the Probus family to live with us only under compulsion. I sat beside her and took her two hands in mine and tried to reach her affection and her understanding. She sat very still, her hands passive in mine, and did not flinch from looking right into my eyes. I told her I loved Marcia and her and Gregory and wanted us all to live together in affection. I said I honored her consecration as a virgin and would not try to interfere with her religious life. She simply watched me as I spoke, repressed any show of emotion, and said nothing. She had not spoken one word to me since that first outcry when she called me a beast and forbade me to touch her mother.

I asked Pelagius if he would not talk to Livia for me. The big Briton shook his head. "You don't seem to understand, Gregory. A consecrated virgin has left her father and her mother to become a bride of Christ."

"I understand that quite well. I have no intention of trying to press her to be less a Christian. I think you who allowed her to take such vows were wrong, but that is past. I want your help—I want any help I can get—to relieve the child of her hatreds."

Pelaguis was impressed. He did talk with Livia, and he was the first one to get any response from her on what course she really wanted to follow. It was a strange course.

"Livia says," Pelagius told me, "that if you become a Christian family, she will forgive and love you. I asked just what she meant, and she said she must remain a consecrated virgin, Marcia and you must live apart in chastity, and young Gregory must begin to study for the priesthood."

"She knows that is impossible."

"If you ought, you can. It is written that a little child shall lead them."

It is hard for a father to know how much of his child's demand is true inner illumination and how much is the compulsion of the wound; but I easily knew that neither Marcia nor I aspired to live apart in chastity, and I was certainly not going to propose for the boy Gregory, at the age of nine, a dedication to priesthood. Boys have their changing ambitions, and Gregory, in his wants of the moment, was like Mercury, because he always had "something to do for somebody," and went "faster than a bird to do it."

For some weeks, even after the first siege was lifted and Rome began to revive, our family life was saddened by this unfortunate schism between Livia and me. I suffered, but in Marcia and Gregory I had much comfort, and I had, of course, an adult's confidence that time and familiarity would tend to ease the situation. Livia suffered in a more lonely way. She made young Gregory a second victim of her anathema. She would not speak to either of us; and once when I was holding Gregory on my lap, reading to him, I saw in her glance that Livia was jealous of him. She became muted, strained and more evasive, and even Marcia began to lose the lonely and harried child's confidence.

Now that the gates of Rome were opened, Pelagius again made his plans to sail for Africa, and Livia told Marcia she wanted to go with him—as had been planned before—to settle for life in Paula's convent in Bethlehem.

She announced to Marcia that she would fast and pray until this request was granted. "Father can kill me if he wishes; otherwise, I shall go."

Marcia, having once seen the child nearly starve herself to death, was alarmed. I asked for Livia to be brought to me at once.

She came. She stood before me, hands clasped tightly behind her back—so like her mother—tossed her red hair once, and looked at me with her intense green eyes.

"Livia darling," I said, "you have dedicated yourself to Christ. It is the custom of some virgins who have done this to live a quiet life, modest, secluded and happy in the midst of their families. I wished you could do that. I wished you could forgive me. But evidently you feel you must go to Bethlehem to be happy. It grieves me that you should think you need to threaten me with self-starvation if I refuse. You need only ask. You need only ask once, and I will grant your request. If you will ask, 'May I go to Bethlehem, Father?' I will make arrangements with Pelagius to take you. If you are not sure you want to go, say, 'May I stay here, Father?' and we will shelter you. It is not a struggle with me, child, but a choice in your own heart."

She was startled. There was a jump of light in her eyes. Her hands unclasped from behind her back, and her arms swung a moment at her sides. She opened her lips and moistened them. Instead of provoking her will to resist, I had offered a major challenge and she faced a moral choice. I was proud of her courage even as I was grieved at her choice.

She broke her will to silence, she humbled her lust for victory. Her voice was very low, but the words were clear. "May I go to Bethlehem, Father?"

"Yes, Livia. I will arrange with Pelagius at once."

I saw tears come into her eyes before the tears in my own made it hard to see. It seemed that I had only blinked when she had already turned and fled from the room.

I made the promised arrangements. There would be some delay, because thousands of people were trying to get out of Rome and Italy now. Looking at Pelagius, I found it easy to see why; that plenteous man had lost so much weight during the siege that now he was a scrawny giant. Pelagius and a friend of his named Coelestius were to sail in about two weeks. They were eager to get to Africa, for Pelagius had written a little book on his doctrines concerning free will and grace, and Coelestius, who was more of a logician, had worked out points, refinements and arguments. They wanted to know what Augustine and Jerome would think of it.

I read the book and told Pelagius, "Your ideas are humane and appeal to me and will appeal to many men as bewildered as I, who want to live as well as they can by choice and effort and reason. But I think Augustine will not like your book. There might be some comforted men, but there would never be a strong Catholic Church, under your doctrine."

But the bland cheerful Briton was confident that he would easily persuade both Augustine and Jerome that we have not inescapably inherited sin from Adam, that children are not born damned, and that ("if I ought, I can!") a man by his own exertion of his will to good can achieve grace, though of course God's help makes it easier.

During these days of preparation Livia watched me with lonely eyes and spoke to me softly little things like "Good morning, Father," or "Thank you, Father."

And then a natural event occurred which revealed the almost incredible loneliness in which the child had lived. For years she had thought she was not like other children and had ranged in lonely power throughout the brilliant regions of her own phantasy. During those irrevocable years of childhood when fortunate children find their richest development in accordance with persons and affections close about them, she had developed at variance with human warmth in the isolation of proud concepts and dazzling illusions. Now she discovered herself bleeding. She was frightened and thought for some sin she was beginning a dreadful death. The third day she broke down and begged her mother to tell her what was wrong. Livia was in her twelfth year now, and Marcia might well have expected these signs of puberty; but Marcia had been through hard and distracting times and had only for a matter of several months had Livia's confidence at all.

However, she now explained to the girl that normal menstruation had begun, that it was quite natural and nothing to worry about. With something of her old good and realistic humor Marcia added, "It is inconvenient, and I wish a better arrangement had been made for women."

But then she saw that all the color had drained from Livia's face, so that the child's hair seemed all the more to blaze and her green eyes were enormous. It was perfectly obvious that she was suffering a profound inward shock. She asked, "Even virgins?"

"Yes, darling."

Then Livia cried out aghast, "Oh, no. *No!*" And she threw her face and arms and young breasts down against Marcia's lap and sobbed in shocking torment.

For she who was special, she who was the consecrated Virgin of

Christ, she who for years had warded off the wounds of reality by splendid and solitary illusions of uniqueness was thus casually caught in the common snatch of nature and saw herself, in the very maturing of the body, like any other girl. She had gathered from slaves' and women's talk some vague knowledge of this commonplace of a woman's life, but she had assumed that a consecrated virgin, a sacred bride of Christ, would never suffer so base a taint.

When Marcia told me, I was pierced with a poignant sense of the child's terrible loneliness and estrangement from the common beat of life, and I wished I could do something to comfort her. But Marcia warned me. "No, Gregory. She is humiliated. If she thought a man knew what was happening to her just now, she would be crushed. I'm sorry she's going away."

Three days later Livia came into the room where I had Gregory on my lap and was reading to him from Homer's *Iliad*. She stood looking at us. I had a strong sense of some need, of some purpose. I made it casual. I tickled Gregory, dumped him off my lap, and said, "Run along, son. It's Livia's turn now."

Livia watched Gregory out of the room. Then she came to me. She stood beside me and said, "I am too big to sit on your lap. That was Greek you were reading to Gregory. I haven't learned Greek."

I pointed to the case. "Get me that third scroll in the scarlet tube. I'll read that one to you."

She brought it, and I took it out of its tube. It was a copy I had had made of Ambrose's oration on the death of the Emperor Theodosius. I began to read. I could feel Livia lean more weight against my arm. She was in acute physical tension. Then all at once she flung her arms about me, pressed her face against the side of my throat, and cried passionately, "I want to live! I want to live!"

I held her close and tight. I somehow understood what she was really saying. I told her, "You don't have to go to Bethlehem, child. I will take care of you here at home."

The spasmodic tension left her taut and limber body. I could feel the fullness, almost the warmth of relaxation spread through her. I lifted her onto my lap, and she sat there a long time, hugging me and holding on to me in a profound silence.

Pelagius sailed without her.

Where Livia now showed her courage was in a spiritual work so much more difficult than any I ever undertook that it is only because I loved her, and by use of sympathetic imagination, that I can appreciate how hard the task was and how valiantly she struggled with it. She who had seen herself as the charmed goddess of her solitary phantasies now tried to live in the midst of the family as a humble virgin and on plain terms of common human interchange and affection. She had to struggle with the anxiety of doubts and with assaults of despair. The illusion that she was a virgin of superior divine choice was shattered, and she doubted both her former dreams and each of her present moves toward sincerity. Perhaps she had offended Christ in taking vows in rebellion and pride; but, being bound by those vows, how could she become a true Christian virgin? She fought against her jealousy of young Gregory. His ease in human affections alarmed her. She had lost those years in which that ease is nurtured and developed, and she was awkward. She suffered setbacks; she had despondent and moody days, and she had days of a kind of radiance when her fundamental beauty of character emerged and shone.

Of course, as might have been expected, she had one of those social misfortunes that increase the fright and redouble the difficulty of one— especially of a child—in such a spiritual struggle. A group of devout women called on Marcia and Livia. Among them was Sospita, an old Christian virgin who had been a lifelong disciple of Ambrose's sister Marcellina. Marcellina had asked for and received from Ambrose many letters on various problems of the Christian virgin. And now this old Sospita, there in company, recited for Livia's benefit the doctrine of Bishop Ambrose regarding virgins who ceased to be chaste and virgins who recanted their vows in order to marry. She made the assumption that because Livia had not gone to Bethlehem there was danger that the child had secret intentions of getting out of her vows or simply of breaking them. Her premise, after Ambrose, was that Livia had betrothed herself to Christ and that if she now wished to marry, then she wished to commit adultery and to be the handmaid of death. Livia had spirit enough to retort that she had no intention of doing any such thing, and the old virgin struck back at the child.

"Ah, but you may. You didn't go to Bethlehem. You have relaxed in the affections of your family, which are worldly affections. You converse with your father. You play with your brother. Who knows what carnal thoughts may yet enter your heart?"

At this point Marcia put a stop to the old virgin's spiritual cruelty, but a lot of damage had been done. Livia had now to struggle also with a sense of sins she might yet commit and with a sense of guilt at each free release of normal affections. She had, as children in puberty do have, occasional vaguely incestuous dreams, and now these horrified her. But she clung with fierce courage to her slowly increasing power of simple human communion with her mother, her brother and me. I taught her Greek and, whereas I read the poets with Gregory, I read the Greek Testament with Livia.

Sometimes a child in the course of such a struggle will reveal her whole problem in one random statement. And so it was with Livia. She said to me once, "Christ wants my real heart, not my imaginary one. I'm trying so hard to find it."

She would have angers and tempers and rebellions in which she would accuse us of trying to destroy her innocence, and then she would humble herself, apologize, and try to regain the lost ground. The time actually came when she began, just a little, to laugh. She had never laughed, but had always been wild and tense. Now her wonderful spiritual efforts were opening her soul to that sort of love which can laugh with warm affection.

And so it was when Alaric, the last time, closed us into Rome and offered us famine, disease and ruin. June was a month of hunger, July a month of despair, and August was the month of death. I will not tell horrible stories; it is enough to say that in such circumstances a human mind here and another there goes stark mad and examples may be found of any atrocity that may be imagined; but in general people starve to death much as they die of the plague, with an incredible resigned patience. The ganging together and the criminal audacity of adolescent children flourished to new heights. They loved to build night fires in the streets or against ledges and battle one another with firebrands or prowl out from their fires to ravage for food. All the gardens of Rome were soon stripped of edible berries and fruits, and a few folk died from eating poisonous flowers or bulbs. The horses and small animals began to vanish, and the desperate cried out to the city officials, "Put a price on human flesh!"

The heat was oppressive, and the stench of unburied dead was sickening. Rats began to attack the living in their own beds.

A lot of people had had the foresight to get out of Rome. The rich ones had closed their palaces and gone off to country estates, even to Sicily and Africa. The poor ones, greater in number, had either thrown themselves on the mercy of smaller towns or had become foraging brigands in their own behalf. This left many a cellar and small house and not a few palaces and gardens empty. The embruted children of Rome seized on such places and set up their little kingdoms and tyrannies. The Sallust people, for example, had fled Rome, and a notable band of ravaging children had taken over the Sallust gardens and lived there a savage and predatory life; they stole, they tortured, they killed, and by their nighttime tribal fires they danced and sang in a tumult of wild and joyous games, and gave strange funerals to some boy or girl among them who had starved to death or died of plague.

All over the city the sexual precocity of children was noted and deplored. But actually in these years of political fissure and social distress—the dying of the Empire—adults, too, turned to the intimacy and self-assertion of sexual excess—whether libertinage, perversion or ascetic negation—perhaps as a distracted defiance of the threatening chaos of public events. In a city gripped by hunger and riddled with plague and haunted by the thought that now was the conclusion of the world, there were many whose hearts urged, "A pledge to Venus, and ignore the end!" Man, a procreative being, may be like those trees which flaunt a last wild blow of blossom in the face of death.

But the kingdoms and tyrannies of children set up at war against one another in the fourteen regions of Rome, I can see now, as I could not see then, were a grim pattern of the dark age to come, with the central authority of Rome broken, and any man of might being king as far as he could enforce his might. Rule now, in what was once the Roman world, is by the force and destructiveness of men of might, and no former province—scarcely any half province—is left a political entity. The children of Rome made for themselves a like violent chaos in the shambles of the great city. And they were helped by runaway slaves, for the anger of revolt and the ache for freedom stirred among slaves, who would murder their masters when they could.

I felt myself a disparate man in this tense and tragic society. I had a sense of status and security only in my own immediate family. No officials of either the Pagan or the Christian party would trust me with any responsible duty. There was a continuous rumor, reaching me and receding and reaching me again, that I, much as rumor had said of Serena, was a confidant of Alaric, an enemy of Honorius, a betrayer of Rome. Even the Probus men, related to me through Marcia, changed the tone and words of their talk when I came near. To be made a disparate man by the mistrust of your fellows, enforced to watch and not allowed to participate, is a real punishment. I felt it.

Livia, too, felt the oppression of what was going on in the city. All these dreadful things set her back into an appalled and guilty silence. It was, she thought, for sins like hers that Rome was being punished. If she were capable of a sufficiently high and pure sacrifice, Rome might be saved. The child prayed and prayed. Flies and other carrion insects were feeding and proliferating on the death of the city, and I would find Livia on her knees in some nook of our palace garden with a swarm of flies and bugs about her as she prayed her long and silent prayers, and because it hurt her deeply to be called away from such prayers I would stand over her myself where she knelt in her white garment, and with a scarlet cloth I carried for the purpose I would fan and flutter the insects away from her bare arms and face.

Then came the fatal evening in August when Marcia, Livia, Gregory and I started from our palace to pay a call of honor on one of the Probus men who was celebrating his birthday. It was to be only a small family affair, and each of us was to bring what he could—a few olives, if we could find them, a bit of bread, a taste of wine.

We went down through the Forum and out toward the Pincian Gate in the direction of the great Anician Palace of the Probus family.

In the Forum as we passed near the place where years ago the Senate had set up a bronze statue honoring me for having fed the city when Gildo tried to starve it—that statue of Julian the Provider—we met with a disturbance. A crazed woman with a starved child was tossing her arms and crying out to that hollow bronze statue of me, "Feed my child! Feed my child!"

People gathered. Our way was blocked. And then the murmur began: "Count Julian is a traitor! Count Julian is Alaric's friend! Count Julian betrays Rome!"

Before we could get out of sight the statue was overturned and its head and arms beaten with stones and broken off. It frightened me to see myself destroyed in effigy by mob passion.

Livia shrank into a sick silence and did not speak all the rest of the way.

When I told of this event the Probus men advised me to remain all night at their palace. "You are one of the most hated men in Rome, Gregory. Especially since you tried to defend Serena from execution. Don't go out at night if you value your life."

Livia watched me with silent anguish.

We stayed in one part of the gardens very late, trying to get cool, for the night had a sullen heat. Old Faltonia Proba made a shocking statement. "This barbarous obscenity ought to be put to an end. The Christian thing to do would be to open the gates and deliver Rome from this agony." The noble old woman sat near a cypress tree which pointed up toward stars, and her aged face shone white in the fragile moonlight.

Her sons and even some of her grandchildren said that they were astonished that one of the last great Roman matrons could conceive such a notion.

Old Faltonia Proba shook her head in the moonlight. "I ask myself not what Rome but what Christ would have us do. Are we not Christians? Have we no mercy for a city in the throes of death and desolation? I tell you, old as I am, if I had but a little more faith I would summon my slaves and lead them in force to open a gate of Rome and end this most hideous prolongation of futile suffering."

I saw Livia, in one of her moments of mute ecstasy, gazing at the old woman.

We argued the point for nearly an hour while the moon went down and the dim stars brightened. We argued with despair, with passion, but with no practical solution to offer. Alaric meant to destroy us; we didn't know how to prevent him.

Then suddenly Marcia was squeezing my arm and whispering, "Livia. Livia is gone, Gregory."

"Did she go in to bed?"

"No. She's disappeared."

Our eyes met, and, as happens between husband and wife concerning a child of theirs, we both understood with profound mutual anxiety that our child was in danger.

We began to hunt for her. It was not a long hunt before we learned from a crippled slave what had happened.

"She is Christ's saint who will free Rome. She is going to sacrifice herself to free Rome."

We got it out of him by degrees. He kept insisting that he would have gone with them, except that he was crippled and could not. If only Livia had touched him and healed him—but before he could get that near to her they had gone. Gone with them? Whom? Where? Why, of course, Livia, the sacred virgin, the child saint, loved by the slaves of that palace, expected by them to do miracles, had called them together, had spoken to them by torchlight, had roused them to follow her, and with their help as merciful Christians to beat down the guards she would offer herself in virgin sacrifice to Christ by opening the gate and being the first to be slain by the Barbarians. She would atone for all our crimes, and Rome would be opened and fed and freed of this agony. At least a hundred of Faltonia Proba's slaves had gone off with Livia to open a gate of Rome.

Marcia and Gregory and I, followed by others, ran out of the Anician gardens and toward the Pincian Gate, which was nearest. But there we found the gate closed and the troop of guards watchful.

We looked at one another in bewildered silence. In that moment of silence we heard the blare of Gothic trumpets rend the night within the walls of Rome. The triumphant and terrible sound came from the direction of the Salarian Gate. That trumpet of the Goths—one and three and then a dozen of their great bull-horn trumpets, blown by huge men of massive chest, even as I had heard them blown in the far reaches of Moesia when Alaric was made king—that wild trumpeting of the destroyers would blare symbolically to the ends of the earth, pronouncing the fall of Empire and the coming on of dark storms of human chaos over the face of Europe.

When the fatal noise reached Jerome in Bethlehem it first drew the groan of ruin from his old Roman breast and, out of Virgil, he compared Rome's night of flame and carnage to the fall of Troy ("Who can set forth the carnage of that night? . . ."). Then, having reuttered the poet's cry of catastrophe, Jerome in various letters flashed his rhetoric, describing the hordes which had swept from the Rhine to the Pyrenees and from the Alps to Rome, and he poured out a sanguine lament for the widows, the virgins, the priests slain, the churches desecrated, the towns burned, and told how horses were stabled at the altars of Christ.

When the sound smote the inner ear of Augustine he began his thirteen-year labor on his massive book, *The City of God*, which is the funeral oration and vast entombment of the Pagan world, arched over by Augustine's passionate and glorious projection of a Romanized and Catholic City of God.

But a herdsman on a hill and a fisherman by the sea heard the sound, too, and their arms hung still, the shock made them silent, the moral ground of action was shattered where they stood.

Philosophers have speculated where the soul is seated, where the affections are rooted, and I contribute this personal item to their researches: I, who had recently felt a deep sword wound in my breast, felt the blow of the Gothic trumpets like a sword thrust in the pit of the stomach. In my mother's womb the nourishment of life came to me through my umbilicus there, and now this death stroke against my Roman world seemed to shock off nourishment at that primitive vital spot. Perhaps a man's brain or heart or soul ought first to be affected by the rending of the moral fabric of the world he lives in, but I felt the blow in the navel first. Then fear and sickness rushed through my body to my fingers and toes and brain.

That doom blare of Empire had to split the night less than a mile to reach us, but our only way around to the Salarian Gate was well over a mile. The Probus men went back to protect their own family from ravage sure to come. Marcia and Gregory and I set off in our anguish to find and save Livia if we could.

We took a back way down into a glen, passing a dreadful place where

many of the city's dead had been dumped, and then hurried along toward
the gardens of Sallust and the Salarian Gate.

Fire in the sky greeted us.

The Salarian Gate had been opened by Livia, leading old Faltonia
Proba's slaves. The Goths were pouring into the city. They had already
begun to plunder and in their plundering had set ablaze the palace of
Sallust.

I pulled Marcia and Gregory through a gate into a corner of the gardens of Sallust. "If Livia wasn't killed at once, the first Goths may well
have brought her here with them while they sack and burn the palace.
It takes a few hours for real viciousness to get going."

We climbed a winding path among cypress trees toward the fire.
When we came within reach of the billows of firelight we saw the main
palace burning. Detached buildings of marble and fine stone reflected
the ruddy glow.

We had hurried ourselves out of breath, but we still went on along
the edge of a terrace where there was a twenty-foot drop to a lower
terrace. From this lower terrace steps led up, some forty paces away, to
our level, and at the top of the steps was a little marble rotunda with
a gilded dome held over it by pillars. There, lit by waves of firelight, we
saw Livia guarded by three Gothic soldiers. While others burned and
sacked the palace, they were holding on to a hostage who might bring
rich ransom.

Marcia cried out, "Livia! Livia!"

The Goths started to their feet.

But then, before we could do anything, a swarm of young Roman boys
and girls, thirty of them at least, wielding firebrands and clubs and
knives, burst yelling from behind an aisle of cypress trees and out of a
thicket of glossy dark bushes. They beat the three Goths insensible with
clubs, leaving several of their own dead, and carried Livia down the
steps. They rushed past, below us, yelling:

"Strangle the Christian traitor!"

"Death to all Pagan Julians!"

"Rape the virgin!"

It was the monstrous public voice of the anguished city and the decadent Empire uttering its cries of pain and anger out of the throats of
children in this climax of vicious stupidity. It was several of the stronger
boys who dragged Livia off, and it was the weaker followers who screamed
their nihilistic screams to desecrate and destroy the child. Other frantic
children were tearing at Livia's clothes with their fingers and slashing
the air toward her with knives.

I snatched up Gregory and started running toward the steps. I stopped as I realized Marcia had run the other way. Then I saw her make an amazing leap, from the stone wall, twenty feet down to the terrace below. I don't know how she did it without breaking her legs or killing herself. But she stumbled to her feet and ran after the wild gang of children. In a few strides I reached the steps and rushed down them, still carrying Gregory.

I heard yells in the downward distance.

I set Gregory on his feet and told him to race after me. Once where there was an elaboration of paths and pools I took a wrong turn, but a scream in the dark redirected me. It was the most terrible scream I ever heard Marcia make. Down here among the cypress trees it was dark, with glowing waves of light from the big fire shuddering fifty feet overhead in the air. I caught Gregory's hand and raced toward the scream. Five or six adolescents almost naked in filthy rags swept past me. One hit me with a club as he ran, and a glitter-eyed girl with wild hair and a splotch of blood across her naked breasts slashed at me with a knife: Her fist and the knife were bloody. I heard others yelling their way off into farther parts of the gardens.

I don't suppose I was two or three minutes late, if that much. But I was not so swift as the naked stroke of violence out of the hearts of these ruined children of Rome.

I found Marcia on the steps of a lovely marble temple before a pool. It was a little temple of serene beauty in the Greek style, originally dedicated to Venus, mother of Aeneas, but Romanized both by the pool before it and by a depiction of Romulus, Remus and the Wolf in the frieze. Within the last century it had been Christianized by the emplacement of a Cross and rededicated as a shrine to Mary, mother of Christ. A fountain played with idle splash into the pool. The cypress trees pointed upward to the tremors of firelight in the upper air which hid the stars. Streaks of red reflection raced across the dark pool.

I who had once boasted that God awaited me on the steps of the morning met God there on the steps of night.

On the steps Marcia sat mute, holding Livia in her arms. Livia's body in its few tatters of bloodsoaked cloth was limp and gleaming in the pale quiet radiance of death. Her neck was broken, and her body had let out all her life through many wounds.

Gregory cried, "Mother! Mother!"

But Marcia did not answer. She gazed at Gregory and at me and sat still and held our slain child in the helpless and humble holding of her arms.

I noticed how wide apart and how still Marcia's eyes really were, with nothing now in them of human pride or worldly desire to obscure her soul; and I saw in them the strangest peace I had ever seen, the peace of final sorrow, of silence and of profound compassion. Indeed, what I saw in the silent beauty of her whole face and serene figure exceeded my knowledge of human grief and human suffering and human peace. There was some ultimate revelation of tragedy there, like an immortal radiance.

As I looked at Marcia cradling our slain child in transcendent and serene tragic humility the core of my mind confessed to the core of my being that my heart was broken and my life had failed. Enduring sorrow set its deep compassionate seal on the flowing sound and silence, color and blackness, form and obscurity of all I heard and saw and felt, compelling this to be the culminating impression of my inner life, bringing to focus all former things, and to be the point of reference for future things, making of all my loves and all their deaths the single, unified and ultimate experience of my life, sealed with sorrow and illuminated by my own profound spiritual failure. I had come to my ripeness in the throes of the world; I was no longer capable of emotional or mystic assertions of faith or hope or radiant communion with God; in Livia's tragic fate and Marcia's suffering and my failure was the piercing presence of God on the steps of night, and the compassionate apprehension of our tragic being flared throughout the human anguish of my heart. Because I loved my wife and loved my child, I accepted, acknowledged, embraced with plain human faith the three great tones that resound the music of God in the breast of man: tragedy, suffering, failure.

My life is a thousand songs, the wanton lyrics of time and chance, the passionate, the comic, the lovely, the gay, but it is God's three great tones of tragedy, suffering, failure that make of all my singing my one deep song.

Until a man has really heard such music of God in his breast, how shall he understand that his life is a song of profound rejoicing?

My life has no other measure; for me these three things, tragedy, suffering, failure, are the substance of love and compose the indwelling and smile of God.

Our whole age, our whole Roman world, had gone dead in its heart because it feared tragedy, took flight from suffering, and abhorred failure. In fear of tragedy we worshiped power. In fear of suffering we worshiped security. In fear of failure we worshiped success. Yea, in fear of the intensity of life that is in tragedy we worshiped the coldness of death that is in power. In dread of the fertile growth that there is in suffering we worshiped the sterile obediences of security. In terror of the healing love that there is in failure we worshiped the corrupt denial of one another that there is in success. During the rising splendor of our thousand prosperous years we had grown cruel, practical and sterile. We did win the whole world. We did lose our own souls.

But outflowing love, and the joy of vital integrity, and the creative indwelling of God return to the soul when the acceptances of tragedy and suffering and failure liberate a man from the sterile grasp of all his fears.

The boy Gregory had turned his face, embraced me, and was weeping against my belly. I put my hand on his head and pressed it there.

Marcia was silent, and Livia was dead.

PART
6

THE RECONCILED

CHAPTER ONE

MARCIA:
THE PEACE OF CHRIST

AUGUSTINE, WHEN I WAS A BOY, POINTED OUT TO ME THAT the two great poets, Aeschylus and Sophocles, did not end their masterpieces in the shattering climax of violence, but, the one in the final play of the *Orestiad* and the other in the final play about Oedipus, surpassed violence with reconciliation, the great reconciliation of man with God. "For in most of our lives," Augustine said, "the tragic climax of violence does not kill us, but only lifts us to our supreme passionate failure. The tragedy should purge our passions, and the rest of our life should be the spiritual part." And, since Augustine was then not yet a Christian, he cried out, "Would God I could reconcile myself with God!" It was Ambrose who later pointed out to me the lyric reconciliation of David and the patient reconciliation of Job. Ambrose told me, "The whole healing of love is our reconciliation with God; all passions less than that are painful and darkly wound the soul: Christ is our love, our healing and our reconciliation with God."

Therefore now, since the violent half of my life was over—and I have lived on as many years after the fall of Rome as I lived before it—what I have left to tell is not the dramatic but the patient part, the serene motions of reconciliation. I neither experienced nor could I wish to invent new incidents of passion, turmoil and drama equal in splendor and tragedy to the part of the story I have already told; and so I write quietly from now to the end.

But I have good things yet in store. I am like some seasoned mariner who, after telling you of the great storm he weathered, refills your cup of wine and talks on awhile in calm reflection about the rest of the voyage and the calming of his heart in the cradle of time and on the eternal sea. For I tell my story not to those few whose lives end in the ecstasy of disaster, but to the many and many like myself who live on their long years toward reconciliation with God.

Stay with me, then, a little while more, for I want to recount the close
of various lives I have mentioned in my story, I want to tell how an old
man's long life approached wisdom and peace, and, most lovely of all,
I shall write in remembrance of Marcia's seeking the peace of Christ.

First, as a man reflects on the afterglow of fire, I look back on the
holocaust of Rome.

I was convinced of the absolute devastation of Rome by Alaric and
his Barbarians. It was not the violent occupation that convinced me,
for, though in Thessaly I had seen these Goths lay waste some village,
gutting every building with fire and killing or enslaving every inhabitant,
Rome was too big for that.

Now they poured into the city of Rome, thousand after thousand.
They burned, they pillaged, they roistered. They heaped up wealth in
the streets and carted it off in wagons. They freed slaves and enslaved
Romans. Although they were Arians, they honored the Catholic churches
and gave asylum and immunity to many Christians of Rome. But there
were countless instances by day and by night of rape and murder, not all
the victims being Pagans. They swarmed the Forum in their wolfskins
and rode their horses in and out of palaces and temples and held up-
roarious banquets in the great baths of Diocletian. Having more desire
for gold and jewels than for captives, they sold and resold Romans by
the thousand. Some of the worst atrocities were done by former slaves
now free to revenge themselves on their erstwhile masters: A band of
rebellious slaves would rise and slay a whole Roman family.

But the city was too big. Where a hundred houses were burned, a
thousand remained untouched. For every thousand citizens slaughtered,
a hundred thousand remained alive and Romans still. It was surely the
most magnificent disaster yet seen in any city of the world, but still
Alaric on his horse could not push over the Colosseum, and one or two
hundred thousand Goths—if ever that many came through the gates—
could not—and did not want to—slaughter one or two million Romans.

Then why was this feeling so certain, so deep, so shocking, that Alaric
and his Barbarians utterly devastated Rome? It was not in the noise
and chaotic splendor of the sack of the city that the real devastation
occurred, but in the quiet, terrible and conclusive destruction of the
thousand-year-old faith that Rome was inviolate, that the greatest civil
society yet devised by man was so magnificent and powerful that it must
be eternal. After all, Alaric made plain that it is not organization and
wealth and power that hold a society together, but faith; and with this
faith destroyed, our society was shattered. During the centuries of our
splendor this faith had grown rotten and hollow, and Alaric's stroke,

which the physical city of Rome was big enough to swallow up, yet burst the faith to tatters.

So it was not by armies of violence that Rome fell: In each heart that ceased to believe, Rome fell.

Even some who hated Rome's grandeur were grieved by her ruin. And we who had loved Rome and the dream of Rome in the ages of man, but had lost our faith and let Rome fall, had great and aching spaces of hollow left in our hearts, and we profoundly wept.

City of my fathers, but never of my sons, it is done! Farewell.

Marcia, I think, in the shock of her tragedy and its revelation of depths of compassion most of us do not know, had not expected to move again, had not expected to have Livia's body removed from her arms, had by no means thought she would be forced to rise up and go on living for years to come. For what soul wants to return to the world's ways after God's immortal wound has pierced it?

I could not save her from these things; they were brutally forced on us by a crowd of Gothic warriors. Marcia did not struggle when they took Livia away from her arms. She made one pathetic sound, not an outcry and not a sob, but a little sound, as if her mind had received the one more blow it could not bear.

Within the hour, herded together with many others, conducted by Goths, I walked out of Rome through the Salarian Gate, a prisoner and a slave of the Goths, with my arm about Marcia's shoulder and with Gregory clasping my other hand. We three fell to the lot of Ataulphus, who still kept careful guard of his highborn prisoner, the royal princess Galla Placidia. He offered me to her as a personal slave, but she said a Roman could be her subject but not her slave. So Ataulphus kept me with Marcia and Gregory in his personal retinue. His children by his wife who had died were with him, and I was made their tutor. "You taught me, Gregory. Now teach my children. Add a new lesson you have learned, that Rome can fall."

For nearly a week of days and nights the armies of Alaric despoiled and ravaged the city of the world, destroying in the blood and fire of this mighty stroke the faith of our world in the rule and order of Empire. It was a stupendous lesson.

Rome fell: What could stand?

A strange thing was said in Ravenna. When they told Emperor Honorius that Rome was in her death agony he said, "No. Roma is well. I've just been feeding her." In his poor stupidity, of course, he was referring to that grand old golden hen I had brought to him as a pullet from Constantinople. But there was a kind of awful wisdom in his error: Cities fall, civilizations break up, but men and chickens go on living.

The blow ruined Alaric's moral confidence; perhaps no one had more reverenced the myth of Rome's immortal might than this man wrought upon by his gods to destroy that myth. His fatal achievement brought the onset of death to his heart.

The great army pulled its thousand and thousand wagonloads of plunder out of the city and moved in slow devouring swarm southward. Old Roman villas gave rest for a while to heavy-limbed Goths who would order Roman boys to serve them feasts on the silver and gold of Rome, while noble Roman girls, now their slaves and concubines, filled gold jewel-studded goblets—perhaps from their own palaces—with the best Falernian wine and served these Gothic masters. Some of the Roman girls liked being mastered by these blond northern giants. Many among us, now slaves, lamented the free dead left behind.

The army ate and despoiled its way all down the coast to the straits of Sicily. It was as if Alaric could not rest, could not govern, and could not build—and yet, having taken the prize of the world, what was there left to take? Heraclian controlled Africa and the grain of Italy. Alaric prepared a fleet to cross to Sicily and thence to Africa. Was there some insatiable love of the sun in the breasts of these ice-born Barbarians?

A tempest ruined the fleet, and Alaric drew back.

Just as Marcia bore marks of difference now, and never spoke and was certainly crazed, so a new thing was evident in Alaric's character. He could no longer communicate with men as of old, neither as a companion nor as a king. He was set apart in some dreadful way, almost like a sacrifice. It was as if the gods had used him for a terrible purpose and he had fulfilled it, and now he asked the gods, "What shall I do?" And while he listened they did not answer, neither could he any longer hear men speak or speak with men, being shut off by the ruin of a world from common things. He often sat, in deep mood, in a gold-and-ivory throne chair taken from the Palace of the Caesars. Alaric died soon, as the foredoomed expire, of a cold and a fever and a little sickness that would not have killed a boy, but laid down that noble giant of the North in his death. He died, I think, of the doom of Rome, which he had fulfilled, and it clove his heart.

Ataulphus was king, and Galla Placidia, a royal prisoner at his side, had deeply reached his heart.

In honor to Alaric, Ataulphus chose me as foremost slave to lead a host of Roman slaves in the burial. Galla Placidia did a strange thing. She, a Catholic among the Arian Goths, told Ataulphus she did not like the poor little Italian priests and bishops picked up on the way. She wanted a man of parts to be her priest, and she persuaded Ataulphus to sever me from slavery so that I might be made her priest. Ataulphus yielded; I was excused from leading the slaves who buried Alaric, and on that same day I was ordained as Galla's priest by a sad and primitive little Catholic bishop snatched out of Eboli.

All the slaves who buried Alaric were slain, and they were many, for this was done: The course of the River Busentinus was changed, and in its damp bed Alaric's sepulcher was dug and lined with trophies and wealth despoiled from Rome. The great king's corse was laid there and covered, the waters of the river were turned back over his grave, and the slaves who did the labor were massacred so that none but the gods might know where Alaric lay cozened by death amid spoils of the city of the world. Son of the North, of the race of fiord and forest and ice, ceaselessly wandering toward the sun and warm South, island-born child where Danube's many mouths pour into Euxine Sea, raised in the pastures of Moesia, the forests and crags of Dacia and Thrace, Alaric the Bold, king, conqueror of Athens and of Rome, now lost to sight forever under the little spill of Busentinus in Italy's warmest South and toward Aetna's fire. Hail, Alaric, and farewell; I always thought of you as a great golden man, tawny golden like a lion, and you were my heart's bold brother.

Galla Placidia said, "I like you better, Gregory, as a live priest than as a dead slave. But I think I saved your life as much out of pity for Marcia as out of any forgiveness of you. Marcia certainly is crazy with her silent griefs, but I see her cling to you like her straw in the flood, and if she lost you she would surely drown in black insanity."

Ambrose often said he had had to learn how to be a bishop by being one, and so I, in my lesser way, learned how to be a priest.

In the slow years during which Ataulphus, king of the Goths and master of Italy, made a vague sort of peace with Honorius secluded in Ravenna, but made it without ever coming to terms for the release of Galla Placidia, I learned the rites and proprieties of priesthood. My true assistant was young Gregory, who had by temperament a sweet and ritualistic love of Christ. My strangest penitent was Marcia, still captive in her grave of silence, except for strange sweet musical sounds she made. All her motions were lovely, but she disregarded her dress and often looked like a peasant woman in old clothes who would age early but never lose her grace. Perhaps language is overestimated as a means of communication—certainly so between man and woman; I learned to know Marcia better and to love her more deeply in her silence. She never in her strangeness did anything angry or perverse, but did forlorn small things that touched my heart, such as singing some gay little tune in most pure tones while tears flowed inconsolable from her wide still dark eyes; or, after she had spent an hour of devout silence on her knees in church her lonely prayer might culminate in soft sweet laughter. I think her soul was always wide awake and profoundly informed, but the surface of her mind, for usages of the world, was stunned by grief.

I had ceased entertaining fancies about life—was it this, was it that, and what did it mean?—for I had a strange, delicate, lost and lovely spirit under my care, and that concerned me more than hatching notions, this and that, about my own soul. Indeed, my soul's dialogue of discomfort was ended; I had grown ripe in the sun and shadow of living; I had reached that point of age and experience where I knew we are mortal by ourselves and find our immortality in one another, where I knew a man has no past and has no future, for I had discovered that being alive is always and only a wonderful and strange participation in eternity. Whether I was slave or priest or bishop or exile no longer mattered, for, since my soul's dialogue of discomfort had ended, I lived in the deep sway of confidence, and the rest of my life could only be the fulfillment of the single spiritual event which was the ultimate goodness of living out my life in an irrevocable love of God.

Marcia bore me a son. In one of those conversations with her in which I did all the talking and she replied by varying the mood of her silence— by close attention I could catch subtle variations, from grave sadness to spontaneous gaiety—and in which we could reach clear understanding in any matter of spiritual importance, we agreed joyfully to name our child Ambrose, and by that name, remembering the great good man of Milan as I did it, I christened the child.

Marcia was like a mother animal with the child—that is, one of those animals which give their own body warmth for a long time to their young. She always carried him and held him and kept him close to her body, and she taught him sounds more like music than like words. The crease of bewildered pain between her eyebrows was eased, and she took to very simple clothing and kept it clean. When occasion demanded, Marcia would read my notes and write me answers; but as for speaking, she knew what she knew and held her peace. Sometimes by misadventure I hurt her feelings, and she and the child would hide for several days in a dark room. I would go in and talk to her in the dark. My voice would reach her in the end, and she would come out.

She came gradually out of the long speechlessness of her mental shock, too. One night she reached out and touched me and said, "Gregory, I

have nothing to say to anybody except you and my children and Christ."
These were the first words she had spoken since Livia's death. Then
she wept in my arms, and after that she spoke to me and to Gregory and
to the child Ambrose, and she spoke to Christ in church and at home.
She was not inclined to say much. She might express a daylong thought
in a dozen words, then hold her peace. She said our Lord's prayer aloud
each morning when she awoke. She never spoke of the past; I never
heard her utter Livia's name. If she saw me restless or disturbed, she
would always say the same thing, "Be patient, Gregory. Christ will find
us."

Ataulphus had pulled the whole nation of his Goths northward out of
Italy and then westward into Gaul. There in Gaul he married Galla
Placidia. I was one of the priests officiating at the wedding, and it was a
splendid affair, combining Catholic, Arian and Barbarian rites. He made
Galla a wedding gift of load and load of the spoils of Rome and Italy,
borne forward and laid at her feet by fifty chosen youths in robes of silk.
Though each of these striplings carried a basin of gold in one hand and
a basin of jewels in the other, the hundredfold gift was but a trifle out
of the enormous Gothic spoils. Honorius and the foolish proud Romans
in Ravenna had cried out "No!" against this wedding; Ataulphus could
never be brother to the Emperor; Galla Placidia must be restored as the
first principle of peace.

But Galla Placidia loved Ataulphus and took the risk of never being
Empress in order to marry him. "I learn, Gregory. I learn," she confessed to me.

And Ataulphus also learned, admitting that I had given him seed of
the lesson years ago in his boyhood. During the marriage feast in Nar-
bonne he said, "In the proud power of my youth I aspired to change the
face of the world, to wipe out the name of Rome and build on its ruins
the Empire of the Goths. But I have learned in these years of destruction that laws are necessary to maintain a state and that the fierce willfulness of the Goths is unfit for the order and justice of a great civil society.
So now it is my ambition to earn the gratitude of future ages by commanding the sword of the Goths not to subvert, but to restore and maintain the prosperity of the Roman Empire. Galla Placidia is now my
Empress to help me."

He led us into Spain to restore that province to the house of Theodosius and had some success from the Pyrenees to Barcelona. Marcia
and Gregory and I did not go to Barcelona with them, but stopped off
in a near-by town which was just large enough to boast that it needed a
bishop. Galla Placidia, who since her marriage no longer cared much

to have me as her private priest, asked me to hold services in the church there, and in the midst of the services she herself set up the cry: "Our bishop! Our bishop!" The mere thought that they might seize as their bishop the priest of Galla Placidia roused the congregation to a riotous clamor of insistence. They took it as certain that a lot of wealth would come to their church along with me. They imprisoned me overnight in a little cubicle near the altar while they sent men galloping off to bring back the Bishop of Barcelona to consecrate me as their bishop.

As soon as I had been forced inside the little room, where priestly garments and some rather plain silver vessels were stored, the wrought-iron gate was closed across the only doorway and bolted on the outside. Then the whole affair ceased to be fierce and became quite remarkable for its humane warmth. I had a good view out through the iron grillwork into the open spaces of the church. Two of the elders brought a bench, a lantern and a skin of wine and placed themselves at the grille to keep me company. They were seasoned and serious men of noble courtesy and of considerable knowledge in church affairs. They imparted to me wisdom of the river, the good fields, the crag mountain and the sky of this their dwelling place, and of the people. I enjoyed sharing their wine and their conversation. The older of the two wore a small gray beard, and the younger, who was at least of sixty years, had a face weathered by Spanish sun and wind.

Finally I told them that if I became their bishop I would by no means abandon my wife and children, but would continue living as a husband, and that therefore the Bishop of Barcelona would probably refuse to consecrate me. With first one, then the other speaking, they considered the matter gravely.

"Even so, we want you as our bishop. We see plainly you are a man of strength, of learning and of good will."

"We follow the apostle in this. To the Corinthians and to Timothy he wrote that it is permitted for a bishop to retain his wife."

"And also to Titus, Apostle Paul said the same."

"Paul said 'If any be blameless, the husband of one wife, having faithful children not accused of riot, or unruly.' I am not blameless, and I have had another wife."

"By the letter of the word blameless there could be no bishops, for none are blameless in this world. And what you have now is one wife. Look whether or not our people accept her."

Marcia had seated herself in soft lamplight on the stone floor facing the altar. She had prayed there for a while. Now she held the child Ambrose asleep in her arms, and Gregory had fallen asleep leaning against her side with his legs slightly bent and relaxed on the floor. He was almost a man, but slept like a child. Marcia was in one of her spells of profound meditation. And both men and women of the congregation came walking into the church in quiet gentleness, approached her, and laid gatherings of flowers on the stone floor round about her. The flowers were golden and scarlet and blue, and their fresh scent reached me where I stood.

The elders assured me:

"When one has spiritual beauty, the people know it."

"You will make us a good bishop and a good bishop's family."

At this point I certainly failed in perfection, for I now desired to be ordained bishop there in Edulius, where the good peasants came in and placed flowers round about my wife and children. This would be a place of sanctuary for Marcia. And it was a wonderful town, too, of fertile ground by a good river, at the foot of that astonishing mountain of serrated crags, lofty, cloven, fissured and wearing a thousand wonders of passing light and weather. Then also, after showing their devotion to Marcia, the people came in small groups to pay their respects to me. The women curtsied, and the men, with clear straight gazing into my eyes, made the slow head-bowing that was of honor but not of subservience.

And with warmth I remembered that I had been born in Spain, at Caesar Augusta, where our Roman bridge of many arches spans the Ebro; it was not far from the splendid pinnacles here of Mons Serratus: Spain was to me a spiritual home.

When the Bishop of Barcelona came about midmorning the church was full, and I was ordained and consecrated their bishop. It was, the bishop told me, perhaps irregular, but he assured me that Synesius of Cyrene, the orator, had just recently been made Bishop of Ptolemais and continued to retain his wife. That was a notable instance, and he knew of other examples both in Spain and in Gaul. So did I.

But these religious matters, which begin by being personal, end by exceeding the man. We are less than God, and God is our only help for it.

Truly I expected during the ceremony of consecration to have a sense or a vision of Saint Ambrose to sustain me, or even, perhaps, the terrible invisible presence of Christ. But it was not so, and a profound sorrow widened out like a well of loneliness in my heart. With my head bowed I wept, and all my being cried out its single silent cry: God forgive me!

Then I heard either the bishop, or One in my heart, utter Paul's words: "Wherefore I put thee in remembrance that thou stir up the gift of God, which is in thee by the putting on of my hands. For God hath not given us the spirit of fear; but of power, and of love, and of a sound mind." And I no longer felt alone.

Ataulphus and Galla Placidia made the church a gift of gold and silver vessels taken from churches in Italy.

I think I began well. I was awed, and I can still remember my first sermon in its entirety. It was this: "God is beyond the comprehension of words. Let us pray." But soon enough I was delivering hour-long sermons like any other fount of righteousness. The people expect a sermon, and the bishop gets so that he likes to deliver one; and I could put together some grandiloquent preachings out of Ambrose, Chrysostom, Pelagius, Augustine, with echoes of Cicero and Plato.

I pronounced a few of these, and then Marcia took my hand gravely and said, "Gregory, you don't know all that about God. You and I are lost. Christ hasn't found us yet. Why don't you be patient and speak simply?"

What I did in my sermons after that for a while was simply to retell the Gospel stories, with not my eloquence but Christ as the hero of each sermon.

The world around us still was rude.

Heraclian, as could have been prophesied, made his bid for supreme power. Once Ataulphus drew the Goths north out of reach, Heraclian set sail with a large force from Africa, landed at Ostia, and started up the road to take over Rome and make himself Emperor. Heraclian had achieved monstrosities of greed. After Alaric sacked Rome many Romans fled to Africa, and there Heraclian caught them off their ships, his fellow Romans, and squeezed ransom out of them. Old Faltonia Proba, taking her granddaughter Demetrias to be a virgin at Bethlehem, paid him a huge sum. Many Roman women who could not pay were sold by Heraclian to Syrian traders who in turn sold them as concubines. His name was odious long before he reached the Tiber with his massive fleet of hundreds of ships. On the way to Rome he was affrighted in a sharp skirmish by a single Roman captain, deserted his own forces, and fled back to Carthage with only one ship. When he landed, those officials who had formerly obeyed him seized and beheaded him.

It seemed that ever since the natural deaths of Theodosius and Ambrose no figure of power and importance could escape a death by violence; it was as if order had died with Theodosius and conscience with Ambrose, leaving the Roman world to a steadily degrading violence.

Ataulphus was no exception. The child born to him and Galla Placidia died within the year and was buried in a silver casket. Then Singeric, brother of the old brute giant Sarus, assassinated Ataulphus and all his children by his former wife. He marched Galla Placidia ahead of his horse, a barefoot slave among his captives, through a dozen miles of hot dust to his camp. He had ruled fourteen days when he in his turn was slain by Wallia, a relative of Alaric and Ataulphus. Wallia promised to restore Spain to Honorius. The Roman general Constantius approached Spain. He was a man with a heavy head which hung down and morose eyes and a sullen melancholy expression; he was able and vigorous, but did not seem to want to live. Constantius ransomed Galla Placidia for six hundred thousand measures of wheat which the hungry Goths needed.

Back in Ravenna, Constantius was raised by Honorius to co-Emperor and married Galla: She was Empress at last! She bore the gloomy Constantius two children before he died. Then Honorius made incestuous advances, and she fled with her children to Constantinople, and when soon Honorius died—a natural death, like his brother Arcadius—she came back to Ravenna. There for a quarter of a century (she died but a year or two ago) she ruled what was left of the Western Empire as Augusta and regent for her children. Travelers who reach Britain tell me that, although she lost all Africa to the Vandals, she has built fine churches in Ravenna. What more could she do? She was able, but she was alone, and the world was lost to Rome when she came to power.

Fifteen years ago her agents found me here in Britain and brought me a letter in her hand in which she asked me to give up my exile and come to Ravenna as her unofficial private adviser. I knew of myself by now that to become the political leader or the spiritual guide of more than those few whom I know intimately and love is but to breed new cruelties in a troubled world; I believed it better for a man to serve and love those few near him than to seek or accept any sort of power or influence over many. I felt that the wisdom of any one man in any one day was not sufficient to be made into a law for mankind on the morrow. I liked what I was doing in Britain and declined Galla Placidia's offer.

Marcia bore us a daughter while I was a bishop in Spain, and I christened this child Marcia, after her mother and with the sweet echo in her name of our lost son Marcus. I had come a long way toward my human achievement of the sufficient peace of a smiling mind, and Marcia was still working toward her greater achievement of the surpassing peace of Christ. She was sure he had not found her yet, but she kept on working in the still places of her heart quietly to achieve a real sense of the presence of Christ.

To say that we were happy would be sentimental nonsense. By our acquaintance with sorrow and some increase in wisdom Marcia and I had earned reverence for that seeking of deep values which is the true desire to lay aside death and see God. We were aware of the wonder, the sorrow and the immortal tragic value of each other's lives. Our association was one of great and quiet depth, in the presence of God and before the face of eternity. It was love of a strength, a richness and a resonance that the young have not dreamed of and that the ascetic do not know. Our mutual and reciprocal sense of each other's humanity was at the core of our united being. We had enough capacity for sorrow for all our years to be as one in the recomforting of grief, in the tenderness of pleasure and in the profound joys of compassion. All the rest of our life together was in essence a golden moment too sound to be harmed by the evanescent humors, accidents and irritations that come and go like bugs and birds and dragons through the daily air in anyone's common living.

The bugs and birds and dragons of course were there. It is one thing, and a good thing, for a man and woman to find their spirits free, in the great realms of sorrow and tragedy, to create with compassion their mutual peace; but there is still the secondary matter of getting through the incommodity of the day. I think any man who loves a woman knows for certain that she is a little crazy, and, perhaps he is thereby relieved of some alarm about his own secretive wildness. The slow dull forms of society and the incessant workings of nature have never fitted any vital soul yet, and something fantastic in the motions of the heart I find is the very root renewing strength to live in the world. A man's path winds along somewhere between madness and God, somewhat crazy, somewhat divine, and human withal. In the matter of the incessant workings of nature, when I simply state that our three children, Gregory, Ambrose and Marcia, for a while in Spain and later in Britain showed themsclves merry, noisy and healthy, so that we enjoyed the vicissitudes of a vigorous family, common sense must know that there were bugs and birds and dragons in our daily air. Marcia could become dead tired, and I could grow exasperated with the roar of our young, and they made us laugh and they made us anxious and they touched our hearts with indefinable tenderness and wonder. Although young Gregory was twenty when I ordained him a priest in our last year in Spain, his natural mirth allowed him to frolic with the two little children.

We agreed that living together in fundamental good faith as man and wife was the most natural, comforting and warmhearted of all the imperfect human relationships either of us had ever experienced; neither of us felt insulted if we chose to quell obstreperous emotions on behalf of the other. Single pleasure has an anxious and lonely face when compared to the warm regard of mutual love. I had learned in myself that single pleasure, or individual willfulness, is only a grasp at revenge for having failed to love, and it never heals the wound; and Marcia was yearning for Christ to heal her wound. Oh, indeed, we dealt each other, as a man and woman will, little blows on the heart and surprises to the mind; but if either of us really faltered in courage or fell too far from peace, the other lifted up and comforted.

"Be patient, Gregory. Christ will find us."

Marcia's brown eyes, her warm face, had really a splendid glow, now that all her hair was white.

I think of no better place than this, so near the end, to recount the fortunes of our children. Two we had loved and lost, Marcus and Livia, he lost to ageless ocean and she lost to the agony of Rome. But three we loved have outlived Marcia and will no doubt live on after me.

Young Gregory was far better suited by temperament than I to be a bishop. I myself ordained him a priest while I was still a bishop, and, having helped us all to remove to Britain and settle there, he is a bishop himself now in Gaul and writes me letters which show, not merely how hard it is to hold up a light in dark winds of violence, but also how right it is for a man by patient and persevering labor to keep on gathering goodness together in a crumbling world. The tribes of Goths and Vandals, Alani, Suevi, Scythians, Huns sweep and struggle, murder and mingle across the face of Europe, and men like Gregory—most of them in the Catholic Church—hold their light against such sway of darkness. What more can a cataclysm of history do to each man then alive than to make him pass through the spiritual crisis of his life? In times like ours of breakup and stress, when the soul is more dramatically on trial than in times of comfort, it is easier to take sides in violence than to mature in humility. But Gregory, by his innate sweetness of temper, understood that any man can choose to be humble, but no man can by his own choice be great. He chose to be humble and gather goodness together with the strength of his life. And since society apparently changes more than it improves, more than it degenerates, there is always a set of ambitious men better able than others to come out on top, there's always a multitude being ruled and abused, and there are always a gifted creative few like Gregory who keep light going in the name of God.

The last time I saw him his arched nose and black hair and swift eye reminded me of his father Claudian; and his sweet smile and the music of his voice were like Marcia's; and by long association he had acquired some of my mannerisms of gesture and laughter and my way of turning a thought over three times, as it were, to find its curiosities.

Our son Ambrose is a man who loves to design and build in stone; he is married and has two children; he has already caught the flight of beauty in two small churches he has built here in Britain, and I think before the Saxons do in Britain what the Goths did in Italy he will be able to shape his vision of God in temples for man's spiritual comfort a few times more.

Our daughter Marcia is married to a Roman lawyer here in Britain who is one of the ministers trying to help Vortigern (a weak ruler) to keep the Saxons from devouring Britain; she has four children and also takes better care of the loneliness and tranquillity of my old age than need be.

Marcia, my wife, is gone, and I soon go, but life of our life and spirit of our spirit will still dwell in the race of men. With all its real tragedies and sufferings and failures, our life together has been better, then, richer and deeper and more creative than that sentimental happiness which is only a dream of detachment from the world.

I liked being a bishop in Spain; I believe I was on my way to becoming a humane Christian; but I was not a good Catholic. I was quite a good bishop in those time-consuming affairs of civil, political, moral, charitable, administrative and personal duties that fall to Church authority in our restless times. My training and experience fitted me for that, and the people of the town respected my justice and my moral authority. I was even good at training young clerics—I could get vapors out of their heads. Toward the people I was a good bishop; toward the Church I was a poor Catholic. I am sure that religion is the first necessity of my soul; I am sure that Christ is the most profound, searching and healing Master I ever heard of or ever sought to love; but I am not always sure that this or that Church holds all the broad and all the lonely pathways toward God. Augustine was indeed, until his death, spiritual Caesar of the Catholic Church, and his remembrance still rules; but some of his outcasts, like Pelagius, loved Christ, too. I mention here only what I heard long after, how this great Augustine was a fearless old man. Old and sick and dying, when the Vandals ravaged Africa and besieged Hippo, he did not flee, but held his place in his church and sought no self-safety from any danger. Where God placed him, there he stood, there he fought, there he built, there he died.

My interest in persons had long ago led me to believe, on the basis of experience, that a man is a man and is not mankind. The body and life of Ambrose will generate one cosmos of belief, the body and life of Augustine generates another; to a Jerome God may seem to shine down from the southeast of his heart, while He shines down from northwest for a Pelagius. God is great enough for men to be various.

It was later on, in reflections of my old age, that I realized it was too bad that I had not fitted comfortably into either the custom of the state or the morality of the Catholic Church; for though God is great enough for men to be various, few men are great enough to be free. Most men, including myself, do not do well outside of an organized morality. I might have done better—lived more happily—if I had ever found and remained within some organized morality not too tyrannous to my soul. But I was tough enough, skeptical enough and so willful as to force myself first out of the state, then out of the Church; but I was never sufficiently creative or inspired to rejoice in my own difference.

I suppose the temperaments of men vary all the way from the comfort of soporific obedience to the ecstasy of unique revelation; and my temperament was such that obedience was an injury to my soul but the joy of certainty in revelation was always a desire never achieved. Such a man may learn to smile or go mad. Saint Ambrose and Bishop Augustine had both of them properly identified my reluctance to obey as, from the Catholic point of view, the sin of pride; each of them had told me that was my trouble; but each of them had also perceived and honored that unfulfilled seeking of God which was the master theme of my life. I was more in love with this world than either of them. My treasures were set up where moths do corrupt and thieves do break in and steal. I was one who had to find the goodness of life and evidence of God in living a man's life in the midst of things as they are. Perhaps it is harder to rejoice in tragedy, suffering, failure, than to rest in obedience or to rejoice in righteousness. But I loved mortality, and so I could smile or go mad.

I began at last to preach my own sermons in Spain. Wallia, warring in Spain on behalf of Rome against Vandals, Suevi and recalcitrant Roman colonials, kept things in turmoil. My uneasy congregation wanted me to explain, in Christian terms, this continual ravaging of cities, hamlets, farms, and my rhetoric was not equal to the brute facts.

When I was asked to define sin I said I thought it was failure to love, and that a man ought to sit down with his heart in the presence of God and learn to accept the moral, mortal and spiritual injuries that life and he had done himself, and begin anew in love.

The faces of a congregation look up at you and ask what kind of a man you are, and the sermons you preach confess what you are. I had a young priest helping me who, from the passionate way he worshiped

Christ, I rather thought was yearning, if only he would admit it, for
Venus. At my time of life and with my fullness of experience I was not
inclined to use the phrases of erotic love to describe the emotions of religion. My confession, in my sermons, was rather something like this:

"I think people differ. Some, like Ambrose, seek fulfillment in a
Christ-relationship; some, like Augustine, in a God-relationship. Each
man had better try to be himself. I am not a great spirit like those two.
I suppose it amounts to this, that some men teach with authority, but
the best I can do is to stir up wonder and surprise. What does a man
want, to be as he is, and have all others and the world perfect to his comfort? Come, man, stir about, look about! How often in a whole life
does a man freely enjoy and experience that fine harmony of the spirit's
gay glory, the body's resolute passion and the world's incalculable hazard
that is the deep intention of our striving? If any man would be free, then
first let him learn that the soul of freedom is the will to give. Had we not
better learn to forgive ourselves most of the time, and love one another, in
the tragedy of the world, the suffering of the body and the failure of the
spirit? I know no final answer to any deep question of humanity; the best
I have been able to do has been to live and enjoy this tragedy of mortal
life in terms of the comedy of my own insufficient wisdom. I have experienced many passages of deep and wild joy, but a man of my temperament is never long at ease in the flesh and the world.

"I would leave parties, dogma, and doctrine to the frantic and insecure; they haven't the heart to live out the day, as themselves, in God's
presence, but must busy themselves at browbeating others along paths of
alleged perfection. I would abide content with the simplicity of the day
and its mystery, still not wishing to bind other men up, now or hereafter,
in the righteousness of my errors. A man can reject outward allegiances
to all organization and still adore Christ and seek God in the unquiet of
his own heart. For a sense of God is the root of spiritual sanity, and love
of God is the flowering of life.

"The life of a man is a smile of God and God's smile is always in motion. The soul of freedom is the will to give. And from first to last I have
been no more than one man who sought God, but as a man I sought Him,
not as a spirit, and in the days and ways of my mortality I sought God,
not in the future, the immortal, the eternal; my seeking, my hope, my
faith have always been now and not hereafter. I suppose with my robust
sense of life and my Roman tenacity, it is in living itself that I have sought
love and joy and wisdom. I have had my lyric joys and have sung bright
songs of the spirit, and also from that deep chorale of tragedy, suffering,
failure, I heard old music of God. . . ."

So it is, whoever begins to preach ends by confessing himself, and a man teaches what he is.

After such sermons Marcia would say, "Be patient, Gregory. Christ will find us."

Marcia's faith was such, the purity of her faith was so plain to me, that I was sometimes lifted up to preach, as it were, her sermon, saying with the apostle Paul, "And all things are of God, who hath reconciled us to himself by Jesus Christ. . . . We pray you in Christ's stead, be ye reconciled to God."

This taught me that I was less noble in spirit than Paul and less pure in love than Marcia, and my last few sermons were my simplest confessions of my own heart, saying: "Grief is the light of the world, love is the joy of the heart, and God is the smile at the heart of life. To experience these three is the lot of man; and to receive them into your soul with the serene acceptance of love is to be reconciled with God."

And Marcia comforted me, saying, "You have grown more patient, Gregory. Christ will find us."

Pelagius found us.

I won't fill a hundred scrolls detailing the great debate between Pelagius and Augustine. There were volumes and letters and sermons and councils, pronouncements, reversals of pronouncements, machinations, intrigue, retractions, recantations, amendments and finally the summoning forth of civil power to enforce the opinion of Augustine as the truth of God. It seemed to me that Augustine and Pelagius were as opposite as this: Augustine said in effect, "Spend your whole life trying to surmount original sin, inherited from Adam, by the evil of sexual procreation— and only the grace of God, through the Catholic Church, will save you"; while Pelagius said in effect, "Spend your whole life trying to fulfill the potential goodness with which you were born, and God will help you." The matter was parceled out in doctrinal points, such as original sin, grace, free will, predestination, concupiscence, infant damnation and I know not what else. It was done in Greek, in Latin and in anger. And another great point became clear, without being centrally stressed: The doctrine of Pelagius, with its emphasis on man's free will and essential goodness, would never build a Church; while the doctrine of Augustine, emphasizing man's corruption, his helplessness without grace and his absolute need of the sacraments and intercession of the Catholic Church for his salvation, would make the Catholic Church the one, the great and powerful spiritual arbiter.

Augustine won over Innocent, Pope of Rome, to his side and cried, "Rome has spoken; the cause is finished!" But Innocent died, and the new Pope, Zosimus, favored Pelagius. Augustine reopened the cause with great force. Zosimus had the Greek preference for human freedom; but, now that he was Pope, he began to feel the enormous pressures of practical administration and gave in to Augustine.

After some years of contention Pelagius was declared a heretic. Finally Augustine persuaded Pope Zosimus to send around a letter commanding all bishops to denounce Pelagius and his heresies and his adherents. Augustine also persuaded the Emperor Honorius to issue an edict condemning these heresiarchs without hearing or trial, confiscating their property and banishing them in perpetuity from any place of Roman rule. Thus Augustine, like a spiritual Caesar, commanded, "Obey, or die outcast!"

I was so small a bishop in so small a place that at first I paid no attention to either of these orders, and no one took note of my negligence.

Pelagius, as the saying goes, "disappeared from history"; but I think it is all right for me to tell now what the sturdy old man tried to conceal then.

It was apt to be considered a Christian sport among certain violent circles in Africa and other places to stone heretics to death. Indeed at Alexandria, only a few years before this, a rabble of fanatic monks had seized Hypatia, who was noted both for her chaste beauty and for her Neoplatonic teaching; they had stripped her naked on the steps of a temple and cut her body down to the raw bones of death with sharp oyster shells as the tools of their fury. At any rate, Pelagius quietly set sail for Genoa to return to Britain. A storm blew his ship aside, he landed at Barcelona. He heard I was near by and came to see me. He was now a large florid shaken-up old man, but he still had his courage. We were at talk in my study when Marcia came in.

Marcia looked at him a moment, then said, "Hello, Pelagius."

It was the first time in more than seven years that I had heard Marcia address a word to anyone except to me or her children or (in spoken prayer) to Christ.

After that she spoke when she wished to anyone. I honored Pelagius for this healing that his presence brought to Marcia.

Pelagius told us, "That Augustine is a terrible man! I was but a toy to his great brain. He has every corner of heaven worked out in irrefutable design. I long to go home to Britain, where a man can be unsure of some things. For, though Augustine's logic, rhetoric and power overwhelm me, my heart still does not believe him. Among the mists, the glad green fields and changing skies of Britain nothing is quite perfect, nothing is ever finally decided, and that is the sort of place where a man can be free to do the best he can for God."

Someone had recognized Pelagius on his way through Barcelona. A delegation from the Bishop of Barcelona, accompanied by a Roman official and Gothic soldiers, came out to see to it that I signed the Catholic letter against Pelagius.

A man misses one of the great events of his life if he never holds to his conscience against authority. I said the spiritual tax of receiving my beliefs from a central committee of bishops was heavier than I cared to pay; that there ought to be some people who knew or tried to know their own minds, even if they are forced into a silent place in society. I was divested of my Catholic authority and told that no place faithful to Rome would receive me.

My remote cousin, Bishop Julian of Eclanum, in a like fix, fought back against Augustine; he was a bold and learned man, and when he finally accused Augustine in this Pelagian affair of falling back on civil power not to prove his doctrine but to crush his opponents, Augustine replied with that worst axiom of arrogant power: "We persecute you to save your souls." Julian wandered for years as an exile and finally died (I think) in Sicily, though I am not always sure of the rumors that reach Britain.

As for myself, in remembrance of my son Marcus I simply did not believe in infant damnation; in remembrance of Marcia I just did not believe that sexual love is corrupt; in remembrance of my father I did not believe in the all-righteousness of a single church; in remembrance of Ambrose I believed in Christ as a teacher of love; and out of the wonders of my own experience I thought a man should neither deny nor fear but ought to and could well love the divine original child at the core of his own being.

Is it not strange and wonderful how each man still tries to find himself the center from which pours all the world?

Marcia was visionary in the matter, for after consulting mystic motions in her own heart she said, "Pelagius will lead us, Gregory, to where Christ will find us. This I know."

Pelagius and I, with Marcia and the three children, made our way to Britain. To our surprise we found the name of Pelagius hated in his native land. We went first toward the western mountains to that monastery from which, many years ago, Pelagius had set out for Rome; and they were ashamed of him there, not for his doctrines and not because they were really Catholics, but because, having pitted himself in high battle, he had lost.

Finally we went to the city of London, and there were surprised, too. We found that since the withdrawal of Roman power a dozen or more years ago, the city was in rapid decline. Trade had fallen considerably, buildings were empty, and it looked as if time would soon eat ruins there. But a place declining toward ruin may also be a seedbed for some future and is at least hospitable toward outcasts. We settled there in a small abandoned Roman villa, maintained our ownership by our presence, and helped one another get along. Pelagius and I, with young Gregory to help us, opened a school, where we taught growing children. Under the guise of Latin and law, rhetoric and religion I taught one thing only, the seeking of God. I never knew anything else to teach. And teaching lasts long in the race. Pelagius joined a monastery in the neighborhood, and we trained boys for religious life as well as for worldly affairs. In time young Gregory wanted to go off preaching, like an apostle on a mission, and so it was that he went into Gaul and became a bishop there.

Our school and our few acres of ground kept us alive. Marcia and the children raised our vegetables, and I was able to get enough pay in money and commodities for teaching to assure our plain living.

Pelagius died, and Marcia and I used to walk in the evening to the oak tree under which we buried him. We would sit there, as in a place of remembrance, on a bench of stone beneath the oak tree. There was a small thicket of pine trees off to the left and a broad field and a clean hill and evening sky stretched and spread out before us.

Our last two children grew up and married, and I watched old age creep into Marcia's face.

There was a convent close by. Marcia began going there for a week of rest and prayer several times a year, and then she would stay even longer. She said, "Christ draws near us, Gregory." And I respected the deepening of peace in her soul.

Finally she went to live in the convent. I did not try to prevent her fulfilling her ultimate needs, and she did not forget me.

I would walk out alone in the evening to the stone seat under the oak tree and would sit there until dark thinking about her in her quiet peace. Sometimes as last sunlight struck the trunks of the pine trees I had the curious fancy that there in the pine woods the foxes of my death, seen-unseen, unseen-seeing, looked at me strangely and sat on their rumps with mystic imaginary triangular faces.

The end was exceeding gentle.

Marcia came over one early evening from the convent. "We have been patient, Gregory. Christ knows we are here."

She wanted to walk to the stone seat with me.

We sat there in twilight and silence.

Finally Marcia said, with a sigh that welcomed surpassing peace, "Christ is with us, Gregory."

"Yes. He has come."

Then I knew by the weight of her head against my shoulder and the final stoop of her body against mine that her life was gone and she would never comfort me again. I sat until dark holding what I had lost. I spoke the burden of my love to all silence that dwelt in Marcia.

"Christ was here. He took you from me with his immortal touch. He did not know me."

FAREWELL!

A MOMENT AND A RADIANCE
OF ETERNITY

I AM A HEAVY ANGULAR SLOW-MOVING OLD MAN WITH MASSY bones and large slow hands; all my rusty hair gone grizzled-gray; eyebrows thick, nose heavy, beard plenteous, broad large mouth, steady eyes looking from far inward with the smile of such wisdom as sorrow and joy have wrought: great age at deep focus and capable of sound laughter rising out of enormous remembrance. For an old man without fear dwells in a place of remembrance where he recalls the original divinity of his own being and that of every man: There he apprehends the smile at the heart of life; that Being is forever; and that the life of a man is a moment and a radiance of eternity.

I am a beggar before God, and I know it, and the world shines resplendent to my soul in humble rags. I rejoice to behold it, and I daily receive alms of wonder at the glory of life. The marvelous light of heaven and time irradiate all the days of my life.

That's one thing. Here is another: Now that I have finished my long story, I realize what I have done; I have uttered one man's acceptance of sorrow and love of God.

What, then, of eternal happiness?

Let me say my say and fall silent. For, despite the boast of any Caesar that he came, he saw, he conquered, this is enough to say of me: I arose, I danced, I disappeared.

It still seems strange to live so many years, so many miles away from Rome. After the masterly sun and warmth and color of Italy and Spain, with the swart and rugged strength of mountains ever present to amaze the heart, Britain is a cool green watery place where a big tree, a clear lawn and an open view compose solace, and it is beautiful to see the clear line of a low hill with a smooth gray sky far behind it, or to watch the splendid piling of clouds in a blue sky on a summer day. And it comforts my old heart to know I shall be buried beside Marcia here in Britain.

The old exile, tranquil and lonely, converses in consolation with God.

Since Marcia's death I have lived out many years in the serene privilege of an old man's smiling mind. I mention those years in passing as a man might say, "Yes, I have worn out a number of old clothes, and have no need of any new garment." I feel the frost of my death in the coming of winter.

Even so, I have kept and still keep a hospitable place where men may come and stay and go as they are so moved, and I consider them all the guests of God. I speak of no great building; my hospitable place is the open temple of the air about me. Buildings are toys of convenience to amuse our childish minds; the most each of us wants to do in the heart's depth is to come freely accepted into another's presence; and when we visit one another we come in search of God. I know now I never called on any man or woman but I thought God would be there. I consider I have a constant appointment with God to learn how to do old needful things in better ways and new delightful things in good ways. This, then, is one way of looking at the end, the meaning and the achievement of my life, and also the hope of all of it that remains: that whosoever meets with me is welcome and may know from my watching and my word that I, too, am seeking God. For when we come to call on one another we hope to meet God; and He is our perpetual Guest.

When Christ came into Marcia's presence with the surpassing peace of her death and resurrection I said he did not know me; and I say I have never seen God so that I could draw His picture. There are those who, reading my story more deeply than others, will say I have lived without faith, basing my life on despair and endurance. But I think that here and there a man more like me may read deeper still and will know that, however blind, foolish and sorrowful my life may have been, I have always at bottom had faith even in my despair, and hope even in my endurance, and I would say that it was in the creative freedom and wonder of love that I have been in no wise magnificent. My love has not been perfect; my love has not been pure. My sorrow for this is very great. I don't know what to call my life except a spiritual failure; I've grown used to that and got over being ashamed of it. My spirit yearned to be perfect, but my spirit, with its dream of perfection, seems to have arisen in the whole man I am and the world I lived in, and the whole man was not perfect, nor was my world, and so my spirit fell short of sought perfection. The great themes of my being—tragedy, suffering, failure—have taught me that my heart can find no rest except in mystery. I accept what I am with mercy, I beg my fellow men for compassion, I ask God to forgive me.

If, in some last moment, my love is sufficient, I shall lay aside death and see God. If not, then I shall die as I have lived, believing in Him I have not seen. This is no dilemma; it is my last two ways of saying that life is good.

And so it is I have said Hail! to my life and to my human fellows, saying as clearly as I could that the life of a man is a moment and a radiance of eternity. And the garment of light that each man weaves and wears is his love of God.

The story is over. I feel the frost of death in the coming of winter. Eternity is at hand. Now at the end I know better what I had to say than when I began to tell it. I have always believed in God; all my life is the gift of this Divine Guest of my heart; I have always sought Him; I have always known He is near; I have never been without Him, yet I never found Him. My life is a fabric of wonder with a pattern of sorrow, and my heart can find no rest except in mystery.

I fall silent and pass by.

An old man listens to eternity.

Farewell!